# Generous Enemies

## Simon Drake

Also by Simon Drake

*Fiction*

Australian Berko

Love Data

10,000BC – The First Geniuses

The Return of the Last Space Explorer

*Non-Fiction*

The Art of Office War

# Generous Enemies

## Simon Drake

Doug sized up Krue yet shook his head. "Major, I'm trying to explain but it's very hard to get it right… I read up on what happens down there just in case I parachute in, land up shit creek without a paddle and you know what. It's not because I've gone mental or been sitting in the stratosphere playing God… Up there you've got to wonder, and Peters – I haven't met him but he'll back me up – you have to wonder who owns what up there. A line is a line and beyond that, in Occupied Australia, it's a million shades of grey. There can never be some U-N peace deal. It's the new Middle-East up there. I commend you for going in there, I really do. Sooner or later we'll all have to go and stake a claim up there or write it off as something for the Aboriginals to sort out."

Generous Enemies
Copyright © 2008 Simon Drake

First published by Simon Drake in 2003
This revised edition published by Simon Drake, 2008

Cover illustration by Simon Drake.

Text set in Adobe Caslon Regular.

ISBN 978-0-9559719-1-4


Simon Drake

27 Old Gloucester Street, London
WC1N 3AX, United Kingdom

www.simondrake.com
publisher@simondrake.com

# Generous Enemies

"All men dream: but not equally. Those who dream by night in the dusty recesses of their minds wake in the day to find that it was vanity: but the dreamers of the day are dangerous men, for they may act their dream with open eyes, to make it possible. This I did."

T.E. Lawrence, Seven Pillars of Wisdom

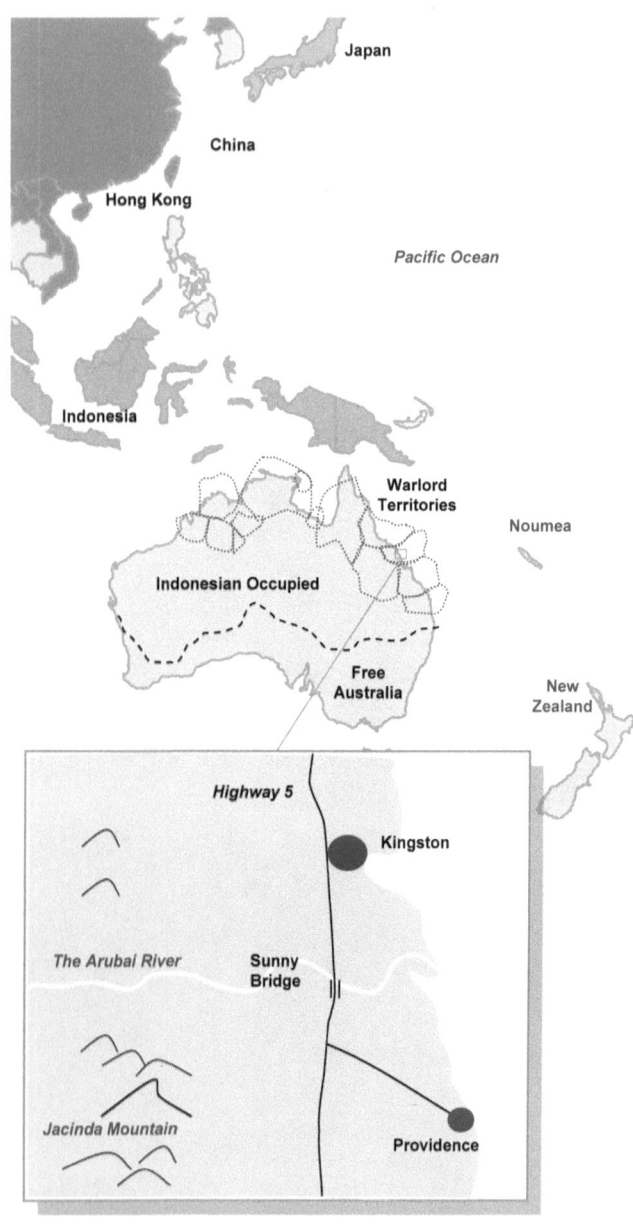

# Desert Surgery

Krue's sleek eyebrow arched up to the clear blue sky, followed by her widening eye, expecting a deathly angel to appear. Her eye pressed against the sniper scope and her shoulder gave a shrug, right up to her ear, pushing in an earphone.

"Angel Five in queue for Voodoo Child…"

Krue tried not to look up; it seemed unreal that in low-orbit, an armour plated satellite was transferring data to an airborne drone, somewhere above her, wheeling into positioning, aiming to where she stared to: the target zone. Relying on hi-tech tools was risky, too many things in the daisy chain were way out of her control, but this was an ace up her sleeve, she had never used it before, and had only ever heard of its use as gossip.

She had seen warlords sweating around the Top End hauling camouflage-draped howitzers, mobile missile-launchers and beetle drones bristling with antennae and gatling guns. The buy or hire, haul and raise hell weaponry were ideal for perimeter defence, geopolitical bullying, small scale acquisition and general mayhem, yet their preference to phallic weaponry on the wide open field brought about their downfall: large weapons were picked up on radar and bombed too easily, jammed by electronics and most of all, jammed by dust. Now for Krue, lying sideways behind a branch in a crevice where the dry earth had opened up, and living there for days on end covered by a bleached net, nibbling dried rations and measuring her diminishing water, she could see hope in the out-of-sight, out-of-mind ordinance, fed on a string of co-ordinates.

"Angel Five in queue for Voodoo Child…"

"Yeah, we'll see," she whispered to the automated call, no-one listening. HQ weren't too open about what the airborne drone carried. That confidential knowledge, she knew, was not worth putting in her pretty head, but the stark warning to keep a safe distance when the Angel Strikes, was.

She drew back from the scope, scanned end to end of the horizon, then edged back to the scope and studied the target zone again. So far, so good.

The target arrived at midday from the north in a well-tuned, diesel, desert camouflaged 4x4. They knew, like Krue, roughly where to stop and after a bit of chasing the exact co-ordinates with their GPS system, they had hit the lode to within a ten metre radius. There were three, looking the part of civilians. One wriggled himself through the sun roof and swung an outdated .50 calibre to the north and remained there, relaxed, sitting back, jabbering. Expecting visitors? Krue, to the south, snorted dust out her nose. Visitors would kick up dust and there were none to be seen. The other two, mercenary prospectors, unloaded metal cases, erected a tripod for a drill, a satellite data link, cleaned out their rifles, trading talk with the gunner. Then one of them swung a sophisticated, low-grade-uranium sniffing Geiger counter over the ground, sweeping, searching, marking a point, sweeping, marking, fixing a diagram, defining the zone. After a solid hour of basic prospecting they were enthusiastic and relayed their success to their warlord, somewhere up north or maybe just over the horizon. This was a career changing event, they may have struck a lode. This was what commandeering foreign soil was all about. But it wasn't a natural lode, Krue smiled, easing herself back into the plan. At the same time she spread the co-ordinates across the Top End airwaves and in a few paying ears, the radioactive fragments were being buried just over there, creating over the weeks a myth that evolved into a honey pot, now cheerfully verified.

Krue nudged the satellite phone from above her breast to mouth, pressed a button and waited. The beeps were long, encrypted dots of data drawn from her, up to the satellite, and down to her HQ, over eight hundred kilometres away in Broken Hill.

HQ answered, "Voodoo Child… Progress?"

"They've hit their jackpot.

"Have they made the call?"

Krue winced. HQ wanted the prospectors to advertise their little uranium prize, call in a crew for excavation, so when they came in and hopefully the local warlord too, HQ could wipe everyone out with some *enriched* uranium.

"They've radioed their patron."

"Good." HQ broke up then came back. "How safe are you?"

"Safe enough…" She had three litres left, four days max. One hundred bullets. What is safe out in the desert? "Why?"

"Parameters have shifted."

"Parameters…"

"Intelligence warning: a Chinese satellite hunter is shifting into low orbit, Angel Five and other birds have to re-align. We're expecting a major disruption."

"Shit. Look, the target zone is as good as it gets."

"It could be premature…"

"Just do it."

"Yes Captain."

She slid the satellite phone back. Nothing else worked this far out in the desert. Back to her scope she saw that the two prospectors stood away from their 4x4, their lean brown arms tense, holding heavy binoculars to their eyes, as they made concentrated sweeps over the lifeless desert. One of the surveyors dropped his binoculars and held a gadget before him, swinging it east to south, west to south, hoping to detect her satphone's signal again. She turned it off. 'Fuckers', she muttered. The other zeroed in on her hideout. He saw the crook of the grey branch and assumed something was behind it. He pointed and gave an order. The guy with the .50 calibre deftly swung around.

Krue wriggled for cover, her eyes resting on some speck of sand. They were under three hundred metres away. Even if she survived the probing bursts of lead they would drive up, and then she could shoot out their tires on the way, but it was still three to one, the distance between them and her *now* as good as it could ever be. How long would it take to pull the tarpaulin off her dirt bike, buried a few metres back, kick start it a hundred times and zigzag south leaving a cloaking cloud of dust? No, she damned them, these guys were smart. She imagined a satellite and a drone, zapping data, adjusting aim, one floating by at twenty thousand kilometres an hour, the other as fast as a crow.

She carefully raised her eye to the scope. They were packing up their boxes and tripods into the 4x4. The gunner at the top was aiming straight at her, a blip of flame came from his barrel. His body rippled. She ducked. The volley cracked the air a few metres to the left and overhead. She looked from the defunct satphone to her rifle. Another volley of shots came over, in a wide spread, followed by another, honing in on her position.

Krue braved the odds and spied through her scope. The gunner with the .50 calibre was adjusting his sights and snarling at the other two. The other two had sheltered behind the vehicle and she could just see, under it, their boots, scuffing up dust.

Krue gritted her teeth, uncorked the barrel of her K-40 Rifle, stretched her arms then propped herself just over the branch. The sun hit her grubby face. With the gunner glaring down his .50 calibre at her in her sights she squeezed the trigger, a healthy fuck-off burst - that missed. She cowered, a cold dread seeping from her core.

The gunner's return volley was still high, but it'd be back, turning her cover into matchsticks.

She rolled to the other end of the branch and turned the satphone on. While it warmed itself up she took aim again. The gunner fired first and sent a spray of lead just over her head. So that's it, Krue smirked, we're all aiming a bit too high because the heat off the desert is magnifying what we see. She deliberately aimed below the vehicle, popping the radiator, and firing another healthy burst, drew the gun slightly up. She did it again, and again, until the gunner caught on and thumped a few holes in her grey branch. The shriek of dry wood splintering, the thump-thump of bullets into the ground metres away, was eating into her mind. She rolled back, burrowed into the crevice, loaded a fresh magazine and psyched herself that if she heard them driving up, closing in, she'd let them have it. But there were no sounds, just the desert, and her coarse breath. HQ had not sent anything to the satphone. She pressed in the ear piece.

"Angel Five in queue for Voodoo Child..." Automated as ever.

They would pick up her signal. There was no escaping on the bike. She readied a grenade. She heard nothing, no yells, no thump-thump, no whining engine. The desert was silent again.

She wriggled along the branch and peeked through one of the bullet holes blown through, the scope to her eye. The gunner was coughing and trying to wriggle out of the sun roof, his smoking .50 calibre limp. She could make out one prospector, then the other, staggering in oblong circles, their hands clasped over their mouths and eyes, their feet tripping over until they fell. One of them raised himself to his knees and in act of defiance stayed there, hands over eyes, gaping at the sky, until like a tombstone hit with a crowbar, he toppled forward and bit the desert. The gunner slumped backwards, his pigeon chest, stringy forearms and flowing beard facing up to the sun, easily mistaken as placidly snoozing, catching some rays, the usual peace time stuff.

She'd already hit their 4x4 a few times but as a test she tried something dramatic: the windscreen was intact until she made a neat hole right in the centre. They didn't react.

She stood up and mutely studied the target zone and the sky above it. Somewhere up there was a drone, camouflaged against the sky, armed with guided canisters of illegal gases, and above it, a satellite. Space, she ran her lean fingers through her hair, was now a mean ass place. She rolled her kit into the camouflage net, rolled that into the tarpaulin and kick-started the dirt bike on the first go. She gave the engine a noisy rev and cautiously closed in, her K-40 resting on the handlebar. At one hundred metres she made a slow half circle around, not venturing closer,  studying the prospectors baking in the sun.

A scavenging bird landed and hopped along the roof and inspected the gunner's earlobe.

"Hey!" Krue shouted, relieved it lived.

The bird glared at her, shuffled along and knew to outwait her. She stopped and remembered the orders from the Instructor at Operations, 'Do not go within one hundred metres of the target zone' and inspected the prospectors, poisoned to death, silent and peaceful.

Yet to truly finish the job she had to show, in case there were still War Crimes Trials and someone paid the lawyers, that warfare was kind and conventional. With perfect accuracy she tapped a bullet in each of the prospector's skulls then made a casually spray over the 4x4. Last was the gunner, it was a shame to break his sunny snooze but the bullet didn't do much, he just seemed to nudge a bit and bleed.

Her next concern were gate-crashers. She spied from end to end of the horizon and saw nothing. She took a satisfying gulp of water and accelerated well away from the target zone. Far enough away to feel innocent she plucked out the satphone. She waited for the drawn out beeps, but nothing happened. She shook the satphone. There shouldn't be too much dust in it. She drew it closer to her eyes. It was on, it had power and was transmitting, but, she tipped her head up, something up there was dead.

# Hong Kong

Ghan admired the hum and bustle cutting through the humid air of Hong Kong. The island was permanently charged and today it was blazing; in the neon-lit interconnecting malls and bars he'd expected global tourists but now it were the excited troops, splurging what disposable cash and emotions they had, making the most of, and some stretching it to the limit, their shore leave. On the streets was the familiar tangy air of the dense, Asian, industrially polluted and garish electrical kind, and now a sweet euphoria was lifting the acumen of the locals; shopkeepers, barmen, prostitutes and pimps, and anyone else with their finger on the commercial pulse, was raking it in. This week was a slice of boomtown in a world of flat, morbid and grim recession. It was also peace town in a sea of pain. Arising from the constant news of carnage and conflict, was the dizzying acknowledgement that history in most of Asia and the Pacific had gruesomely ground to a halt, reset itself and was evolving unmolested, and now, from today, it seemed there was real hope in the air: Looking down from Victoria Peak into the harbour, over to Kowloon, then staring out to the sea, Ghan studied the majesty of the Third Fleet.

His daughter tugged at his hand, "Daddy! Are you really going out to sea?"

His eyes shifted left, right, then he slyly checked behind; a few tourists and many troopers like himself, forming rivulets through the crowd, jostling onto and pushing against the railings of the viewing platforms. There was a small chance, but he swallowed hard, picked his daughter up and hugging her, faced her to the fleet, pointing out to the larger vessels. They were anchored in a defensive diamond formation, sparkling and bristling with the latest technology, and although Honk Kong was neutral, the world knew that to touch it and the rest of the West was liable.

"I am. I'm not sure which one I will go on but you choose one, and you remember it, can you do that?"

She nodded, picked out the nearest (a Jiangwei II, freshly painted, a row of sailors in white standing on the bow, a new radar up the top swivelling madly) and shut her eyes and concentrated.

Ghan smiled, he looked up to the sky then down at the tram coming up again. Packed inside were young men. He recognised a few.

"Daddy, why are they waving at you?"

"They are in my Brigade, they serve under me."

"Do I serve you, too?"

"No, I serve your mother, and you – but," and he whispered into her ear, "I serve you for ever and ever."

Digesting that concept, time and servitude, in such a young fertile mind, was hard work. She fell silent and stared hard out at the ship, then the others, and at a helicopter touching down on one of them.

Ghan's wife returned. Her expression of joy at the holiday had washed away in the night and now she was foreboding, unashamedly, yet prosaically smiling. She knew too who some of those troops looked up to.

She said, "I was chatting to some of your officers, they were buying postcards. They are very excited."

"Many of them have never been out of their own province."

"Colonel Chiang was there too. By himself."

"Deafening solitude is his kind of music."

Her brittle smile morphed into something real. "He talks to me."

"He trusts us."

"He *knows* us."

Ghan slowly nodded up and down, meditating almost, until his daughter playfully made a swipe at his bobbing goatee, so he swung her into his wife's arms and clasped the railing before him and glared at the towers of Hong Kong, then straight over the fleet, and to the horizon of the sea. All around him were the *zzzt* of digital cameras zooming and translating light and form into binary, the cooing of people and the quiet respite of others, contemplating, like Ghan, what lay over the curvature of the earth, where patchy reports of horrors were beamed from. He exhaled, blushed, turned and saw that his wife and daughter were frozen too, fixated, alone in their thoughts, unable to extract from myth and hope what they wished for most.

His daughter, with all the naivety and impatience of youth broke the spell, "How far away is Australia?"

He took her back, positioned her firmly on his forearm and with his free hand limply cuffed her mouth and drew her closer. "Where did you hear that?"

She shook her head under his hand.

He held her jaw up. "It's a story, a little story." He checked left, right, left again. "Ice cream?" He removed his hand.

She didn't nod. She didn't squeal with delight. She just sat on his arm, kicked her legs out, a fierce stare trying to penetrate and travel beyond the horizon (not knowing yet the earth was round) and to what lay there.

"Will you come back?"

"For you," he swallowed hard, "I would swim back."

Ghan was alone in the elevator for the long ride to the top, the longest ride he'd ever enjoyed. When the polished steel doors opened at the top floor bar he was blinded by the morning sunshine, then stepping out, nauseous at the smell of stale cigarette smoke and spilt alcohol that had seeped into the carpet. It was a tidy bar, fit for the playboys and elite, but empty as a tomb. He saw Chiang had been there awhile, comfortable in a couch set to a table, smoking, staring smittenly out to sea. Crossing the freshly mopped dance floor, Ghan inspected the windows, floor to ceiling plates of glass, and through them the other wonder; fields of tower blocks stretching from behind the fancy sky-scrapers, filing the island, rows and grids gone vertical. Who exactly lived there he dismissed with a shrug and sat down across from Chiang.

Chiang's eyes shifted from the sea to the table, and he blushed. "You thought you would come early, to be alone, and enjoy the view?"

"Yes."

Chiang slid his lighter into his cigarette packet and made to grab his folded up newspaper.

"Stay," Ghan commanded, "We all need a view to clear the mind." He settled into the soft leather cushion. The bar had seen many hard nights, he could almost hear the local Hong Kong syndicates cutting their deals, and before that the diplomats and ex-pats of the West drowning their homesickness. He rotated his head back to the sea and counted the fleet, not so much brute force, just protective power: two frigates and five destroyers to escort ten cargo vessels. And there were submarines too, not the diesel kind to boost the numbers for small scale regional bullying, but the nuclear type, sleek, quiet and primed with civilisation-levelling payloads. And there was one, taking on fresh supplies from a rubber dingy, sitting heavy as lead on the ocean when everything else the same size or smaller, bobbed like toys. Civilian pleasure craft drifted up to the perimeter set by the Water Police, appraising the huge grey hulls and exotic armaments. A horn would blare and the civilian craft would turn before the buoys, leaving a small wake away from the attraction.

Chiang looked appraisingly at the newspaper then up to Ghan, "Have you kept up with the news?"

"Just television; kids stuff mostly."

Chiang lit a cigarette and shifted the newspaper to Ghan, "It's official now, Indonesia has requested support from us to police their territories. Clandestine activities will continue, as ever, but it is a step forward."

Ghan opened the newspaper, it was a local high-brow mouthpiece, keen to smother up the pains of nursing Taiwan back to the bosom by proving Hong Kong's transition wasn't that bad, obviously censored as much as the rest, but endorsed by the local entrepreneurs. Ghan browsed for a few minutes, noted a few articles and closed it, placing it squarely in the middle of the table.

"They're sending us down there to eliminate the rogues," Chiang grinned.

"And not to face the Americans?"

"Our prayers are answered…"

"For the moment." Ghan could see the elevator had gone, and was returning, rocketing up forty floors and in a minute his Captains would spill out, perhaps soothed by the bottle and the brothel, and now anxious to venture out. Ghan had heard from his Two Stars peers news that might never make it into print.

"Do you know about the satellite-killers?"

"I heard something," Chiang's eyes narrowed to the tip of his cigarette then out to the sky above the sea.

"A new kind of war to command space. Some craft have been knocked out of orbit, others wrecked, or obliterated into a thousand pieces."

Chiang emitted a distorted chortle and inhaled.

"Cloud of fragments, just like shrapnel, spray out but unlike on earth, nothing falls to the ground, instead this debris stays until it drifts down, and is damaging those that survived."

Chiang nodded, tapping one foot, his eyes now locked on to the fleet, "So the West's edge has been blunted?"

"Intentionally yes, so too ours."

Chiang squinted at the fleet's radar domes and wiry antennas, and the expanse of sea to cross.

"When we get to where ever they send us, and we land ashore, deployed and securing what we know not," Ghan stroked his finger tip across his chin in a small arc, "We may be out of contact, or reliant on old means; radios, relay stations. Fifty years of technological advance, been turned back in two hours."

Chiang was immobile, stubbing out his half cigarette. "It must have been some show, up there," he kinked his head to the heavens then made a slow droop to his feet, "But it doesn't change much down here."

"Perhaps."

"How many know?" Chiang asked.

"None."

The elevator arrived, the doors opened, the Captains' amazement at the view stunned them and then seeing Two Stars Ghan, they gave a whoop.

Ghan stood up, one hand out to the arrivals and the other out to the fleet in Hong Kong's harbour, tilting to the sea they would vanish across, "Comrades, come!"

# Outside Broken Hill

At first glance of the parched camouflage sheet draped over the still curvaceous body one would have assumed death, dehydration or hypothermia. From a distance it would appear as an insignificant dot on the dry desolate landscape that stretched for miles. To the statisticians, they would add the casualty into a database that recorded the loss of most of a generation.

To the boy on the camel, staring down at the sun kissed brunette hair protruding from the jumble of concealed limbs, hopefully his second sense, the one of dread, would retain its place of defeat. He stroked the coarse hairs on the neck of his camel and straightened his back surveying the lay of the land. His wary eyes saw to the ends of the shimmering horizon and coupled with the carbine slung diagonally across his back, could shoot anything out there in a matter of seconds. He waited, slumped forward in the saddle for a good minute, turned to check his flanks, then slowly back the way he had come and waited another minute. To the north, scavenging birds hopped about a mangled carcass of a long dead kangaroo. With their large black wingspans, hawks drifted on thermals rising up from the baked land, circling directly and patiently above his objective.

"Hey miss," he called, the tremor in his voice waking him from the trek into isolation. "I know you aren't dead."

A crisp breeze tickled her exposed skin. She pictured the rising sun and imagined the progress she would make in the day; walking painfully hunched into herself, staggering into the coolness of morning, struggling with the first pangs of thirst at midday and collapsing, waking, wandering east for shelter, failing, curling up in chilled agony in a rocky crevice beside some inedible low-lying shrub.

"Hey Miss," the boy called louder, and then unslung his rifle, made another long look around the flat land, the ranges stepping up to the north, the rising sun lighting the crowns of low shrubs a vibrant, pastel, oily green. "Don't be playing dead on me. I know you're alive."

He quietly peeled the crinkled khaki sheet off Captain Katherine Krue. She was cuddled into herself, the broad shoulders crankily hunched up to her ears and collar. Her army uniform had been trashed; cotton frayed, loose faded buttons dangled by threads, yawning crevices opened in the leather of her battered combat boots.

As the crisp morning sun blinded her she groaned and buried her head into the crook of her arm. The dessert swallows me. We are one. Passing through my lips is cool water, droplets soaking into my dry swollen tongue. Oh God it's good.

"*Nah nah nah nah* you don't!" the boy withdrew the wet tea-towel from her flaking lips and greedily protruding swollen tongue, "You been dying real slow too... Takes longer to get better. You had all the time in the world to die so now you got all the time to get living. You watch. I've seen worse get better quicker but then they go back to nothing... Sick again... For what?"

Though utterly exhausted, she portrayed a strained glint of thanks for the friendliness the boy exuded. He was captivated by the scene and inspired to tell his Uncle Willy and together they would paint it on the rear of a door and leave it there as testament, on its hinges, to bridge the mystics of dreamtime and the realities of wartime. The boy patrols a waypoint, is heading back, and finds a warrior woman. They are two-days ride west from Silverton, south of Broken Hill. Her food is gone. She doesn't really know how to live off the land. They say her friends skirmish way north around the old uranium mines. Some don't make it back, but she came out of the desert alone. For those that died their spirits remain part of the desert. Many more would have come into Broken Hill but helicopters, though they look around a lot, can't find aviation gas, they can't rescue these warriors who think they know the land but they don't. This is as far as the boy will travel for further west is where starved strangers with guns wail at the moon's china white beams cast on the desert's endless sandy ripples. You would have to be crazy to walk out here, he smirked, and not know a thing about how to survive. With a towel dampened by bore water he cleansed the muck from her eyes.

"Thank you," she croaked, though it sounded indecipherable.

He then blew the grit out of the barrel of her rifle, practised aiming it on a watchful hawk above, then slung it diagonally over his back. Next he crafted a small fire by her side to brew a large pot of tea and brown sugar. He then erected a small camouflage tent and watched over her shaded body or out to the sun-baked land. Throughout the scorching day he fed her chocolate mashed into a paste, a pulped apple, and a grub he found poking its head out a hole. By sunset her eyes opened alertly and she found herself helped up and propped on the rear of the seated camel. After the sun's fiery retreat to the west an onslaught of perfectly sparkling stars were sprinkled across the sky. The boy stroked the camel's head to the east and feared his passenger was paralysed by a tick or a big brown snake's venom for when her head tipped back up to the heavens her face was blank and morose, jaw sagging, the eyes wild at the stars dazzling above.

He nudged her with his elbow.

"Uh,"

"How long?" he asked of her retreat.

"Eight days," she croaked.

"I reckon you could have made ten. Eight's O-K eh? That's all right. You're alive – that's even better."

She closed her eyes and fell to sleep. She awoke again at dawn. In the distance the land was desolate, ranging from black to shades of pink, and flat, yet when she watched the passing ground it was craggy and harsh. The boy artfully navigated along a thin path between bare hills and rocky passes, whispering to his passenger that she was going home. She murmured that she already was.

# South China Sea

Ghan's gesture to his own captains came back full circle. Prominent on his mind for the first days at sea was the farewell at the quay, dignitaries of Hong Kong, the wealthier of the troops' families, and the mandatory batch of political types were pressed against the barriers waving the brigade's dragon flag, cheering, singing, yet those with an investment of love were set apart; intermittently their farewell façade would drop, and in its place, an inhospitable glare took over them; the profit from this entire venture could be their ruin. Ghan had wondered, from the eyes of his own wife, if she felt that way too. His daughter, too young and shielded to understand, was probably the happiest little girl in Hong Kong that day, but her mother was something else. Was it superstition, or some higher order at play, coming from not only the mothers, but the wives, the sisters, and the male relatives of the departing troopers. It was as if they knew not to expect them back in a hurry or in one piece, at least. The newspaper editors and television presenters chatted that it was only a regional inspection, home by New Year, but who believed that, except maybe, his daughter. The more he thought about it the more it weighed him down; was fate decided in the black hole they were shipping to? So he paced his cabin, stared for the spare minutes he could out the porthole to the sea. Sometimes a lone seagull, flying beside the ship, would stare back at him, both of them flushed along to what was drawing them, yet one only needed to flap it's wings to exit the slipstream. Thankfully there were duties. Some of his troops were seasick, in his mind, a symptom of something other than the poor food and pitching. There was discipline. Planning. Information.

Four days to sea he was summoned by two military police, escorted to the deck and whisked to a frigate by helicopter, body-searched, and entered the cabin of General Zhing. Before Ghan could observe the layout, Zhing's pale flat palms and splayed fingers flipped back through the air like a fish's belly out of water, arcing towards a long leather couch staged before a wall that was covered in a white screen, the screen illuminated with a projected real time map of S.E Asia and the locations of all units, land, naval and airborne. Ghan giddily sat down, grinning down his boyish excitement, yet adult enough to acknowledge the counterweight deep in his gut. The un-announced invitation to spend time with one of the top brass didn't happen on training missions, or on Sunday cruises throughout the region. Alone with Zhing (a once in a life-time opportunity), he studied the live map, and in that silence the weight unsettled and began to rise.

After basic and abrupt formalities Zhing spoke to the map, "Many things have changed. We have these means, but there is still the fog of war." Somewhere in a mainframe the new data of unit locations was updated, and the map changed, new points to focus on and new directions to ponder. Sea lanes were covered by small craft and submarines, divisions were amassed all over Taiwan, and a reconnaissance bomber was pushing into the lonely expanse of the Pacific. Zhing keenly watched its progress, awaiting a discovery, his mouth mumbling, "So let's start with what troubles you."

Ghan, stoical and statuesque, said, "Do we have a reliable satellite fleet for the tasks ahead of us?"

"One in four, for how long… If 'they' had done their messy work a week from now, maybe that would be beneficial, but so soon." Zhing's wrinkled face dropped, half contemplative, half despondent. "How are your troops?"

"Well enough, building up courage. Fear of the unknown induces sickness, so I make sure they are not idle, as best I can."

Zhing's wiry eyebrows raised and he smiled.

"They are ready, if that's what you must know,"

Zhing slapped a hand on Ghan's shoulder, "You have told me more than any technocrat in a similar position could tell me in ten years and a billion emails." He shuffled about his expansive cabin, answered a silent yet flashing phone, barked a few orders, went to a refrigerator and fetched two beers and two glasses. As he sat down, poured them and said, "When I was a boy the only entertainment I had was the town square. So much change and everything keeps changing. In one corner, after dark, the men with the splinted spirits and addictions would gather. They made me laugh, but when they made me cry I found better things to do. No revolution, no red book, no dollar note could change them but they are there for a reason: Great Lessons in Life. One night the guitar man, one leg in bandages, who knows why, hobbling on crutches for pity, I don't know, was playing his songs. His guitar was old and patched up, and he was terrible, singing like a woman twice widowed and crowing for a third. But they put up with it, they had nothing else, and one of them had a dog. It began howling, howling like a beast betrayed."

Again, on the map, unit positions were updated. Zhing ran his finger up to his fleet and loosely drew a route south. Picketed along the route were submarines, and stations Ghan guessed as spy vessels.

"The man with the guitar, he said, 'Shut that dog up'. And the others went along, 'Yeah, shut that dog up or we share it, our stomachs are empty' and then the owner said, 'It's my dog and it does what it wants!' so the guitar man, put down his guitar and took up his crutches and hobbled over to the dog owner, 'Shut that dog up – I'm playing!' and the owner he backed up, trying to defend himself from crutches, screaming, 'It's my dog and I like the sound it makes!' So the guitar man hit the dog owner with his crutches."

Zhing took a hearty swig, smacked his lips, seemed to forget where he was, checked the map, massaged his forehead and continued.

"So the dog, his head hung low and his tail still, seeing his master under attack, you know what he did?"

Grinning like a boy, Ghan said, "No."

"He scampered away into the shadows. Gone. His master was pinned down on the ground. But the dog came back, jaws wide open, closing right on the guitar man's good leg; and down he went, screaming, waving his crutches but the dog and his master, by then, skipped down the alley, singing."

Ghan asked, "Did that make you laugh or cry?"

"Ha!" Zhing elbowed him playfully in the ribs, "It kept me awake, I begged my father for a dog, but that wasn't the point."

"Yes."

In the middle of the map of the Pacific was a speck of live data; the reconnaissance bomber began to wheel north, peeling off from its previous course to a glowing, now fading, radar signature: Surface vessels in wing formation and a title appearing as it was typed by an analyst in a backroom: *US 7th Fleet: Battle Group.*

"Ahhh expected... They are watching from the sidelines... They have lost too many and that old weary giant is tired. That's what they say. Or it could be oil and resources: they can't get it and now they claim not to want it. Isolationism takes a strange pride... The question is," Zhing enthused, "In this new world, who are we? Playing our guitar or howling at the noise."

"There is no answer, only contemplation."

"True if you are unsure of who you are." Zhing stood up, went to the map, and keeping his shadow off the east coast of Australia, planted his finger on a region and drew a circle, "It was the man that could walk away that made me laugh, yet in life we can't always play our parts."

Ghan clenched his teeth, scrutinizing the region so far away, so remote, so volatile. No training could prepare him for this.

"I will not be sailing so far south as I'd like to," Zhing cocked his head up to the 7th Fleet, a pocket of ocean sprinkled with metal fins, "They might chase us down, and there is so much to attend to." His hand brushed against Australia. "Yet, you will not be so alone down there."

"How so?"

"Most men are obedient, like their dogs. They can't wander far. But you and three other Brigade Commander will be beyond that, there is no master you can conveniently call in to right the wrongs. You, my friend, will be master of all before you."

Now Ghan burnt, bright and hot with pride and the humiliation of susceptibility to it, and gulping down the last of his beer didn't dampen the flames.

Aged as ever, Zhing continued, "It's not so bad, you know. Many men lie awake dreaming of what you will be undertaking. They are restless, right until the end, but have done nothing. They wake, feed the chickens, die happy, never knowing their true worth." Zhing fetched more beer. "I have thought of you, especially you, for a reason you will only come to understand much later: First comes the Mission for the Motherland, then the Mission to Yourself. They are intertwined. They give, they take. Men die, many more may not return." Then Zhing made a double-take; stooping to place the beers on the table and as if to lay on a final bereaving commitment to his brave junior, then standing straight as a rod, digging his bony finger right into Ghan's sternum, commanding, "You and I live the curse 'May you live in interesting times'. The path of your brigade is down a one-way street; actions will make history. In a sense your life is over Ghan, you are history, now live it."

Zhing sighed, slapped a hand on Ghan's shoulder and sat him down. He opened their beers, made a silent toast and watched as Ghan sipped.

"It's not so bad, it may not be that bad. All this might blow over. Your brigade could be extracted out and back home in months," Zhing yawned, "You never know in this world, ever."

"… Yes."

"You must understand," Zhing spoke squarely to his man, "Where you're going, to make history, to clean up history and enforce civilisation on barbaric senility, I and many others, want you back."

Tipsy, on deck, waiting for the helicopter to take him back to his ship, Ghan made sweeps of the inky dark for the fleet and then up to the stars. South. Full steam. History. He knew where they were going, most of the 'why', obviously the 'how'. Yet he'd been there, maybe not the same cities or regions, and they knew he'd been there and seen the bright lights, so to say, and wouldn't he be tempted to live on there, to defect? He filled his lungs with the sea air. Why not send someone who had never tasted the delights of the West? Unless of course, where he was going wasn't the West, it was something else.

He mused, stoic and sober, pondering the West; It was a state of collective minds, he decided, and when the minds broke down it was just a wasteland. And of history? There is little history now. Hadn't a Chinese fleet, six hundred years ago, explored Australia? Or was that myth, adorable as nationalistic banter, yet the available evidence inconclusive. He was not the first to venture so far, yet his lips parted and widened, and his teeth were bare to the salty spray, this is *my* history.

# Sydney Town

She artfully snaked through the crowd lining the parade route along George Street. Unfurling streamers floated down from skyscrapers. Jubilant cheers rang up the walls of the congested bustling city. Civilians, the young, too old, returned, or too important but left to carry on the struggle behind the lines, poured out of their offices to see the passing of the latest gladiators: A battalion of babies marching before the grand architectural statements of corporate fanfare, Martin Place, heading for an army fleet of diesel armoured trains down at Central Station. Drones were in the air and the undercover police were sweating it, the crack of an obliterating suicide bomber hadn't broken the city nerves for a month, and the parade progressed with a festival radiance.

Krue, six-foot-plus in boots, saw over the bobbing heads of the swarm of civilians. In the rich morning sun the parade went on with a fresh heroic impetus. She shied from the lure of community hype, settling for seasoned anonymity, but was jolted from the quiet of her mind as the jolly crescendos, *"Good luck! Farewell! Safe Return!"* pounded the young passing soldiers, hit a chilling apex, capped by plain roars from patriotic well wishers. A departing soldier with bold green eyes fell out of step as what had to be his lover, a petite brunette radiating a lustre of youth and complete devotion, excitedly ran up, squeezed him, sucking a lasting wisp of love with the locking of their arms and smashing of lips.

The crowd stood on their toes in merry awe, misty eyed, then the boots kicked forward. The girl wiped a tear from the corner of her eye. Krue's lips kinked, it was enticing and exhilarating, the rush of love, to miss, to love again, but all that bullshit was on hold. The breath of sweetness brought another onslaught of mob cheer. The soldiers proudly heaved a fancy glossy banner over their heads: *Alice Springs Relief Battalion*. Brave and strong, ignorant of their fate, they were off. It was little relief to Krue's eyes. She'd been there. To think back to that time would only give her a nauseous headache. Was it the gas they used or the stench of death it caused?

She slipped through the crowd, heading further up George Street, towards Circular Quay, thankful to escape the dispersing crowd and found her mark. She stood before Australia Square; a grey cylindrical forty-eight floored building, blasted with sunlight, a monument to peace time economies. At ground-level the electronic doors were repeatedly tripped by four old women sparingly sipping tea out of styrofoam cups having just enjoyed watching the battalion march by. Krue stood in front of the glass foyer, studying in her reflection the tight immaculate uniform issued only two-days before. Behind her had marched the fodder, to her sides chatted the old timers. In the middle stood her mirror image on the heavy glass, her enveloping stare admiring a new apparition; the newly appointed Major, gracefully tall, savagely yet clinically scary, a contemporary noble in the savage art of war, proud in action but silent in mind.

She rotated her profile and followed the curves of her jaw leading down to a finely round chin, then up the commanding line of her Romanesque nose, to her finely cut eyes and sleek, streamlined eyebrows. The roll of the genetic dice had served her well; three Anglo and one Asian grandparent had blessed her with a silky appearance: long coils of brunette hair with golden tips, deep blue eyes with dashes of silver in the iris (making them altogether paler at dawn by the sea or in acts of defiance), a curvaceous tall frame tight with lean muscles, and a well-rounded mode of simplistic, though very unattainable to the average punter, graceful style. The month in hospital had restored her well from the skeletal, scatterbrained, infertile wreck that walked in there.

The elderly women chattered slowly and profoundly about the parade. Krue knew to listen to the old dears; catch a dash of their wisdom and mix it with life for another generation or two.

"Much the same, really."

"I saw the boys of the *HMAS Sydney* do the march… In forty-one? Didn't know what they were in for."

"None of 'em did. Nor ever do."

"Singapore. All over again."

"Didn't happen then but it sure as hell happened now. God only knows why we've been kept around."

"First time wasn't it, was it? Off go the boys."

"They're not coming back."

"They don't know that. Didn't know about my father until it was all over."

"You think the names will be in the papers again?" asked the shortest of the elderly, "Uncle Archi, that's how we found out about Archi. Always one to leave with only a nod, so be it."

"Otherwise no one would know," one exclaimed and then bounced with calamity, "Off they go together. Fight'n wars. Dreadful business."

"At least they're not fighting each other. See them all do some good."

"All of the buggers'll do some good – Black, Yellow, Towel Heads, Wogs, Snobs and Yobs too."

"Well, what ever happens the blacks might be the only people left on this dry old land – they know what to do'n'all. Who knows, they may have seen it all before."

Krue clicked her heels and made for the electric doors. As the old women raised their tea to her she gave a quick return salute and beaming smile then smartly made her way inside. The doors rolled closed behind sealing her in a vacuum of silence.

In a lavish boardroom high in the sky worked Colonel Smacker and Brigadier Tolken. Pre-War they were high-rollers sitting on blue-chip boards, prestigious committees and slumbering hedge funds. They were the fanciest of corporate dressers, their image of opulence bench-marked to respect and responsibility regardless of their true prowess, logic and ego-driven aptitude to stretch the longest lunch. Come the thunder and mobilisation of war they were slotted into the ranks of those who look out the windows at the bombers creeping across the sky, the frigates, submarines and ferries cutting through the harbour weaving a criss-cross of widening white-wash, and stare with stony scrutiny at the crowds in the streets below, and to each square foot of wing surface, cubic centimetre of hull, litre of rocket propellant and mouth to feed, attribute a cost, check it against the mountain of debt, plug it into a master plan and play, tinker and hope there was still enough to go around and deliver a favourable outcome. But when there was a glitch in the system, when something wasn't adding value, or it was sucking too much, it was Tolken and Smacker who implemented more than economic orders, their niche realm was salvaging, grafting or liquidating.

Smacker stood by the expansive window, using the flood of fresh light to review the manila folder. Colonel John J. Smacker was forty-something with flaking skin, looked about sixty-something and carried and a terminal illness that screwed with his haemoglobin. He stiffened and looked up to view Sydney, thankful for the depth of distance to aid him like a tonic for his thinking. He admired the concentric blue ripples on the harbour, the smog stained yellow tiles of the Opera House, the great curved spine of the earthen grey Sydney Harbour Bridge and the sweep of the harbour.

Brigadier Tolken sat down at the boardroom table and playfully typed away at his laptop. Usually he spoke to the machine in his patient manner and it handled the rest but for succinct correspondence he solely relied on his brain and fingers for conveying the privacy of his thoughts. He was the older, wiser and softer touch in the Tolken-Smacker team. Tolken could not always explain his military duties to his wife. It overlapped from counting beans to bodies. He had nearly finished the calculation of how much to charge the United Nations for the latest fiasco, but as if they will pay, really. Blame would have to be appropriated first. Someday he'll receive a medal for this and other conniving activities and literally no one will have security clearance to know why or what he accomplished. There will be no parade in front of the plastic-flag waving masses. They'll want to forget his doings. And if we do lose, he grimaced and tapped away, if I can't get out to New York or some obscure South American villa I'll jump out that bloody window even if I have to shoot my way out. I'm fried, he shrugged, but at night I sleep with a calming satisfaction; I make a difference.

Smacker sat down, thinking of the next briefing. His withered, thin fingers formed into knotted fists as a distinct memory hit him like a brick – the wild cobalt eyes of that maniac sent to a beach of slaughter and horror – an event Smacker and Tolken were now facing the consequences of even though they were a thousand kilometres behind the stagnant frontline. With a flicker in his eye Smacker pictured a nuclear strike over Sydney; which buildings would fall, would the water in the harbour rise in a column of steam? Wouldn't that alleviate the state of six million hungry, useless, wailing individuals penned up in their self-prescribed ghettos? If given warning, could he escape? Did he want to?

Tolken's eyes locked onto a recent sentence, his fingers poised, his lips mouthing the rephrasing.

Smacker shakily asked, "Do you think we could have ever really *understood* him?"

Tolken frowned down his inferior's peculiar frailty. "It's too late for hindsight: I rate it up there with laziness. Idle minds are the playground of the devil and that precious hindsight. I don't have time for it. Now you make me think of him, it's on the record I recommended him for the job; young, devilish, perfect. You travelled up the coast with him. If he had turned then, would you have known?"

"He changed, up there." Smacker cleared his throat, rambling from an over-exaggerated memory, "He'd never left there, I believe. In the very early days I was cutting my teeth with Army Intelligence in Far-North Queensland, he was up there, just another Reserve Officer, feeding back the reality of what was really going on, and the first units to really hit back. Knowing what they saw and faced... All that mayhem of starving refugees and foreign soldiers forging something *alien* to us at the time, I wonder if that was the seed…" he nonchalantly explained only to fire himself up, "We lose it then we send him back! No wonder he's off the rails. A wildcard!" He shuddered and pretended vague interest in some visual anomaly on the North Shore skyline and robotically drew himself to the window.

"Wildcard…" Tolken absently commented.

"Always the wildcards," Smacker muttered to the grandeur of the city, his eyes roving from towers of commerce to the inner-city ridges crested with red-tiled roofs, distracting himself – hunting in the thin shadows between the walls for a weighty resolution.

"Heroic and decorated one at that." Tolken whistled lowly and tapped away, deliberating on what goes wrong and more importantly, he shed his frown with a delighted smirk, is harnessing the maximum effectiveness from the players who survive having outlived failure. A cornered animal fights to the death. Tolken straightened his face and gave Smacker a stern look over; Everything can be fixed, even from the comfort of behind the lines.

A knock at the door sent both men into a few seconds of reprieve.

Smacker slowly bee-lined to the door then briskly opened it, "Come in, please."

Krue entered and computed two classy Military heavy-weights at a black marble boardroom table. Her stride was like a precision instrument, every movement effortless, sitting opposite them, holding an auspicious presence, placing her beret in front, enveloping their stares.

Smacker sat next to Tolken. Their eyes were as wide as dinner plates and slowly shrinking to size. Their fingers compulsively tugged for the request sheet, assuming they had received the wrong package, but in no way wishing to make a complaint.

Krue's curt tone purveyed a mild defiance, "Sorry if I'm late, gentleman."

"Brigadier Tolken, and, Colonel Smacker," Tolken said, and then with a casual and charismatic charm, "You gave us more time to think."

"Major Kathy Krue." She leant over the table to shake their hands. "Lieutenant Manning posted my profile. You received it?"

They nodded. They knew her record but not her. The profile they dug up from Canberra was an extensive anthology; eight de-classified (excluding five too sensitive) geo-political critical missions ranging from target acquisition, to saboteur and assassin, documented extensively by pre and post-mission intelligence reports.

She was in the prime of her twenties and they knew, as with previous participants, those that burn to shine are like the candle that burns twice as bright – for half as long.

"Busy outside?" Tolken asked, faintly interested. "I could hear some street fiasco."

"Sending off parade," Krue altruistically smiled for the people, "Relief for Alice Springs."

"They'll be off to Darwin then," he quipped.

Krue flatly replied, "I don't think so."

"No?" Tolken raised his bushy eyebrow. "Amuse me, please,"

"They won't make it to Darwin this year. They'll be bogged down on the outskirts in an intensive guerrilla war waged by armed refugees operating under the local Warlord – some scar-faced tyrant searching for a fabled plutonium El Dorado in Kakadu. Gentleman, let's get to business?"

"Yes, certainly." Smacker's hands smoothed over the folder positioned squarely on the bare marble table. "Due to the urgency, the importance of the region involved, I'll be blunt. We have a low-profile yet high-hardware target."

Her eyes narrowed to the folder then sprang up to them; welcome to my world.

"We just need to restate some facts. You've been operating beyond the frontline for the last eleven-months, between Darwin, Broken Hill, the dead centre?"

Usually they gave her the orders from dusty bases, maps over a fold-up table, with days to discuss strategy. Once it was in-flight to the drop zone, cruising low across the Simpson Desert. But above Sydney the level of classification multiplied proportionally and significantly the risk and severity. She liked the brassy feel up here, the imposing comfort of wealth, the physical elevation above the masses, the knowledge that a diplomatic levelling of the eyes can draw as much weight as a discharged bullet.

"Dead centre, it's out there," Krue innately joked.

Dull response. Old Tolken and Smacker were strictly facts men.

Smacker continued, "Targets?"

"Communications, headquarters and personality sabotage in arid environments are my speciality."

Smacker continued, "Using marksman, air-strikes, guided missiles, drones and chemical weapons?"

At the word chemical, Tolken uneasily clasped his wrinkled hands.

Krue interjected, "If you're intent to delete a target – it's all *science* – mathematics."

"I see you studied physics? You'd like to continue that, after all this?"

"All 'this' has changed everything."

"True." Smacker noted a line in the text. "Wounded once."

She winced, shifted herself forward as if seated uncomfortably, "Early days. Once bitten – Twice shy."

Tolken sardonically chuckled. "Isn't that the truth."

"And in your experiences, from either side of the line, do you know of an Indonesian bounty on your head?" Smacker informed her, observing her eyes and hands, then formally pressing on, "It's the first for a white female too. And I'm talking not just Islam, it's a wider appealing bounty, a very fanatical bounty. If anyone will actually pay it out is another matter. The *notoriety* is what concerns us the most."

She looked straight out the window and crossed her arms, her silent sigh filling the room. Her targets were key players of the invaders, some she had even known on a short personal basis, many she'd paid information for. A bounty was just plain karma.

"I guess I've had it coming. No, I didn't know."

"Well, it makes you a liability. The weak and desperate and spies will close in and sooner or later all the technology and expertise in your team's arsenal will count for nothing." Smacker paused then fired up like a coal furnace, "You see Major, out *there*,"

Krue's eyes zeroed in on his idiosyncratic facial twitches; a pinched cheek, a half bitten lip, a curled up nostril. As if he'd ever been beyond here. If he had, he'd cut that crap and seep back to reality – everybody has an un-posted bounty. But then he showed her something that she could never forget. From his folder he slid out a facsimile of her sketched portrait set in a crude *Wanted* poster. She could not read the variety of Asian characters labelling her crimes, names, height or traits. She only saw herself as depicted by some artisan paid to enhance her into a majestic and seductive creature that was not to be trusted yet its curvy flesh and polished skull worth its weight in gold. She wondered if she had met the artisan, was it some friend of some warlord she lied to and destroyed, was it from a photo they had taken in a moment of courteous behaviour to the brave young diplomat from the vanquished nation?

"You are a complication to regular strategic procedures." Smacker stated nauseatingly categorically into her facsimile. "Notoriety supersedes you and will undoubtedly come back at you."

"Right," she snatched the facsimile and grinned at herself.

Tolken added, "Katherine, we take these matters very seriously…"

Her voice was anxious, direction blurred yet brightening, "Does that make me inoperable? I'm grounded? An exit?"

"No," Smacker guided her, "But a change of scenery is as good as a holiday, they say – and for the better. Every Indonesian soldier, refugee and civilian from Darwin to Alice Springs to Broome and across to Mt Isa would know of your escapades so we've organised to move you elsewhere."

She felt giddy. "I understand…"

"And, we're acting on new information and responding: Occupied Australia needs a new yard for you to roam. We know you've just recovered from a decisive and tough mission and now it's time to get back on the horse."

Krue reflected on the circumstance. With a bounty for her scalp, capture by hostile units no longer meant military imprisonment, rape, or a mid-afternoon execution. Indonesian superiors would claim a hearty price for her alive, she would be en-slaved to the lunacy of their disintegrating war machine, a prized possession and caged star of a Jakarta Propaganda Circus.

She rattled her finger tips on the table. "How much is the bounty?"

"Fifty thousand, Euros."

She scoffed. "Punitive."

Smacker brazenly flared up, "Fifty thousand is the highest we've heard of!"

"Maybe it is – but it doesn't reflect the damage one has caused. It should be a measure of the damage you can still inflict in the future."

"I *see*," Tolken leant back, and in an anxiously agreeable tone, "We all crave to be known for our true worth. But when has the world ever given that to anyone?"

Krue shrugged. Be happy with the notoriety.

Smacker didn't understand perceived worth, nor want to. "Ignore the fifty-K. It could be ten or a hundred, it doesn't change the facts – you're formidable and that will not be wasted."

Tolken embraced her with a pleasing smile, "You see Major, given your history you're exactly what's required: You *make* the Mission,"

And with a precision salesman grin Smacker continued, "Exactly. Now, about your contact with Indonesian military commanders operating as warlords," Smacker eyed the response in her eyes, reminding her, "They have constituted most of your targets. We know you've been in contact with a variety of adversaries up the Top End. We know that your craft extends from saboteur and assassin to un-official diplomat." He grinned his thin lips into a tight smirk, "Playing them off one another, so to say."

Krue felt an icy fear run through her legs. Now she's *so* right for it. She insipidly spied her superiors as more than glorified messengers for a much higher brass reporting to righteous wig-heads at the Hague hammering the need for humanity and order. They were so keen for her they just had to add on the personal dimension, her dirty laundry was a lure and hook: Did they want her out of the Top End due to her habit of meddling in affairs too far beyond what they could ever have perceived? Is this her reward for ingenuity and excellence?

"Major," Tolken wet his lips, "To enable us to understand *your* experience, define what you know of warlords, and speak freely."

So she spoke eloquently but blandly factually, "After Indonesia's major trade routes to the north were jeopardised by warring South East Asian nations they looked to the south... The Indonesia Navy had to defend its vital trade routes to the Australian continent and hence became easy pickings for our submarines. The fate the of Indonesian Army on this continent was sealed. Their supplies from their bases off-shore stopped. Partially stranded, self-sufficiency by the invading population was a means of survival. Once they could eat properly they upgraded from barbaric antics to fierce self-determination and if they continue to evolve and prosper, organised states and cultures seeking legitimacy will flourish, as some have. The elimination of particular warlords is a directive based on our military strategy and not to be confused with a criminal activity. Do not misconstrue my diplomatic quests with an underlying rogue element *up there*. I know where my allegiance lies, gentlemen. Yes, warlords and merchants have charmed me as I them – but look who sits before you – in one piece."

Tolken sucked in his cheeks and with a casual wave authorised Smacker to continue.

"Buy beyond dictatorial force, how do these warlords operate?"

"Operations depend on the resources in the region they hold. Most of my targets were just entrepreneurs mining diamonds, gold, uranium, bauxite, trading slaves on the side. Once they found a raw commodity they'd try to refine it, ship it out in bulk, trade it for weapons, food and the usual bits and pieces of infrastructure. Humanity is ingenious or cancerous, depends how you view it."

"Were they all military personnel?"

"No... You don't have to be; some are ingenious civilians out to make a buck... But mostly military, turned mercenaries, yet tied to the high command somewhere. What else are they to do out there stranded by their own army? The produce naturally goes back into Asia on smaller vessels disguised as nomadic sea-faring refugees."

"We understand there is a fierce rivalry?"

"Again, depending on the resources in the region. Dead ground is dead ground. Fertile valleys are prized possessions but the teething problems of these new arrivals has subdued. It's more political than feudal. That's how I came to penetrate their lines. The politics of preference. They're so desperate for acceptance in the foreign world – the world outside their warring territories and the undefined borders. They're content with protecting their spoils from outsiders of all types – but most commonly it's themselves they have to fear."

"Of your elimination of such warlords, were any civilians?"

"My orders were sabotage of foreign targets on Australian soil," Krue snapped.

Smacker sensed the distress, "Yes…"

Tolken intervened, shamelessly playing the coach-cliché, "Together we're a Team, Major Krue. And as a Team we'll be open. There's absolutely no leeway for confusing of agendas and right now we're just trying to adjust you to the difficult nature of what the nation has been confronted with. The elimination of military and civilian targets are merely benchmarks enabling us to qualify you as an appropriate player in the following scenario."

She smugly smiled. Deaths as benchmarks. What they wanted, snug in their armchairs a hundred metres up in the sky was another willing participant to the tactical merry-go-round at the top of the geo-political pyramid. Consequently, by playing such parts one steps past and above the normal selection routine. Who knows where this leads, but when it's finished, she'll have leverage over them. This must be her final flight in and out of the firing line.

"Go on," Krue accepted the game.

Tolken slid a folder from Smacker, carefully fingering out a grainy black and white photo and gave it to Krue. "It's interesting, to say the least… Do you know of a General Sumatra?"

General Sumatra, a grainy study in black and white, half-criminal, half-entrepreneur, brewing his own brand of trouble in what was an abandoned Western beachside backyard. For all the curses fired straight into his narrow black eyes, bounced back his principle – he was right. Any man that smiles for a kneeling photographer, wearing a weathered Indonesian General uniform, Pearl Colt .45 peeking out of a leather holster, and with two play-bunny Asian mistresses at his side, should have reason to believe he was the Shit. He had the Winning Poker gleam in his cheeks and wild holy cannon eyes that lined you up for a nasty death. Behind him were his troops, some rustic regular army Indonesians with uniforms, others the skint sun-tanned refugees with an assortment of guns celebrating today as a pseudo-revolutionary-militia-day with one principle – enforcing the King's golden words. Sumatra's prowess and mean sneer looked as though he loved it all – and it wasn't a pose. The power, the clear sub-tropical sky overhead, girls under his arms, all the possessions in a tribal sense of the self-made man. He could afford to act the part, because he was the part. He was bona fide Warlord and loving it. Intelligent minds love power vacuums.

"Central Queensland Coast Kingpin," Krue recognised the face. "Queensland was not my field of operations. And, he's dead, so they say on the intelligence grapevine – the usual confessions from tortured prisoners. I've heard it's a massacre zone for newly arrived refugees. Some fabled *white devil* took over. A tropical paradise for South Pacific pirates…" She peered into the photo. "I have to say though, there's so much disinformation germinating from all corners of Occupied Australia that I can only believe what *I* see…*Out* there, I mean."

"Very wise, especially concerning Queensland," Tolken said with a drawn out breath, anchoring the severity of his command: "We want you in there immediately."

Krue suppressed a shallow sigh. The man in the photo now came to her as a humorous caricature of a lost soul but a worthy soul to remember. He once held a history in his hand and that was more than a million other men had to offer this world in the thousands of days at the peaks of their lives.

Tolken continued, "Central Queensland Coast, into a region around a small town called Providence. You're right: He's dead. And now it's his replacement that worries us."

Behind Sumatra, bobbing over his shoulders, were his cheery faced fans and loyal subjects; refugees with guns and high hopes peering into a lens that to them promised some form of immortality. The photo relayed the message that Sumatra had it all under control and all the other scene stealers would never amount to anything of historical substance.

Tolken decisively tapped the folder, "To be more direct, it's the capabilities of his replacement; the personality is bloody irrelevant."

She tossed the photo aside, her brow crossed, ruminating. "Warlords are not easily replaced. They're predator minded entrepreneurs that serve to replace anarchy with order. Easy to say, painful to do. This replacement is following in Sumatra's footsteps. They write their own rules with the same pen."

Smacker twitched into a defensive mode, "True... Yet this is different. *He* knows our tactics... We can't dislodge him so easily. This replacement is also wanted by the United Nations on charges of International Piracy."

Krue tsked, "*That* he will wear on his sleeve. The U-N has no place in the new world. Is he part of the *Black Tide*?"

"There are connections," Tolken affirmed, almost apologetically, "But the replacement knows our weaknesses. He *is* our weakness. He's so evasive not even the Americans can pin him down with satellite coverage. Rival warlords haven't been able to lay a finger on him, we thought they were just trying to rip us off but no – He's a very tactful tyrant. He's made it into east-coast folklore and it's tipping the regional see-saw. We tried to reel him in, gave him incentives, but it doesn't work. Major Krue, after lengthy consideration, you're our best shot."

Krue felt suffocated in her chair. Like the marching boys this was another suicide gig. All line up. All run forth. All lay down.

Smacker calmly continued where Tolken left off, "His power-play is the stealthiest we've seen. His armed forces are impossible to calculate... He could be concealing a hundred or five-thousand militia and we wouldn't know. It's like he's invisible so our superiors shy from handing sizeable resources over to us to chase a ghost."

Krue speedily interjected, "This replacement, is he a tactical threat to our frontline?"

"Well, yes. Behind our front lines too!" Tolken boorishly thumped at the table with the divine authority of a pocket preacher. "The global community – those that do know of his atrocities – want him done away with immediately. Australia has to wash her hands of him. It's a disgrace Major Krue, a terrible mistake by our strategists, I might add."

Krue imagined she were in the same boat, alone, up there, in an invaded Queensland, on par with the devil, in the sub-tropical heat, like all the rest.... "Whoever he may be, why eliminate him? He's obviously taken the reigns of Sumatra's little enclave up in the middle of Queensland. It's surrounded by other warlords and starved Indonesian Army Divisions... To knock him out would create a power vacuum. And where our frontline is, Brisbane! As if he's going to attack... Surely if he is as sinister as you say he is, the odds are he'd be expanding inland for the minerals and cattle. His survival hinges on his ability to trade. He's a warlord making it work out of anarchy. The Indonesian Army is too weak to attack him – Why should we?"

"Because he's a multi-layered danger," Smacker testified with a refined frown, "He's set up a new frontier, free trade, black markets, shipments departing from his port all through Asia and back again full of weapons. That's how he buys defence – always keeping ahead. Before, he was benign problem. Yes he maintained order, a barrier so to say, between us and the multiplying messes of the north, but the near future," he smartly professed with a stately tone, "Is the greatest peril. The rush of people from the north hasn't stopped, it's only evolved."

Krue probed, "Does he attack us?"

"No." Tolken said, "But will if provoked."

"Well, our forces can't possibly retake that land. It's been tried and failed. Queensland is their country, still open to any raving refugee the disintegrating world has to offer. It'll take at least ten years of hard slogging and crusading genocide to return the population back to anything like pre-war. Hard times are ahead either way. Why kill him? Who wants it other than bleeding hearts in the U.N.? What's the cause?" Her face was burning from a reckless embarrassment but she tightened her fists. "These are factors I have to take into account on every mission. I'm not taking your case apart out of sheer indulgence – I need a point to focus on. Statistically I'm cannon fodder with tits, so I need reason to believe before I go in anywhere."

Smacker eyed Tolken who said it slowly, bitterly, the cliché of the coach saving the best for last, passing the folder to her, exhaling, "Because, *he* was one *us*."

She opened it expecting the usual desert grid maps and satellite photos of hidden headquarters in gullies and rock-faces. But no, a crisp photo of a Caucasian man in an Australian Army combat uniform at work in a mobile armoured personnel carrier headquarters. Radios nestled in the back sprouted cables like vines, strained Australian Reservists in the background lugged ammunition crates through a smoky semi-forest. Although it was obvious he was busy, surrounded by two wounded aides and outdated communication equipment, he still had time to look at the photographer with a warm smile, beaming a sharp confidence from piercing, precise, cobalt, blue eyes. He was playing it up, laughing at himself for being in this dangerous predicament, knowing this could be your last second, it could be his. Krue shuddered. He was fine boned, using sly visual wit to portray an aura of magnetic power in the midst of the fog of war. Peering closer, his face was soft, sincere.

Back, he was chiselled like a work of stone, austere and commanding. A caption read, *Captain Peters.*

"Taken years before," Smacker explained, "At that time he was one of the frontline tactical geniuses defending the Queensland coastline. Indonesian Forces eroded us all the way to Brisbane, and if it wasn't for his type, they may have done it in half the time. Once a fine man."

She was entranced by the photo and asked in a muddled croak, "Who is he? I've never heard of him."

"He's your warlord." Tolken announced, a grumpy sigh of relief fuming from his chest as he sat back in his chair and studied Krue's inoculation to the madness trembling in her hands.

A simple photo, a minute before, a no-one, an anyone, with guts, and now she was suckered into the majestic illusion of a warlord. A white man? She placed the photo squarely in the middle of the table next to her beret and ran through the extremes of possibilities. Smacker and Tolken patiently brooded at her countenance and hesitantly prodded her to speak by directing their piercing stares at her skull, trying to read the fine print running across her mind.

"Major, feel free to ask any question you like."

She tapped her index finger into the space before them, "He is one of us, doesn't attack us, unless provoked. His region is defended by his means. How he chanced to replace Sumatra and re-engineer his forces is another story. But why go out of our way to eliminate him? Look at us, sitting here high'n'mighty. I need reason."

Tolken whispered his thoughts, "A simple reason…"

Smacker spoke in a dark classified tone. "Nuclear capabilities. You think because he's raided a few ships in the Pacific he fears international reprisal? Not worth it right now. That's piracy, chicken feed, and punishable as one lives by the sword, dies by the sword. And so what if he's guilty of genocide, the over-populated world has been bubbling over to all the major coastlines and no-one can claim to have saved every single refugee. Besides, over-population is this generation's as much as the next generation's problem. It will get a lot worse before it gets better. What we've got right now is a rogue nuclear player."

Krue sat impassively. "We fear him and he fears *us*."

Tolken spoke rigidly, "He won't fire on us. He won't fire on the Indonesians, they're weak and couldn't amass enough confidence to take a swipe. It's all anarchy up there, no established government or society. Year zero in some places, like history was swallowed up, spat out and what we have now… Non-compatible, they say. It's living on the edge. We know the regional muscle of his arsenal are short range missiles. He has a wide range of warheads; napalm, high-explosives, maybe gas." Tolken sullenly spoke down his shirt, seemingly pushing his breath across the table to Krue. "Then there are the killings. Yes, mass genocide to curtail the influx of refugees. That is a secondary issue." He sat up, recomposed himself, his eyes never leaving Krue. "Somehow he traded in a Beijing Ninety-Six: an inter-continental ballistic nuclear missile riding on a mobile launcher platform, hauled by a heavy haulage truck. The missile was made in Taiwan, programmed to home in on Beijing and shipped throughout Asia by the Black Tide to classified dealers as a message to China not to destroy Taiwan or face the consequences from any number of hidden locations. Up until a few months ago China hadn't broken the peace and this Beijing Ninety-Six was one of the last to be tracked down and destroyed. Now the urgency of a benign situation has became precariously dangerous."

Initially she struggled to make coherent sense and then her eyes widened. "You think he'll attack China with it?"

"Major, it's not will he…." Tolken explained, "It's that he can. And we fear that if his cohorts can alter the guidance system he can lob that nuclear warhead anywhere from Los Angels to Tokyo to Jakarta to Beijing. It's war all around the Pacific Rim and every chief including India, Korea, China, Indonesia, Taiwan and Japan, have ruled out the use of nuclear weapons. After India and Pakistan's tit-for-tat nuclear match, easily culminating into half a billion casualties in the next decade, the global village, although not publicly, is united on not using weapons of mass destruction."

"So who is to say he'll use it?" Krue argued. "Unless in defence."

Smacker prophesied. "His region is stable: command is based in the coastal town of Providence, trade flows in and out from the deep-water port of Kingston to the north. If an invading force were to throw itself at his region, who can accurately predict his reaction? He's been bent, Major Krue. Day one of this war he was first into the action. He's been captured, rescued, and back in the line. Defeated countless times and victorious for his stubbornness. Hardened to the bone… Yet, never for an instance think we owe him the right to exist beyond the means that forged him."

Krue's eyes squinted and she tried to shake away the confusion. "So are *we* pushing him over the edge?"

"God no, but China is." Tolken's pace slowed and his tone deepened. "It's the only superpower at full capacity. They're already restoring order in Malaysia and creeping south. They've got a hell of a lot of cleaning up to do, and there is a pact, all un-official, that the U-S is staying out of it. When it comes to taming religious insurgency, rounding up pirates from the sea lanes and wiping out rogue nations, the Chinese have raised their hand and why not? They've got the units, trained, armed and deployable. They've been given the mandate and they've been watching the action and they have a hit list, so given some warlords' positions the Chinese will move into Queensland and make a point. It's lightly defended and packed with resources." He furtively threw up his hands, "After that, who knows what's on their card table? Half their game is confusion! The other half is gaining leverage!"

"And an ounce of prevention is worth the pound of cure," Krue confided.

Smacker continued, "Think, if Colonel Peters was attacked and he lobbed his pride and joy at them, they could retaliate a hundred times as hard. We're talking global stability. Now it has to make sense."

"Certainly. And if I'm caught, what would his reaction be?"

"Would he kill his own kind?" Smacker asked her.

"Is he one of our kind?" Tolken proposed to Smacker and Krue.

"Well, as he doesn't strike his homeland – I suppose it's not worth it, the guilt," she comforted herself.

"Right." Smacker agreed.

"So what are my objectives given the China scenario?"

"The elimination of his present and future nuclear capabilities by whatever means possible," Tolken said, cementing Krue's next bout of war.

"And," Smacker expanded on a friendlier note, "The elimination of Colonel Peters's present and future capabilities as a renegade."

Krue blinked. "I'm free to adapt to the nature of my mission?"

"Freedom granted solely to you," Tolken widely smiled. "We wouldn't have such a flexible tactician such as yourself unless we thought you were qualified."

"Yes," she replied sagely. Krue knew her target – a renegade of a different calibre in a new region. Regardless of how unstable or sane he was, *they* wanted him six-feet under and more importantly *they* were prepared to create a power vacuum because it's simply safer than *his* threat.

"Very well then," Tolken said, fatigued but exulted, "You're up for it, Major Krue?"

"Of course... It appears straightforward, the identity, the situation... But I have one question," Krue looked out to the clear blue sky, the expanse of the glowing harbour and the city spread out to the horizon, then to her new superiors and their reflection in the dark marble of the polished boardroom table, "How did Colonel Peters ever become a warlord?"

# Two Years Ago...
# Creating Warlords

Once sleep was a vessel for dreams; flimsy nightmares, aspirations and heroics. After tasting all three for real, sleep slipped into a new realm: a flood of trauma. The twitch of one foot in a new combat boot awoke the other. He winced. The rifle pummelled his shoulder. Comrades retreated across the half-destroyed, yet still standing, Story Bridge. It was semi-sunken into the river forming a giant and steep V, the last bridge to be blown on the Brisbane River, the last viable access to the south to be urgently destroyed. Behind and above him on the iron railings were snipers fresh out of a sharp-shooters course methodically firing into the approaching Indonesians and the smoke they beat before their advance. He yelled up, "Retreat! Retreat!" they waved back down, their searing eyes widening, mouths screaming, "Fucken oath!" and immediately clambered down.

The young Captain Peters then heard the heavy drumming of an Indonesian armoured car's machine-gun peppering the southern side of the river from a position on the cliffs at New Farm. This was a triumphant moment for them. The bridge was partially destroyed but troops could cross, and given some work on by cranes, would roll across numerous expendable light tanks. He yelled to the northern side and the few stragglers to race to safety, "Any more?"

They cried to the north, a city drowned and stained by smoke, "Dead!"

He raced forward to drag them through the silty river water, calling, hurry, hurry, the thunder in his voice igniting the last ounce of strength in their drained bodies to clamber up the mangled bridge to safety. Once all were out of the sunken V-section of the bridge and he could see none of his kind alive to make the journey from the northern side, he squatted in the rising waters keeping the ear-piece of his radio dry.

"X-O Captain Peters requests the High Fliers," he called and searched up into the heavens for vapour trails, chalked and fading into the sky, highlighting the presence of mammoth bombers on standby.

"Er," the radio replied, some kid aged seventeen, a shaking high-pitched male voice, "G-two says they've been pulled out, Captain."

"... Put him on then!"

In the seven seconds between switching over to G2, Peters spied the green dome helmets of the Indonesian army crawling along the fractured road barriers at the northern approaches to the bridge. If they kept their momentum they could cross the bridge in less than ten minutes. He fired a three-shot volley at an excited scout who then scuttled away. Peters scanned other approaches, fired warning shots, but what use, he wondered. Seven popped their heads out from behind railings and beams reconnoitring a path across the warped bridge. Sweat dripped from under his dented helmet and flak jacket, the thick ceramic plates of which where thumped into his chest cracking two ribs as he took a shot and was slammed backwards, his helmet flying up into the air, landing downward in the water, floating along. Winded, he bobbed in the wild flowing waters and drifted like a piece of flotsam, over the crumbled road of the slanted bridge and rolled against a submerged railing. He squirmed between the iron lattice and hence off the bridge and into the river, sinking, yet his hand reaching up and out like a periscope, steadily holding the ear-piece coiled around his thumb. When he eventually surfaced and rolled onto his back, as if dead, he spied the Indon soldiers storming his bridge, their guns firing forward into Australian soldiers, many of whom were without ammunition. He placed the ear-piece into his ear and found the microphone drifting by his collar. He blew the water out of it, groaned at the grip of pain on his left side, his eyes fixated to the silhouette of the crumpled and majestic metal frame of the bridge set against the thin smoke drifting between the pock-marked high-rises in the centre of the shot up city.

"G2!" he whispered. The water lapping against his body, the weight of his fractured flak jacket sagged him down.

The kid came back, "Captain!"

"Call in the strike: Story Bridge."

"Say again, over."

"Call in the fucking bombers on the fucking Story Bridge now!"

"Right,"

"Blow it now!"

The poor kid, somewhere south in a bunker and watching the war unfold on a computer screen twisted around to G2, who spoke briefly to an Air Marshal, who placed a call to Tactical Air Wing, who explained they'd already despatched the only FA-18 with half a tank of precious aviation gas and even more valuable, a trio of 250kg bombs. All the while Peters was swept by the river out to sea, the bridge sinking from sight. On the northern side he could see Indonesian reserve units prepare to cross. He wondered if it would be better to be washed up on the northern bank and captured, or washed up on the southern bank to recuperate for a few hours then fight the retreat again, or just to float out to the peaceful blue sea. Then time stopped. The ripples on the river flattened and the sky was white from end to end. A thunderous cry. The bridge disappeared, as something from the clouds obliterated it, punching its middle V section safely from the fixed spans into the muddy bottom. The demolition threw up an ugly spray of hot metal fragments over a kilometre radius. Twisted iron beams and rivets showered out so Peters submerged, wriggled from his flak jacket and lay in an under-current, praying the barrage of metal would not find him; praying that after it had ended and he opened his eyes the sun would illuminate the path up to the surface and the moment he breathed, some sharp eyed conscript from a foreign country with a cloned telescopic sight would not take great fancy to his pinkish face, bluish lips, wet haired head, gasping like a shrieking ghost for air. As his legs panicked and thrashed, his eyes rolled open to an air-conditioned atmosphere rank with his own perspiration. He gasped and wiped the sweat from his forehead.

"Callaghan," he murmured, "What's the time?"

No reply.

He lay on a steel bunk bed with a flattened pillow folded under his neck, his head tipped back, his eyes scanning the dull metallic ceiling above. He had not seen the bridge since, since what, he wondered. The recurring dream born from over a year ago? He breathed slowly, patiently, in, out, his long slender fingers tracing loose loops over the dashes of scar tissue on his forearm, stomach, ribs, including a nip above the knee. He finally felt to his face and the inch long welt crossing down and into the shadow cast under his high cheek bones. The touch of each wound reminded him instantly of a former age of recklessness that won him survival and thus escape that enabled him to now utilise all the hard-won learning for his eventual return. For revenge? he cajoled, bitter and sweet? His eyes squinted closed and for the first time in his life he felt truly scared, yet unable to fight the fear, he embraced it, for on this new morning he understood the eminent reality of what was prescribed to not only himself but a hundred other souls. He extended his arm to the ceiling and without feeling the cool metal eerily sensed the cold depths out there in the universe where we roam once we are, well, he shrugged, spat out and retired from this tired old world. Spiritually he had already left the world and the terror that binds it. What more could it throw at him? A conniving smile formed on his normally stern face, his body was revitalised with a new vigour that shone from his crystallised blue eyes to his finger tips; he was ready to die, again. His was the business of death.

He swung off the bunk and saw the bed below was empty and messy. His second in command, the cocky Captain Callaghan, would be in the mess hall. With mechanical precision his palms flattened his combat uniform, opened the cabin hatch, and he moved smartly down the gangway. By the way the naval crew stepped out of his way or performed a casual salute, pushing under their breaths with a tinge of honour the welcoming words, "Morning Colonel Peters", Peters felt all the more lighter yet stronger, like a well crafted steel. When he looked into their eyes he was confirmed that they saw his acceptance that they may never see him again, in fact the entire crew on this frigate discerned in a uniformly accelerated notion that Colonel Peters and his Task Force Seven may never be seen again, for they were, and there was no other way to describe it in communiqués or gossip but to stress the truth, one-hundred and one men were to sink into the void, the murky anarchy and wilderness of Occupied Australia.

Colonel Peters made his way into the mess hall, reassuring each man he locked eyes with that the new day would run to plan. He was well known, admired and cheered by his men. He ate at a separate table with his lieutenants and second in command. Earlier that night Peters had stood tall and mighty, delivering a going-over-the-top speech to his soldiers. They're geared up for it and he knows when it comes to hitting that beach the first ten seconds decides your life; the next fifteen minutes decides the battle; then the rest of the day is yours. But maybe it's completely empty, the local defenders are diseased, or hiding in the bush, or dead and buried by a nameless epidemic.

At the table sat Doc Nelson, Lieutenants Weller, Jenkins, McCallister and Captain Callaghan. All except the latter had seen true action. By the directness in their mannerisms and the coarseness of their eyes, Peters knew they were sturdy, hardened and reliable.

Doc Nelson didn't eat fast. Medical school interrupted by frontline postings had cut all notions of a promised professional occupation and subsequent lifestyle in half. He was forever caught in the act of learning without ever graduating or feeling comfortable in what he was doing. His nervous eyes shifted timorously sideward to Captain Callaghan, an inappropriate second in command.

Peters planted his elbow on the table, drew his hand to muffle a cough and covered his mouth, remaining in this manner studying the newcomer who spoke candidly to whoever at the table was listening.

Callaghan, oblivious to the sting of combat, and with hours to go, was rolling out a lame joke: "So this guy, he's sitting there, and his wife comes in and says, 'Honey, do you think I'd look better with bigger breasts?'" Callaghan belly laughed like he'd been there before, knowingly under the steady watchful eye of all at the table even as the frigate listed a few degrees. "And he says, 'You know, it really doesn't matter – they're fine' and then the wife rolls her eyes doll-like and the guy thinks *oh fuck* and says 'You don't need surgery' and she rolls her eyes again – it's all become some big drama now – and he says 'Listen, I've got an idea. Twice a day, rub toilet paper between your breasts, up and down, and that will make them bigger'. The wife stares at him – you know," and Callaghan had the table enthralled though they hardly showed it, "She's not believing but she's clutching at straw and she says, 'O-K'. A week later she says to her hubby, 'It's not working!' and he says 'Give it another go!' and she gives it another go... Now a *month* later they're having dinner at some fancy joint and she slams her fist on the table. 'Right, twice every day, I've been rubbing toilet paper between my breasts and nothing's happened! They're not even a millimetre bigger!' so the guys nods, sizes her up, and says, 'Well it worked on your arse!'"

They laughed. Peters surprised himself that he was slyly snickering. Callaghan appeared content with his tale and either unaware or extremely aware of the shifting moods of men before battle, in total hiding some greater thought than that of the approaching carnage he would be thrown into. Apart from his aptitude to humour he was the one element of Task Force Seven that Peters was not impressed by, yet on the decree of a higher order had to accept the man as a professional, though in no way an equal. He was personally chosen, like Peters, but obviously vengefully dumped by a higher brass as the appropriate man for the job. It wasn't a glitch in the database that sent Callaghan here. Must have been a serious bug under a General's skin. Callaghan was as experienced as killing as a virgin to fucking, but that's not to say the virgin in Callaghan hadn't been interested in drawing blood.

"You're a funny one," Peters wryly added.

"Being funny is just a bag of luck, I say." Callaghan assured all, reached out and drew his mug of tea to his chest and swirled the tea leaves for the entertainment of his stagnant eyes.

In the first year of the war Callaghan was one of the last able-bodied men not to be persuaded to join up. Then the government systematically conscripted the worst case pacifists into cannon-fodder to join the expendable baby-boomer battalions on a miserable frontline in the deserts facing thousands of maniac staving Indonesians. It was more mortar pits launching gas canisters than guns and trenches but just as dangerous. "The hell with it, we're all in it now. One big croc-hunting family," he admitted disdainfully to his transient peace-loving girlfriend. She did not move from the window in their lavish apartment overlooking the rich, deep, green glow of Elizabeth Bay in mid-afternoon. The glare of the sun through lace curtains glowed behind her. Her sudden blinking appeared slow. She was resolute he would not come back like so many before and to be. She had seen him minutes before in her arms on their bed and that's what she wanted to remember; the happy James Callaghan with the wondrous smile, the bold innocent eyes and his long arms hugging her like a warm juicy vine. Before departing for Canberra he lunged at her and kissed her madly then forcing her off himself, exhaustingly begged, "Sweety, I'll be back because I am not going anywhere where there's *bullets*. Quote me on that." Yet her stare was strictly out the window, she half-nodded, only proving her disbelief. He was as good as dead. That's how it goes. *Fuck it*, he grunted, which was as much a cry as *fuck you* and ran out the door.

His nature was actually far from pacifist, in contrast, the eternal optimist, which in order to survive and flourish, involved conflict, but not murder, killing and all that. He bribed his way into Officer Training then bedded a widowed bureaucrat to secure a plush tactical operations position in Canberra. There he sat out most of his war building a mystique of technical importance based on the software at his fingertips. From minuscule cameras imbedded in weapons and drones he had seen missiles strike capitals and troop ships, he watched with fascination the ghastly satellite images of cities and ports eaten by fire-storms. This wealth of vision and information did not grip Callaghan with fear of the world, for yes it was an awful place, but someday it would all end. He saw the means to which the people of the world would go to achieve their lasting peace, and though many were failing with silly attempts at mass destruction, those that succeeded did so with minimal effort and expenditure, married with a clinical precision in timing. From the safety of the Australian Defence Headquarters nuclear-proof bunkers he imagined himself dictating campaigns of terror, assassinations, mass troop movements, and even salvation of civilians in besieged towns. He saw the worst of this dirty war yet the dirtiest his hands had been were when he shifted the greasy lever on his ergonomic chair or slid his fingers up the dress of any willing lass. But, man can delude and sidetrack himself as long as he likes until his true calling comes knocking: The higher order of the institution he wormed so well into did take notice of him, weighed up the merits and debits, and abruptly rejected him, not with a demotion or promotion to a dead-end role, for his worming warranted something distinctive, and in this day and age, something rewarding of his previous exploits. It was at 10:37AM, a Thursday, pay day, pacing from a potential squeeze in Urban Resources to a fellow-opportunist mate in Pacific Strategy on the seventh underground level below Parliament House when two Australian Secret Intelligent Organisation heavies coming from the other way convivially smiled then yanked Callaghan by the collar into an adjoining hallway, down another hallway, into an elevator, out, around, left, right, and into an interrogation room. They had little time for his staged, abhorrent, muddled fright.

"What's this fellas?" Callaghan squealed, sizing up and recognising the two suited bastards, one tall and one short. He could tell by their leans and overbearing prances that they were a well practised duo with broad slanted shoulders, the offset thanks to a limping artificial leg each, probably veterans of the same landmine or drink-driving accident. He could tell by one look that they saw through his professional mirage of competence, his "profound efficiency at interpreting satellite communications" and all that whiz-bang stuff that had nothing to do with what the system had marked him for.

ASIO shorty grunted in a terrifically perfected, throat-curdling, horrifying tone, "You're leaching days are over: You're now working up *north*."

"North?" Callaghan sighed as if *they* should know there were no postings up north that *he* knew about. He always imagined the dreaded Australian Secret Intelligent Organisation hallway attackers were a public service myth to keep the government employees eternally fearful about base security, privileges with free coffee and dedication to their respective departments, but no, they existed for a more sinister reason – disposal.

"We've got nothing going up *north* beyond Brisbane – and I'd be in the know! We've lost it completely!"

"Not so Romeo, *you* lived there up until you were eighteen. Your type lost it and now *you're getting it back!*" ASIO shorty continued, scripted and punctuated with rasping breaths, all the spine chilling elements of a man who takes his cue from obscure gangster movies.

"You've got to be joking mate! I'm not the combat type."

ASIO shorty shrugged, non-committal. "We know that, *Sunshine*."

"You mean Queensland don't you… It's fucking banana country full of savages! Have you heard the shit going on up there? Fucking Jesus *Christ* wouldn't go up there and heal the blind! What can I possibly do up there, in the service of the country, huh?"

The taller ASIO man leered, his eyes like drill bits screwing with Callaghan's head, "It can't be as savage as staying here: You think your D-N-A is better then the rest of us? You think your sperms have got *promise* up all those loose cunts you make habit of?"

"C'mon, I was fooling around! Really! I do it partly so guys like you can live your lives through guys like me, O-K?" Callaghan grinned smittenly but it wasn't reciprocated. He tried scratching his head in some sorry contemplation but his hands were bound too tight. "I see," his voice lowered, "North. Where? Amberley? So who requested my skills up there?"

ASIO shorty hastily assured Callaghan, "Not one person in particular."

"Right."

"Let's just say you've been granted that request for a transfer… A bit of a holiday in *Queensland*," tall ASIO enthusiastically added, "You'll remember it if you think hard enough,"

"I requested it?"

They thumped him playfully but nearing vital organs.

"O-K, fuck it! What's the drill!"

"Some *Top* Secret Mission and yes, we're living our lives through the likes of you! Hilarious! These postings come up once in a lifetime! Your friends upstairs must love you a hell of a lot," ASIO shorty congratulated his prey, "Fine, fit men are hard to come by these days."

"Rare as hen's teeth," ASIO tally seethed.

Shorty sneered into Callaghan, "And their virility and cunning can be used in *many* ways against our friendly tenants to the north."

"Oh you mean *that!*" Callaghan shrieked. "But I'm no good at that sort of shit. You've got the wrong guy, I'd, I'd be a liability! I'm weak! Get some Commandos! They do that! I know what you're getting to – don't bullshit me – I'll come back you know, and I'll come back and send *you* up to check it out!"

ASIO shorty paced up, one long leg clicking on the floor, the other dragging lamely behind, his stubby manicured hands held Callaghan's head to face the dark light of reality, "You don't understand... Who says they want you back? You got no fucking idea what you're doing up there. You're heading up there to stay *and* with a promotion *Captain* Callaghan."

ASIO tally grunted, "Didn't have to fuck your way up for this one, *shithead!*"

Callaghan felt the ugly sting of karma. "So, I got a one-way ticket to fucking anarchy-world? But who'll take my place down below?"

"Face it Callaghan they need *you* in the field," ASIO shorty bellowed, eerily pointing his index finger right between Callaghan's beady eyes, his other hand harshly thumping his artificial leg, "You too can be a hero! Think of it as *redemption.*"

"Redemption," Callaghan moaned flatly. He imagined himself collapsing forward into a foetal mess on the floor.

ASIO tally echoed the sentiment of the moment with a twist of brittle compassion, "Sometimes great things are called of *little* men. You're the Man."

"Jesus. I'm the man now? This peer pressure crap," Callaghan retorted, "I'm a pussy! C'mon, you guys are tough. You go! You guys are the stressed out fuckers – You take the holiday! What the hell is this about!"

They slapped him about some more and threw him in the belly of a Hercules destined for Sydney. Task Force Seven had its Admin & Communication and Second-in-Command. He could forgive the bitter sweetness of becoming a team-player in a military pyramid, he'd just have to work harder at the game. Logic assumed he'd over done it with a prominent lass *again*, and she got temperamental, guilty (only a matter of time before they do), betrayed their lust to a higher order, aka her other-brass-half, and that's how he was magically transferred. Once he accepted fate that someone wanted him to die he took on the position quite cheerfully; he was getting lethargic in his role anyway and now was perhaps the time to crawl out of the cement caves. Two million plus Australians were six feet under and the Indonesian army was, from what he could discern of the mountains of data he absorbed in his stint, spent and not going much farther. There were un-explained issues, but, scratching his head over it and with little room to manoeuvre, this just might be it: *Life.* He'd eluded the frontline so far and bar the fact they were going deep behind enemy lines in a vulnerable and covert operation it could be a bit of a trip. The tropics. Get some good sun on his pale skin. Imagine lazing on a beach when there's Rest & Recreation! Transmit the logistic and tactical info to the intelligence experts and let the reinforcements carry on the hard slug. When the military objective turned into a political subject he'd be there playing spy-boy. In the mess that was rolling his way, he would adapt, make it a blessing in disguise.

Peters brooded over his men cleaning the last scraps of breakfast off their plates. With the majority of the men fed and returning to their appropriate berths in the guts of the ship to strap on their packs and say their prayers, the mess hall was left strangely empty.

Doc Nelson, Lieutenants Weller, Jenkins, McCallister and Callaghan instinctively remained at the table with Peters, each man nursing his coffee or tea, awaiting some final word or detail to finalise the landing at dawn. Colonel Peters, running his eyes over the laminated map of the coastal town of Providence before them, absent-mindedly drummed his fingers on the table.

"No change in the weather," Callaghan announced to break the strain of anxiousness, "Same old sunshine."

Peters tapped at the stretch of golden sanded beach on which the town of Providence sprawled and pushed against, "With the amphibious landing craft arriving at sunrise and the helicopter drop-off points," his fingers then plotted two points inland from Providence from where he and two platoons would converge into the centre from, "We can easily simultaneously penetrate Providence and secure it."

Callaghan sat smugly in his chair acknowledging the plan. Too easy.

"Word is that the frigate's Captain, Mackenzie," Peters nodded his head to the bridge of the ship above them, "Is under considerable pressure to leave the area A-S-A-P. He's trusty but testy."

"Is there a new threat?" Callaghan asked, suddenly fearing the frigate in which they travelled could be under threat *now*.

"It's unpredictable up here," Peters squared up Callaghan, "But what it means is you and Doctor Nelson will be landing on the beach with Jenkins's first platoon in one go."

"Can we all make it in one go?"

"You'll have to squeeze in," Peters told the two concerned. "It'll be a rough ride ashore but it gets us ashore in one hit, then the navy can be on their merry way."

Callaghan immediately felt dread strangling like a vine from his frontal lobe through his gut to his seedling sized balls. His *virility* had now cornered him into a beach assault on an enemy-held-town on the middle of the Queensland coast, a thousand kilometres from the frontline, a town no one knew much about. Still, it could be worse.

"Intelligence update?" Wilson asked.

Peters tucked one hand under his armpit, the fingers of the other rubbing the jut of his chin. "Usual chit-chat; a few armed refugees. The small garrison in Kingston, the port to the north, are over an hour away. We'll handle them next. Ambush. We can only see how it all pans out." Peters stared off to some distant point, his face partially aghast and frozen, either processing eventualities or missing his mind. "It's been awhile since a real force was in there."

Callaghan noisily placed his mug on the map, "Can I ask a simple question?"

Peters flickered his eyes at the landing points on the map. "Shoot."

"The strategic significance of Providence – I know it was a resort town pre-war and it's still intact – but now it's practically the same except a warlord has been known to lay-up there."

Peters's eyes zeroed with renewed interest to the map; the thin lines of streets, a loose distorted grid centred on an intersection with roads running west to the Great Dividing Range, south to Brisbane and the frontline, north to the Cape, and east, a few hundred metres, to the beach, where the amphibious landing is set for an hour from now.

"We don't know exactly where, do we?"

"*If* there is, he is our target. We're controlling the region."

"So I gather," Callaghan continued, "That the enemy is the warlord and militia, and remaining conscripts…"

"Anyone that points a gun at us, yes."

"And those that don't?"

"We disarm them."

Weller, Jenkins and McCallister were equally interested.

"Peacekeeping?"

Peters's intentional silence drew out Callaghan's inquisitiveness.

"O-K, peacekeeping was a joke… It'll be a pushover."

"Well, don't hold back."

"Fine, I won't: The port of Kingston to the north – that's a strategic target and could easily be bombed – like Providence – I'm surprised they weren't raised to the ground when we retreated,"

"When we retreated through there," Peters reminded the table, "We had no time."

"Yes, time…" Callaghan mused on the concept of time and distance and focused on the map, this isolated town. "And the resident warlord? He's hardly a military force. He trades from the west through his port to the north and he keeps the borders tight and all I'm saying is that he is an enemy, he is an invader, but there are thousands of men and women living there now, and what are they?"

"What are you saying?"

"I'm asking in a broad sense what do we do with these people – our Liberation – once we've taken out any armed resistance – what next?"

Even before he could answer, from Callaghan came a suggestion derived from fact.

"I mean genocide, Colonel. Warlords use genocide to control the population up here; they all do. Are we going to hang around to deal with that scenario?"

"At this stage, I don't know."

Weller, Jenkins and McCallister sat as if passive, but slyly smirking at their preference to defenceless refugees rather than gun-toting militia. Callaghan looked up to the ceiling and the white glow of lights then to the mess hall: Now his virility has bundled him with barbarians! His skin crawled. All signs pointed to hell.

High on the frigate's bridge peering into computer monitors, Colonel Smacker stood out as a pesky and contagiously nervous figure under the feint red lighting. Navy crew sat at their posts, checking sonar, scans, satellite photos, intelligence reports, and radio broadcasts. They were engrossed in surveillance and paid him no attention.

He mused to the frigate's Captain, Mackenzie. "Do your people like this Special Operations stuff?"

Mackenzie stroked his greying beard and spoke with an old-world flavour, "Just another day."

Smacker stiffened. "These things seem piecemeal, but they're worth it. We're safe off the coast, I can assure you of that."

"That, you never know." Mackenzie advised in a deadpan voice, soft as the rumbling of the ancient undertows where many of his sea-faring forefathers lay. He stepped closer to the impatient guest that he had only recently succumbed to accept on the bridge. "And in Providence? What assurances can you vouch for there?"

Smacker flicked through windows on a computer screen, his narration disjointed to the images displayed; outdated aerial photos and reports. "Indon Army up here isn't organised at all... Population: Refugees. Starved mongrels. Some warlord having it over them. Low-key zone, really." Smacker's hands minutely trembled but were splayed in a congratulatory form, "We need some offensive, and this is it." He then painfully rolled his eyes down to the inner of the ship as if digesting a brick. "Task Force Seven don't look much but they're a litmus test... If things go well, after this operation we could launch a campaign and the coast could quite easily come back. Liberation!"

"And re-enforcement units?"

There were no other naval ships on radar for over five-hundred kilometres. Back-up was essential for any assault. Off the coast of Queensland where few frigates had reason to patrol alone, Mackenzie suckered down on his upper lip and intuitively lapsed into military thinking. He was another cog in the fleet. They greased him with a low-key East Coast command, the odd tough job, heroic commendations for his command and sailors. Everyone was doing their bit and through that productive guise it didn't concern him either that the rest of the Australian Navy was taking positions on the other side of the continent for a larger assault. The Pacific, named for its supposedly pacifying waters, suited Mackenzie for this chapter of the war. He knew to take the cargo Task Force Seven this far up the coast and launch an assault by air and sea and sail back to Garden Island in one piece. After his helicopters have landed minus their cargo of men, and as the last foot hits the beach, his vessel is free. This is his reality. Smacker had not answered.

"You can keep all you want classified but I still need to know, or I'll find out later – so what's the point."

"Highly Classified." Smacked echoed, at pains with the word's binding blindness.

"My only inadequate quality is a conscience – remember that."

"Captain Mackenzie," Smacker lamented, "This is a joint exercise of extreme importance... Don't go biting your golden hearted bunny yet." He swiftly leaned into Mackenzie's ear, whispering in the relieved tone of a fellow conspirator, "This is nothing more than a *diversion*."

Mackenzie quietly leant back. "Obviously...Wasn't hard for me to figure but do they know?"

"Would you tally-ho into there if you knew?"

With a tight nod out to sea, the invisible inky shore, Mackenzie understood, "And what happens to them when we're gone?"

Smacker shrugged. "Ask the volunteers, Captain. They all jumped at the chance to go in. We screened them too," he rubbed his hands together, "All crazy: certified burnt-outs, suffering P-S-D, a few criminals, you name it, they got it. Wouldn't want them on civvy-street, if there ever will be a civvy street."

The damned: Mackenzie sickly smiled, because not only were millions of naïve refugees sailing to their deaths in Australia, now the whites were too, plugging that gaping black hole and here he was, on the bridge of a ship of war, at the event horizon, amused.

"And how do I phrase this in a report?" he asked callously, more for annoyance.

Smacker grinned, "There's nothing to say beyond the simple fact – Task Force Seven is landing at Providence. They're technically migrating there. How does that sound?"

Mackenzie made no sound. He listened to his crew as they listened to the digital traffic on the airwaves and the sounds of the sea, their vigil, their participation, their methodical calm awaiting and pre-empting the next contact between two worlds: the West and the Rest. What would it be, he wondered? How would it unfold? At what point should he flee? There were degrees of destruction that still made him shiver, and up here, there were rumours and ideas he had never had to verify or understand, that made him shiver even more.

At the same time, in Providence, the local warlord, General Sumatra, pondered if the *Asia-Pacific War Zone* would carry a story about him, titled *Dynamics of a Warlord*. It was all up there in his head, day and night, evolving into a juicy epic, week by week, the mess that fate had dealt him becoming easier to explain. He could make it poignant and touching, the tale of his fortunate life and this little region, into something worthy of erecting statues too, and maybe even a flagpole at the United Nations.

After evacuation of the remaining mortified population of stubborn elderly, die-hard hippies, partially-disabled, welfare recipients and few remaining demented tourism operators in face of an unstoppable invading army, Providence became a ghost town. Usually quaint seaside towns were torched by a low flying F-111 fighter bomber's afterburner yet Providence remained intact because it was of very little significance. After the Indonesian Army had painstakingly fought to expunge Australian defenders from the coast the resettlement of Providence and surrounding regions fell to a truly creative, optimistic, entrepreneurial and ruthless individual. The assets of this character are what makes men and women, through strength and ingenuity, forge history into their statement of affairs rather then read, write, or reflect on it from the vantage of idealistic youth or the hindsight of one's twilight years.

General Sumatra's upbringing was the customary rags to riches journey; slum birth, factory boyhood, teenage solider rises to officer status and sits there for decades, and under the looming clouds of geopolitical meltdown in the Pacific, a quiet promotion in a well bribed institution.

He did see the trouble coming, couldn't identify the outcome (who could?) and was content to let it roll on. Worthy history *is* chaos. The shift didn't appear as some said with this attack or that, it grew quite naturally and it was the fault of none. There were food shortages, too many mouths and too many large families, limited land, a spluttering environment, so the poor peasants and workers were upset. The rich were slaves to cheap labour's leverage over the global market, and the political elite inhabited an international scene, believing their place of privilege would never end, and if it did, there was always a First Class Ticket to somewhere else. The religious folk (Sumatra's pet hate) demanded a type of neat moral change that echoed sulking in the dark ages. Democracy, 'the experimentation' as the intellectuals scoffed, was a fad and for the poor and religious mugs, the feudal system had never vanished, it had only been expanded, re-branded, and was as much a rip-off as it ever was. And that's when it started. Riots. There was no one supreme force, it was not a binding and blinding ideology or a better god, but some poked their fingers at technology. Then came the cyclones that shredded paddy fields, the droughts in India (they had sucked dry their water table and were plunging nuclear heaters into the Himalayas) and criminals rising to power elsewhere. Next, the maddened and angered people began the great shift. They were escaping collapse of societies, and in the fear the rumours flourished, the finest finding agreement, and that cemented vision and imagination into direction, and for millions, their compasses pointed south. At the same time, Sumatra knew to bribe his way up and let his colleagues get on with over-throwing their impotent government.

He never liked Australia. A desert. Droughts. An Anglo population. Arrogant. But the refugees didn't mind. They crawled out of their huts and cement towers, bought the flimsiest of boats or paid all that they had to ever so eager fisherman, and formed a steady trickle south. The Australians were prepared yet outnumbered, and after weeks of playing kind and hoping for a diplomatic solution to a non-diplomatic situation, there was nothing stopping the deluded refugees. Overnight single junks turned into flotillas and the families turned to tribes. They were barred here and there but hope still pointed to the most open of coastlines - Northern Australia. In the beginning the whites put up a gentlemanly show, part humanitarian aid and camps, part military cordons and control, and with a judgemental world watching they couldn't exactly sort out the problem as they'd liked to. Then came Indonesian civilians pillaging what they could under the guise of refugees, setting up camps, escaping as much as anyone else and creating a new existence, and when they really were starving, struggling against the wilderness and shot at by Australians, what was the Indonesian Army to but make it legitimate? A government should be the arm of the people, and the legs.

The invasion was planned in a grand style; the covert infiltration into Australia was shielded by a very public display of politics; appeasement, denial and accusation, soaking the world's attention, leading to a blitz, and the mandatory use of refugees as a cover and buffer for all things strategically important. In reality it was very un-organised, but it went ahead, sloppy as hell, catching the under-resourced and over-whelmed enemy un-prepared, proving that chaos and luck can outwit western methodology, power and technology. All the while, Sumatra played his hand with an impeccable, cool style. When the first surge over was purged and things looked settled and less of a slaughterhouse, he made another bribe. Getting to Australia nearly cost him his life twice, which could have been an omen, but by then, the machine was in motion. Everyone wanted a tiny bit of the action but a fat slice of the great southern pie.

When the great moment came for conquest, for there is no other way to describe what ardent adventurers believe when they set forth, General Sumatra led two thousand conscripted soldiers from Darwin down the highway towards Alice Springs, and short of that destination radically east across the barren red deserts to Mt Isa. Here General Sumatra saw the new tycoons rising from regenerating the sabotaged mines and how a stately fortune is amassed in times of conflict. Refugee labour was cheap, and with them were many educated types. And, having risen from a gutter, the accumulation of wealth was never far from his mind. But orders are orders and conquest is movement.

He led his two-thousand men east towards Cairns. It was on this stretch from scorching desert to drenched tropical mountain peaks that their numbers were eroded by random bombardment from high-flying bombers, sniper attacks from Aboriginal guerrillas, and the treachery of deserters sneaking off into the night never to be seen again. There was no reprieve in their destination of Cairns; the foliage thicker and greener, water clearer, and the diseases of a snow-balling population of refugees, soldiers and prostitutes so festering that after some rudimentary celebration for coming so far, Sumatra quickly pulled his unit south, ahead of his Division's schedule. Happily back on the road and by the sea, their feet accustomed to long marches and their arses used to long rides in trucks, Sumatra tallied the losses and gasped at the remainder: One thousand and five hundred men. He decided that this land, and even though he had only seen Indonesian Occupied Australia, was deceivingly beautiful to camouflage its harsh and rugged nature. He was devout that what force he had left he should not deviate from their objective and hence quickened the pace down the humid Queensland coast towards the frontline. The distant sounds of heavy artillery shifted south as they marched forward to chase it. Then their lean legs suddenly faltered, reverberating with the sound of roadside explosions and machine-gun fire rolling over the sugarcane fields. It was on. Nothing set-piece and classical, more insurgent, like the Dutch ditched effort to hold Indonesia. Still, there were ripe banana plantations on the hills, even though the sound of war was carried by a pleasing tropical breeze. His superiors, praising his fervour to chase the battle, found favour in their General, in fact they found favour in their hundreds of Generals commanding at that time, about six hundred thousand soldiers on Australian soil.

Sumatra's men comprehended that they were on the crest of the wave of their nation's advancement the day they came face to face with those wearily returning from the frontline. The latter were the wounded, hobbling north, tight-lipped about the 'mince-maker'. A few stared to the new-comers, mouths pursed into *Ohhs*, miming words of wisdom that could only be understood when one faced the perils that had scarred them so. This worried Sumatra. Sometimes an entire battalion would retire from the front, carrying each other, men dying on the roads, and his men would drag them into the fields for a hasty burial under some craggy foreign tree, home to laughing birds that fluffed their feathers with delight.

What General Sumatra and his men found most disheartening was the sight of a panoramic natural paradise torched of its previous

Western identity and the charred frames were all that remained of once accommodating houses on freshly paved streets. This land of conquest was eerily abandoned. Many soldiers had embarked on this journey to find their house, to bring their family out, but now that all they saw was ruin, their attitudes changed to an immediate and attainable objective to thrust their covetous vehemence at. The lure of the frontline tugged at many a man's heart for surviving en-route to battle was a journey within itself and as a bonus, survival and the ultimate clash, was a holy invitation to triumphantly face the enemy and hunt him down and overrun him and find his promised lands and houses in their pristine state and capture them intact. Then their turn came.

On a sunny morning, on the two lane Highway Five that runs past Providence, General Sumatra advanced his remaining one thousand and three-hundred men into a funnel-trap set by a steadfast Australian Army Rearguard Platoon made up of young vicious women. As the ambush revealed itself Sumatra followed doctrine and issued the appropriate orders to physically attack the enemy positions in a sparing and teasing manner, so that in time the beleaguered defenders would expend their supply of munitions. Then General Sumatra would order his attack, circle them, capture a few, and claim a victory. However, as his first major battle unfolded the bulk of his eager force condensed into terribly excited blocks and ignoring his master strategy, honed in on the enemy dug-in on either side of the highway, rapidly charging straight into the strategic loop of machine-gun nests, some of which were already failing, the defenders apparently either out of bullets, wounded, dying or clearly running, screaming like beleaguered sirens and for a moment General Sumatra saw victory amid failure of order. With the tempo and taste of conquest before them, and assuming the defenders spent so easily, General Sumatra's uncontrollable unit launched themselves en-masse at the un-womaned positions.

For a few minutes it was before him, a routing out of the military textbook, history to be written without complication, Sumatra's men on the precipice staring at the gems and rewards of success, until five Australian helicopters fitted with MetalStorm one-hundred-rounds-a-second 20mm cannons and laden with a tonne of ammunition fresh off the boat from South Africa, ascended from behind surrounding low lying hills and combined their firepower with the dug-in machine-guns, now dutifully back to life again. In under a half-hour, half of General Sumatra's men were struck off the list of the living, many where they sought cover. In an act of ultra-efficiency his superiors disbanded his unit by midday. How could he be a tactical force? Yes they had reached the frontline and in a bloody effort moved it a few hundred metres in twenty-seven minutes, but now only two-hundred men remained, tending to five hundred wounded. The next Indonesian battalion to inherit the tempo stepped over the carcasses of their brothers and resumed the battle. The Australians booby-trapped their machine-gun emplacements and ran south to mastermind the next trap. The next unit to spearhead the mighty Indonesian Army triumphantly marched south down Highway Five leaving Sumatra and his sorry bunch by the road huddling in shock and awe, awakening to a very uncertain future.

But General Sumatra wanted none of that. If this was war, then it was over for him. He led his vanquished men in a straggling column east to the sea in hope of finding food, water, perhaps a stream to capture fish from. Something simple. Instead he found Providence. It was a gem, an intact and abandoned seaside town untouched by a low-flying F-111's afterburners.

With time to ponder the horrors of death and the futility of war he dipped his toes into the caressing low waves on the golden beaches and sniffed the Pacific sea air, marvelling at how Alexander the Great must have felt upon conquering the known world. In conclusion there was little comparison. Alexander was hungry for more whereas Sumatra had conquered as much as he had ever wanted. General Sumatra thus assumed responsibility for the region. Then the Indonesian High Command gave him their blessings, for he had bribed them well. Regional Commander Sumatra converted the town bank into his Military Headquarters for Providence. As part of the war-effort he would oversee the trade of local produce, and uphold the law, and much more. Some troops, and others drifting back from the frontline nursing the stumps of their missing limbs, lay down their rusting weapons to plough the liberated fields. They were the first settlers.

As word spread through Asia of conquered lands all along the Queensland Coast ripe for farming, the hungry mouths in the millions of slums grumbled with a maddening envy. Refugees of all sorts from the furthermost reaches bought their passage and flooded south through Cape York to grab the last free-land in the world. The rapid population explosion had not been expected by the Indonesian High Command, the magnitude of such never seen before in the history of planet earth. Divisional Regional Commanders in captured Australian territories found themselves increasingly isolated by their weakening High Command and inundated by a mass of diverse, demanding, brain-washed and hungry refugees. Hence, in a flurry of geopolitical risk-management the High Command acknowledged that their own generals were warlords, and the only means to control the numerous regions on their maps.

Warlord Sumatra found himself in an opportunistic position. He was technically in the middle of the Queensland Coast with exotic and primary industry bounty in all directions. He set about to make himself a king not for greed, fame, or the spoils of this costly war. More so, blatantly, because he could and being in the position, right that he should. His paradise was a thousand kilometres from the static frontline extending from Brisbane to Adelaide. Far away in the region of Providence he was a new man with a new home. His sea-faring navigators plotted routes through the Great Barrier Reef. Engineers and surveyors cleared roads and rail lines to coal mines and wheat fields to the west. Farmers reaped a succulent harvest from sugar fields. He exported produce to the starving of South-East Asia and imported weapons to defend his lands. He employed healthy minded refugees as farmers, militia, road-makers, nurses, teachers, and bureaucrats. His development of infrastructure grew with the influx of reliable merchants. His region stretched two hundred kilometres south and north, five-hundred kilometres west. He had regular sea-merchants to his port town Kingston to the north, a radio station, a postal system. By importing expensive radio equipment and training his regional militia his kingdom became a network of intelligence and thus strength. In a year he had re-ignited a civilisation. If only his childhood friends from the slum (especially those who inflicted cruelty on him) could see him now. Yet, of the influx of population and his position, he was surprised that even his mother would not live here in her son's kingdom. But that was, given the larger picture, a minor issue.

Casting milestones of success aside, his persistent cause of migraines were incoming refugees. The initial cause of migraines was related to that horrific morning when of all things, one of his own mortar shells fell short and knocked him flat to the ground. For most of the failed attack he lay listening to the helicopters and their *whirring* machine-guns mowing down his men and the puncturing of their soft little bodies or *tacking* of their helmets. When his vision came back he sat up and where he last saw over a thousand men triumphantly poised to demolish the imperialistic Australians, he found a Valley of Death. Over a few hundred scrawny metres a thousand men bled to fertilise the weakest of soils. They flocked to heaven in one giant band of pearlish Angels, and remembering their translucent wings flapping against the sky, he understood their Death to be his new Birth. And now, with his feet firmly on the ground, or in the sand, this was one man that strangely knew too well the exaggerated price and value of human life.

Every week, trudging alone with a monk's guise or in processions by the thousands searching in biblical proportions for the promised land, starved, diseased and miserable refugees demanding *their* share stumbled into his region, sometimes their ranks swelling with the unstoppable roar of a flooded river. He herded the sick, the starving, the doomed and the fanatics like sheep into the palm of his hand – the Providence vice – and when the pits were dug a hundred metres long and three metres wide behind some obscure hill on a serene horizon, in they went bulldozer style after the guns had mowed them down. Of what bureaucracy he had, no account was kept of those unaccepted of Citizenship to his Region. Over twenty-thousand, forty, a million if he tallied the work of his neighbouring warlords in this sunburnt country.

He cringed and rolled in his sleep. His mistresses rolled to the sides of the bed for fear of being crushed under his large bearish frame then slid their hands under the covers like heat-seeking missiles for his warmth.

Every month or two he witnessed the dilemma. He watched his militia toughen themselves against the scared, pale and frozen victims. The captured creatures were utterly helpless and in a final act of defiance shone an intensely holistic glare of anguish to Sumatra and his militia as the weapons discharged and eased the pain. Having travelled thousands of miles, optimistic and brave, vital ingredients for humanity, Sumatra felt saddened of the reward for their trials. He felt saddened for the world. But, he contemplatively sighed, in one alley there can only be one tough cat. And under that cat are only so many cats that can feed off so many bins. And what of humanity, some dared to ask in shrieks before they flopped into the pits. Humanity, he coyly smiled, humoured at the prospect of humanity growing out here as some vibrant flower does in some precious green-house in the lavish perimeter of some kingdom. He would turn away and face the sluggish clouds trekking across the sky, an arrow formation of birds flying the other way, or the crescent of the silvery moon. Note, the guilt does not linger and die, it submerges and disappears to strike again.

"But can I feed them all?" he asked the still and cool night, remembering that some were cannibals, some had to be cannibals, and for all those that came there were un-imaginable terrors driving them here, terrors and evils and miseries that he alone could not fix. But he received them, in his lap, with his finger on the trigger. What bad luck, he huffed, and fell into a brooding silence yet the wind blew hard and he heard the freak rise and fall of a helicopter's blades chopping into the air. He wiped the instantaneous burst of sweat from his forehead and knew he had drifted to that horrific morning and that sound, that beating of the air! The sea of red soaking into the most weakest of soils! What grows there now? Weeds! He awoke. What is a dream.

The younger of his mistresses, Jintana, automatically stoked his chest, her small fingernails lightly clawing at his bare flabby skin, yet her stroke, though pleasing, was powered by necessity to please, not the true love of a woman who operates on amorous instinct.

"It's just a dream... Dreams come and go... What did you dream about? I dreamt," her soft voice fluttered at the image revolving inside her mind, "Catching the butterfly in the garden and chasing, floating over the ponds with the goldfish. There are no walls. Sleep, sleep."

Sumatra rubbed his bloodshot eyes and squinted at the barely visible curves under the sheets in his giant-sized bed. Silence.

"Just a dream..." she whispered, her breath and silken eyelids falling on the satin blue pillow.

Sumatra settled. Jintana and Qiao devotedly cuddled up to him. He softly patted their buttocks, feeling the soft tight skin on his coarse fingertips, the body heat rising into his palms. The two mistresses were the antidote to the rigours of the climate and the title. Yet they were not at his side purely for indulgence or the strict art of prostitution – they came to him for protection. For all their cunning, grace and beauty they were vulnerable creatures. In one sleepy move he glided their hands back, wriggled forward and leapt off his giant bed, landed on one leg and nearly toppled over, draped himself in a flowery cotton shawl from his father's ancestral island and shuffled to the balcony. Four stories down was the moonlit beach and silvery waves washing in then sweeping out to a horizon of jet black. The surf rode low and he sensed a thunderstorm. Farmers need rain like tanks need petrol. He smiled for a brief second to the god that had partially covered the brilliant stars of the heavens with silvery clouds, glowing with the moon's shine.

He lived in the penthouse of Providence's only holiday beach-front unit that was taller than two stories. It was a quality structure built before cheap materials and cheaper business sense ruined the hearts of standard builders. From the fourth floor vantage point he could walk the tiled balcony and study the sea stretching north, east and south out from his kingdom. Facing the cool breeze and soaking the panoramic calm he instinctively thought of a drink to suit the mood; the anaesthetic purity of cheap Bourbon. It had been smuggled out of the U-S of A by Marines, sold in the Philippines for women, and lugged by pirates to his Port Of Kingston. After a quick fix he poured another and settled into a comfortable chair, by an art deco lamp and read the latest issue of *Asia-Pacific War Zone*, a monthly magazine he could trust for an independent view of geopolitics. It was published by the *Black Tide*, a Triad and Yakuza hybrid networked from Singapore that had many interests in the new world opened before them.

He wasn't pleased to read that the U.S. would export another five hundred Tomahawk cruise missiles to Australia. The round-eyes could knock out his little penthouse with the push of a button. Obviously one day he would have to hide in the mountains from fancy missiles packed with explosives, but so far the appeasing Australian diplomatic efforts hadn't hinted at such slyness. It was more like, 'We know who you are and what you do, keep on doing it because *we* can't do anything, but don't think you're a hot shot'. Next article concerned the latest sightings of the phantom Task Force Seven. He saw a propaganda photo of a column of troops cheering and smiling on a street in Sydney, the man leading the procession standing adroitly tall and stern, a veteran, though still youthfully enigmatic. In some immature moment of fascination he studied the face and imagined he were him, he were crusading again, and diligently read the article. All he could make of the articles was that whatever this Task Force Seven was, there were spies living off feeding false information of their exact whereabouts. Some say they are starting from the top down by securing Port Moresby, Cairns or Townsville. Others say they plan to land north of Brisbane, circle around and take that. Some say they are already here, having parachuted far north into the Atherton Tablelands. In war and peace the ear on the ground hears all the things people throwaway. As always, reliable information is hard to find. He read an essay, *The Emerging Chinese Moral Dilemma*, but the passages and tone were too hypothetical and vague. Not even those leading the counter-revolution knew where they were going but the country seemed quite content to embrace *any* change. Some feared an aggressive China, others pressed that it was a typically cyclic transgression. A European think-tank was even so bold to predict that China was the only power that could bring peace to the Pacific. Whatever, he shrugged, if it comes to the crunch, you can't fuck with China. You just roll with the flow, duck the blows, or find somewhere else to go.

On the bed Jintana arched back in her sleep as if struck by an arrow from behind in a dream.

Sumatra sat still and silent, smiling over her. It was four AM and he was keen to read more. He was far away from the busy workings of the day. Staff questioning him, nagging for silly answers to sillier problems, but his decisions were vital and if he let one idiot make one idiotic decision he could have riots, or worse, a full-scale uprising on his hands from neighbouring warlords throwing excess diseased and unwanted refugees armed with machetes and ex-army rifles down his way. His power was a ring of steely discipline interlocked with other rings forming a near impregnable and impressive chain of security. As soon as he surrendered his barbaric right to any force, mystical or real, his region of control would tether and fall apart leaving a people impoverished of leadership. They would be easy pickings to a flood of new arrivals. It was his boldness to take on the role of warlord that had held this little world together. He was the gravity and every soul in Providence knew they were suckered to him – and grateful for it. If they didn't like it they could face the bullet, head south into Raoul's Free Trade State, trek way west into the deserts, east into the seas and the sharks and pirates, or North to General Kai, a gentleman much like Sumatra, but not as forgiving.

A chilled breeze blew from the sea and as he mechanically counted the strategies of days ahead the satellite phone rang. He lurched up. The ringing noise would disturb Jintana and Qiao.

"Yes?" he yawned, trotting the length of the balcony, scratching his buttocks. "Romano? … No, I'm awake… I don't sleep anymore. Is it urgent?"

Romano spoke urgently, Sumatra's tongue being his second language, "Very important! Very! I'm at the bank… I'm coming up!"

Sumatra guessed the reasons for this early morning appearance by his Chief of Militia; armed or diseased refugees sighted in foothills mauling cattle, or bandits, drunken pirates or rag-boy outlaws causing trouble in the brothels of Kingston? Outbreak of new viruses in the hospital? Sumatra rubbed his stubbled chin. Another day. How long can this madness go on? He waited, sitting down but hunched over, his head bowed, hands clasped together before his knees, his mind ruminating on how good it had all been; the ride here.

Romano's sandals slapped up the internal cement staircase followed by two militia, ex-soldiers who, when all three entered under the gaze of Sumatra's personal red-eyed guards, nervously stood before the warlord with an apologetic glare that quickly evolved into a suppressed jealous stare at the two sleeping mistresses seen through a half open door to the lavish bedroom.

Romano was a robust forty year old Philippine with a slight beer gut, a kind heart, a community and ground based instinct for life, but the sincerity of an ex-bank robber turned fugitive then refugee, and now naturally, Chief of Militia for the province of Providence. He was heavy in bulk, his head weighed forward by a large, though flat nose and drooping chin populated by some scrawny wiry hair. Add to that the weight on his brow as the thoughts of his heart ballooned in his mind. Most times he was leaning forward, which to any man was an indication that Romano was keen to head-butt or kick some butt. This outward appearance worked like a ruse, similarly his craft of manipulating a sense of adorable stupidity. With these characteristics and relying on some intelligence rarely did he face trouble – he delegated militia to stamp it out. Romano had seen the death in these parts and proudly added to it, yet not in a psychopathic way, for his simple wholesome heart lay in a bare farm where he tried to play farmer with dreams of growing plantations and actually settling this new lands rather than spilling the necessary quota of blood to keep the population in check. However, his failings as a farmer were offset by his wage as Chief of Militia in Providence, which on par with Sumatra's friendship, made the personal arrangement and fulfilment of service a dependable commodity.

The militia at his side were typical stranded soldiers, given a third-hand military tunic, a Kalashnikov rifle and an imported Iranian or French grenade that may or may not work. They were usually young men or older boys and incredible naïve to politics, ideals and geography, in want of hot sex more than anything, luckily picked out from the doomed refugees and now waltzing around Queensland as supposedly the best men for defence where life was precariously cheap. The loudest attraction, apart from the abundance of refugee women they would all one day be able to pick from once the war clouds dispersed, were the lives they led as compared to maturing in the slums back home. In the New World they were the men they had only seen in movie posters and comics. They were the villains and heroes, and though tainted by blood, it was better than dying in an outbreak of an unidentifiable disease or caught in a genocidal slaughter, or as Sumatra knew and cautioned them, caught in a reign of murderous gunfire from flying machines.

Sumatra wriggled into his Generals tunic, appreciatively implying, "Providence never sleeps… True warriors never sleep."

"Yes," Romano's voice panted from the rush up the stairs.

"Keep your voices down," Sumatra kinked his head to the bedroom. "So to what do I owe this pleasure?"

"Fishermen from the reefs… They saw a…" he threw his hands wide into the air encompassing the length of the beach outside, his round cheeks puffed, "A long boat… No lights."

"No lights." Sumatra's eyes narrowed. Submarine? Ship adrift? Plundered, the crew and captain slaughtered, what becomes of a gigantic boat under no control? "Heading?"

"*Nowhere*. Anchored. *Strange* voices – whispers on the winds."

"Pirates? Or traders with valuable cargo?"

"It's been there since eleven last night." Romano continued, "I say like Navy? They can't tell. I say does it blow smoke? And they say yes." He sniffed the air. "Diesel."

"Hmph. Diesel power. Bring the radio," Sumatra beckoned them out to the balcony and sat on a squeaking banana-lounge more suited to Jintana or Qiao's petite bodies for sunbathing.

The two militia placed a standard army field radio at his feet. He carefully looked out from the balcony. Out in the sea there was nothing but impenetrable darkness and the low roar of the waves crashing, each set drowning the previous roar. A man can read the sea. If he had a lighthouse, or a radar, yes radar, then he could see into the night! Then he could read between the lines. Then he could project his power into the trading routes. It would cost another ten thousand US to buy satellite coverage from the *Black Tide*, why hadn't he bargained it down to eight?

"Maybe we go to the bank?" Romano cautiously suggested, "*Black Tide* may know something."

Sumatra's hand cut into the air. "*Black Tide* want *more* money…" He tuned the radio to a known pirate frequency. "H-K, H-K, wake up, wake up."

"Jemmy might not be awake!" Romano fervently cautioned.

"Bah!" Sumatra swore. "He's a pirate! He works nights!"

Romano backed off.

The radio crackled: "H-K's ready for bed."

"Jemmy!" Romano cried, astounded.

The two militia felt in awe at the radio: H-K Jemmy, Hong Kong's most notorious pirate, the Chinese Navy pin-up, Sea Faring Enemy Number 1!

"… Jemmy," Sumatra began solidly, "You have been awake all night or are you just waking up?"

Jemmy recoiled. "All the same to me." In his sea-side hut with boat-ramp, he burnt the midnight oil masterminding anarchy on the South East Pacific. Over maps he plotted interception and rendezvous for one of his many speed boats, plucking small to medium-sized cargo ships from sea lanes and looting more than safes. He was after goods of all sorts, and with a crack team could deliver a cargo ship into Sumatra's deep-sea port of Kingston.

"Clear your mind of the past Jemmy. We are brothers here and I would never do to you what I did to Phan-Duc… You will tell me the truth… Brothers in Trust…"

"Brothers," Jemmy knowingly hesitated, "On *circumstance*, my good General…" What followed was his trademark snide laugh, a spine chilling death note, "Ha, ha-ha-ha," and then as if he wasn't finished amusing himself, "Ha *hee* ha!"

Sumatra coltishly barked, "Have you fired on the Australian Navy again!"

"… No! I keep away… Always…"

"Do you know something I don't, but should?"

"I heard from Xian, just an hour ago, he saw on the radar so he turned it off right away…"

"What did he see?"

"It must be navy. No other ship would come. It's was passing Providence, Xian said. I didn't really believe him."

"But you do now, because I'm calling you!"

Jemmy lit a cigarette, thumped his table then spoke into the radio, "Why disturb a sleeping bear? You made a deal with them, yes? No?"

"I make no deals!"

"I trust *you*," Jemmy spoke in a jumpy negotiating manner.

Sumatra fumed, "Bah! If it's your fault they're here… *Disgrace* Jemmy! There are many who value our deal better than you!"

"No! You – Me, good trade always!"

"Good! So, what is it?"

"Must be navy ship. It will move on. Maybe."

Sumatra spoke squarely, "Jemmy, because of your friends you know more. Tell me!"

Jemmy purposely brooded over the airwaves, holding down the transmit button as his eyes skimmed from his maps of the Coral Sea to some sexy young thing expired in a hammock beside the rickety doorway that led out to the rowdy streets of Kingston, "I'd be ready if I were you. But don't attack it; bad for business."

Sumatra's voice tightened. "What?"

"Phantom Task Force Seven, don't you read the *Asia-Pacific War Zone*?"

"Bah! Do you believe that Jemmy?"

"You don't scare easily,"

"What do you mean!"

"What can I do about it, General? My boat is in the dock and my men are drunk or with women... Not a good night."

"Scoundrel!" Sumatra cursed. "You know!"

"I can't rob their navy. *Black Tide* say a frigate left Sydney two weeks ago heading north. That's it."

"O-K!" Sumatra slammed down the radio and bellowed to Romano, "It's an Australian frigate! The fools in Jakarta should have warned me!"

"A frigate?!" Romano stood perplexed. "What is that?"

Sumatra wrung his hands, un-able to exactly translate pure military terminology, "A Battleship! Wake the militia immediately!"

Before dawn the wailing of the night militia awoke the regular militia. They stumbled out of bed, slung their guns from their shoulders, and buttoning up their shirts and pulling up their pants, wondered what the commotion could be about. Bandits? Looting refugees? Before breakfast? They assembled outside Sumatra's Headquarters, the ageing but well protected bank in the middle of Providence. Romano stood on the steps, holding a lantern to his face, briefing them with great hysteria that an Australian War Vessel was waiting at sea, using night as its cloak, to stage an attack. Low chants celebrated the special occasion, cigarettes passed freely into nervous fingers, they drunk from a communal pot of tea. The poorly trained and brained militia boys could be up against a conventional army. With Sumatra's months of propaganda looming in their hearts this could be their big chance to show the First World that the New World were an efficient and brave force to be reckoned with.

The civilians of the town, awoken by the noise, peered from windows hoping for a false alarm. Mothers led their children back to bed. Events like these were usually settled with some gunfire to sweep the streets of marauding refugees.

Meanwhile, Sumatra paced the balcony of his penthouse sipping coke and bourbon or green tea, and smoking his favourite 555 cigarettes. The repeated frowns and confined short-steps of his frustration only served to increase an imposing grip of irritability and trigger the dull thud of a migraine. It was too dark to see out to sea. He tried penetrating the wall of darkness, knowing it would recede with dawn's golden-pink blazing touch, but he only felt it embrace and envelop him. He stood back for a minute, closed his eyes, and strained to hear above the waves. Footsteps. Tank armour. Jintana and Qiao in the bathroom. Bombs that fell from the sky a year ago. He can still hear the whistling. He can see red dust clouds blowing over and choking the man in front.

Past the master bedroom and into the en-suite, Qiao lightly stepped out of the shower, wiping steam off the mirror to see the reflection of the nubile Jintana stepping into the shower cubicle behind her.

"What's your hurry?" Qiao asked in a contrived tone.

"I can't sleep." Jintana turned on the hot water and tipped her head back into the thin jet of steamy water. "Everyone's awake. At the bank the militia are ready. It's early and unusual."

Qiao closed the bathroom door and knowing the roar of the water would drown out her words to those outside, spoke softly and precisely to Jintana. "The refugees... I have heard of none lately."

"Good," Jintana sang thankfully from under the water. "We were the first."

"... Maybe there is no war?" Qiao turned to the figure in the shower, raising her voice, "No war no more?"

Jintana laughed sceptically. "Oh it can *never* end, they say."

"They say many things," Qiao turned to herself in the mirror, smiled with bobby pins held in the corners of her lips and propping her silky black hair into a bun, talked sternly to herself and Jintana, "He's worried. New people can only be opportunist. Do not trust any man."

Jintana pretended not to care or understand from the feeble security of the shower. Qiao had been Sumatra's mistress the longest. She aided his mental and emotional health, whereas Jintana, younger and not so blemished by age, was the sexual sponge with many more youthful years before her, years which weary Sumatra would not be able to take full advantage of. That deal in itself was momentarily fine for Jintana. Why waste her sex on a lukewarm bag of bones and meat?

Qiao flashed her eyes to Jintana's blurred figure behind the glass door. "You be careful."

"For what?"

"He doesn't know what's coming from the sea. He hears things. *Black Tide* say things. Many have been waiting. They talk. The round-eyes will come – ha! No one knows and only the smart expect nothing,"

"And this 'nothing', it calls for us to look our best?" Jintana swiftly and guiltily added, knowing Qiao had began the first steps of her thirty-minute beauty ritual usually reserved for lunching with Sumatra.

"Maybe,"

Jintana turned off the shower, wrapped a towel tightly around her body and spoke to Qiao's misted reflection in the mirror, "Who would come by boat?"

"Pirates," Qiao wearily assumed, drooping her long slim limbs to her sides, "Trading cheap jewellery or guns or opium for women!"

Jintana embarrassingly shunned the poisonous words, "Never!" For a few seconds she felt herself traded again, sharing a metal hull with soldiers and tinned food as her new captor steered a course for the next outpost. "Sumatra only deals with Jemmy – the rest die."

Qiao continued, an inkling of opportunism forming the framework of her smooth countenance, "However, foreigners will value us differently," and added buoyantly, "Wealthy Westerners... So we..."

"Yes,"

"We be good girls. But remember!" Qiao menacingly demanded, "We are Sumatra's girls first and foremost."

"Have I thought otherwise?" Jintana had not seen a white person since setting foot in Australia. It almost seemed absurd that they still existed, though this building with its large bathroom and bedrooms and expansive practical kitchen was a surreal remnant of their luxury, rightly appropriated by the more needy, like herself, a simple mistress and her protector, a powerful warlord. Yet these surroundings seemed synthetic, and if not that, tainted.

"No." Qiao flatly replied. "But you will. Many men have different tricks to take our value – Sumatra's value."

"Women too?"

"Women too."

"And we will know who they are very soon?" Jintana compliantly smiled to Qiao and with nimble steps shuffled to the bedroom and sat on the bed combing her hair, serenely staring out the window to the dark sky. As seen through the half open bedroom door, the glow of the lamp in the dining room inside dimly illuminated Sumatra on the balcony. He stood resembling a nocturnal statue with a soft, yellow, congealed expression, contrasted by the dark sky above him.

He blinked and unhinged himself, turning a half circle as if to shake off the strain or vigorously swirl the liquor inside his body to dilute the migraine in his head into submission. In a follow-up reaction he flicked half a cigarette over the balcony, rubbed his forehead to mash some answers into place and grumpily sat down on the squeaky lounge chair. To his side was the field radio, large and bulky but good for the distance. He checked many channels and found only the chit-chat of rogue Taiwanese fisherman out in the seas.

"General!" came the call from the front door.

Two of his ex-Army Captains arrived, walked the perimeter of the balcony like inspectors and lit expensive cigarettes, yawning, stretching, pretending that they were not sleep deprived or annoyed. They sniffed the sea-spray and waited for Sumatra's eyes to deviate from the impenetrable sea. They could see through to Jintana patiently drying her hair. Steam crept out of the en-suite door, followed by Qiao's soft singing.

Sumatra cast his arms to the dark, his eyes and tone leaden. "An Australian Naval frigate is out there."

The Captains imagined out there, trusting Sumatra's instinct, reminding themselves that he was protecting an enclave of society and microcosm of civility from the ruthlessness of the outside world.

"A patrol?" Captain Tran said.

The other, Captain Yip, scanned with heavy binoculars, and seeing nothing but a void, shrugged. "I am not guessing." On the northern horizon a blurred band of feint salty spray was illuminated from behind by a bright, stationary, shimmering planet. "If they come close we can harass them with rockets."

Tran signed, playing the scenarios out in his mind. But where to begin?

Sumatra turned to them, face full as a moon, eyes wide and wild, "Can't you two feel it? It's an attack! Jemmy said it's Australian frigate. That *dog* didn't tell me it was there earlier. 'Good trade?' – Bah!" He grunted. With his hand shaped like a heavy pistol he shot the vague outline of the moon. "Pow! Pow! I'll have him in the gutter biting garbage with a bullet in his brain!"

"General," Yip sympathised, "Jemmy is a man of deception. Show him his own reflection and he wouldn't recognise himself!"

"True,"

"And he says one warship, one *frigate*, that's all."

"One frigate," Tran progressively refuted its value, picked up the *Asian-Pacific War Zone*, leafed through and easily reacquainted himself. "It can't be Task Force Seven. They'd use battleships and aircraft carriers and bombers. Anything less would be suicide."

Sumatra clenched his fist into a club and thwacked his own leg, listened to the sea and heard a grinding stillness. Regional security was threatened. The frontline may be a thousand kilometres away but right here, right now, was the possibility of an assault by an unknown and unchecked force. His military resources around Providence were for protecting the land; mines, train lines and farms. What army would dare navigate the Great Barrier Reef? How many ingenious pirates and villains had made great progress and snared their flimsy vessels on coral? And further out, the Pacific Ocean, to Sumatra's limited seafaring standard, was no foreigner to war and peril.

"They might land on my beach," Sumatra grunted indignantly.

Yip ran the calculation: "To attack Providence? An amphibious assault? It's a remote-"

"Why?"

"One frigate… Two companies maximum…"

"If I see it at dawn," Sumatra's mouth snarled back revealing his crooked teeth biting into the fear stained air, "I'll send a missile at it!" With his index finer he drew an arc from outside his town to out to sea and then a new thought gripped him, "The missile trucks! Where are they?"

"At the mechanic, next to the bank," Yip replied.

Tran objected, "But no use against frigates, General. We would need armour piercing."

"So I need anti-ship missiles? How much? Where?" Sumatra groaned, "You see, I can't afford all this. I am not some industrial power, bah!"

"The French in Noumea might have some anti-ship missiles?" Tran suggested. "I can go to the bank and call them."

"Are they good?" Sumatra asked.

"French missiles are excellent. Exocet – new variations. Anti-submarine missiles too, very nice."

Sumatra was tempted. "Can they be used against people?"

"… No."

"I have no time for an arms race," Sumatra said then brightened with another idea, "And Malo!"

"The *aboriginal* is not to be trusted."

"Where is he?"

"He's *walking*," Yip testified, unsure what Malo's farewell words meant.

"Where?"

"Walking about." Yip folded his arms in an act of heavy concentration, "He goes nowhere, Sir. He just walks around the country and comes back."

Sumatra's eyes levelled out to sea then up under his skull, whispering, "He knows something, I know he knows, I know Jemmy knows and,"

Yip's hissed, "Listen!"

Qiao's subtle singing became louder and most agreeable against the slowly crashing waves and then something indecipherable, or was it their hearts, beating faster and faster, closer and closer, came from the sea.

"Shut up!" Sumatra yelled to Qiao. She shut up. Then he heard the militia noisily stumbling from the streets to the beach, arguing about how best to fortify in case of an improbable attack. Sumatra scurried through the unit and returned with a loudspeaker and hailed down below, "Silence! Silence!"

Followed by Romano calling back up, persistently, "Sorry! Sorry!"

And Sumatra's shrill reply, "Silence or I shoot you!"

"Yes – Sorry!" Romano called, barely audible, and could then be heard disciplining the militia with curses that stung like a whip.

Sumatra stood on his balcony gyrating his head to the night. The eyes of Jintana, Yip and Tran now held on him, questioning his nerves and sanity with their youthful guile. He frowned, this is what becomes of a man who kills too often! Then, disproving his impertinence, carried on a gush of wind, came a thudding that chilled him from head to toe; the helicopter's blades resonated through the unit, shaking the mirror in the bathroom, the glass rattling against its aluminium casing, Qiao's perplexity amplified as the reflection of her eyes vibrated before her. Tran and Yip's heads intuitively yanked back and their mouths widened in awe as the flooring on which they stood rattled and the foundations reverberated. A helicopter flew directly over them, vanished over Providence, then peeled to the north, rattling the town in its wake. As if leaving a vacuum, sucked from the south came the thudding beats of another helicopter, skimming across the waves back out to sea.

"Seahawks," Yip marvelled, then bowed to his feet, frozen in fear.

Tran swallowed hard. "If it comes back, do we… What do we do?"

Sumatra jutted his chin up to the sky, he cast one fist out into the air then thumped it against his chest. The militia below readied themselves for the invisible enemy. Yip and Tran shared a curious glance; an alliance in fate and an insidious desire to flee, yet Sumatra stood solidly facing the heavens and if they were wrong he would hunt, castrate and hang their bodies from telegraph poles. He was ruthless but fair on matters of honour.

Qiao hurried out to the balcony wearing fluffy slippers, a full-length silvery dress, fervently puffing a freshly lit cigarette propped in the corner of her mouth, carrying Sumatra's pressed olive green pants, a polished belt, leather holster and pearl handle Colt .45 in her long, slender, soft as velvet, hands.

"Thank you, darling."

Then in pure automation Captains Yip and Tran helped their warlord dress into a general and by the act of such gratitude he regained his professional composure, the hot-blooded smile returned and the memory of minor victories flooded back. He was General Sumatra again. Once dressed, he held his loudspeaker to his lips and shouted down below, "See they try to scare us! They try! They must try harder!" which was met by cheers, so he continued tightening the tempo, though in the back of his mind ran the dim and remote view that this may be a scare, it may be nothing, but at the very least it united his people, yes, "We are united! We are ready!"

Qiao's hand motherly stroked his hair through to the silver tips, "We are ready, General, we are ready."

On the bed, Jintana lay on her stomach, squinted her eyes shut and clasped her ears with her hands. But she could still hear the militia noisily forming a line of defence behind the beach, as if given a license to deconstruct Providence, tearing down fences and anything else half solid to make barricades. Rarely were they called to arms so close to Providence, and at such an eerie hour.

"Jintana!" Qiao fumed, "Dress! Hurry!"

Jintana distressfully rolled off the bed and landed firmly on her bare feet, opened two drawers from her personal wardrobe and jutted her lip out as a sign of clear confusion. Are the visitors western? Helicopters. A real navy! To sink pirates into a watery grave! How should one appear? An expensive prostitute or an exclusive princess? She folded her arms, frowned, and examined herself.

Meanwhile, Qiao searched under the giant bed, dragging out belts of ammunition and grenades, carting them to the balcony and returning to lug out a sizeable rocket launcher, casting rudimentary scornful stares to Jintana, "Dress yourself girl!"

"I am!" Jintana replied and in her own time carefully picked through her clothes. Even though Qiao, taller and flat chested, was not quite the plaything, she appeared the most daunting and demanding like a dynastic Queen! Qiao's perfect execution of this position typecast Jintana into anything other than fellow Queen, and Qiao's experience and gravitational upper-hand went so far to suppress Jintana's individuality and spirit into that of a chambermaid. This catty presumption and acceptance by both parties was a logical and momentary default yet in the face of intruders, potentially disrupting current values, Jintana felt a charge of vibrant insolence ignite her mind. She settled on a golden, silky, knee-length dress with an embroidery of a dragon over her heart, and a pearl necklace anchored by an opal above her breasts. She was now a princess. This land, she smiled with glee, now has a sense of royalty, and lineage, deserving of respect!

On the balcony Sumatra stood with his hands firmly on his hips, grinning, facing the horizon and the sun, barely rising out of the sea, its rays extending along the horizon. Low clouds appeared to edge higher as light slipped under them. For a second of brilliance, silhouetted against the semi-circle of orange rode that mysterious frigate, passing through a puff of smoke expunged from its sleek bow. It was a beautiful sight; the mighty sea at dawn, and riding on it, one of man's highest forms of technology, a ship of war, as one, until the high-pitched scrape of an incoming shell landed a few blocks inland, the shockwave rattling the penthouse. Sumatra just grunted, reached for his Colt .45 and fired three shots at the frigate, roaring until he was blue in the face to the awed militia below, "Prepare for Battle!"

In a fluid succession three shells hit the beach in a line  and expelled plumes of smoke. Sumatra, his face contorted, peering over the balcony, understood the use of smoke and yelled through his loudspeaker, "All militia to the beach!"

The Captains, using the elevation of the penthouse, patiently watched the smoke puff out and up and drift, so in the fresh light illuminating the sea, they could see, surging to where the waves rush in and out, a sharp grey line cutting through the surf. They braced themselves. The line elevated, a wave fell, revealing a slanted metal object, the front of a landing craft, its profile low and dark, powering towards the beach.

Sumatra, stupefied, watched the landing craft cover the last yards through the shallows and lower its ramp to the hardened wet sand. He saw the barrel of a tank. Militia fired wide shots then straight at the tank as it rumbled onto the beach. Soldiers in dark camouflage uniforms followed, swallowed by a smoke screen, their frequent, solid bursts of bullets obliterating whatever they happened to hit.

Sumatra fused into a perfect synergy of anger and order, calling out, "Militia cover the beach!" He ached and gripped Captain Yip, "My missiles! Where!"

"Ready, Sir!" Yip replied.

He pointed to the landing craft. "Kill it before it goes back to sea and brings more of them!"

"We can't fire at the beach! We'd destroy this building too!"

"Bah! If worse comes to worse, exactly!" Sumatra glared from the tank, to the landing craft, to the soldiers it expunged. Three more shells landed in quick succession, smoke mushroomed over the beach. Sumatra gulped as he heard the familiar clank of tank tracks edging closer. Then in an odd unison, Qiao and Jintana shuffled onto the balcony cradling in their little arms a heavy, shoulder mounted, rocket launcher.

Qiao explained, "The Russian one still works!"

"Ah!" Sumatra's index finger rubbed the trustworthy Red Army markings and activation switch. In one move he swung it up and balanced it on his shoulder, breathed deep, exhaled and steadied his aim on the lone tank. The whites taking cover behind it would scatter. His militia had already shot some! Impressive! Sumatra fired. The clink-clank of the tank tracks and its turret machine-gun peppering the dunes fell silent as the tank absorbed the rocket yet moved progressively forward. Sumatra saw flames shoot out of the entry point then chunks of hot metal sprayed into the air. A few desperate and wounded whites yelped. The ground shook. Sumatra stood on the tips of his toes, the raw energy of a battle raging charging his soul. The beach, below his penthouse, was the setting of a triumph. Flashing before his eyes came the arduous journey arriving here. They had tried to stop him even as he left Sedak Port before reaching Darwin! Had they succeeded in the desert, never! With one mighty gush from the wind the smokescreen thinned revealing hunched Task Force Seven soldiers sprinting for cover from the beached landing craft and their precious tank exploding, again! Militia perched in defensive positions, behind the beach in houses, units, from behind trees and dunes, shot at the darting targets with a magnificent show of joy married with primal terror. One Australian soldier sprinted back to the waves; a mad dash escaping the flames that completely devoured him.

Sumatra observed the battle unfolding, smug at the demise of the tank, devout to decimate them all. Jintana and Qiao returned from the bedroom carrying an antique U.S. M-60 machine-gun and obediently propped it on the balcony ledge. Sumatra took the women either side and rolled his head back, gurgling a devilish laughter, "See ladies! Revenge *so* sweet!"

As machine-guns from the attackers and defenders raked the battlefield Jintana and Qiao dropped to Sumatra's knees and cuffed their ears. And to make Sumatra feel all the more greater came the sounds of wounded Australians sprawled on the finest sands on one of the most beautiful beaches he had ever seen.

On the landing craft packed with one tank and fifty men, Captain Callaghan had shuffled his way to the rear of the tank, next to Doc Nelson and Lieutenant Jenkins. He had been upfront, and relatively new to the force braved himself to stand there with a few tight lipped men who were obviously veterans of many a battle, yet in no way inclined to boast, or even recount, especially now that any second as the ramp goes down they could be in the firing line again. Doc Nelson and Jenkins, by privilege of rank, had secured the area behind the solidly built German Leopard tank. Jenkins shut his eyes, listened to his ear-piece, deciphering the garbled messages of third platoon, on the outskirts of Providence, poised to infiltrate. Above them the pink glow of sunrise erased the glimmer of stars. The men, first platoon and miscellaneous sections comprising half of Task Force Seven, stood shoulder to shoulder in good spirits, yet during the pre-dawn silent ride from the frigate to the beach, the salt spray slapped their cheeks, sobering them, and the knots in their guts tightened.

Jenkins checked his watch, "Fifteen minutes to make it into town. Peters will be waiting there – have it secured. Remember," he called to those with radios, "Radio silence is crucial until we get smack-bang in there,"

"That's two-hundred metres – roughly." Callaghan imagined the direct route though urban territory at dawn. Piece of cake. He imagined Peters and the other fifty men of Task Force Seven abseiling from helicopters before dawn and silently infiltrating the sleepy town. This, Callaghan smiled, may be a fine adventure to partake in! Imagine an office job ten stories below in a nuclear proof bunker with stale air-conditioning when one can live this, to land in occupied territory, to shift the boundaries of history. He brightened when around him men were reflective, pointing out crucifixes across their chests.

"Yes," came Jenkin's delayed reply. Standing on the tips of his toes, his grey-blue eyes scanned over the tank (its exhaust now a slight discomfort) and the front ramp of the landing craft, to the beach they were approaching, section by section. He saw flat tin roofs, trees, a few bewildered skinny local beings staring incredulously out to sea, and a four storey building. Apart from the throb of the craft's diesel engines and the anxious shuffling of men, he heard nothing, then a strange voice, carried on the wind from the beach, like a gargled bark. The landing craft gave a slight shudder as they hit a sand dune, yet powered on closer to shore, a slight swell rocking it back and forth, the heavily laden men swaying, squatting down, braced to charge out. Then the shells came screaming from the heavens and layered the beach with smoke. A gun fired, that strange voice, shells. Wild cries. It was, he panted, *over*.

The Helmsman, steering from the rear, bellowed, "Ready! Ready, now!" yet as his vessel nudged the sand again, and he scanned the terrain, his voice abruptly changed to a blistering yell, "Contacts! Contacts!" and patted his helmet securely on his head, his fright followed by a rumbling of weapons spread out along the beach. Bullets that hit the landing craft sounded a large metallic thud and ring, those that flew overhead were like a whip cracking.

The men knew there was no element of surprise. They gripped their K-40 machine-guns, ready to level them, trusting only in firepower. The front ramp lowered taking in a gush of sea water. Bullets ricocheted off the tank. The tank's turret machine-gun, aiming into a smoke screen, fired only intermittent bursts at what the gunner thought to be an enemy, and hopefully not that of their own soldiers, somewhere in the town. He could not see a definable force, just skinny brown bodies dressed in an odd assortment of clothes and boots, matched with differing weapons. He took aim and made a lengthy sweep.

Jenkins hunched into himself, scanning the beach, urgently radioing the frigate, "*Overlord, Overlord*," the tank engine rumbled and roared, "We're hitting the beach and it's HOT!"

Callaghan raised his head an inch to stare over the aft of the landing craft to the rising sun and the frigate, *Overlord*, being the call sign of Colonel Smacker, overseer and proprietor of this operation. The front cannon discharged.

A corporal yelled to his squad, "Incoming – Ready – Any second,"

The shell dropped on the beach and bled smoke.

The radio blurted, "*Overlord* here, come in *Pow-Wow*."

"This is *Pow-Wow*," Jenkins said in a controlled manner, "Directed enemy fire coming in from the beach… Maybe twenty small arms… Need covering fire, rip up the dune-line! The dune-line!"

Then the Helmsman yelled, "Go! Go! Go!" and was shot where he stood, behind his wheel, leaving the charge of his flat hulled boat up to his Ensign, who didn't know what to do except watch the Leopard tank launch into and out of shallow water, up to the smoke covered beach, fifty men crowded behind it, firing bursts into the fog that enveloped them. There was considerable smoke cover, and some slight distance was made, yet in one gush of nature all was gone revealing half of Task Force Seven under the sights of hundreds of local militia crouching out of beachside houses, from under houses, clinging to tree branches, or noisily clambering on roofs.

From the bridge of the frigate, Smacker's gaze was pressed to the beach. At first the smoke infuriated him, he couldn't see the action beyond the landing craft, and when the smoke blew up the coast, it delighted him to see that his project was way beyond concept and planning, it was a reality; his little men were running up the beach and though some stumbled (their packs were heavy) and didn't get up again, the majority were making ground and the tank fired a salvo into the unseen enemy. Who were they, he cursed, the mismatched flashes of their guns bursting, concentrating on *his* men. He stood erect, quiet and dismayed. Seconds lasted hours. More than too many men weren't getting up again. He could see the tank providing some with cover and then it disappeared in a puff of orange flame, sweeping men up like rag-dolls and hurling them back into the sea! Even the seasoned Mackenzie lapsed into a state of suspended morbidity. The tank's magazine of shells exploded, lifting it in the air, spinning, landing facing lengthways on the beach. As if snookered, the turret popped off high into the sky with the fury of a ballistic projectile, flames gushing out at the decapitation point. Threat detection crew panicked as an un-expected bogey popped on their radar and by default they classified it as an incoming missile. Alarm bells rang. Evasive manoeuvres were the solution. The turret vanished into the waves as the frigate executed a full-speed U-turn.

Colonel Peters estimated he was five to six hundred metres from the beach, and nearing the centre of the town, took a left when the rest of the squad he was leading continued on. He back-tracked but they'd moved through, fanned out, perhaps confused, yet continuing. The streets were empty. The barrage of noise from the beach was irritating; it was obvious what force was winning, and to anyone who couldn't decipher the sounds, their recklessness would multiply the mayhem. Still, Peters pressed on, into another street, surprised that the houses were so intact, most windows were glass and not old board, and that women peered at him then ducked out of sight. A dog sauntered past. He felt exposed. He slipped through a gate, crouched by a fence, squatted, trying to think and calculate what to ask over the radio, waiting for the rest of the platoon to catch up. And then he heard light footsteps and saw sets of small bare feet, two, then three, plus a fifth, all children, coming from behind a house. The oldest was six and they were all shades of races. They looked at him with wonder, and wary, like a pack, retreated when the battle from the beach hit a deathly high.

"Hey," Peters called softly.

The children, hiding under the house, wide eyes watching him, mimicked his word: Hey. Peters stood. They were amazed by his height, a giant, armed to the teeth. The eldest wriggled out, stood up and pointed straight to the beach. O-K, Peters nodded, and took off.

The tank was a burning wreck, soldiers torn to pieces with it. The rest charged forward until a barrage of bullets from a fence line behind the dunes mowed down the first few. The survivors flung smoke grenades at the fence and shrapnel grenades over it and carved petty foxholes in the fine dry sand with their quivering hands. Some bravely squatted and aimed at whatever moved. Then the re-exploding tank flattened them down, tossed a few who were too close into the air and sliced them open.

Callaghan's first plea was for his face, the heat from the tank had burnt him yet the blast had thrown him into the low surf. His heart rocketed from his ribcage up to his head and now bounced the inside of his cranium at a thousand times a second. And he was deafened, wet, cold and partly flash blinded. He felt himself over; shrapnel in the leg. Bleeding. He slammed another magazine into his K-40.

The K-40 was Task Force Seven's mainstay rifle. It was a Belgian arms manufacturer's core stream of income, its customer base 'disaster-impending' Western nations in need of something a bit more persuasive than what the rest of the world could afford. The K-40 ammunition was caseless 5.56mm bullets and frangible; able to penetrate steel but not a human torso; it would only explode, creating holes where wounds should be. It was the best lead-spitting, rapid-fire, flesh-buster that money could buy. "The K-40 is the tool for personal maximum-incapacitation. Gone are the days of just wounding the enemy so he has to be hospitalised to inflict primarily logistical damage – *that's Cold War Mentality*. Now it's Hot War Mentality, over-population is the problem, the K-40 is the solution," chirped the sales Rep, enthusiastically welcoming Australian arms buyers to the well-equipped stand (complete with high-calibre foxy PR ladies) at the *Euro Kanone Fair* in Antwerp, pressing the international salesman grin. He need not have bothered. There was an emerging market for tools to lever against the hordes that traditional M-16's and Steyrs couldn't budge. The K-40 was a smoother big brother of an Uzi blended with the dreams of a few ballistics engineers. A gun-designer's utopian creation; 300 metre accuracy with a mid-length rifle barrel, and with a firing rate of five shots a second with over 120 caseless spuds in the magazine. The K-40 pierced and obliterated nearly anything: A real fucker.

In one act of defiance, and to enable those on the beach to crawl forward for cover, Callaghan performed a feat previously unimaginable: He stood up and faced the enemy positions and in three long sweeps showered them with bullets, slammed in a new magazine, and did it again; though his heroic arc of fire now wider. He had little idea what he was aiming for. If he hit the blurred skinny figures it was a bonus. Those at ground level certainly ducked for cover. Then from above a heavy machine-gun began to draw on him. He jumped this way and that; it followed him, insisting he was next, pumping into the sand, until a roll of smoke from a smoke grenade concealed him, and Jenkin's stern voice ordered: "Follow me!" A scattered volley passed between their torsos.

Callaghan, Jenkins, and three young privates crawled across the white sandy beach under the last wisps of the smoke cover, under fire, through a haze of heat, over dead and wounded comrades, for the burning tank and the protection it might offer. They heard chirpy Asians cocking weapons from behind the fence line and in beach houses, moaning white men, and a curt voice issuing commands through a loudspeaker, pounding incessantly from above. A succession of grenade shockwaves displaced windows. In this confusion of mayhem and death, plain logic was the key to survival, Callaghan announced to his plummeting soul. A bullet shot off his helmet. In a half second of clarity he saw it roll into the sea and fill with water. It took an eternity, but was only second, to sync with his predicament. The most obvious factor, he concluded, that led to death, like those on the wet sand, was in proportion to whoever out there can aim at you. But who could see through this new layer of smoke? Is it leaving us again?

"We ain't got long," Jenkins panted. He'd run into the smoke, gathered dead men's ammunition and a shell shocked Doc Nelson, who now rinsed his bloody hands in the sand, a roll of bandage discarded at his feet.

Callaghan whispered to his smoking gun and the warped side of the destroyed tank they hid behind, "Who's on the ball – who's gonna' get 'em!? I'm gonna get 'em! They're *fucked* – *all* fucked,"

"I'm ready – I'm fucking ready!" a private devoutly yelled.

"Give it to them!"

"Marcus!" Jenkins cried and dragged in a newcomer, crawling on all fours through a wash of smoke to the tank.

Marcus glared at the path he had weaved from the landing craft to the tank. "My fucking God! They missed! They missed me!"

"Anyone hit?" Doc Nelson asked, and finding no replies, winced at those in contrast on the beach, their half-concealed figures shaking with shock, rolling in agony, or limp.

Callaghan paternally embraced his gun and peeping over the smoking tank carcass, any second now, the beach would be back to normal visibility as the wind banished the latest smoke screen. Heat from the wall of the tank wasn't too bad. Heat. Touch. Feel. Enemy fire. Fence line. All around them machine-gun sprays and single shots raked up and down, or drawing circles in the beach through a grey-yellow haze; the last of the smoke coiling with the cordite clouds of spent K-40 cartridges. Out to sea the rising sun blinded his eyes of the frigate's presence.

"Overlord, Overlord!" Jenkins called into the radio, "We're pinned down, sir."

"Pow-Wow, who am I speaking to?" Colonel Smacker replied full of courteous urgency.

"C-O of first-platoon, over."

"Attack that beach! Attack that beach!" Smacker's voice yelled until Jenkins changed frequencies.

"Peters this is Jenko,"

"Grenades!" one the privates yelled.

Four lean arms hurled grenades onto the beach, too far. They rolled on the hard wet sand into the water. As with all things second rate only two of the militia's grenade's exploded, throwing up a spray of water and sparkling sand.

The voice from the loudspeaker congratulated, "*Yah! Yah!*"

A wounded man on the beach begged, his twisting lips and words incomprehensible, then threw his clips of ammo to those defenders behind the tank. The smoke cleared. Three militia finished him off. For the living there were twenty more meters of beach to traverse before a line of sand dunes, a few meters beyond that, splintered wooden fences, yards of decadent bullet-holed beach houses and two-storey units. Centre stage, a prized vantage point for the enemy, the four-storey brick unit. Militia with second-hand farm boy weapons perched on balconies, cautiously out doorways and windows, from behind dunes, like monkeys clambering in and out of structures, firing with the fervour of regular revolutionary heroes at anything that dared move without first consulting heaven. Looking up, Callaghan distinguished order reigning from the top level of the intact penthouse; khaki helmets, a bobbing lock of long silky black hair set against the orange glow of dawn, and a general of sorts flaring his nostrils at the beach.

"Attack!" Callaghan screamed and sprayed his K-40 from top to bottom of the unit. The three privates selected single men, taking bites from each target before moving to another. The whirrs of their guns purred soft and deathly but only scratching at the numbers assembled before them.

Jenkins squinted at the dwindling silhouette of the frigate, "Overlord! Overlord!"

No reply.

He called into the radio, "Peters! This is Jenkins! If you can hear me,"

The voice from the loudspeaker barked a new range of orders to the militia.

Callaghan peered over the tank to see the line of buildings. Militia faces were pressed against rifle butts, aiming to the wounded, popping them off, one-by-one. He checked his K-40 and hosed fifty plus bullets, cutting a swath, but where one militia fell another appeared, taking up the former's rifle.

Jenkins yanked him down behind the cover of the tank to slap him across the face.

"Save it, Capt'n!"

Jenkins then knelt closer to Callaghan and Marcus, "We need support. This is no way to die! It isn't right!"

The frigate rode across the rising sun.

Callaghan took the radio, "Smoke screen... Or an air strike... Overlord, come in, over."

A rocket launched from a rooftop skimmed over the beach into the landing craft. The deck groaned, buckled, and an ammunition crate was blasted by a geyser of flame. With each rippling of bullets the militia cheered.

"*Overlord!*"

"I tried," Jenkins clenched his fist. "They're not even returning fire. No smoke screen!"

"Must be coming in for another pass," Callaghan yelled into the radio, "*Overlord* this is *Pow-Wow*, over."

"*Pow-wow*, what's your condition." Colonel Smacker replied over the radio, retaining a calm, steady, naïve fixation, that he really was a thousand miles from the action. "Looks like errr, you're pinned down… Has the attack *stalled?* Over."

"Shat on, *Overlord*. Where's the smoke screen? We have above forty-percent K-I-A. We are dying! Get the chopper to do some damage!"

Enemy shots clinked at the tank.

Militia shouted, pointing out the few remaining wounded targets.

Callaghan continued, "Shell all the bloody buildings, smoke screens – I don't care! Call in an air strike!"

"*Pow-Wow*," trickled Overlord's reply. "Second and third platoon could be in the area. Your landing craft, is it operable?"

"Destroyed! *Overlord* – what's your story. You're a warship damnit! Get to War!"

Smacker was short and precise, "*Pow-Wow* we're *ahhhhhssessing* situation."

Callaghan could see the enemy's eyes wide as golf balls anticipating an old fashioned tribal slaughter. He tenaciously zeroed on the frigate, a look of disgust brewing into treachery.

"You're fucking turncoats! We need support here!"

General Sumatra, perched on the balcony of his penthouse, leant into and swivelled his prized M-60 machine-gun, chewing through belts of ammunition, spent shells spitting out and falling at his feet. His two mistresses shook with fear and retreated inside. His aim was poor, direction scattered, but it was effect and the militia were enthralled. Not sure what else to shoot at, they simultaneously unleashed a barrage of bullets at the frigate. It appeared to zigzag in order to escape, turned side on and shot back one ill-aimed shell from the front cannon then smothered itself in a smoke screen.

"Overlord!" Callaghan shouted into the radio, "Get your arse back here!"

"Ah… Ah… Coming under heavy fire, Pow-Wow, have to pull out!" Smacker croakily replied. Around him the bridge was a mess, all crew at battle stations, the tinker of flying lead impacting on the windows leaving coin sized craters, a man on deck dragging his limp leg up to a hatch, a rise in temperature under the collar as the air-conditioner faltered as all power in the ship surged to the most important functions.

Mackenzie turned to remark at the holes punched into the glass panels overlooking the front cannon, "More bark than bite – Damage reports!"

"Radar equipment's down sir."

"Radar?"

"Yes sir,"

"And radio – primary mast sir,"

"Switch over. Sonar activity?"

"Nil, sir."

"Fine, fine, double the spotters and rake the shoreline. Colonel Smacker, we're still operational," Mackenzie enthusiastically announced, "We don't need radar for this shit."

Smacker stood rigidly glued into his binoculars, scrutinising the beach, and at the same time trying to block the disastrous elements; panic radio reports from first platoon on the beach, no word from those inside Providence, phosphorous tracer bullets racing from the beach, a haze of grey cordite, a landing zone littered with dead. One landing craft completely written off, blazing, the remaining crewman leaping into the shoals only to be dunked by bullets and then knee high waves. A fucking catastrophe. He'd read first-hand reports of these disasters and always wondered about the state of the authors.

Mackenzie elbowed him, "We *should* level out the dune-line,"

"And take out our own too?! Catastrophe… Fucking disaster." Smacker posthumously grunted and threw his hands in the air replicating some immortal ancient god's hissy fit. "Wasn't meant to be like this! They are a diversion – but this is… Where's Peters!"

"We can lay down some fire," Mackenzie insisted. "Level that line of houses."

"What, and become another casualty? This ship," Smacker seethed, meaning himself, "We have to retreat for deeper waters!"


"Overlord!" Callaghan begged into the radio. He watched above his head as hundreds of bullets raced through the sky towards the fleeing frigate.

"Too hot on the beach, Captain." Colonel Smacker stated. "Taking heavy damage!"

Callaghan twitched, "You're telling me! You can't leave us Overlord!" He checked the battlefield again; the enemy on the pickup. "It's sabotage! This is *your* career fuck-up Colonel! Do something NOW! Do something! Cover the beach!"

"Say again, over."

"We're pinned down," Callaghan dismally replied then revitalised his tone, "We need… Covering fire!"

Smacker saw the smoke stained beach and a hundred angry incoming shots. "This is *Overlord*, I repeat – We're under heavy fire."

"You can't Smacker! *Slack* bastard!"

"Face it, Callaghan, you're expendable. *Overlord* out…!"

With one arm Callaghan aimed his K-40 at the fleeing frigate and joined the barrage of the militia, standing into the salty breeze of the sea, his teeth chattering with the soft relaxing vibration of his K-40 spitting a hundred rounds out to sea. With his other arm he pressed the microphone of the radio to his lips and screamed, red-hot and raw into the radio, "I'm nailing your schemish ass right now – *Errrrrrrrgh!*"

Jenkins pulled Callaghan to the ground, "Snipers!"

A mix of bullets flew through the air where Callaghan had stood. The firing rate subsequently died. The militia's little excited voices chattered with supreme delight at their latest show of defiance and the retreating frigate to prove it.

"What now?" a Private asked. "Look at 'em run! Navy faggots!"

Callaghan kicked the radio and swore to the sky, "Mongrel!" then grabbed the radio, mothering it, "Peters! Talk to me! Talk to me! We're on the beach – if you can hear us – we're fucked! Pinned down!"

No reply.

"Who's alive out there?"

"None – they're, I can't believe it they're just,"

"… Dead."

The battlefield fell silent, though punctuated by a few wounded moans, militia scuffling behind pock-marked fences and houses ready for more. Then from high in the sky at the penthouse flanked by peeking girlie eyes, General Sumatra's poor English was put to the test through the loudspeaker, edgy at first, then gaining in bravado, "Task Force Seven! … No fight! No weapons! Surrender! You will surrender!"

Jenkins swayed his head, his ears ringing.

"No surrender!" Callaghan hollered back then quietly reminded his comrades, "These animals can't even be classed as an army; I don't think they'd know anything about prisoners of war! Savages! Look at 'em! See 'em – watch it he's taking aim again,"

A volley zipped over their heads for the frigate.

"Fucking warlord country sir!" Marcus moaned to the dunes, "You know," frenetically ducking from a predicted spray of bullets, "Fucking crazy chopping off cocks shit! This isn't liberation! We've been double-crossed. This is…"

Doc Nelson added, "*It. This is it.*"

Another eerie silence followed bar the drained wounded in death throes.

"I am General Sumatra!" the voice decreed from above. "No escape! Your life: No value. Surrender only."

Callaghan gasped, "What?"

A dying soldier on the beach wailed, "I'm dying… Help me! I'm dying you fucking cunts!" until a single militia shot silenced him.

Marcus, accepting the stench of his own flesh cooked for the local savages, decided, "He's got us, *knows* we know it,"

Jenkins cocked his K-40. "Steady boys!"

The weeping private grasped for words and proudly proclaimed, "They'll skin us… Savage refugees! All of 'em cannibals!"

"That's all very gutsy…" Callaghan remarked and peeked up to the militia, "We can wait behind this tank," his beady eyes danced about, "Those dunes, sit all fucking night and swim out to sea and paddle up the coast! Or we can wait for Peters!"

Doc Nelson snapped, skimming his eyes over waves twirling at the edges of the bombed out landing craft. "They can outflank us on the beach,"

"Colonel Peters – where's he?" Callaghan berated, "Fucking madman isn't 'ere to be mad!"

They heard no other fighting except from the beach and each in his own perverse way imagined Colonel Peters and the others caught in a similar trap to what they had just encountered, yet so much worse, because they did not hear guns or screams, they heard nothing, they heard the silence of death. Their sombre eyes drifted to the horizon, the frigate, retracted back to shore and a thin film of clear water racing up the wet sand, swirling around the limbs of fallen comrades, dragging a rinse of cherry water back into the most beautiful sea in the world.

"Surrender," Doc Nelson mumbled, "Worse than this."

Callaghan argued to himself, "Couldn't do it. Who knows what it's like up here? Fuck! On the count of three, we go over and mash their fuck'n faces."

A bullet pinged the tank. A few militia cheered at something out of sight. A freak wave washed to shore and on its return drew out a dead soldier.

Jenkins gripped Callaghan's forearm, poignantly peering through him, "You've seen fuck all… It gets worse before it gets better – chill the fuck out."

"Well, we got to waste 'em all," Callaghan panted.

Jenkins grimaced. "You're out of your fucking mind."

"No!"

"We got time,"

"For what?

Jenkins spoke clearly into the radio. "Third – third this is first – first. We need, we need…"

No answer.

General Sumatra's voice rose again, more pressing and angered, "I give one minute. You decide: Fight and die, or surrender. Both ways, I win."

A spray of bullets probed their position, most striking the tank.

"Surrender," the private moaned, yet his fingers tightened around his weapon. "We *gotta* surrender."

Doc Nelson fumed, his body curled into itself behind the destroyed tank, "Crazies… Torture us for fun. Fucking fanatical bastards!"

Jenkins peeked over the tank and scanned the battlefield, darted his eyes up around the penthouse balcony, then to the militia, cautiously stepping out from behind their defences. Some had half buttoned plain tunics revealing scrawny rib-cages dotted with tattoos, or faded shirts from the factories where they use to slave. Around their necks were beaded necklaces, crude crucifixes, sunglasses hanging by nylon string, or shark teeth.

Callaghan knelt behind the tank and clasped his hands together. "Yea though I,"

"Quit it," Doc Nelson intervened.

"I'm praying that whatever we do, it's peaceful," Callaghan muttered, "*Jesus* Christ save Us! And I aren't even Christian – *fuck!*"

Jenkins ducked his head behind the tank processing his last sighting of the militia, "Some of them are. Look."

Callaghan sheepishly craned his neck to see.

Jenkins pointed two out. "See them fuckers up there – yep, yep over a bit."

Resting their elbows on a veranda in a shot up house beside the units, the two beady eyed militia stood with the semblance of Gemini-brothers, the smoke from their rifles still coiling out of the barrels, into their unbuttoned shirts, up their chests and off their little sunlit silver crucifixes into the air.

"Some of 'em got Jesus crosses 'round their necks, see!" Jenkins persisted.

"Typical Christians killing Christians." Callaghan ground his teeth.

"Don't matter who we're dealing with," Doc Nelson said curtly, "See the loony up the top. Sadistic."

Callaghan couldn't believe his eyes. That sadistic bastard had two women at his side, a few uniformed cronies, a patriotic band of mongrel fighters, and a penthouse on the beach. "Warlord," he croaked, "Oh shit, it's all true."

Jenkins said, "What?" and expected a realistic answer but rambled on, "Why they stopped shooting? No ammo? Why? It's... Shhh!"

High on the balcony, the surreal trio were set against the peach clouds of the diminishing dawn. They were discussing, counting down, the two Captains monitoring the progress of the frigate.

"Whoever and *why*, he's it..." Callaghan spied the accompanying women once again, cruel witnesses to one man's misery and sweet comfort to another. "Maybe we can surrender. We've played our hand. We're fucked. You're right – heroic antics are *fucking* stupid."

Doc Nelson scolded, "They'll cook you up in a flash!"

"Bull!" he rested on his knees, scowling at the frigate running for the centre of the Pacific, then turning hopefully to shore, "It's been his fucking sporting day. That's it. He's won, why shouldn't we surrender? We owe it to him! He's probably got third platoon strung up like us! Captured or something! We've been fucked over – right? I ain't attacking or defending this beach for *nothing* no more. There is no reason, that's it. No reason."

They looked to the ends of the beaches where sea spray and horizon merged into a haze of grey, gold and blue, coated in a thinning veil of white.

Jenkins attested, "He just wants a clean shot at us – easier for him."

"Yeah, and he could lob over grenades right fucking now." Callaghan huffed. "Listen... We're alive... At least we can decide what happens next, even if it is only for the next ten minutes. What more can a man ask for?"

By the dismay of their blank faces he guessed, not much.

All sign of manhood vanished from Jenkins's face, his voice flattened into a degraded state, "Captain, I am not taking orders from you,"

"I'm not ordering anyone,"

Jenkins grinned sardonically, "So you're making it a free choice."

"We don't have much of that," Callaghan pensively grinned back, "Just watch."

Jenkins grimaced: "You're *nuts*. Go die."


Callaghan exposed himself with his gun raised high over his head and walked away from the smoking tank, over three dead soldiers, with the posture of a proud, lanky, giant. With each footstep padding on the sand the bullets could strike him down or within an hour he'd be a grated mess shredded by jungle-natives with cheap Taiwanese Bowie knives and a hunger for Western white-bread flesh. Or burnt alive. Slavery. Sold as a slave through South East Asia... Poor White Trash Eunuch on the international Flesh Market. Callaghan imagined the amused mind of a warlord perched at the pinnacle of anarchy in the depths of this black hole. What is the etiquette for invaders in apocalyptic territories? Do they believe in the charter of the United Nations or is it solely up to the erratic mind of the local witch doctor sprinkling whacky herbs into a cauldron?

Then Jenkins stood, Marcus hobbled as best he could, then came Doc Nelson with his blood stained hands, then the privates who tightly gripped their K-40s over their heads, followed by ten other survivors from the beach, all precariously gathered before Sumatra's penthouse.

"We surrender," Callaghan called up loudly and clearly in a plain, strong and plausible tone, betrayed by his cocky way of staring up to his captor and slyly winking at the mistresses, "As one can accept that in battle," he swept his hand widely to the line of militia training their weapons on him, "We are no match against an overwhelming force." He encompassed his palm face down to his comrades, strewn over the beach, reflecting their calm in death. "I am in awe of your tactical brilliance! That is the sore truth we have learnt."

Sumatra growled through his loudspeaker, "Bah! Look who comes to me! See your men dead! You Are Dead Man! Why let you live?"

Callaghan knew well the body count; maybe fifteen Task Force Seven soldiers left standing in puddles of their own urine, shuffling closer to him with heads bowed in shock. Thirty something were the remainder, cemented in a mix of coagulated blood and dry sand as the tide retreated. Somewhere was the second and third platoons of Task Force Seven probably carved up into little pieces by savages and served steamed and wrapped in cabbage leaf. He looked up to Sumatra, his consternation completely ignorant of the appalling stench of death around him. "I am the surviving Commanding Officer of Task Force Seven and ask that you, General Sumatra, accept our surrender on this ground we have so bravely tried to take from you. Do that honour and our fate and respect is yours."

Sumatra grunted with satisfaction. For the first time an enemy had been ritualistic and polite, and in his long stretch from fist-fights behind the petroleum plant to buttering up government low-lifes the decency of simple respect was a prized honour. These prisoners in his hands were a perfect addition to his collection, another side-show of entertainment for his people. He could interview them on the radio station then all of Occupied Queensland would know of Sumatra's status; a man capable of throwing the imperialist whites back out to sea!

"Stay!" Sumatra proudly announced, pinched the arses of his two mistresses, slapped his Captains on the shoulder, then marched downstairs to the beach of Providence. With a jolly stride, his short legs thrown into exaggerated and excited long steps, he arrived onto the dunes, calling in his native tongue to the militia perched in the shot-up beach houses, *People of Providence, Victory!!! We are Victorious! Come! Rob the dead! Guns! Coins! Belts! Socks! Gold teeth! Hand them over and I will reward you accordingly!*

"How do we split the loot?" Romano eagerly asked.

Sumatra paused, "Fifty-fifty. First militia kill the wounded, then loot only when I say… The prisoners are mine. Understand?"

"Too fair, General." Romano made a shrill whistle.

Callaghan watched with a fusion of morbid fascination and fearful awe as militia swarmed from their defences, disregarding their own dead and wounded, to plunder the dead and wounded of Task Force Seven. The militia, aged between fifteen and thirty worked hard and fast, some armed with pliers, some selfishly carving their knives into a dead soldier's pockets rather than waste precious scavenging time to unbutton or unzip. On the occasion that a victim did offer protest, a plea for help or a feign weak fist in a scavenger's nose, the knifes were directed, easily shared between scavengers, into the dying mens' jugulars. From this pitiful sight Callaghan's eyes recoiled to a patch of sand before him, his long shadow cast onto it like a marker for the militia's royalty to stand from and briefly study him.

Flanked by his two Captains, General Sumatra stood infallibly impressed with his work. Behind him stood his two mistresses, Jintana and Qiao. They possessed a dry grace but radiated smiles sweet as ice-cream, their presence seamlessly gliding above the sourness of the dirtied and grubby half-clothed militia on an air of polite contempt and pristine poshness. Callaghan glared obstinately at their false civility and for the rest, formed a sneer of streetwise insolence.

Sumatra was five-foot-three of muscle and dynamite, a bloated demon, leering up to Callaghan, brandishing bold black eyes, stretching his cheeks back, a victorious grin revealing gold tapped teeth and a smoked yellow tongue. He levelled his Pearl Colt .45 to the young Callaghan's fair skinned forehead, cocked the weapon and expeditiously pulled the trigger. It happened so fast that Callaghan, jaded by carnage, failed to squeal before the customary dull *click* of the striking hammer on an empty chamber.

Stuntman, Callaghan muttered to himself, feeling warm urine creep down his inner thighs. A fucking trickster. No one told me I would die at the age of twenty-six, like this!

"Surrender?" Sumatra grinned at the K-40 high above Callaghan's bowed and cowering head. "No soldiering for you! Goodbye soldier!"

Callaghan shamefully registered the implications and felt a simplistic urge to swing the K-40 above his head into his captor's nose.

Sumatra played up to the K-40, "How much? Ha! I buy? One life for every ten rifle!"

Callaghan raised his back and grimaced down, "We ask for fair treatment, General Sumatra. As you can see," jerking his head to the sea, "We were deserted by our cowardly Commanders."

"Bah!" Sumatra threw up his hands. "They run like dogs from me! Me! ... Maybe you failed them? What do you want *me* to believe? What should I tell my militia? They are the winners... You... What are you, huh?"

"Sir, we are fine soldiers... Deserted..."

Sumatra scrunched his brow, swayed his head and openly admired his militia plundering the dead as a shepherd is happy to see his drought stricken flock drink from an oasis. He squared up to Callaghan, in the taller man's shadow, and in a quick glance compared him to his fellow survivors, "Your mistake is to talk too much." He reached up to grab the K-40 but could only do so when Callaghan lowered it.

"You like?" Callaghan saw delight in his eyes and symbolically handed over the K-40, "We can always get more. *And* the ammunition. Always *more* where I come from."

Sumatra pulled the beautiful weapon into his shoulder and ran his stubby fingers over the smooth butt, warm stock and air-cooled barrel. Tears nearly bubbled from his eyes at the symbol of power he now held, and now empowered, swung it into Callaghan's sternum and pressed the trigger. *Click! Click! Click!* Qiao rushed to Sumatra to comfort him from the anger that the gun was empty, and on realising this, Callaghan collapsed to the ground, pale in face, his arse emptying into his pants. Sumatra gestured for Qiao to step aside whilst he cursed and called, '*Romano! Romano!*' but Romano was nowhere near and then he clicked his fingers for Captain Yip to lend a pistol. Around the beach the militia delightfully searched the bodies and packs for valuables: food, technology, clothes, especially quality boots. Sumatra, with Yip's gun in hand, heartily kicked Callaghan in the ribs until he looked up and their eyes met.

"I will take care of your men," Sumatra lied, "by killing their infidel leader! No more talk for you!"

Callaghan felt nothing, no shock, just numbness, creeping from within and radiating out.

And still Sumatra talked, his Asiatic chatter briefly directed to Yip and Tran as if showing them how to execute an imperialist scum, the do's, the don'ts, etc.

"Just fucking do it!" Callaghan cried, "Fucker!"

"I do it!" Sumatra snarled, training the gun to Callaghan's chest.

Qiao stepped closer and peered over Sumatra's shoulder either because she wanted to see the death for she needed the vision of violence to calm her anguish at the white man, or she loved Sumatra, and would follow him to the ends of the earth.

The bullet, Callaghan realised from behind his closed eyes, would not come until Sumatra was satisfied with trickery and entertainment. So Callaghan, as a lasting gesture to the female species, eyed off for three strenuous seconds the gold clad mistress with the opal necklace, staring a few feet back from his own execution. Her face was unresponsive, impenetrable to demands from the doomed. But his final seconds, she blinked and recoiled, were not met with fear. He was feigning a smile, aware of death and all that, and the great nothing that lies beyond it, but still there was light in his eyes. Then as they locked, her frightened countenance fighting Callaghan's ridicule, he grinned and looked up to admire the sky, now blue, and glimpsed a familiar figure perched patiently on top of the penthouse. Callaghan gave a confused look of recognition and welcome wave, whilst the figure took aim at him, maybe to do the job properly.

Sumatra paused in his prancing, intrigued at his captive, then followed the wave of Callaghan and saw up to his own penthouse balcony and recognised the stern face from the magazine, the facade of this Phantom Task Force Seven, staring down at him with no trace of cruelty or malice, only a clinical precision aiming, a virgin K-40.

Callaghan heard the familiar *whirrs* criss-crossing the beach from the fence line and above. He saw Peters set against the sky precariously leaning over the balcony carving Sumatra to bits, the tall mistress flopping to the sand too, then directing bursts into the two Captains as they tried to run away. Before the ill-prepared militia could retaliate the men of second and third platoon, having taken them by surprise from behind the beach, had mowed them down with an admirable destructive clarity.

Callaghan remained on his knees, cold to the core, monitoring the gold clad mistress clawing her way towards Sumatra and stopping short of embracing what was left of him. Her eyes wavered from the dead, her master, and rival and friend Qiao, to the next living man, Callaghan, and there they remained fixated: in this world she needed imminent protection.

After the firing ceased and even the wounded that dared to moan were quickly silenced, the remaining men of Task Force Seven solemnly crowded around Sumatra and Callaghan in a wide circle, their eyes searching for what few enemy remained. Peters picked him up by the shoulder and brushed sand and bits of Sumatra's flesh and tunic off his face. Callaghan seemed fixated on the surviving girl. She seemed fixated on him, yet from the corner of her eyes would scan Peters, then down to her Sumatra and Qiao, two lovers interwoven, a gruesome mess.

Peters narrowed his eyes to the frigate retreating to the horizon, judging the distance and speed. "I heard some of the messages… What happened?"

Callaghan stepped past Peters, clutched at Jintana and politely held her by the back of the neck, a renewed strength motivating his tongue, "They left us… That bastard Smacker… They watched us die! We had to surrender! The warlord has us pinned down! She saw it all,"

"We can believe her?"

"She was up top,"

Peters studied her.

She didn't know what had been said, what memory of the morning, most of which she wished to forget, would be of value, nor how to portray it, but Peters believed her.

Callaghan seethed, "Smacker – he knew… He knew *something*."

Peters kinked his head to his dead soldiers, the warlord, and called to his second and third platoon members, "O-K, get going back in, secure the town perimeter, I'll be setting up a H-Q in the centre! Go! Watch the friendlies! Any nasties drop 'em! Go! Go! Fan out!"

What remained of Task Force Seven darted off the beach and secured the town. Along the way their weapons silenced the few men standing in opposition.

Peters studied the beach, end to end, and said to Callaghan, "What else does your little friend know?"

Callaghan felt under his grip Jintana's angelic face, tilted to the remains of Sumatra and the taller mistress. He turned her head to his. "English?"

She nodded, yet in shock, could not speak, or knew little English yet needed time to remember its structure, and once her linguistic value proven to her new captors, could be assured of her life.

"Don't let her out of your sight, let's go."

"Sure – give me a minute," Callaghan spoke for the survivors from the beach, "We're, well, I go to wash my pants out."

They advanced. Peters, Callaghan, this strange woman in gold, Doctor Nelson, Lt Jenkins, and the shaken survivors from the beach. Task Force Seven's other Lieutenants, Weller and McCallister, secured the town. In total, sixty men. Forty lay dead on the beach, alongside over a hundred militia. This was not Peter's ideal of acceptable losses for an attack, yet in this new venture there were no proven rules to break.

The few blocks from the beach to the centre were civilised, and though stray bullets (mostly K-40) had torn through houses and punctured windows, the residents were gripped by fear of capture, imprisonment or worse. Young mothers, the cream of the crop, Peters noted, with their babies, children or teenagers, emerged onto their verandas and ruefully examined the gladiators warily marching down their streets. The air the white men carried conveyed to the locals the stench of Sumatra's death. The locals did not smile, and they did not frown, or run scared. Their acceptance of rapid change in their town, many of whom who would find their dead lovers or brothers or tormentors on the beach, was in direct correlation to the change they had faced in arriving here. Uncertainty as a backdrop was the rule, security and comfort, the exception. So their eyes fell from the new soldiers to their yards, the new growth of recently planted herbs and meagre crops, and the hope for a new form of peace to replace the previous.

The centre of town was deserted. Peters stood with his K-40 ready, examining the best structure to assemble a skeleton headquarters. Turning back to the survivors he sensed that due to the disaster they had encountered that morning, their nerves would not be back for days, if not weeks, so any guidance or assistance asked for would be met by whimpering or misunderstanding. To his surprise, Jintana's nimble hand pointed across the main intersection to an old sandstoned bank, her other hand, the index finger, rubbing the opal on her necklace.

"Something worthy, huh?"

Her hand dropped to her side and she stared intensely at the bank.

Peters saw from within its dark depths, behind its glass bullet proof doors, a rush of flurried movement and instantly squatted to his knees with his gun raised.

"Contact!" Jenkins called in panic, he and the other soldiers following Peters's movements.

Unannounced, or due to ill-timing, three seasoned South Pacific bandits armed with shotguns, hauling heavy hessian sacks, ran from the entrance and down the five or so steps to the road, and upon sighting white soldiers, froze.

"Boys, cover me." Peters raised one hand in a friendly gesture and walked towards them, "Peace! Peace! This is my town! You answer to me! Put your guns down! Down! Peace!"

The three thieves shared a brief look of worry then whispered some ideas, the favourite of which led to their immediate executions. Callaghan clearly obliterated one, and once all three were down, joined Peters in inspecting their loot. Jintana kept close, tallying, crudely explaining, her ease with her captors growing with their accelerated progress.

Callaghan glared at the dead bandits and their sacks, the thin hessian frayed and breaking under the strain of lugging numerous crudely shaped bars of gold. He knelt down and touched the cold metal.

"Everyone else fought it out and these guys... Thieves!"

Peters remarked, "There's more than just a few agendas in this town."

"And that's something *different* we haven't taken into account."

"Meaning?"

"This place is a warlord setup and we, well, we can't just waltz in expecting what we think as civilisation. This is it, this is..."

Peters appeared to not listen, enjoying a brief respite, his face soaking the sun, his eyes closed, "We're a military unit, Callaghan, we have orders."

"Orders? Up here? After what I saw?"

"We are the order up here."

"But *here* isn't what we'd like to think it is: Liberation: Shit."

A soldier called from down the road, "Colonel! We found some missile launchers on trucks down this way. They're ready to rocket!"

"Bring them up…" he called back and mumbled to Callaghan, "Asymmetrical war just gets crazier…"

From a block away shots rang out. A Sergeant screamed "Hold your fire! You hit a friendly! Hold it!" A woman screamed. Her neighbour cried then subdued herself.

Peters nudged the gold with his feet and said to Callaghan, "Sure, this is unexpected, worthless to us, but let's get this inside."

Jenkins and Jintana followed.

Between the sandstone walls and behind the glass door they found an intact bank. Mauve carpeted foyer, lined with a row of tropical patterned cushion chairs, stretched out to an old-style hard wood counter and tellers. Passing behind this obstacle by way of a narrow gate, the four silently entered the rear administration area of desks, filing cabinets and computers, ergonomic chairs and plastic pot plants. Branching off from the plush environment to the left was an office, separated from the bank by a large stained glass wall. Inside, Callaghan found a desk and imagined the 'boss' of this establishment hard at work day and night, a family portrait sat on a corner beside a tray of standard though crude documents; certificates and licenses. More importantly, Callaghan favoured the chair and slumped in it, staring to the empty chairs on the other side of his desk. Peters called him out.

The rear of the bank was divided into two equal sections and contained the true wealth; information and communication, and the by-product of commerce. On the left side a room was decked out floor to ceiling with radios, satellite links (a cable running to a concealed dish on the rear of the roof), and modulated, reliable and robust computer hardware, the complexity of peripherals feeding in and off them more relevant to Callaghan than Peters. The second half of the rear, as Jenkins discovered, revealed spoils that surprised all but Jintana, was a walk-in vault the size of a small room. The walls were six inches thick, and inside, sturdy steel shelves were erected to store complex parts for what Callaghan guessed as circuitry for missile systems, polished pine boxes containing unsorted, rough diamonds and opals, nuggets of gold, faceless silver coins. Other boxes contained currency, ranging from yen, euro and US dollars, roubles (forming by far the largest pile) and lastly, a small wad of Australian $100 dollar notes. Peters, a man of war, trained his attention to one side of the vault that stored an assortment of weapons: a crate of North Korean anti-personal mines, two Stinger anti-aircraft missile launchers, gas masks, a new biohazard suit wrapped in plastic, a few antique handguns (that probably didn't work) and a Semtex H hand-held detonator. It felt healthily heavy in his hand and he imagined the radius of its high-powered explosion – twenty metres of blast and two hundred metres of shrapnel? Enough to bargain your way out of any diplomatic nightmare. Jintana's hand clasped over his and under her meek strength and cautious stare guided the detonator back to the shelf.

"Don't move an inch!" A Private yelled forcefully from outside, "Watch it! Hands up! Up!"

From under a desk came kicking and scuffing, then a gagged man's plea for mercy. All present rushed around it, dragging him out, the crescendo was Jintana's recognition, "Romano!"

Poor Romano had suffered at the hands of the bandits, obviously a rifle butt in the mouth was not suffice so they gagged him and knocked him out, kicking him under the desk while they escaped. If they shot him they might have alerted the militia during the confusion of the attack.

"Who is he?" Callaghan asked Jintana.

"Chief Police!"

Jenkins pulled off the gag, Romano immediately pleaded in pidgin English to Jintana and shook his head when she cross-examined and when all seemed square, both looked up to Peters and Callaghan.

"Was he part of it?" Callaghan asked Jintana.

"He know nothing! Nothing! He came to call more militia and they," her arm arced to the dead outside, "Thieves come!"

Romano explained, "I, peace keeper! Chief!"

"You're what?" Peters intervened.

Jintana answered, "Chief of Police – *militia*."

Peters fingered Romano's sternum. "You work for me now. I am the Boss Man. I am the General. I am the new Warlord."

Romano gravely nodded, his eyes searching in Jintana for the story of Sumatra's fate.

Satisfied, Peters escorted Callaghan into the privacy of the separate office though their looks of wonderment were seen by all through the stained glass wall.

"I'm shaky – I'm fucking shaky,"

Peters scoured the bank, "Settle a bit will ya. Want to see what they're waiting for. If he's Chief of Militia then what's he doing here – that gold must've been on his mind. All our guys on the beach were done for, right?"

"Yeah,"

"Small change in the scheme of things… Are you O-K?"

Callaghan paced about the desk and saw in the reflection of the glass the drenching of blood in his uniform, "Sure… Sure… I can handle it… I can't explain it. It…"

Peters sat quietly in a guest chair, rubbing the nuzzle of his rifle into his fringe, parting his short hair.

Romano glumly sat on a desk, his head in his hands, the full impetus of the situation hitting him with each of Jintana's words.

"Callaghan,"

"Yep,"

"Before I ask what happened on that beach, I saw you surrender," Peters said. "I know it wasn't pretty down there."

Callaghan bit at his lip remembering the gunfire, the pleas, "What *ever* it was it's fucked with my head. I can't remember surrendering, I can't,"

"Doesn't matter. Intelligence was wrong. I infiltrated this shitty town and found those with guns at the beach pinning you down so when you did surrender and they jumped down to the beach it wasn't hard to take up their positions and," Peters guilelessly laughed, "Mow 'em down. Fucking idiots."

Callaghan's stood still as a statue. "Them or us?"

"Them… We're alive. Saved your fucking ass,"

Callaghan wrung his hands together, "What, I owe you something now?"

"Are you joking?"

"Forget it." Callaghan threw up his hands in confusion and searched the office for cigarettes.

"Captain, next time you do surrender, you ask me. Got that?"

"Yeah! If you could break radio silence – break fucking procedure – as some humanitarian gesture when your own men are fucking dying just to jump into this shitty fucking bitch of a town!" Callaghan screamed, his hands flexed, eyes burning to those outside staring in, deflecting their gazes.

Peters grinned, "Want a punch in the head?"

"No."

"Then relax... If you don't you'll end up a stretcher case and up here,"

"I could handle being a stretcher case... But I'm alive!" Callaghan brilliantly and wickedly laughed, brimming with sarcasm, "In this paradise! That beach! And with these fucking friendly people! Look around! We got civilisation... Liberated! Right here where it isn't meant to be!!"

"Whatever it is we're here, and for us we maintain order and you," Peters testingly decided, "are freaking out."

Callaghan was motionless, trying to freeze the blitz of thoughts pinging his mind. "I've never seen combat: I never wanted it. Now... Here... This,"

"This place, I'll let you know now that its true nature will show its pretty face sooner than we think. Can you deal with that, Captain Callaghan, or do I have to lock you up in some pit with the lunatics?"

"Of course I can handle it, the adrenalin is driving me mad!" Callaghan sang, rummaging through the office and finding a precious pack of cigarettes, held it before Peters, "Look!" He scratched the plastic off a pack of *Parliaments*. "Jap cigarettes! Fucking like a tourist resort! I can *relax*."

"They're not fucking Japs!" Peters dismissed Jintana and Romano, the dead militia on the beach and the pacified locals in town.

"No, sure they're not... Don't you get it... Look around."

Peters took a long look around. Callaghan's crazy senses were crazily making sense. Peters's men were returning the gold in the hessian sacks back to the vault and Jintana, clearly Thai, conferring the realities of their new fortune to Romano, clearly an opportunist refugee come good, offering her a consoling tone and casting suspicious glances to his new rulers.

"But where are they?" Callaghan called to the empty chairs in the bank, then "Oi!" and Jintana obediently entered the office. He saw that the hem on her golden dress was sprayed with dried blood.

"Yes," she said bluntly, her piercing stare shining from a coarse straight face.

"Who worked here?" he pointed to the commanding chair behind his desk and the emptiness of the bank. "Who? Where?"

Jintana's slender little arms held an imaginary rifle and aimed towards the beach, recoiling with shot then pretending to fall forward into a bullet.

"All fucking dead," Peters stated with abandonment, exited the office and seeing the bank was secured with two of his soldiers at the front, stood at the top of the outsides steps and received the wildest shock of the Liberation.

From inside he had not heard them, or his mind was so devoured to fitting the pieces of this 'shitty town' together to form the characteristics of a military target matching what was briefed to him, namely something of considerable military value worth not just forty men or more, but the entirety of Task Force Seven. Now before him, parked on the road adjacent to the bank, a truck fifteen metres long carried four missiles, laying horizontal and cradled, which in five minutes could easily be pointing to the sky. His eyes narrowed at the warhead, the unmistakable red-ring on the tip denoting a North Korean brand. Gathered around the truck and missiles were locals, carrying pineapples, bananas, bread rolls, and offering them to his soldiers. Peters grinned, they're making peace, until he saw his own soldiers handing over what money they carried into war, for fruit, stuff that grows on trees! He was about to yell an order but Lieutenant McCallister alighted from the truck and bit into an apple handed out by little jubilant refugees come local boys. Peters stood perplexed by the missile truck. In strategic terms it was insurance. In technical terms it was completely outdated; that make and model were prone to explode in mid-air. If that's the way it is to be around here, he impulsively shrugged, I'll need some hardcore sledgehammer equipment to outdo the efforts of my predecessor. He observed the intersection's instantaneous activity.

Across the road stood a pub. A set of short, near identical Vietnamese sisters with silky black hair in bobs, the publican's daughters and waitresses, hurriedly buttoned up their French patisserie blouses and opened for trade. On cue the entire town had awoken. Yes the morning gunfight created a racket and set the precedence for a new beginning but few took the signs as imminent catastrophe. Obvious in local style shone the ethic of hard work coupled with simplicity and servitude. A few militia who had missed the morning's quarrel fronted up to the steps and held their rifles up to Peters, begging for work. A diesel utility crawled through the intersection, its rear stacked with produce: fish, coconuts, crates of goods. These, Peters thought, would have to be traded into this shitty town. How did this work? Why is this a society? Can't it be some quagmire of pain and suffering and genocide as he had been gravely forewarned by the brass yet refrained from scaring his men, and now, rightly so.

Callaghan stood beside Peters, gladly smoking his cigarette, staring from the fresh morning sun to the nouveau civilisation, a smile devoid of cynicism or parody, just plain appreciation, plastered across his face, "Fucking unbelievable shit this is. Fuck the elections for Mayor – hit the beach with a one-way ticket."

"Take a breather,"

"Peters," he explained, "Look at them. Now they know the situation don't they! Bet you never inherited something like this before, eh?"

"Inherit?" Peters stood perplexed.

The locals filed past the bank to glimpse their new ruler, his counterpart, and acknowledge that Jintana was up there too, and now Romano. And the white soldiers had not harassed or raped any of the pretty women yet, but that will come. And afterwards they will understand it's easier to take a wife, or two.

"Yeah,"

"Captain, call *Overlord*. We've finished Phase One."

"I did, the radios in there work."

"And?"

"They're not coming back, Colonel. Trust me."

Peters twisted to Callaghan, suspecting mutiny, "What are you saying?"

"I told them, the town is secured, got some signal guy saying they're pulling out to deep water, radio silence about to commence. There was something in his voice, you know. *They're* not coming back."

"No, you're *saying* they're not coming back," Peters fumed, stormed inside and found the radios, all modern and working. He sat down and tuned to the right frequency and set about patiently calling in. The static was deafening. He tried alternate frequencies. Nothing. He pleaded, cursed, demanded, but nothing. Callaghan called him to come out. Doc Nelson was in a rush, about to turn on his heel, claiming to have found a half-decent hospital to treat the few wounded. Peters nodded, at least that was sorted, and glumly sat at the top of the stairs of the bank, for all to see for most of that morning, issuing commands, meeting locals, and in between he was not reflecting on the score, the riches, or the local townsfolk parading past appearing subservient to their new junta. Instead, he was brooding on his predicament.

His first successful calls to his superiors were short, sharp and without remorse. Their replies were excuses and hints the next offensive by the Allies will surge out of Brisbane up towards Providence. Victory, Colonel Peters! Victory! Hold Providence! For it is freedom amid anarchy! A ray of hope! At the same time word came of an attack on the other side of the continent, the bulk of the navy and army reclaiming dessert.

Not some pitiful attempt, he figured, accepting he was a diversion, and pitiful at that. What did it achieve? Understanding the abandon of not only himself and his men and through their actions, the civilians of this apocalyptic outpost turned paradise, Colonel Peters methodically assumed a supervisory role. The regional borders of Providence were intact yet doomed to decay by bandits and competing forces. Within days of arrival and with help from those locals that saw benefit, Colonel Peters had recruited a new militia, continued the region's trade, and for strategic insurance purchased medium range ground-to-ground missiles and other necessary weapons from his new friend and known fiend, Jemmy, the local pirate.

To Captain Callaghan this was all very exciting but draining. There was liquor here, but never enough to drown in. He burnt his blood stained uniform on the beach and now wore hemp pants, a faded Hawaiian shirt and an akubra hat. He resumed his sit-down, all-important role in an air-conditioned office at the bank. When farmers or merchants needed a loan to purchase machinery or buy slaves, they came to Callaghan. When miners wanted to bank gold dust or nuggets, they came to Callaghan. When Callaghan had exhausted his patience dealing with peasants he logged onto his computers and played the share market via a satellite internet connection riding on a rogue satellite linked to an understanding French trader in Nouméa. Acquiring foreign capital and sizeable reserves was the only way to purchase real military hardware, and acquiring skilled personnel (those educated enough to evade death) assisted him in this task. He was no longer working for the government, the prime minister, the people, the honour of a country that had abandoned him. He often emailed to those still alive and easily tracked down around the world, including his two ASIO hallway attackers, that he was the number two man for a third millennium Warlord. Who would have thought. More importantly, who would have volunteered.

# Ceasefire in Brisbane

Corporal Matthews's eyes skimmed over the murky waters of the Brisbane River to the opposing bank's mangroves. Dense branches of sunlit leaves dipped lazily into the water, contrasted by their dark roots fingering in and out of the thick silty mud. Serenity of nature injects a meditative and spatial dimension yet for such a pleasing view Matthews's state devolved into a pained anxiety.

He observed that swept along in the mighty current of the ageing tropical river were smaller currents, insular ebbs and finger sized whirlpools, careening between muddy brown boulders covered in moss, and the disintegrating fallen trunks randomly jutting out of the mangroves. Insects skimmed the surface faster than his eyes could follow, birds systematically skimmed the insects. He'd seen a few prowling feral cats on the banks paused on the rocks, still as a statue, then smartly dipping their paws for a catfish or an amphibious lizard. He saw a body rise to the surface, tunnels had been mauled into it by crabs or some other creature that lurked in the belly of the river, then simply float away, peacefully out to Moreton Bay and then the deep blue sea.

Matthews was concealed well enough, and this being mid-morning, felt the first flush of humidity stick his khaki shirt to his back. He inhabited a homely token bunker by the river bank. The corrugated iron roof was covered with sandbags and old gum tree branches. The walls were older sheets or iron, painted olive green and now peeling, there was no door, just a space to crawl through. Through a horizontal slit he observed the river. The slit was wide enough for a trio to poke their weapons with ample space for swinging elbows and spent shells discharging. His eyes searched for movement south across the river, which was actually the northern side. This and an assortment of other technical aspects of this campaign caused annoyance to his otherwise pragmatic and practical mind. He and his battalion were in a pocket of a river that curled itself down from the Great Dividing Range down to Moreton Bay. His Commando Company, posted immediately after finishing training in Victoria, felt like strangers in a stranger land. The weather was beautiful, constant, the nights crisp and clear. The Brisbane River coiled like a snake. When it stormed, a mass of debris would flow out to sea: plastics, bobbing bottles, branches, twisted junk food wrappers, and the latest deluge, war debris – a category within itself. He could crawl out and stretch in the open air and poke at the water swirling by but few risked it. Every trail of debris has a source.

However the river tirelessly wound through the city the situation remained the same: For over two years now, the enemy were on the north side, and the Australians on the south. But what predominantly annoyed Matthews was the denial of his requests for a ticket into officer training, and that today was the third day of the ceasefire. Before it any man that dared pop is head out in the open was liable to catch a sniper's bullet between his teeth. The ceasefire extended along the Brisbane River from the mouth to some obscure point inland and had been agreed upon by tired Generals after a nasty month of sinister activity. Matthews had not killed anyone yet, though he swore he'd winged some raggedy figure hauling a frying pan, scurrying between pock-marked buildings on the opposing riverfront. The in-activity of a ceasefire translated to Matthews as a forfeit of his chance to prove his prowess. Although it defied all moral sense ingrained since he learnt to listen and evaluate the concept of harmony, this was meant to be a war, and it wasn't happening. During training he heard an abundance of stories of young diggers given half his training, slaughtering scores of the hordes with antique weaponry. Additionally, short of denying Matthews with sport, a ceasefire postponed an eventual victory. Each force had its side of the river. All he was left to do was look out from his bunker to the flowing river and imagine.

"Matty," the radio spoke.

"Yup."

"… Nothing?"

"… Wadda you reckon?"

"Fucking nothing."

"Yeah."

He placed the handset by his side and slouched. On the first day of the ceasefire both sides emerged and lugged out the dead, some completely sunken, from the muddy mangrove banks. Funeral pyres lit up the night and the stench rolled up river. Matthews had been here for half a month. His squad of five was down to three, including himself. None had died which was good for morale, it was dysentery. That's it, Matthews reminded himself, enough bitching about the ceasefire, the dysentery, what next? The girlfriend. Tanya had wanted to enlist alongside her lover and fight, but due to diligent study in her formative educational years she was holed up in a laboratory in Tasmania perfecting something top secret for the military. Matthews imagined her black hair platted into a sexy coil and resting on the bone that pinions the back of the neck, shoulders and spine. Her eyes would be scrutinising down a microscope, as he'd seen her with the textbooks or over the stove, muttering something in Italian to a microbe or a microchip, or the rising gnocchi.

Tom darted from the street, through the abandoned riverside house and into the backyard where their bunker observed this straight section of the river. For Matthews, this little command filled him with some elation – he controlled range, space, a field of fire. He had a bees dick under one hundred and eighty degrees view and thus excellent frontage of the opposing southern bank. Tom kicked at Matthews's long legs before crawling inside behind him.

"Are we on?"

"No fucking way,"

"What's into you then?"

"Corrie got one!" Tom grinned and pressed his palm to the warmth of the billy. He was a runty lad, same age, with a nuggety face blasted by the freckle shotgun and topped with mongrel blonde-red hair. To the untrained eye Tom appeared a nice boy, his gutsy boyish pranks tolerable, and his soul trustworthy.

Matthews discerningly observed his prized Private. Tom, and this was wildly known in the platoon, seven days ago shot the guts out of two Indo's with one slug then laughed it off as luck.

Matthews inquired, "One what?"

"A root. What'da'y'a think? A pay rise? A handjob off the C-O?"

"Where'd he get that? Did he catch a ride down to the Gold Coast? If he's AWOL it's you and me covering here,"

"Nah Matty!" Tom smugly crossed his arms. "Got one right here in West End."

"Bull."

"No bull."

"Yes *bull*."

"Think what you think – *I* couldn't give two shits."

"It's like that then? Something opened up I don't know about?"

"Yup."

"How much?"

"A fidda."

"That's cheap. And what do ya get?"

"Couldn't say," Tom shirked, "Haven't been there myself. Working up the courage."

With that said both young men settled back into their respective slouching positions and lazily searched for the enemy across the river. They where adequately concealed from losing their brains should the firing begin again, as very few hoped. At the far right end the river curled around to the north. Standing directly across on the opposing bank were residential unit blocks between five and twelve levels high. Between them stood stately houses, run-down and shot-up, and tall gum trees with sagging branches of beautiful greeny-grey leaves, a few twisting walkways and driveways leading to car parks and a road. To the left side across the river they marvelled at the sandstone top of the Great Hall of the University of Queensland. The pock-marked and ransacked library peeped over a chewed on cavalcade of rich leafy trees that lined a ring road that paralleled the river as it curled south. Being situated off-centre on the straight of an S-bend or any bend didn't matter in the stakes of who can see who. Sniper activity was not confined to those directly across the river even though accuracy was more precise. One could shoot up or down the river. When there wasn't a ceasefire bullets were coming from differing ends of the river, random levels of units, and from inside half demolished houses. Most of the unit blocks had taken random hits from skewed anti-aircraft fire, intentional hits by tanks, and the sporadic rocket attack by a helicopter, should a particular structure advertise its threat too well.

Ceasefire.

"I reckon if they keep this up it'll all be over by Sunday."

"Yeah Sunday next fucking century," Tom corrected.

"And this root, and remember you don't know what she's actually like," Matthews questioned his friend, wishing he had packed some hand-held computer game or trashy novel, "Or do you?"

"Nope… But you wanna' a bit?" Tom slyly winked. "Maybe it's fifty 'cause she's, you know, working on volume of sales rather than servicing a bourgeois clientele."

"Where'd you learn to pull out big words like that?"

"… T-V and the newspaper."

"Gotchya. You are so full of shit."

"Prove it."

"If I could I'd only feel more sorry for you,"

"You're not even half the bastard you try to be, *Corporal*."

Matthews complacently shrugged. His eyes skimmed along the opposing bank then vertically up the largest unit block they'd nicknamed the behemoth. There must be at least a platoon hunkering down in there. Last night he saw a few candle lights waving on walls, and shifting across were shadows, the enemy.

Tom watched the university, perhaps envying an education then cynically smiling at its slow destruction. Three flag poles atop the Great Hall now flew one red and white Indonesia Flag and some foreign Regimental Flag of the starved khaki fellas across the river. With ease he levelled his sniper rifle, breathed slowly, and lined up the Indonesian Flag. Matthews had seen Tom do this before and it would be a stroke of brilliance or fluke should Tom knock the flag off the mast with a single bullet from half a kilometre away. The minutes crept by.

"When's he coming back?"

"Don't know."

Kill the time. Matthews perched himself up with the binoculars to officially scan the units of the behemoth. If he could spot their spotters now, then when the 'cease' had been decapitated from 'ceasefire' he'd know exactly what to take out first. Perhaps they were already trained on to this hole in the ground. Surely on the night of the expected *massive* attack they knew a few positions to obliterate.

"Pull my finger,"

"Pull it yourself."

"Moralist."

Tom preferred to fire from obscure crevices, inside rooms inside houses that were partially destroyed or appeared dangerous to enter. He took the risk to avoid exposing himself. One night he claimed five kills but it was stormy and everyone knew lightning and rain plays tricks on a man's eyes. In the brilliant electric flashes a man sees purely what he wants to see or just what he fears.

"'Gonko' down the end is in hospital." Tom stated matter of factly to arouse superficial interest.

Matthews didn't know Gonko, but with time to kill he'd like to get to know him well, and mocking disbelief, argumentatively replied, "*Bullshit.*"

Tom's retaliation yarn in his trademark discreet tone (though no one was around for fifty meters in either direction) sounded honest and all-too-important not to be taken seriously, "Captain Smith wanted to keep it hush-hush right? Oh 'Gonko's got malaria', something *fucked and stupid* like that. Even Papa Smurf doesn't know."

"Malaria?" Matthews waved an imaginary mosquito away, "As if."

"Yeah – so Harris comes back – you know Harris?"

"Kind of," Matthews lied.

"Harris is wheeled out – stitched up and that – copped some frags in his nose and cheek – ugly bastard anyway – so he's rolling out of the ward and there's Gonko, 'Hello Gonko', looks over 'im, 'They get you up the arse 'cause I can't see a bandage *Mate*' and Gonko taps his temple and is speaking like a geriatric," Tom pretended to dribble on his shoulder, trembling his hands like twigs on a dying tree and rattling himself awake, "And Harris says 'Snap out of it – what is it – let's go to a real hospital you and me mate' and Gonko just lies there, 'duh-duh-duh!' Exact words."

"He's faking it."

"Well, it gets interesting."

"Anything'll interest me."

"Harris heard the nurses talking and they wouldn't touch Gonko until the Doc said 'it wasn't contagious'."

"Oh bullshit."

"*No* bullshit."

"So what is it?"

"Don't know." Tom replied and turned away to gaze the river, imagining the multitude of nasty diseases that lurk in the belly of ancient rivers to drown men in sweat with.

Matthews refused to believe until he saw proof. Now more than ever was the right time for contagious mental diseases to strike.

Tom filled the billy up and thumbed in two used tea bags. "Can I borrow twenty bucks?"

"…Going to get laid?"

"Might."

Matthews hated them asking for it in that whiny impervious moan like $10 would fill the hole in the ozone layer or feed a starving family for a generation.

"We could go for a group discount," Tom replied to the uneasy silence, "If you're interested."

Matthews shooed him away. *Tanya, come to the front!* He quietly hid his eyes behind the binoculars making slow horizontal sweeps of the levels of the behemoth. He steadied on the lines of the brick work and the bullet marks, shattered windows, a blood smear now and then, khaki washing on the balcony. Hold on that. Wet khaki, black socks, green underpants. Inside the unit, the light difference from outside making it very dim, Matthews saw the domesticated creatures. An Indon was making use of the day to wash clothes, skin and cut up a golden pineapple on a table with a machete and offer a half to a friend who stood there yapping away, casting furtive glances to this side of the bank, then sucked on pineapple, wiping his chin, excitedly yapping away, took a bite, and shut up, brooding.

Tom leaned to Matthews's shoulder. "Eh what you got?"

"Two. Behemoth. Five up, two across."

Quick as a flash Tom trained his rifle. "Yeah – yeah – oooh, nice one *Maaate*." He spoke to those in his sights. "Hey good looking – look over here… That's it… Big fucking smile. Cop this,"

"Don't bother." Matthews lamented and leant back. "My brother's in an Abrahams Tank pushing the Indo's back to Darwin. Says he just runs 'em over. Squish squish. They get stuck in the tracks and only a high-powered hose gets the mulched bone and shit out. But there's fuck all water up there."

"Where's that?"

"North of Alice Springs. In three months Darwin will be back in Oz hands."

Tom glared south to the northern side of the river. "Doesn't do much for us here."

"But it's better than here," Matthews dully admitted, contrived, "A *fucking* ceasefire. What type of war is this?"

"A shooting war."

"Why aren't we shooting?"

"Because no one wants to die right now."

"Right now?"

"Yeah right fucking now. I don't wanna' cop it. You know what?"

Matthews checked the small flames licking about the small twigs and the heat scalding the metal base of the billy, "What."

"How about *you* get a root. Fifty bucks. Honest, you'll feel a million dollars. She's not that bad, I'm telling ya."

"I'll wait."

They waited. Silence. Water trickling. The wind. Clouds moving across, the sun sinking.

"Wait for what?" Tom asked.

# On the Wings of Eagles

Krue touched down at Amberley Airbase, less than one-hundred kilometres south of the frontline. A reign of missile attacks had dissipated in the preceding months but a random allotment of sizeable testimonial craters remained. Off the tarmac were misses; wide circular rough edged sludge pits, partially full with rain. A few large bunkers were half-destroyed, some of the hangars skeletons; blackened, hard iron foundations. Different causalities but similar reminders were crashed jets, crumpled Hornets, blackened Phantoms, half a stealth bomber ("Did the other half disappear?" ran the base joke) and a wing-less Hercules closest to the other side of the runway, twisted and crumpled like a rolled up newspaper chewed by a giant, bored dog. The remnants of the frenzy of attacks during the height of the invasion remaining by the runway puzzled Krue until the thought struck home – they remained there because they represented the many more that never returned. They represent what we can still be.

She turned into the chilly wind and hunched over quickening her pace. Overhead the clouds were sickly grey yet retreating, sinking into bands of gauze wrapped around the blue-grey mountains sitting on the horizon. A light rain swept over and quickly dispersed. She swiped the cold water from her cheek and shivered. Her fellow companions on the flight were high-ranking, shipped in for an emergency intelligence briefing. In-flight they were flipping through fact sheets on Chinese hi-end hardware; naval anti-aircraft systems, including submarine based, low-orbit, satellite detection and striking missiles, and Russian ECM capabilities. Once they landed they piled out and hurried to a control tower, its base protected by a low wall of sandbags and anti-aircraft gun emplacements manned by thinned-out baby-boomers drinking lemon tea.

Krue had never seen a base crowded with destroyed weapons of war, old guards, full and ready armament trailers, tired ground support crew, pallets of this and that, nor a major base so close to the frontline, and was easily taken by surprise by her new contact. He was an excited, tall, lean, prematurely weathered pilot by the name of Doug Wellington. He shook her hand with school-boy joy and shouted something about following him in the direction of his thumb. She couldn't hear. Fighters were taking off, one taxing onto the runway while another thundered down it. Airforce guards relayed calls from a pillbox nearby. A suicide charge of sappers had infiltrated the perimeter last night and the race was on to nab them. Some lay buried in mud, breathing through a straw, and at an opportune moment would emerge and sprint towards a jet ferrying to take off. She followed Doug behind the tower, through a tight maze of supply pallets that led to a spacious maze of old shipping-containers connected by thin blue wiring. Airforce grunts stopped to admire Krue's long legs; skipping over puddles, leaping over her own reflection set against the bellies of grey clouds. They watched her mysterious profile; her figure hugging jumper and pants, ankle high jump-boots, the small bag on her back, a new K-41 gun hung from her hip, and her audacity to wear such thought provoking attire, an obvious testament to her role, something which many guessed and few knew.

"Here!" Doug rattled his fist on a metallic door and swung it open.

Before stepping inside Krue saw that the base was littered with these metallic-huts.

"You like 'em?" he called inside, his voice coming back and fronting his face into her, "Wouldn't rust in a million years out here."

No, she swayed her head and stepped in.

"It's a briefing room, take a seat," he said and didn't seem to notice she couldn't hear as a jet buzzed the base, "… is a good toilet and then a bunk and it's home sweet home."

Inside the air was damp, and once he'd closed the door and flicked on the lights she saw that the container was softened with basic tiled carpet and an electric heater. Detailed maps hung on the metallic walls, office chairs were left haphazardly, an imposing high-definition flat screen sat central on a make-shift stage. Doug led her to the front row, sat her down beside him and purposelessly toyed with a remote control. He spun it around between his fingers and over his knuckles for show. When he realised Krue's astute young mind was not fazed by quick tricks, he asked, "Rough ride in?"

"No. What happened here? Run out of space?"

Doug lingered on the practical explanation and struck for the absurd, "It's an introductory phase of seasoning the base battlers to imprisonment – should the nation falter. Most of us have money riding on both outcomes."

"I see. It looks like a port here."

"Yes well… Indon saboteurs. By giving them so many crappy structures and targets to choose from they go nuts. In the old days they knew what to go for – hangars, generators, fuel depots. They knew what hurt. After the mess hall was nailed the base commander said No Way. We deny them the booty and offer," he unfurled his palms to the carpet tiles extolling the greatness of this cavern, "A wide range of equally shittier targets."

"Fair enough."

"Tonight they'll try again: Suicidal fuckers. They don't do it for religion anymore, they just *do it* – no reason required. Losers."

"Great. I'm out of here once I'm finished with you."

"Sure," Doug relaxed and seemed profoundly proud of himself for entertaining, bemusing, and freaking Krue out. "Just one of those spooky things around here, Major."

"Thanks, but I'm quite capable of scaring myself."

"Lieutenant Manning was blunt and a bit shifty," Doug explained, "I didn't understand what you're actually doing."

Krue scoffed. "He's a messenger boy for the big shots."

Doug spoke in a firmer tone, "Sure. But why do you need me?"

"Precision bombing of unidentified and un-located targets on the central Queensland coast."

"Needle in a haystack stuff." An untamed spark lit Doug's sturdy eyes yet his voice brimmed with sarcasm, "Sounds *wild*."

"H-Q said you're the one."

He pointed his remote straight at the computer screen, "Did they say why?"

The screen awoke to the flickering and silent digital image of a high-resolution long-range camera that sat in the belly of his F-111 fighter bomber and zoomed in on where the Navigator steers the ordinance.

"No. Just orders."

"Cool. This allows me to introduce myself without blowing my whistle – which I will do, unintentionally, mind you."

"Good for you."

Krue watched the screen. It was his show-reel. From high in the sky peering down she could make out thousands of invading troops laden with field packs and rifles slithering up wide, open, white, sandy beaches as crystal blue foot-high waves washed hundreds of squad-size canoes ashore in assault waves behind them. This was one of the first runs on the Indonesians on the day when they really invaded. Her first impression was 'target': There were thousands. Who do you shoot first? It was an entire amphibious brigade making their first break.

"It's all about dispersing destruction," Doug animatedly explained, "A science within a science."

Krue could see the invaders grouping, NCO's pointing directions to take into the wilderness, every man eager to flee the crowded beach. A single targeting circle appeared in the middle of the screen. The image frame vibrated as turbulence, minuscule anti-aircraft fire, and other bombers pounded the combat zone. Bombs drifted off his wings. Fins and laser guidance clicked into action. They sailed down like torpedoes to the targeting circle then whoosh, a bright white brilliance. The glow receded, and those thousands of ants disappeared in the blink of an incendiary mushroom cloud. The canoes were alight, overturned, rolling in green-grey surf that slowly cleansed itself with each steamy wash.

"My first missions," Doug said overtly profoundly. "Old days. They said my body-count was an easy thousand a day. It was hairy. Lucky it didn't take long to wipe out their air-support too."

"What type of bomb was that?"

Doug's tone fell into that sarcastically dark classified mode, "Prototype. Oh I don't know the names but they've got better. They use a midget uranium trigger on some hard core dynamically flammable gel that explodes out like an electrified spray of napalm – sets the air alight but fuck-all fallout."

"Cool."

The next footage was an overhead, daytime, low-level view at mach one, decelerating over fringe shanty towns of a mammoth 2nd world metropolis somewhere in Indonesia simmering under an equatorial sun. Krue relaxed, taking the full sensation, speeding above grotty brown rivers clogged with rickety frail wooden jetties, moored junks, and thousands of grey dinghies. The haunting shadow of the jet passed over old paved streets packed with darting bicycles and frozen pedestrians pondering up to the heavens. Then appearing quickly were warehouse roofs, street stalls and markets, power-poles, their lines crossing over advertising billboards, roof-top washing lines and hanging plants, a sea of tin-shack ghettos, shanty slums, a thinner but slicker musty brown river, then plotted suburbs with traffic jammed streets and traffic-lights. The speed slows. Dirty-grey factories puffing on black chimneys, columns of civilian and military supply trucks blocking double-lane streets, queues paused at half-built and half destroyed bridges on their way to trade or embark from the wharves.

Naval vessels flying the red and white flag were tied in a logistical mess at larger wharves. Pine crates and pallets of gas drums were congested and piled on the jetties in neat zigzagged rows. Personnel and civilians ran wild like lost children scattering at the roar overhead, taking shelter from the mighty beast cutting apart the sky with its threat of volcanic fury. The target circle arced across the screen and neatly locked on to a drab-green cargo vessel recently refurbished as a troop transporter. On deck the boxed in tanks and kneeling troops fired into the sky puffing up a collective cloud of cordite. The port had come to life with a hundred or more dazzling sprinkles of weapon flashes. Sweeping trains of flak tracked the centre of the lens and missed.

Krue could feel the hearts pumping. Doug smiled to himself and patted his knee. A missile dropped from his wing and gracefully swerved down. Those below froze in astonishment. It hit the ship, silence, then came the blast from inside and the shock waves from secondary explosions tearing more carnage than the missile itself. Tanks sailed through the air as the ship, laden with ammunition and fuel, exploded – snapping its spine, twisting the bow, rolling into a shallow watery grave. The dock was hammered by an instant blow as if Allah's fist had pounded and left a crimson mark – all *that* must die. Flaming bodies flopped back to earth and into the polluted waters.

"Impressive," Krue referred to the screen, "But I need to see something a bit more accurate."

"Major," Doug wooed, "I've got that too… This stuff is my 'Best Of Collection'."

"Cute. Does your 'Best Of Collection' include missions over Providence?"

"Providence? Not yet, I guess. Keep watching."

The next of Doug's clips were more symmetrical and sadistically sterile. A dirt-track stretched vertically down the screen over a red dusty landscape. The camera panned over a column of troops, again like ants, but in two unsuspecting neat rows over a kilometre long. Each man may have been spaced ten meters apart in tandem with the opposite line, but the weaponry poured on them equated for that. From Doug's wings large torpedoed canisters sailed to earth, one after the other, splitting open and trickling a flock of yellow brick size bombs down along the track and a few hundred metres above the enemy. A systematic line of rings of flame decimated the troops, dispersing them like spontaneously combusting, cart-wheeling seeds, blown into the red desert.

The next scene was shorter, blurred by night-vision, almost deceivingly perfunctory in its nature. From the wide view of a suburban street, people casually waltzing on its footpath smoking cigarettes, zoom in on a house, zoom closer to the half-open window of a rear bedroom overlooking a quaint backyard. A forearm sized missile sailed through the window into a room and minutely exploded leaving the remainder of the house unscathed, yet obviously smoked out. Doug stopped the video, emanating a pride of his surgical skill.

"Assassination," he explained, "Strangely more titillating than wholesale carnage."

"Who's your navigator, bombardier – the one that guides the stuff through the windows."

"Will. He's off base catching up with his wife. Check this out," Doug displayed his hands to Krue for at first she figured as a nail inspection. His palms were face down, fingers evenly spread, and on closer inspection, right up to his arms, further down to his toes and apart from his growing grin at Krue's surprise, he was as calm as still water.

"I see. Cool Hand Doug."

"The fine line between sloppy bombing and a surgical strike."

"Absolutely," she agreed.

"It's an exact science," he boastfully conceded, "Just like towns called Providence."

"So you know of Providence?"

"Birds eye view only. I've seen millions of recon pictures of the human tides in those regions and the measures the renegades up there go to quell the waves." Now his hands sympathetically took the form of surf levelling out to a dead calm.

"The waves?"

He pressed the tips of his fingers together and contemplated. "Imagine thousands of refugees get taken out by a missile. You know you don't think it's real until you zoom in and see them tossed off the road." He lazily saluted the previous footage. "See that's legitimate; military orders for military targets."

Krue unerringly stared him down, "You've hit refugees?"

Doug sat back, slapped his knee and laughed. "No, but yes if they're in the way, but I know whoever you're after, does. Am I right? Yes? Get use to it."

Indifferent, yet intrigued, Krue bit her lower lip, drawing it over her lower teeth in a spasm of text-book horror. She'd found her man.

"I'm going in to take out one of the Warlords," she told him, "Peters."

"Colonel *Patrick Peters*. He's like Peter *Fucking* Pan. Good luck."

"Luck's not on my agenda. I just need to know that when you get the call you can deliver. Don't expect genocide… Just a strike on a command post and a few missile sights. I'll jam it into not more than one sortie."

"I'm there!" he cheerfully volunteered and enigmatically winked. "What I showed you before, and knowing where you're going, don't think too hard about it, I just wanted you to know the scale of things up there."

"You mean every single day you kill a thousand men with the push of a button? The war's not like that anymore."

"That was early days – I agree. These days my zone is Queensland Coastal and the Indo's have melted into the bush like natives. Sure I get to nail a few ships in the Coral Sea but the old days of mass exports to heaven are over. I guess God's still processing them. We should have bar-coded them down here so up there it'd be more efficient."

"*Right.* Back to my mission. What do you think of Peters up there and his region of Providence?"

Doug folded his arms and recalled the war from the cockpit. Who fired what. When. Why. "Not much – I can't... I don't think I can actually care, if that's what you want to know."

"Have you ever been on a mission to destroy any of his forces?"

"Never."

"Why."

"There was never a reason. I guess that's changed otherwise we wouldn't be sitting here... I've never had trouble flying over Providence and I hope not to. Everywhere else some crackpot is only too happy to let off a few rounds, sometimes a SAM to try and catch your tail and they miss because they're poorly trained, starved maniacs with second rate equipment."

"Peters is not a threat to you."

"Exactly."

"By not threatening his region you're allowed safe passage?"

"You got it."

"But you are committed to my mission?"

"Orders are orders."

She looked him over, past the good looks and concealed sneer; he enjoyed it and though he couldn't admit it to his superiors because he was addicted to the rush, he wanted out. His compulsion to kill was not natural, and on the grand scale, better orchestrated by the insane. But now he was a virtuoso and given the choice of tools at his disposal felt the need to further perfect his method.

"What do you know of Peters's Militia?"

"A handful of Scud-like stuff, maybe a Beijing Ninety-Six, and a militia trained by watching *Rambo* movies, but you never can be sure. Who serves him hides themselves and they've got a wide area to move about in. I wished you good luck because he'll be hard to find. Even though it looks all bush, it's populated, farms tucked away here and there, many places to conceal nasties. He's got a million places to camp out in."

"I'll get him," she adhered confidently. "I arrange it so they come to me."

"That's classy."

"That's my speciality. Has anyone bombed Providence or the northern Port of Kingston?"

"Not yet. They're not drop-off or exit points for Indonesian Units and the most I'm aware of is their economic value. See contrary to the 'big picture', the 'strategy' laid out by those who think they know the east coast deal – for goodies and baddies – is that free trading ports will cause military juntas to fall to the controls of a free market and then heal old wounds. Until that changes as it will, merchant towns are counted as civilian targets. True opportunists will dissolve Warlords. Trade brings peace, and so on."

"Even though they're behind the frontline?"

Doug sized up Krue yet shook his head. "Major, I'm trying to explain but it's very hard to get it right… I read up on what happens down there just in case I parachute in, land up shit creek without a paddle and you know what. It's not because I've gone mental or been sitting in the stratosphere playing God… Up there you've got to wonder, and Peters – I haven't met him but he'll back me up – you have to wonder who owns what up there. A line is a line and beyond that, in Occupied Australia, it's a million shades of grey. There can never be some U-N peace deal. It's the new Middle-East up there. I commend you for going in there, I really do. Sooner or later we'll all have to go and stake a claim up there or write it off as something for the Aboriginals to sort out."

"True." Krue obligingly complimented his frankness, "Who knows, if you get shot down you might join me?"

"Let's do it!" he lampooned her. "We can hang-out by the beach and trade my pistols for mangoes. We'd be dip our toes in the sea. Yeah. Don't tempt me."

"I'm in no rush."

"My call sign is *Blue Tongue*, Major Krue,"

"*Blue Tongue*. Mine is *Voodoo Child*, and for now, 'Katherine' is fine."

"Katherine…" he tasted the word, measured her eyes, and shifted forward. "So you're the one to go up there and sort some order. Very impressive but very dangerous. Are you 'removing' Colonel Peters or just taming him? What's it to be?"

"Um," she noted his candour, "We'll see,"

"And I want you to remember something because now I'm responsible for you in some ways,"

"How could you be responsible for me?" she recoiled.

Doug grinned, a nasty sadistic glint shining in his eyes, "Listen, when you call in the strike keep a *wide* berth from Ground *Zero*. That's all I want you to know. I'm a clean operator but sometimes," he pointed up to the sky, "Word comes down to make a thorough job of a target. They like to be extra sure they get what we're after."

Krue inclined her head in thought, "Then my friend, you should know that the surgical skill you stroke in the sky I weave on the ground - Maybe your services will never be required."

"I've never heard *that* before." He sat back with his arms crossed and legs in an open V-shape to Krue. He couldn't decide if he was hot for her looks or in sheer awe at her will to clean a mess he was thankful to witness from several miles in the air. "You're such a piece of work aren't you?"

"They all say that."

He winced, "Damn! When you get back, drop by."

"You think I'll get back?"

"I'm your guardian angel in the sky. You'll be back. First up, how you getting up there?"

Krue paused, unbuttoned her bag and passed the transport documentation to him. "Looks like no-frills out of Brisbane, what do you think?"

Doug scanned the document. He'd seen a few of them previously, run off from a template; sending bodies up north like popping daredevils out of cannons at a fun fair. "Archerfield. V-L-O. Yeah, they run a gutsy flight... Gets you up north quick, but a bit bumpy crossing the line. If it's tonight," he said elatedly, "I'll be your escort out of town!"

"Fancy that." Krue, in an act of efficient scheduling, extended her right hand to shake with Doug, "It's been a pleasure."

As their palms touched, Doug feigned a jolt from her enigmatic soul and slyly winked at her, his words pressured and precious, "I mean it. Make sure you drop by when this is over, Katherine."

"If you can prove yourself up there as good as you say you are, sure."

"You're on."

# Viva Brizvegas

That afternoon all eyes were fixated on Corrie. According to his grandmothers' chattering, Corrie was a descendant from head hunters of the South Pacific. Cannibalism in a family was something to be proud of, plus being a mix of Maori, Munga and Irish, he was a bulky lad, medium height, and knew how to enforce his articulate skill of spinning a yarn with glossy, bold, black scary eyes streaked with cat scratches of orange.

"And she was going down on me for five minutes an' I'm saying Hey Miss, get ready, and she didn't get it, and her mouth was full, and then I moved her around a bit. Ka-ching. Snoop Doggy-Dog would be proud. The mattress stunk like a porn mag in a Young Offenders Institution. Gag. Afterward she says, 'So unreal. You're the one.' Not a slut. Not like the meat market in the Cross."

Matthews had heard Corrie's sex stories after a bender in Kings Cross. They had a similar ring. That was two months ago. Ever since then the Commando Company had trudged its way up towards Brisbane looking for the shit and finding nothing but this, the sniper range and now a ceasefire. And a shag if you were lucky.

"An' then she gives me change from me fifty. Ace."

Tom piped up, "Less than fifty?"

"Forty. You believe that? 'Cause I'm 'the one'."

"Sure!" Matthews implied that Corrie was full of shit.

"Anyway, so I give her the ten and say I'm saving up for next time!"

"Not bad!" Tom rubbed his hands and delightfully turned to Matthews, "Not bad at all!"

"Fuck off!"

"C'mon Matty," Corrie cackled, "You need to get a load away. It's written on your fucking forehead. C'mon mate!"

"Yeah. Without one you're a fucking royal cunt to serve under," Tom sneered. "We'll chip in if you've been sending your money to ya' honey."

"I respect you two, right..." He threw his hands to his head as if to lift it off and hurl it into the air. "There's nothing *going on* around here! No women! All cleared out! And it's a fucking ceasefire!" He leant out of the foxhole and wailed across the river, "This is all *shit!*"

Corrie pulled his superior back down to the earth, "*Settle* on bro'. The Engineer girls can be obliging if you give 'em the right smile, you know that 'are-you-thinking-what-I'm-thinking-but-no-one-knows-we're-thinking-it's-just-you-and-me-now-on-your-knees!'"

"And if you're an officer!" Matthews protested.

Tom lit a cigarette and fanned his hand at the smoke, then them, "And a gentleman… Let's not forget *that* drawback, perverts."

Matthews cursed. The sun was setting. At night they could move about and although the ceasefire prohibited sniper activity, there were reports of the odd angry shot let loose. On the radio he spoke to his platoon commander who had not changed the 'sit and wait' order.

"Who's cooking?" Tom asked.

Matthews shrugged, "Scrounge around and I'll fix something up."

Corrie grimaced. "Yeah?"

"Well I got nothing. Last night. Remember?"

"Yeah."

"Tom, nip up to the sergeant,"

"Nah – call him."

"Doesn't work. You gotta go up and hassle some tucker," Matthews explained, "Otherwise all they send down is crap."

"Yeah, in a sec."

Tom's eyes slowly ran along the opposing bank. His mind weakened at the twinkle of glittering golden sunlight on the ripples of water. He wasn't feeling hungry enough to go up the hill. Apart from the itch in his pants there was nothing he needed to please. He instinctively ran his eyes up the behemoth. There was movement on the third level, first from the left. He raised his rifle, peered through the scope and spied two Indons cuffing cigarettes, setting up a heavy calibre machine-gun on a tripod, feeding an ammunition belt into it from a large plastic crate. It was either carelessness that they were seen or audacity to be seen, or sheer luck that Tom caught them in the act before they would cover the shot up doorway through which he saw them.

"What've you got?" Corrie asked.

"M-G. Two. Three up. First on the left."

Matthews perched himself at the slit with his binoculars. The celibate strain in his veins had subdued. His breathing was extraordinarily calm. In half an hour the sun would be gone. Maybe this was a set-up for tonight. Maybe this was happening all along the river front, maybe there is no honour and all we want to do is kill each other until there's no one left.

"Tom scan right, Corrie left."

All three were at the slit searching for signs; figures hauling ammo crates, normal scout posts unattended, the absence of smoke from cooking fires trailing from behind buildings.

After five long minutes Corporal Matthews called for sightings.

"Zero."

"Jack shit."

"They've either pulled out or gone to ground – in which case they're up to something. Ceasefire my arse," he gritted and nabbed Tom's rifle and took careful aim. The two man machine-gun crew across the river had finished the setup and now looked over their work with a degree of pride. Both were thin, short, and as Matthews breathed in, chuckled to himself that they hadn't had a square meal since leaving the Indonesian Archipelago. Must be mad with hunger and stupid enough to show their silly little faces to the outside world, smoking too.

"Corp' you can't," Corrie whispered and placed his hand reassuringly on Matthews's shoulder, "We'll get 'em latter."

"Settle." Matthews quietly replied, more to himself. "Just letting them know we're watching." He slipped the safety catch off. "Tom, range set?"

"Yup," he gulped.

"Cool." Matthews breathed in, this is for bombing the *HMAS Goulbourne* and killing Auntie Tracey, out *ahhh*, this is for fucking up Trevor in Darwin, in, and this is for – fuck it – the explosion from the barrel cracked across the river and echoed back. One of the machine-gun crew hit the floor. The other sat atop an ammunition crate, staring out to the river and the glow of orange clouds on the rippled surface and then collapsed in a heap beside the assembled machine-gun.

"Through the heart." Tom commended Matthews's finesse.

"Fluke." Matthews retorted with the huff of a seasoned hunting gentleman. "I was aiming for the space between them,"

Corrie scratched the back of his head. "I'm real sure they know it was a mistake, eh?"

Matthews held his satisfied smile and handed the smoking rifle back to Tom, grimly stating, "Ceasefires Are *Hell*."

"The C-O should know, I reckon," Corrie said. "Just for a report. You got one. We got one. They have some big database they put everything into."

"I don't think they'd care," Matthews shrugged. "Just one conscript. There's loads kicking the bucket on the front every day – Trillions of the buggers wishing they'd cop it so easy – through the heart."

"You make it sound like a love song… Well…" Tom sat sullenly on watch but the sun now slipped behind a thick pinkish thread of westerly clouds. The behemoth was completely darkened. A torch light lit up in the unit of the dead man. Another torch waved around then foolishly out to the river as if to isolate the offenders. Seven minutes later the torch bearers rechecked their bearings for the opposing bunker and aimed their rocket-propelled-grenades.

"Anyway," Corrie grinned, trying to de-pressurize the situation, and cuffed his cigarette, "Why do Queenslanders wear thongs?"

"Gee. Why's that?" Tom asked.

"They can't tie shoe laces!"

"Lame!" Matthews concertedly laughed, "That's as crap as the one about the,"

Tom hissed, his hand slicing through the air about them, "Shhh!"

A few metres outside the bunker the first rocket landed. Then the second. The two explosions blew the roof off the bunker and flattened the three petrified men inside to the dirty floor.

"Out! Out! Out!" Matthews scrambled out, up the backyard to the half demolished house. Bullets picked about, zipped past his ears and hit a retaining wall. A flare sailed up – he saw his reflection on the pock-marked wall. He loomed larger than he could imagine himself and was crash tackled by Corrie into an empty swimming pool basin. Two more rocket propelled grenades landed in the bunker, guttering it, leaving a smoking crater and ring of fire.

"Tom!"

He splashed in the river, cussing, having leapt the wrong way.

"Get out of there – They got night scopes!"

Tom ran up the bank, skidded in with Matthews and Corrie huddling in the bombed out swimming pool. From every second unit of the behemoth came tracer shots bearing down on them. Chips of tiles and cement flew from all directions, the house before them creaked. A mortar crew from their side of the river added to the ever growing crescendo. Tom rushed into the house, through it, and out onto the street leaving wet footprints on the dusty floor. Matthews and Corrie soon followed, cut and bruised, ecstatic to have survived and huddling in the new safety. The street was protected by the houses facing the river.

"Holy Fuck." Corrie gasped.

Tom stooped to kiss the ground, "We're alive!"

Their riverside suburb of Hill End was soon in on the act, the sound of bunkers and foxholes all along the river opening up with pre-aimed fire. Consequentially machine-gun crews on the high ground initiated high-carnage payback.

"Hear that?" Tom cuffed a hand to his ear.

From a ridge before them, its elevation commanding a view of the pocket they inhabited, a machine-gun emplacement came to life sending half-second bursts of hundreds of slugs to positions across the river.

Corrie shuddered, "Mince-maker."

Out of the early evening confusion and half-light the platoon's Commanding Officer boomed, "Matty! Matty! It was your crew! Wasn't it! I heard the first shot! I heard it! And what's this!" His index finger pointed to the heavens and the tracers of machine-guns crossing the night sky, to and fro.

"Sir!" Matthews stood up. A flare sent from the enemy sailed over, illuminating his C-O striding up the street, fuming, the Staff Sergeant at his side, and another imposing figure of career changing prominence.

"What happened!"

"Captain Smith!" Matthews gaped at the imposing figure, yet answering to his C-O, "Surprise rocket attack!"

"Who fired first!" Captain Smith waved his arm about to the dusky clouds above and tracer shots whizzing from the river front, now dipping dangerously closer to head height. In an adjoining house, what remained of a broken window, shattered.

From halfway up the ridge, in another bombed out house, a cranky voice bellowed for his mate, "-that fucking stretcher!"

At this point battle-front discipline became secondary to personal safety. As the bullets raced over they were returned and soon enough the entire stretch of river honed on the positions they'd meticulously spotted for the last three days. Men on opposing sides of the river would pick each other's muzzle flashes out and form duels until one was either hit or burrowed out of sight. Captain Smith dragged the Corporal down the street, into the dip of another and screamed abuse. Even this became dangerous. Mortars began to fall on both sides of the river. One hit the tin roof of a house, went right through, and blasted out the five walls and a dunny door.

"Back!" Captain Smith screamed to the Corporal, "Back to the River! Defend your post!"

"Yes Sir!"

"Go on! Privates – get back!"

"They nailed our hole, sir. They got us!"

"I know! So get back there! If they're swimming across – you'll be there to meet them!"

The ceasefire was officially over. Captain Smith slapped the Corporal across the face and left him to the Platoon C-O to boot.

Captain Smith ran north up the ridge onto its spine, Dornoch Terrace, which ran up to Highgate Hill, a major vantage point of inner-city Brisbane. On his zigzagged walk up he could see the extent to which one simple shot, and he'd heard it, and the subsequent rifle crack bounce back to the southside, excite an entire river stretch and now howitzers in Woolloongabba were lobbing shells into Fortitude Valley. In an accumulative measure of boredom it was as though a three day ceasefire had been too much. He turned his head to the north and the central business district of Brisbane. What glass still remained on concrete towers reflected the orange, pink and red glow of the disappearing sunset. The bridges that once spanned across the river were all torn to bits. He wondered if he'd ever get to the other side, if he'll ever get out of here, if he were better off in another division where ground was taken in a mighty offensive and a man, and a woman, could feel a sense of accomplishment. Whereas here, we rot. And Corporal Matthews, no wonder he wants out. No bloody wonder.

Captain Smith arrived at his Command Post completely drained. It was atop the hill and in a half demolished terrace house. Back at his desk the orderlies came in with reports. Two wounded from a direct hit on second platoon. The engineer convoy from Holland Park had halted. Nurses at Princess Alexander hospital were hiding in the bottom level of the car park. Urgent. Dispatch three commandos for a confidential insertion mission up north: The battalion stamp at the bottom.

Captain Smith called up battalion, "Papa Smurf please, Captain Smith... Fit and fine... ... A concentrated show... Yes Sir... ...It's not probing... They're up to something... ... ... Uh-huh... ... Three? Old hands or green?"

The Battalion HQ was not far away, concealed in what was once a jail for fraudsters, thieves, rapists and murderers. Boggo Road's thick walls could supposedly withstand a wide assortment of weaponry and up till this point had.

Colonel "Papa Smurf" Starkey sat at his desk, calmly talking into the radio, "Three you can spare. I'll send a jeep down to pick them up."

"And what are you doing with them?"

Papa Smurf turned discerningly to Lieutenant Manning, sitting on the other side of the desk, "Not sure. Brass insertion up north. Just hurry them up. They're leaving tonight. Call in if anything pops up Smithy. Out."

Manning breathed easier.

Papa Smurf observed the visitor, Lieutenant Manning, clean shaven, nice haircut, shot straight out of the big smoke, groomed to be a back-office general, wispy internationalist, strategist for the new world order.

Manning sipped on his scotch, tersely flickering his eyes around the thick timber supporting a thick roof that held up tonnes of brick and more wooden supports. This was the first time he'd heard the War. Even in this chamber it sounded amplified. The hairs on his ears prickled to the sound of booms from north and south and then the whine of a descending bomber. As soon as the 'final three', he had termed them, were on their way, he would be back to Sydney for a new posting in the newly formed East Coast Naval Battle Group. But will I survive, he pondered.

"Are we safe?"

"Safe as houses."

Manning nodded. "So how can you ever feel safe up here?"

Colonel Papa Smurf stroked the thin white hairs on his chin, sparingly sniffed his scotch, flimsily unfurling his fingers to the heavens. "It's a numbers game." And clutching the numbers from the air around him, re-affirmed the principle between life and death, "Numbers. But I wouldn't bet on them."

"Certainly not."

"Now, what is it really like up north? Are you in the know? Word gets around *that* little camp fire."

Manning rested his glass on his knee, sedately enveloped in the quest for an adequate and honest answer for the frontline commander of one of the most grizzly patches of the Brisbane Line, "I think that's it – we hear things. All a mess of numbers," he finished with a falsely content smile, "Numbers. Spiralling. And Random."

The signals sergeant burst through the door, "Spotters report two Indon battalions heading out of the city.

Papa Smurf winked back as she about turned down the hallway to spread the word.

Outside, an incoming shell struck a wall. A creaking sound and gush of a muffled shockwave painted Manning's face white as a ghost. Dust, sitting on rafters and coating walls, was shaken free and hung in the air like frozen static.

Papa Smurf exhaled, stood, donned his helmet and flak jacket, "Get back safely. Brisbane won't be pretty tonight."

"They're attacking?"

"An attack I can handle but they've been planning something different for days. Good evening, best of luck."

In a crude dark underground bunker, water stagnated in a thin greasy film on the cement floor. The walls were cold earth and zapped any warmth in the air. Krue re-fitted a blanket around her shoulders and read using the illumination of a perfectly still flame atop a cheap white candle. She turned over page 97 of 99 on the combined reports on her target, Colonel Peters, formerly of the Australian Army, though in her reading there was no official dismissal of his services. The 'target' encompassed much more than his flesh and persona. There were his fellow Task Force Seven Soldiers, all listed as missing. Included in the report were their photos taken weeks before departure. She could see the crows-feet spreading from the corners of their eyes and the erosion in their hollow cheeks. Though they achieved a smile it appeared in hindsight a frank welcoming of an unknown peril, or, Krue imagined, a weary notion of retirement to fate, fate something that few men control yet one, now and then, holds the reigns of.

Page 98.

*It is strategically inconclusive if a tactical invasion could dismantle the myriad of forces of influence in the current geopolitical climate of Occupied Queensland. There are serious implications in recovering resources-rich and highly strategic terrain. In the foreseeable future there will be more cunning and less obvious 'ventures' by foreign powers to lay social or economical claim to sections of Occupied Queensland. Refugee populations will no longer move from impoverished region to another. Faced with geographical overcrowding, limited resources and practical knowledge of how to manage the land, an equilibrium will surface. Present settlement rates of refugees in coastal areas of the mid-coast of Queensland have reached crisis point. Overcrowding in 'civilised' centres has led to outbreaks of disease and with the fear of spreading disease through an isolated lawless land, regional commanders have resorted to wide-*

*spread systematic genocide based on the health of a group of people, rather than race, religion or other discriminatory indicator. The crisis is a continuum of cycles; overcrowding, disease, culling, renewed settlement thus an influx of populace, overcrowding. Until adequate measures or circumstance arise that facilitate the management of the flow of refugees there is no solution bar the present solution. Peace requires economic stability. A population overload creates anarchy. The genocide of refugees emigrating to Occupied Queensland is a self-saving measure by established forces in the area. Neither the country of origin of the refugee is outraged or the newly established civilisations in Queensland.*

*In contrast the introduction of Col. Peters as a Warlord into the regions afflicted has caused considerable mayhem in many international circles. While it's politically convenient to overlook that a Third World dictator may commit genocide on races in his own nation, it's politically dangerous and internationally deplorable that an un-sanctioned Westerner should implement genocide on refugees, as his Asian predecessor (late Gen. Sumatra) had done. As numerous nations are at war in South East Asia, the majority of warring nations are content to redefine the value of refugee populations in accordance to their own varying needs based on basic supply and demand, politics, religious and other forms of prejudices. In contrast, the operations of Col. Peters in-appropriately reflect Australia's role in regional population control. The greater the perception that Australia and her citizens and forces are a regional player in genocide, the greater the mandate by Asian nations to annex sections of Australia from the Western World's geopolitical influence.*

*I hope this information has clarified the need for immediate action to Brigadier Tolken and counterpart Colonel Smacker.*

*Yours sincerely,*

Krue stood, stretched her legs, checked her watch, paced around the table and inclined her head to watch moist crumbs of earth descending from the loose trestles in the roof. The earth reverberated. Above ground was either bombardment or rush-hour. The aluminium hatch to the room flew open, the candle light flickered, three lumbering figures formed up, the door shut, the candle light regained its stillness. By this soft light and partially in a darkened corner, Krue quietly pointed to the dirty commandos then to three bare student chairs positioned around the candle lit table. They shuffled around and sat, one sniffed, another sighed. The ride in must have been rough. Krue sat at the head of the table and waited for the feint rumble from above ground to recede. The three young men were exhausted and carried rifles, a half full pack, helmets, flak jackets and water canteens. For their youth they were very subdued and servile, or maybe it was her commanding and imposing presence. In their faces they looked twenty-one or more, but their agitated, frenetic motions projected their real age, perhaps nineteen.

"Major Katherine Krue," she quickly introduced herself.

"Corporal Matthews."

"Private Tom Gale."

"Private Corrie Chip."

She sat down and examined them. Corporal Matthews held them together; his mouth was expectantly open, ready to defend or ask, his eyes roving the room for clues. Tom was the runt, perhaps the most dangerous and sneaky, not for a second letting his sniper rifle out of his grip. Corrie was the muscle, with intelligent eyes, his baby-jungle-face on a huge frame but emanating a fresh primalistic glare. For Krue it was imperative to take an instantaneous liking to her new crew. She had no other choice. They were young, time and guidance would fix the 'dumb' element, therefore they could be moulded into exactly what she wanted – Krue's Crew.

"We might be needed back at the front soon," Matthews nervously and righteously advised her.

"You won't miss it a bit."

"Major, is this an interrogation or something?"

She laughed lightly. "Why do you say that?"

He eyed the bare earth walls and candle, "This is a bit severe."

"Yeah." Corrie piped up.

"Silence!" Krue hissed and then politely to Matthews, "Why? An interrogation would be… What did you do?"

"Nail an M-G man: It was me or him,"

"Hold it," she wizened. "Who were you to report to?"

"The Military Police and some Lieutenant rode us down here," he explained all that he knew, "They dropped us off and pissed off quick."

"So who sent you here?"

"I think Captain Smith sent us. Maybe as punishment. Is this a prison? We haven't been told anything."

"Stop." Three Commandos had arrived on time. They wore the uniforms, they'd done the training. "Why do you think you're here?"

"We," Matthews rolled his eyes over his comrades, "*I* broke the ceasefire."

"Ceasefire?" Krue shook her head. "So the Captain sent you to me?"

"Maybe to get us out of the Company," Corrie suggested. "Everyone's gone bonkers. I heard someone got a mental disease."

"It's contagious," Tom added with a smirk.

"Shut up! … Maybe," Matthews embraced the darkness in the corners of the room, "We're actually safer in here."

Krue's eyes circumnavigated the rim of the puddle on the crude, uneven, cement floor, then zeroed on the candle. No one up here knew her. She was a nobody. A body bag waiting for a body, like these three sacked Commando, if they were of that creed, and they had been trained, and they weren't that expendable. They were clearly drunk on the rush of endorphins released from a sporadic shattering of their nerves. We are a recipe for failure, she bit her lip, glaring into the soft light. This is an on-key death note, a country on its knees, doomed, and this is our last-ditch effort.

"Major, are you all right?" Matthews kindly asked.

She was infuriated and refrained from yelling some obscenity. She sportily clasped her hands and forced a single perfunctory smile to precede her stern words, "I requested three commandos trained in infiltration for an assassination mission on the Queensland Central Coast."

Matthews, Corrie and Tom's jaws drooped to the floor and a dumb-founded glare distorted their faces.

"I think there is a mistake," Matthews wistfully advised.

Krue frowned each of them down. "No mistake – we've been shafted."

He suddenly agreed, readying to rise, "Shafted? We should,"

"Stay where you are Corporal!" Krue growled. Her voice was fluid, forceful, and terrifying as any career drill-sergeant. "You are what I requested but… Action? Seen action?"

"Front line," Matthews said.

So Tom added, "Nothing like hand-to-hand or strangling,"

"Shut up." She could cancel. You can't cancel this. This is it: All the good men are dead, plain and simple, or up north.

Matthews asked, "Can you explain precisely what we're doing here? I thought this was some disciplinary action."

"Fuck your ceasefire Corporal!" Krue shouted. "Let's have an understanding… We're going in, we're completing our objective, we're returning…. You're to ask no questions as to why. This is my Mission. You're here for the ride and to protect me."

A brief silence fell over the room. Above ground large Chinook choppers were touching down.

"You're taking us on your Mission?" Matthews asked, puzzled. He could not fathom a new routine so quickly! Or, he glared at Krue, he'd be another thousand miles from his darling.

"A targeted assassination,"

"Targeted assassination?" he struggled with another bafflement.

Krue rolled her eyes. In her dry tone she exacted some precision, "Assassination of a regional commander: a Warlord."

"You're an assassin?" Corrie half choked.

To the three youngsters she appeared daunting, spiced with high voltage sexuality and totally dominant, yet they just couldn't picture her plunging in a dagger.

"Yes."

The three clenched their fists, spelling the word in their minds, twisting it around, but still completely unsettled.

"This is my ninth." She moved to the end of the dank room to three large metal cabinets. "We'll be shipped out in half an hour. I know this is all rushed but let's just say, some serious geo-political shit is going down. There's just enough time to fit out and brief you on the terrain,"

"Major?"

"Yes Matthews."

"We've come straight from the front. Is it possible to eat and clean-up?"

126

"No," she opened the cabinets. "Up north we'll be out of this time zone – you'll be in my time zone. I'll see to some form of down time depending on how low a profile we keep." From the cabinet she handed around the equipment. First satphones. "One for each of you. Basic satellite phone with a GPS trackers so our superiors know of our whereabouts. Green button is standard tracking. Red button, and all of you pay attention, is target activation – what ever co-ordinates you put in with the red button on get wiped off the face of the map. Once we locate the target, or it's moving we update the co-ordinates. It's the most practical method to complete our mission. Best of all we can plant it on a moving target but trust me, you don't want to be near it when the shit comes down."

Matthews turned the satphone over in his hand, "Handy." It was surprisingly light with a flip-top screen detailing their global position in longitude and latitude.

Krue slipped a satphone into her left breast pocket. "Private Gale."

"Tom, Major, is fine."

"Krue, Private Tom, is fine for me too… You'll have the radio. Multiple capabilities. We can make contact with almost anywhere in the world when routed through our H-Q in Canberra and Airforce frequencies." Krue then handed out personal two-way radios. "Good for five to six kilometres depending on terrain. Enough standby battery power for a week."

"Is that the duration?" Matthews asked sharply, his eyes trapped on her behind.

"By my planning, yes. Shorter is always better though. Now, note: Turn off your satphones. There's no need to have them on. Next, ordinance." Krue passed 9mm berretta handguns and new K-41 rifles. Next came rations for two weeks, the usual assortment of camouflage creams and netting, torches, knives, grenades and two claymore anti-personnel mines. "I assume we're trained in all on hand?"

"Yes Major," Corrie and Tom sang excitedly.

"Absolutely," Matthews announced and watched the change of shadow on Krue's backside as she shuffled to the table; one cheek was full and womanly, the other marginally deflated. He rubbed his tired eyes.

Krue laid out on the table a detailed map of a section of the central Queensland coast. On the coast was Providence, seemingly unimportant except for her slender hand redrawing a thin neat red circle around the outskirts. Stretching twenty kilometres to the west were farmlands, back roads and then the foothills of Jacinda

Mountain, the most prominent and daunting form on the tail of the Great Dividing Range as it eventually trailed off much further to the north. She neatly marked an X on the western side of the mountain and stood back.

"We'll be dropped in there early tomorrow morning. From there we'll be ascending Jacinda Mountain on the ranges, observing, and then moving off the mountain, infiltrating through the farm lands, staking out Providence, finding our targets. It'll take as three to four days to get there undetected. Questions?"

"Do you have any intelligence reports of who is between there and here?" Matthews traced the distance between the X and the circle.

"Yes but it's mostly unreliable." She pointed to the port of Kingston, north of Providence. Between the two towns snaked the Arubai River. The road between the two towns was Highway Five, crossing the river at Sunny Bridge, spanning over the Arubai. "There's the main trade routes. Cargo is shipped in and out from Kingston into Providence. We'll briefly monitor their trading routes in favour of immediately searching for our target and his main strength, a mobile missile launcher."

"Scuds?" Matthews blinked.

"Some of those, but not on our agenda," Krue said. "We're after an inter-continental ballistic nuclear missile."

The trio apprehensively peered into the map. Somewhere in there was an inter-continental ballistic nuclear missile. It was surreal, like a training exercise played on simulators in dark rooms like this.

Matthews spoke timorously, "On the map it looks like a Sunday Picnic but from what I understand you're saying this area is a breeding ground for World War Three."

"This is World War Three. We're an insurance policy that one day there may be a World War Four."

"What?"

"That's right. *What*. We're dealing with risk, uncertainty and high stakes."

"So, our target is a Warlord, he has got nukes and that's our objective?"

"And his assassination."

"Cripes," and still suspended in disbelief, "So which is primary and secondary?"

Krue looked down to the map. The contour lines of the Great Dividing Range and the sheer twisting ridges of Jacinda Mountain formed a jaded question mark in her mind. With any luck the two targets would be bundled together and Doug could wipe them out with a cluster of 250kg bombs. Plain and simple like three from her previous eight. She wondered if any of the top brass had seen this through, had predicted that her team would be in-experienced, and had supplied her with some larger game plan. Was the strength of this effort in true proportion to the strategic importance? But all that was left were the conscripts and the young, who until the moment Indonesia invaded, saw combat as a field of pixels on a computer screen. She moved from the map and sat down. The trio watched her, politely turned away and dutifully packed their equipment. Regardless of their youth and an intact innocence, she fondly noted, they were disciplined and quiet.

"If you have any questions beware," she said, "Currently I'm short of answers."

Matthews rubbed his dirtied hand up the side of his face. He could feel embedded specks of tiles and cement. He could feel the whoosh of the grenade and thick reeking mud on the banks rising up to his nostrils as he cooked breakfast. Then it lifted as he observed his new boss, on a chair, flipping through a report. She wasn't speed reading, it was more like absent minded study while he and his comrades readied themselves.

Ten minutes later the door to the room flung open. An Airforce woman dressed in overhauls, earmuffs on her head pinching her brain, and wiping her snotty nose with the edge of a wooden clipboard, hoarsely screamed, "Operation *Voodoo Child! Voodoo Child!*" as if she'd been working in a deafening factory all her life.

Krue lazily saluted

"You're up!" she pointed to her watch. "Five minutes! Five minutes!"

"Chop-chop!" Krue clapped her hands and tossed the report into a tin bin in the dark corner.

They hastily packed and walked up the cement stairs into the underground tunnel. The woman in overhauls shone her red torch to the earth roof and about turned, hollering, "Follow! Follow!" She led them up a side passage, stopped, turned, handed out ear plugs, checked they were four as marked on her clipboard then booted out a hatch into the night air. A thunderstorm had passed over in the last hour. The tarmac was a muddy field. She threw her arm out to five fixed wing Vertical List Off (VLO) Bombers taking on weapons.

The night roared with the whine of their jet engines warming up. Weapons crew raced to fix bombs and missiles to matt-black wings. She jogged to the centre VLO. The pilot remained in the cockpit, nodded his helmet-head, then yanked his thumb to the belly of his jet. A three-step plank dropped into the mud. It led up into what should have been a bomb-bay but was now altered for a human cargo of five. Up they ran, jostled for space, sat, buckled up in flimsy canvas chairs and peered ominously out thick perplex windows set in the fuselage above the front edge of the wings. The woman in overhauls popped her head in, and though no one could hear her scream, they could tell it was a cross between good-luck or get-fucked, twice over, then thumbs up, salute, see you next time! The plank automatically rolled up sealing the crew inside. It was pressurised and still deafening.

"Can you hear me?" Krue yelled.

"Yeah – you're over there!" Matthews pointed directly to her.

"No! Can-You-Hear-Me?"

"No!" he shouted.

Two rotating jets either side of the fuselage pivoted thrusters to the ground. Between the cargo area and the cockpit was a hatch big enough for a pygmy to crawl through. The co-pilot pushed it open and passed ear muffs connected to an audio panel in the cockpit. The team hastily pulled out the futile ear plugs and clamped on the ear muffs. They heard a one-way intercom, could not say anything, only listen to the pilots yapping to each other or to other VLOs, but could not hear the replies from other craft or themselves.

"Clear aft."

"Clear."

The thrusters' partial ignition rumbled the craft. A heavy coarse nauseating scrapping sound levelled out to an even grind as the mix of oxygen and fuel shifted to the optimum fiery rocket mix. The VLO shakily lifted off. Its jets sent up a sharp spray of dirty water then smartly baked the mud into a hardened flaky clay.

"Okay okay," the pilot yanked up, his oblong helmet head swaying as he checked his flanks, banked left, his dry voice narrating, "Up up and away… She's hot to trot."

The co-pilot came to in an over-friendly enthusiastic manner, "Human Traffic… Welcome aboard… Could passengers refrain from serving their dinner up, please."

Krue thrust her thumbs-up clenched fist through the hatch into the cockpit. Out the windows the crew could see by the short spouts of solid flames from other thrusters that the flight of VLOs were lifting off and forming a loose arrow formation over southside night time Brisbane. In the distance, on which side few could tell, the soft glows of ground fires reflected on the bellies of slow moving, sluggish, low-level clouds.

"Good to see Major. Good to see. Sorry you're muted. These things aren't cut out for the five-star treatment. If you're sick give us the thumbs down but don't open the plank in the belly. Just suck it up, we say."

"Form up."

"Before we proceed to the L-Z we're sneaking north over the river for a run on Indon spotter emplacements... As you may or may not know-"

"*Sinbad* move in... *Thunderbird* up up yup," the pilot steadily narrated.

"there's action up and down,"

The pilot's voice broke in with a brief surge of angst, "Since the ceasefire was broken at sunset all Hell's broken loose!"

Krue thumped Matthews in the arm. His heart was thumping. As Krue looked to the cockpit (and couldn't see anything) Tom and Corrie reached over and punched Matthews in the leg. He wanted to slam them all but quickly wondered if Tanya could imagine him now, cooped up in an airborne coffin catapulted across the river. Did she receive his letters, did she have the patience to decipher his horrible hand-writing? She said letters are better than emails. Could he write one now? He fingered the satphone in his pocket.

"So we're to pipe it down. Captain T-Rex is our Flight Commander, the best pilot around,"

"Say again?" Captain T-Rex said blandly, to another jet or his co-pilot, it wasn't clear.

"But has a poor landing record."

"Enough of that, Magnus."

"Okay. Sit tight Commandos. You may see some flak – don't worry they can't aim for shit – there's a fire extinguisher under each seat. Okay? These babies are armoured plated – fitted out for nasty urban environments."

Krue thrust her thumbs-up fist through the hatch again.

Captain T-Rex's lips smacked, sounding like a whip of wet leather, the dryness of his voice exciting into a high-pitched gasp, "What, no ring on that pretty hand?"

Krue thrust her middle-finger-up-fist through the hatch.

"Okay – that explains it Wild One," and then to the flight forming up in the darkness. "Fifty metre low-level. Ten... nine... eight... seven..."

"*Blue Tongue's* up top," Magnus noted with a relieved sigh.

"*Blue Tongue* this is *T-one*, over."

Doug replied, and like replies of the other craft whizzing about in the night sky, could not be heard by Krue or her crew.

"Roger... Warning to Flight... *Blue Tongue* is pounding Mt Cootha with a, um, concentrated cluster bombs at some nocturnal anti-aircraft ... Snakes in the Grass. Give 'im some distance. Sound off."

"Countdown."

"Down. Six... Five... Four... Three... Two... One... GO."

The g-forces were terrific as the VLO shot forward. The Human Traffic sitting in twos with their backs to the fuselage facing each other were tossed rearward, sat back up and braced as the VLO carved into the sky. Their legs lifted, heads rolled, the light in the belly switched off. Through the portholes they could see the shifting dark horizon, blurs of isolated fires below, and the first tracers shots of the night leading off into pitch black. For the petrified men they only had to take one look at Krue's delighted and infectious glee of this shared experience to comprehend that they were travelling in style to some exotic hellish pit. They saw her lips move but couldn't be sure if it was 'this is fucking great' or 'can't wait for this mate'. They nodded 'yeah – yeah' and quickly twisted to stare out the porthole windows. It was better to look out than in, solely because they could.

"Hit the deck *Sinbad!* Follow the Leader down river..."

"What'd you think of that barge – them Indons trying to surrender ..."

"Aw it was funny... Coulda' done better,"

"G-O says it's adrift and burning in Moreton Bay,"

"Yeah, well, fucking surrendering on our shift, they deserve it. Hold it... ...... Repeat ......E-T-A?"

Krue and Matthews saw in an instant, forever burnt into their minds, a view down the darkened river, bright moonlight peaking from between the clouds reflected on wide ripples, the circular ripples under the criss-crossing of pink and white tracer shots. Incendiary mortar shells ignited fires on opposing banks, the flickering flames danced on the water, curling up to the oblong reflection of a fire storm on an incinerated Mount Cootha, subject to *Blue Tongue's* ferocious temper.

"Mig contact is back," Magnus alerted. His breath shortened then corrected itself to a calm rhythm, "Popped up over Stradbroke Island coming in *fast*,"

"I'm on it."

The jet smoothly yanked back, slid off to the right then dropped a hundred feet then dipped forward, faster than before.

"Bearing?"

"Zero-eight-seven. Skimming over Moreton Bay… Two Migs…"

"*Blue Tongue, Blue Tongue* are you on call…"

They waited.

"Two Migs coming in from two-nine-eight, confirm!"

A few seconds passed. The crew thought of dropping out and becoming pilots as soon as they returned. The VLO slowed and seemed to halt in mid-air, pointing down to earth searching for answers.

"V-V it. … *Bye bye baby goodbye… …*Nope it's an A-A."

"Armed. Locked on."

"And the Migs – circling like sharks?"

"Yeah,"

"Flight – Migs approaching – close in… Tight. This is good. Hmmm *mmm*."

"Hold it T-Rex. Got it… Three – *tuh-woo – wuh-hun!*"

From under the VLO's wings twin rockets fired up and shot to earth. The VLO ducked, swooped, and then followed the snaking Brisbane River again. The team saw the banks flashing by, fires guttering houses, muzzle flashes from tree tops, coils of smoke, a collapsed steel bridge kicked deep into the river.

"SAM site in the C-B-D… … *Thunderbird* – you're what? … God's speed Thunderbird."

"Let's do a run." Captain T-Rex's hand waved into the belly, a complacent gesture as if to say, what do you think you can do?

"Make it hurt."

"Make 'em bleed for *Thunderbird*… Confirm *Blue Tongue*,"

The VLO swerved barely metres above the water's surface then pulled up over a broken highway bypass and shot between two battle damaged mid-sized skyscrapers into the dilapidated centre of Brisbane. The city was alive with sporadic shots, messy anti-aircraft flak, missiles and flares zigzagging casting shadows of VLO's on the fractured buildings facades, then a spray of signal flares, some hitting buildings and deflecting into ruined streets. Krue stiffened at the Indonesian defenders' antics; reckless panic.

"Up top. Up? Up?"

The VLO vertically rose to the top of a gothic-stylised but war-gnawed skyscraper. On top, ten Indonesia soldiers with an empty surface to air missile launcher darted down a fire escape. Within seconds the rooftop was terrorised by the VLO's front cannons.

"Maybe ah, rocket down the centre, Captain."

"Magnus, sadist *and* optimist. We aren't paying for this."

The VLO lifted directly above the rooftop then dipped straight down to it and fired its rockets. The rooftop caved in. Several levels below exploded out sending glass, frame work and bodies into the enemy held central business district. The VLO swooped off the rooftop into a ballistic turn up and out of the danger zone. The pilot's breath calmed then spasmodically raced.

"Flight go tight and hide – Mig Attack!"

"South – south-east – three – thousand – closing."

The VLO dropped back into between skyscrapers as enemy Migs, ex-Soviet fighter jets, circled the city waiting for VLO's to venture from the protection between the buildings. Bullets rattled the fuselage. Krue thrust her thumbs-down-fist through the hatch.

"It isn't moving – sitting on Queen Street – taking fire. Shit."

"Port – port small-arms,"

The VLO rotated, lined up the offending attackers hiding in an eight story office complex and fended them off with scattered searching bursts of cannon fire.

"Okay – next…. *Mick* what you got on Riverside?"

The VLO rose, peeked from above and spied the land. The crew in the belly saw the burning city, the glows reflected on thousands of fractured windows, the orange ripples of fire reflected on the river, a burst of yellow exhaust from two Migs persistently roaming the city waiting for the VLO's to venture from the cement woods.

"Hold steady Flight – Two Hornets on the way."

Twin sonic booms shook the VLO.

"In or out?"

"Out, for sure… Migs gone?"

"Gone T."

"Check… *A-M-D* what you got from Highgate Hill?"

Two more rockets fired from under the wings, swooped to the ground and obliterated the foyer of a half destroyed hotel. As the building shook and crumbled, wounded Indonesians, fearing a complete destruction of their makeshift ward, leapt from various windows down to the messy streets.

"Enjoy your stay in the Sunshine State. *A-M-D* say again, over?"

Krue looked to her crew. They were scared, like herself, and questioned if they were expendable to be taken along but it was worth it. Tom and Corrie's eyes were glued out the portholes and when the VLO wasn't throwing them around with g-forces, they boyishly pointed to explosions and macabre scenes.

"Excellent. Anyone for a Mig sighting? Vanished?"

"Hornets pursuing them out to sea, T."

"Fuck'n A. Flight – this is Captain T I'm off to an L-Z… Carry on search and destroy…. *Blue Tongue*, *Blue Tongue*, high-level escort ready?"

The VLO dropped fifty metres above street level and smoothly powered north.

"O-K, threats, anybody found a threat."

"Nil. Coast is clear."

Tom's two fingers formed a quick thankful cross across his heart.

Magnus threw a tab of sea-sick tablets into the bomb bay, "An hour, ladies and lads…"

"Yes *Blue Tongue*. Major Krue?"

Krue again thrust her thumbs-up-fist through the hatch.

"She's the one Bluey… Okay we're going up. Up." The VLO steadily gained altitude. Left behind was the city. Outside the portholes the moon shone down on a ruffled silky blanket of clouds.

"Ten thousand. Set, sonic boom. We're outta' ordinance so we should make Mach One… Ready. Human Traffic sitting pretty?"

"Yeah T."

"Let's do it. Hold tight."

At full thrust the VLO shot forward, gaining in speed, rattling, the crew fearing the bomb bay doors would drop open and they'd fall to the ground and be mashed in a paddock but BOOM. Krue managed to catch some sleep at the speed of sound.

# A Day In Kingston

On Gallipoli Street in the Port of Kingston, James Callaghan thumbed through the last button below his collar. A flush of sweat broke out under his silk shirt. He admired the Chinese Tailors for their handiwork then mused to himself that he admired many men for their handiwork. He strolled to the wharf with Jemmy at his side, both stately men checking their dress and proud strides. A sharp appearance, Callaghan knew, was what separated thieves from merchants, even in the tropics where an intolerant environment dictated fashion.

Merchants prowled the streets early in their new, cheap, light clothes, bartering deals and eyeing Callaghan to catch him in a 'good mood' for a 'good deal' that Jemmy had promised over the final shout of cheap bourbon from the night before at some vice abiding venue. 'They go hand in hand!' Jemmy gladly professed of Callaghan's renowned good moods and deals. However, the cautious merchants saw that the head wheeler and dealer was far from smiling. Rather, a quaint annoyed glint emanated from the typical smiling face at some abstraction few could interpret.

Jemmy waffled on about deals to open throughout the day, "And bananas from south and north."

"We have our own banana farmers – they'd riot if we bought elsewhere. Half their sons are in the militia."

"True," Jemmy simultaneously pretended to now understand and quickly offer, some other deal where he was party to the profit, "My boats can ferry fish in – deep sea. No freezing. But can we fix the ice machine?"

"At your expense. But I'm not feeding fish to civilians or refugees: give them brain feed and they'd wake up! They can catch it them-fucking-selves. We got food; we need hardware. C'mon, we'll see the Ruskies off," Callaghan cocked his head to the northern end of the wharf.

"What about bulk coconuts?"

"Are you nuts?" Callaghan sighed. "Luxury. Who the hell has coconuts?"

"Kang San."

Callaghan shrugged at the name of the latest refugee-oddball to roll into Providence, the *zone*. "That Korean," he reminded Jemmy, "Some say they're the French of the Pacific." He remembered meeting the guy yesterday and in the muddle of sorting paperwork at the Trading House, what's coming in, going out, and have they been paid and who gets the rest when they eagerly return, this funny little moon faced man was spinning an uncanny life story, an excuse for his existence where it was widely known that in the Port of Kingston, who cares where you've come from. As long as you're healthy, smart, and trading something valuable, you're fine.

"I have never been to France or Korea," Jemmy played naïve.

Callaghan said boisterously, "Frog legs and dog legs is what they eat over there, respectively. Frog legs, not too bad. But dogs…" He looked over his shoulder to the merchants cautiously at the corner of a red brick warehouse, each spinning into another then spinning into another trying, to organise some mindless chatter amongst themselves to dispel the notion that they were waiting for some signal to pounce on Callaghan with their unbelievable deals. He confused them by inclining his head to the sky, staring at the serene beauty of a lonely high-level cloud travelling from the sea. The merchants then spied to the near empty heavens, pondering if that was from where Callaghan took his cue.

"He sold munitions," Jemmy added. "And said he can get more."

"The world is awash with fast-talkers selling unreliable weapons; like when do they have to test their gear in a rolling street battle?"

Callaghan then remembered with a notion of epic romance that Kang San's story was very compelling, proving truth stranger than arguable fiction. Once a poor fisherman and idle party man (communist) in North Korea, Kang San reached an age and disposition that he was destined to fail in both ventures: He would never bring home a big catch to free him from debt and inverse to the over-fished sea, the party was bulging with apprentice leaders, back-stabbing comrades, all easily suspected of 'revolutionary activities' and paranoid of a silly execution, such fitting finales for communist die-hards. Six months ago famine approached, nothing new in that, but this time there would be no relief from the world at war. Kang San escaped from where there was nothing left with nothing but his boat; and what's the great story about acquiring that great vehicle of mobility in a time of plunder?

Callaghan imagined him bravely riding through the naval war zones and cyclones to the Top End then trading exotic things all the way down the coast to Kingston. Kang was in the admirable position to go and fetch more produce, trade, and save. It seemed very admirable and legitimate. Cute too, and, as far as Callaghan knew, Kang wasn't in the business of 'blackbirding': ferrying refugees to an inevitable doom or into the laps of slave traders. Crowded market, that sport. After meeting Kang, Callaghan had remarked to Romano, "It's like he's a real survivor. This impresses me Romano."

"Impresses me too," Romano lied, couldn't give two fucks for some obscure Korean. Romano had seen it all, and then some.

"And when he's in Providence," Callaghan tweaked Romano's elbow, "Keep an eye on him. All that glitters is not gold."

"Very wise. All that glitters is *not* gold." Romano practised his English.

Romano rubbed down the gold by asking around. When Kang first docked at Kingston he paid for three months of mooring with wads of crinkled Yen. In a time of anarchy, any forecast paid up for three months was welcome. Then he immediately started circling the edge of the markets, making inquires and contacts, and let it be known he had eight crates of 5.56mm NATO rounds; a bit different and risky from the stock standard 7.62mm for the AK-47 (or cloned variant), but there *was* a niche market: Some traders offered M-16s; the Western made weapons representing a form of class among Pacific scoundrels and mercenaries, and horded crates of 5.56mm, perhaps waiting for the whites to show up again and begging for ammo with bars of gold. But, as Task Force Seven had shown, the whites had evolved in weaponry, and who in this part of the would could supply a hungry K-41? Still, 5.56mm was better than nothing, and an almost perfect, strategic, calling card. So, after a week, Kang made a killing, and was now selling fruit to the few bourgeoisie: the prosperous merchants, farmers and foreigners. But for his nouveau wealth, he dressed like a dag. Then again, Callaghan chuckled, Jemmy was by far the worst dressed man in Providence. Jemmy had true pirate traits, tattoos galore and a nasty blowtorch burn across one cheek that only the drunk and suicidal dared to ask about. His dress sense was time warped: 1980s TV cop, *Miami-Vice*. He hardly shaved, his narrow jaw festering with a sparse three-day growth. His fraying grey suit was once *coultre*, now a joke.

Kang, being spun off the merry-go round of global change and keeping some personal abstract integrity, could have easily been mistaken for a middle-class tourist lost in an Amusement Park. His cheap and out-dated Pentax camera dangling from his neck was a utensil hardly worth stealing and very unpractical. The closest shop to develop photos was in Noumea. Callaghan assumed Kang's use of tartan green slacks, creamy T-shirts and the foreign beer baseball hat, was an intuitive use of 'objects new'. With childlike wonder he did not stress at the wardrobe unfolding before his eyes as he fled North Korea and strict Party Regulations on street dress. Like a madman with creative flair he traded trades and images and evolved: The arms trader looking like a fruit seller looking like a tourist. Callaghan noted Kang was a character, a jumbled puzzle, and the sooner he lost his absurd image, the sooner he could fit in with all the other gutter-sniffing, flesh-bartering, wretched merchants, slithering in what can be best described as their *natural environment*.

On this pretty morning it were the sailors to strangely look Kang over. On the northern wharf was moored a medium sized freighter fitted out as a bulk cattle ship. It was a sulky old thing waiting for its crew of Chinese looking East Russians to return from a beer guzzling and semen-thrashing-night-out in the steamy red-light district of Kingston. Hung over, they were barred from boarding their glorified rust-bucket by a grinning Kang San and his tray of fruits.

"Scurvy!" he taunted at their perilous journey ahead. "Oldest illness of the seas! I have the cure!" He chanted in English, strained with an imitation American TV twang. In each hand like breasts he sported his medicine, ripe prickled golden pineapples with a crown of razor sharp green leaves. Kang San held his head like a noble as the sailor's red eyes avoided the golden tipped spikes. For the sailors, the brothels in Kingston supplied the bed, the breakfast, and the girl from the night before to serve it.

Stepping next to him in quick-time, Callaghan and Jemmy mockingly admired the rusting hull of the ship before them. It resembled a Stalinist wall. Distaste spiced their lips but for varying reasons.

"Helps constipation!" Kang yelped to the last of the boarding crew.

"Where's coconuts?" Jemmy demanded. "You said coconuts! At twenty for a dollar!"

"Sold! All sold to General Kai in the north!" Kang San apologised profusely.

Jemmy livened up but Callaghan calmed him, "Forget it."

"Why?" Jemmy asked, staring insolently to Kang, "We had a deal to sell coconuts!" He found no audience in Callaghan.

"Really Jemmy, you got coconuts for brains?" Callaghan stepped to the edge of the wharf and stood firm, fists clenched, annoyed at the shades of rusty red, cadmium orange, revealed on the underside of flaking white paint layers on the hull before them. "See that dodgy upkeep! Ruskies. I bet the cattle die, I just know it. Halfway back to Vladivostok they'll start hacking into them, or run out of hay, you reckon they got enough?"

Jemmy could smell the dung from the cattle on the freighter and glared dumbly at the foreign Russian lettering on the hull, character shapes welded three feet high, not quite as neat and precise as the lettering K-O-B-A-N-T-A on the vault at the bank. The vault was a stationary object, cold and shiny. It wouldn't be moved anywhere. Alternatively the Russian freighter, obviously not the flag ship, was a shuttling craft for the trade that makes the vault so stationary. He squinted up to the ship's name, *Dzintra*. Jemmy as a pirate enjoyed a free reign of terror on anything other than trade in and out of Kingston. If he stepped over the line Peters would skin him alive. He made a mental note to pass the word to his brethren from here to Papua New Guinea to lay off the *Dzintra*.

"Jemmy?" Callaghan raised his voice. "What do you think – can they survive?"

"Livestock – I know nothing," Jemmy said.

Callaghan was dismayed with the Russian freighter. Cattle dung was mashed into the wharf and work teams had tried to wash it away yet for all their efforts only mixed it into a putrid slick coating. They were deliberately messy to claim a few more days work to clean it up. Seven dollars a day. Callaghan's inspection of the Port of Kingston was part civil and commercial intrigue, enforcement of discipline and ultimately safe-guarding the takings of the week back to Providence.

"They bought at a good price," Jemmy squinted up to the vacant bridge of the *Dzintra*. He waited a second for any of the crew to appear. None. An evil glow flickered in Jemmy's pirate eyes. "Easy prey."

"You would too." Callaghan screwed his face tight, "I know these cheap fucks." He threw his hand over the length of the ship. "I'm only concerned about their mechanical upkeep for two reasons."

Kang looked on with interest as Jemmy paid full attention.

Callaghan held up two fingers to state the weight of his words, "One, that rust bucket could easily sink right now. Consequence, we would lose use of this wharf. That'd leave us helpless. It'd be counted as sabotage by Peters, and all of 'em, they'd be shark meat. Chop chop chop. Next best port is Townsville, and the great Buddha only knows if we can tackle that outpost. General Kai's the number one up there for good reason. We're not keen to flex our militia until we source new hardware. Arms races are *shit*. You know, wouldn't it be good to own an orbiting laser cannon? In my old underground days, I saw some tech guys testing one on unsuspecting Indons preparing to attack a supply column. Spooky. The power to take, without a sound, controlled from above and over the horizon. We called it the Grim Reaper."

Jemmy, suffering Callaghan's effusiveness, bowed his head to the rickety wood of the wharf scratching the few mature hairs on his chin. Jemmy was the preferred weapons dealer to Peters, and orbiting laser cannons, were obviously out of his league. He hastily prompted Callaghan, "You don't have to deal with Russians. There are others. Two?"

"The Great Barrier Reef." Callaghan ran his eyes along the waterline. Fragile ripples lapped against the rusting hull. Flakes of red metal floated like discarded bonsai leaves. "If it spills its load in transit, huge oil slick on the coral reef. Now I know pretty fish don't give me visual orgasms," he grabbed his crotch, released it, "It's the standard you set. It's good to be good,"

Jemmy paced about wondering what Callaghan's punch-line would be.

"The world is always watching," Callaghan summarised.

Jemmy's two-way radio cut in. "Excuse me," he said and took the call.

Kang casually pranced towards them and semi-rotated his pineapples before Callaghan's eyes, "Yes! Somewhere somehow someone sees! How about a pineapple for the wife?"

Callaghan cast a defying glare to Kang, "I have no wife."

"Oh – she seemed very devoted to you."

"You were in Providence?"

"One day ago."

Callaghan smacked his lips at the pineapples. "Make big bucks? Huh? You'll be a millionaire soon. Next stop, Sydney?"

"No… It is good here. Friendly and safe." Kang humbly inspected his fruits, explaining, "I go into Providence, today, you know anyone who buys fruit?"

"Yeah, the starving. Why do you need to go down to Providence?"

"I know some people."

"You're a friendly kind of guy, huh? Just don't go near my woman."

"Your *woman*," Kang's voice lowered.

Jemmy, burning with caprice, interrupted, "Coal! I have a buyer for coal."

Callaghan quickly remembered the return on investment to be realised from the western warehouse, full of all that coal, shipped there two months ago from a newly acquired mine. "Fruit and cattle: Soft commodities are pains in the arse! When?"

"The buyer is different," Jemmy gracefully dismissed Kang and the rusting Ruskie freighter by sniffing at the clean sea air from an opposite direction. "His ship is sailing in from South America."

"What? They've got plenty of coal."

"No... He won't go back yet. My friends in Singapore are trading to him. He can stop here, load up the coal, ship it to Singapore then trade on."

"Two sides to every transaction. And how did you get to know of this? *Black Tide* buddies?"

Jemmy tensed on that secretive pact, "But the buyer – Toro – has already arrived. He's up with General Kai."

Callaghan cursed. "*Kai.*"

"But Kai has not much to trade in bulk. And Toro needs to trade something valuable up to Singapore, coal is filthy but he is desperate."

"Understood."

"I can call, he can travel down and if you make a deal, when his ship comes in, it can dock."

"Sounds like a plan. Well, I would like to meet him, yes."

The *Dzintra's* Captain Tzinksi strolled down the gangway hovering a lit match over a wad of tobacco thumbed into a black pipe. He knew Jemmy and Callaghan by mere introduction. "Morning," he greeted, a calculated washy growl. With a mild dosage of arthritis in his wrists, a wisp in his husky voice and a mole weighing his left eyebrow, Captain Tzinksi stood in true sea-dog character. Raising that eyebrow in surprise, wheezing his lungs and involuntarily shaking his working hand he bade farewell, "I leave with morning tide." Puff-puff... Wheeze.

"Great." Callaghan nodded. "See you next time you're in warm waters."

Kang chanted to Tzinksi, "You buy fruit? Long sail to Russia?"

"You American? You sell Pepsi? Goes with my vodka." Tzinksi wheezed to Kang, who froze and sucked his cheeks in ready to reply. "They say Kingston is the freest port." He leered directly to Kang, "True, Yankee?"

Kang laughed off the mistaken identity. "I'm Korean!"

"Hmph." Tzinksi laughed. "You remind me of a man from Hong Kong. But we're all the same in Kingston. No?"

"Providence is better, it's the Capital." Kang sang on Callaghan's behalf.

"Of what?" Tzinksi lazily waved to Callaghan. Tzinksi looked over the roofs of warehouses to a drooping ultramarine flag limp off a mast.

"Providence." Callaghan yelled in a drawn out annoyed manner. "It's a state, our state. Your master is dealing with *us*."

"And Providence is the Capital of Providence? So that's where my Master's money flows to," Tzinksi grumbled and jerked his elbow to his rusting ship and the two hundred cattle in its hold, "Not cheap. *Noooo* friend."

"They're disease free." Callaghan called up to the plank. "They'll breed like rabbits if you treat them right."

"And if they die," Tzinksi wagged his wrinkled finger, "Will I know why? Why should I trust *your* word my friend?"

"You're a veterinarian, aren't you?"

"What is that?"

"You're an animal doctor?"

Tzinksi managed a laconic laugh and withdrew his finger, "*Nyet!*"

"Neither am I, but I can assure you the cattle are good quality. You paid top dollar for them. Expect the best. Before you go, you still trust us as much as when we first met? Yes? Maybe. No?"

"This is *first time* into South Pacific." He sucked hard on his pipe. "I say we have enough to feed the cattle and with the wars they are precious animals. Very hard to buy elsewhere. These times are hard for many people."

Jemmy sympathised. "It's those Yankees."

Tzinksi huffed, "It's everyone. China and the Viet and the Jap." From then on he rattled his politics in Russian, non-stop, half gibberish that he was, for half a minute. They couldn't understand so he futilely threw up his hands and made his way back up the gangway stopping at the top to shout down. "Mister Callaghan – of Providence!"

"Yes Captain?"

"My Master, he knows a good deal."

"I bet he does. He's your Master."

"And if he gets 'no good deal', then you will be dealt with. Very bad. He knows many men in many high places."

Callaghan summarised, "Great. Tell him, likewise… Captain, *bon voyage* back to the northern hemisphere!" And when Tzinksi was out of sight he leaned to Jemmy, "As if those bastards are welcome back! Fuck? What's this world coming to? Who is his Master? What's all that gangster shit? Is he really trading for Russia?"

Jemmy faced his back to the ship, a simple gesture that skirted Callaghan and Kang to his side to hear what he had to say, "If he really was who he was he'd make no threat – he would just do!"

"So?"

"Who knows who he works for? He trades. Maybe for the Chinese?" Jemmy cast deep suspicions over his shoulder up to the empty bridge. With that said they left the wharf heading towards the Trading House of Kingston. It was not uncommon to arrive and be swamped by all sorts of merchants and traders masquerading as legitimate capitalists rather than behave like the vigilantes that they were. Lieutenant McCallister was out the front under the shade of an umbrella kneeling over an open crate of rocket launchers. The seller, one of Jemmy's men, pointed to the dull-coloured explosive heads.

"They take out tanks – they take out navy too,"

"Only patrol boats," Jemmy corrected his man.

"Patrol boats too," the man nodded to Jemmy then down to McCallister. "Fast boats too."

"Heavy and fast. Right."

"How much?" Callaghan asked, leaning over, recognising the weapons and suppressing a laugh.

"Two thousand dollars – everything." Jemmy spoke for the crate and another smaller crate of warheads, "Very good buy."

"Very good," the man agreed.

McCallister looked up to Callaghan, the two whites sharing an instinct to drive the price lower.

"Fourteen hundred, looks like fourteen hundred."

"Eighteen hundred," Jemmy staunchly replied, "No more!"

"Hang on!" Callaghan called to those assembled before the Trading House, took one look at the crates and flashed his five fingers three times.

"Fifteen hundred then," McCallister told Jemmy.

Jemmy bitterly accepted. He could have easily got two-grand if he'd gone south to Warlord Raoul but only one grand if went north to Warlord Kai. He left the Trading House, leaving his man to collect payment, and noticed Kang was hanging around trying to sell his fruits to anyone interested. Jemmy's pace quickened. The gathered merchants would spend the best part of the morning hassling Callaghan with tantalising offers. Jemmy despised them; middle men trading off middle men and he was too, but for only half the time. Sometimes, like today, he would have to go hunt for the stuff and make the contacts with the real players. At the far end of the Port of

Kingston, on the lowest of rickety wharves, he entered his warehouse and shouted abuse at two of his men slouched dolefully playing cards talking about their next Black Tide tattoos.

"Get up! Where's the map! The radio! You think I started pillaging the seas on the land! No! Up!" He kicked one in the buttock. "We need trade! Look at this warehouse! It's empty! Empty *no* good!"

Five minutes later they were monitoring the radio and plotting ship locations on the map. Jemmy retired to his office and sat on his tattered leopard skin couch with his hands interlocked behind his head, his feet on a fraying silky cushion, staring at the black nylon bra of some clumsy prostitute, hanging off the wooden chair he had molested her on. She was too willing and submissive for his liking. She would not be a good mother, either. He closed his eyes and dreamt, or remembered, it all blurred into one photographic exhibition tainted by erotic poses, of the women he had fucked in the last few years. In one hand he held the temptation of the flesh and though it be satisfying, it in no way diminished the paternal instinct to feel the flesh of one of his offspring in his other hand – to bounce a baby boy up and down. Now his thoughts were to teach his unborn son not of the sea but of something, Jemmy shuddered, something he had no idea about. Maybe something as absurd as peace.

"Jemmy!"

"What!" he barked.

"Toro, the owner of the *Margarita*, he asks of the coal."

Jemmy sat up feeling the blood rush to his head. Where does all of this lead, he wondered. When does it end? When did the rush of pirating wear off and leave a brave man a vanquished lonely character with no family, only cold-hearted criminals as company. Jemmy dreamt of hitching a ride on Toro's ship on its eventual return to South America. Jemmy could take his gold, his bonds, his coins and a shipping container of weapons and become a new man in a new continent. That's it, Jemmy smiled, it has to lead somewhere. He would also take a woman of his choice.

# Unconfirmed from the Edge

Below deck Ghan and his Captains stood around a high bench, pens in hands, sketching approaches to potential strong points between two foreign towns. Ghan circled behind them, observing their meticulous minds at work determining the appropriate reaction considering the great unknown. What were they facing? Who really knew. But he drummed the manoeuvres in their minds anyway.

Lieutenant Ling entered, stiffened to attention and held a folded transcript out to Ghan.

Ghan nodded and beckoned the eager Ling to sit with him and began reading.

"This morning?"

"Correct," Ling confirmed, "Irrefutable proof, too."

Ghan snorted some phlegm through his nose and braced himself. The report was from an operative outside of the primary target. The operative, code-named Flower Two, used a satellite phone. But something about Flower's manner betrayed his condition.

> *I tried to gain access to the port but 1000+ displaced people were foraging for food. As I was using them for cover, I suffered with them. Militia shot at us to keep us away. We could see warehouses and traders, livestock, cargo and containers of coal but we were kept back. A local Militia Commander called 'Romano' had come to us and gave his word that we may find food at a later date, but he could not specify when or where. Many of us returned to the woods. At night there is fighting – starvation has turned many men and women into animals. I did manage to climb a hill and look to the port and saw one medium sized vessel. Hungry, I came across a party who has escaped from the north. The Militia in that region had been clearing their territory of all displaced peoples. The next night more displaced people came. I am still hungry. I have begun eating grass and am sick. I saw the vessel at the port from a distance being loaded with livestock. I tried to venture in alone but was chased away. I am very weak now.*

Ghan folded the transcript and slid it into his pocket. "Who else has seen this?"

"No one, Sir."

"You read it?"

"Of course – It's valid intelligence. We're monitoring not just military information but social intelligence too."

"Does Flower Two ask of our arrival?"

"No, he would know not to."

"But," Ghan glanced over to his Captains, "Desperate men do desperate things: He's out there, and if people found out who he really is, they would begin to speculate."

"What do you suggest?"

"What is Flower Two?"

"Military Intelligence Operative. Basic military training, specialising in communications."

"We must sever contact with him."

"When?"

"Now." Ghan nodded to himself. "He is desperate, he will trade anything he has for food, including the dearest of information. Next time he sends a message, do not reply. Do not let him think we may help him."

"Yes Sir."

"That is all."


As expected he tossed and turned in his sleep. For hours the thoughts ran like multiple stock tickers across his mind. Eventually he was physically tired enough to doze off and half an hour into that his guard woke him.

"Urgent meeting with General Wing, five A-M."

Ghan reached for his watch but the guard read off the time.


At five Ghan entered. Zhing was either anticipating breakfast or something else. He was excitedly following across his large electronic map the envisioned route of some vessel as shown by a girlishly thin but super intelligent Naval Officer. There were quick introductions, the Naval Officer pointed to a lonely ship, edging out of the depths of the Pacific, now entering a point halfway between Vanuatu and Fiji. Its route had been tracked, first picked up after leaving the South American coast, and now apparently about to curve in for New Caledonia or head straight on its current latitude and hit the coast of Australia, and on that area, Zhing's eyes twinkled.

The Naval Officer explained, "An all-purpose trader, small container ship, lightly armed. Owned by a bankrupt corporate listed in Bermuda. Intercepted communications reveal that it has been linking with Singapore and *Black Tide* listening posts."

Ghan stepped closer to the map. A quasi pirate, the benign kind. In its vicinity wasn't much in the way of traffic, but a Chinese Kilo Submarine lay in wait between Vanuatu and New Caledonia.

"We have been following the web of communications and the ship has confirmed a new destination." The Naval Officer tacked his finger on the coast of Queensland. "Here. A Port. Kingston. Subsequent communications called for radio-silence."

Zhing grinned up, "Ghan a change to plan: we move forward by three days."

"Yes Sir."

"If all goes to plan we can master a Greek Strategy – The Trojan Horse."

"*That* ship?" he sneered at it on the map.

Zhing nodded, "That is being organised, it is possible and it serves our purpose. Fortunately for you it's going to where you wish to go, and for us, it's cut off contact – obeying radio silence."

The Naval Officer nodded. "Our sub," he pointed to it, between Vanuatu and New Caledonia, "Will intercept and launch an assault group. Once we have control of the vessel we can begin the necessary logistics."

"The perfect cunning cover," Zhing professed, "And, it saves this fleet from venturing so far south to plant you there."

"I understand, Sir."

"The timing is tight and the risk is high, but the surprise we gain, invaluable and overwhelmingly superior. See Ghan, you are making history."

# On the Plains...

Stripped to the waist, tanned and sweating, Lieutenant Jenkins stood on the barren hill staring strenuously at the crisp, golden countryside with a frank, strained, smile. Around him ten militia knelt on the hill curiously examining blackened tree branches. Sweat dripped from brow to nose. They gulped precious purified water from hot canvas canteens. The interpreter, Jenkin's only bridge of communication to his second rate militia, radio-man Rachi, poked at the obvious disturbances on the bare, low hill.

Rachi enthusiastically guessed, "Come from the sky. It burns!"

The militia looked up, inspecting the thin ghost clouds for precious rain. A lone circling hawk spied them from above. This was black man country and even then black men weren't here.

Jenkins could smell the ash. Last night a giant blow torch had kissed the ground. The bare hill was protected by a thin ring of grey gum trees and wide enough to land a helicopter or jump-jet; and gone as it came, leaving few clues. From the scant shade on the hilltop and spying in all directions were plains, a rolling golden sea stretching to the horizon, except to the east, where the ranges were and Mt Jacinda stood tallest, an obtrusive anchor, few defining features, just a mass of rock, gullies and a jagged crest that sometimes snared the clouds. Militia sauntered over the hill looking for tracks. Rachi passed his radio handset to Jenkins.

"D-Man. Found a landing zone," he despondently transmitted, "As you said."

Peters replied full of vigour, "Good. See if you can pick up a trail; it might be eight hours old, but whoever touched down in the night might have been careless. Out."

Peters's mobile command was in the depths of a sub-tropical ravine snug on the other side of the ranges north of Jacinda Mountain. Sliding east off the dividing range were the sugarcane fields, fruit orchards, the farmers, and then Providence. He scratched the back of his neck. The morning was moving too fast. Out in 'bandit' territory there were reports of a lone whining jet touching down then up again. Even his crew at the bank had picked something up; an incoming aircraft, zipping out as it had zipped in. Peters knew all of what it could be, but feared most what it should be.

The back of his armoured personnel carrier was equipped for the communication needs of a rogue state guerrilla warfare commander;

multiple pirated satellite linkups, a low signature radar-radar, close-range eavesdropping capabilities, and a short-range missile guidance system. A satellite-dish on top sucked data from the few rogue satellites he shared leases on. The available information was viewed on twin screens. Next to the APC was one of his infamous camouflage-netted missile launchers. Slotted into the truck's tray was a cross between an American cruise missile and a Soviet scud – a Panasonic Fudo (*Fudo*, an age-old mystical fierce-faced impartial judge and chastiser of wickedness). It was Made in Taiwan under license from Japanese designers. In its heyday it was cheap, flooded the markets, and stored by smart arms dealers and countries like Australia and New Zealand. Now ninety percent had been used, it was superseded and the remainders favoured by nomadic terrorists with room to move - namely a road on which they can drive undetected. Given a target Peters could make a crater fifty metres wide. To protect this mobile force of terror were his personal body guards, the Tonkas. Twenty of these elite tribal lads, well accustomed to the darkness of a jungle, drank green tea and smoked tight rolled-cigarettes with their fine bony fingers. When they were deep in the mountains, they were deep together, and together they were as cunning and able as a pack of wolves.

In contrast to highlander warriors was the dutiful Eric, happily glued to the two screens, content to sit next to banks of hardware and dangling loops of bunched serial chords. He contentedly tapped at the console, under the guise of scientific vigil, mastering 'Surface-to-Surface Missile Guidance Software V12.5'. Its compatibility with the guidance circuitry of the Fudo enabled Eric to plot multiple and moving targets. He was a hired soldier but had never fired a gun. He was nineteen and too young to know exactly where fate had taken him. As careers go, his was that of adaptation like many a hired educated hand fleeing war zones and ending up in Providence. Eric the zit-nerd at school preferred jerking-off over the parabolic symmetries of Manga babes than unbuttoning gingham skirts of perky-breasted, awkwardly fretting, school girls. He had acquired the dirtiest digital porn collection in class and held an advanced electrical engineering certificate by the age of 17. After these accomplishments passed, the bad-boy tech-head realised that there was more to life than programming computers and digital smut. Matter of a fact, there were trillions of worlds out there that a virtual community can not compete with. He had a skill, and that as his trade, set forth to see the world. As the computer-jockey ventured further and further from Hong Kong and as the exodus morphed into a war it became a means of survival to apply his skills at any price. Through sorted connections the *Black Tide* came to him and he met Jemmy in Saigon. Jemmy knew of some people that needed talent. Shipped out on an antique ex-Soviet submarine, destination and fate sealed under 200 feet of water, Eric landed in Kingston and within days was a systems operator for a rogue nation in Australia. He launched missiles, was a valuable member of Peters's team and preferred these out-of-town missions and hanging with the soft spoken security of the Tonkas than to rounding up refugees with Romano and his militia.

The Tonkas were calmly waiting for the signal to take on whomever had landed down on the plains. Their sullen brown eyes peered through the darkness of the lush tropical surroundings. Peters trusted them, because in contrast to Eric they had little knowledge other than hunting in a jungle. But similarly to Eric, their expertise landed them a secure job.

Eric reported, "Fudo ready for blast-off."

Peters checked the screen displaying a digital map of the region; anxious to read off a location, "Excellent. Now, what's really out there?"

Rachi was with one of the Militia, squatting by patch of crumpled grass, just off the knoll.

Jenkins arrived, "You got something?"

"Maybe. It goes north, north-east" Rachi pointed from the semblance of a track to the direction it appeared to go, straight through the grass.

"Let's do it." Jenkins called out to the Militia, all flogged by the overbearing sun. "Smarten up slackers. Can't hear a word I'm saying, can ya'? But you know what I'm thinking."

Rachi snarled a short authoritarian burst to the militia that made Jenkins jump. Rachi's report back to Jenkins was just as quick, "We move on Boss."

"Sweet… North-east we go." Jenkins hollered, "It's a chase. And a woman for the man to nail a rat. A woman with big tits or a young one with pointy nipples. Shy ones maybe. Tell that to your militia buddies, Rachi."

Rachi stalled, "Huh?"

"A woman for the man to make the first kill,"

"For wife or girlfriend?"

"One-night wife. Tell them with six hours of daylight left I want to bag one rat before dusk. Someone has to get sex for all that it's worth."

"Dusk?"

"It's when the sun goes down!" Jenkins wearily explained.

The militia, in a sorry bout of dizzy unification, turned to Jenkins with sour long faces.

"And if we don't get anything today we chase into the dark. How about that Jungle Bunnies?

Night was six years and two litres of sweat away.

"We find water?" Rachi asked.

"Maybe, only if you know how to drink it." Jenkins took the lead and onto the plains. "A woman… big tits… Tight…" he dreamily called and sipped sparingly from his canteen.

Rachi translated but the militia were only partly humoured. Many had wives and children. They needed the money from soldiering as worth thus a secure reason and existence *not* to be disposed of like some hungry human vermin waving a machete.

Jenkins trooped on. Who landed on the hill. Where were they *going*? East were the ranges. Was it a recon patrol, which meant, in a few months, or a laborious year in Peters's self established nation, his former kinsman would return? Would they punish the abandoned men of Task Force Seven? He slowed his pace and focussed ahead, searching the dry golden plains for any sprouting greenery signifying even the most humble of dirty puddles to sip from.

Mid-afternoon. After trekking over the golden plains for several hours Krue's crew settled down to rest and observe. They lay in a diamond shape a few metres apart covered in the waist high grass on the northern slope of a low hill. Further north of the hill under a hundred metres away was Krue's point of interest, the single railway track linking the coast to the outback. With her binoculars she followed the track east as it disappeared into the ranges, and according to her maps, snaked in and out of passes, then down to the coast and on to Kingston. Out west the track disappeared into the endless golden plains. Scattered over the land trotted the odd famished animal: a kangaroo, a meandering rabbit, Corrie even spotted a slim, yellowish dog, its skin stretched tautly over a bony rib cage.

"Dingo." Krue answered for the shy inquisitive city boys.

Corrie smiled. "Don't look no domesticated dog to me." His vantage point was lying at the top of the low hill, making slow wide sweeps to the ends of the horizon. He could hear Krue's soft voice talking to Matthews and Tom something he deemed unimportant, but he half-listened, more content to view the wide open land and wonder if he had ever been out this far in this huge continent. Though there was not another soul to be seen. His grip tightened on his rifle.

"Trade," Krue said in an educating manner, "is their only means of survival… We move along the train line at night. It's a direct route into, through and off the ranges into Kingston and from there south into Providence… We may encounter some riff-raff, who knows… Where there's trade, they're there. Some will be helpful. Some just want to claim your ears."

"Ears?" Tom asked.

"White-boy ears," Krue explained, frowning at the heavy sun reddening his cheeks, "If they do you in they take an ear back to their chiefs. Claim a bounty."

"Why didn't we just land in Providence?" Matthews asked, "Or right outside?"

Krue's gentleness of contemplation added an air of wisdom to her eventual explanation, "The Town of Providence relies on what's out here. We watch it all. There's something unexplainable about the wait in the hunt… If you see a cat, or any animal, they sneak up on the prey and move in a stealthy manner right up to the final moment and then, like a spring uncoiled – *ouch*! It's in this time – our enforced isolation – that we can become part of the land so that when it comes to take out our target – it's the land that swallows him, or it, or her," she figuratively frowned, "and then we sink back into the land. It accepts us, for we are part of it. To bust in there kicking down doors is a sure-fire way to end up fucked up."

"Yeah," Tom involuntarily fidgeted with his earlobe.

Corrie, now concentrating on the ranges to the east, had found himself hanging on Krue's every word and giddily smiling. He continued his observation to the south and noted a strange anomaly, a set of thin dark trunks standing out of the grass, the branches of such drooping to and swaying in the wind. He blinked, glanced down to his rifle, and back again. For seven seconds he patiently spied the tedious but direct movement of eleven soldiers. One, obviously taller, a bronzed whitey, was the leader knowing exactly the bearings to follow. He said abruptly, hinging on perversely cheerful, "We got a greeting party!"

"Corrie," Matthews cautioned.

Corrie only placed two fingers to his lips and pointed to the south, "Eleven man patrol."

Krue wriggled through the grass and studied the patrol. Her face was panged by confusion. "Out here...?"

"How'd they know we're here?" Tom wondered aloud.

"Set up the claymore," Krue ordered and with her binoculars glued to her eyeballs, observed the distant pursuers weaving through the grass. "They must have found our drop zone and tracked us. They're prepared."

"Who are they?" Matthews asked.

"Doesn't matter. C'mon Corrie."

Part of Corrie's pack was a claymore landmine, a delicacy of thousands of tiny ball-bearings caked into a layer, behind that, a layer of explosives with a charge. "Sure," he said, then realised he had spied them before they spied him: what if it had been the other way around. What if-

"Hurry," Krue cursed him, her measurement of distance and line of fire spilling from her mouth in a strange dreamy whisper, "Up there, come there and contact – down – down – down."

Her men looked to each other with alarmed gestures. Why not continue north and outrun them? As if requiring a cue, Matthews sharply nodded to Corrie and Tom.

"Boys, they're good," Krue paused to rethink, "Could be tribal, but I don't think Aboriginal... Lucky, or professionals... Or both..." In her mind dwelled the prospect of an easy peace; a meeting of warring parties and breaking of bread, but in her heart burnt ferocity. "We'll take them out."

"Spot on." Tom absolutely agreed, watching Corrie cautiously unpack the claymore.

Corrie crawled just off the top of the low hill through the grass and faced the mine to the direction of the oncoming patrol. The trigger was a simple switch at the end of a three metre wire. He uncoiled it, and once all was set up, nestled comfortably to his spot and observed. The pursuers had not changed their course over the plains, and though fatigued, were determined. Then it hit Corrie, a tightened stomach and like his counterparts, his mouth was dry. His trigger finger cramped when there was no reason to. His arse loosened, and thankfully, only a wet fart escaped.

Tom lay by his radio, with one ear-piece in, listening to static and weak bursts of a rough Asian dialect. Matthews lay snugly in place fondling up his rifle. Aim for the belly. Aim for the belly. Or the small of the back. Crack. That's the sound it makes. This is not the river. He wanted to stretch his body, expunge some energy, but concealed and cramped he could only grip his rifle tighter.

He said, "We don't know who they are."

Krue's voice was shallow, "If we pop up and run, or if we pop up and wave our hands, and they're not sure who we are, well, don't take the risk. Not here."

"Claymore armed," Corrie said and breathed heavily down his tunic, completely afraid, wishing that it would all be suddenly over in one *whoosh*. Then run. Like crazy.

"They can track us through this." Krue ran her slender fingers down the golden grass. "We have surprise, that's it." She thought of the photo, the young Peters, if it really were his playground. "He's sent an armed greeting party, who knows what might be next."

"Who?"

"Our target," Krue told Matthews, "is trying to flush us out."

"… Wouldn't you?"

"Yeah." Didn't Doug warn her of the absurdity up here?

"He – whoever you mean, would want visual verification first, of whatever he thinks we are." Matthews then perilously added, "They work for the same Warlord, yeah?"

She twitched at the ranges to the east, "I'm sure."

"They'll see us soon – if they're good."

Krue played her bottom lip between her teeth and spied through her binoculars again. They appeared third rate, and by the hunching of the shoulders, tiring. The white leader moved like a seasoned professional. It wasn't Peters. Eleven verses four. Plus the claymore mine. She checked the position of the mine and its spread of devastation provided the prey followed the trail.

Corrie described the patrol with stringent distaste. "Aren't Regular Indons. Just Sunday troopers. We can do it, we got to."

"Never underestimate them." Krue cautioned.

Jenkins could see the slight hill and a railway track disappearing behind it. He stopped and plucked the radio handset off Rachi's back.

"Peters. I'm nearing the railway track, trail still heading north-east. You got my position?"

"Keep on it," came Peters's digitised reply, tracing his finger on a computer screen from Jenkin's position to the railway track. "Hmm. They might be using it as a guide. They've got a head start but you're covering ground a lot faster. I want them taken alive. We need some bargaining power."

"Understood, but there's no shade for miles around. The militia are a bit dehydrated."

Peters growled with impertinence. "In two hours I'll send the jeep down with water, just keep on that trail!"

Jenkins, suffering exhaustion and deprivation from a civilised society, turned to his companions. The militia's disinterested faces revealed that the dizzy sensation of dehydration had already set in.

"Peters, I'm moving on but we might be stepping into a trap."

"True."

"If I find them, and they're nasty, can you lay on the heavy stuff. The Militia aren't up for a serious skirmish," Jenkins faced away from Rachi and said quietly into the radio, "And I don't really trust them. You know they run if the firepower is too much."

"Understood. If you can see whoever it is that's out there and they're something substantial – I'll help out... And I know I'd be destroying the evidence so I'm trusting you. Got it?"

"Right as rain. Out." Jenkins handed the radio handset back to Rachi and called in a livelier voice than before, "Spread out, advance, and keep your eyes open. Spread out! Advance to the railway track!"

"The white guy?" Corrie asked in an imperious tone, "Who is he?"

"Mercenary." Krue whispered.

Tom lined the figure in his sights, "Not one of us, 'eh?"

Krue lay and tried not to think; us, them, the in-between.

Corrie cursed, "They're spreading!"

The loose line of militia was meandering apart, edging forward, guns dangling from their shoulders to waist height and their tired faltering eyes probing ahead.

Krue's heart raced. In seconds the militia would be too dispersed from the arc of the claymore's spread.

"Corrie – hit it!"

The charge, in his fist, was wet with perspiration. His thumb held on the trigger. Nothing happened. Had his sweat seeped into the charger?

"Fuck!" Krue hissed but was muted by the blast.

The militia patrol were shredded by thousands of ball-bearing shot out in a peppered wall through the heavy afternoon air. In mid-stride they dropped into the grass, perforated, paralytic with pain.

"All down?" she asked abrasively.

"Yeah – No!"

Six wounded militia rolled over and sat up in the grass to glare at their hostile surroundings. They were in shock. What happened.

From the small hill ahead a spray of metal had come gouging eyes, taking off noses, shattering bones and filling torsos with death. Their heads swivelled, yet pain had cemented their looks of astonishment. Several militia had gagging chest wounds and punctured throats. They were chewed up. If there was Leadership they were in no state to hear it. Jenkins was dying but thought he had been spared from the onslaught. His back had been to the blast as he twirled around to harass the slackers into action. His buttocks had been shredded, his back pierced, and something else. He dreamt a devil's hand with spicy hot fingers dabbing into his cranium and feeling only coldness, then abstract visions of the old family when he was a man's knee high, and distant wrinkled relatives rocked on chairs and young cousins crawled on floors, dragging him to and fro from consciousness. His heart slowly thudded along, the heat on his limbs receded, his sagging body snatched by a grimy chill that in its later stages became quite pleasing. Around him, his blurred view limited to being paralysed face down, head turned left, was swaying golden grass set against a bright blue sky.

Rachi blubbered, into the radio handset. "Raaachi, Colonel Peters...."

"Where's Jenkins?" Peters asked, aware that a drowning man was on the line.

"He die! Colonel,"

"Rachi eh?" Peters asked squarely, "Where. Are. The. Enemy?"

"Bleeding, Colonel... My legs... My neck."

"Who are they, Rachi?"

"... ... Dying!"

"Have they escaped?"

"No," Rachi drew his knees to his chest and shivered, "I see nothing!"

"Jets! Was it 'landmine'? Boom from the ground!"

"I, I," Rachi purposely held down the handset signal and gaped to the apex of the low unassuming hill at three figures, parting the grasses, minutely rotating their torsos as they picked off targets until the echo of their gunshots ceased and for a fraction of a second they steadied their aim, bearing directly on him. "We walk into them – *ugh!*"

Peters dropped the radio receiver into his lap and wiped the corner of his eye. Jenkins was dead. He didn't need visual verification of the shot up corpse or a signed and dated death certificate. Gut instinct: The militia patrol was taken out. And he'd ordered them straight into it. He placed one finger on the computer screen at the last known location of Jenkins, guessed how far they'd moved since, then the range from which some explosive or landmine then rifle fire had finished them off. It was an area near the railway track. He circled the area with his finger, dotted the centre and then with his other hand clapped Eric on the shoulder. "Lob one in there."

"Can do, Boss." Eric's hand drove a mouse, which directed the cursor on the screen and with one click came up with the exact longitude, latitude and elevation.

Peters climbed out of the APC and ran to the missile truck. The Fudo was three metres tall and a half metre wide at the thrusters. It didn't look like it'd clobber much but the warhead was high explosives, equivalent to over a tonne of regular TNT. Peters checked the Tonkas. Their distant stares were acknowledgement that something horrible was happening.

"Count down!" Eric rushed out to watch the missile swing into action.

Its driver, an ex-Task Force Seven soldier, Wayne, harassed the Tonkas to clear away, "Stand back! Keep going! Back! She blows big!"

They heard the mechanical whine of winches on the truck pulling the Fudo fully erect up to the sky. The liquid fuel began to warm. The rocket engine ignited.

Peters smirked. "Teach those internationalists not to step into *my fucking* back yard,"

The radio chirped. "D-Man this is J-C. Over."

Peters reached around and grabbed the handset. "J-C, what is it?"

"D-Man... I heard Jenkins before. And Rachi? Is everything O-K?"

Peters growled "They got wasted. I'm sending a surprise over the range as we speak."

Callaghan gasped. "That's... It's pretty dry out there..."

"There's cyclone activity off the Solomon Islands, moving south. It'll be raining cats and dogs by nightfall."

"Sure..." Callaghan paused, trying to make his superior recap. "Couldn't you send in the Tonkas? They're crafty. What's out there anyway?"

"Jenkins and his patrol got the bullet," Peters stated uniformly. "Whoever did it: Fucked. I'm, um," he palmed his eyeball to squeeze his thoughts together, "It's whoever dropped in last night, out."

"Oh. Oh dear."

"Ten seconds to go, Sir." Eric reported.

Wayne again shouted to the Tonkas, "Get back! Further! Trust me! Go on!"

Peters stood well back as a marker for them to stand in line with. The missile blast made him blink and in the awesome seconds as it pushed itself up into the air and powered up to the heavens, an odd feeling swelled from his gut to his heart and slumped in his throat. When the missile was out of sight and en route, his heavy proud hands began to uncontrollably shake from the tips of his long fingers to the hardened knuckles.

Krue squatted, her cheek pressed against the rifle. Corrie had moved twenty paces into the kill zone, checking for survivors. Matthews and Tom stood by her side.

Corrie called back, "K-I-A. All of 'em. Shit. That was close, that could've been,"

"We move out," Matthews said agitatedly.

Krue stood up and turned on the spot, her stare despairingly sweeping the railway track, "There goes that plan."

"What next?"

"Shelter and water," she spun to the east, the ranges. "We can get there by nightfall."

Tom, surveying the ranges and the clouds sitting level with them, saw a dart's shifting shadow on a cloud's lining as it passed before another but then it peaked above the clouds altogether. He yelled abrasively, "What? Look! East and high! Is that what I think it is?"

From the ranges, passed well above the clouds now, a chalky arc drew up, thickening and puffing, reaching an apex then keenly bearing down.

"That's…" Krue trembled, trying to label the technology and in a flash it came to her: "Fuck! Run!"

Matthews looked in all directions and saw no cover, one kill zone, Corrie kicking a corpse, and cried, "Incoming!"

Corrie was still admiring the dead – they were dead and he wasn't.

Krue screamed, more to Corrie, "Run!"

He stiffened, turned, followed Tom's pointed arm, and saw something dropping from the sky.

They scattered, running, they didn't know where but just away in their direction and space, knowing they couldn't be getting that far and that they wouldn't hear it, and it had to be what they thought it to be, and it was all a matter of how big it was, how mean it was, how the fear kept them running and running and no matter how far, it wouldn't be enough.

The flash of heat was followed by a shockwave.

The ground opened up and shook. Time, matter and senses were warped, some of it obliterated and re-shaped as a static haze. Krue woke seconds later. The rumbling receded. She was flattened forward into the soft grass. Her head ached; wild throbbing and metallic adrenalin. Then a spray of vaporised, now cooling, soil and rocks came raining down. She flinched. Bits hit her and bounced off. She couldn't see. Her hands felt for the water canteen and leaning back, dribbled water into her eyes. Dust and grit, some stinging, trickled over her cheeks and under her collar. She rolled on her side, washed her eyes clear again, squatted up and blinked at an alien world.

Wobbling and bewildered, she stood, checked her kit, cock-eyed at a wave of flames, spreading out from a crater a hundred metres away. She'd got that far. All around her grass smouldered. The wind lifted up the smoke whisking in fresher air breathing life to the fires, casting the afternoon into a premature and artificial dusk. The sun was up but it was just a dirty light bulb.

"Hey!" she yelled but couldn't hear anything. Just ringing and an ache. She turned and gagged in terror at pockets of fire spreading, linking together, enveloping, surrounding her. Even her uniform was smouldering. She picked a path through the patches of burning grass.

Matthews, somehow closer to the crater, skipped over the flames and caught her from behind, screeching, "Run into the wind!" He was bellowing at the blast zone and how close they were to it. His face was red, one eye involuntarily winking, his other eye searching for a path.

It was hard to find the wind, but it was easier to flee the fires, and once on the circumference of the fallout of the hottest debris, breathing fresh air and frantically eyeing the sky for another, they saw Corrie, on his haunches, well clear of it all, rifle raised, petrified and expectant of a sudden attack. Krue waved both her arms at him. He shook his head, picked himself up and cautiously trotted over.

Matthews called out for Tom.

Krue trained her binoculars to the smoking pit: a silhouette briskly skirting patches of flame, making his way north, then changed to south. Matthews looked to Krue, she pointed and in he went.

When Corrie arrived, un-touched by heat but shaken by awe, Matthews had led Tom out. His face was lit up, a giant merry grin pinned from ear to ear. They couldn't hear what he was saying but it looked like, *So* fucking close!

Colonel Smacker briskly whisked down the Canberra corridor rhythmically slapping his thigh with a rolled up statistical report in one hand, the other held a cup from which he slurped jasmine tea from, nodding forward with Mrs Benson's stride as she abstracted the latest priority email.

"Australian National University reported nil tectonic disturbances. Airforce spotted a large explosion, Fraser Island Radar Station: medium sized missile surfaced north of Jacinda Mountain ... Traversing roughly thirty kilometres south-west to Major Krue's last position."

"Oh my," Smacker smarted, thrusting his security badge to two Armed Guards (forgetting completely who he was with) and entering the Control Room ten stories below Parliament House in Canberra. "This is preposterous! We've grovelled to Peters and look what he does! We need payback!"

"Nothing has been confirmed as yet," she calmed him. "We've contacted US Tactical Air Wing in Guam," Mrs Benson persistently continued to keep the Colonel up to date, hearing a new report via an earpiece, "They diverted a B-nine to the impact area. It's not a nuke... possibly a Fudo."

"Peters: at it again! And Voodoo-Child, have they reported it?"

Mrs Benson stood still, in-between banks of operators and their computer screens, her eyes roving for the one feeding her information, her mouth responding, "Where we last detected them, *is* the impact zone..."

Smacker's jaw locked. "*Christ.*"

Peters quietly smoked a cigarette at the back of the APC. "We got 'em, set half the fucking countryside on fire, but we got 'em! Tell me they're cooked."

Eric nodded. "They're cooked. Whoever it is must have copped it."

The radio buzzed. "D-Man this is J-C, come in, over."

Peters tersely answered, "They send 'em in and I knock 'em down ... What is it? Over."

"Well," Callaghan spoke calmly to himself as an example for Peters, "You got to send someone in to check what happened out there."

"Oh I will. We'll just let the fires die down."

"O-K. Well I'm heading back to Providence now. Farmers are still reporting bandits in Highway Five, and seeing I'm loaded to the gills with you know what, could you meet me on the way?"

"What am I, you're girlfriend?"

"Um... You're the one who needs a girlfriend, fucker. Just meet me on the road."

"Understood. I'll be down soon."

Peters placed the radio back and looked through the rich leaves of the forest canopy up to the belly of greying clouds passing over. Was it rain, or smoke?


Flower Two heard the distant explosion and wandered out of the gully. Perhaps it was a sign. He hobbled to the stream, picking up an aroma of cooked meat, and double fortune, a familiar language. The party, filthy and hungry, nibbled at the scraps of some odd marsupial. Flower Two had dreamt of snaring a wallaby but had lacked the ammunition. And, he'd lost his gun one night.

"Please, you must feed me."

They looked at the intruder with caution, the leader aimed a rifle.

"Please, feed me. It is very important that I survive."

They half laughed. At least they had humour.

He said, "We share the same tongue."

"What does it matter, so far away."

"It matters,"

"Where you from, the mainland?"

Flower nodded and cupped water from the stream and lay on his side. His stomach ached. His mouth was dry and inflamed.

The leader said, "We escaped Indonesia: too much trouble."

Flower's hand flung out to the last of the roasted animal, "Feed me. Maybe you can go back... Please."

Hungry as they were, they laughed again. This lunatic was a mess of skin and bones. And persistent.

"Indonesians forced you out because you are Chinese," Flowers told them.

The leader nodded. "We had no choice. There are many like us in these hills. Many have no choice."

"We knew.... The Pacific rim needs to be stabilised. Soon,"

"You are Chinese, a refugee too?"

"I am Chinese Military Intelligence." As if to prove it, he took from his pocket his dirty satellite phone and a small solar-panel wrap, unfolding it, and hoped to re-charged the battery. "They must call me,"

They laughed again, but were tired as well, of running, starving, foraging, dying, and now this lunatic's jokes. Someone tossed him a cracked bone.

Flower ignored his phone, took a twig, dug out the marrow from the bone and licked it up. "Thank you. Thank you. You will be safe."

"Safe?" the leader shook his head. "Everywhere we run to, we run from. The lies we have been told, all are liars. Go here, go there, they say. Lies."

"Soon our Army will be here." Flower said. "Safe, all safe."

They didn't laugh. They'd heard a lot of hope but nothing as grand as this and it did set them thinking. But he could so easily be a spy for any of the Warlords – General Kai was half Chinese and look at his preposterous hospitality! Many were rounded up and sent to slave in a mine!

"And when do you think the Chinese come?"

Flower assured them, "Soon. I *know*. They do not contact me anymore."

# The Hunger

"Look at this beautiful land! Totally awesome scenery," Kang gaily sang, his dialect warping as he was caught off guard by the splendour, revealing an *Americanesque*, or more precisely, an West Coast dude bubbling to break free.

Callaghan's ears had prickled before but he had more pressing things on his mind; calamities assumed bulbous proportions, some popped, atomised into the air while others simmered, anchoring his thoughts for days, weeks or months. Kang bumming a lift to Providence was not something to get worked up over.

Kang, cheery and windswept, continued, "No wonder so many people want a better life here. It's so fertile."

"Want and Have – the extremes meet here." Callaghan ruefully scanned the terrain, it was scenic, it was sub-tropical, it was worth it all, but, he smouldered, not so good if you're dead.

The jeep was driven by a beefy, loyal, militia henchman named Creton. An intellectually-sedated crony but maturely tempered driver, he was a fat Bhuddasque nondescript mongrel Asian who didn't say a lot but knew a lot, and even then couldn't act on the lot. He drove well, deflected bullets with his ample lard and underlying muscle and observed with not one but two wonky eyes. He could crush skulls with his bare hands and crush hope with mean-ass, though hardly synchronised, deathly stares.

Kang's titillating glee continued, "Where I come from, North Korea, very cold. We are outcasts in this world and here we are in a land of plenty! It has opened my eyes! You know, five years before it was so cold we ate grass. My Aunt died and authorities said: 'Feed her to the dogs – fatten the dogs to eat in the winter'. No State Cremation. She was a hero in the war. Very strong woman. Tough."

Callaghan peevishly asked, "Which war?"

"The war." Kang shrugged, stretching his arms out to cover the rear seats of the jeep. "A long time ago."

Callaghan turned to him, "When?"

"Sixty-seven," Kang shot back. "She served under Ho Chi Minh!"

Callaghan stiffened. "And she was from North Vietnam or North Korea?"

Kang straightened, rightly offended, "Korean! Pusan!"

"And Uncle Ho was from North Vietnam. So unless she was North Vietnamese Army… What was she doing there?"

"Viet Cong." Kang answered, his accent faltering, his complications with English increasing. "Her life like love movies. Like on TV... Not that I have seen. Only propaganda films. She married into Korea – my uncle. They met at a the Communist Party *party* at the end of war."

"*What* a party. I can imagine all the hilarity."

"Yes... No more jolly green giants to shoot. Very happy."

Callaghan was tired and stressed but admittedly Kang was fun; it was an intriguing little story, a breather, told by someone half interesting. It almost touched Callaghan until he remembered the outcome: An inglorious demise, eaten by dogs. There were plenty of those around here, and today he could be a magnet for it. At his feet was a fortune, immensely larger than what the optimistic likes of Kang could ever possible muster; $60,000 in US Dollars, a few re-issued million Yen, seven silver ingots and thirty gold ball-bearings, all the takings for the week from the Port of Kingston. So presently he felt like a fat juicy target for lucky highway bandits. As the bounces of the jeep wobbled Creton's flab the staggering cash prize remained perfectly still as if bolted down. Callaghan pinched himself. *Why confuse myself with illusions of death?* But what of Kang, Callaghan yearned, playing the chummy and naive card. Little stories. Painting a picture of himself, the harmless guy in a cruel world. Callaghan didn't know how long he'd drifted, how far they had travelled, and the jeep was unexpectedly slowing.

"Captain, hey Captain..." Creton lifted his index finger off the steering wheel, derisively examining a rabble of starved humans up ahead, moving to the side of the road, "More *Imports*."

Callaghan drew his pistol, "Careful they don't jump us."

The rabble were withering, wandering in a strange land in a stranger time. On sight of the jeep they placed their hands out together as a symbolic, grateful and begging ploy, thankful, celebratory smiles unzipped their dry, brown faces revealing sharp yellow fanged teeth and creamy, sickly, swollen tongues.

"What the... Stop!" Callaghan ordered, his mind accelerating with an inspiration, "Never *ever* seen them before..."

Normally they scattered into the bush or flopped dead as if instant United Nations aid was the only answer. Some just stood awaiting execution.

Creton pulled the jeep next to the fifty starving wanderers, couldn't see them as a threat, then brandishing a bearish smile passed a bunch of bananas to a lean and bony woman. She was graceful and gleeful with thanks, somewhere in her late fifties and as agile as any girl among her tribe. As a group they were uniquely dressed like exotic islanders, just hungry as hell and out of steam. To this, Callaghan became confused. Yes, technically they were refugees. Their clothing was a mix of fine weathered silk sarongs, quality leather sandals with very distinctive weaves, wreaths of wattles as crowns on their heads, and fraying Indonesian Army surplus packs on their backs. Therefore, Indonesian Islander Refugees picking at the fauna. Several of the women had possum skins sewed together as herb bags; enough local grub was there to shame most half-caste aboriginals. Callaghan looked fondly on adaptation.

"Hey Kang. Give 'em some of your fruit. If you want to hang with the Providence Hierarchy you gotta' learn how to be a humanitarian."

"Will they pay?" Kang frowned at the penniless refugees, "What are they?"

"What do *you* think?"

Kang swayed his head. His voice shakily probing, "They are lucky to live −and for how long? My fruit is to sell in Providence. Customers are demanding."

Callaghan felt like throwing a well-aimed punch into the man's nose, "Haven't you starved, ever? You could barter your fruit right now for one of the women." And on an even lighter note, "Or your own harem." There were twelve decent women, between fifteen and twenty, young, exotic as Asian Islanders go, but ghastly thin with yellow bruises tainting their skin. He picked up his radio, calling, "D-Man pick up... *It's me again...* Found some feral friends. Highway Five north of Sunny Bridge."

"Friendly," Creton noted of the ripest and deprived females. "Need shelter..." He snickered to himself, some sick suggestion in his head to the tune of his fat ugly cock busting virgin hips. His wonky eyes projected this to them, yet the girls stood there, mute and afraid, their minds fighting the prospect of a premature death.

Callaghan passed over a water bottle, absently staring off into their chomping graters. The tribe expertly peeled Creton's bananas, their widened mouths revealing their chiselled sets of pointed teeth. The children, straight toothed, took small bites of the food and passed it on. The elders would only eat once the children were fed. The cramps in their swelling bellies slowly receded. They chirped some form of thank-you, thank-you. Kang succumbed to the refugees and carefully placed one of his three crates of fruits on the road then slithered back into the jeep watching them share the fruit.

Callaghan watched Kang, the man was upset, as if he'd never given charity before. Strange to get this far without it.

Kang then fumed, "They are sick. Could they breath airborne diseases?"

"Airborne diseases. Oh, be very afraid."

"It could be true. I have seen many sick!"

"You're very educated for a Commie. You know, you are probably the last of the Communists? How does that feel? Guys like you get recorded in history."

Kang shut up, feigning some worldly embarrassment.

A refugee coughed. Callaghan eyed the offender, a middle-aged man with blistering lips, crooked chiselled teeth, and a feverish daughter wrapping her entire hand around daddy's one index finger.

Kang asked, "What do you do with them? How many crates of fruit do you have? Why not just give them plots to farm?"

"I saw you as a great believer in caring." Callaghan shot back.

Kang grimly grinned. "It is my trade."

"A tidy little trade to get you *this far*." Callaghan kept on the heat, "What'd ya' make of the Russian captain?"

"Not to be trusted. He threatened you too!"

"I take them all with a grain of salt. Now, what to do with these wretches."

"You shoot them?" Kang suggested and sniffed at nothing.

Callaghan let his head fall into his palm, baffled by the depths to what Kang could know. He swayed his head, put his pistol in the jeep and stood on the road, looking up and down. Shoot them.

"It's not that simple," he explained and heard the hum of an approaching jeep. It was friendly (who can source diesel anyway?) and he recognised Peters, Doc Nelson, and two militia boys, hurtling down the road. Peters took one hand off the steering wheel, gave a friendly wave, calmly braked, grinned at the surge of inertia, slowed to a roll and came parallel to Callaghan.

Peters ran his eyes over the wretches and with similar sentiment squared up to Callaghan, "What'd I tell you about making new friends?".

With a flick of the arm Callaghan imitated checking a precision watch on his wrist, "That was quick, Racer X."

"Yeah, been lead-foot'n… Had to bring up the Doc; heading north to lay on the charm to some pineapple farmers about contraception. They're popping them bubbas out non-stop."

"I see. Could you spread the message globally?"

"Maybe, but I am not the Pope or Allah."

"Hey Callaghan."

"Howdy Doc. That cream cleared up my jock-rot."

"Me too." Peters scratched himself and inspected the peculiarities of the refugees; they'd been crafty with the local flora and fauna. "These are the ones?"

"Yeah."

"So, what's the deal?"

"I was just… Thinking,"

Peters interrupted, "Don't scare me,"

"Sure… What have you been doing lately?"

"I was trigger happy, maybe paranoid, but it works." Peters raised himself and scoured the sides of the road to be sure there weren't more refugees, not more of this distinct tribe, but the other type. "I'm gonna' have to do a roundup again. Rat Riddance Week, again. A new wave came down from the north – must have survived from Kai or the others. Never, ever trade with him again. We'll need to make the refugees real welcome before we get them out."

"Before we get onto that, hear me out."

A giddy tribal teenage boy leaning on a machete for balance was still smiling at the speedy appearance of Peters.

"Sure… Crazy teeth," Peters shivered. "Chew through your throat in minute."

"Exactly. They're different. What do you reckon, Doc?"

Doc Nelson alighted from the jeep and circled the tired tribe. "Sick and starving." The women fidgeted, tugging what children they had left, closer. "Wouldn't wanna' touch those teeth. Might fall out."

"This guy was asking about airborne diseases." Callaghan introduced Kang to Peters and Doc Nelson. "Kang is from North Korea."

Peters cocked his head back, "You were selling fruit outside the bank the other day." Winking at Callaghan for fun, "Trying to chat up Jintana too."

"Jintana?" Callaghan marvelled. "Well, well, well! Grease on in, Kang. For a North Korean Commie drop-out you got some real talent."

Shunning the attention, Kang explained, "I only try to be friendly. Go about your business, there are needy to be taken care of."

"Teach English too?"

Kang nodded. "I learn fast."

Callaghan drooped. "And that Ruskie Captain made threats to me."

Peters licked the corner of his mouth, "Maybe he likes you? Receive payment?"

Callaghan kicked the bag at his feet.

Peters eased back in his driver seat. "C-O-D is A-O-K." The tribe watched his every move with hopeful interest. Peters tossed them a banana cake and smirked as it was handed to the most needy, the children. "There are reports, you know, trouble-makers *are* coming into Highway Five." He scanned the tribe, studying the sincere glare of an elderly woman, "But I don't think these travellers fit the bill."

Doc Nelson noted, "They're trusting."

"If you look closely at their dress, it's unique. Some culture highly advanced for Islander life. Cool kids," Callaghan cheerfully added. "I'd say they're civilised, more than fundamentalists could ever be. With some food in their tummies I reckon they'd be funny little bastards, quite possibly, fair minded citizens."

"You like 'em? Is that it? Favouritism to anything but the mediocre?"

Bravely, "Well yes. They have culture, plus, a psycho over-bite."

"Can they survive?"

"Possibly." Doc Nelson answered. "Creton, ask them where they are going."

Creton sorted through all the languages and dialects he knew. The man with the daughter replied, using a clumsy meta language, answering Creton's questions: *Who. From Where. Where's that? Next to? I see. And going?* Creton jutted out his lip in contemplation, probing another question and returning to Peters, "Fraser Island. They say they originated from Dasal Island off Borneo, and that of the Indonesian soldiers that are kind, the word is Fraser Island would suit this tribe best."

Peters laughed and flapped his hand to his heart, "That's right. Just look at a map and point."

"I don't think you can farm much on Fraser Island. It's a monolithic sand beast," Callaghan stated categorically. "Biggest in the world. They'd need a fertile playground to keep 'em out of mischief."

"Ain't farmers… They're hunters!" Peters sympathetically grinned. "Jacinda Mountain. Perfect stomping ground."

"Jacinda?"

"Yeah." Peters laughed. "We need some eyes and ears there. It's staring us in the bloody face - Islanders are Highlanders now. If they can live on Jacinda Mountain under my rule it's another blanket of protection. They'll learn that it's *their* island on lease."

"Too cute to kill," Callaghan gratefully clasped his hands as a meagre pray to Peters, and then to Kang. "Given some nourishment they'll be fine individuals."

Kang enthusiastically agreed, "Yes. Promising. But are they cannibals?"

"They need meat," Doc Nelson suggested, "Something light to begin with, say chicken. Then build 'em up to devour sheep and kangaroos."

Peters bleated like a sheep, "*Bahghgh*!"

The children laughed, shyly pointing him out as the funny one.

"Ah a sense of humour," Callaghan stroked away his fringe. "Goes a long way further than miserable factory-hands from ghettos."

Peters tucked his fingers into his armpits and felt a guilt-free satisfaction, "You know, saving lives is the natural urge. I really didn't feel like the usual *killathon*."

Callaghan echoed the sentiments. "Naaah."

Kang then asked complacently, "And who do you kill?"

Peters's casual absolution was coupled with crudeness. "City refugees; the millions booted out of Jakarta and Manila and all those crap places with no idea. Peasant battery-hens. They've been kicked out, offered all kinds of deals and easy passage and when they get here, what do you think this is, a charity club? They eat the crops. They rape, loot, and procreate like rabbits. Diseases take a good chunk. But too many are armed and preach with their guns thinking they can take land by force. They're not an army. Problem solving, as I see it. You could say they're all in need and full of heart, but when the critical mass is too much," and his eyes briefly narrowed on Callaghan, as if they had shared a joke on the matter.

"Fuck 'em."

"Exactly. I've thought about it a lot. There's no need to write a fucking manifesto on it all, one historical note is enough: The Shit Happens. Why are you so interested, friendo'? Scared? What are you doing here? Sounds like you're searching for something and not too different from the rest."

Callaghan added pensively, "It's O-K to be scared…"

Peters's smouldering eyes rested on Kang.

"My story is long," Kang inclined his head to the road to formulate an adequate answer for Peters but was cut short.

Callaghan said, part jovial and rightly irate: "He's a spy."

Peters grinned, "Interesting… *Very* interesting."

At the gentle foothills, the eastern approaches of Jacinda Mountain, Peters gathered his flock of new friends. "I will call you the Fang Tribe," he told them. Unified and partially clothed with excess supplies, they understood. The word 'fang' did not exist in their language or any other associated dialect, but Peters was quick to explain and Creton translated using a hybrid meta-language: pigeon. "It is rare that I save people, and I tell you as I feed you today, that you protect me tomorrow."

The Fang Tribe were overwhelmed. After four months stumbling south from Cape York they had found land and more valuable than that was a king's trust. They looked to the summit of the mountain, a rocky ridge. Wisps of cloud caught on jagged peaks above dense gullies. Lush forests spread from the base. In there, life spanned from hundred year old trees to 24 hour life-cycle insects. In between, hidden in the dark soil and rolling throughout the valleys, was survival.

Peters told the Fang Tribe, "I provide protection that we should be thankful for." He stretched out his arms to encompass his region, including the sky. "You will warn me of those who trek on your land. I offer you a feast to give you strength."

The sun had set on the other side of Jacinda Mountain. The rays pierced the smoke from the plains and lit the clouds behind the range a brilliant and stained grainy red. The Fang Tribe kneeled, facing into the sunset and Peters. He held a burning torch above his head, the trails of smoke twirling into the wind.

To his side Callaghan saluted and kicked his toe-cap to a full forty-gallon drum, the centrepiece of the event.

"Ready?" Peters asked its doomed occupant.

The drum was filled with water and stood on a neat bundle of dry branches bedded on a thick layer or kindling. Gagged and bound, in a semi foetal position, submerged but breathing, with onions and potatoes, chillies and zucchinis bobbing at water level before his popping pupils, trembled Kang. Tears ran as he sobbed over the hack-sawed rim of the drum to the Fang Tribe waiting patiently. Peters knelt at the base of the drum and lit the firewood. Kang would howl but the apple gagged in his mouth wouldn't budge. His eyebrows wriggled like worms.

Peters stood erect, grimacing through the smoke wafting up from the wood down to Kang's begging eyes. Peters turned to the Fang Tribe, "You were starving. You had faith to be kind to Captain Callaghan. You are rescued."

The Fang Tribe agreed unanimously that Callaghan was a decent fellow.

Peters stood firm, like a monument, and the true depth of his nature came rolling out with thunderous words, "You can pray to your Gods, the Old and New, as much as you like, but you are here now. You live here. You will obey my One Commandment!" He stood immaculate and sharp in his old uniform, the piercing blue eyes few of the Fang had ever seen roving over them, "Trust no one, bar me!"

Kang's mortified shriek was muffled and violently swaying his head, ached to scream up to the stars.

As Creton was putting the finishing touches on the translation, Peters could say no more and the Fang raised their heads to see how the stew was coming.

Callaghan circled the drum, his arms tightly folded, his brow raising as each new tangent kick-started a supernova of thoughts. He spoke with a crisp undertone of sympathy. "I've met three North Koreans in my life. Truth is stranger than fiction. They were not idiots. I'd say they were pretty much on the ball like myself. They were paler than you, and they were, I guess, real dodgy fucks too." Feeling the warm water swell from the base of the drum, Callaghan continued, "You came as an interesting surprise, so what we're doing here is symbolic – sometimes Peters, more than myself, feels the need to give something to the world." He thought to the smoky sky. "At the very least you'll remember your own death as incomparable to anyone or anything you've ever known."

"Callaghan, you could spin shit for hours," Peters reached to Kang's head and removed the gag, "Sorry."

Kang coughed and spluttered. They'd gagged and hog tied him at the road, and all through waiting for two trucks to pick up the Fang, shipping them here, preparing the fire, and the show of humanitarian fanfare. His tongue poked from his lips to taste fresh air and his eyes switched between his captors. He spoke with a nasal and antagonising American accent, "It doesn't have be to this way! *Cough! Ergh!* The water is getting hot! Time out!" He struggled but couldn't break the ropes binding his hands. "This is not sane! You are *not* barbarians! You're good guys! You've proven it!"

Peters dipped his hand in the water and lapped it against Kang's ears, "Pissed your pants yet?"

"*No!*"

"Good." Peters tasted the water. "I want to know one thing,"

"What?"

"Callaghan was right. You aren't just some lucky chap – to be here you've got to have a friend in high places."

Kang indignantly looked down into the water.

"So lucky-*unlucky* you. A spy, soon to be a boiled feast for third world monkeys. *Wipe out*, dude."

"No… This is a mistake… Let me explain… I can't die this way!"

Peters observed the sunset and the washes of red and orange, a reflection, he smiled, of his own impenetrable anger. "But you can."

Callaghan winked to Kang San and then at the Fang, "Cannibals?"

The Fang Tribe nodded, big smiles, wicked teeth, gnawing hunger pains.

"No… You two, are… Gawd… It won't help you!" Kang bobbed his head forward towards the Fang Tribe. "What about humanity! I'm from a civilised country, man!"

The Fang Tribe's teeth chattered, hungered by the trek, and so close to starvation. Plus the supplies Peters brought, tents and pots and pans! These white people were very good people! Callaghan watched them watching Kang who watched Peters. Callaghan couldn't decide what turned him on, was it the Fang, Kang or the pretty sunset? The diabolical blend or the thought of the aftertaste?

Kang stuttered and the heat made him sweat, "I'm boiling alive! You're a Westerner! Who do you think you are: Warlords are not barbarians!"

Callaghan whispered, "*But it helps.*"

Peters swayed his head. "You're right, I guess. I don't know what I am anymore. But by feeding you to starving displaced persons, perhaps I'm the Red Cross? Nice Christian virtue. Maybe Sunday School got to me eventually."

"O-K! I get it!" Kang kicked inside the drum. "What do you want to know?"

Callaghan leant into Kang's face, "You already know."

"It's Colonel Peters."

"Nothing about me?" Callaghan cross examined the helpless man.

Kang shook his head.

"So, you think I'm a soft cock?"

"Help me, help me explain." Kang's tears streamed down. "I'm not going out like this! We can work towards *positive* outcomes. You will get nowhere doing this!"

Peters cleared his throat and spat to the side. "We know *that*. But you're stewing because we can't trust you. Do they pay you well?

Who and how much? I just don't pick you as a fool for a competing junta, that's all."

Kang wailed to the sky, "My name is Chris McDuncan!"

"An Asian with an Irish name? Don't bullshit me! What are you?"

"I'm C-I-A! What else can I be? Get me out of this, please!"

Callaghan whistled down. "And the rest of you?"

"Just me. Believe me," Kang pleaded, the fright in his voice was exhilarating, relieved to hear himself squeal rather than spin lies. "You can call them! Email, fax the bastards! They'll pay for my release! You need currency!"

"Currency?" Peters huskily laughed. "Do we?"

Callaghan's execution of a Gaelic shrug was synchronised with a disbelieving, "*No*."

"When I call them," Kang muttered, "I can get you an offer..." Now his chin was up, out of the scalding water. "We can offer information on Indonesian and Chinese movements."

"But we buy that information," Callaghan said, "Sometimes direct."

"O-K. Listen," Kang neared feinting, "The C-I-A wants to know what you're doing... That's all. Hard information."

"We tell their Australian counterparts all the time," Peters said.

Callaghan, offended, added, "And why didn't you just call? Pick up the phone? It may be a world of anarchy but it's still *connected*. People just don't communicate anymore!"

"No..." Kang stiffened and levelled his eyes at Peters. "No... It's more complicated... It's about the Beijing Ninety-Six,"

"And?" Peters cocked an eyebrow.

Kang cried. "Disarming it."

Out of sight of Kang's panting and moaning, Peters un-holstered his pistol, slid off the safety, turned and with his face grim, expediently discharged a bullet into Kang's sweating forehead, blasting brains through the back of the cranium into the stew. They floated on the top like a broth. Kang slumped, head back, warm water filling his mouth, blood trickling out of his nose and into the water.

Silence.

The fire crackled.

Peters holstered his pistol. "Creton, are they really cannibals?"

"They say I could feed them for a month!" Creton laughed to himself, holding in his gut and trying to spread his infectious laughter to Callaghan and added as a sombre after-thought, "So I might lose weight now."

"The teeth." Callaghan whispered back, admiring the Fang, "They got to be. See 'em run their hands over their bellies over this poor bastard."

Peters stood facing away from the submerged corpse, "You have to wonder if this is how they cook 'em though. Seems wasteful and typical of us whitey bastards."

Callaghan studied the mess riding the top of the brew, "Can't fix that."

"Those Fang must be laughing their heads off at us. Dead-shit cooks, that's what they're thinking. Couldn't even cook a sausage in a fry pan."

"Peter, can we just get the fuck out of here?"

"Sure we can." Peters moved towards the jeep, waving farewell to the Fang Tribe. "Remember: You will eat no farmers, and none of my militia. Beyond that, I don't care."

Creton translated, sure that they understood these valuable points, then, "Anything else?"

"Yeah, I'm sorry about out our dismal cooking method."

The Fang Tribe agreed unanimously, although fearful of openly ridiculing Peters, that boiling of human meat was wasteful and not as succulent as roasting it. Peters, Callaghan and Creton jumped into the jeep. The Fang Tribe respectfully bowed until the passing of his presence. Creton gunned the jeep out of the foothills through the plains into the farming plots heading for the coast and Providence.

Peters looked over his shoulder to the vanishing flames of the fire, "You know what?" Figures danced around the over-turned drum, a pack of men dragged Kang to a circle of women with machetes momentarily raised over their heads. "Just another day's work." Peters froze as the women decapitated Kang and descended on the limbs. "For all of us."

Callaghan snorted, "And for the covert kind? Those who got Jenkins?"

Peters turned to the front. His eyes followed the rise of his knuckles, one hand restfully in the other. "I'm sure I wasted them. Nothing could escape that."

"Sure. But the price we pay," Callaghan explained, "One missile, if that's the price of protection, we have to make a lot more money. I need to make some deals. Kang was easy, one bullet, but the others, whoever they are and what they were doing – that's expensive insurance, what were you fucking afraid of out there?"

Peters remained silent.

"Because they nailed Jenkins? Are you fucking losing your marbles? He was one man and two-hundred or two-fifty dollars worth of militia! It would make all the more sense if we knew what was destroyed out there – *what* of the fearsome enemy there really was. One *what* or a hundred *what* you don't know."

Peters cringed, "Is that all of your petty bitching?"

"No... Yes."

Peters briskly changed the course of the conversation, "What of the bonuses? What of the trade in Kingston? Tell me one good thing, that's all I ask."

"Trade *is* good," Callaghan smiled, really smiled, for the first time that day, a hint of sarcasm propelling his voice. "And we certainly made a statement to the big bad world. Kang – McDuncan *what-the-hell* he really is."

"If I had a camera the Pentagon would be receiving a lovely postcard: cooking tips from the Foreign Countries."

"They'd love it."

"They're wasting time with choir boys... This is exactly what I was on about two months ago, I'm a marked man now, not only locally, but globally."

Callaghan felt a relief in exclaiming, "*Boo hoo*. You're marked? *I'm* marked."

"We all could have died a long time ago..." Peters saluted the dark road ahead.

Callaghan rolled his head back and sighed to the twinkling stars, "And today we gave freedom to those who deserved it. Who gets to do that, organically, without the paperwork, on a whim, and feed them."

"Charming. Now you know what stands out in that glory?"

"Oh the glory!" Callaghan compulsively retorted, "A Nobel Peace Prize is coming your way in the mail? That kind of glory?"

"Not quite."

"Those glorious teeth? How about those chompers! Scary fuckers. We could open a tourist resort."

"Not yet," Peters snorted. "But that spy,"

"Oh, Mr positive-outcomes-send-me-to-hell, please Sir."

"Yes. He's proof that the big boys fear me, not just scummy Warlords."

"Hang on, let's be serious. One loner sneaking into our little world that we fingered out is nothing to lose sleep over. Sure the nuke upsets them but don't take it to heart. They've could have wiped out

Providence and Kingston years ago, but we're civilised, they're civilised, nothing serious has come up yet."

"No, but now it's personal, that's what. They want *me* dead. I'm telling you, McKang was lining me up for something. Me and the Nuke are One."

Callaghan laughed, "Really?"

Peters laughed back, "They want me so badly. Dead cold, that's it."

"I want to go in the bath. Glass of champagne in one hand, girl in the other."

"No listen, it irks me; it's personal. They could have called. Talked."

"Sure, we always listen... But they're not against you, it's your statement. That's what it's about. The World is at War. Don't inflate your ego because you're a drop in the ocean compared to the heavy shit up north."

"To McKang I wasn't,"

"Why?"

"I'm the rogue. In the beginning, it was bad. They were like, 'Task Force Seven survives. Sorry. We'll get you out... Fend for yourself.' And now I'm the anti-Christ. Moved on. I've traded beef for a nuclear weapon."

"I set up *that* deal and *you* get the credit," Callaghan scratched at his chin, grating his teeth, "Is there a bounty... If you hadn't turned his brains into cannibal soup we could have asked a few other things."

"Maybe I was a bit, you know..."

"One Nuclear Armed Beijing Ninety-Six is nothing. General Kai's got two,"

Peters gritted. "See, I bet he doesn't."

"He is full of shit. But fuck that. In this new world *evolution* is our policy."

"And part of our evolution is self-protectionism, including lots of nasty shit the big boys don't like," Peters wryly reminded himself, "I just feel we're at a point." His hardened eyes stared up to the congested heavens. "We've done a lot of bad things and it can't go on forever."

Callaghan added, "But outside our region is an environment not of our making – I tell that to Canberra. I tell them to fuck off and leave us alone. They get righteous about it, paint you as the cunt of the century."

"I'm the Bogeyman." Peters acknowledged up to the Milky Way, "This wholesale killing by numbers will go on and on but I don't want it, we got to evolve."

"You didn't start it. Creton, how long has killing been around?"

Creton didn't know. It wasn't on his list of comparative thoughts of the day. He resumed picking the wax from his ear and wiping it on a banana leaf whilst driving the dirt track into town.

Peters felt normality again. "What were you trying to say before…"

Callaghan clasped his hands together, "Well… Yeah… That nuke. The fact a superpower sends some CIA-dude to find out where it is means they want it destroyed. What if you get taken out as well?"

"They try anyway."

"They can try harder, and they will."

"O-K. It validates what we've been doing all along. We are a nation, remember, and they don't like it but they're not taking the risk. We have a right to defend ourselves."

"True, but it's getting complicated. You're right, we're at a point, we can go either way."

Peters clenched his fists, "So how the hell do we get peace?"

# Communication Breakdown

After the strike, they hurriedly crossed the plains, wearily scurried into the rugged foothills at the base of the western side of Jacinda Mountain, and slipped into the deeper cooler gullies, leaving the smoke stained air behind. The moisture seeping from low lying clouds sedated them, meagre streams trickling between boulders satisfied their thirst. They then scaled uphill to see the hell from which they had escaped.

Propped against trees, with dejected stares to the lake of orange and red still burning below, they were thoroughly exhausted, aching, still in shock, and thankful to be alive. The dazed lull that understandably prohibited any attempts at conversation was a sedate collusion of what all of this meant. Krue kept her mouth shut the tightest. In that smitten pit, they had escaped both the evils of man and nature. Down there was testament to the lengths Peters would go to when protecting his land.

At dawn the rain blew over from the coast and swept the plains and now the clouds were off somewhere else. The progress of the fire was easy to see amid the golden plains – it had spread evenly and left a stain, engulfing about three kilometres from its epicentre.

This mission, she swallowed hard, is a winner-takes all stunt, just a notch below a kamikaze ride. The top brass throw her at crazed warlords and he throws back missiles, the cost of which was probably the same as her pitiful bounty. Still, impressive. She sipped from her canteen and swallowed vitamins. Her eyes were content to stare despondently to the stain, yet her stomach tried to expunge the tablets.

Tom was on watch, his back to the west, staring spookily up the wooded slopes of Jacinda Mountain. He munched a muesli bar and sniffed oddly at the wind.

"Tom," Krue whispered softly.

His eye traced a route up the mountain. "We're going over it, right?"

"I want to reach the peak by afternoon. On a good day we can observe the entire coastal region."

"Aye…"

"Did you sleep?"

"About three hours." He shrugged off sleep altogether. "I don't plan on sleeping until we're back – wherever we go back to."

Krue looked over the short solid fellow with a decent degree of compassion. "You were in Brisbane?"

"Temporarily... Thankfully... But sleep don't matter until we're back. Don't think I'm a nutcase, but I like it out here."

Krue breathed the mountain air, "Rest, you'll need it. You'd be surprised how it can catch up on you."

He winked.

Krue had her pack by Matthews's slumbering body (if he was asleep, if he could sleep, if a thousand thoughts weren't running through his mind and he had merely closed his eyes to rest them and hopefully his brain and his fingers weren't involuntarily tapping a message into the satphone to his lover in Tasmania). In one arm she carried her handgun, in the other a khaki hand towel. Her tunic top buttons were undone and her belt off.

"Washing up?" Tom asked her.

"There's a stream down there – yes. If you hear this," she tapped the handgun against her thigh, "Bring in the cavalry."

"Sure." He yawned.

"Ciao." She stepped over the boulder he observed from and disappeared down a ravine a few meters in front. As she descended, knowing she was slipping off the ridge she planned to lead them up to the summit on, the air became thicker with chill and astonishingly refreshing. She picked her way down, found a damp animal track and cautiously stuck to that. She knew that an animal track leading downhill would lead to water – and there it was, a wide pond fed from small streams that had trickled from crevices on the northern side of the summit. The immaculate still surface reflected with the clarity of a mirror. She inquisitively peered over at herself. She was blackened from head to toe. She could, she amused herself, be mistaken for a native. She neatly stripped and folded her clothes on a bank of pebbles beside the pond and then inch by inch, so as not to send sounds of splashing to the placid depths of the ravine, slowly submerged herself. The chilled water electrified her. It was difficult not to shake vigorously but like cutting herself intentionally or drinking herself to a stupor, she could control herself, including the thoughts that race between practical and pragmatic. When she was finally underwater, the pond being only a few feet deep and she lying on and holding herself to the pebbled floor, she meditated. One minute. She calmly surfaced and breathed deeply. With short hard strokes she washed the ash from her skin. Her true glow, the natural tone of her genes and the odd sprinkle of freckles from days at the beach, came back. How that seemed an eternity ago.

She stood in the middle of the pond, arched her head back, and wrung the water from her hair. From behind her in the dark ravine a twig snapped. She spun around. A sapling swayed as something had shot away out of sight. In one leap she landed on the pebbled bank, naked, aimed her handgun to the sapling now straightening itself to the stillness. She cursed. This was exactly how wanderers meet their death: Alone in the wilderness with not a soul to hear their death throes.

Her men were awake, poking their fingers into tins of ham and pea. Krue emerged from the ravine looking clean, and to the surprise of her men, a decade younger and full of urgency. This was the first time they had seen her cleansed and in the freshness of morning.

"Major Krue, I never knew you're so," Tom began to drawl and yawn, rubbing his eyes, until Corrie thumped him one.

Krue silently sat with them but her smile was faltering.

"You alright?" Matthews asked.

"Fine… Don't get too comfortable."

"We move out?" he asked.

"Something spooked me down in the ravine."

Corrie's eyes despairingly ran over the plains below, "Any furry little animals down there would've fled up here."

Tom added, "Sure is quiet."

"Too quiet." Krue said. "Let's go. You guys can wash up top, promise."

Trekking up the mountain was a chore but rewarded by panoramic views. With patience and exploration they wound their way around the mountain and by midday rested under a meagre waterfall: an over-glorified trickle. The men quickly stripped and washed the flakes of ash and grime. Krue, isolating herself on look-out, had no intentions of hearing what the three could whisper about as they went about their business. If anything was to be taken from the preceding afternoon it was the sweet taste of life enjoyed only by the living. By late afternoon they had reached the rocky summit and concealed themselves with weather beaten branches. What water they had bottled on the way up would last a day or more which for Krue, was the duration of their stay.

Before sundown the sky was clear and the visibility perfect. From the summit, east to the coast was roughly twenty kilometres, and consecutively from the base of Jacinda Mountain's foothills were rolling woods of gum trees that abruptly ended on flat fertile ground, cleared and poorly fenced paddocks, rows of tilled soil, new crops, lonely farm houses, dirt roads, broken telegraph poles, and further to the coast, a few hills and dips, woods, then the tiny settlement of Providence. Seen through binoculars it was a low-lying town, bar the odd prominent beachside building. Most visible structures were intact, which impressed Krue. The majority of the townships in Queensland had been burnt to the ground by the retreating Australian Army. Her assumption was that this area, including the tight cluster of buildings seen in Kingston to the north east, had been overlooked in the rush. Between Providence and Kingston she could see the sun reflecting on the silvery snaking Arubai river. As it curled closer to sea the vegetation on opposing banks thickened into dense impenetrable mangroves. Out to sea she could see nothing, her eyes were tired. She nudged Tom to check the radio.

Matthews, Corrie and Tom were thankful, the cool Pacific wind blew onto their clean faces. They had seen a lake of fire and now the calm blue of the earth, coupled with the elevation, granted a heavenly view down to little mortals on little farms and roads. The sub-tropics impressed the young soldiers. Here was terrain they had been taught about and now the textbook tips made sense. Down by that River, the Arubai, Matthews noted on the map, would be leeches, crocodiles, fungal-infections between toes, possums to snare and feast on. The jungle, the young Corporal eagerly and joyfully smiled, I'm gonna' fight in a jungle! He grinned to Tom and Corrie to share his vision yet they were staring out to sea or running their eyes back and forth, up and down, systematically scanning the terrain. I must be slacking, Matthews thought. I'm overwhelmed that I'm up here. I'm so far away from the Battalion C-O and that runt Captain Smith (who sent us here, didn't he?) that they would not know if I type a quick message to my darling. An anonymous text message, who is to stop that?

"Hey, I got something," Tom pressed the radio to his ear. "Isn't ching-chong... It's English... Very feint." He placed a notebook on his thigh and wrote what he could comprehend. "It's a repeat... Over and over again... And music... Awful music..."

Krue and Matthews waited. The wind picked up.

"Done." Tom read the note to himself, and again, then folded it to pass it on, "Major, you better read it."

"Thanks."

"What's it say?" Matthews asked Krue but simmered intently at Tom.

Tom looked the other way, squinting, trying not to think or believe.

Matthews watched Krue re-read the note.

She was curt. "If I had had time I would have told you before at the airfield,"

Matthews cast her a sudden, hurtful, questioning stare.

Corrie had acknowledged as he ran through the smoke with the flames licking at his ass that he was in fate's hand, a safe hand, and there was no other way to comprehend it. The faster you run, the smarter you plant those feet and don't trip, the safer the hand to guide you in the now. And now he had God. God has just jumped up recently like a puppet at a show and it wasn't a particular bright fluffy brand of God. It was just "God", man, he imagined explaining to those who could never understand Big Corrie's change of spiritual heart.

Krue sombrely watched over Providence, but with the young eyes and minds seeping into her, she read in a dry factual tone verging on mockery, "Colonel Peters, Warlord of Providence, is offering food supplies to displaced peoples. Go to Highway Five south of Kingston. Come out of the trees and we will feed you. This is not a lie. We have food."

She handed the note to Matthews.

He read it and passed the note to Corrie.

"Colonel Peters…" Corrie fathomed and turned to the peaceful scenery, "That's a white name."

Matthews swayed his head, dipping it between his knees and made some swipes with his index finger into the dusty surface of the rocky summit. Conceptualisation can be a real bitch sometimes. Without looking up he said, "So Major, you know this Colonel Peters?"

"I know little but what I do know is he's it. He's an Anglo Warlord gone berko up here."

"Streuth... Must be *fucked up*... What else can you say about him?"

"… Not much."

In absence of truth, imagination creates a monster. Her men didn't have to know everything, but by the same token, what had Brigadier Tolken and Colonel Smacker led her to believe?

"He's our primary target," she confirmed their fears, "A rogue warlord, like any other."

Matthews bit at his initial hysterical intrigue, "And the nukes? Are they part of the mission?"

"Secondary target."

Matthews ruffled and felt the urge to lift Krue out of her nest on the summit and throw her off the edge into the ravines below. His eyes half-squinted, his top lip involuntarily quivered, his normally eloquent fingers cramped around the K-41 in his lap. It was not uncommon for mutiny. Twice Krue had thought of fleeing her own superiors, and even now, she subconsciously was.

"Everyone, turn your satphones off."

Matthews scrutinised her, "They'll assume we're missing, or dead."

"Missing," she corrected, "It's a precaution, just in case they're being monitored by third parties." She then turned to the distant sea and scanned from end to end with the binoculars. It must be surreal for them, she sighed. She felt their stinging eyes on her back, then their exchanged glares of distrust, ganging up in a typical wall of testosterone.

"Major," Matthews interrupted her.

"Shhh... I've spotted something." From Providence, a lot of radio communication came out, too much for just civilian chit-chat. She spotted the tallest building, right on the beach and close to the centre of town. She dreamt of an easier life, living down there, morning and afternoon swims, watching evening storms from the balcony, sipping cocktails after a seafood dinner.

"Major,"

"What?" Krue said through clenched teeth.

Corrie and Tom boyishly grimaced at each other.

"I don't care why we're assassinating... It's part of the job. That's what we're taught to do."

Krue faced him. "And?"

Matthews pried, "We're going down there..." He craned his neck at the little farms they would encounter first. "So I'd just like to know who this Colonel Peters is. I'm just getting the hang of shooting who I'm meant to... See, taking out a white-fella is an extra leap I'd never imagined before."

Krue rubbed her eyes, composed herself, suddenly muttering, "He's not any ordinary *whitey*: Colonel Peters is a renegade."

"A renegade?" He bowed away wondering why he ever asked. Why not just *not* know? Shoot first, ask later.

"He's posing a strategic hindrance – a big fucking problem," Krue fantasised, "To the superpowers out there around the Pacific Rim who see him as a," yet she couldn't find the words.

"And they reckon he's gone berko?" Matthews thoughtfully intervened. "Who wouldn't go fucking mad up here? From the shit I've heard it's a recipe up here."

"Correct. Power vacuums. Refugees. Warlords. Genocide. Politics. But we're not just a few ingredients, we arrange a better outcome."

"Because he's plain *mad*."

"With his finger on the trigger of a nuclear weapon. But don't you worry Corporal," she proudly reminded her men, tapping her finger once on her handgun, "I'll be doing the dirty work."


Canberra, a picturesque day; a stark blue sky reflected on the calm lake, idle trees home to descending formations of birds. Colonel Smacker and Brigadier Tolken shuffled down a hallway, straightening their uniforms, arrived at Mrs Benson's office and put on a mood of urgency. They collapsed into comfortable office chairs, facing her, yet staring out the window to wet pink wattles illuminating a garden. The two men had aged years in days. In contrast, Mrs Benson brimmed bright and cheery in command of her office, adjusting a wattle in an hour-glass vase on her desk, soaking the stork deeper into sugary water. There were urgent requests from heavy duty diplomats and global news producers on her desk yet her eyes patiently sized up her visitors.

"What's into you two?" she asked benignly.

"A touch of confusion." Tolken said.

"I see." Mrs Benson's fingers ran down the sides of a small sheaf of papers before her, skim reading, "Time is of the essence... Briefly... Infantry progress through New South Wales and South Australia is well ahead of schedule. Light armoured are probing deep into the Northern Territory. Opposition is described as 'starving and useless'. It seems the last of the Indonesian forces are routed and hungry. God knows what their morale is like. This is the first optimistic news in a long time, the tide is turning. It hasn't been released publicly though."

"It could turn back." Smacker's eyes shifted to the next page she read from.

"Not down there.... Next... CIA, Head of Special Operations called me up before he sent me this email. One of their Operatives was making excellent progress up north, tracking down the Beijing Ninety-Six, getting to know Colonel Peters and Captain Callaghan,"

"Really?" Smacker glowed.

Tolken quipped, "Do tell!"

Mrs Benson's index finger skipped lines of text, "He frequented Kingston and Providence... Masquerading as a business man... *Sounded* promising... Good intelligence... But now vanished."

"Vanished?"

"Close, but no cigar, as the Americans say." Mrs Benson flipped another page. "I suppose he's more K-I-A than M-I-A, until further notice... Now, this one..." She placed it before them. "Progress from our side?"

> TO: OVERLORD
> FROM: VOODOO CHILD
> ALL IS WELL. SAFE AND SECURE.
> MADE CONTACT WITH LOCAL
> MILITIA. ESCAPED MISSILE
> ATTACK. FEAR HIGH LEVEL OF
> MONITORING BY LOCAL
> WARLORD. WILL COMMUNICATE
> ONLY WHEN NESSECARY. HAVING
> A SPLENDID TIME.

"Major Krue seems to have made contact in a very provocative manner," Mrs Benson adjusted the wattle in the vase, tilting it to her, symbolically raising her voice, "So I suspect Colonel Peters will still be standing in the way of the Chinese for a while yet. Any ideas?"

Tolken cringed. "Naval Intelligence paints a very bleak picture... The Chinese are moving in. The savvy diplomats say they're 'cleaning up' the war. Bullshit. But that's why our progress against Indonesian has been easy."

"That's accepted." Mrs Benson expressed dismay.

"It gets worse. Chinese Naval vessels are moving into the Coral Sea. There's enough tonnage to land a division, perhaps a small army. And there's three attack submarines, advertising their presence."

"They're not after a war. Easy pickings is what they're after." Smacker insisted. "And they're making a real run of it, straight on the heels of the Americans. Do you have any word on Darwin?"

Mrs Benson said smugly, "Disaster. Chinese Recon Forces gained a foothold but failed to secure the port. The locals sent them back into the sea. If this is their idea of Global Policing, they've got a lot to learn. We've authorised high level and high intensity bombing on strategically sensitive pressure points like uranium mines."

"Excellent." Smacker smiled. "But they'll be back with twice as many next time. They should have stuck to communism instead of that crypto-capitalist crap. Who knows what they are now."

"Still," Mrs Benson re-iterated, "Colonel Peters has to be removed."

Smacker re-read the message, amusingly biting his cheeks, "If our bet on Krue doesn't work we'll use saturation bombing of Providence and Kingston." Having spent many a restless night with his arms behind his balding head, he gleefully imagined a strike on Providence; a fighter bomber's front cannons criss-crossing the streets, high-explosive bombs mashing the flimsy buildings, or maybe just gassing the fuckers. Then concoct a midday firestorm over Kingston. That'd hurt Peters. "We know the options and appropriate solutions," he stated authoritatively.

Mrs Benson spied his glimpse of apocalyptic vision and promptly diverted their train of thought. "Are you thinking Krue will miss the chance?"

Smacker's eyes shifted to his superior.

Tolken brooded. "Possibly. The Queensland coast is open to attack by the Chinese in the name of Pirate Policing and Colonel Peters is on their hit list. There was a low-level diplomatic meeting last week, here in Canberra and it was verified, un-officially of course, so... Yes it's up to us." He quietened, "We can't trust him either. We could explain to him to lay off, but he won't."

Smacker agreed with a firm nod.

Mrs Benson's voice became brittle: "We must contact him again."

Smacker *tsked*, loudly and out of order, but tolerated.

Tolken frowned. "We've tried... There always arises a point of contention, you know,"

"The situation is getting critical. It's also in our nature to hear what he would have to say. Regardless of egos and policies, we have to keep the lines of communication open."

Tolken appeared to suffer for lack of air, gasping, flexing his jowls, "Of course... Yes... But *he* won't come back to our side."

"Try again. We need some hold on him – somehow. Get someone to call him up and try."

Tolken nodded. "The specialists in Intelligence can do it... But there's not much to say, as a military option we're in no position to give Providence any protection. China can easily poke around Queensland, easy picking is what they'll get and that's their favourite currency for leverage. It's out of our hands if they run into Peters."

Smacker positively added, "But not the hands of Krue."

"What we don't know yet," Mrs Benson craftily rationalised, "Is should he be informed, what position he'll take. It might knock some sense into him."

The next day Callaghan accepted the call. The act of accepting the call was a two-pronged pain. One, they knew he was willing to answer, and thus locate him (at the bank, where he could be reached most days, via an underworld telecommunications network) and thus clinically kill him. Two, he appeared approachable. Peters, out in the jungle herding refugees, had posthumously laid down the law: Do not play approachable with them.

Comparatively, Callaghan had a rational heart. He sat in his office sipping coconut milk forming a list of requirements.

Jintana sat directly across from him taking notes.

"Toilet paper,"

"Toilet paper," she wrote, scrawny though legible longhand.

"If you can source some, I don't care where, but we don't have any. Haven't had any decent stuff for weeks. Where did Sumatra find it?"

She shrugged. That task would have gone to some clerk, which she now was, partially.

"And Doc Nelson reminded me yesterday – bandages. Enough for ten thousand wounds, ten thousand rolls, I guess."

"Bandages."

"But speak to him because medical terminology is an exact science," he attested with a wistful smile acknowledging that Jintana would be radioing to prospective distributors and importers in the New South Pacific. "They're all too happy to trade what you're after but at inflated prices and terminology. When I asked for surgical gauze I received Band-Aids decorated with *Simpsons* characters whistling tunes. Not very adequate for exit wounds."

"This afternoon I'll see him at the hospital."

"Excellent."

"Callaghan," Eric called urgently from the door.

"Yep,"

"For you – cold caller from Canberra."

"Ah." Callaghan deliberately held his eyes up in the air for the duration of his thoughts; I'm in the middle of a meeting, we couldn't find Jenkins's body so we couldn't bury him, don't be approachable. Make them wait. They'll know about the missile strike, maybe they'll be upset or rub in a little victory like dog shit into a new carpet.

"Put them through?" Eric loosely pointed down to Callaghan's desk phone.

"Yeah." With one elongated wave he thanked Eric and beckoned Jintana to leave.

"Why are some calls personal?"

He sighed, "… Jintana,"

"Yes," she strangely blossomed, thankful that he would assure her.

"Do I ask what you dreamt?"

She expected to be ambushed by some cryptic answer; an immediate non-answer. A riddle full of clues which she would have to assemble and dissect, consulting her English dictionary.

She said, "You should."

"I don't because there are things I don't want to know."

She was captivated by the dark streaks in his blue eyes. In them she could see her smile reflected back.

"And when you do tell me your dreams, are they real?" He lifted up the phone, winked at the flashing light signifying the waiting caller, routed through the digital radio, beamed up-down over the earth.

"No, not all the time."

"So like this person that wants to speak to me, things I say may not be real and you won't know the difference."

She immediately thought of a woman. This was, she decided, not her usual self. But she was in love, blindly, faithfully and unashamedly in a strange land where life was cheap. Is this Woman one that Callaghan left behind? Did they work together in the capital? Does he promise to eventually return to her? To her the capital appeared as a grey, horrible and inhospitable place. She huffed out of the office.

"Hello there!"

"Uh yes… Hello?"

"Yes, hello! It's Jimbo Callaghan speaking."

"Captain Callaghan," the voice was irksome like the torment of an amateur head-job. The voice also had the professional edge of the contemporary diplomat trained in specific mind-altering methods based on old fashioned wheeling and dealing, just repackaged into something slick, fancy, corporate and forceful. For the voice is a high-level man in the government, not some rusty ageing General leaning over the plotting board or his aide or their intelligence officer or even the Prime Minister. This is the voice of blunt commandments, zero appeasement, abrupt challenge, and flowery, idle threats, yet strangely reversed and appearing the opposite.

"*And* who the fuck are you?" Callaghan pulled his legs up and purposely hit them hard on the table.

"That doesn't really matter. You know who we are." The voice played 'concerned', "How are things in Providence? Safe?"

"Let me see…" Callaghan spied outside the glass walls of his office. Yes, everything was fine. A few new merchants were in the foyer, two of the Thai girls were explaining the banking arrangement, Eric and Marcus toyed with their computers (probably listening in) and Jintana sat at her desk brushing her hair, staring at herself in a compact mirror, though one eye distractedly and obviously on his own eyes. "I think I'm safe. Are you safe? Is the world safe from another Ice-Age, a hit by a comet, or good old fashioned plague? Did you snack on doughnuts or chocolate covered Anzac biscuits this morning? Are you in that impenetrable bunker underneath Capitol Hill in lovely Canberra?" He closed his eyes. "Or lunching at Manuka? Will it be the Barramundi with Goat's Cheese or Veal Scaloppini? Or maybe you're in a vegetarian cafe, living the lucky life choosing what to eat whenever you want with no concern for the other five billion, oops, four billion scavenging souls."

"I'm actually underground in the Occupied Australia Affairs Department... Some of your old Team are here."

"Oh," Callaghan skipped a beat and tipped his head back, "*My* team. Gee, that takes me back. I feel all, what's the word?"

"Reminiscent?"

"No, *nostalgic*. My ol' team. Whacky fucking dooh."

"Yes Captain Callaghan. They're doing fine you know, just fine. Do you remember Jenny Woodward? She remembers you."

"Brunette... Short and voluptuous. Tasty. Yeah, Jenny Woodward. She was a bit of a babe if I remember correctly. Not too shabby at all. Laughs like a galah but hey, I'll never hear it again."

"She was asking after you," the voice attempted to chuckle, setting up a punch line.

"Is that because I gave her a broken heart but she got a promotion?" Callaghan double-chuckled, "So you're all safe down there? Her too?"

"Yes,"

"Are you in Melbourne? Sometimes these calls originate from Melbourne, and you're a mystery guy, so I never truly know, eh?"

"You know I can't give out that information, but I can lie,"

"Just lie then, I'll see through it,"

"I'm at a call-centre in Antarctica. It's the safest place on earth. The U-N Reserve is here. All eighty-seven nations."

"Sounds like they lost a few members recently. And now they're setting up shop in Antarctica!" Callaghan spun in awe, "That's amazing! You know we can still hit Antarctica with our nuke, she's good for it. Peace of piss. If we can't vaporise you or them, the thermo-biblical flood will drown you."

"And we can always take out Providence with a five-hundred kilo bomb."

Callaghan feigned a bout of sobbing speechlessness, ".... You can't. That's... Horrible! It's against the rules! *Bastards! There's civilians here!*"

"Unlike Peters, we play by the rules. We won't do that."

"I know you *don't* but you'll never get him – like I'm fucking disposable aren't I? I run the civilised part of Providence, so *I'm* innocent," he was now demanding, bohemian and defiant, "So don't go givin' me the bomb-you shit because I know exactly where to find you. We probably worked together? Is that why you do it? Because you thought I was a bit of a wanker, no really, a big wanker, now I'm up here and you get to feel juicy about making me squirm. Bomb this precious little town. Fuck You. Stock up on radiation tablets, homo."

"And...?"

"And this Jenny Woodward. Trying to remind me of some attraction that never existed,"

"She's married now, Captain Callaghan."

"Oh yeah? Who?"

"Some American Airforce guy. A real slick mick smoothy."

"Fucking Yanks."

"Yeah," the voice easily agreed, "But we buy their weapons – we're a franchise of themselves but dictated to by a slightly different government."

"And as if their weapons are anything grand though," Callaghan forcefully cut in, "It's still the Europeans that make the good stuff and the rest have to rip-it-off."

"That's true. But Callaghan, I want you to know that it'll be an American Cruise Missile that slams into your little bank – sent by Australians."

"You really want serious payback: Real ugly shit from you know who."

"And how is our Mutual Friend?"

"He certainly isn't your friend. He's your mutual enemy, and he's my mate, though we never really got it on. So I guess I'm in partnership with him."

"And...?"

"And ....? .... What?" Callaghan echoed the voice.

"He's trigger happy. We saw the crater, west of Jacinda Mountain."

"Crater? You've been looking at the Moon, mate."

"It's there Callaghan. We heard your distressed call. What was Peters aiming at? Did he get who he was aiming at? It sounded scary out there."

"I know he was thinking of you when he launched the missile, that's all I'll say. Why, who should he have been aiming at?"

"Nobody."

"Bullshit. You've got a team out there, don't you? A little surprise."

"Oh sure!" the voice arrogantly dismissed and initiated a new subject, "Does Colonel Peters know that we've made plans for your return? Is he O-K with that? Do you need to send in a letter of resignation to him or do you need a covert operation to airlift you out?"

"Hmmm," Callaghan licked his lips, "I don't know. I did talk to him last week and if my memory serves me correct he said it's cool. Yeah it's cool. He says that sometimes I'm only as good as furniture – fucking furniture. What type of connotation is that?"

"Nothing. Just wearing you down. Do you suspect some type of mental problem with Colonel Peters?"

Callaghan knew the ruse, "He's lost it. He's so fucking insane he doesn't know what he's shooting at. You would not believe what he's about to do."

"What?"

"Oh," Callaghan sighed as if it all was plainly too much to bear, "Population control of some feral refugees turned bandits and looters. It's us or them again."

"Same old excuse," the voice commented flatly.

"If he doesn't do it they do it to themselves. It's the Christian in us, you know, fucking around with other cultures that just happen to walk God's Earth."

"I'm a non-believer," the voice stated with fake authority. Actually, the voice was a Catholic hard-core from way-back and would never escape its grip, especially now that the voice worked for the Australian Secret Service.

"So, is that it? You're reminding me of our fuck-up, that Jenny is married to a yank, and you're a non-believer."

"Yeah."

"Nothing to do with the major power vacuum left behind in the wake of the U-S fleets retreating back to the homeland?"

"Yeah, that too," the voice relaxed (a ploy within a ploy).

"You know what I reckon?"

"What?"

"The Chinese are not conquerors. They're smarter than that. They've been kicking pirates for thousands of years – and now I'm on their hit list."

"I don't believe you. You're a nobody up there, Mister Callaghan."

"You reckon? Get your Mandarin or Cantonese speaking lackeys to look up w-w-w dot new china anti pirate brigade and I'm there. Photo and all. I'm number seventeen on their list. Makes me misty-eyed and proud."

"So you think the Chinese would really come all the way down to Providence in the name of policing the waters of the South Pacific because the U-S Navy tactical strategy of retreat is really an invitation for the Chinese to rid the waters of pirates because they're too lazy to do it themselves?"

"Um… I can see you've been sitting around the Conspiracy Theories Board Table so Yep. See the Japs use to keep the pirates in toe before World War Two. The Japs didn't fuck around. But the Chinese do it to get bribed. It's all leverage to them."

"Captain Callaghan," the voice stated with authority and all the graveness that comes with a seasoned negotiator hitting the punch-line. "All we want to know is what will Peters do if he meets the Chinese."

"Sell beef to 'em."

"Beef?"

"They're hungry for commodities. Peters has nothing against the chinks. Why should he? He hates you guys."

"Why does he hate us?"

"When you left us here we ran out of toilet paper and you fucked up the war. He says you guys didn't have the guts to stop them. He says you guys gave it to the Indonesians. Very un-Australian, he says. It's not just you but the whole system. He's bent on this shit. Now we have to clean up the mess and take the blame. Fair call? You should have him along to your next inter-departmental Monday morning conspiracy theory meeting."

"Can I speak to him?"

"Sure, I'll put you through," Callaghan groaned and flicked a few buttons. He was tired now. It was the same monthly call and he'd try. It always ended up the same. The voice would be transferred to Peters, out with the jungle bunnies, usually busy.

"Hello,"

"Colonel Peters."

"Colonel Peters, your Captain said you were available. We um, we were wondering what your China Card is?"

"My China card?"

"Yes," the voice said.

"I'm not playing the China Card. What the hell are you on?" Peters grinned.

"Nothing. What are you doing at the moment, Colonel. China is on the move. It's serious. I'm sure you know about it."

"What do *you* think I'm doing?"

"We don't know, that's what troubles us."

"Tell your mates in Canberra, Washington and Brussels that I'm killing a nasty nomadic tribe up north. Or do you want me to send them south to New South Wales? Free Australia? Melbourne? They're friendly people."

"That's not the issue,"

"Not the issue? Fuck you," Peters cursed, "What's this China Card shit? You're trying to glamorise diplomacy. They're not threatening to execute *you* as a pirate!"

"No,"

"And if the Chinese do start closing in on my turf I know you'll be telling me before they do, right?"

"Absolutely," the voice pledged. "We don't want you throwing some megaton into the face of the world's largest army."

"Well that would be silly-sally suicide, wouldn't it?" Peters sighed.

"You're not the type to suicide."

"No, but you might be... Did you know I've got five thousand genuine refugees south of Providence who would be tickled pink if the U-N could shower them with canned food?"

"I thought it was six thousand?"

"Some ran away, some joined my army, some died. But they're there."

"And you'll let them die?" the voice asked as if Peters would.

"No. They're O-K. Don't mean any harm. But I've got enough trouble all over and I'm not bullshitting you."

"Peters," the voice sounded dismayed, "You know we can only give aid to nations recognised and party to the Geneva Convention,"

"I know. Fax me an application form for this Convention. I'll make the grade."

"It doesn't work like that."

"No shit. I'll send 'em down your way then. Is that the way it goes, mate? You can have as many refugees as you like."

The voice sneered, "If that suits your fancy."

"Well it does."

"And I advise you against it," the voice forcefully spoke as if acting on some higher order, "We have our own refugee problem – citizens in their own country, do you remember them?"

"No. I'm not party to that anymore am I, on account of being left for dead up here." Peters continued, "Do you ever give up? Six months ago it was the threat of India, and then for a while a New Zealand Amphibious Assault wanted to visit. What next?"

"There is international concern, it's growing."

"Like a human tide?"

The voice, the non-descriptor personality of the Government, became terse. "Pardon?"

"You know what it is,"

"Yes, we know. Atrocities and genocide are catalogued by the United Nations, your options for avoiding serious,"

"Serious what? You going to come and personally whisk me away to a War Crimes Trial? You think I give a shit?"

"Well, it's a humanist question, isn't it?"

"Asked by those who don't have to deal with it. You got no idea about what goes on up here, at all. I've got prime real estate in the dustbin for humanity, and that is something you'll never have to work out. Good Bye."

Peters hung up and rested. They worked him up, it was good, good to let it go, but it never worked. There was no peace, only a show trial and imprisonment. Whereas amid the anarchy, there was freedom, at another price. They could taunt him all day long yet they had never reminded him of his first time – the very first time he had taken out innocent civilians in the fog of war.

Years ago, a lifetime it seemed, he and five soldiers had spent an entire week laying dormant in a dry range ringing a drier basin of hardened red earth way out west. The expansive terrain would be the setting of a clash of Indonesian and Australian light tanks. Naturally, the anticipation of metal on metal was a ploy by both sides, a temptation, of which to take advantage. Peters's mission was to observe what and where supporting Indonesian Forces would be in his allocated section of the inhospitable range. His squad hid as the first Indonesia patrols swept the area, checking the caves, the hills, anything intrusive to their operations. After a day they gave the all clear. They stayed and escorted twenty surveyors who climbed the hills and stood staring to other hills and in between, glimpses of the vacant basin. They wiped the sweat from their foreheads and appeared plainly disheartened at the prospect of setting anything permanent here. Then came the General. He marched defiantly into his section of the ranges, threw his arms about in a wide grand encompassing gesture, settling one swift fist on the impressive fortitude of a saddle rising out of the wilderness. Within a day an Indonesian Artillery Battalion came to settle.

Out of the dusty desert they came, a cautiously moving column of trucks laden with about a hundred fresh soldiers, canned food, stale water in huge rubber bladder bags, mortars and cannons and anti-aircraft guns, mobile radars, and a wide-eyed European TV Crew. By night the next day Peters and his team had manoeuvred and concealed themselves in a neighbouring knoll with slightly better elevation and strikingly uninteresting features. There they sat it out in silence, a stint of mediation, observing the contours and movements of their new target. The saddle was roughly three hundred and fifty metres long, two near identical smooth bare hills with a dip in between. The soil appeared rich, supporting a few ancient gum trees and a retreating cover of thinning browning grasses. After three days of observation Peters recognised that before him was more than an artillery battalion destined to support the battle in the basin, this was the clandestine headquarters masquerading as a punitive firebase, and refraining from taking even the most tempting and pleasurable of sniper shots at them, fooled the Headquarters Staff and the soldiers that they were undetected. This fostered good spirits in the Indonesians - They knew that when the set-piece titanic battle over the range and below in the basin took place they would be delivering the munitions into the whites and making the all important difference to a now seasoned war. For Peters, who knew the staging of events and the ritual retreat of Australian Armoured Companies for safer harbours, he was content to observe the Indonesians existing under an umbrella of false security. They had not been fired upon. Maybe it was something to do with the resident European TV Crew attached to their headquarters.

The Europeans (dressed in the latest stylish NATO desert camouflage) comprised of two blonde-bearded cameramen who kept to themselves and admired the unbaked land; a sound engineer who spent most of his days recording the sounds and goings on at the firebase (bird calls if possible); a tall blonde ski-instructorseque organisational type of guy who wore permanent sunglasses and a sleek Israeli flak-jacket and tried to scrounge the more interesting soldiers and officers for an interview; and finally a short busty brunette, no doubt the star reporter roughing it out in the Aussie outback with the invading Muslims, earning her stripes in the media world. Europe was starved for a non-US point of view and would go to extreme lengths to find one, often using their hunger for independence as a passport into the 'other-side'. The Europeans could be seen posing the fanciful news girl in front of the artillery emplacements or around mortar crews or outside the camouflaged headquarters tent and its sand-bagged walls, the stern faced guards eyeing her televised pouts. The blonde guy, pluming his shoulders about, would move her about, then the cameraman would point for the news girl to step here or there, the blonde guy nodding and the newsgirl would, well, tell the news. Sometimes, if the wind was blowing right their voices were carried from the middle dip of the saddle to the knoll that Peters and his men stealthily inhabited. Peters, akin to hiding from Indonesian patrols and having been pissed on once (as he hid under a layer of dry foliage) had grown super-attentive to sound and sight, obviously smell, and wind. At dusk the Europeans would fix their satellite dish to the stars and beam to Paris, Berlin, Stockholm and everyone else in the syndicate, a special report from Occupied Australia. A fondness for her sensuous voice did foster, the dialects and languages she knew, the stern news terminology, all thoroughly confusing yet entertaining, made him wish that of all the destruction to come, she could be saved.

Soon the set-piece battle's true character would show; the Australians would feign an advancement, the Indonesians would naturally charge at it, and buzzing from all around would be anti-aircraft missiles and flak at the allied bombers. By midday, when the Indonesians would think they were ready to squash the punitive Australian force in one swift manoeuvre, there would be some special display of fireworks to wipe them out. Peters knew nothing of what it was yet for the last six days had begged - using the shortest of coded messages - for an adequate response to his burning question: what will be available for Hill 209? Who could tell what would be available on the day? One strike by an already stretched high-level B-11 bomber? A pack of helicopter gunships totting uranium studded bullets? Eliminating Indonesian anti-aircraft emplacements was paramount to success on the ground yet until the very last day, with only twenty minutes to go, was Peters given an answer: One Fudo – loaded with a napalm warhead. Very suitable for this dry environment.

Now it all made sense. There would be no allied air-assault on the attacking Indonesians. It would be a textbook reign of terror.

Nineteen minutes to go. Peters knew the saddle like the back of his hand. The southern higher end (hence Hill 209) was a compact fortification of trenches and sandbags protecting the headquarters, and living around it in foxholes carved into the shallow trenches were the bulk of the expectant virgin soldiers. What the headquarters were leading over there, two hundred metres away he didn't know; maybe the entire affair? There seemed to be an abundance of Officers, five at any time escorting the Europeans, showing them how well their island of firepower was defended from above and below. See how impregnable it is. Ringing the northern mound of the saddle were the artfully camouflaged heavy artillery, five guns in all, an anti-aircraft missile battery prominently in the middle. In the dip of the saddle were concealed rudimentary bunkers, full of missiles, shells, munitions for the soldiers, precious food, stale water. Trailing off from the dip on the western side was the access, an old steep fire-track now very worn down and expertly guarded by beady eyed soldiers. The walls of the saddle ends were impossible to climb or to flee, thus well defended from the typical roving Australian saboteurs. These cliffs, ranging from thirty to fifty feet, were flat-faced and slippery, unappealing to even the most prolific of rock-climbers.

Fudo was the sick fantastical name for an otherwise perfectly boring missile (the Panasonic Fudo Mk I). As a forward spotter Peters could not control the acceleration of the Fudo as it dropped out of the atmosphere but he could program where it should drop to and from which direction, the angle of its descent, and as one can imagine, given an error margin of fifty metres, wind direction, contour of the target surface, calculate the flow of napalm, usually a billowing egg-shape sometimes a football field long, and how the flame will spread. fifteen minutes to go. He could see that already the saddle was alive with activity as around them, on other saddles and hilltops and in gullies in the ranges surrounding the basin, alarm bells were ringing. Something was up. Their satellites were obviously working today as they detected not the launch, but the Fudos, at the peak of their apex in space. Only one was the sole property of and hence guided by Peters.

The Indonesians and Europeans were excited by the prospect of action then apprehensive of what form it could take. Either the Australian tanks had run away early or had not made a peep - meaning they had run in the night. Currently there were no claps echoing around the ranges signifying missile strikes. Fourteen minutes. The European crew, sensing that finally they were in a war zone, fought with each other over which end of the saddle would be safest should the Australians attack with sniper-fire or helicopters or those missiles they hadn't been warned about and never would be, given the tightness of their escorts. Instinctively the busty news girl, in her stern voice, forcefully pointed to the dip in the middle and the fire-track leading down into the hot wilderness below, but the escort of Indonesians officers shook their heads and suppressed her impatient desire to flee the saddle. Just come into the headquarters tent. We have a bunker underneath. Besides, if anything nasty does happen, we don't want you to see it. You're here to make us look good to the world out there, not wasted.

Twelve minutes. Peters, though wedged in a dead log that he shared with blue tongue lizards (he paid rent by way of sultanas), managed to look from his digital radio, feeding in targeting data, to the Europeans coerced into the camouflaged headquarters tent, then scratch his head. The General came out, threw his arms about, was briefed by an artillery officer, and spied despondently around the terrain, finally resting his eyes on Peters's knoll. Peters heard the news girl's shrill voice again, professionally upset, the blonde guy barking back. The wind came from the east. He faced them from the west. He could direct the Fudo to the south end and hope the spray of flammable jelly would spill to the north, or vice versa, but he could not stop the wind from washing flames and embers over to his observation point. Either way he would have to flee fast. It would be wise to take out the fire-track to trap them up there, and yes the wind would only blow the fire over, into his face. His only other option was to hit the dip from the east and see if his final cunning plan would succeed. Whatever he did, the fire would fan in his face given time, and given time, he would be running. For the next week the ranges would be alive with abandoned, starving, angry Indonesians.

One minute to go and he saw the Fudos, a speck, dip out of the stratosphere to the east, a point above the planned set-piece battle that would never eventuate. In a few seconds the harmless speck grew into a dispersing grainy blob that split into eight separate Fudos, aligning themselves to individual paths, arranged by eight other cunning individuals hiding around the ranges spying on the intrepid and daring make-shift Indonesian Armoured Division.

"C'mon baby," he whispered from his cramped, hot, dry, hiding place. His five soldiers, concealed in similar conditions only metres away, had not spoken for days bar purely military speculation; numbers of enemy, positions, officers' inspection routines, who is the European news girl? Will Peters take her out? Oh God I haven't seen a woman in months. Is she there to stop us from taking them out? Is that it?

"Where's my baby?" he panicked as his Fudo slipped into a lonesome ghost cloud for what seemed an eternity then dropped out and reaching the programmed point dipped its nose the prescribed degrees, inclined to come in from the east, and zeroed in on the dip, the eastern side, at the lip where the fire-track descended to the wilderness below. An emergency horn blared from the headquarters tent. The crew manning the anti-aircraft battery, probably with some early warning from their own radar and understanding the nature of missiles, broke from their slit trench beside their missile turret and ran at full-speed for the fire-track. Good for them. The other soldiers raised their helmeted heads from trenches and panicked – why where the anti-aircraft guys running so bloody fast? They have to know something. Back at the headquarters tent, a few curious officers who had never seen the real war before bravely ventured out and raised their pistols to the incoming missile. Maybe they are actually experienced, Peters muddled, and knew that this was the last chance they had. Their punitive pistols had a one in a million chance of downing the incoming Fudo. It stuck home with an almost inaudible thud and unleashed rolls of fiery napalm over the dip, filling the fresh tunnels that led to the new bunkers, boiling the water cans, melting the stale food-supplies into the dry soil, heating the casings on the missiles and shells in storage. The crew who ran first were swallowed whole by the hell.

Peters expected a fantastic and immediate series of explosions and remained perched out of his log, braving the initial blast of heat that bronzed his face and his prolonged strained expression of anguish and disappointment. Like a statue he lay there on his elbows listening to his five men quickly assemble themselves to flee the scene. They were even wondering why they had come. One man, as shown, was required. Perhaps that they were with Peters and now knew his tricks had originally made them volunteer. They turned for a tentative second to the fiery dip, the men at the cannons staring at the flames then burying their shells in the ground, the officers at the headquarters screaming at the soldiers to do something. They rushed to the glowing and advancing edges of the flames with blankets and thrashed at the fire dancing through the dry grasses. As planned, the easterly wind pushed the flames from the dip along the eastern sides of the saddle, over the northern and southern ends. In a few minutes it would all be a blaze, and after that, a barren black saddle. There was no escape down the fire-track, it was on fire. The dip was a successful inferno. As the first heated shells exploded, followed by anti-aircraft missiles hissing and blasting and rupturing the ground, those brave men who tired to dampen the fire fled to their respective ends of the shrinking safety on the saddle, unable to flee down-hill. The General shot some cowardly soldier and did not need to order the rest back to extinguish the abominable heat.

Thick grey smoke blew up into the air and was palmed to the west overhead. Peters, glad the shells and missiles were exploding, packed his gear, carefully stretched his legs (to avoid cramps from being cramped for so long), and remained a few more minutes to examine the final outcome. The headquarters tent became a mecca of doomed talent as high-brass, middle-aged characters with boyish postures and ferocious tempers, ran about and ordered coughing and blackened crumpled-faced soldiers with cindering uniforms back into the fire to extinguish it, but a gush of wind blew hard and the men disappeared in smoke, some never to be seen again, the wind carrying away their rasping and coughing. Peters waited. The smoke whisked away revealing amid the mayhem the Europeans at the edge of the saddle, escaping from the smouldering headquarters tent, picking their way along the rocky edge, discarding their equipment and peering off the rocky lip to the wilderness below. They seemed to jump with excitement when they found what resembled a path off the island of fire, but nearing the craggy steps, they looked and pointed forcefully down the flat-faced cliff and stood to attention with solemn disappointment, hands in each other's hands, turning their heads to the approaching fire, then back to the unobtainable wilderness below them. It was a fifty-foot drop and already some Indonesians tried yet who could tell what success is. No man can survive the wilderness with a broken leg. Those that trekked into this barren land would never trek out. This was the set-piece battle.

Peters felt Private Lance tugging at his collar, "We're out of here mate. We'll be cooked," and pointed out to Peters that fire had begun to leap off the saddle down to the dry gum trees below and soon their knoll would go up.

Peters turned to him, "One more second," and turned back to the saddle but it was covered in smoke so thick the source could only be a complete envelopment of crackling flames and a gushing fiery wind, drowning out the doomed cries of those purposely suffocating to death, rather than die engulfed by fire. He heard men jumping, their final wailing screams a wild shriek to the world they had known and loved, extremely loud and upsetting, ending with, as they hit boulders and craggy rocks below, nothing. As Peters ran he imagined the news girl, how she would sound as she went over, but he heard absolutely nothing.

"Colonel Peters," Vince called him from the roadside, then compassionately louder, "Peters!"

Peters snapped awake and dreamily strolled across the empty road to under a tree and recognised an elderly woman from the Fang Tribe standing a good two feet shorter than Vince and the other resting militia. Peters looked around; up and down the road, even up into the sky. They were south of Sunny Bridge taking a breather. He was masterminding Rat Riddance Week and this woman had found him. Of all the thousands of spots he hides to evade the hundreds of assassins and spy planes, she finds him, and greets him with a gratifying chiselled teethed smile and a frail warm hug. His first thought was that they want food and as his body exhaled in her light grip she stepped back and smiled up to him, her bony finger pointed right into his heart, his groin, then to her lips beckoning him to hear her words.

"Um, Vince!"

Vince sauntered over and stared at them incongruously, "Yeah?"

"How did she find us?"

Vince, like Creton had previously, searched through his knowledge of languages to find some match with her and after a few minutes had an adequate answer. "She knew we'd be here. She's one of the Fang Tribe Callaghan told me about, isn't she?"

"Sure is,"

"Evil teeth."

"Well intentioned though."

Experienced militiaman Vince studied, "Has Malo met them?"

"He will. Have to teach 'em bush tricks soon. … I think she's trying to say something. Can you translate O-K?"

Vince gasped at the woman's gyrating teeth as she smiled to Peters, then Vince, then specifically to Peters, and spoke slowly, acknowledging with sideward glances that if Vince was trying his earnest to translate her precious words and was he keeping up. She didn't mind the guns hanging from their shoulders or the rabble of grubby refugees under guard further down the road.

"She says the fires – they saw the fires, from the Mountain, late at night."

"From Jacinda Mountain – where I sent them,"

Vince verified with the woman and she patiently continued.

"She says the man you fed them – bad meat. He caused *bad* sickness in their stomachs, many of them had to lie down in the bushes and rest."

The woman burped and winced at the smell of her own imaginary flagrancy, fanning it away.

"Right," Peters blushed.

Vince excitedly continued the translation, "Early the next morning she and some other women went searching around the mountain for food. When they saw the land to the west on fire they were scared,"

The woman appeared frightful as she explained.

"Had you sent them to a land of devils – was it a fitting destiny to live bordering a devil's lair? Then the rains came and they knew that their gods were still with them and heard their prayers."

"Hallelujah." Peters nodded. "Yay for gods. Where is this leading, we got rounding up to do,"

The old woman sniffed the air, her clickety chatter never ceasing.

Vince persisted, faster. "She went around to the other side of the Mountain, and knowing you're one commandment, she saw,"

The woman pouted herself and mimicked the voluptuous features of an adorable female creature, lapping water over her face and alertly staring out her surroundings.

"A creature covered in ash – born of the fires, beautiful as the black of night and as she washed,"

The woman grabbed Peters by the wrist and pointed to the underside, the fairest of his skin.

"She became a white woman."

Peters chortled, "A white woman?"

The Fang woman ruefully nodded and continued.

Vince's translation became more detailed, "She is very strong with long arms and long hair and moves through the forest like a deer. She has three servants – two white men and one who is of some tribe she knows nothing of. All with fire sticks."

"Like this?" Peters unslung his imported, fresh out of the factory to supersede its former version the K-40, an ultra-light and clinically nasty K-41.

Her eyes lit up and she nodded, patting the weapon, then recoiling at the foreign feel of flesh-busting cold metal, continuing.

"They came over the mountain, but the Fang did not eat them or kill them,"

Peters rounded on her, "And *why* not?"

The woman now began a fanciful picturesque explanation, dropping and raising her shoulders, half gyrating her hips, pointing to Peters's heart and groin and eyes and staring at Vince, hoping he understood.

"She says this woman – she is for you. She is born of the fire. She says everyone knows that you make the fires so, any woman that comes out of the fires has to be *your* bride,"

"Well bring her in," Peters told her.

But the woman said nothing more, her expectant face tilted to Peters and then cocked her head back to Jacinda Mountain, just under a day's walk away.

"Is that it?"

She spoke slowly, her eyes fixated at Peters.

Vince continued, "She is happy you know there is a woman for you. You saved the Fang. They saved you a woman. They wouldn't dream of eating your bride. She must return now. The woman is coming to you."

Peters looked to the distant eastern slopes of Jacinda Mountain, "And where is she now?"

Vince asked. The woman expressed she didn't know and said one word.

"Gone."

"Gone?"

"Is that all?"

That was all. Peters watched her swiftly trot into the forest. Hopefully she would make it home before the sun fell to the west. Vince was amused then solemnly thoughtful. Peters tilted his head to the range, trapped in thought and dreams, letting them guide him to serenity.

# Emelda

Emelda loved to chatter. In the kind face of Katherine she could find solace, companionship, stories of similar hardships, and an enlightening understanding of the world. They had little in common (geographically and culturally) but the local gossip was hard for Katherine Krue to find; intelligence depending on how she deciphered it, and it was Emelda's trust that poured this 'intelligence' into Krue's lap. Why should Emelda care, it was her day, she the Queen with eloquent fancy foreigners in her court.

From her wide loving brown eyes dancing in time with her flapping, expressive limbs, she shone an open heart to them. They were not dirtied refugees starving for mutton, muddy-water at the least, or to share a single rotten banana. These visitors drank her husband's beer, smoked her husband's tobacco, and were charmed, dignified and relaxed enough to put their feet up on his favourite old table. They were real men, free, far removed from the scavengers darting through Providence. More so interesting, a woman as their warrior leader. Emelda was instinctively concerned that her visitors may be operatives, Western Rats, but clean and well dressed like a wolf in sheep skin. Once she had witnessed a sick refugee cover himself in the bloody skin of a dead cow to sneak into the pig pen. She scared him off by screaming hysterically and firing her pistol into the air. He scurried over the back fence and was later tracked by the militia and buried in a shallow grave then dug up by a pack of marauding dingoes at night and torn limb from limb and who knows now. Who knows. She could easily call the militia now. However, their aura radiated calm and at the core, a steely security. They could be trusted. They were, to her disbelief, Australians, and amazingly, they were not the abandoned type.

"Another beer?" Emelda asked.

Tom and Matthews looked to Krue. She swirled the dregs in her first bottle and speculated if another would blur her judgements. It was a smooth sweet home brew with a challenging and exhilarating chilli and ginger aftertaste.

Corrie smacked his lips and placed his eye to the opening of the bottle and spied in, "Whoa. Good stuff eh?"

"Yeah." Tom drained his beer.

"I think one is enough," Krue told her new friend Emelda, "We are on duty."

"Yes," Emelda agreed, and cautiously monitoring her English, "Tea? We have Papua New Guinea coffee too. The merchants mix a good blend."

Krue intervened, "Tea is fine."

Emelda shuffled into her kitchen, and humming a Philippine Slum tune, boiled water on a gas stove and set five pristine white porcelain cups on a wooden tray. Her kitchen was well stocked, and with one servant at her beckon, she was a master of the feast. The servant for this afternoon was out with her husband.

In the lounge, the windows opened to let in the cool coastal breeze, the crew followed the path of the air as it swept through from the eastern side and out the western windows, over the fields and paddocks and up to the Great Dividing Ranges and Jacinda Mountain. Their eyes sombrely rested on the peak, thankful that during their descent they avoided contact with those crazed savages enjoying the beauty of the view.

"Do you need a hand?" Corrie called into the kitchen.

There was no answer. Krue motioned for Corrie to go into the kitchen and put forward his question, one-on-one. He stood, and leaving his pack and K-41 by the couch walked into the kitchen with a homely, doey smile.

"Can I help you?"

"Too late... Summer *so* hot." Emelda feigned expiring, picked up a tea tray and led Corrie into the lounge.

"Thank you Emelda." Krue smiled at the sight of more refreshments.

Emelda held the tips of her fingers to the spout of the teapot as she immaculately filled five cups to a uniform level. On the tray were home-made biscuits, "Please try them," she said. A flurry of hands later and all that remained were sticky crumbs.

Krue uncurled her hair and shook her mane free, sat back, and admired Emelda's creation. "It's a nice home you have, well decorated."

Corrie added with uncharacteristic profanity, "Very unique."

"Oh yes, thank you!" Emelda giggled. To Krue, "A brush?"

"No, I have one." Out of her pack it came and was quickly put to use. "So how long have you been here?" Krue asked, tentatively tugging at knots in her hair.

"Three years maybe."

"Three years...?" Krue echoed, intrigued.

Emelda's tension of the years showed in her drooping cheeks and weary eyes. "Yes. Three long years. Plenty changes in that time, more change than in my entire life in Manila. Who would think that us – good people from different countries – can make war for such little reason. But it's safe here," she emptily testified.

Matthews dipped his biscuit into his tea cup and with crumbs on his lips asked, "So it's good being in Providence? Peaceful?"

"It's a hard-won heaven. I have my husband to thank for much... He's made sure that we always have our farm. Without it, we would be Rats!" she said, looking depressingly at the window, her sad reflection blinking back.

Krue queried, "Rats..."

"Refugees who come with guns." Emelda sipped her tea. The china clinked on her front teeth. "You don't know?"

"Oh, refugees!" Matthews jovially agreed. "I can imagine. Millions of them."

"Now we're all refugees," Krue said in a stately and altruistic manner, easily gliding the brush from her temple to the tips of the locks of hair in her hand. "I don't think one culture owns this land – it owns itself. We're just visitors."

"But in the now it's the future that matters, for the kids to come afterward," Corrie counteracted. "I mean for a sustainable future."

Krue cast him a displeased stare, wondering where he had received such an exemplary practical education on utopian foresight?

"Or," Tom tipsily piped up, "The owner is in the *now* – you know, like who is there at the time. I don't go back to me old flat and say hello – let me back in you bastards!"

"If you left your TV there you would," Matthews added.

"There's that saying, ninth-tenths of the law is about property."

Emelda politely smiled, dumbly and gladly agreeing. "Yet so many come to survive but only fight. Can we all live here, so many?"

The five sat and pondered. Anything *is* possible.

She was confused and felt rude, "Sorry – I mean how many more can live here? When does the land say 'No!'."

Krue answered, "It has... Not everyone can live here. That's why we have a war over paradise. We're fighting for the sake of the land," and with a partisan nod to Corrie, "the future."

"Never thought nice beaches could cause so much trouble!" Tom joked.

"And food," Emelda congruously added, "They are *so* hungry! If they really had no food where they were from, they would be dead already and have no energy to come here where many starve. Here is plenty but too many people. Trouble. Too much. The hunger."

"Is that why Peters is so popular?" Krue asked.

"He stops Rats from eating our harvest. He knows he was a refugee. Like his great-great grandfather, a convict in chains sent by the British Empire! Terrible people! … We are all outcasts."

"Outcasts." Krue noted.

Emelda said, "He will keep Providence from harm. We have had only one disease since he came!" She held up her one stern finger then turned it into a show of force, "He is our only hope for peace – true peace for those that will fight for it."

"And you believe in him?"

"He keeps his word… In town we have electrical power, we have unlimited supply of batteries," and added proudly, in her childish understanding of English, "Made in Taiwan."

"I see." Krue forced herself not to laugh.

"So what brings you here?" Emelda asked, now comfortable to approach the basis of this interlude. She recalled only an hour ago… Hanging out the washing, odd, because normally the servant Hoochi did the chore. But he was in town, they needed every able bodied Providence Male to stop a large flow of Rats north of Sunny Bridge. She took on the washing duties and it reminded her of old times, and due to her height, she reached up to the line from a sun-bleached red plastic milk crate. Out in her yard, singing in the freshness of the air, she felt magnificently alive. Then these soldiers came in single file from across the sheep paddock. She did not feel threatened, she did not reach for her pistol. Emelda thought it was a lost Task Force Seven patrol. She'd never seen a uniformed women soldier. This woman approached with a warm smile, a lazed tired salute, and gestured in plain English for the easiest path to Providence. Emelda's heart went out to the exhausted woman. At least they would both be extra safe with the men and their guns.

"Providence." Krue replied.

"Business?"

"My business is to see Colonel Peters."

"To see Peters?" Emelda harped, "He sees hardly anyone these days. Many men have tried to take his life. Thirty-seven times so far. Even one of his Task Force Seven men tried – but no! The dog traitor is dead!"

"Thirty-seven?"

"That many, true, true," Emelda concluded, "They fail. It is not right to kill a good man, bad men die doing so when *once* they could have been good."

"Who would do such a thing?" Krue asked with an excitable ignorance.

Emelda shook her head. "He harms no one, oh, but oh! the Rats... And the Yankees and Chinese do not like him because he has too much power. Too much? Not enough! He can only do what he can. The West, they have their own reasons and power to do too much."

Krue shifted in her chair, "Was it as good with General Sumatra?"

Emelda clicked. "Why do you ask, have you come to live here?"

"Maybe," Krue placed her brush into her pack. She suddenly felt the apprehensive eyes of her crew on her bare arms and neck, and the way her groomed hair sat over her collar.

Emelda looked over the soldiers with a teasing smile, "Many good wives for all of you in Providence... Not Kingston... Many whores... Good men make this land a paradise."

Krue sternly added, "We're here to make sure it stays a paradise."

"Yes, yes, our paradise." Emelda spent a few seconds adjusting to this warrior woman's thinking, "You mean to save the paradise?"

"If called to."

"But from what?" she smiled at the soldiers.

"Change. Another stronger warlord. It happens."

"It does. My sons," she held up two fingers. "The Philippine Army. So brave fighting Revolutionaries. They died fast. We try not to think of it, we are farmers now, living off the land to feed the many." Emelda fluttered her eyes towards the heavens. "We hope and work for peace. We protect our borders to save ourselves and the land. Oh to see the rivers clogged with dirt! Fields weak and dry! We must love these lands."

"Well put." Krue complimented Emelda.

"This is our home now!" she exclaimed rightfully. "I have no other home, gone!" Her hands played out a simple spread of explosions, the carpet-bombing of Manila, "The bombers destroyed everything. Who sent them who knows? To kill the Revolutionaries, the corrupt Government, us?"

"And you have other children to look after?"

"No more." Emelda bowed her head and placed her hands over her belly, "Barren."

She looked as though she could have been pregnant, the wide chubby hips would have been ideal. She pushed her thin black hair away from her face as sorrow welled below her eyes. Then the familiar sound of a car engine caught her ear and brought a smile to suppress the tear.

Hoochi drove. They moved through numerous paddocks. Romano opened and closed the cattle gates. Some may say it's a tedious and precarious chore left to staff like Hoochi but it gave Romano a few seconds to walk into the different fields and brood over neighbouring crops. He observed the growth in the area, the spread of potatoes, pineapples, tomatoes, small plots, or large fields yet to be planted. His eyes followed the rich red lines carved into the fertile plains. If he were lucky a local young woman may be out or just passing by in a loose cotton sarong. Approaching his own land he saw nothing fertile or grand of a farm or of any rural existence, except, his home. A large, well-kept, one storey Queenslander on stilts. This may be a flood plain, be assumed. One day a rain will wash everything away including their crops. Why plant them then, he shrugged. The house will always remain.

"Let's go." Romano half enthusiastically said as he slid back in the passenger seat after closing the last iron gate.

"Yeah!" Hoochi floored the accelerator, spitting gravel. "Sorry boss!"

Romano thumped him in the arm. Next time he would take the wheel. Hoochi was a good servant, fair soldier and Romano treated him well, but Hoochi was also a young man with a fever for speeding and dreaming of women. Easily led astray, Romano wondered if young Hoochi knew much of where or what they were and fortunate that it all should be so. Or was this just another stop-off point for Hoochi in his merry travels, the life and times of the lucky-faced refugee with a halo over his head. How Romano chanced upon Hoochi was a tale set in one of Peters's first epic measures to rid the lands of the unwanted, of which Hoochi was part of. When the Rats were brought together, not for judgement, just slaughter, Romano noticed this young starved man not on his knees cursing his captors, but making a flimsy shelter in the woods. That, Romano motioned with his hand to the militia, was one of the few souls worth saving. Romano had Hoochi hog-tied and whisked away so he wouldn't see what happened to the rest. At the home, Emelda quickly chalked down the duties and chewed Hoochi's ears off with family stories which didn't quite matter anymore because there were no living family left.

Romano rattled off some finer points, "You have a room in my house and if you're to drag any women there you ask me. No women that have had too many men! Not good for cock! Makes cock *angry* and *sore!*" He obviously spoke from experience.

"Thank you boss." Hoochi embraced Romano.

"Romano." Romano corrected, "And what do you plan to do with your new life?"

Hoochi didn't know. So far he'd been island hopping and landed here.

The front door was swinging homely and open. That's odd thought Romano, because no visitor's vehicles were out the front. He tip-toed up the front stairs and heard a range of polite voices inside. The neat civilised conversation in clear English made him slump with embarrassment at his meagre knowledge of the tongue. He could see a firm fair forearm resting on the edge of the couch, everything else somewhat a dark backdrop to this white skinned limb and its ginger hairs catching the afternoon sun. Their talk was eloquent, he could smell his beer burped up, they were engrossed in some conversation he would have little understanding of. Educated visitors? Romano walked in with Hoochi tailing behind carrying an AK-47 with as much prowess as an apprentice gladiator.

"My husband," Emelda boasted cheerily, rising like a well-tuned flower to introduce, "Romano!"

Romano's first reaction was confusion. Three young Australian soldiers armed to the teeth relaxing in his house sipping tea, their (his) empty beer bottles on the table. Hoochi looked on with lazy envy, and then stiffened to a macho militia attention eyeing the woman in uniform sitting on the velvet three-seater with Emelda. This mysterious woman was another serious hit in the gut for Romano. Had he not been invited? She had a relaxed posture and like the soldiers, ritualistically rose to greet him. She seemed quite thankful, with a full-toothed wide delighted smile and fluttering eyes, that she, they, could finally meet him. Their uniforms were grubby and stained - Thin yellow grass and prickles clung to the fabric, the whiff of dung was blended with traces of acrid smoke.

"Major Krue, Australian Army," Krue proudly introduced herself, shaking Romano's stiff hand.

"They've come a long way," Emelda explained as if amused. "Their clothes, phew!" Sniffing, momentarily tugging at Krue's tunic towards the washing room, "You must wash! Long time in the fields and mountains. Smells of campfire smoke and bark."

Krue pretended to wipe away a blush.

"They travel far to see," Emelda told her husband, "The Colonel Peters."

"Oh," Romano thought, as if that made it a lot easier to deal with. "Lucky." He wiped his brow with one crooked index finger and turned away to hide an excruciating glare. Once recomposed he smiled as genuinely as possible. "Ooh a very busy day. You've come to the right place. Very fortunate for you. Very. Anywhere else and you may be," he held an imaginary knife up to his jugular and sawed away, "Bad luck."

"Fortunate," Krue winked, "Extremely." It wasn't fortune. She knew Romano was the best connection to Providence she'd seen in the last three days whilst observing the area. He drove the most expensive ute and owned the laziest farm with the most home electrical appliances. He didn't slave at the land like his neighbours, the working families ploughing the fields under the sun with their strained backs and weathered straw hats. Romano made a living elsewhere. Krue's crew had hid in ditches, under hail bales, and up trees and were nearly caught out several times by farmers going about their duties. The prized snippet of information was from Corrie sliding against the side of the house last night at nine PM. It was bedtime for the majority of farmers but from this house he had heard a male talking into a field radio to the object of their mission, Colonel Patrick Peters, 'D-Man'. The next morning Krue had decided she had had enough voyeurism of petty farmers. Her approach to this house, this contact, was to be as friendly as apple pie.

"Is it just Peters you want?" Romano asked her with an artfully assuming grin.

In return Krue smiled a seductive glint and in one quick move slid her hands between her knees, alluring Romano and Hoochi's greedy eyes down there, then quickly clapping her hands before them as if immediate action were required, "Yes, that Colonel I've heard so much about!" She looked out the windows, expecting his awesome greatness to materialise on the horizon, "They say he is elusive – but I must see him. As you can see I pose no threat."

Romano's left nostril hooked up betraying the amused smile he had successfully forced in a contemplative frown. He shook his head. "He will see *you*? I can take you to Callaghan, but Peters, a busy man. Up in Kingston, out west, Mt Isa three weeks ago, who knows? The four of you will wait. Even Callaghan, *very* busy."

Krue paused to fathom the disappointment, "We're here to do business with Peters. It's very important."

"Ah!!!" Romano cheered, perfectly cloaking his immense suspicion, "You will see Peters *through* Callaghan."

"I've invited them to stay the night, darling?" Emelda told her endearing husband. Romano couldn't care less. In the scheme of things, it's better to have the infiltrators in your house than lining you up in their sights from a barn window.

"Is there room?" Krue politely asked, "As you've guessed, we're all-terrain, sleep anywhere, really."

"We have spare, beds, warm water."

"Thank you so much Emelda,"

"We have a bath too."

Krue shone, "You are wonderful. This is all so unbelievable!"

Emelda shunned the attention, "All of you such hard days before and ahead."

"We make a good meal!" Romano announced proudly, "Emelda is a good cook."

Corrie passed an excusable slight fizzy burp, "Do you need any help in the kitchen?"

Romano hardly believed the decency of these visitors, how charming and nice. "Can you kill a lamb?"

Krue didn't know, she'd forgotten her survival training. After too much desert, living off ration packs, hospital silver service, and there it is… Scurrying for a hole, a feral rabbit bounding in her sights and the last bullet is in the chamber. She stiffened her back and swallowed the strange flashback. Where the fuck did that come from?

"I do." Tom boasted, stood and unsheathed his knife, "Where is the kid?"


She was only sixteen. Everyone wanted her. At the Relief Zone she'd be easy pickings for the tough scavenging men who claimed to be Good Natured Slave Traders but rumour had it that they were not. They were like the rest of them, depraved, murderous of their own kind, religiously fired and the worst of the money hungry bastards that walk this earth. She was not even part of their creed; removed more in mind than in geography. But why had the ruling Warlord supplied free food for this assembled mass of mislead people? There were cartons of apples, oranges, chickens running around with their heads chopped off, and roasted kangaroos hanging from trees. She greedily fed herself and escaped past the ring of the Warlord's watchful militia because something told her it wasn't right. She was fed, now run. Keep running. The bush was rough, the tall grasses like razors, a spider web wrapped around her face, yet she remained parallel to the road, heading south until she came to the river and saw the most beautiful reflection of the sky on water. She crouched at the northern end of Sunny Bridge and listened. Silence. The trickle of pinkish and blue water. She darted across the bridge and dived into a ditch. A jeep sped past her heading north to the feast; the congregation of displaced people emerging from near and afar adding to the enveloping vibe of prolonged misery punctuated by a short-lived feeding frenzy.

"How many?" Callaghan winced, the wind flicking the tips of his fringe into his eyes.

"I can't say." Peters explained, "But they're just like those fuckers that came out in Winter,"

"Nomadic Fanatics?"

"Kind of. If it was us coming to them I'm sure they wouldn't be as half fucking charitable as I have been."

Callaghan nodded, "Lucky we'll never have to find out."

"Whoa mate, in these times never say never. That's why I'm taking over tonight. I sent Romano home… I think the work is getting to him. He'll be back with the spirit next week."

A few minutes later, just beyond the point where they had befriended the Fang, Highway Five ran into a sunken, dry, oblong indentation in the land. The two lane road had space on either side thanks to parallel, dirt-track service roads. As they dipped into this indentation Callaghan felt a welling in his chest as he saw that the mass of refugees gathered there was nearly as long as the indentation in the terrain, under two hundred metres. That, he summarised, was a few hundred more than expected. Militia placed cartons of perishable food in the middle of the crowd on the road and patrolled the outskirts sending back any person who tried to wander away. All in the name of charity. The roasted kangaroos were gone, so too the smell, and if one stayed too long one would smell the faeces. At the southern and northern ends of the crowd the road was blocked prohibiting riotous attempts to break out. At the southern road-block the militia lazed, sitting on drums of crude ethanol, smoking rolled cigarettes, eyeing potential trouble-makers in the crowd.

"Get off – No smoking there!" Peters pointed to the drum. "Ka-Boom! Not for you to Ka-Boom! It's for later!"

"Yes!" the militia man said, but didn't move. He didn't speak much English.

Peters slapped him across the cheek and turned to another militia man, "Fucking tell him – no smoke – gasoline – for boom-boom later! Okay!"

"Yeah boss!"

"And get Vince back here, where's Vince!"

"O-K boss. O-K!"

Peters led Callaghan into the crowd, "I know this is blocking the road,"

"No shit," Callaghan disdainfully replied, the efficient running of trade from Providence to Kingston being his pet. "If it continues unabated the merchants will become nomads and take their trade elsewhere. Don't mess with the rules of the free-market: Keep the roads open."

"No shit. Check 'em, they get suspicious – they've heard – they know what we do, they have to. Sometimes I think I've seen them twice," Peters rambled, "It's the same guy with the lucky face coming back for more or the same mongrel mob that missed out first time but here they are!"

Callaghan discerningly looked over his friend. "I don't think so…. Maybe you spend too much time in your little hide-away."

"It's the first time this is happening *so close* to my little hide-away."

"And this is the closest we've ever massed such a circus of bandits between Kingston and Providence. Your Warlord buddies up north are getting slack!"

"I don't know what they're getting but it's not slack. Scared. Like *these*." The crowd Peters was referring to were the worst case of the refugee crisis. They had come from all over South East Asia, and as Callaghan noted, a group from the Middle East and Central Asia had made it and formed an uneasy alliance. They were oppressed or starved or poor, yet left the love and bosom or the hate and pain of their home, survived the treacherous sea, ran the gauntlet of pirates and pseudo-pirates, arrived to a foreign land, starved some more, found food in the fields where nothing much grows, threw up, ate grass, a kangaroo or two, trekked this way, starved, someone fed them on the way, companions fell to strange infectious diseases, then came the rumours, hope, courage, and short-lived salvation.

"Waste management," Peters cursed.

There were distinct sub-groups, but throwing them together under the weight of fate, meant they had a cohesive purpose, and were easily subject to ruling by a brotherhood of forceful villains who happened to be bestowed with Charisma and Guns. As a united throng they focused on demands and ultimatums from the new lands they trekked into and now suddenly they were all herded here for food! Glorious food! Somewhere in the mêlée Peters searched the faces of the gun-carrying refugees for the leaders who had not risen to a podium or dared introduce themselves even as a token gesture of thanks. He watched what could have been a ring of leadership; five capable men who cupped their mouths with their hands, knotted together, kneeling, discussing some course of action or conspiracy as around them their followers gossiped or ate what was left of the food. Peters walked to the men but they quickly hid their old rifles under their shawls and dispersed into the crowd. The crowd even seemed sympathetic to them; a mob of angry women dressed in plundered mis-matching garments blocked Peters's way and demanded something in a foreign tongue. He turned back to find Callaghan and stumbled into a dark, limping, dirty figure that revealed itself by briefly tipping its broken straw hat back.

"Malo!" Peters gripped the man's forearm, it was black as black could ever be, "You don't know how good it feels to see you."

"Keep your trap shut or we won't be feeling *shit*," Malo joked gravely, "They like that white fella meat – oooh yeah." Malo kept himself distant like a leper and motioned Peters to follow him towards Callaghan.

Callaghan had forced himself to look at the assembled and united people, shoulder-to-shoulder, surrounding him. Why had they come here, can they be saved? For what? *Why me*, he smouldered. Their eyes spoke of the hardships getting to this patch of road in the middle of what, he threw up his hands in confusion. What can they possible find! He waved at the familiar sight of Peters, led by Malo, who was well concealed in his disguise of dirty rugs and shabby clothes.

Peters fronted to Callaghan, "There are some real baddies in this bunch – tough nuts who'll stab you in the back in the name of some whacky god."

"This is not a religious cause, though a bit of god might shine the way," Callaghan replied. "I call it catastrophic desperation."

"And what do you reckon Malo?"

He spoke down, his eyes shifting to the motley refugees, "Bad stuff…" his throat curdled with disgust. "Nothing them blokes like about black fellas. Us aboriginals won't let them in out west. No way."

"Why's that?" Callaghan asked slowly.

"They aren't refugees," Malo spat to the ground, "They paid a lot of money to get here, sold the wrong deal. It's a fucked up tribe. They got some leader but since it's you that's feeding them he don't wanna' be shown up."

Peters nodded. "The sting of pride. Did you try chatting to him?"

"Yeah," Malo outstretched his arm, and without showing his face, revealed a cut below his little finger, "Said he'd cut it off if I didn't tell him how tough you were,"

"He wants to take me on?"

Malo nodded, his eyes searching the crowd, "He's got black hair and a grey beard and he thinks he's a Heavy Weight Championship. One on one he'd knock you flat, eh. His fella' got them guns too. Dirty bastards too."

"So what's he doing now?"

"Getting fed, what'do'you reckon? You're paying, too."

Peters placed his hands on his hips and studied the refugees, somewhere in there was a small time competitor, from another land, bent on some cause. He said to Malo, "You better clear out of here."

"I will, just wanted to know you white fellas are doing us black fellas a big favour."

"Understood, Sir."

"See ya, then." And Malo was gone, slipping through the crowd and into the bush.

The two white men stood watching, and were also watched and identified as the mysterious Saints who provided the means to temporarily fend off hunger. However, Callaghan and Peters were not chasing reverence. With their guns slung over their shoulders, sweat dripping down to their sandals, shadowed faces hidden under wide straw hats, their scrutinising gazes were after reason. The more they searched the greater in tune they had to be, and simultaneously they felt a suffocation, ignited by a simple sight.

"Hey look,"

"What?"

"See that?"

"Fuck, let's head back."

Centre to the crowd where the cartons of food had been devoured were now the sick, and the sickest of the sick praying and begging, stripped to rags, breeding only disease and pain with the exasperated pleas for attention and miracle cures. Armed refugees, acting on orders from a mysterious leader, herded the sick into the centre as some ploy, and though compassionate, Peters cringed. It seemed an invitation for any good natured Christian to investigate, yet deep in the middle of the crowd, would easily fall prey to any knife wielding assassin or single bullet. Callaghan and Peters promptly headed back to the road-block.

Vince was in charge. His lean and leathery professional soldier face searched into the crowd for souls who wanted to be saved. They usually sensed what was going on and came forward offering some service. Vince could pick the worth in their eyes from a mile away, but sent nineteen out of twenty back.

"Vince."

"Colonel… Captain Callaghan," he greeted them plainly.

"You've got them roped in pretty well," Peters commended, "They're not exactly subservient given their circumstance."

Vince drew on his Camel cigarette (standing a few metres from the gasoline drums), "And they don't take orders easily."

"Meaning?" Callaghan anxiously asked.

Vince exhaled, "The woman and children are related to the men, they're all bandits – looted to get this far."

Peters spied again. Yes, the women glared at Peters with a vague suspicion yet partially concealed by false thankful smiles. The world's still a stage, he reminded himself.

Vince continued, "We could send them to a farm but they would fight with other farmers."

"So we've understood," Peters said, "They're more pain than they're worth."

Vince let his free hand fly up into the sky and dive over into the centre of the crowd, "What time do you want the strike?"

Peters looked over them. The sun was setting. They'd scatter away during the night, it was natural to find shelter. He should take the radio, call Marcus at the bank to relay the message to Eric.

"Hey I got an idea," Callaghan stepped forward. "Spread out more food for them, right in the centre. That'll charm them. Don't want what happened north of Kingston again."

"No way," Vince recalled with a shudder.

Peters half laughed. "Got to be kind to be cruel. Touch down in ten minutes, gentlemen?"

Emelda had slaved in the kitchen chopping vegetables, buttering pumpkin bread, sprinkling fresh herbs and checking the roasting lamb.

Romano contemplated the meaning of these nice professional visitors, *so* trusting. They were in the two spare bedrooms in the four bedroom house. He could spike their dinner but things could get complicated. He tried radioing in, but Peters and Callaghan were in the field. Romano, for now, didn't want to raise too much of an alarm. It could get messy, not just complicated.

Hoochi holed himself in his quarters, a little baby-blue bedroom that caught the morning sun. He sat on his bed thumbing through numerous tasteless, messy, pornographic magazines. He had the routine but little energy to make use of them when on the other side of the wall he heard the lapping of water in the bath, grumpily accepting that she was to see Peters, but first Callaghan, and

Callaghan, the eternal optimist, would want a good poke at her. Hoochi gritted his teeth, didn't Callaghan already have Jintana, when would he stop? Was it true that Peters's girl died out west? Tough commanders get some tough love around here.

Krue sunk herself under the warm water. A bath, by God, this mission was telling her something cryptic about water.

Romano tried the radio again, Marcus replied that Peters was setting up a strike. That was serious, and Romano felt relieved to be absent. He left the radio on and wondered how they'd set up the kill zone. Old style gathering in the bush? Too violent, too many escapees and witnesses to hunt. On the road was good, easy to clean.

Emelda drummed her fingers watching as the sun set to the west, the pinkish glow on the bellies of the clouds, remembering the rains.

The soldiers were setting the table.

Romano slyly pottered about.

Hoochi's dream was to barge into the bathroom and fuck the tall white woman with as much fury as a Hong Kong banker high on cocaine and drunk on a soup of ground tiger's testicles and oysters.

She stepped out of the bath and slowly dried herself. Her skin had come back smooth and fair. She could beat her body and it would bounce back like elastic, or so youth led her to believe. Her torso was whitening in need of some sun. She dried, tried on a borrowed dress and arrived at the spacious dinner table right on time.

Hoochi exchanged his displeasure with Romano, who stirred and glanced from his head of the table position, to Krue at his side, breaking the bread before passing it down to her soldiers last to be served. Krue's uniform was drying out the front. She wanted it clean, which irritated her crew that they couldn't clean their uniforms but her strict instructions were not to bother yet. Krue wore one of Emelda's old summer dresses, a billowy frock decorated with miniature strawberry cartoons. She made a wholesome thanks to her homely hosts. Her free-swaying breasts pushed against the light fabric, the hint of nipple caught Romano's observant eyes.

Emelda incessantly chattered, "It gets so hot sometimes," and pulled at the front of her own blouse to shift the air and see if her nipples could poke too.

"It'll be much hotter soon." Romano smirked, "Maybe so many fires and so many wars heats the earth. Always more wars. "

Emelda chirped, "So hot sometimes I see the mirages." That spooked them all. "I see trees up close, cows and pigs at wells." Was Emelda going cuckoo in the heat? "Is real as you before me!"

"Get a pool then." Tom suggested, "Cool down in the Summer."

"What else do you see?" Romano asked his wife. "The aliens?"

"No! Things in the heat, very hot. I see what shouldn't be seen, you know?"

"Out there?" Matthews jerked his head to the open window. "I have an explanation." All heads turned. "You see a mirage is heat in the atmosphere and it distorts how we see things. It can make the atmosphere a magnifying glass, or a telescope, so you do see things that exist and in reality they are further away than what they actually appear. The cow and pigs at the well do exist. If you're not hallucinating, they *have* to exist."

Delighted, Romano took heed and recounted with the deep heart of a local who has lived in these lands for generations. "The Van Family, west at the foot-hills, have two wells and pigs, and cows…"

Emelda clasped her head, "See I am not crazy!" and then high-pitched, "Thank you my love, thank you… Enjoying your meal?"

"Ooooh yeah." Corrie complimented her, "I haven't had a good feed in months!"

Matthews preferred a dry tone, "Marvellous Emelda. Where'd you learn to cook?"

"My mother." Emelda said, "Romano loved her cooking too."

"Bet he did." Krue smiled.

Romano locked his eyes to a point in space, his ears tuning in, and then all at the table could barely hear a tiny voice from his field radio in the master bedroom: *"Fudo lock-stat set. Will advise on countdown. Out."*

Tom asked first, "What is that?"

Romano said, wearily, "Colonel Peters."

Emelda pushed a slice of lamb across her plate, her fork scratching the china, and proudly added, "Romano has met him many times."

"I work with him."

"There have been thirty-seven attempts on his life," Emelda boasted.

Romano shrugged, "He is lucky. And smart. And,"

The voice on the radio was stern: *"Militia units north of Sunny Bridge take cover. Countdown – one minute."*

Romano suddenly stood up and heaved himself to the back door. "We will see it!" He beckoned for all to follow, smirking, "Come! Peters strikes again! Hurry!"

"Oh quickly!" Emelda scurried in her husbands footsteps, "It's as fast as shooting stars!"

Krue left her half-finished meal. Her soldiers wiped their mouths, unsure, following. All rushed outside into the yard near the washing line. Emelda arced her hand to the inky night sky. In the southern distance was a flickering blast-off, then a missile glow, slanting up to the heavens, levelling out, thundering north against the belt of the silvery Milky Way.

Tom gasped, "I *know* what that is."

Romano kept his eye on the missile. "Follow it!"

Post apex it began a direct decent for thirty super sonic seconds and disappeared behind a set of low hills far to the north. They stood in silence. A white burst flared behind the hills, briefly vanquished the stars from the night, then receded, leaving a vibrant, diminishing, orange glow.

Romano stood smugly next to Krue as she stood in her summer dress, observing the trajectory. It came from the south, near the coast.

Romano raised his arms to the sky and seemingly sinister but blunt with the peculiarity of fact, "Peters! Protector of Providence keeps his word!" To Krue, the most jovial he had been that night, "The man you wish to see, he might not be so busy *now*!"

Hoochi chuckled, in the dark he could smell her fear.

Krue nodded, almost respectfully, of the fires ignited all those miles away, illuminating plumes of smoke. "It looks all very impressive but what was he aiming at?"

"The Rats!" Emelda explained.

"Rats… I assume he has much to fear from them?" Krue asked Romano.

He didn't answer. He faced the night with a sense of rigid accomplishment.

"It's protection," Emelda explained, taking Krue by the elbow, dutifully leading her upstairs, "Word spreads… Soon there will be no refugees coming. None! We can live like those that were here before!"

"The aboriginals or the whites?" Krue asked her, "They had peaceful ways."

"Yes, peace!" Emelda rebuffed and seating Krue at the table, "What more does one wish for? But there is no peace in a crowded world! How could peace be with so many people!" She laughed at the absurdity then regained her composure, counting on one hand, the years of peace she knew here as everyone else picked up their forks and stared hard at their cold meals.

In the kitchen Corrie and Matthews washed dinner plates. In the bedroom sat Tom and Krue cleaning weapons and packing, mesmerised by the second strike. Around the house Romano stomped, a nervous habit, fulfilling his domestic duties as chief ape. Emelda oversaw the washing, Hoochi vanished to his room and magazines. Romano cringed at Krue's early retirement from the night, surely he should keep all of them up with beer and thus tire them for the days to come. Krue had politely weaned her way to the bedroom.

Krue's satphone beeped: A request for an update. She methodically arranged a reply in her head. Is it befitting to report an act of genocide without seeing the evidence?

Tom unzipped his pack and checked his supplies. "What's it to be?"
"Not sure."

His eyes vacantly swept out the window to the twinkling stars, imagining the missile's descent again.

Krue typed her message. "Maybe I've got to speed things up."

Tom scanned from star to star, locking his eyes on the dimmer ones for three seconds at a time. Sometimes one can see satellites; pin-head dots of orange light slowly moving across the sky as they orbit mother earth. Krue hurried with her message as outside Romano frequently paced up and down the hallway. Tom wondered if he saw a satellite, was it receiving Krue's message – a tin can with solar wings up there – their only link to the civilised world.

> TO: OVERLORD
> FROM: VOODOO CHILD - KK
> KK PROCEEDING TO PROVIDENCE
> SOLO TO LOCATE PRIMARY.
> TEAM WILL OBSERVE HIGHWAY
> TRAFFIC FOR SECONDARY.
> RAAF MUST RECON SOUTH OF
> PROVIDENCE, COAST AREA, FOR AT
> LEAST ONE SURFACE-TO-SURFACE
> MOBILE MISSILE LAUNCHER.

Tom leaned over and read the miniature screen, absorbing it, playing it out in his mind. "You're splitting?"
"Shh," she elbowed him. The satphone beeped; transmission successful. She re-read the message, pressed the delete button and her body hung slack.

"You're going in there?" Tom scolded with a stubborn, new found vexation, initiating an instant neck and cheek blush he could not suppress with all his youthful innocence, "That's crazy shit, Miss,"

"Oh don't be so surprised! What's a mad man going to do with the baggage of a diplomat? Think about it."

"I'm not baggage,"

"That's my point. You guys are dangerous. Keep your distance."

"But you're not a diplomat! You could be shark bait by sundown tomorrow. It's crazy!"

"It's not crazy. It's the only way to get close and personal."

"And you reckon going it alone is a risk worth taking?" His arms flailed in a wild crazy manner that seemingly embraced a wholesome object before him which in his mind was their crew as a united and dependable force. He protested, "Why not stick to the system! We're to protect you! We've made it down here with you and now you want out?"

"Shut up. There was never much of a plan and there are two tasks. We are this far together for reason. Tomorrow, under Corporal Matthews, search and destroy Colonel Peters's launchers. See the launcher tonight?"

"South."

"It wouldn't be anymore. Move on Highway Five connecting Providence, Sunny Bridge and Kingston. Monitor it. When you can," resting her hand on the trusty satphone, "Send information, text only. I wouldn't trust having full length conversations either. Canberra would only confuse you in the reply."

Tom sat on the bed in heavy contemplation. "Shit. And what if we track him down. Do we nail him or his missiles?"

"Only if they're nukes."

"A nuke." Something to wipe out a city with. Jesus. "How?"

"Call in an air strike but keep well away from the target."

"Don't worry about that. But him… What if we get close to this guy, do we do him in?"

That, Krue didn't know. If they found him could they tell if he had killed her or likewise seriously taken heed to the demands she would make? She unbuttoned her shirt and from her neck untied a thin leather band. Attached to it was a smooth thin silver ring dull with sweat from over the years. She placed the ring firmly in his hand and held his eyes in hers in a majestically inspiring stare.

"If you boys are good enough to kill Peters, you'll be close enough to see this on his pinkie or index finger."

"Major," Tom absurdly halted her, "Are you fucking serious?"

"Damn right. When I see him, I'll be telling him to wear it only if he makes a truce to destroy his nuke. If he won't, I'll not even mention the ring. A sign of trust, and if I can come around to it, by God he may even be wearing it for protection."

"So he should."

"No need." Krue said, "Once I see him, he'll know there's more. They'll be searching high and low. You guys will vanish. Keep in contact with H-Q... Colonel Smacker... But don't respond to ludicrous orders! I'll be safe with Peters. That's one thing I'm sure of."

"He's been shooting missiles like firecrackers!" Tom swung away to compose himself. Before facing her, he plainly asked, "And you trust him?"

"If he's wearing my ring, I do. Besides, the missile tonight was genocide. There's rationale in there."

"What do you mean?"

"You see where it hit?"

"Kind of."

"Do you know its target?"

"We were his target – don't forget that." Tom crossed his arms, hugging into himself, and spoke apathetically, "So it was refugees tonight, you really think that's the truth?"

"I do. I've seen them by the thousand looking so hopeless. When there are too many he gathers them together in a herd, hands out food – they're all starving,"

"I can imagine that. Hungry buggers."

"And once they're together he drops a tonne of napalm on them. Nasty stuff. People in extremes don't go to extremes for the fuck of it."

"Miss, you're brave. I can't believe it."

"I have to," Krue restfully repositioned herself on the bed. "Do you remember what Emelda said? Thirty seven attempts on his life? He's no fool."

"And if you become thirty eight?"

"If," Krue cautioned, "Well then don't be thirty-nine, forty and forty-one. Don't let Canberra dictate your death. It's their fuck up and they know it."

"And what if you're missing in action or," he gulped, "Dead?"

She flipped her hands out, exposing her palms to the Gods.

He slipped his index finger in and out of the ring, entranced at some bizarre prospect of romance with Miss Death Wish. "Means you're a married woman, then? Some lucky fella took you off the singles market."

She flicked her head back, emitting an ecstatic laugh, "In *this* life?"

Tom knelt before her and reassuringly gripped her hands, "You don't seem like the marrying type." He practised placing the ring on her wedding finger. "Sorry, that's your business, right?"

But then she wiped a baby tear from the corner of her eye and toyed with the ring and half-choked on her words, "Never married."

"This war business?"

Krue confided, "I guess so… Not what you think… He'd be alive and well… After the invasion the fucking typical European ran back home."


At Emelda's splendid breakfast the hearty soldiers feasted and paid homage to the woman of the house as Krue fakely smiled, ignoring Hoochi's suggestive retarded friendly winks to a bout of impossible too-late sexual play. Romano wore clean light canvas slacks and a blue singlet with a pelted-rabbit bush hat, cheerfully helping his wife in the kitchen, eager to rush into town with the soldiers as booty as if this was how he played every regular day.

"How long will you be in town?" Emelda asked of Romano, adding, "It's Market Day."

"Oooh," Romano wondered, his eyes craftily darted about the room then finally settled on his wife's questioning smile, "Much work to be done, so busy! New traders come, makes old dealers unhappy, new militia to train,"

"Can I come?" Emelda asked.

"No room in the ute. Bumpy ride, smelly too… I might bring back cow manure," and with a scowl at his vacant fields, "For the crops."

"There are markets every weekend?" Krue asked, looking immaculate in her clean uniform.

"Yes, and they get better each time as Providence grows." Emelda pottered around her kitchen serving seconds to the soldiers. "More for you? More?"

"I'll bring back many fruits too," Romano boasted, "Juicy. We should grow pineapple too."

Emelda stopped in her tracks with a sizzling saucepan in her hands and stood transfixed to the fields of their farm, some half ploughed and abandoned, others flat grazing land for a flock of sheep and several cows. "You find out then," she told Romano, "I know nothing about pineapples. Ask the farmers at the markets."

Or, farming, Krue noted, tracking Romano's stony stance as he too searched the fields for purpose. Hoochi remained washing the dishes as Emelda farewelled her visitors from the front stairs. They kissed cheeks and she nearly shed tears as Corrie, Tom, and Matthews lazed in the back of the ute and Krue and Romano sat in the front. Driving through his property the soldiers took turns in opening and closing gates along the dirt tracks leading between low hills, past other farms, through a bubbling stream, more farms, then off a small ridge down to a bitumen road crumbling after years of downpour and neglect. At a juncture with Highway Five a signpost read Sunny Bridge North, Providence South. On the road south tall swaggering gum trees and thick dry bush loomed on either side concealing ground too rocky to farm or clear.

In the front they drove in silence, the driver and passenger digesting their breakfast and thoughts. The ute passed farmers pulling carts of produce, a shepherd and a cattle-dog pushing a small flock of mangy sheep to town, and then three tall women trotting along with baskets of fabrics balanced on their heads. As they rounded a bend Krue noticed the rugged land on either side. It was a rough rocky buckle, probably the iceberg tip of un underground load of granite peaking through the earth's crust. Krue quickly remembered from her geographic study of the area that this mass of rocks and crevices would be an ideal nest to hide or escape through. She unsheathed her pistol and placed the barrel to her forehead, quietly turning and urging Romano, "Slow the car or I'm dead."

Romano jolted, fearing for her brains self-blown through his ute. "What is this! What!?" he belly yelled, portraying betrayal that he should share a ride with a suicidal maniac. His broken English sounded almost perfected, "*Fucking* crazy woman!"

She lowered the gun, resting it over her leg, "Thank you."

He jerkily slowed the car to a halt. From the corner of her eye in the back of the ute, Tom snapped Corrie and Matthews into action.

"Why? Why?" Romano stammered, pulling the ignition key out then flapping his hat about. "What is this!" He twisted to see her soldiers menacingly staring back at him.

"Would you have stopped if the gun was at your head?"

"Yes!"

"After the hospitality you've shown us, it just wouldn't be fitting. Get out."

Romano broke into a sweat. "You can't!" Surrounded by brutish soldiers, and acting the extremities of the intimidation, he placed his hands forgivingly on his head. His gun, slung off his belt, was not touched. "I'm a citizen! You know that! It's against the con-con…" He damned himself for not attending more of the English classes they held in town, "*Conumism!*"

"What?"

"Geneva *Communism!*"

"Shut up. It's Geneva Convention," Krue corrected him, "And fuck the United Nations. You know that."

"I'm a farmer! You can't shoot me!"

"Hey Romano, you walk thirty paces down the road. And take your hands down, no shooting, no scare. Understand?"

Upset, he slowly nodded, sheepishly walked thirty paces down the road. Oh to lose this catch! They would steal his car, leaving him to walk the distance, tail between legs, right into Callaghan's office to hear his curses: "I am an honest man! And look! Rats!" Romano then felt this was his end, after rounding up so many refugees he would finally meet *their* fate. How does it feel? How, he squirmed, does it feel? Life, life is understanding that what you do to others is done to you!

"Major, sure you want him bumped?" Matthew asked, finger on trigger, his barrel trailing Romano. Don't aim for the belly: Aim for the head.

Krue glanced to Romano's back, determining if he could hear. "Hell no. We're separating."

"Say again?"

She shook Matthews's hand, "Corporal Matthews I wish you the best of luck. Tom knows the details, take off now," she pointed to the rocky side of the road, over a low crest and to the unknown route of their escape, "You're going bush."

"Right now?" Matthews faltered. "Here?"

"Scat," she hissed and then to Tom, "Remember the ring."

"Major, you can't!"

Krue endearingly clasped her hand on Matthews's shoulder, her invasion of his personal space filling him with such immediate embarrassment and realisation that he had just endured a lesson that he sunk away from her light grasp only to immediately crave it again.

"Go," she said quietly.

Tom, biting down a cheeky smile, led Matthews and Corrie off the road and immediately scaled the rocks. She listened for their trudging through the dry undergrowth and as they slipped out of sight and sound she called haughtily to Romano, "Oi!"

He turned to her, muddled. Less the soldiers, he breathed an immediate air of relief.

"Going into town?" she called, pouted her chest in her clean uniform, "Give us a lift, Farmboy?"

He looked to the black hole of Krue's barrel in line with his gut, "No guns?" He meant, no execution.

"Yeah, hell, sure I got guns." Krue replied and jumped in the ute. "C'mon! We're going into town! Yee-haw!"

They drove in an uneasy silence, taking a short exit off the Highway for Providence.

"You," Romano snorted, "Brave *and* crazy – but here is not the place to prove it!"

"It's my country and I'll do whatever I fucking want."

He thumped the steering wheel and turned to her, a giant grin stretched from ear-to-ear, in his eyes a sincere glint of the parody, "You're right. And you're *very funny too!*"

# Paradise

Driving south they passed farmers making the same pilgrimage as Romano but their flimsy horse drawn vehicles were burdened with produce for the Providence Markets. Coming into town along a half-tarred and half-gravel road, Krue saw a disused, wonky, railway crossing, and a service station selling crude diesel, the proprietor waving a morning welcome to all that passed. The first inhabited houses were converted cottages with simple verandas made of bamboo and local timbers supporting thatch roofs, hard wood decks, thin blinds and hammocks. It was an innovative clash, they had adjusted to the environment and weather, improved from what materials they had, giving the society a certain pride. Local women and children coolly moved on the streets at total ease with their surroundings. Krue saw no distinctive dominant race. There were shades of yellow, brown, white, some olive, a few solid black skins smiling, brandishing flashy white teeth. Youngsters skipped about, playing hopscotch with chalk on neglected footpaths, nagging their pregnant young mothers for more chalk or a mango. They wore a mix of clothing: funky western T-shirts made in sweat shops, cotton sarongs, patched up hemp slacks, rubber thongs, cheap leather sandals, ex-army boots, sampan hats and baseball caps. Machetes were casually hung on the belts of the young men, pocket knives dangled from the necks of kids. The odd militia man, an oiled AK-47 hung over the shoulder, a grenade tied to his belt, a radio clipped to a shoulder strap, patrolled the streets directing farm traffic to the markets. Three bandaged men smoked cigarettes in the ambulance driveway of a medical centre. Doc Nelson, the first white man she saw, stood over them, inspecting their healing wounds, noting their progress (or the volume of casualties) on a clipboard. There was no ambulance, only a jeep with no cargo. The tray was scraped with reddy-brown rust, and on second glance, it was pooled. Rust doesn't pool. Blood coagulates.

"Is that a hospital?" Krue asked, glimpsing Doc Nelson as his eyes fell to a flower bed at the front of his hospital. Little bright yellow flowers opened up to the sun in contrast to a dying champagne coloured rose.

Romano, self-conscious to be seen with this woman, acrimoniously nodded, "Yes... Yes... Maybe your soldiers go there... I have been there. Doctor Nelson *very* good man." He turned to her, shoved his index finger in his mouth, stretched his lip out and exposed the inner of his cheek, "They cut out a *parrot*."

"Eww.... *Parasite*," she corrected him.

"Parasite... No pain now." A purposed pause gave way to a more direct tone, "You think you are brave. Your soldier boys too. I think you know fuck all: I do this, I do that, I know where I stand but what are you doing here?"

"I'm going into town on business to see the 'ruler'," Krue cheekily replied and pointed into Providence. "You don't understand why I'm doing what I'm doing because it's not your concern. Don't worry my friend."

"Friend," he frowned. It didn't sound right from her lips. "I see many men, many women, I see them before and after. I see good and bad. I see you and I think you come to *destroy*."

"Wrong Romano. I come in peace."

He slumped glumly behind his wheel, edging through the light traffic. He said, "Callaghan drives me crazy... But sometimes he says good things... 'The road to hell is paved with good intentions'."

"Touching, in retrospect."

Romano sighed. Just deliver her and be done with it.

Krue knew the layout of the town centre from satellite and drone photos and was pleasantly surprised by clean swept streets, multi-lingual road signs, trained militia men in place of traffic lights. Merchants and bourgeoisie in their fine threads strutted past the assortment of stores, now stocked with goods and services appropriate to the economic-ecosystem of Providence. In a row were businesses: farm machinery, labour-hire (with several Kanakas loitering out the front, thumbs in their pouches of tobacco), and a chaotic but well stocked supermarket; fruit, vegetables, smoked meats and imported luxury foods. At a make-shift pharmacy, herbs were lined up on the footpath. Women knelt to sniff and rub the plants. They called to their children not to run crazy on the road. A shoe shop's wire stands were packed with casual sandals, synthetic paratrooper boots, outdated but favourable runners. Next to that, Providence Radio Equipment, a no-nonsense sales and repair service run by two ex-Task Force Seven retired soldiers, both suffering variations of post traumatic stress disorder. On walls between shops, blue posters flashed a slanted silhouetted profile of a lean figure – the benevolent dictator Colonel Peters.

Krue appreciatively smiled at the propaganda and it reminded her of her own printed fame – the wanted poster advertising her bounty. On Peters's posters words ran down the margins in a variety of languages. Civilians strolled straight past the posters, although some adventurous children pulled funny faces at the deeply set eyes then charged to the waiting embraces of their mothers. There was nothing sinister about the town; heads of provincial provocateurs were not propped on telegraph poles, hobbling petty or political criminals were not tied in barbed-wire and paraded before the poverty stricken, rotten fruit throwing underclass. Krue saw people of all sorts meeting and greeting, shaking hands, going through the motions of morning chatter.

At the main intersection of the town, Romano pulled the ute over in front of a one-level sandstone building. Krue noticed the peculiar *Dead Head Pub* across the road. Patrons sat on the shaded footpath breaking bread and sipping teas. A short squarish business man inside the pub, facing out, sat at a window ledge, patiently observing. By his peculiar stoop and scurrilous gaze he stood out like a dangerous player. He was not of Asian decent, but his skin and features were dark and serious. Krue then remembered what she was, and at this distance she turned profiled to him, pouting minutely but enough, as Romano waved her up to the five stony steps leading up to the sandstone bank. A ten metre tall jungle of antennae equipment towered from the roof. A plain ultramarine blue (like the background of the poster) flag fluttered from its peak next to a satellite dish. Militia guards at the front sipped tea from steel mugs, wealthier locals chatted at a basket stall next door. With a quick whisk she brushed any loose locks of hair into place, re-tucked her shirt in, glanced a line down her reflection in the front glass doors and entered, guns and all.

Inside she felt the weight of money and as the thick glass doors swivelled closed behind her she felt entombed in the thick sandstone walls. It was a *real* bank, and after a quick look over the walls for security cameras, she saw pockmarks of bullets. The layout of the bank was divided into two parts. The front was the foyer. Farmers sat on cane chairs, scribbling down figures on papers. They were smoking flimsy rolled-up cigarettes, chewing sugarcane stems, fanning themselves with imitation akubra hats, and in one united front, appreciatively browsing the arrival of Major Krue. In her clean uniform she felt as if she had stepped off a private jet and was a legit business woman rather than an assassin crawling out of the bush. A few farmers stood in a line waiting to be served at a counter. Behind the counter and the Thai staff, and this was were Romano led her directly, were the back offices of the bank – the nerve centre. With each step the reality clawed at Romano's pride as a protector; he was leading the enemy straight into the hub of Providence.

Jintana was seated near Callaghan, entering data into a laptop. She had noted Romano's familiar walk in her peripheral vision and cast a friendly smile to catch his gaze and was immediately offset by his fraught face. A taller Caucasian woman, lean, a bit muscular but still femininely alpha, stood by his side, her smartening stare sizing up Jintana and the entire layout of staff, weapons and strategic points. She was also a gliding beauty with sun-kissed hair and smooth skin, right to her finger tips.

Jintana could not compute it. She had seen many Caucasian men, too many, and few white women: They were rare sights where she had worked and if she did see them it being professional and practical nature to suspect their feline intentions.

"Major Krue." Romano quietly told Jintana, pointing into the office, "To see Captain Callaghan, on business."

Jintana jumped with blood-boiling envy and verified, "Captain Callaghan?" then shifted to an uneasy compliance, "Follow me, please."

Krue was led directly into a large office with glass walls. There was a large desk, maps of Queensland with neighbouring Warlord borders clearly marked out in a thick red pencil, dotted lines wavering above and below the borders proving Peters's warlord finesse. Marked in blue and green pencil were trade routes from produce point to market. Pinned black string spanned out of Providence up to the port of Kingston, then through the Coral Sea on to Noumea, New Zealand, Port Moresby, the Solomon Islands, Bougainville, Jakarta, and one line spanning east into the Pacific and off the map, the destination listed as a longitude and latitude. She turned to peer through the glass wall. It was thick, tinted, and had taken a bullet near the roof. It was certainly bullet-proof yet would not withstand an entire magazine. She summarised that this old bank had stood long before the war yet renovated to the corporate banking open-planning trend. One could imagine people getting the sack in this Manager's Office. How polite. Krue could see beyond a few desks manned by the Thai girls, a large metal vault, so large one could walk into it, several could huddle in there, making an interesting capsule to escape bombardment.

Next to the vault was a small room crammed with computer screens, hardware, cords, and some smooth young operators. She saw two white men, one of which was certainly Captain Callaghan, who according to the official documents, was Missing in Action.

Obviously Captain James Callaghan had not entered the afterlife or wandered the wilderness. In the databanks under Canberra were over a thousand hours of recorded radio and satellite telephone transmissions by Callaghan as he communicated with various trading agents operating for neighbouring Warlords. The other white man was another Task Force Seven survivor, Marcus. His back was hunched up to a large flat screen, scrutinising maps and reading snippets of intelligence. The other operator was Eric. She guessed he was one of the lucky refugees to be saved, a genius welcomed. His puny voice had also been recorded and until now there was no face to match to it. They were engrossed in monitoring Peters instructing the militia, wiping the evidence of last night's massacre off the map. Reports were pleasing. Few survivors were rounded up, briefly interrogated and systematically executed where they stood. In a few days bulldozers would clear the stinking road. For now all trade would have to sail from Kingston to Providence by smaller vessel or take back-roads.

Grunt work, Callaghan sniffed, the bitch of regional self-protection, the primal process of establishing order, the knock-on from waste management. Some days he wished there was a magic button he could press and the monkeys would fly from the caves and descend on the baddies and eat them where they stood and a day later the monkey shit would fertilise the farms and so on.

Krue detected her first impression on Jintana. Krue admired Jintana, the doll was discerning, and though hardly at ease with Krue's presence and trying to appear indifferent, she became something completely different again. As a base for persona Jintana had all the trademarks of style and grace, which Krue could trust on a universal level. Jintana wore a gold leafed sarong, very neat and tidy on her petite body. Her hair was up in a tight bun skewed together by two large expensive silver pins. Krue tried to guess the class and ethnicity: Upper-middle? Vietnamese? Thai? She was lean, high cheekbones, honey glow smooth skin, thin black long hair, and a discipline in curt mannerisms that would make a geisha envious.

Jintana dutifully leaned into Callaghan's ear, "You have a *white* visitor."

"Sure," Callaghan said, engrossed in the computers, and then to Eric, "Any hiccups call me over, cool?"

"Cool."

Jintana swiftly lead Callaghan to his office. He entered with his arm around her waist, the tip of his thumb rubbing against her hip bone, then stopped and stood abruptly straight upon seeing Krue.

She sat in his office facing his neat desk, admiring *his* map of Queensland. Holding a confident pose promoting a spirit of plain and clean clemency, her thankful glint to Jintana then zeroed on Callaghan with an interrogating depth until it became too obvious and shrank in intensity to a pleasant courteous smirk.

"Morning," Krue said.

"Morning," Callaghan chided, and to Jintana, pleasantly, "Thanks, I'll deal with her alone."

"Yes James," Jintana cast a sweeping stare down to Krue and retreated back to her tasks.

Callaghan promptly sat at his desk across from Krue, tensing with the familiar inkling he was being watched by the *voice* yet this was not the pretty face he imagined, not that they hadn't tried tempting him with things pretty. He was not the type to *not* admit to himself that a beautiful women was fucking gorgeous but certainly fell short of flopping to the floor in a salivating and humping heap. Callaghan then imagined all the nastiness that might lurk inside her mercenary head as she calculatedly locked eyes. Not too shabby either. Proudly stepping up and forward he outstretched his hand, "Captain James Callaghan, Task Force Seven Second in Command and Governor of Providence."

Fluently, full of morning bounce, Krue charmingly introduced herself, "Major Katherine Krue, Australian Army. Formerly of Army Group Centre; Target Acquisition Unit, now an Army East Coast Diplomat."

"Really? You're shitting me?"

"No, and I feel better for getting it out of the way."

"Target Acquisition." He was thrown back to the desk job, sitting at the screens, watching the war as pixels, yet she didn't look like the indoors type. That could only mean she played out *there*. "You know, that's really neat," he raised his index finger not to her but to a point between them, "Because you're a girl. I like that. It's hot."

"Oh. How very 'modern' of you Mister Callaghan." Looking out to Jintana's desk and the Thai bank staff, "Your fancy personnel seem in order." And further admiring her surroundings, nodded favourably as the office was immaculately organised for the position of Chief Bureaucrat.

"As they should be. I trained them in 'civilised business'. Before I came along they were using abacuses." He gave a wry smile. "That's irrelevant though… What are you doing all the way up here? For diplomacy! What a word. I'm diplomatic. I juggle everyone's shit all day."

"If you see it as that, yes." She pressed on in a politely agitated tone, "The obvious questions, who and why I'm here, are easy to guess. They are not assumptions nor should you look into them too much. Seeing your position of importance is in proportion to intelligence, we won't beat around the bush."

"No, let's not. *My* time is as precious as yours." Callaghan understood the graveness but loved the game. "You know *exactly* what you're doing here and given your level of importance in the mightily perceptive war machine you'd know my history and all but enough of that... This is the first time *I've* actually met a frontline assassin. One look at you and I know that's what you do. How did they ever get you up for it? I'm not denying what you are, I'm just asking out of interest."

"When the men were being conscripted there were women who wanted to go 'frontline' and they – the army – hand-picked a thousand of us and took it an intelligent step further: *Behind* the frontline."

"Wow. Selected. Special training. What was the burn-out rate?"

"About half."

"Hmm. Five hundred in the field. Lose a few here and there... Retrain some more lasses. Let's say there's at least a hundred female assassins lurking about. And did you volunteer to get in here?"

Krue shrugged and actually thought about it. "Did you?"

"I'm with you, baby... They wrap the do-or-die stuff up like Christmas presents. Exciting stuff. And what is it like, squeezing the trigger or stringing a guy up with piano-wire?"

"I don't share my thrills."

"O-K. But given a knife you could launch yourself over my desk and providing I was a fucking slow idiot you could do me in. In how many seconds?"

"You? Three. Add another forty-five before you actually clunk out."

"Gotchya."

"You find this amusing?"

Callaghan aroused himself with a volley of howlish laughs. "Yesss! I know of your type and I've always wanted to meet one." In an annoying and invasive manner he peered into her eyes, blinked, and unable to magically decipher from her soul valuable information and raw emotions, summarised, "You're one of a kind, I'd like to freeze you so future generations could know that you existed."

"What a cliché compliment."

"Did you know that it was those Europeans and their bizarre chivalrous religions that removed women from warrior status?

Thousands of years ago it would have been no big deal for lasses to move around in packs and hunt and kill and gather... Peters will absolutely *love* you, providing you don't try to tap a bullet in his skull," and he idled, studying as that particular comment orbited in Krue's head, breaking her most profound quality, calm. He could see it ricochet behind her eyes, spinning off the inside of her cranium. She dropped her eyes and purposely fidgeted with her fingers, and then waved both hands in front of Callaghan's face.

"First and foremost I come in peace."

"Oh we all do! But you shoot to kill: Just another nasty piece of work."

"I come in peace," she consciously reiterated.

With a pistol hand he shot his own heart, "Do I make the grade?"

"My superiors made no mention of you."

Callaghan pondered, a quaint Cherub's grin colouring his cheeks: "Those brass dudes must like me then! They like you too; letting you in on the top secret circus. Now they got you roped just like they had us *in* for the dream – Liberation and freedom and all that vision."

Krue gyrated her head to scope the workings of the bank and bullet shatter at the top of the glass wall, "Yet you've chosen *this* from that vision and found yourself a peculiar freedom."

"Oh yes! This is freedom! I forgot! *How* one masters the art of forgetting. But it wasn't my vision to be revisited by visions, the inescapable things most of us should never ever have to witness. Have you survived a massacre by crazed militia armed with the most rudimentary of weapons and rusty machetes?"

"We could trade tactics in those situations."

"You are funny. But the brass really thought we were goners – and we were in a way – they left us to fight it out. We're not fucking Christian crusaders nor revolutionaries but Peters changed that and now look! We *are*. I'm so happy you've come here as a diplomat because it means you understand that what we have created in this enclave in the middle of savage sunny Queensland is order that demands civilised respect. It makes me feel so damn good!"

"All is true," and before she could continue Callaghan rattled on again.

"So now they send you to tantalise Colonel Horned Peters to be a global good guy rather than annoy everyone with his bully tactics. That's the shit, isn't it. Anything else is sugar coating. That's why you can walk in here and be so coy about it. Good on you, girl."

"... Not quite."

"See from the gracious goodness of your little ol' heart you accepted this mission with the faith that you were doing your bit for world peace? Was that the vision?"

"I'll not deny it was sold on those merits – considering the stakes."

"And after this Mission of Great Importance did they promise something greater?"

"No, but I like to think I'm destined for greater things."

"But this is great, Major Krue! What are you complaining about… O-K… Let's get back to reality because we kill people here, lots. So many there's a queue at the Pearly Gates. One of those Middle Ages Saints came to me in my dreams and you know what he sounded like?"

"I have no idea."

"The *Fat Controller* – Ringo Star. I can't believe it. Look at me, can you believe it?"

Krue did. Callaghan was a firm lively man, five-eleven high, high I-Q, high on life, 'up there' with the insane but his feet firmly planted on the ground. And with every fit of this insanity it invaded his handsome face, scrunching it up in some eternal spasm of pain at the world. By the end of the decade he would die, not of anything in particular, something would get him in the end and he knew it. He brought it on. He was not fit for the job. She crudely and empathetically cringed at him, *Who would be?* Is that not part of life? Becoming the job thrust onto you? She frowned for him. He was sinking, fast. He brushed his hair from its side part and forced himself to face her.

"And *what* was that morose face about?" he snarled.

Krue fumed at his outlandish behaviour. He was an excellent specimen, titled Victim of Prolonged Genocidal Exposure and Social Isolation. She clasped her hands together and cleared her throat, very lady-like, "What we've been discussing here is entertaining, but I urgently need to see Colonel Peters."

"Yeah, well: I'm evaluating you. But don't worry, he knows you're here. He has eyes and ears everywhere. Omnipresent kind of guy."

"I have my own eyes and ears too. You think I waltz in here with nothing more than a bluff and a rifle?"

"Depends on your bluff, cowgirl."

"No bullshit. I know exactly what I'm doing but meeting you is a surprise,"

"How grand."

"So, did Colonel Peters get who he was after last night?"

Callaghan's brow crunched together at the point above his nose and pursed his lips out, sarcastically saying, "*Big deal*. The body count was up from last time. A refugee gold rush is on, hundreds more flooding south and in such a hurry!"

Krue was pale, part emotion, part shock: All previous evidence could have been illusion, but this man...

"So how did they put you up to this?" he asked, a contrived mockery of the stupidity she possessed to be here. "Seriously. Every month we bury some idiot trying to nail the 'beloved' Colonel Peters. To us we know it's a new month when we shovel on the top-soil."

She dropped one shoulder, inferring defensively, "I'm not out to kill him."

"Yeah. Right. You're not that type of girl."

"Well, I was," Krue proudly informed him, "Routinely I would track down my target and eliminate the ability that pissed my superiors off in the first place. This time dirty-tricks aren't my game. I've come in peace."

"Hippy chick in the asymmetrical war zone. *Nice*. It's a reality." He sat back in his chair and re-arranged the new thoughts in his head. There was no way he would let her see Peters right now. An assassin, singing peace. He yawned at the high-powered rifle by her side, snickering at her free-spirited hugging and shooting concept of 'How to win friends and influence people'.

"Regardless of what you think of me, I have a job to do."

Callaghan looked dismayed, perhaps bored. "What pisses your superiors off about Colonel Peters?"

She wondered if it was worth it, or it was the wrong piece of information that would implicate herself further into a dangerous predicament. Even her stalling at this question was registered.

"Oh... Go on, Miss Global Defender!"

"Nuclear capabilities."

Callaghan quickly rebutted. "As culture and defence evolve, it's a regional leader's ultimate insurance policy."

"And you think Providence has a 'high culture' granting validating it an exclusive elitist armoury enforcing a thin freedom and short-lived peace from the woes of global change when the world is at its most vulnerable? Don't forget we are a world at war and things can blow out of proportion very easily."

"In a nutshell – Yes. That's it! See Providence is a product of global ruin," Callaghan preached with an air of historical identity, "Part of the unnamed new order, I say. Even you have admitted this by coming in peace to deal with us."

"So when do I see him? It's imperative."

"To what? World peace again? Give the world peace and it throws it up."

She nodded, her glare brimming with a subdued scorn.

"Colonel Peters is a man of few visitors," he mused. "His favourite haunt is a little hut deep in the forest between here and Kingston, or he could be visiting neighbouring Warlords discussing the waste-management procedures of excess refugees. They're all in it together. He's hard to track down. If he *was* easy pickings you wouldn't be here - he'd be catching cruise missiles between his teeth during his sleep."

"He shouldn't have to hide," Krue said. Callaghan didn't care. She continued, "I'm sure I'll be a welcome visitor, wherever I may find him."

"I'm sure you would. I'm fair, Providence is fair, you can certainly bring your case to him, after all, that's your only objective, isn't it? Some 'reasoning' where reason has never been before? How poetic and believable. But is that the pick-up line before you slip a boot-knife into his jugular?"

"I told you, I'm here to reason with him, peacefully."

"A true idealistic pioneer, Major Krue. It impresses me. Do they know you're doing this out on a limb? I bet they wanted you to play the suicidal patriot to fix their mistake. Is that what you realised you had to be so you changed your tune?"

"Just by being here I'm expendable and I choose my destiny so, yes."

"You choose your destiny... Don't we all," he reflected. "Just a point though, and I'm not trying to be a facetious little bastard but whoever sent you here – Was it Grumman or Tolken?"

"It's irrelevant who sent me here."

"You are such a sneak," Callaghan slapped his hand on the desk. "But, the sluts who sent you here did it to be done with you. They don't like you." As if to prove his point and charisma he menacingly snarled at her. "They didn't like me so they sent me here! Do you like me?"

Her pose was dull and apathetic. "I don't know you. So for the moment I have to admit... No."

"Oh that's just *excellent*. Bravo. It's better this way just in case we have to send your ashes back to Canberra as some gesture of politeness." He tapped a button on his phone, commanding: "Jintana..." Then to Krue, "Miss Global Defender, I'll arrange your

Age of Reason with Colonel Peters. Could be a few days though, seriously. There's some shit going down up north."

Krue protested, "A few days is too late. The sooner I see him, the greater chance he has of living."

"So it's like that?" Callaghan rejoiced with racy fervour, "Impending doom! You're an *act*."

"It's no act."

"I tell you what," he shifted closer, leaning over his desk, "A little something between you and me,"

"I didn't come here to make little arrangements."

"It's just step one… Establish some trust… You hand over the gadgets you use to contact the brass, and I'll try and help you meet my brass. Deal? But you can keep your weapons, in these parts, even your enemies need weapons."

Krue's nostrils flared as she ran the calculations. Isolation vs. integration. She placed her satphone and two-way radio on the desk. "Deal."

Callaghan swiped them into his top drawer. "Progress. You know I've worked down there, I'm not going to play with your equipment, O-K, it just makes us feel a bit easier. Got it?"

"Sure. I trust you. You have to trust me."

"We'll see… Jintana!"

Jintana entered the office, wary of Krue's sudden iced gaze, "Yes James."

"Do you like the beach?" Callaghan chirped to Krue, "Sea air?"

Krue politely eyed Jintana, "I'd never say no to a beach."

"You'll love this beach. It'll give you a feel for what we're all about."

"Is it the-"

"Where Task Force Seven found its destiny? Sure is mamma. You can look hard but you won't find bronze memorials to sacrifice and vision. Jintana, take Major Katherine to the Penthouse… Five Star accommodation."

"Thank you."

"It's Sumatra's old haunt."

Jintana held her tongue and led Krue from the bank, without a militia escort, across the intersection and east towards the beach. Jintana knew the route too well, every pace, and felt too timid to even breath near the graceful stride of this warrior woman. Krue had come to Providence, and unlike many, possessed and radiated a glow that she was just a visitor to the region: her true life destined for elsewhere. The civilians looked to Jintana second now as the tall foreigner dazzled their eyes. Jintana's path from birth to here was as rocky as any soul thrown into the winds of change so she wasn't overtly or gravely envious of Krue.

At an early age, as Jintana's breasts pushed out, it would only be a matter of months before she'd follow her older sisters into no-frills prostitution; an institution binding her existence to the mattress. She had managed to avoid taking it up fulltime but then a playboy dolled up as a reluctant but promising Naval Officer sprinkled glitter in her eyes. He seductively kidnapped her onto his disembarking troop ship and invited her to a new life in Australia, that of the mistress of a conquering general-to-be serving under some amazing established war hero. The prize outweighed the contradicting circumstances and she agreed, totally ignorant of the war in progress. When the first torpedo struck the Officer was never to be seen again. The ship shuddered, slowed and rolled, there was smoke, the order to abandon, the emergency lights faltered and even though the rush to the deck was swift and orderly, all around her men were wailing and drowning in their heavy uniforms. Usually a man's eyes would see one thing in her, flesh, the flashes of their brief orgasms in their eyes seemed as trivial as urinating. In the Timor Sea she saw that men were actually petrified souls and it took an incident, in this case drowning, to free their real spirit. Her perception of man was rising as they were sinking and then Sumatra pulled her onto a drifting piece of debris. Men would try to claw her off and climb on but Sumatra kicked them off, shot a few, protected Jintana like a child, explained the great war hero whose army he was part of was a fool for crossing the Timor Sea at a time like this. In this perilous moment Sumatra, apart from snarls at men as they tried to crawl onto the floating debris, was full of smiles and praise of life. Three times he'd crossed this sea, he'd never do it again. Six hours later they were picked up by an over-crowded patrol boat and sailed on to Darwin to regroup. Sumatra found is unit and as payment for saving her life she became his mistress. The trip from there to here was another saga, and then when he died, in a purely automated move she came to Callaghan. If it wasn't Callaghan she would have been bait for pirates or rape for bandits. More than once, behind Sumatra's back and persistently behind Peters's, Jemmy had persistently practised his crafty art to rope her in to yet another new life across the seas but his brand of glitter was stale. She was perhaps the most beautiful creature to adorn Providence, and she was alone.

Krue would be isolated in the penthouse atop the beachfront four storey unit block. Jintana nudged the door open, cautiously looking inside with a grave face. Krue sensed a ghost lurking inside like a wet mist clinging to the patched up painted walls. The balcony had some resemblance of battle; patched up cracked tiles and brick work, the tips of K-40 ammunition poked out like nipples in the walls. In the living room was a lavish setting; a large smoked glass dinner table, four pine arm-chairs and a lush sofa stretched with a tartan print, a large sleek black television, the ominous blank screen reflected the blue sky outside. It seemed an amusing modcon out here in the depths of this mission.

Jintana shuffled to the bedroom and stood awkwardly to attention at the queen sized bed complete with fresh white linen, falteringly commanding, "Sleep here."

Krue fell to the bed, tossing her pack and rifle aside, sighing, "Oh my god I can't believe this – Luxury!"

"Maybe," Jintana said with a taste of tenacity, "It is for special visitors... Much different when General Sumatra was here."

"So, the original warlord lived here?" Krue eyed a sliding door to the bathroom and then flicked back to Jintana. "How long?"

"On and off... When he was in Providence we would be here."

"Surely then, I would think it would be reserved for Colonel Peters?" Krue questioned, and as hierarchy flowed, this maid had been passed to the Chief Bureaucrat. "As order goes?"

"Sometimes." Jintana opened the wardrobe and shuddered at its emptiness. "Here is too obvious for assassins."

"Who said I was an assassin?"

"Romano."

"Can't help gossip. But I'm nothing of what he says. On the contrary I'm the sitting duck up here," Krue noted, "And it's mine. Catch twenty-two."

"Catch twenty-two? What is it?"

"It's when they put you in the squeeze."

"They?"

"Anybody, anything. Life."

Jintana attentively listened, her eyes diverted to some insignificant patch of sky.

"It's to describe a tight situation. You can do one thing but it'll come back at you later and the only other thing you can do to get out of your problem will also screw you. It's good as bad. If you do anything good, there's a bad consequence. Question is, can you do anything bad to get something good? Oh Jesus it's a muddle. Not a very optimistic saying."

"You said it." Jintana reminded her, a hint of compassion in her strained tone. "That's irony."

"Ironic, yes…" Krue complimented her. "So, do you know how long I'll be here for?"

She replied vacantly, "When *they* decide."

"They?"

"Follow me."

They moved to the balcony to take in the sea and breeze. Facing out to sea their separate recollections of the horrors on land seemed to vanish. They looked down to the white dunes. White wash curled around the ankles of a lone boy casting a fishing line out over the soft waves.

Krue pointed down to the stripped hulk of a half-buried tank, "And that's where it happened?"

Jintana said nothing, her chin resting on her chest, her eyes restfully closed.

Krue looked further, north up the beach, to a canal opening and the masts of small vessels passing through, "Some fisherman?"

"They are not fisherman."

Krue squinted. "You're right. I see no nets."

"They say there are merchants or fishermen. You know what they catch?" Jintana softly snarled, "Pirates, slaves, pussy, weapons and profit."

Krue turned her back to the sea, looking through the living room to the doorway. Standing like a dimwit was a large militia soldier loosely holding his rifle and a padlock. His eyes were locked on her and even as she looked away, his pupils followed her evasive twitch, "Can I help you?"

No answer.

Jintana turned on the man as if commanding a precocious child, "Creton."

Krue's stance was equally solid as the visitor, she sternly asked, "*Bisa berbicara Inggris?*"

Jintana answered for Creton. "He knows English."

"Hmph," Creton grunted. "Jintana, come out," and shaking the padlock and key, "I guard."

Jintana clutched Krue's hand, "I am downstairs… You are staying here. That will be their way."

"I see." Krue intimately mocked a pleading groan as Jintana's hand withdrew. "Don't be a stranger. Maybe we can bake cakes or something?"

"Yes," Jintana was confused.

"Someone will bring you food from the markets." Creton told Krue, stepped aside for Jintana's exit and then closed the door. She heard the clunk of the padlock, the pocketing of his key, and the sitting of his fat arse on a creaky wooden chair outside.

"Shit."

That was mid-morning. She checked out her accommodation. All very well, considering. No nasties, like bugs, spy holes and trap doors. First scan of the beach she studied the tank, burnt out, just sitting. It was Western, not some cheap developing nation tinfoil tiger, but something solid, European and wasted. Well, she shrugged, they're busted up tanks everywhere in this country. She sat inside and tried to think.

This wasn't prison, yet. It was Club Providence, sea views and a television. She showered, cleaned her weapons and imagined that she still had her satphone: Opt for rescue and they'd probably swarm Providence with a fleet of Seahawks blasting the town to splinters with 20mm armour piercing bullets. Let hell break loose. Right now would be a worthy time too, as from the streets of Providence, from what she could see from the balcony, it was Market Day.

Women travelled on the hard sand of the beach from market to home with potatoes, kangaroo legs, watermelons and bundled cloths balanced on heads. Many used the beach as the easiest path. Krue imagined the bartering paradise in Providence; a crude market meshing the new, the recent, and the *old* world. Then she imagined herself, if so desired by her captors, cast to the bounty hunters. Disgruntled, she unleashed the fury of energy; one hundred semi-naked sit-ups on the balcony. It drained her. Sweat dripped. She took her bra off then her pants and relaxed under the afternoon sun. Wearing only underwear and feeling the awakening of nakedness she wondered if a spy satellite could see her now. Fresh sea air cleansed her mind. She objectively thought of Callaghan as a conduit to *madness*. She could see it happening to herself given the predicament and what Jintana saw in him, she had no idea. Yet then again she was not Jintana, and did Jintana notion that she had a decision in the matter? Irrelevant. Krue smiled. At the very least Colonel Patrick Peters knows I'm here and they're treating me with luxury, though confinement, it's a mark of respect. And that box that says I'm too beautiful to kill, it's just been ticked.

# Strangers

Morning sunshine fingered into a serene gully north of Sunny Bridge and east of the impact zone. Peters, with thirty of his Tonka and a few militia, lay in wait by a trickling stream. Far down the stream, resting on a pebbled bank gently inclining into the clear waters, was the objective of the morning; the last of the loose order that had bound the refugees and bandits into the doomed rabble. Peters spied though his binoculars at the dishevelled leader, a wide forceful man from some Middle-Asian Republic carrying a Kalashnikov and a rocket launcher over his shoulders. Around him twenty of his best, survivors in reality, and a few younger men, squatted around a blackened possum roasting on a fire. All had ashen, sad, faces, burnt clothes, some nursed their scalded skin in the cool waters of the stream. They were emerging from shock. Something nasty from the sky has obliterated their people. Was it God or Man? They'd never thought themselves so valuable to warrant such acts, and now having run into the harsh wilderness, were completely uneducated and ill-equipped to tame it. Many felt they were being judged, yet fought this fear with logic; God is watching, and let's not forget, Great. So it was Man.

"Is that him?" Peters offered the binoculars to Malo.

Malo gave a cold nod and shrugged off the binoculars. Malo's Zen with the bush was the fusion of genetics and upbringing. He saw through the foliage and down to the stream. There was the large leader of the refugee throng of yesterday, a bit burnt but otherwise fit, leaning sideways staring despondently at nothing. Malo raised his hunting rifle. The militia followed suit. Peters preferred to watch through the binoculars. Malo struck first, right between the eyes of the leader. The militia raked the bank, decimating the enemy, without touching the possum. Silence descended. The stream trickled, a twig snapped and a bowed branch whacked back into place. There was always one survivor and he or she could take out five militia on a lucky day.

"There!" a fifteen year old militia boy pointed into a dark patch of bush.

Malo had already trained his rifle, fired, and overtly satisfied, called down to the possum. "He'd be ready 'eh."

They crawled forward through the bush as quietly and slowly as they arrived. They surrounded the bandits, crept in and checked for pulses. Malo carved up the little possum with his bowie knife.

Militia gnawed at the thin scraps of meat. Peters was brimming with pride but spoke softly, "Now we split. Half of you spread out across Sunny Bridge for any runners." With his boot he nudged the head of the leader. "Neat. We don't want renegades running around out there bent on revenge, got it?"

Between minuscule bites and chews they nodded.

Peters than made a call to Callaghan.


Callaghan picked up the phone and relaxed to hear the familiar morning welcome of Peters. After the preliminary update, Peters pressed on, urgently, "Yesterday that new trader arrived in Providence Town from Kingston. His name is Toro."

"Jemmy sent him to me." Callaghan said. "Think it's worth it?"

"If it's serious. Jemmy and him have conspired something on the side so I want you to see what you can do with him. If we can move cattle or coal or refugees it'd be great. How's the currency?"

"Enough."

"How much is enough?"

"I'll do a recount soon. What's on your shopping list with this Toro character?"

"Helicopters."

Callaghan rasped, "They're fucking expensive. At least a million for anything good. Plus a pilot or two."

"I know. See what you can make out of this Toro. If he's come this far he'll want to make something substantial out of it and if he's connected as Jemmy says he is, well, who knows what can happen."

"Easy… And one more thing,"

Peters intuitively paused to test Callaghan's strained voice, "What?"

"Someone came in from the west, yesterday."

"Uh-huh," Peters's attention was snagged by a volley of shots from downstream. One of the militia had nabbed something. "Sorry, continue."

"They came in from the other side of Jacinda Mountain."

"Cheeky; what's their game?"

"It's an Australian Army assassin posing as a Diplomat wishing to see you to broker some non-nuclear deal. It was too open-ended for me to take it seriously."

"Why am I not surprised?"

"You will be surprised," Callaghan hinted, "Pleasantly surprised."

"You think they did Jenkins in?"

Callaghan gulped. "Add two and two, what do you get? But there's something else I can't put my finger on-"

"All this sounds unrealistic…"

"I know. Not a very impressive way to come into town talking peace."

"Listen, I haven't got time for that shit. Just kill 'em."

"… Sure." Callaghan slapped his hand to his face and wiped it down. "I'll talk to you later about it, looks like this Toro is here!"

"O-K, I'll be busy today; cleaning up."

"Understood – Out." Callaghan dropped the phone onto the receiver and leant back, his hands splayed, kinking his head and releasing a peevish sigh. God only knows where Peters is right now, tracking scummy parasites of the upturned globe. But, truth be told, standing outside the office door was an apprehensive Toro, now led into the office by the good natured Jintana.

Toro's childish grin punctuated a proud and sneaky ovular flabby face. Gone was the scurrilous gaze seen at the *Dead Head Pub*. He was dressed in a red gingham shirt, designer jeans, aviator sunglasses, Italian shoes, a giant belt buckle, a silver crucifix around his neck, and chunky oblong rings imbedded with green jewels on his thumb and little fingers.

"Captain James Callaghan!" he spoke with a South American accent that proved itself to be versatile and well practised with English.

"Toro! Finally! Good to meet you!"

They shook hands and sat. Toro's eyes did the usual roaming about the office but found nothing of interest. Apparently, he visited much more intriguing warlord offices or drug cartel bunkers, who knew.

"So, first time in Australia?"

Toro's voice was husky, from either smoking Cubans cigars or shouting orders at imbeciles. "No… No… Many years ago I visited the Gold Coast… Melbourne… Noosa. Very nice. Beautiful beaches and birds that sing. I saw whales too. Sea World. Very nice. Sometimes *like* America."

"Really?"

"Believe me."

Callaghan smelt a rat. First up was that Major Katherine Krue marching, not waltzing, into Providence, and if she only knew that Peters wanted her dead without even personally evaluating her. Now there's Toro, waltzing in to trade. If he was any good at trade he'd have little need to come to the Port of Kingston and even then why does he come down to Providence? He was either a typical spy/assassin/operative or an illegal arms or drug trader or an avid adventurer with a death-wish.

"Where are you staying in town?"

"The *Dead Head Pub*. Funny name," Toro grinned, "Is there a story, why?"

"No idea. But I can make one up."

Toro nodded, shrugged and waited.

"And where did you come in from?"

"First Townsville, then Kingston."

Callaghan tapped his finger lightly on the table. "How did you get into Townsville?"

Toro vividly recounted, "First I sailed to Fiji with my ship. It sailed on but I flew to Vanuatu, and from there I flew over."

"You flew over. With whom?"

"General Kai has connections. I think maybe his bankers are there. He is a nice man too, but charged me too much for the flight. And he had nothing good to ship or to trade. I was not happy, so I'm here, down here."

"And how did you get here?"

"Jemmy has a man, he drove me through some back roads. I heard about the people, and the bandits, and you know, I understand."

"Well, in some places the shit happens."

"Sure," Toro dismissed the event, remembering the militia rounding up the refugees he had passed on the way.

"Now," Callaghan rubbed his hands together, "Explain to me in the simplest of terms why you've come down to Providence. Long way, isn't it?"

"What do you mean?" He was suspicious. It should have all been sorted.

"Why are you here?"

"To meet you about the coal! The war is one thing but trade must go on... I have a ship coming over – the *Margarita* – to deliver the coal for the *Black Tide* in Singapore." He beckoned up to the map of Queensland, expecting his ship to be bobbing across the Coral Sea.

"It's dangerous... They tell you that?"

Toro masked his mouth with his gold-ringed hand, admitting, "They did... And they said they know when the war moves, and how to avoid it."

"The *Black Tide* told you this?"

"I know some from Venezuela. They put me in contact with their friends, I had to sail, people want to trade... And now it's my first time here, during this war, and because you're a gringo I can tell you... With the rice mafia I don't know who I can trust," his eyes moistened, "You understand?"

"That, I do: Too well… You're in a tight and desperate spot…"

Toro nodded.

"Don't trust me, or Peters, except for a few certainties,"

"Certainties?"

"Truths. The truth. We can load the coal only when we've received payment from *our* Black Tide buddies. But, between you and I, we want to buy too, we want helicopters – not quickly – but if you're making this a regular trip."

"Helicopters. Hmm." He wondered how the hell he could ship in helicopters. Be *interested*. "And what are the helicopters for?"

"See," Callaghan pointed up to the map of Queensland and their enclave, enlarging every quarter, "Walking is too slow."

Toro laughed. "Funny guy. I understand…" he made the point of thinking hard and shot back a simple question, "But is it safe here? What if the war comes again? *Black Tide* say 'Come, come, good deals everywhere, good trade'. I don't know what to think. They say 'many ships were sunk in the war and ships are valuable' so my ship could make good money shifting cargo. True?"

"*Yes* if you know the right people and play the right games. I'm sure you're experienced with the nature of the industry."

"People, they are the same all over the world. When I heard that here was good, I decided to try."

"So you came over here just like that?" Callaghan clicked his fingers in the air.

"Oh no!" Toro scoffed. "Not so *simple*. My own country – I say not – they want me to go to prison. Prison! Ha! Once I was a billionaire! Politicians and judges in my pockets. Now prison! Forget it."

"A billionaire?"

"Sure. I tell you one thing, funny man, making the first billion is the hardest. I made many great deals with the Americans, the Columbians, the South Africans, then the currency change and the deals and the corrupt police and the politicians and my cousins in the business, they go under, and I had to cash in everything! Now I start again. Things are a bit different."

"How different?"

"Just *different*. I mean, I had the big chance with the big shots, but I tell you, funny man, I missed oil. I saw it coming and I did nothing… So I said, 'What did the big shots do before they were big shots?'" Toro nodded to the Pacific Ocean on the map, "I got two ships, they're my babies now, and the ugly one – *Margarita* – is out there, heading for Kingston. The coal. But don't screw me because I'm desperate,"

"Never,"

"You know, this is what it's about," Toro dipped his stubby finger between two imaginary jaws, "Someone doesn't want something and someone does. Put money in and take money out. In: Out." His smile was genuine. "And a little here and there and it adds up after a while."

"We speak the same language."

"But I ask you… Jemmy would not tell … And the Colonel was busy,"

"Yes, very busy right now."

Toro's eyes danced up and down the map, left and right across the desk then pleadingly to Callaghan, pinning the white man down, "Is it safe here?"

Callaghan posthumously declared, "Safe as it'll ever be!"

"And where did the big war go?"

"Toro, the war never left!" Callaghan said with a cheerful twist to the severity, "This *is* the War! Look, if it wasn't here you wouldn't be here."


The next afternoon Krue was hurting. She was insane for surrendering. In a colourful reflective moment she imagined running a million miles an hour with the bush rushing by, a darkening blur as she wound through secret ravines, up to Peters as he twists around to defend himself and she plunges a dagger into the man she saw in the photograph and with all her bodily strength guts it.

She sat on the balcony listening to the sea. This was, she sensed, a place of pain, and as if to answer, Jintana slipped through the front door and quietly sat beside Krue.

"Hello."

"Hello. Make yourself at home."

Jintana checked to see Creton closed the door, "No one can hear us. No-one."

As if to test her words they sat in silence and listened to the waves crashing on the shore below, the locals down below, the wives of the militia and their children playing in the dunes, the mothers washing clothes and chopping vegetables on wooden boards, chatting about prices, weather, and the state of their men ploughing the fields or patrolling borders pencilled in on some rudimentary map.

"Jintana?"

"Yes,"

"This town," Krue spoke up to the blue sky, "I *feel something* here."

Jintana's petite little arm extended up and her index finger curved down to a spot on the beach.

Krue saw the wreck of the tank, sand brushed by the wind leading up to dunes matted with thin grasses, and an endless stretch of beach.

"General Sumatra died down there. Colonel Peters killed him; he was standing where you sit when he fired. I was down there,"

A shiver sprinkled up Krue's spine.

"A strange morning. The white men come from the sea to this beach. Sumatra was ready. He knew. He was smart. He killed many," she sighed, "But Colonel Peters came from behind. No-one talks about it."

"A sore point?"

"And here," Jintana flapped her hand and encompassed the town and region behind the coastline, "Peters killed many very quickly – he had to. Have you seen dead men? They stare up at you like this," Jintana easily turned dead, frozen in some crumpled discarded-doll form with an eerie gaze to the heavens and a benign smile for those on the ground, her own mockery of the state igniting a ruffle of laughter from her new friend.

"I've seen them," Krue admitted, "But I never hung around. Who the fuck wants to look them in the eyes? It's hard enough as it is."

Jintana comfortingly crossed her arms over her chest, leaned against the balcony and looked from the beach to this visitor, she saw a ruthless hope in Krue. "I did. It helped me understand them,"

Krue stiffened, "I see."

Jintana placidly monitored the retreating waves on the beach, "You understand the flow of these lands. There is love in some places but in others, the death."

"It'll all end one day."

Jintana objected. "Peters and his men come, they conquer, as Sumatra did. We think peace and yes I live in peace but the killing goes on. No fault. It was not Sumatra's fault, it's everyone who comes. Anyone who comes here comes to kill and destroy. Do not forget that."

"I'll try not to." Krue felt a fleeting solace that the town somehow rested on her shoulders and her saving grace was to see it survive. Yet there was nothing exemplary to say about it. Jintana's complacent quietness prompted Krue to say something to fill the void but she could still think of little. What she could explain, as in her purpose, wouldn't help. But in Jintana's resolute way it was obvious she was one that survived the chaos that covers these lands, like a hapless butterfly floating between volcanic eruptions it may have triggered.

After lengthy minutes Krue asked, "Did Peters and his Task Force Seven try to leave?"

"They couldn't. The boat they came on," she pointed out to the deeper waters on the horizon, "It was strong but did little to help. It left them here, abandoned like refugees! Then no Sumatra meant no order and Peters, he became the Warlord. He had no choice. James thinks it funny – a cruel joke – I don't get it."

Team Smacker & Tolken's doing, Krue fathomed. They left Task Force Seven here thinking Peters would fade away into the wilderness and die a bearded freak battling it from a cave like a rabid revolutionary. Instead he prospered. He had blossomed like an invading weed. She was here to rectify a mistake. She wasn't an assassin, or an idealistic, self-appointed, glorified diplomat grasping for recognition. She was a gardener.

"Some jokes," Krue explained, "Are better when you don't get them."

# Extremes

Twenty meters back from the muddy southern bank of the Arubai River, a cluster of elephant sized granite boulders jutted up in contrast to the dark, murky, mangroves. Matthews squatted between the mammoth boulders aiming the stubby aerial of his satphone to the heavens, half praying that an allied satellite would swing over in low orbit, and half calculating if the bursts of data from the gadget could warp the fabric of his brain. He was sceptical of their concealed position, wary, and tired. One night had been enough. They were readying to shift but first a brief check-up with the brass, listening to their wirelesses, thousands of clicks south beyond the anarchy.

Matthews kneeled, blessing the satphone's signal strength as it maxed. He licked the beaded sweat from his top lip. He counted. Seconds was all it should take. The weather was extremely humid, the heat promising to be stifling. Come on space junk. I'm calling you.

Then his heart jumped - he heard the lazed yet ghoulish *aaarrrk!* of a crow, then nothing, and looking about saw only putrid bubbles oozing from the mud and crabs sliding down their holes. Tom and Matthews, both wrapped in camouflage, cradled their guns. They heard a foreign grunt from young lungs. Boots and athletic limbs skipped up the other side of their mammoth boulder. The intruder sighed; relief. Looking up, Matthews and Tom fell under the shadow of a militia grunt precariously balanced atop the boulder, delicately aiming his AK-47 into the depths of the neighbouring mangroves. He was lean, wearing imitation Chinese Army Arctic white and grey cut-off trousers and a dirty black tank-top with a *Pepsi-Cola Taste the Difference* faded decal on the back. A tin flask dangling from his shoulder dripped glistening water down a rusty chain attached to the screw-on lid. The grunt excitedly fired, three bursts, the last on target. The high-pitched yelps of his victim came from near the riverbank. Then came his young, hunterly, gloated, primal, grunt.

Alone and concealed, spying the boulders, at one with stinky brown mud, rich barks and oily leaves, Corrie breathed steadily watching the grunt saviour the puffs of gun-smoke, computing the strange sense of accomplishment for hunting something so tame and how it moistened his eyes. Corrie opened his mouth, *"Aaaaarrrrrk."*

The grunt turned and saw no crow on the branches. He swung his rifle, trailing the victim, now crawling in the mangroves. He cursed and dangled his smoking barrel to his side. "*Coooo eeeh!*" he sang to the dense maze of twisted branches and loneliness. No reply. With a few meters height he soaked up the view of the silver sparkling tide drawing out from the Arubai River and the muddy edge of its northern curling bank. Dangling from his neck were plastic yellow sports binoculars, stamped with a cartoon logo golf ball whacked in mid-flight. He studied the riverbank, relaxed, unzipping his fly with his free hand, pissing off the rock careful not to hit his dirty boots. He neatly rotated east, thinking about what's next, trailing the winding river to a thin band of stagnant blue sea on the horizon. Perspiration fogged the eye-piece. Urine trickled down the boulder. He blew air down his shirt and released his binoculars, hung them off his neck, and peered down to the sturdiness of his two feet; I'm pissing off a rock. It's hot. Got that Rat. Total $2. One more bullet will do the trick. This is *the* life. How's my footing, got to get off the boulder. Two blue-eyed charcoal-smeared whites with raised rifles are looking at me.

One hissed a deathly curse, "Mine!"

The grunt had no time to train his dangling rifle on them. Corrie, concealed by branches and a slanting decaying log, acted first. The grunt's shoulder blades were pummelled, his body thwacked over the dark wet space between the boulders. Waving in his leap, shards of splintered rib bit out of his tank-top slicing through the crappy detail. The binoculars spun around his neck as he slammed spread-eagled on the other boulder. Tom yanked the body down, paused at the grunt's wheezing, then slit his throat. The eyes squinted tight and with the approach of death, sprang open.

Matthews held his breath. "Shat his pants." He kicked the grunt's legs closed and pressed OFF on the satphone, "Ready?"

Tom thumbs-upped, popped his head over the boulder to Corrie's direction, who smartly waved all was O-K. Corrie curled his hand over the hot barrel and nervously parted through the clinging mangroves. He hadn't seen what the bastard had shot at, just heard a wounded body dragging itself though slushy mud.

TO: OVERLORD
FROM: VOODOO CHILD
(CPL MATTHEWS)

VISUAL VERIFICATION OF ONE
MOBILE FUDO, REFUGEES NORTH
OF SUNNY BRIDGE ANNIHILATED
BY MISSILE STRIKE.
PROVIDENCE MILITIA HOLDING
ARUBAI RIVER (AS BORDER LINE?).
NO CONTACT WITH MAJOR KRUE.
OTHERWISE, NOT DETECTED.

Matthews kicked the grunt's body deeper under the boulder into a crevice of moist urine. The unseen victim in the mangroves moaned, high-pitched and abandoned.

Matthews hoarsely whispered, "Corrie! Sort that out!"

Corrie followed the whimpering. With his knife drawn and the tip of the matt black blade guiding him to the irregular crawling sound coming from behind a large twisted mangrove trunk, he crept closer feeling totally alert, wired, and then paradoxically, impotent to kill: His eyes ran down skinny knees, thin calf muscles, and mud-caked old grey gym shoes. The laces were loosely and stickily twisted around fallen twigs. Further peeling himself around the trunk his knife grip became sheepishly limp at the sight of long-black hair tossed over bare, yellow shoulders, and smallish teen breasts pouting under a skin-tight cherry and white polyester polo shirt stretched over corrugated ribs. A wide smudge of blood stretched from her thighs to the torn denim jeans shorts clinging to spread-eagled legs, splatters leading up to and from her bitten tongue crawling the corners of her quivering mouth. She crunched up her shirt with a painful ferocity, half covering her exposed guts. Corrie edged forward, empathetically placing his hand flat on the crown of her head, running his grimy skin over her thin black hair down to her collar bone. He expected the welling of a tear from her as an acknowledgement of his sympathy at the vulgar mess ripped open in the congestive heat under the salty leaves. She glared at him defiantly. Corrie felt clammy and scared. He removed his hand, staring down to her ripped body. By the meeting of their eyes at her wound, they knew it was over. Shivering, eyeing off the dull knife, she tilted her head back. He cuffed her mouth, drew the blade to the bruised exposed neck smeared with red and brown mud, and paused. The girl was a mess, rotting to the mangroves before his eyes. He was intent to make one clinical swipe. A quick slash at the exposed throat. Deliver the mercy. By the tip of his index finger he felt a pulse, her burning cheeks against the coarseness of his thumb, a salty tear rolling over his knuckles. He tensed, hurtfully drew back his knife wielding arm, squandering another way to erase this wreck from his memory. She squealed hysterically through his fingers and ferociously bit deep into the thinnest skin on his palm. He held in his call of pain.

"Pssht!" Matthews crept into the mangroves.

"Wild bitch!" Corrie flung the knife and dropped his knee on her chest, palmed her head with his free hand as she bit harder. Then she gripped her rake thin hand up to his throat scrunching at it like a sponge. His eyes bulged. He couldn't slam her in the head with his fist, not when his knee slipped down her torso under the shirt and into her. The fumes made him wince and pulling his bitten hand away, her jaw only clenched harder. He launched backwards, tossing her a good metre through the air before her head flicked and she broke the vice not without tasting his blood.

Matthews silenced her with a neat shot to the head.

Massaging his hand, squeezing out blood, Corrie stood in turmoil.

"Fuck it." Matthews pitied him, pointing her lifeless body over to the boulders. "Drag her next to the dead fella."

"She!" Corrie picked up his knife indicating slicing of the jugular. "She wanted me to do it!"

"Let's move." Matthews ordered. "It's not your fault."

The girl was thrown to the side of the grunt, both nudged between the boulders. Tom aimed the AK-47 into the sky. "If anyone's listening, we'll make it sound like a victory for them,"

"Sure," Matthews stooped to pick up his pack, "We sprint two klicks south." He impatiently cast his hand over the dead duo between the grey boulders, "These make it fuck a loads hotter for us."

Tom fingered the AK-47 trigger. "Let it rip, Chief?"

"Go for it."

Matthews and Corrie scurried into the mangroves leaving Tom to finish the job. With one eye closed he sprayed the girl with bullets from the grunt's AK-47. He left them, their limbs thrown over one another in a weak embrace under a cordite cloud, the two dead heads of messed black hair and blue lips barely touching.

Aided by a cool sea breeze, Peters heard the volley come from the east. He heard twin volleys creep from the south yet nothing from the north where the missile had landed. He stood in the middle of Sunny Bridge, spanning the Arubai River, staring down to the silty waters flowing out to sea. Behind him his militia patrolled the bridge. He could smell the foulness of the missile's effect and he pondered falling off his bridge, into his river and sinking under the tide and ending up in the cleanliness of the sea. He could hear relief as militia led a single file of women and children across the bridge to a pasture of safety in his deep south. He clearly remembered the road of slaughter they had passed through. What had spared them? They hadn't come with the dead. They were a mix of wanderers. Is that what they do – move on and on.

"Hey," he called to one of the militia. "Ask them, why they are running."

He did. He returned. "She says she just follows."

"Follows."

"But why run now. Everyone is running."

The militia man didn't understand or knew too well. He had run once. The reasons were many and varied.

"Peters!" Vince called from the southern end of the bridge. He stood by a jeep flexing his hands preparing for a lengthy drive. "You'll be late for Raoul."


Jemmy bound his hair in a net and at the helm of his twelve-metre long 'fishing' boat equipped with over-sized engines, a front fifty calibre machine-gun, equipped with surface radar and one anti-aircraft missile under the Captain's armchair, leaned into the dusty fuel gauge. He was thinking of the approaching point of no return in the Coral Sea where he would have to return or find himself falling short of Kingston or Providence, adrift, prey to the likes of himself. His crew of seven were on deck scanning the ends of the horizons with binoculars and at intervals turned their faces to him with nothing but questioning stares for the unexplainable lack of prey to be seen upon the sea. Jemmy made the weekly patrol at the request of three coastal Warlords, from north to south, Kai, Peters and Raoul. Typically he could expect to encounter two or three boats and once he came parallel he could grade them as merchants, refugees, or fisherman. Amid the great blue he had heart for there are unwritten rules of humanity whilst at sea. Merchants would be directed to Kingston or Providence. Fisherman were exactly that and rarely proved otherwise. Refugees were directed far north or south, or if they were extremely tight faced and vigilant, he would rightly tell them to go back north or face the bullet.

"Jemmy," one of his pirates excitedly pointed to the north east.

Jemmy casually left the wheel to his trainee pilot and sauntered to the bow. On a bearing of thirty-seven degrees was prey. A warm fuzzy feeling grew as he refocused and identified a vessel, possibly a freighter, and if it wasn't armed to the teeth, he could raid it. He called to the trainee pilot to set a course to trail the vessel. It was moving sluggishly. What if it was full of something valuable like ore or oil? Imagine commandeering that and sailing it through the treacherous waters to Hong Kong! Imagine the currency! He would buy an apartment in Kowloon and sit out the chaos! He would sell the latest of technologies, forge steel patents for factories in China, play the stock markets then lavish and ravish the women! They would stare at him with wonder and fascination for he was what many men wished they had been – a plunderer of the sea and survivor to tell the macabre tales.

A half hour later the first characteristics betraying the true nature of the prey appeared as flotsam. The lanky spotter perched on the bow inspected an oblong patch of drifting debris; charred floating wood, a floating corpse dressed in a thin cotton robe, three empty plastic milk bottles tied together, and under them, anchoring them, a fourth bottle tied to and full of fresh water. Jemmy had seen this before and if the first assumption was right he assessed the situation as follows: some small vessel had been run-over, possibly as it sided up to a larger vessel in the hope of rescue. He had seen this before, more so up north. The floating body was fresh, he guessed from last night (it was now midday) and the culprit is over the horizon.

"Three more!" the spotter called.

Jemmy called to the trainee pilot to take them in for a look. The boat made a small deviation and eased off, drifting to a larger spray of debris. With both hands holding a hooked pole Jemmy leaned over and prodded the floating bodies. Miraculously they were together. Had they died only minutes ago, hand in hand, and now floated, face down, inseparable by the mightiest of the seas? He saw it was a man, his wife, and their teenage son, all of coastal Vietnamese descent. He felt surprisingly ill at prodding their bodies, the act a mark of disrespect but he continued because though they were flesh and blood and related, the sea should separate them except he found their feet were tied together by a thick nylon rope. He lunged the pole in to drag up the rope and in doing so raised three sets of prunish legs out of the water into the blistering sunshine. With the rope in his hands, weighed down by the legs, now revealed up to their thighs, Jemmy inspected it. It was nice rope, new and shiny. It would not be found on some decrepit craft used to shuttle poor and desperate refugees. Rarely does an entire fishing family go to sea. There is nothing worse than losing an entire family to the sea during a war. He looked over them for any other significant signs but only saw the backs of their heads and as he angrily tugged at the rope it twisted the body of the son so that the head bobbed, rotated, the shift expunging a flow of cherry coloured sea water from the exposed finger sized hole in the temple, just above the ear.

Jemmy's nostrils flared. Executions of sea-going peoples was severe. He assumed with a grumpy sigh, in this sea was competition, raiding small craft, looting, killing, and so on. Very unnecessary too. And they were close. So close he stood straight, discarded the rope and its legs back to the water and sniffed the sea wind. Another pirate at play? Or maybe some tribe from the Solomon Islands?

"More!" the spotter pointed to the south east.

"How many?" Jemmy called.

"Two!"

Jemmy told him to check on the freighter they trailed.

"It comes this way!" the trainee pilot delightedly called from the bridge.

Jemmy felt himself rocking with the waves, thinking about the trainee pilot's glee and watching it sour. The engines coughed and abruptly stopped, yet the craft still glided through the water and would soon be at its mercy. Jemmy stormed up to the bridge and slapped the trainee pilot who cried that the pumps were clogged. The mechanic was called and as he tinkered with the valves Jemmy became increasingly aware of the rocking to and fro. This was a sign; before the cyclone, the ravishing storm, or bad news. He spied the freighter. Yes it was civilian, approaching, sitting very low in the water. His radio operator had reported no transmissions. It was just a mid-sized cargo ship. It wasn't the *Dzintra*. She would be long gone. Maybe it was the incoming *Margarita*. He scrutinised the slowly progressing shape and when it split and formed two distinctive ships he thought he was *dreaming*. He held the bridge and steadied himself. One was smaller, almost of frigate size, moving from behind the other. It drifted apart then powered into an abrupt turn away. He spied hard. It was battleship grey.

"Pump is good now. One hour O-K," the mechanic called up, guessing the time they could further spend on roaming the seas before the next malfunction.

Jemmy lit a cigarette. In a few hours he could be in range of them, and who they may be was now none of his business, as it was in his best interests that he was certainly none of their business. With renewed appreciation to the trainee pilot he politely ordered, "Back to Kingston."

"Fast?"

Jemmy hunched around his binoculars, the cigarette dangling from the corner of his mouth, seeing that the frigate peeled itself to the east and the cargo ship slowly moved south-west to the Queensland coast, and possibly where he was going. He stood up and sucked hard. Complicated.

"Make a slow turn, nothing sudden. They are watching us."

"Who?"

Jemmy had no idea. The trio in the water might.

"What will they do?" the trainee pilot asked.

Jemmy nudged the trainee pilot aside and performed a steady slow turn east out to the wider ocean then due south as if following the coast down and once he had triple checked his bearings would break east through a narrow gap in the Coral Reef for Providence.

"They come!" the spotter called, now at the aft of the boat.

Jemmy lit another cigarette. A speed-boat, chasing him, had come from the frigate but as the frigate sailed further east, then north, in a zigzag pattern, the speedboat changed course, and like Jemmy's wide turn, would return to safety. Jemmy wished for dark clouds, typhoons, for safety. He was a pirate with a high-powered craft that fished for easy profit. He was not a navy. And why did that naval vessel execute a zigzag as it sailed away? Do they fear submarines? Which side is it on anyway.

"Jemmy!" the spotter's head was transfixed up to the southern sky, pointing out seven thin and white vapour trails of mammoth jet bombers so far up they were just specks of black on bright blue. They headed north in formation with enough payload to destroy a civilisation or two.

Jemmy's chest tightened. He'd seen those familiar etchings before.

Callaghan stood inside the vault with his hands on his hips, proud and vindicated. Inside the vault were an assortment of treasures, relics from the past, oysters from the sea, microchips for missile parts, wads of foreign currency, bars of gold, silver, precious jewels. He had the exotic stuff valued by one of Jemmy's trusted *Black Tide* friends in Singapore using on on-line camera. Adding to and by far the greatest contributor to the wealth was the value out of the vault that had made it to the free market and back in the form of protection; not just guns and grenades, but megaton.

Produce, the sale of cattle or coal or diamonds or gold or slaves was paid for by hard currency, US dollars, gold, or funds transfers to one of the many bank accounts Callaghan had aligned around the wonderfully huge, complicated, desperate, globe. He managed money in and outside of Providence. He had organised the most educated echelons of the welcomed refugees, now citizens, to handle playing the stock markets from Hong Kong to New Delhi to Zurich via the French dealer. With that money and weight of investments he had bought weapons of mass and punitive destruction. He evaluated their reserves of foreign currency in numerous global bank accounts, onboard private vessels shuffling their hard currency to ports for trading, and that in the vault. Smirking, he stepped out of the vault, swung the heavy door closed, locked it, and feeling light as a feather moved to Jintana, stoking her shoulder and then sat in his office. Four million dollars. Thanks to the governance of trade and labour of numerous resources, and sizeable booty thanks to the late and great General Sumatra, Callaghan was a millionaire. This would not have happened had fate not sent him here. Accomplishment is esteem. For a few minutes of his life, he sat in his chair, feeling like a real man.

Then Marcus said gravely from the doorway, "Wake up, we've got trouble,"

"Trouble?" Callaghan cackled, amused at the very essence of the word. "This is a world of trouble! Enlighten me. Show me a meteorite hurtling through space for earth – now that's trouble."


On an insignificant island off the coast from the thin border between their regions, two neighbouring Warlords sat with their feet dangling in the crystal clear water, low waves lapping against a beach of golden sand. The island at its peak was a metre high at king tide, an adequate ovular patch of sand inhabited by budding palm trees and an exposed coral crop. At its edge were a series of intermingling atolls lush with tropical fish and the finest colourful offerings of the Great Barrier Reef.

Peters sipped at his gin and tonic, amusingly observing the speedily melting ice-cubes under the sunshine. He swivelled his head to their only means of escaping such a beautiful barren outpost; Raoul's ageing Iroquois helicopter parked at the far end of the island. Raoul and Peters sat side by side on banana lounges on a slope of beach that Peters childishly imagined as running thousands of kilometres into a trench in the middle of the Pacific. Their bare feet floated on the sea. They stared out to the dark blue horizon.

"It's a tragedy that one day this will all be gone," Raoul removed his stylish rap-around sunglasses to reflect on the island as if it would disappear but not in his lifetime. "All good things must end." He reclined as far back in his lounge as possible.

"So it goes," Peters softly chided, swirling his drink, "So it goes."

They were men of few words. Both wore bathers, their clothes in the helicopter, and came to meet here every month or two, to basically chill out and discuss regional affairs.

"I was wondering if I could borrow your doctor at some stage. Nelson, is that his name?"

"He's no doctor," Peters freely admitted. "Not in the traditional sense. Can't even perform an appendicitis. Can clog an exit wound, that's about it. Why?"

"My sister-in-law," Raoul worried, "She thinks she has cancer. We have a doctor and she seems to think so too."

Peters reflected. "That's unexpected."

"Unexpected...?" The tips of Raoul's thumb and index finger stroked his cheeks down to his narrow jaw. His sister-in-law's approaching death clouded the urgency of the meeting with his favourite adversary.

"I'm sorry to hear that." Peters closed his eyes and soaked up the sun. "To die like that in this day and age. I'd forgotten how normal it is..."

"Ah you're right. It's fate... Plain fate... How's the mine?"

"Working. Took some time. Had to hire refugees as miners. Extracted a lode of brown coal and Callaghan says we can sell it. Got some buyer coming in. The geologist tells me there's another year worth. Hard to know, until you dig it all out."

Raoul swallowed a tightness of pride. *His* geologist had said six-months maximum. Well that was the way when you deal in things that can't always be accurately calculated pre-trade. It was plain business to sell the mine.

"Lucky you. And how many refugees have come down?"

"Five or six thousand." Peters cupped water and sprinkled droplets over his chest, watching them slide down his ribs. "Not counting a few hundred gone bush to join the thousand already starving there. Push them in far enough and give them enough time, they either die or de-evolve into cannibals, just like the brain eating monkeys that we once were."

Raoul soaked the radiance from the serene blue ceiling they shared then to the sunlit crests of subtle waves washing against their shins.

"And you?" Peters asked.

He breathed the clean sea air. "Six thousand. The same. They came in through the west. They had bypassed Providence on account of your, how shall we say it,"

"My reputation precedes me?"

"That's it!" Raoul praised his friend and minded himself for another few minutes.

Peters lazily rolled his head to the helicopter again. Standing under the shade of the limp rotor blades were two of Raoul's guards; spicy Pakistani ladies in khaki shorts and tunics, stripping down to their panties to snorkel off the island. The pilot, a lean bearded veteran from Burma, scoured the skies with binoculars, searching for seagulls, or planes, anything, sipping a can of coke. Beside him stood the party's only esky, packed with precious ice.

"Callaghan said the transport for the coal is from South America. Says he has a cargo ship. Probably loaded with narcotics."

"South America," Raoul frowned, "Tin-pot dictators and drug barons."

"If he can ship me in a few helicopters, he can take away coal, bulls, sugar, kangaroo skins. I don't care."

"Yes, you need air power." Raoul's fist flexed then relaxed, calculating the adverse affects of a localised, low-budget, high-stakes arms race.

"Don't panic... But it'd save me money. The Providence Region is too big to be relying on militia and jeeps. Too big."

"I understand. You'll need it armed. There's Russian dealers in Asia."

"Russians. But the supply route down this way is the problem. If we can get a link across the Pacific, maybe you and I can prove international legitimacy."

Raoul smugly played his hand into the water. "Dream on, *righteous whitey*."

The pilot called up to the sky, then to Raoul, the sky again, his quick-fire foreign jabber jolting Peters.

"What's going on?"

Raoul's eyes dreamily meandered up to the sky, stopped and sharply focussed: "I think... It must be... The bombers are back."

"The same formation we saw this morning?" Peters spotted them, high up, crawling across the sky drawing thin white lines that soon puffed out.

Raoul nodded, counting, "One, two, three, four, five... Hmm. Six."

"And seven went north. We both counted."

"And only six go south. Interesting. I wonder what they were bombing?"

Peters frowned. "The usual shit. Wipe out an industrial city. Vaporise a dam. Must have come from Amberley... We'll find out soon enough. If they lost one they'd be hoping it was worth it. Worth over fifty million a piece. Something *is* going on up north and the big players aren't afraid to take losses."

"I hope not." Raoul gracefully flicked his long dark fingers into the sea, up to the slight sea breeze, and touched the tip of his chin and in his educated manner asked, "What do you think of the recent refugees: the armed *menaces*. They're bold to come so far and expect so much."

Another minute passed as Peters formulated an answer. Raoul was from Pakistan, educated in Great Britain, arrived in Australia hot on the heels of the Indonesian Army, and how he came to be the most civilised of Warlords would remain a mystery. Was it maniac disposition to concealed ruthless behaviour or plain good business sense? Peters had detected a trace of fear in his lowering voice. It always sounded as though it could be stronger or tougher but it didn't have to be. Now it sounded strangely terse.

"Desperation, Raoul. The driving force is beyond our comprehension or control yet it is our enemy – an unknown enemy, maybe the next war, a new kind. These wars won't stop yet."

"It takes money to wage conflict."

"A bankrupt economy doesn't mind."

"But how many displaced people are there?"

"Billions. The first wave of refugees came in search of the promised land with the will to settle, accepting a few of their kind would die doing so, and displacing the original inhabitants. Just look at me. Fair enough."

"I was ridging that first wave, I guess."

"Yes. But the population overload isn't over yet. The second wave know it's not all peaches and cream. We're dealing with the tough ones. They're not the charity cases you can trust anymore."

"I arrived for the peaches and cream," Raoul proudly smiled, waved to his lady guards, then flapped his heart, "A humble trader of foods and clothing! I wonder if I would do it *now* though. Violent as all fuck, *now*. Wouldn't last a minute."

"Exactly. Because in the *now*," Peters eyes narrowed to some distant point on the sea where it meets the sky and both dissolve in a thin misty band, "They're running scared as their homelands expels them.

World War 3.0 and 3.1 was cake, easy to grasp and conventional almost. World War 3.2 – It's nastier. Bitter. And we're at the forefront."

"They are so motivated," Raoul sat up on his elbow and thirstily sipped his gin and tonic, "It's useless. You think they would know,"

"They do, but they know if they stay where they are they die. If they flee south following plain ignorance, and ignorance is *bliss*,"

"Bliss, surely bliss is not starving in Australia, the most inhospitable place on earth! Surely."

"Who knows? Who wants to?"

"And this ignorance – what drives them to be ignorant? Many fear you – they are not foolish – yet they come through your region."

"For all *my* fear, a much greater fear is driving them down here."

"What?"

"I have my suspicions."

"And?"

"It's out of our hands Raoul – It's on the way. It betrays its advance by the dust it kicks up as it marches forward. That's the generous nature of our new enemy."

Raoul kinked his glass to Peters, and both twiddling their toes in the beautiful ocean, saluted with a tone of professional gentlemanly respect, "To our new enemy…"


The following morning Krue waited patiently for Jintana's company, and by sunset she was still alone and drifting into despondency. After fifty push-ups boredom nagged her to a new extremity. Cross legged, blank faced, she faced the large TV. With one press of a button the world's media glared over her slender body. For hours she thumbed away, picking from thousands and thousands of hours of programmed consumer sludge. It was a good service, and she guessed the supplier pirated content from the optical tubes of the globe and zapped them out to a select client base. She navigated her way through Nordic pornos, Ukraine folk-art shows, 1960's 16mm wildlife documentaries, and a galaxy of washy predictable movies about New York Cops. That was fiction. For the blur between fact and fiction there were an infinite array of equally depressing news reports, updates, specials, flashes, and profiles by bland authorities with set hair and dressed in designer suits. "Sri Lanka sends a grateful message to South African United Construction Pty Ltd for donating 20,000 tonnes of cement to cap one of India's eight bombed out Nuclear Power Plants… Pakistan accepts Red Crescent Aid as a ferocious nuclear winter fogs kiddies eyes, bloats stomachs and recedes hairlines on cows, camels, and government leaders. Hawaii is the hive of the United States Naval 7th Fleet, ready to picket the Pacific from Alaska down to Midway, Pearl Harbour, New Zealand and Brisbane. This line of steel will stem the red stain from seeping into more western soil and sea lanes," Krue's thumb pressed and pressed until the screen was shimmering static: the fuzz of the big bang that looked like it was coming around again.

Krue's brow creased. The media was all static, but with the absence of human interaction she needed it. She was sedate, restless, "a Welsh Parliament sits… North Korea's bumper rice harvest… rehabilitation centre for failed suicide bombers opens in Jerusalem. On offer is counselling, poetical political education… Italians in Palermo flock to a vicar's van rear window to marvel at the Virgin Mary's silhouette… Brazil enters the space race for only thirteen minutes… Virus sweeps through Internet… Influenza wipes out eleven-thousand in a remote highland region in Laos… News Flash: Advance Chinese Special Assault Units have taken Darwin and restored order, eliminating Pirate Activities. Similar operations underway: Airborne attack on Townsville in North Queensland. Order will be restored. UN approves by two votes. Thank you and good night." She couldn't sleep that night – but she did. It was a dream of not being able to sleep.

Sleep, Matthews sombrely reflected, oh what joy, unless you're on watch. Sleep was once perfect, Tanya would wriggle under the covers with the tip of her cold nose on his chest and remain there still as a statue until dawn.

Presently, the rising sun's golden lustre illuminated the bush. Over his shoulder, Corrie and Tom were dead to the world. Who would want to wake now, Matthews smiled. It's the most beautiful time when our dreams from the night are fused with reality. Back to Tanya. Her little head would kink up and nuzzle under between his jaw and neck – a perfect ball and socket fitting. Then her hand would glide down his side towards the one part of himself that woke before the rest and now he felt that particular neglected part angrily awaken. Glad to have you back, but when do you get action again, he sighed. He slowly stood, stretched, and wondered which direction to take to go urinate in the beauty of the freshly sunlit bush. His paces were short, quiet, and once in the unexplored bush, he felt strangely uncomfortable. He was in semi-light, before him were tall ancient gum trees, connected by silvery spider webs that had collected more than their fair share of flies and bundled them into slivery little bubbles. Mind the webs, he shivered. He ducked under one, moved to a small clearing, and unbuttoned his fly. Steam rose from the urine. To diminish the sound of piss on hard earth he pointed the stream around the clearing and winced as the soft splattering moved from long grass and dry soil to something hard – like a rock – and leaning forward, the first rays of sunshine collecting on the clearing – saw no rocks, only pale grey bones of jumbled skeletons, a dozen or so. The dead, he kept on peeing, from years ago. How many forgotten years ago? Just the dozen? White or yellow? Black? There was no flesh. There was no memorial. This isn't desecration. God no. He put himself back in his pants. Big breath – don't let them know. Retracing his steps under the web and onwards he felt the chilling calls of the dead freezing his back. Scary stuff. If anything was scary, he shivered, that was it. Though it doesn't now, it'll haunt me. I think I'm going to get out of this alive and if I don't, who can ever say I was never, ever, truly alive?

# The Day of the Dragon

Jintana rolled off Callaghan's chest and lay assembling her thoughts.

Through life she gave it her best and it handed something better back. She was once bright eyed, bought and sold, found and lost, over and over, now in Providence, she had a man. Life was crazy, sometimes it would have been best to be born simple; a bird, a fish, free and wild. But everywhere and everything had become wild for everyone and her man, he wasn't running anywhere. He cuddled up to her and lay with his ear to her chest. Her slender hand stroked his hair. He sat up, straddling her and leant forward embracing her head in his hands. She looked so sweet and lost.

"James," she whispered, "I don't want this moment to end. Never."

"It won't," he enveloped her, then sleepily tighter. "Come wind or rain, it won't, or even a Chinese Invasion. Never."

Her body jolted and her eyes crossed. "What did *you* say?"

"Oh... dream talk... I had some weirdo vision."

"Dream talk." Her eyes congealed to scornful lie detection sensors, "You came home very late – you were at the bank?"

"Yeah..."

"You sleep well?" she demanded, her English failing as she grew suspicious.

"I did," he pressed his cheek to her breast.

"What happened last night? The *Chinese*."

"Oh." He rubbed his face. "The Chinese are up to it now."

"Tell me!"

He didn't know how to begin without sounding besotted.

"What they find wouldn't be of much use," he snickered, "Asia's been tearing at each others' throats like a pack of bitches for years now. The Top End is just as fucked."

"James!" Jintana pleaded.

"Baby... I *think* the Chinese are invading Australia. It's Policing the Pacific or Plundering Plutonium, I don't know. I was always predicting *it*."

"Huh!" she nearly choked.

"It's not that bad..."

She turned to the windows and the clear morning sky. "No... James, will they come here?"

"Couldn't. And if they did we'd have at least a month warning. We are so far away from the action it'll make Peters jealous not to be able to clobber them."

She slid her body away and closed her eyes. "So we have a month then."

"What?" Callaghan protested. "If they come we're running for the hills baby. My gun-toting days are over."

"Where?"

"We could go south,"

"Past Brisbane?"

"If they take me back."

"Outlaw," she lamented then smugly corrected, "If you were not an outlaw *I* would be dead."

"Yeah... Dead. Cute, but dead."

"I don't want to die. I want to live, James. Even now we are not living. You know why?"

He set about tickling her. "You're alive! More than we'll ever be!"

She didn't retaliate with delightful screams. She sullenly pulled the sheet over trapping them in a whitish atmosphere of breath and sweet bodily smell.

"Jintana, you have nothing to fear."

They lay in silence. Seagulls fluttered by their window. Local children chattered on the beach.

"Fear," Jintana muddled.

"Once you know fear... Then there is no fear."

"Then why is Katherine here," Jintana raised her hand to the unit above, "She is not a wanderer."

"She won't be here forever, her days are numbered and she knows it."

"Do you mean she will die?" Jintana venomously protested.

Callaghan's face screwed into a tight consternation, "No. She's just not the type you kill... I think she knows that too."

"Does Peters want her dead?"

He relaxed to a placid honest gaze, "I don't know."

"Can you find out then?" Jintana asked. "I like her. I am her friend."

"Friend?"

"Yes – I have few."

He coiled under the sheet and hidden from the morning shine could barely see her bold eyes. Jintana had a sheer gleam of anger to hide. He'd never felt so aroused in his life. He teased her again, "What about me, aren't I your friend?"

She pinched him. "You know what I mean."

"I'll find out," he comforted her, "I need to know too. Let's not forget, Peters would have her dead unless I stepped in. Fool that I am."


Creton opened the door for Callaghan's brisk entrance. Krue was alone on the balcony, bare feet up, pants rolled up to her shins. She had no warning, only submerged like a brick in the back of her mud-pool mind was the foresight that she would be called. She had been here a few too many days too long and now the mission was getting critical, and like being trapped or imprisoned she had even forgotten how to converse.

Callaghan boisterously sang, "Good morning Major Krue!" as if he were trying to wake a corpse.

She shook her head, momentarily muddled, "Thanks for knocking."

"Politeness is for those who have time to dissect its virtues."

"... So, what?"

"Ooh... Let's see if your tongue is sharp as you look."

"For what?"

"Nothing to do with me, Miss Global Defender. Today's your *big day*."

"Oh." She moved into her bedroom to find her boots.

"I'd take your gun too, Missy, if I were you." Callaghan explained, "We're going to see real wacko' country. Refugees are noted for taking pot-shots from within the woods. They're feisty," and on a determined sarcastic note, "Now you'd think they had time to practice politeness being visitors and all."

"Don't worry, I've seen action. Didn't you, before you came here?" she asked with one arched eyebrow.

"Amazing," Callaghan comforted himself, "Hard woman strikes *again*."

"So who finally got their fucking act together? See if your ego testicles are as big as you talk, Captain Callaghan." She slid her rifle under her bed. "I trust in your company I'll be safe.... The Chinese haven't invaded here, yet."

He grimaced, patiently waiting on a couch for Krue to emerge from the bedroom. She said the 'China' plus 'invade' concept with too much confidence. She marched out dressed in her uniform pants, a tight black T-shirt, and collared shirt loosely draped over her forearm hung below her gnawing disgruntled stare, ready?

Callaghan snapped out of his trance, "Ready for anything, Missy."

Riding in a speedy topless jeep, Krue cherished the break of freedom and rush of air palming off her face. Marcus drove, beside him sat Creton. Behind them were Callaghan and Krue, both unresponsive and subdued. She had nothing to speak directly to Callaghan about, he was lost in his own little world watching as the bush and fields passed by, staring into oblivion with a complex frown chiselled into his face.

Two argus-eyed militia squatted in the back, ready to fire a volley into any suspect figure fatefully lurking by the roadside.

Krue didn't know if it was the strangeness of morning, adjusting to the light blue skies and their contrast to her unit walls, or mix of travelling company, that depressed the need for communication. The bulk of her guarded thoughts were angled to meeting with the fearless leader of this warped paradise. Standing in his shadows is Callaghan, a nutcase. Living at ground level with Providence that was understandable. To meet the leader, the Master of Providence, could be more of an diplomatic minefield/nightmare than with its second in command. To conqueror lands and trade beef for nuclear firepower was a masterstroke only an insane and desperate entrepreneur could deal. To weave the fabric of a civilisation was genius. What a team.

Crossing Sunny Bridge and the scenic Arubai River she suddenly sensed Peters had been hard at work on the most vulnerable approaches to his Empire. Maybe they were heading for Kingston, the money-making heart of Peters's Monopoly Board. Citizen Peters, an admirable evolution from Soldier Peters. In wars the winners are the traders in the peace that settles, even if they were defeated. Marcus slowed the jeep. Krue's senses jumped with the change of gear. She smelt a filthy wisp of ash, lurking on a slight breeze. Then the distinct aroma of rotting meat curled up into her nostrils. She shuddered at the wall of this complex freakish stench; confusion gasping for reason, how can anything smell so revolting?

"You smell that?" she asked Callaghan.

He disdainfully grumbled. "Meant to smell like victory, isn't it? Over population… That's all I smell. Surely someone knew, so many years ago, with all their policies and well meaning interventionism and all that crap, that it'd come to this. We see it, they don't, and-"

Marcus cringed, "*Please!*"

"Oh, you've heard my rants all before? So why don't you tell it to *him*. Stick it to the man, the big man, he's hearing all the world's problems one-to-one!" Callaghan laughed and shut-up as the smell sunk into him again.

Krue observed. The trees at the side of the road were healthy but deep in the shadowed forests were fallen trunks, swooping birds and a few human bodies dead where they'd been shot. Turkey shoot, she figured. Turning to her fellow travellers, none appeared phased, only dully staring northwards monitoring good progress with a vacant glare – not wanting to *think*. Only the two rear guard militia appeared alert, the wind parting their thin black hair, their fingers on their triggers.

Callaghan crankily moaned, "I *will* burn in hell for this, not all of it, just a bit, a little bit…"

Krue spun to the road as it dipped into a basin. The smell hit her like punch. They were driving into an ashen clearing, and covering the road and lesser roads running parallel on either side, was an oblong blending black, grey and brown, slick. She felt nauseous and turned away. They drove past clumps, quickly recognised as remains of the incinerated. Marcus slowed the vehicle and ran his eyes over burnt clothing wrapped around blistered and bloated bits and whole ballooned bodies. The road ahead was a messy obstacle course comprising of too many corpses, thrashed under a long-gone fireball, leaving a pungent mark.

"The road," Callaghan warned him. "Keep ya' eyes on the road."

Marcus dodged carcasses and progressing forward, were larger clumps, little and big, mangled piles. The sight was as overpowering as the smell.

Callaghan held his breath, "Step on it."

Marcus turned back and joked, "You think I like this little Sunday Drive?"

"No… I had no idea this was still here…"

Marcus accelerated and concentrated on carefully navigating the devastation - driving over the lesser of it.

Krue cuffed her mouth by pulling up her shirt and witnessed the mess through seething squinted eyes.

"Incendiary works fine." Marcus noted the burnt clearing and shrivelled crisp skeletons. "Don't leave no crater. God was with them, burning them quickly."

"The adverse effect is… Nowhere to throw all the bodies in to. Haven't cleaned it up." Callaghan snapped and picked up the radio, "*D-Man. D!*"

Krue crucified any remaining scent of morning innocence to purposely study a clump of corpses, not the crows pecking at them, forcing to determine what they were. One large, one medium, two small-medium, one small and crushed. A nuclear family. Hundreds of such tight groups, and around the clearing, bodies with intact torsos and limbs and craniums. Thousands like a packed, rank cemetery, soil and coffins eroded by the blink of time revealing a communal batch of global specimens preserved in a state of putrescent decay. The road was longer and longer, hundreds and hundreds more. Missile strike. Coming down and scooping them up to heaven. This, Krue shuddered, was as close to home as any maniac would want his dirty work. They are convincingly more desperate than the desperate people they devour.

"Why hasn't this been cleared!?" Callaghan shouted into the radio, crouching, shying away from the muck outside the vehicle. "This is a trade route from Kingston to Providence! It's the Grim Reaper's Bowling Alley! Who the hell wants to cart produce along here?"

Peters's unforgiving voice came loud and clear, "Say again, over."

"Yeah mate, could be a bit late. Might get bogged in body parts *Deeeee!* Hard yakka lugging supplies this way huh? Don't see no bulldozers and cleaners. Wasn't this all meant to be cleaned up? What's the story?"

"It's a sign." Peters said. "There could be more. See you soon."

Callaghan placed the handset back, sat forward and cursed the man, "You hear that? Could be more... Maybe he is doing this as a little gesture to Major Krue! What does he know about you? Nothing! Bad Karma at the least, if not, lack of tact and grace. I'm sorry Major, I think he has it in for you."

Krue probed up to the sky for mental distance and found her mind sedated by the tranquillity of the distant ranges, "Maybe he's scared?"

Callaghan sat, humbly stroking his chin, thinking.

Krue had never seen anything like this genocidal massacre. The buck stops here. Who could warrant such a greeting? It wasn't only Romano, Callaghan, Peters and their warlord buddies. The farmers, merchants and civilians of Providence all had something to say about their new found freedom.


At the wharf in Kingston the deal was on. Toro and Romano shook hands and waved to the approaching *Margarita*, sitting surprisingly low in the water. Toro's jaw dropped in horror – she was meant to be ballast. Maybe she is taking water, sitting lower because of the storms. He bit at the knuckle on his middle finger. She may be damaged, and obeying radio silence, may be damaged by the pirates or the storms or the damn coral and why didn't I stick to trading in the Americas! He swayed his head in disbelief and wholesomely smiled at his ship, "Ah so good to see her! How long before I can board, I have not seen my men in weeks!"

Romano made a guess, "Two or three hours then it will dock and one of my men will check. We have to be sure there are no 'extra' passengers,"

"You mean refugees?"

"Anything."

"Excellent!" Toro ecstatically shook the shoulder of his new friend. "I'll go back to my hotel, get my stuff, dress nicely for my crew and be here in two hours.

"Sure... Be here."

"See you soon." Toro strolled off as high as a kite yet deeply and privately burdened by his ship. What is a man to do if his ship takes water and the Captain has not radioed ahead but they have arrived, yes they are here.

Romano slowly walked to the Trading House. The head clerk closed his prized possession and chief reason for employment, a laptop into which he tapped in all the trading data, relayed to Callaghan at the end of the day.

A young runner darted up the front stairs into the main office. "*Margarita* sighted coming from the north!"

"We know." Romano thanked the runner and sent him off on another errand.

"Romano," the clerk called. "What's with the continued radio silence?"

"I don't know, radio in and tell her the spy planes can see her destination now."

"O-K. And she knows when to dock?"

"Straight away."

"How soon?"

"Two or three hours. The owner, Toro, will be there to greet them."

"I tried contacting the ship, Romano... Do they speak English?"

"I don't know. I think so."

"They don't reply," the clerk fumed, "No manners!"

Romano shifted his stance on the creaking boards of the antique Trading House. Sometimes vessels feared radio contact as they came into Kingston. Communications were monitored by foreign agents. Owners of vessels could be held responsible for some of Providence's Crimes.

"It's no problem," Romano told the clerk, "Toro is no saint where he is from. Is this the only one for this week?"

The clerk grunted. "China's actions have stalled traffic all over the Pacific."

"Yeah, they'll be sunk!" Romano reasoned. "This *Margarita* is probably being very cautious. A new customer."

Lieutenant McCallister entered carrying a clipboard and a torch, wiping sweat from his neck, "I just heard,"

"*Margarita* comes soon."

McCallister noted the name. "She's late by a day?"

"Well," Romano shrugged. "The owner – Toro – He's not that smart."

"Met him this morning. Seems O-K. Isn't she ballast?"

"Yes."

"Sitting low. Carrying something, I reckon. I'll be first to inspect."

"Sure," Romano agreed. "I think the deal is O-K, so we'll be loading the coal on with the trucks."

"Excellent. I don't think we should have that ship hanging around here too long – with the shit going on it's a target."


The hut was half-concealed by golden green vines and had through the decades sunk into the forest like a permanent fixture. It could only be found after tediously negotiating a narrow winding dirt track that coiled up and down through ravines, buzzing at sections with swarms of insects. Leading away from the hut, and hidden to the untrained eye by bustling bushes, ran an animal track, snaking three-hundred paces down to a secluded stream. It would be a half-hour before they would arrive, so Peters made for the crystal clear water trickling from the foothills of the Great Dividing Range. Dangling a towel from his forearm, brushing away leaves, and laying it over a log, he inhaled the clean air and naked, tanned lightly from head to toe, smiled to the leaves and branches of the canopy swaying against the bright blue sky.

He stepped into the stream, jerked at the chilled water, then dived forth. Upon surfacing he felt revitalised, the iced tingling eating away the taunt strings of angst. Rat Week had been a scorching success. Surviving refugees fleeing back north with tales of genocide would deter the aspiring new waves of opportune immigrants. They might even scare potential invaders, though the progress of the Chinese Army would be curtailed by its habit of logistical in-efficiency; history had shown they weren't the crusading invading type, commercially yes, but guns, no. They may not even want to venture into the Region of Providence, he decided. Their over-stretched supply lines would snap and dwindle, disintegrating from their cautiously minded career Generals.

However, the Chinese were on the Australian continent, and having taken Darwin, and by last reports some pockets of Far North Queensland and Broome in Western Australia, anything was possible. How far could they push themselves? What was driving their thirst to envelop a quarter of the world with their standard of order? Food for the masses? Minerals to make shitty cars, bicycles, clock radios and the second pair of sneakers for a new bourgeoisie? It wouldn't work. Importing western culture is cheaper than invading it, but like reheating a cheeseburger in a microwave, it'll never taste as *nice*. So ultimately, should it happen, do they come to trade or to come in peace and shoot to kill?

Peters's warm body alone would never heat the chilled stream flushing by his body. He swum in playful circles, stood on his head mid-stream, poking his slithery feet above water like periscopes, the tips of his toes feeling the cool mountain air. Dull grey fishes darted past his eyes. Surfacing, he floated in silence, satisfied. Providence, a quirky religious name given to a town 200 years ago, still living up to it's name. He sunk to the pebbled bottom leaving a soft wake sucking leaves and a thin film of surface dust down with him.

Mrs Benson's last email had drilled right through Smacker. He swivelled in his chair and arranged to meet with Tolken. Smacker worried. Mrs Benson was hammering for results and obviously the powers above her wanted the whole thing cleaned up yesterday, yesteryear, whatever. Smacker printed off the last piece of information he had received.

With the second invasion of Australia yet to show its true nature, surveillance of foreign communications was stepped up. Submarines dotted along the Queensland coast tuned in to sea and land. Smacker read the transcript, scrutinising, imagining…

> *Recorded: 10:05*
> *Location: Providence Region, Occupied Australia.*
> *ASIAN 49: She's a tall, good looker. Beautiful breasts like big juicy mangoes. Watch out.*
> *PETERS: Hmm. You think she knows what happened to Jenkins?*

*ASIAN 49: Maybe. She's says she's an assassin that comes in peace! She's a piece of work too, Jintana says. You gotta' see her. You got to decide it.*

*PETERS: Sure. Callaghan is bringing her up this morning. I'll have a little chat, see what this is about. After that I'll come down and check on the ship coming in. Callaghan and I want the coal shipped.*

*ASIAN 49: I'll see you here.*

*PETERS: O-K*

*ASIAN 49: Let's do a late lunch then.*

*PETERS: Sure. Out.*

Smacker arrived at Tolken's office and saw him reading the same script.

"No one gave her the right to become *friendly* with *targets*."

Tolken paced the window-less dull-grey room, dreaming of their plush temporary offices high in Sydney. "She's been out of contact for too long..."

"Desertion?" Smacker feared with a face that rolled up into itself like smelling shit on his top lip. "She was up for some leave. They break, those psychos. Send 'em up on recon' or insertion and the isolation gets to them. They set themselves free. I feared this would happen."

Tolken disagreed, "I don't think she's the tanning or depressive type. She's alive and well, carrying out our Mission, doing exactly what we wanted."

"But *beyond* us!" Smacker insisted. "She could contact us."

"What can we tell her except our need for results?"

"We could tell her not to eliminate Peters, if the call came."

"It won't," Tolken wrung his hands.

"She's split – she split from her men, she's split from us," Smacker decided. "What else do you think she's doing up there? It's her little holiday, I tell you."

Tolken rested his head in his palm and groaned.

Smacker tapped the transcript on his wrist. "See this is them playing with us – they know we're listening. They know who she is, what she is, why we sent her up, and how to play her. I bet."

"Hold it," Tolken pulled himself together, "Her role is critical to regional stability. She's dependable and expendable yet she's all we've got. We sent her in there because she can be trusted."

The dream of a firestorm burnt in Smacker's cold mind. "Well either way we don't need her dead or alive when we have the power and strategic necessity to raise Providence to the ground and wipe,"

"Smacker!" Tolken snapped. "It's not the town, it's the man. What if she is alive, think about it."

Gripping the transcript, eager to tear it up, he seethed, "You think she is? For how long… She's walking right into their trap."

Tolken questioned his inferior with a sanguine frown.

"Colonel Peters and his merry band of vigilantes. He knows what's happening to her. We've lost her."

"Smacker, *you* have."

Smacker stood silent, rigid, the flames in his eyes flat and calm, "I'm sorry, it's China. They're moving in faster than the Indonesians did. If we took away the value of Providence and Kingston as tactical targets worth invading, the Chinese wouldn't go near him at all. Would they?"

"True," Tolken rebutted, wagging a cautionary finger, "Yet he'd still be out there causing havoc for us."

Smacker settled, a sneaky smile holding him together, "We created him. We destroy him."

"And with Krue, we will. At the end of the day it'll be her call or ours." Tolken's face became deadpan. "We'll deal with it when we get to it."

The forest, north of the massacre, was well patrolled by Peters's Tonkas from wandering refugees and assassins like Krue. The sentries at the turn off from Highway Five viewed her uniform suspiciously. Callaghan assured them with a nod. She executed a neat two finger salute. They sank into their hidden positions, eyeing any additional movement on the road. The jeep hit the dirt track and was enveloped by the forest. Krue stared into the dark tropical depths and felt it staring back.

"Spooky these parts. Hey Marcus? … See, this is Peters's garden." Callaghan clarified dryly, as if he were a tour guide. "The man has a mountain… If it wasn't for him Providence wouldn't be a civilisation. It'd be some pirate pit. But he's brought Christianity without uttering the word Christ. So it's fair and just he's owed a mountain, a forest… It's called Christians Forest. No idea why."

The sun vanished behind dense canopies, its presence left to picking its silky fingers through the leaves. Her eyes reflected the seclusion, her sight unable to intrude beyond the impenetrable fauna lining the winding road, "And it is not Providence's? This garden?"

"Do you see any farmers here?"

"No."

"Great defence though... Commands Highway Five, to the north is Kingston, and south, Providence." He smiled wondrously at the condensed forest. "Isn't it grand? Beautiful?"

"So, all the missiles are up here? Nestled in the dark?"

"Too obvious." Callaghan responded boring and elusive as if she should've known the missiles would be far away, concealed from the prying lenses of satellites and spy planes. "And what kind of conceited, doomed question is that, Major?"

"Inquisitive."

"Yeah," he joked, "We'll be telling you if the big one's are up here. Sure baby. From now on, it's pretty much the man's word up here. Hell I don't even know where he keeps his prized nuke..." He suddenly faced Krue with a sureness and an almost retarded leer, "But why should I care? It's not my finger on the button, is it? Just don't make me die for the privilege I don't have."


He sat in the hut at a hard wood table and humble as a monk peeled an orange, neatly arranging the pieces on a side plate. He cocked an eyebrow upon hearing the whines of the jeep's engine grunting around winding inclines and then the strained torque holding the weight of the vehicle down narrow bends. If there were any unfriendly visitors in the jeep, Peters was sure his Tonkas stationed in the forest outside would have ousted them. He took a kettle from a stove and dropped three honey-lemon teabags in and added chopped ginger. The jeep pulled up outside, right on time. He stepped out of the hut, swinging open the door, brandishing a curious grin.

"Hi there!" he called to Callaghan then saw her: She was striking and stern, her cagey surprise hidden by a warm, comforting and stately countenance. He looked away. The wheels were wet with rich soil, the rims dotted with a fine silt. Scraped on the side of some of the panels were deep red smudges. And by the gaunt pale of the woman's face, he knew what it was from.

"Howdy Partner." Callaghan alighted and embraced Peters. "Taking an extra Sunday eh?"

"Yeah, ha ha."

"Colonel." Marcus greeted, waving with the euphoria of a friendly neighbour.

"G'day Marcus. All is good?"

"Fine thank you."

Peters drew in a deep breath, opening the door for Krue, "And guest of the month – Major Katherine Krue."

She laid her hand in his, "You sound as though you already know me."

"Let's say your reputation precedes you,"

"As I envisaged," she guardedly assured him, beaming with confidence.

Between them was a transfusion; the formal virtues of politeness, and then Peters's enigma ballooned before her. His bold eyes honed on her wide dark pupils, prying into her mind. However, in recoil, Krue could see she was no victim of this emotional tyrant. She was hardened enough to keep a good two feet away from his elementary mystic benevolence. After all, enemies are overtly generous with the approachable offerings of the cream of their personalities.

Peters stepped back to view her in full. She'd come all this way like a disciple, all the way up to the mountain retreat. She had mixed-genes, a few freckles, a lush Caucasian female frame, something he had longed for yet it never registered until now. She was tough. Intelligent. Carried only a pistol, no knife, not even a notebook, and was here to talk. So why hadn't she even tried to assassinate him? And if the Gods had sent her, as the Fang woman professed, what be her real purpose or was it as superfluous as the legend of her birth in the sea of fire?

"I thank you for coming to see me." Peters let his statement hang for her to answer.

It came from Callaghan, "Her directive is to kill you on sight – so she's got to see you, yeah."

Peters singled her out with the tip of his finger, "Into the hut," and turned to Callaghan and Marcus, "This is business as usual."

Krue followed Peters into the hut.

Callaghan and Marcus stood straight faced. After the door closed, they scratched their heads.

"It's like some," Callaghan scoffed, "set-up of military fruit cakes!"

Marcus was frightened. "Yeah. It's-"

"Weird?"

"No, it's... I'm sure he'll fuck her over. Has to. What's her story?"

Callaghan rested his hand on Marcus's shoulder, "Mate, women have two superpowers – the power to be late, and the power to interfere with the present, future and past."

Peters passed his hand over the plate of oranges before seating himself across from Krue. "You can never be too sure when some illness lurking about out there chooses to pull you down into the grave."

"Guess not," she expeditiously contemplated it all and took a piece. It was succulent and juicy. Juice trickled from the tip to the back of her tongue. The grisly misery of the ride and the arduous struggle of the days, the bleakness of confinement and mental madness in the penthouse, plus roaming the wilderness, were momentarily swept away. She wiped her sticky fingers on her thigh and studied the hut.

The ceiling was low, the walls made from planks of dark grey black-butt, a native wood spawned to weather hundreds of years or more. Altogether it was glum balanced by an ancient presence, confined into a tidy square three meters wide. His assemblage of retreat equipment was lined against the back wall: folders of maps, a laptop computer wired to a hi-tech satphone, a handgun, a knapsack, one netted bag full of bananas, oranges, avocado, a pineapple, and a grenade. A sexy Italian hunting rifle hid in a shadowed corner. Peters's elbows were planted firmly on the table, his head fixed in one charismatic broad inviting posture, his pupils piercing up the stairs of Krue's imagination.

She fidgeted her hands between her knees under the table and turned sideways to a fractured window. Thin luminously white cobwebs clung like mist in the corners of the frame, bridging all sides. Outside was the subtropical forest, dense, dark and contrasted by jewel-like patches where the sunlight diffused into a murky-green glow. She had never felt more safer or alone, secluded from the lenses of the spy planes in the atmosphere and satellites in orbit, deep in dangerous inaccessible territory. She felt the tip of her finger compulsively circling the rim of the plate and with her eyes on her finger, if she looked up, he would see, and they would know her ease to be in this predicament. For a few seconds she even thought she didn't have to go through with this, enjoy the serenity you fool, but he had to go through with this, and he had built as much anticipation as she had. The irony struck her.

She relaxed and looked to this man with a firm resolute stare. He sat back, signifying in disguise the need to get down to some serious talking. So she indolently shrugged, smiling fondly up to him. He was an exemplary individual which all the study into his dossier had made little sense.

"You're a soldier," he nodded to her simple uniform.

In her tight t-shirt, she shrugged. Peters's eyes veered to her shoulders, skimming down the sides of her chest and then back up through the middle of her breasts, up to her hair, silky brown, soft and bundled in a rough pony tail at the back, a few stray sandy locks curled and bounced playfully about her ears.

"So are you... And I think you've accomplished more than you were ever required to."

"I do too. I've missed quality compliments. I've craved them from decent and respectable peers – which number very few up here."

She frugally laughed, a congratulation that made Peters straighten as she spoke, "Yes, in isolation the only strength an individual has to offer is itself."

He bluntly added, "And when you're by yourself you can't lie to yourself forever... Pride. Is that what brings you here?"

"No."

He meticulously continued, "I know what you're capable of; military and feminine intentions, so casting those aside, I want to know what we can give to each other – apart from an early death."

Krue played it cool. "Reason... That's my gift."

"Wonderful." He tipped his head back and briefly closed his eyes, springing them open to force a congenial stare, "On that note, some reason: You look very refreshing I must say, considering your journey here." He looked away. She was, he seethed, a moral dilemma. What a weapon. He turned back to her, "You are perhaps the bravest and most intelligent offering of reconciliation I've seen. It took me a while, thanks to a few kind words from those you've met along the way, to understand that."

"Thank you," she smiled. Then the rotten ribcages and pecking crows lapped over her like an emerging nightmare. "To get here, was a contrasting trip though."

"I imagine so,"

"And not an isolated event."

His fleeting disapproval dissolved into a patient explanation, "What you saw is as old as anything in the bible and long before that. It's a primal instinct based on what we can term as excess supply and demand, but not something passé like ethnic cleansing. I'm glad to enlighten your mind to the worst of what Providence provides given this point of world history. Where did your journey to me begin? I want to hear your *story* before you underestimate me."

She stretched her legs under the table. She imagined the black marble boardroom table was before her and the photo of a younger Peters, when he was fresh and lacked a crueller profile. It only took a few seconds thought and mandatory research before her focus was misconstrued. He wasn't like the others and she wasn't a novice either. Tolken and Smacker should have seen the folly in sending her here. But up there with the dark grey harbour bridge spanning a greenish shadow over the sunlit blue harbour and the twinkling ripples catching her eye as she stood to leave them, her arms cradling an abundance of questionable intelligence material, intimate respect did not exist. It was a glimmer hidden in a shadow. Wasn't she the best? Didn't that make her the most susceptible to admire the ruthless and evolve to form a level of professional respect? She quickly moved on to something non-comparative, something he couldn't have seen, or better, something bland that should be in common.

She stated categorically, "Brisbane."

"It's falling, finally."

"Grinding itself to death,"

"*They're* grinding themselves to death. That's why I accepted the offer to go up here. To escape the mince-maker. Next contrast, please."

"The wife of your Chief of Militia, Romano, is a fabulous cook and complicit to murder…" She chuckled, "Captain Callaghan's been under the sun a wee bit too much but I think he likes this predicament, would be lost without it, I presume you too…"

"That much is true. Is that what calls you here then? The prospect of peace and serenity in the mountains? A little holiday from the frontline?"

She smartly continued, "To lavish in the pleasantries of a tyrant? No. Did you ever imagine that you would end up as you are? You've done well Colonel Peters. You are a creator of many great things. I like that."

Peters posthumously honoured himself then soured for her benefit, "And creation goes hand in hand with destruction. Considering the manner in which you have arrived today, forgive me for the mess. There was a surge into my lands. If I had known such a fine lady was dispatched to enlighten me to my necessary evils I certainly would never have done such an act. At the time, when you have the power, it pays to flex it, because you bloody well have to regardless of the consequences. They would've taught you that, Major?"

"*I* wonder if you've earnt that power. We've been wondering that. At what point will your power destroy yourself and many more and is it worth it? That's why I'm here."

In long winding swabs he traced his forefinger around her aura, "Such is reason, from someone brandishing intelligence and wit, to dissect a good man as he has done to himself countless times before, your gorgeous and generous smile reinforces my own feelings,"

Krue's front teeth clinked as a constrained, over-acted look of disgust flushed over her. "You can't hold out like some gentry of the criminal race or a cult warlord."

"No shit," Peters grimaced. "Did you think you could really kill me?"

"Yes and *noooo*," she whistled down to the table and straightened her back to sit at full height, "And if you must know, it has come across my mind that maybe I should have."

"But now you're a Diplomat," Peters challenged the myth, "Or some kind of Army Reconciliation Messenger? I mean, you're too darling to suicide or just rub salt in old wounds."

"Maybe this *is* my suicide mission."

Peters was muddled, or appearing to be. "Well, you're qualified for both but you've failed. I know exactly where I stand and for what... You can't change my mind. But what are you? They've sent you up north into this filthy wreck of a land to bring the one white fella with his head out of the sand back to ground. With old-fashioned reason! What a ploy! You're a messenger! I don't shoot pretty messengers."

Krue tilted her head back beaming with pride then rocked forward, head lowered, "I'm sorry Colonel Peters, the only message I know is the statement: I'm your assassin."

The duo trotted down the path to seclusion, lay back, and switched their radio off. Callaghan dipped his toes into the stream. Marcus lazed, head back to the Sunday sky seen through the canopy, dreaming with his arm as a pillow.

He asked, sincerely and innocently, "And Jintana's the one?"

"Absolutely," Callaghan admitted. "I'm over chasing the rabbits." He patted his stomach. "Does a great grilled kangaroo. Far out man, wait until it happens to you."

Marcus postulated, "I have to see it to believe it... Adoration is the key. Money and gifts don't buy that... And did you see the Colonel? Haven't seen the man so like, Ah! – alert and aroused."

"Flirting *fucker*." Callaghan carefully hinted. "Maybe he's got something for this Major. She's basically a tuff cow. Like he's cool, and it's shallow, treat 'em mean keep 'em keen. He's pulled some weird shit for her."

"Like what?"

"Like keeping her alive. I argued to keep her around – he would've easily seen her six feet under."

"So, you think she's good for him."

"She's good for us," Callaghan analysed it all, relieved to have admitted it.

"Why?"

"Oh you know: The Shit."

Marcus watched a flight of birds taking to the sky from a gully further up the mountain and disappearing into the north eastern horizon, somewhat hazier than he remembered. "I know. Peters definitely needs a new tangent. It's been growing on him."

Callaghan faced up to the sky, "Of course he's out there a bit, wouldn't you be? He's got the finger on the pulse. But I don't know about this 'recluse' shit. Interaction, keeping the lines of communication open – it's all necessary otherwise we turn into cannibalistic monkeys – especially in these parts – this fucked up world. So I'm happy he's chatting to her – she's the first intelligent signal we've seen from Free Australia."

"A bit of sanity, huh."

"Call it that. At a cost. Ol' Peters needs some of that from an outsider. He could be scared of death. Thinks his number's up." Callaghan sniffed the clean air. "Why else would you hide up here?"

"Well he hasn't alone in being scared. I hit the beach thinking I was dead, and here we are..." Marcus became subliminally poetic for a tech-head. "I get confused in my sleep that when I'm dozing, having bizarre dreams, that that's my old life... And what we're living now runs like another dream. I wake up sweating. I'm reborn." He laughed at the absurdity. "Born again in an illegitimate nation!"

"Why you worrying then, Marcus?" Callaghan playfully thumped his friend, "Didn't you know, you don't get out of life alive?"

"Oh it's not about that... That's old news. Now its what's about to happen." Marcus stretched himself to the sunlight and yawned, "You see it jacked in to the information highways. Me an' Eric hack and scrounge for info'."

"Maybe you're too wired?"

"That's a constant condition, but we've picked up heavy shit."

"Explain,"

"The Chinese have been selling the US dollar and the Euro – like they don't need it. It's scary. Financial meltdown in the making. Shit like that can lead to global depressions,"

Callaghan snickered at the smoke and mirrors. "Which can only be undone by something momentous like a war – a war that re-shapes the globe. The Chinese do have the tentacles and they are strangling the rest of Asia with their causes, anti-pirates I don't know, but I guess if it cleans and binds the world together again, free trade will bring peace. So who knows where it can lead. We can't discount the benefits because it looks like complicated mega-death deals. At the heart of it we're ready to wheel and deal, aren't we?"

"Sure," Marcus agreed.

"The Chinese don't make a show of it, though. They don't invade a country out of their own borders. They just trade their way in. Maybe they'll do a bit of policing but it's because they have to, and if they don't, the trade is fucked and then it's renegades everywhere. For the great cause and accumulation of wealth the Chinks rely on the ambition of their own people to go somewhere, settle, reap rewards, send the kitty back home. Much nicer than a lot of other nations."

"What are you saying?"

"China's filling the power vacuum, giving order we hope, in a void of plunder. Every half millennium they step in to the world's affairs." Callaghan felt the joy of the scenic view dissipate as a greater fear grew in his heart, "And we are forgetting that in this situation," and his hand passed between them like a marauding shark fin, "We must play legitimate if we wish to survive."

"Legitimate? But we're a drop in the ocean!"

"Not," Callaghan winked to the hut up the trail, "According to her."

"You're blindly out to kill me, right?"

"Assassination is my first directive, that's what it boils down to."

"So you came to talk some sense into me. What girlish trait possessed you to do that?"

"Exactly that. You've achieved much, given your predicament... So I decided that as you were beyond the normal means of, how do you want me to say it?"

"Relating?"

"No, god no... Neutralising."

"I was to be neutralised. I like that. It's good. Go on."

"I was chosen because I have experience in dealing with varying *situations*. I chose my way as it's how I accomplish things. I respect you, perhaps too much," she cast hurting eyes, "And relate to your isolated predicament. I'm proud of what you've built here. You are the creator and destroyer, yes, but someone who also stood up in a time when many fall back."

"And now a messenger disguised as an assassin to compliment and consult me on my future sits at my table."

"I had to change myself to get through to you," she urged.

"But what do you do now?"

"Reason! Call it character assassination!"

He frowned. The thoughts were in a cloud above his head and when he looked there for an answer he only found nastier questions bearing down on him. "Who do I owe reason to? What's this reason I suddenly have to grapple with?"

Krue stammered, "You don't get it – you are not over the edge. You're only doing your duty. You can't go on like a dictator, it may have got you here but it won't take you any further!"

Peters agreed. "All this advice from an outsider? Well, why don't *you* keep the gates closed from the north?"

"Why don't you go south, back to my side?"

His head fell forward and was caught by his palm then quickly pulled up again, "You know what they'd do… I'm not one of *you* anymore – same for Callaghan – that's why he's here too."

She pressed on, "And what makes you think the world hates you so much it can't have you back?"

"I don't want it back! This is my world here!"

"So you have to preserve your world," she proposed, "And apart from protecting your land from over-population, do you really have to threaten the rest of the world with weapons of mass destruction?"

"The statement is this: I for one will not let this patch of earth be trampled over ever again by some conquesting nation!"

"So Providence is behind you?"

"I'm a dictator," Peters ruefully explained, "That's all there is to it."

"Surrender your most dangerous weapon, that's the base line."

"But it keeps the peace."

"Has it? You've never threatened with it and it brings me here to do you in. Does it do your cause more harm than good?"

Peters sat dumbfounded at her simplicity. Then the intense fixation washed over him as easily as he had pushed in the button and with a simple sigh to the sky neutralised the masses. The demonic indulgence, his persecuting laugh, came out as bold as brass. "This is incredible. You come up here full of praise and expect me to throw away the only mechanism I have for absolute defence in the name of, what exactly is it? Global fucking harmony? Do you think I care? We are not from the same world Katherine but now you're here, Welcome! There is no way out! So now I've met someone who wants real peace but at my expense! So fuck me – No way! What do we do now?"

"Reason, that's all you have to do," Krue urged.

"Fucking reason," he lamented, "You think… Do you know what I am?"

She sat silently waiting out his banter, unsure where it would lead.

"I create order and the side-effect of that gracious act is not the right or will, but the practical necessity to have to destroy! So after thinking with my eyes wide open and then *waking up* here of all places and forging an existence with some of the most vicious and savage maniacs in the world you want me to give up my protection so," and he paused in surreal disbelief, systematically levelling the cruel scorn in his mind onto her, "So the world can invade me! Are you serious? Have you actually observed what goes on here, how graveyards sprout the finest and richest of flowers! And now I see you, it's not your accident to be here is it? It's someone's order, perhaps their mistake – that's your fate! Live it! You've been sent up here to die with the rest! Is that why you came?"

Krue felt the chill. Early stages was the Grim Reaper's frail hand passing overhead with the ease of a casual wave that zapped the warmth from the soul. She'd felt it twice before, once in the desert and nearly dead from dehydration, the other when they had raped and bound her ready for execution until some thug decided it be better to have his way with her again, but alive rather than a cooling corpse. In both circumstances she was rescued and narrowly escaped heaven or hell or re-incarnation or zero. Here, nervously peering out the window to avoid the now demonic glare in Peters's unsettled head, she saw only the murky depths of an impenetrable forest, another alien environment to die in.

She compulsively pinioned the question back to him. "Regardless of what happens to me, what in the world can you do now to make your little world a better place?"

The second benefit of climbing the tallest of gum trees at the peak of a pocket of rough ground surrounded by marches and mangled shrub was escape from mosquitoes. The dangerous element was that should contact be made, the man in the tree was easy pickings. Tom volunteered, being shortest, most irate at mosquitoes, and additionally because Corrie and Matthews had started, under the pressure of the mission, to be mates and he felt they should build on this without his friendly guiding hand.

It took him an hour to climb the tree unseen though there was a relatively small chance any of the militia were out there. On the odd chance they were, and they were actively observing the trunks of gum trees for short white men covered in hessian and twigs and branches and dried silty mud, Tom could be shot well before he could defend himself. After he had layered his limbs and camouflage over the contours of forked branches and under the shade of the thin leaves he made concentrated sweeps of the approaches to his pocket of land. At night it would be an ideal camp away from the marshes and the mosquitoes, the annoying pests a special genetic version from the Arubai River. He scanned for objects of interest. The Great Dividing range, and in particular Jacinda Mountain, though beautiful, was too far too warrant a comprehensive study. Closer, and more important, was Sunny Bridge. He could easily plot where it should be to the north west but could see neither onto the bridge or the road. Now the object of this little tree-climbing expedition was nonviable he rested. He ate a strawberry energy bar and sipped his chemically purified water. The hand radio clicked.

"Yeah?"

Matthews reminded, "The Port, Kingston."

"Sure." Tom turned his hand radio off. A message came through that morning from Canberra asking them to 'pro-actively' investigate the cargo on an incoming ship to the Port of Kingston. As if, Matthews agreed with his two Privates, they were going to march north when Krue was missing and their confidence crumbling. So Tom twisted on the branch, facing the north east, and trained his binoculars in the direction of the Port of Kingston. After minutes of excruciating inspection he turned his hand radio back on.

"Why'd you do that?" Matthews softly scorned.

"What?"

"Turn it off?"

Tom said genuinely, "Didn't want you to annoy me."

"Fucker... Find it?"

"Fuck'n'oath. Must've taken a few hits. The Port is *smoking*. Burning up like Delhi. It's fucking cooking!"

"What, exactly?"

"Buildings'n'shit."

"What's on fire, can you see?"

Tom scanned again. There was the miniature little port and the twinkling fires between the little rows of warehouses dwarfing little buildings and the huge ship berthed in the small hazed harbour. He could see the bridge, a section of the bow peaking from between two structures. Smoke blew over again, grey voluminous clouds that originated from Kingston. This is amazing, he winced. Is the heat of the day playing tricks on my eyes? He wiped his eyes, shut them restfully and called into the hand radio.

"Give us another minute, right?"

"… Sure."


Peters begrudgingly listened to Krue.

"Declare yourself neutral."

"This *is* a neutral land. It's every man for himself. In effect, every warlord is neutral around here."

"What about a free trade region?"

"I am," Peters frustratingly replied. "All neighbouring warlords are free traders by default. You don't see us throwing up tariffs."

"I don't understand," Krue held her finger tips to her temple, "You have established a new, unrecognised, fair country based on free trade and neutrality, bar acts of genocide,"

"Correction. First, define genocide and self defence. These acts of self-preservation I am not alone in committing. I and participating Warlords, a guild if you call it, act the same as any other instrumental arm of the United Nations but our role is waste management,"

Krue shuddered, "Whatever."

"I really don't understand why you're here. I don't know why so many want me dead. I'm minding my own business."

She stared at him deadpan, "With a nuclear missile hidden away as bargaining power, I don't think you're minding your own business. You've stepped up the ladder into a whole new game of self-determination and you have to prove yourself without it to become legitimate."

"Wrong; you're preaching old-world geopolitical rules. I don't flex my nuclear muscle and oppress. I don't threaten with it unless in defence. I bought it because the price was cheap, I had zilch currency and they were hungry and I had beef," he snaked his hands together, "Deal! That's how the world works! It came to me!"

"So why not sell the nuke back but into good hands?"

"Then I'm vulnerable." Peters frantically gestured to Krue, "What are you trying to win me over for? Deprive me of my weapons in the name of Insurance for World Peace? It's a ruse. That's it – play the global emotional hand. Who are you to raise me to greater stakes yet tie me down at the first step?"

"At stake is regional stability."

"I read my *Asia-Pacific War Zone*," Peters joked, "On the chopping board is the lean new juicy world. It's so delicious to the many mighty powers out there roaming the Pacific and Indian Oceans! The war is far from over and I can't stand back and watch. I have to kick it into place *my* way. I'm a player in this mess! I compliment Australian regional security. They know that!"

Krue was adamant, forceful, and relentless; "Your actions could trigger a domino effect. One little nuclear weapon leads to another. You are responsible for too much and no one likes it. Don't forget that you are white. Your sole action would be seen as an act of the white race."

"No, that's old-school righteousness. What you are you saying is, per head of capita, the people of Providence don't deserve nuclear weapons?"

That jarred her. "*Yes*."

"This is a place of nouveau freedom. It wasn't voted on, I conquered them, they took me in. I'm in control. They love it."

Krue said, "No one's trying to take that away. And my honest opinion is your determined path of defiance for nothing more than a unified rabble – it could be any rabble anywhere and it'd be the same righteous you leading them – is destined for the trash heap."

"Aren't you catty!" Peters proudly interjected. "Trust me Katherine, there's only a few players I have to fear … The Yanks are piss-weak. They'll probably try and line me up as a puppet once they get their shit together."

"And China?" Krue asked, casually.

"Whoa now there's a question in a question! Without them there could be peace around here. The latest refugees are fleeing them, I know it, so now it's my problem. Their exporting their problem to me. Oldest trick in the book. And I clean up the mess so that the rest of Australia doesn't have to."

"If China steps in, what are you going to do about it?"

He comically applauded her. "Nothing. I'll be playing the China card real cool... I'm so far south and how isolated do you think the Chinese will be if they get here? They're in a difficult situation even at their triumphant best!"

"Regardless of their predicament, as a rural leader your directive is to protect your lands. If it came to attack from a foreign power don't attack the rest of the world for the benefit of petty Providence. You're responsible for more than your little enclave. Maybe you should set a standard?"

Peters prattled, "That is such an altruistic thing to say it makes me sick."

"It's something to consider, especially to your people. They'll be the first to suffer."

"But how unique are my people, and really, how valuable? We have a history a year and a bit old. Austria, a thousand years old – and they spurned just about everything from symphonies to fascism. We can be *that*."

"But right now you understand how valueless your people are, and you want to defend them? You're betting on a culture of substance to rise from this muck? What makes you think that even you'll survive this new age of disorder – *intact*."

"Disorder *is* order." Peters smiled, quite insanely. "Look what exists here, the soil beneath your feet, smack bang in the middle of a continental black hole. It's a sold out block. The World Bank can't touch it. Australia abandoned it. Tell your brass bosses that I'm looking straight ahead carving an entirely new existence and I have the freedom, granted to me being in the latest *terra nullus* to pop up out of war – and this is true war because war *is* change; history and borders and peoples – and on that note what I earn from the scrap heap, I should keep."

"Did you really earn it? Did your people earn it," Krue asked, "These lands?"

"You think surviving miraculous acts is something you don't learn from?"

"No."

"I am what I am," Peters explained, "And I'm doing what I feel someone should do. Stand up, cement the dam on your doorstep and carry on as a free soul. Now, you have to understand that."

"I do."

"Do you forgive me for hanging myself to that fate?"

"No."

"Thank you." Peters sighed relief.

"So be realistic, what chances do you have?" She could tell by his resolute snared grin, it wasn't working.

She wasn't working.

She would have to kill him.

# Enter, Two Stars Ghan

Out of rolling tunnels of black and grey smoke coiling over the reverberating wooden wharves where the *Margarita* had docked, swarmed platoons, rapidly spreading into streets, splitting into adjoining streets and paths so that in a matter of minutes, Kingston was secured. The assault was a blur of bobbing helmets, discharging rifles, and bayonets cutting into the smoke filled streets. Those who dared resist were left in the gutter.

Enter, heels planted firmly on the wharf, Two Stars Ghan. His polished black knee-high boots were lined with brass zippers. His olive green trousers were rolled up to mid-shin, decorated with double golden silk-stitched seams, enhanced by a swipe of gun-oil staining the outer thighs like a horse rider's whip-lash. A lacquered black leather belt carried a golden embroidery decorated pistol case. His tunic was tinted with a rose dye, conjuring the sense that he was nasty as he was holy. The gold and silver five star medals glinting from his right breast did not detract from his countenance of suppressed aggression, parallel in spirit to the stares of stone archers sealed in their tombs for a thousand years of darkness.

His trimmed, thin, black goatee, jutted out and curled under his prominent chin, groomed and clipped at the end by a small jade clip. His thin and sleek moustache curled along the contours of his sleek angular lips. A finger thick lock of braided, ivory black hair curled from the rear of his otherwise smoothly shaved cranium.

Kingston burnt. For Two Stars General Ghan, life and destiny were periodically unclear but now with two-thousand troops, thirty-eight tanks and his Primary Target taken within bone-crushing minutes, Zen was awfully clear.

For the occasion he adopted a smug and correct stance. His firm hand moved from the hip and levelled flat to the rickety wharf at his feet. He knelt and with his other hand took from his thigh pocket a tongue-red notebook embodied with a cubist Dragon hissing puffs of flame and bearing down a fork on unseen prey. From his breast pocket came a polished metal pen cast from melted Tibetan Monastery Bells. *Let their spirit live in the words*, he wrote on the first page.

Colonel Chiang watched with envy at the troops still filing out of the ship and charging into the unknown, and with adulation to his master, "Your memoirs?"

"No." Ghan sniffed the acrid smoke, "History."

"Yes, history!"

"Before those who were not here paint our history in their favour to their taste, I shall write my own."

Behind them, their mother vessel *Margarita,* was berthed. It had been a daring and mischievous mission utilising much more than Zhing's cunning and tactical brilliance. The ship was captured rounding Vanuatu by a Commando Team from a submarine. The captured crew from Chile, more mercenaries than seamen, interrogated, were promised a ticket home, then once their loose tongues had betrayed their master's plan, were promptly fed to the feisty sharks of the Coral Sea. The ship was steered north. Ghan's Brigade and three naval ships had already broken from the fleet, charged south at full steam, and intercepted the *Margarita.* Overnight they performed a logistical feat: The transfer of 2000 men, and thirty-eight tanks, at sea! They then continued the ship's journey, escorted by one frigate for a day, and obeying radio silence, flying the flag of a scoundrel Cross-Pacific Trader, sailed straight into Kingston. The oldest trick in the book!

Once the wharves were secured, were the cargo doors lowered and the bulk of the troops and tanks swarmed the dock. General Zhing's last message was still ringing in their ears: *Go Forth for Prosperity. Liberate the Bandit Lands. Cleanse the Western World of its impurities. Return and Retire!*

Ghan could not help feeling a bit smug, and then some. And, it felt good to be back. He knew firsthand of the gold that lay in reefs under and above ground. His fondest memories of Australia was the Gold Coast. Golden sand for miles. Internationalist tourist mecca. He visited several times on business, studying the working habits of a high-tech industrialised country. He travelled to Sydney often and marvelled at a culture so different to his own, the air so clean, immaculate freeways, gay city streets, tidy and classy women, towering glassy buildings. He also added to the economy, (something he couldn't tell the Party or the wife about) the most sexually exhilarating moments of his life were in numerous high-rise apartments in control of (fake) tanned, (shock and very fake) blondes, sometimes two (junkies) at a time. Prior to his golden experiences was the near forgotten history of his great-great-great-grandfather and his cousins who had come to the tip of Queensland in the late 1860's and returned with many ounces of gold yet more heavier stories of hardship. The Chinese were easy prey at the hands of bigoted whites and the ferocious spear-throwing black men, who allegedly preferred the taste of yellow flesh to white. That was how one of his great-great-great-grandfather's cousins remained here, here! He stamped his foot on the dock. He was back.

But of these fond and nostalgic memories he forged himself a mask of pure ferociousness. Kingston was his and with very few Brigade casualties! His superiors radioed the Tri-Victory: two brigades had captured Townsville and Cairns many hundreds of kilometres to the north. Ghan stroked his goatee knowing that distance in this country need never be a burden. The isolation worked as a conduit. For the first time in his life, or any of the lives of his troops, they were uncoupled from the physical links of their Superiors. Now free to use the elements in the wilderness to their advantage, a surge of independence invigorated him from head to toe. This is the furthermost southern advancement of the Chinese Empire in all of history! He tapped at his satphone a special official message for General Zhing:

> To: Supreme Commander, General Zhing,
> The Port of Kingston on the eastern coast of
> Australia is now occupied by the Chinese 177
> Brigade. History begins with small
> enterprises.
> General Ghan.

"Read this," he showed the message to Chiang.

"Very good. Send it now!"

Then Two Stars Ghan stood firm and brassy, hands on hips, three-quarter profiled to the sun as the smoke cleared for two military correspondents, kneeling on the wharf, sizing up the hero in their viewfinders. Within minutes the images would be zapped to Beijing. Fresh plumes of black smoke running to the skies formed an excellent backdrop for his commanding statuesque pose, soon to transferred to slides that would be mounted on billboards around the country, beside portraits of Mao Tzu Dong, Deng Xio Phing, and General Zhing. Ghan wished he could live this moment for the rest of his life, but he blinked, life is just that – blink and you miss it.

Yet this life had been waiting for him, for he had forged it. His appallingly bleak childhood comprised of standing on the cold cement floor in the middle of a production line, slaving under fluorescent lights six days a week, growing from boy to man, watching the coiled scrapings of metal falling to the floor from squeaking grease-deprived lathes, or prodding the cooling pinkish plastic on phallic moulds in the state-run vibrator factory. Who knew where these perverse products went to – but someone had the money to pay for them. Such beginnings are rewarded with a trade from which to move up with. In later years he became Foreman of a Reebok sweatshop which enabled him to study at night and hence improve his offerings to the world. Next posting was manager of an imitation brand of fluffy toys, then with the help of his new wife's political connections, he managed a team of information technology specialists to develop an anti-Internet ionising cannon. After tasting some success against capitalist merchant banks he found that the bubbles in his champagne would never be as radiant as those rising in the West. And if he couldn't have the West, what good was it? He about turned from the lunacy of imitation and the deconstruction of Western trends and technology and offered himself to the army as a newly emerging climate of *real* conquest swept his country. After sinking knee deep in the mud, the years of arduous training with the Army's finest, and biding time in Party meetings, moments when it all seemed a waste, those times away from the wife and lone daughter, now it was all worth it: To make history.

The ringing telephone obliterated her afternoon nap. Jintana looked to its incessant buzzing, filing her scattered thoughts away, as she probed to the nature of the call with a tired, "Hello?"

Jemmy was urgent and insipid, "Come to the bank, quickly."

"What?"

"The bank! Come!" And he hung-up.

It was Sunday, usually few were at the bank except smart technical-militia manning the computers. She hurried, bewildering herself: Callaghan is in trouble, Jemmy has caught him with that woman... Or Rats have murdered her lover! No! No! No! She looked a fright running all the way there, right up the sandstone stairs and through the glass doors, "Tell me! Tell me!" she pleaded to Jemmy, standing by Eric at his computer screens and radios.

Eric sat entranced at the information assembling on his screen from news websites; headlines, sound bites and videos drew him closer until he was speechless, the whole picture before him, yet unable to describe it

"Cairns, Townsville." Jemmy seethed from Callaghan's office, stabbing his trigger finger at a map of Queensland. "*They* said it could never happen!" The venom seeped from his skin. "*Very* bad."

"What?"

Jemmy stepped out to confront her, "And Kingston."

"Kingston?"

He marched out to Eric and cursed the world map on the wall by the radios. "No land has been spared. They're here now. *My* Kingston!"

"China?" Jintana cried.

Jemmy threw his hands into the air. "They'd been threatening for years!"

"What's Peters doing?"

"He doesn't know." Jemmy placed a stern hand on her shoulder, "You know what this means? We swim or sink…"

She imagined riding the wave of anarchy, swept with the tides again.

"We have to move…"

"Yeah, and fast!" Eric, faithful to the Providence core, shrieked.

Jintana skipped to Eric's side, "Call Peters… Call James! China has come!"

"Peters's radio is off," Eric changed frequency, his voice frail, calling into a sea of static, "J-C, this is Providence."

"Where are they?" Jintana shrieked, "Not up there? They can't! Major Krue, what has she done!"

"Nothing!" Jemmy gripped her wrist, pulling her limb down, plugging her into the floor. "They're in Christian's Forest… Romano, he's in Kingston. No word from anyone. The Chinese could be everywhere…" He pulled her into his venomous lecherous grip, "We don't have time, Jintana. You now what this means?"

The teenage Burmese prostitute was nicknamed Anastasia. She did not know what the name meant, nor how it came to be tattooed in English on her upper back, over a single red rose, after her mad affair with a lucky-faced, shipwrecked New Zealand Merchant Seamen who washed up into Kingston, and made it out again. Stranger things do happen. She slipped her US$200 into a clear plastic sealed bag with other currencies. With the help of a smudge of Vaseline she then slid her savings up her vagina, suspicious of Mr Toro, straightening a silvery tie to himself at the full-length cracked mirror. She tucked in her shirt, shaking at three fresh bullet holes in the wall sprinkling dust to the carpet each time an explosion rattled the town outside. Out the window on Gallipoli Street, smart marching Chinese troops rounded up the surviving locals of Kingston; bashed pirates, compliant mercenaries, cursing whores and begging civilians.

Toro sweated profusely, yet appeared profoundly ignorant of the rifle shots escalating from the outskirts of the Port. The Trading

House across the street, where he had been yesterday to discuss deals, crumbled as flames licked the grenade-blasted foundations. The clerk lay star-fished in the front yard, his steel-rimmed glasses slanted across his jilted face, a machete skewed through the laptop on his torso and into his heart. Toro placed a mobile phone strategically on his belt. A grenade blast, followed by a more serious secondary explosions from a neighbouring warehouse, rattled window panes. He brushed falling dust off his peach shirt. He polished his deck shoes on his expensive navy blue trousers. He heard tanks firing cannons again. They were chasing shots. Invading armies have to cease fire some time.

"*Safe* those rice queens said... Assholes... Liars everywhere... But it's just a war zone, it is the world us usual but drunk on everything," Toro calmed his nerves, sizing himself up in the mirror, "See – Hey girl! First time for everything. Please relax... Don't you worry a thing. I've seen it all before."

Anastasia swayed her head. She dressed conservatively for her profession, more like a beauty-queen prancing as a factory worker; dull matching pants and tunic, her hair refreshingly layered on her shoulders. She said something incomprehensible and thought of jumping on the bed, jumping up through a manhole into the roof and hiding in the rafters, but they had set fire to other hotels and brothels, why would this one be spared?

Toro measured himself in the mirror again, side profile. "You don't speak Chinese do you? What type of country has two languages anyway. Cantonese, Mandarin? No Spanish, eh. You think they smoke dope? Soldiers smoke dope? Lots of dope and cocaine where I come from. Every culture has its vice." His smile was pinched in place. "Maybe cocaine is better than opium. I give them the *taste* test."

She listened to screams outside, a woman crying in pain next to her spilt cart of dried meats. A tank roared past. An execution squad did their business. A body flopped against a wall and to the pavement.

"Girl! We will deal them something! Every man wants something another man has, you should know that,"

Anastasia made no reply. Approaching footsteps in the hallway made her deathly still.

"Ah my dear, Kingston has charm. The Chinese will see that,"

Anastasia saw through the cracked window; smoke hovered above the streets and between the warehouses, before the bow of the ship, blanketing the sun. She held herself in her arms, "I knew this town was *bad!* I hide!"

Toro palmed his hair back and watched it bounce up again. He raised his eyebrows. "From my years of surviving dictators I tell you girl, hiding won't last you long. I show you how *we* survive. Stick with me and you'll be farting through silk."

Anastasia scorned, "Please, let me hide!"

Toro huffed, "There is no hiding. What a screw-up, I can not believe it! I walk right into a war zone! What fucking *luck*."

"I'm hiding,"

Big rubber boots on little brown feet busted down the door. Three young troops faltered at the entrance, studying the bedroom. They edged in, two cornering Anastasia with testosterone fuelled glares while one senior sniffed out Toro. Toro pointed to his steel suitcase on the bed. The soldier warily opened it, western documents: typed lists and timetables, crude maps and photocopied graphs. Toro waited, smiling impatiently, staring at the senior soldier.

Gallipoli Street ran to the wharf, and closer to the sea, the more prominent buildings stood; red bricked cargo warehouses and a pub. Walls were lined with propaganda posters of Peters and his symbolic three-quarter stately profile. Immediately troops set forth joyfully tearing them down and spitting on the image. Paper burned, ashes flaked and wafted up to the smoky grey sky. Toro and Anastasia were marched towards the wharf against the grain of the captured populace treading the road out of Kingston, heads bowed under the gaze of trigger-happy troops.

Chiang called them over.

"Help me!" Toro embarrassingly outstretched his steel briefcase to the prominent military officer.

"You speak English?" Chiang asked falteringly.

"Yes! English? Spanish? Portuguese? English!"

"Good." Chiang tilted his jaw up, "What is your crime?"

"I... I am a *good* man!" Toro heaved his chest. "Deal! I make the deals here!" He stomped his foot on the pavement. "No fires! Please! You destroy good supplies!"

"Come!" Chiang spun towards the wharf, "Rank? Position?"

Toro followed at his side, peppering his details to Chiang's cold shoulder. "Investor. *Billionaire!*" He held his mobile phone out. "Ring my embassy, they're not at War! Chile, peace! I'm a major trader from South America!"

Chiang apparently agreed and categorically stated, "China is not at war with any country in South America!"

"Yes!" Toro rejoiced and pressing buttons, his phone beeped thrice. "China," he laughed, "*We* didn't expect your presence for weeks… How successful of you!"

Two soldiers escorted Anastasia from behind.

"My secretary… Knows the parts." Toro pointed from her to the individual warehouses and stepping around a corner onto the wharf, delved into pragmatic boasting, "I trade everything an army needs. Weapons… Medical supplies… Coal! Tinned food." He tugged at Chiang's sleeve. "Maybe uranium, Australia is open to the global market now. Think of the opportunity! Think of your generals and presidents will praise you!" Toro turned to a more severe and commanding man. "Hi, I'm Toro!"

Ghan's look of surprise swung from the bandit and narrowed to Chiang prompting an explanation. Toro shut up and artfully diverted his attention elsewhere: A thin grey haze hung over the *Margarita* docked at the wharf, flying the Chinese Flag, manned by Chinese troops, its sharp bow right out of the water cutting the smoky haze in two. It was early by a half-hour! They hadn't told him! It was…

"Oh fuck! You mother-fuckers stole my *Margarita!*" Toro swore under his breath, mortified, and wobbled to the edge of the wharf to the hull. He had had it painted before leaving to impress new clients. Rigidly pointing to the ship's bridge he cursed to Chiang, "I have protection under many, many international treaties, that's my ship!"

Ghan sniffed pure loathing down the back of his throat and briefly noted something in his notebook.

Toro wiped a tear for his *Margarita*, then screamed, "Give me my ship!"

Ghan pocketed his notebook and rested a hand on his pistol holster.

"Forgive!" Toro shrieked to Chiang. "Translate for me! I help you! See, I trade with you already!" And pointing from his old ship to his old body, "You owe me money for that! Then we trade again!"

"*What is he saying?*" Ghan asked Chiang.

"What are you saying?" Chiang shot in English to Toro.

"*I* deal! Huge trader! Please let me help you! Food! Minerals! Tractors! Military Supplies! Bullets and bandages!"

Chiang to Ghan in Chinese, "*A corrupt capitalist begs like a crypto-Communist peasant.*"

"*He is really a merchant?*"

Chiang frowned, "*He says he can trade many things.*"

*"He would sell us the rope to hang him with."* Ghan reached for his imitation Colt-45, re-engineered, named in memory of one slick holy leader: The DengXioPing97. A monster bullet in the chamber spied down the barrel to Toro shielding himself with his shiny steel suitcase. Discharge. The suitcase was punctured in then popped out like a reverberating drum beat. A lead tip struck into the sternum of Toro. Winded and gasping, he fell backwards, dropped his steel suitcase and landed with a thump at the edge of the wharf. Their boot kicks sent him over. He splashed into the warm lapping waters of the Coral Sea. Splashing and choking, he saw his suitcase above, opened up, tossed down in pursuit. It landed and quickly took water. Paper, documents, business cards, old worthless notes and pens settled on the water, riding on swirls of his blood. He wasn't sinking though, one hand was sliced on a barnacle encrusted pylon and the other steadied against the hull of his ship. One corner of the steel suitcase jutted out of the water. He coughed on the salt and blood. A pivotal change on the ship from the movement of the last three tanks and four crates of fuel supplies off the *Margarita* caused it to pitch, rolling into the wharf. *Squish.* On the rebound roll Toro surfaced mashed into the hull at the waterline. From above, Anastasia peered down and convulsed, only to be yanked by Ghan's hand clutching at her hair.

*"We speak the same tongue!"* he screamed into her face.

She could understand limited English and mouthed the word which Chiang, though a few feet away, was quick to pick up and intervene.

*"What is it you wish to know, Ghan?"* Chiang asked.

Ghan let the girl go but pushed her to her knees before them. *"Pirates. Where will I find the pirates that have plundered the Pacific!"* Chiang asked her.

Her explanation was to point the precise locations of their haunts; the specific warehouses and whorehouses but when she stood and looked for landmarks she saw nothing but smoke and flames, ruin and decay. Her hand cast itself there and quivered not for the loss of pirates but for the lack of buildings to identify them by, and hence, the lack of information she could provide, and thus the diminishing value of her life.

Krue understood the trappings of his self-prescribed destiny, if there was anything as remotely romantic as destiny. If his life was a spark of change then the total output would be scattered dust.

They sat in that inhibiting silence. Tolken and Smacker said with superstitious tyranny and the ease of distance that Colonel Peters was a Mad Man. Beyond that trivial piece of data they were nuisances, and in contrast, Callaghan was a showcase of madness but possibly saner on the inside; perhaps closer to both extremes. What did it matter. Mad together. Access to a long range nuclear missile. Smacker and Tolken could push some buttons and have Doug zooming above the earth in his fighter bomber or cruise missiles (much more advanced stuff than Peters could ever buy on the black market) raining down. An escalation of Madness and Waste. She was a cheap utensil to alleviate the severity and to this point she had failed. If there was nothing for her to reason or kill, her value sitting here in a remote forest thousands of kilometres behind enemy lines, was zero. And the three innocent young men still out there? Part of the deal. What of the millions who perished since the war erupted thanks to the wills of men and women with simple ideals based on tribal self-preservation. All part of the deal. Less than zero and sinking. She felt colder than the Antarctic and stiller than the deepest lake.

Peters said, "You decide who you're standing for, then how to save yourself."

"You know where I stand."

"Far from where I am, then."

She was obediently silent. What power and radiance she once possessed now drained through the soles of her feet into the wood floor of the hut and seeped into the rich soil below. She felt a weak voltage running through her arms, enough to lift her hand and drop it on the table, her loose, limp, fist and dejected eyes pleading brinkmanship, and if that was not accepted, servility. Deep inside her mind she schemed, how long can this act last. He's not even looking. His eyes are out the window calculating some steamy symmetry of his little prehistoric world, some unexplored aspect that once reconnoitred, humanised or neutralised, will add to his jungle belt of rights and armaments.

A knock on the door rattled loud and furious.

Peters stepped past Krue and grudgingly opened it.

Callaghan, seeing Krue facing the other way, tugged Peters outside and closed the hut door. He gripped Peters on the thicker part of the forearm, "Now you hold yourself steady," Callaghan's eyes were red rimmed, "A Chinese Brigade have taken Kingston. There's nothing we can do about it."

Blood just drained away from Peters's face.

Krue opened the door and gasped at him.

Callaghan hissed to her, "Listening in: spying witch!"

"I heard. Kingston, wasn't it?"

Peters groaned; exhaustive yet acidic. He gripped his fringe and spun a tight circle. "*Fuck!* ... How?"

Krue stepped to their sides, re-evaluating, numb at why she ever thought Smacker and Tolken were *full of shit*.

Callaghan's normally senile mind was now strangely sane and calm. "They hopped a ride in one of Toro's freighter. Sneaky. That's piracy, the righteous fucks."

Peters's fists tightened. *They'd* attacked. Empty re-assurances from underworld diplomats. Insufficient warning from his own country. And the balls, of whoever *they* were. Or, the writing was on the wall and he'd never wanted to read it.

Callaghan chattered incessantly, "It's the full show: mechanised too. Might be paving the way for bigger things. McCallister copped it first – rolled over by a tank. The little shits sure have *nerve*. The guy who radioed all this in *died* on the radio – that mousey little clerk at the Trading House. What'da'ya'reckon?"

"It's insane..."

Callaghan shrugged, apathetic and calm, "It's the shit, isn't it."

"We were a diversion... Perhaps it is time. Anglos came, now the Orients. They aren't the first and they won't be the last. I'm an educated Aboriginal now."

"Don't react just because," Krue felt propelled to intervene, but Peters cut her short:

"No chance Missy... Callaghan radio Eric and a Fudo launcher ready to move. Go to the bank and be ready to deal something to a Chinese advantage. Try and keep the people calm, if the Chinese see the civilians running they'll know to come in and mowing them down won't be a problem. We've got to show them how relaxed and sane we are... Play it safe... We're cool, because we've seen it before, right?"

"Right," Callaghan said. "Actually, *we* haven't; personally I mean."

Peters slammed his fist into his hand, "This is what happens up here, we were *right* all along... And escort Major Krue back to her lodging. Place an armed guard on the door at all times. I want a clean hit at these invading bastards at all costs. She's not to leave at all."

"She'll be secure."

"I'm harmless." Krue testified. "I've given to you what I can – you can let me go."

"How harmless that you've failed diplomacy?" Peters spied the forest for the seedy eyes of her snipers. "You're got options. They don't send you this far to talk..."

Krue's pretty faced scrunched in anger, "I've tried and this is how you treat me?"

"Frankly I don't give a fuck; Get out of here." He pointed to the jeep and turned to Callaghan and Marcus, "Send a message off to the Chinese Third Fleet and any listening post, their embassies, anyone. 'Do you know what you're dealing with?... Please consider, Colonel Patrick Peters, Commander-in-Chief, Providence.'"

Marcus repeated the message in his head, turning the key to the car ignition. "Got it."

"They'll understand?" Callaghan second-guessed. "We don't want no reverse politeness with the Asian mind game?"

"It'll work, they listen, they have to... Do the Chinese know what I'm lunatic enough to do, Katherine?"

She shook her head knowing they didn't, they wouldn't care. On the geographical landscape, what can one rogue player matter to a nation of over a billion?

Peters deftly scrutinised her, and just as quickly lost all patience, screaming with rage, "Get her away!"

# Escape

Stun grenades. Staccato raking. Shells *tinking* on cement and rolling. Pirates scurried out, blood trickling from their ears, flash blinded, taken out with a rifle butt to the head. Troopers, some only sixteen with a twelve-inch bayonet, guarded the streets shooting escapees on sight. This was another year of living dangerously. Romano ran. He kick-started a moped, zoomed out the backdoor of a warehouse as troops kicked their way in through the front, skidded back alley corners and came face to face with a stationary tank. Its turret faced sideways minding an adjoining street. The front machine-gun swivelled and sputtered. Bullets shredded the moped's front-wheel, the fuel tank pissed from three holes and flared up. Romano run, Romano run, behind the flames, between the bullets, escaping the troopers steadily moving block by block, taking light casualties but they don't care – they have the flame inside them.

Running. On the outskirts the sense of desertion haunted him. He ran. His heart ached, he might keel over, they would silence his huffing, run, foot after foot, through the sweet smelling orange orchards on the south side and make for the road. Some militia must be there to sniper, lay explosives or at the least check out *what* was going on. So much training must not go to waste. So much running. A spray of bullets whistled widely over his head. Just strays. Keep running. They want you to stop and he did, dazed and confused by the roadside, only two kilometres from the centre of crumbling Kingston.

"Duc!" a woman cried from the bush at the side of the road, "Duc!" but the beloved "Duc!" was nowhere to be found. She ran inland, into the bush, towards the mountains.

Romano crouched in a ditch, one hand groping at his aching heart, the other holding a branch over his body, spying; Troopers moved house to house and rounded up civilians. He was keen to escape but now feared snipers picking him out. Patience. He lay down, let his breath catch up and trailing that his guttered mind…

A surprise attack. The *Margarita* came a half hour early and sided straight into the wharf as if piloted by a maniac. Before Romano could oversee the boarding party, or find out where Toro was, a side cargo door swung open and sharp shooters appeared from the deck. He ran. Many of the dock hands couldn't. His boarding party were caught completely in the open. He ran through Kingston wailing, rustling off-duty militia, anyone, then tried to find the rocket-launchers but it was too late. The ship expunged thousands of over-eager troops, firing their rifles at anyone. To fight was suicidal. Many of Jemmy's pirates, staying in numerous brothels, were trapped and tried to shoot themselves out. Romano heard their obstinate howls of anger and abuse. But they couldn't survive and surrendering was the only way other than burning to death. The Chinese, as they eat everything of the dog, shot every flea.

Romano's only hope was to run south. He spied again. Mercy! Good Lord Mercy! A shabby column of a hundred or more civilian prisoners were marched out of the town until their many captors, from the comfort of tanks and houses, blew a whistle and the procession halted. The civilians then simultaneously buckled at the knees, flicked down to the ground by a giant's invisible finger, and lay still, sprawled out, or crumpled into themselves. Then the sound of concentrated bursts of machine-guns rolled over Romano and he squirmed into his ditch. A few of the young militia were running through the surrounding bush, loud and heavy, clumsy and fearful.

"Pitiful," he cried and defiantly stood. No bullets came. It would be a long walk to Sunny Bridge then into Providence. He was a refugee again.


As the jeep traversed through the ashen clearing Krue was intrigued at the clean-up eating at the carnage. Two bulldozers worked in tandem digging holes at the side of the road and scooping them full of charred remains. All was in action and as they were driving through, the radio spoke.

"*J-C* this is *D-Man*."

"Yeah."

"You'd be at the blast zone. Slow down."

Marcus slowed and suspiciously eyed Peters's voice emitting from the radio.

"Leave the bodies on the road," Peters posthumously decreed, "As a *sign*."

Callaghan moaned to the radio handset, "For Christ's sake! Not this again! You don't get to smell it!"

"Don't worry, I have and I will again. It's for the Chinese," Peters gritted, "Show them global liberators how nasty this place can get. I wish I could drag Smacker for a tour of domestic duty… Leave a dirty reminder permanently stained on his fucking face. Do you hear me Smacko? Do you hear? I am nuking Canberra. You slack ass white *cunt*."

"Um – settle mate," Callaghan replied. "Marcus, stop the car."

They stopped. The bulldozers hadn't worked their way along more than a tenth yet. Krue wrapped her shirt around her mouth and nostrils.

Callaghan leapt from the vehicle with a tea-towel tugged over his mouth, cursing, waving to grab the attention of the bulldozers.

"Will the Chinese come through here?" Krue's voice was muffled, "On this road?"

Marcus shuddered. "I guess. What have we got to stop them? It's the most direct way to Providence... The fuckers got Kingston; *we're next.*" As if with seconds to spare he toyed with a pistol, poking his eyes down the barrel, "You think so?"

Her eyes hung to the north eastern horizon; smudges of smoke blown west, and adventurous crows flying high and heading in for a look. "You never know in the fog of war."

He spat. "What they want anyway? Peters said the Chinese are far more superior, thinking ten times ahead... For what? This cesspit?"

"Here is halfway for them to Antarctic; all the plutonium and fresh water this side of the southern hemisphere." She stomped her foot, "And there's enough minerals here too. There's a lot we don't know. A lot of reasons why we've been sent to these places which we have no idea about."

Marcus wisened up, "Yeah?"

"And for what it's worth, I was the insurance policy to see Peters *not* having to face the Chinese."

"... You sure fucked up." He griped his steering wheel with renewed angst. "Now I don't feel so bad. He *is* here though, who else would stop them from finding out what is really here?"

Krue asked him, "You think the Chinese are that far advanced that they come all this way for one renegade and a mountain of rotting bodies?"

The pieces of Marcus's own little jigsaw loomed large and heavy in his mind but half put together, the others dangling on piano wire before his eyes. It'll all come together, soon, he told himself. And then in a blink, it'll all be gone.

Callaghan returned to the jeep, the bulldozers ceased their work and rumbled south, the drivers cautiously turning to check out the north for *the shit*. He said, almost gladly or perversely, "I guess Kingston isn't on the delivery run no more."

"To Providence?"

He shuddered from his final study of the dead to permanently scar his mind, their legacy a reminder that this was his work, "Air-conditioned office, hell yeah, home-sweet-home sea-breezes, step on it. Providence *awaits*."

"While it lasts," Krue dismayingly added.

Callaghan's teeth grated. "Or while you last."


In Providence the news spread like wildfire. However, at the *Dead Head Pub*, the end of civilisation proceeded with a more casual air. Jemmy sat on his rounded stool, staring out through the window over the intersection of Providence, drumming his thumbs on a table. The town was simmering under a steamy midday sun. Usually people idled about, swaggering under the heat, and today they were frantic. Most had been refugees and knew that what they had escaped had only snowballed and followed them. They were busy shopping for supplies and bartering for emergency transport; rides on trucks, old bicycles, passage on a fishing boat. Others stood at corner, listening to, or explaining contingency plans, worrying for the future, not sure where to run to. Their trust, Jemmy noted, was still anchored on the bank: rock solid, guarded and grand.

Jemmy projected the conflict and tried to estimate the timing. One civilisation closes, another opens. He'd seen a few. Then the nifty footed youngster, a buck-toothed, cheeky, messenger, humble adolescent orphan to the world, darted through the wake of a cruising farmer's ute, cut across the road straight into the pub, past the bar, and slightly out of breath nudged at Jemmy's sleeve from behind and then into his ear, "I *find* him!"

Jemmy scanned from the bank's walls and steps to search the flow of people for a sign, "Where?"

"I told him... He's coming, soon!"

Jemmy turned to the boy and suavely winked. "How much?"

He panted, "One dollar, Australian."

"When?"

The boy said excitedly, his palm out to Jemmy, his eyes staring at the man standing in the doorway, "*That's* Malo!"

Malo, off-duty, but thinking hard, breathed an air of rugged independence into the pub like a reverse air-conditioner unit. His faded blue singlet was covered by a tight, unbuttoned, champagne silk shirt grubby from caterpillar-crawling through the bush. From his taunt gut down he wore faded green light cotton trousers, a thin leather belt, and matching sandals. Strapped to his belt on a light but high-tensile chain was a professional hunter's pistol that Jemmy had once bought from a Yakuza drunk in Port Moresby.

"Malo!" Jemmy welcomed and scrutinised, could not see any other weapons, and beckoned too warmly, "Take a seat, please! We have much to talk about!"

Malo nodded he would.

Jemmy paid the boy up, who fled outside to peek in from the wall adjacent to the window sill.

Malo hooked his head to a new pretty waitress behind the bar, his scurrilous gaze then circling the establishment, his attentive ears tuning through conversations: two try-hard pirates by the door planning their boat trip away from the Chinese, three farmhands whinging at a table counting coins and damning torrential rains and igniting the idea of trading food to the Chinese, and three merchants arguing, tucking away their wallets, assuming they'd be all equally squared up. The new Cambodian waitress glided like a temple dancer, descending a tray of cold Asahi beers to the merchants, spun on her heels to pluck an empty glass from Jemmy, kinking her head, motioning she too saw the street-smart boy hiding by the window. Malo didn't care. He saw Jemmy, who was a third to half drunk, looking the better side of miserable.

The Cambodian waitress closed in on Malo, her full lips expressively practising rudimentary English, "Big Tron night-woman next door says you after a wife." She pointed down to herself. "You like?"

Malo looked over her admiringly, "I'd take you away. Far away. So far you vanish. You want that, sister?"

She squinted at him, her hand held contemplatively between them, and still jutted her hips to him; They say his type have been in these lands forever and ever.

"What can I get you?" she asked, sweetly.

"The dark stuff."

That she couldn't understand. He pointed to an earthy non-descript bottle standing by the sink, then sat next to Jemmy. They quietly monitored the panic of the populace with equally experienced and distant stares.

"Here we go again," Malo said distractedly.

"Round and round."

Malo understood the foreigners in a simplistic context; inexperienced nomads in a land that had been home to nomads for thousand of years. One wave after the other. If they don't kill each other, Mother Nature will.

"You never told me what you did," Jemmy asked, one hand lifting off the table suddenly weighing up his words, "What you did, before…"

Malo proudly slapped his thigh. "I did a lot… Mostly I was a Jack of all trades, brother. A tracker. A jackeroo. Tour guide 'round the Olgas. I know me *way* from here to Darwin and down to the bite."

"And your name. They said it meant…?"

"*Mah-Low*. It means trusted boomerang," Malo bullshitted.

"So your real name is Boomerang? You always come back?"

"Nah. But it sounds good." With a low hiss he passed off further explanation. "What-ya-want? The kid ran half a mile to find me."

"We've seen this all before… It's a tight position." Jemmy patiently lit and puffed on his little cigar. "Do you run or stay and welcome the new friends? … Who are the Chinese… Maybe they are here because of people like me…" He then studied a familiar jeep arriving at the bank. "And now… Watch…."

Callaghan alighted and with one scream sent the jeep to the beach, driven by Creton, two militia guarding a white woman in uniform. Callaghan ran up into the bank. The two militia guarding the bank stepped down to the road and summarised what they could; they smelt fear from the north. The pedestrian population shuffled along, a smouldering anxiety weighing their stride.

"So what?" Malo grinned. "Never seen a white sheila before 'eh?"

Jemmy half smiled. "I've seen many… And I see her and think… Well… What do you know about Kingston? Maybe we can never go back."

Malo *tsked*, dropped one shoulder, accepted a drink with a wink from the Cambodian waitress.

"It does not worry you?" Jemmy pressed yet without staring directly at Malo, just the bank, its prominence over the intersection, they way people looked to it as they passed by.

"Me'n'you bin 'ere with Sumatra. Don't get no fuck'n ideas because the whiteys are running the bank. Them good fellas… Like you'n'me… An' now your yellow mates are up in Kingston hosing your fucking filthy fucking pirates out to sea and you, you lick ye' lips 'cause you're a fucking *dingo* sniffing the arse of the carcass," he scraped his lean finger into Jemmy's arm, "I don't see nothing dead so don't go sniffing yet."

Jemmy faced him, "I can trust you, Malo, to speak truthfully."

Malo raised his drink in manly salute.

"And, I want to know what you will be doing if the Chinese come."

Malo sipped and startlingly straightened his back. "You thinking I'll 'ave a party here, waving a fucking Olympic flag?"

Jemmy fickly laughed and stubbed out his little cigar.

"I seen you thinking," Malo continued, "An' your mates, in Kingston? They laughing too?"

"Probably dead," Jemmy answered, painlessly and certain. "Everything I earned for three years... Burning. Smoke. Or stolen now." He sniffed the clean air and lit another cigar. "*Black Tide* say Chinese will rid the Pacific of pirates,"

"Why they do that, huh?"

"*Black Tide* no more pay money to Chinese Army. '*Black Tide* must save face now. *Black Tide* is too strong to depend on China!' they say." Jemmy's subtle ridicule settled. "So many of *Black Tide* will be sacrificed to save those," he exhaled up into the air, "who run us from high above."

Malo mumbled, "All the *bull*shit I've heard in my life!" He brooded. All the lies. All the talk. Then the urge came, strong and serious: Go walk-about again, way out west past the mines and between the desert warlords and into the gorge where only the blacks live because only the blacks knew to live there and no one else was allowed, even the prettiest and innocent waitresses from Providence.

"So what will you do?" Jemmy asked. "Fight?"

"Nah. I duck them bullets an' gather a stash."

"But you are the best bounty hunter and a rich man. Rich. I have sold you the best guns,"

Malo meagrely rolled his eyes.

"And you have *big* stash?"

Malo shrugged. "I'm saving up for a new receiver for the TV. We get fuck-all reception out there. Snow, they call it. Can't watch snow all day out in desert country. Makes black fellas *angry* as bull-ants."

"I get you a good one!" Jemmy promised, "Two hundred channels! More!"

"Nah," Malo held up his hand, "I don't need that shit where I'm going."

And that was all Jemmy was after.

Malo spoke short, "Just keep ya' head down and don't be sniffing what you shouldn't, eh?"

Jemmy dipped his eyes then reflectively back to the bank.

Malo thumped him on the shoulder, "You're a smart fella' so don't fuck with 'em. They got the guns now, they wanna' die fighting for *shit*. You go back to your own with what you got – ya self. It's better than nothing, eh?"

Jemmy blushed and turned away but Malo called him back, offering a sturdy black hand to shake.

"Shake on it brudda, c'mon, for you, so you can keep alive."

They shook.

Jemmy's gaze drifted to the sky and the feint scent of salt, whispering, "Thank you."

"But you wanna' know who the white sheila is?" Malo spoke down to him, "She's something special. Don't sniff her out. *Never*."

"What?"

"She's a bad lady," Malo stood to leave. "She got shit coming."

"You're going?"

Malo glanced down with a look that he had marginally better things to do.

"I'll see you later then."

"I'll see you when the storm blows over," Malo's voice thundered in celebration, saluted the waitress, and strolled outside into the sunshine.

Eric typed the message, triple checked it, felt a pang of cheekiness and scrunched his face up in consternation.

> To: Chinese 3<sup>rd</sup> Fleet HQ.
> From: Providence HQ, East Coast Australia
> Do You Know What You're Dealing With?
> Please consider,
> Colonel Patrick Peters,
> Commander-in-Chief, Providence

It looked plain and impersonal on the computer screen. He printed one copy and emailed the digital version to every Chinese military headquarters and embassy and United Nations outpost around the world receiving scraps of transmissions. In one swift move the global village heard the lone whimpering voice bellowing against the local bully. Jintana quickly realised that it could work, but what combined force has ever stopped China and how would it happen now? For the sake of one defiant dictator, master of an insignificant civilisation, population ten thousand?

"Now they'll know he'll retaliate." Eric boasted.

Jintana's hands folded into themselves. She stared dejectedly to the Map of the World on the wall. The tyrant's power is not the voice of

312

the people, it is the roar of his weapons. China knew better than to ignite a rogue. Similarly, could China actually care? This was the furthermost they had ever ventured and were bound to fail sometime sooner or later... When, and to whom? No. China rotted from the inside first. And how long would that take? Jintana rushed from the computers to Callaghan's desk, laying her head in his arms and whimpered.

Callaghan tersely stroked her hair, "Be strong... Together,"

"For how long?" she croaked between choking tears.

"Silly Jintana." Holding her head in his hands, his voice soft as caramel, he spoke into her eyes, "Together we are one and I know for myself *I* don't plan to die. Safety! Happiness! Think *that* and it will come! Go on, think it! Believe it!"

She cast him an absurd stare. He'd never seen the sinking ships that she had, or the refugees on the over-crowded ferries rejecting those swimming in the water and their pleas for help. Here was the definitive split for two lovers. One trusted the roll of dice for it was fate. The other willed the roll of dice for fate is what he made.

"I am in love with a crazy man," Jintana admitted to herself.

"Oh, come now baby," he held her closer, trying to cheer her up, "Sane guys, the nice ones, always finish last. I'm sure you of all people should know that."


Peters sat alone in the hut, gathering his thoughts.

Who had been in Kingston? He reached for his radio, "Romano, Romano." No reply. "This is Colonel Patrick Peters, all Militia Units in Kingston report immediately to me." Nothing. A void. A vacuum. Something filling it.

He thought about nuking Kingston. Too close? Sure it would be off-limits for a few years but hey, if he didn't send them the message now, why wait? But, he cautioned himself, then he'd have nothing to bargain with. He'd be another bandit with a gun and a touch of charisma. He tried the radio, flicking through frequencies. To his surprise there was the inquisitive chatter of Chinese, sharpened by military discipline, arguing, possibly over what to do with a captured radio. They were excited.

He said, "Can. You. Hear. Me."

"Hello?" Chinese chattered in the background. "Hello-hello-hello?"

"Colonel Peters speaking. How. Are. You."

"Colon-el Pee-tah."

"Excellent. O-K."

"*O-K.*"

"Listen. Colonel Peters has a message."

"Message?" It was someone familiar with English.

"Yes. A Message."

"Who message?"

"My message. Colonel Peters."

"Ah. Yes. Please message..."

"My fist.... My. Fist."

"Message. My fist, O-K."

"My fist jammed..."

"Peters's fist, jammed..."

"My fist, that's me, Colonel Peters, jammed up your ass. O-K?"

"... Your fist jammed and pumped up your ass... Ahsoo... No.." The voice conferred with its pals. "No... Your fist, jammed and pumped up *my* ass. Is that message?"

"Yes." Peters grinned. "You. Like. It. Like, That!"

They paused, conferring again, and then fast paced and horrified, "You suck cock! Ha! You pirate! Die now! Pirate of Pacific! We kill you!"

"Oh," Peters quietly raged, releasing with a calm, deadpan, questionable funny line: "You are a smart-ass. I. Like. You. I think you're funny."

"Funny? Ha!"

"Fucking hilarious!"

"Yes! Funny! You. Suck cock! Ha! Pirates will die!"

"I am going to kill you all. You will all die. I am going to kill you all. Colonel Patrick Peters will kill you all."

He then changed the frequency back to his normal one and laughed to himself through ten seconds of radio static.

Eric, loud and clear, spoke on the radio, "*D-Man* what was that on channel twenty-two?"

"Communication with the enemy. Psychological Warfare."

"We're monitoring it... *J-C* heard it and reckons you didn't get a load away."

"With what?"

"The Major."

Eric's radio changed hands to Callaghan, "Gimme that... That was really good. You *Pirate of Pacific*. Arse-fucking *nutcase*. Now they've got a moral and poetic licence to kill you."

"What! Don't you lecture me about diplomacy!"

"No really... That was great. You told them they'd die."

"Messing with their minds," Peters proudly rallied. "If you're not giving it you're taking it."

"I know that, but don't you think you could make a slightly different impact? Something, perhaps… Approachable?"

"I know!"

"Say, are they meant to be our friends, just maybe, in the future… As a remote fucking option? I thought maybe that bitch should get to your head just a little bit? No? Yes?"

"Don't worry – its reverse psychology." Peters yelled into the radio. "See they're listening in right now, I bet! They would not know what the hell we are up to. Codename: Two-six-one. Position: Classified. Status: Active. Weapons System: One Beijing Ninety-Six! Target: it's a surprise!"

"You mean they're eavesdropping? They've been doing that all week." Callaghan muttered. "Warning to all sneaky bastards: We have the Princess! Her little diplomatic quest has gone nowhere! Thanks for trying *losers*! Where's my shotgun? Aaaagh! *Bang Bang!* There goes the neighbourhood."

"Yeah. Funny one. I am about to kill my Captain Callaghan! He is not complying with my Marxist doctrine! Did my urgent message get sent, Globally?"

"*D-Man*, message sent."

"Estimated reply time?"

"As if they care, Pacific Pirate. Come back at fifteen hundred?"

"Can do… And if you're listening China, I'll nuke your bony little ass if you come an inch closer. Now, I'm going to take a peek at Kingston."

"Are you sure?"

"How else are we to know what they're doing."

"Anything else?"

"Yeah, M-L-T three. Position Five."

"Five?"

"Five." Peters verified, "That's all."

"Are they still listening?"

"I hope so. I'm going to kill you all, incinerate you, burn you. I am a nuclear power. I'll be seeing you sooner than you think."

# Victory

Two Stars Ghan surveyed the damaged warehouses lining the docks of Kingston. Supply staff had tallied thousands of crates of food, two-hundred cattle penned out the back, five trucks, twenty-seven cars. Coal, enough for at least one shipload home!

"A healthy prize." Chiang commented of the pillaging.

Ghan smiled, "Yes, but it pays little for our conquest." He turned to ogle. Metres away, two troops stiffened to attention, guarding Anastasia. She sat cross legged, nibbling a pear looking at all going on around her. Troops hauled assortments of captured weapons, maritime and trading equipment, plus crates of bruised fruit on their shoulders. Anastasia shuddered with fright as a tank rumbled up Gallipoli Street fluttering the brigade's flag: the red and black dragon spitting fire, tied from the aerial atop the turret. Her captor looked fancy in his fine uniform. His index finger and thumb stroked down his jaw, correcting the strands of his goatee.

He spoke, "Chiang, despatch this message to the company commanders... 'We must not destroy this town. It is no longer a den for pirates. War is about control. We have stepped far from our borders to maintain order. A spider's web is intricate."

A runner arrived from the Intelligence Unit, saluted, handed Chiang a slip of paper, and stood, watching his shadow on the road.

Chiang read, huffed and proudly sang, "De-coded orders from headquarters: From General Zhing." Chiang read ahead.

Ghan felt the satphone on his hip, was it no longer secure? Were the satellites down? And now a message from HQ via an inferior? What if they were to restrain him just as he had tasted the sweetest victory of many to come? They could order his force north to link with the brigades that had taken Cairns and Townsville, hundreds of kilometres away... Leaving Kingston a bare outpost! Ludicrous! He would have to raise the town to the ground in his wake as his testament!

He ground his teeth, "Well?"

"A salute to the skill of the troops in the One-Seven-Seven Brigade and especially your tactical genius," Chiang said, passing the slip of paper to Ghan, "And our next objective."

Ghan read, and patiently re-read. Right. Well, it was obvious. You wish, you receive. His heart beat in great bounds. A muddled smile scarred his face. "This coastal town of Providence, is it a port?"

Chiang had to think. He'd read up properly a week ago. "It's the capital of this region, as declared two years ago. Bandit territory."

Ghan pursed his lips out, "Headquarters wants us there within a week."

Chiang mused. "Many kilometres of dense terrain... Intelligence reports two hundred local militia and twenty Australian Mercenaries."

"Well," Ghan said, smugly satisfied. "We rest today. Tomorrow and the day after that we will prepare to amass on Providence." His arms expressed the situation as if painting a large sweeping hieroglyphic picture, "General Zhing sees the world from above; he directs our path from afar but does not complicate us with the overall nature of his true objective. As our objective is now Providence, those pirates and bandits we are chasing, their annihilation will be our next victory. Perhaps it is better to not know the full extent of what we will confront, it is too late, our path is set, for we know where to go and nothing shall stand in our way." As a lasting symbol he tapped at the unknown, in his temple. "Such is our war."

"Beautiful," Chiang commented on his superior's prose, "Very beautiful."

"I have a new message to be sent to our men,"

Then Lieutenant Ling sprinted through the busy streets, leaping over crates, and found his General, "General Ghan!"

"Lieutenant Ling," Colonel Chiang acknowledged, "Speak!"

"I had radio contact," Ling wiped sweat from his brow, "With the enemy."

"The enemy?" Two Stars Ghan growled, "Explain!"

"A Colonel Peters claimed he would kill all of us." Ling's clenched fist was tiny but awesomely displayed the threat. "The white devil is unstable, a sadist perhaps."

Two Stars Ghan crossed his arms and coldly spat. "Spread the word, our next enemy is more depraved than the simple peasant pirates we wasted here. Our next objective is a town called Providence. We will be welcomed by the civilians! Liberation! We were sent to rid these lands of Pacific Pirates and Bandits – we will be greatly rewarded! We have a mission like no other!"

"Yes Two Stars Ghan!" Ling chanted.

Ghan then saluted the *Margarita*, "Now, how long before she is loaded and ready to sail?"

"You wish it to sail?" Chiang asked, how would they get back home without it, "Where to?"

Ghan frustratingly vexed himself, "We will send the coal home. As we cleanse these plentiful lands we must not let our comrades back home miss out on the spoils of conquest! It would be a great dishonour not to." Ghan settled himself and reflected on matters of honour. He curled his hand into a tight fist. This mission, this history, had only just begun.


Peters slammed the heavy wooden door of the hut and locked it. Regret swelled in his heart. He may never see this sanctuary again. In his strategic plans the lush forest would fall out of his new defensive line, the Arubai River to the south. He hoped that as the Chinese may wander the ravines and sip the cool waters they would eat the berries and wither from the poisons. They know nothing of the dangers lurking here. Three Tonkas arrived in a jeep. He leapt in and patted the driver on the shoulder, "Kingston."

"Is it safe?" Vince asked. "I see smoke and hear many guns. Few leave."

"I have to see it."

Turning onto Highway Five they travelled at a cautious speed studying the human debris flowing out. From the outskirts of Kingston fleeing residents carried meagre belongings in ruffled hessian sacks. Peters passed by them, saluting their fear ridden faces and pointing south with refreshing dignity in defeat.

"You will pass through a road of death but fear nothing for walk on to Providence, cross at Sunny Bridge!"

He knew about pompous dignity and that his own people were refugees in their own land. Nearing the Port of Kingston the flow of people on the road became thin. Peters spied smoke rising to the heavens from behind low-lying hills and he knew that beyond them were the ruins of his trading town.

"Drive at twenty-klicks an hour, if any Chinese show their faces, raise your hands... We're a greeting party."

Vince nodded, fearful but trusting, placing their weapons out of sight but within easy defensive grasp. The jeep peaked a hill and stopped. A freakish sea wind from the east lifted the hairs on their heads, as before them they focussed straight down the road to the sparser fringe of Kingston. Further along stood organised town blocks and houses and generous yards, some buildings bleeding clouds of grey and white into the sky. A tank cannon boomed, spitting a shell out of town to some unknown target. Peters took to his binoculars and scanned the closest buildings for signs of snipers. Of what troops he saw, most were content to stand warily at defensive points and junctions on the outskirts of the town and from this distance, apprehensively point him out. In the denser centre, troops carried supplies, two tanks halted at an intersection, their daunting cannons raising up and down into the sky like two birds squawking. Peters scanned the road running out of town. He saw dead bodies, civilians cunningly crawling into ditches, and a lone familiar weighty man dashing from tree trunk to tree trunk, at the side of the road, diminishing the threat of a sniper bullet in the back.

"Romano," Peters winced.

In the town there was a ceasefire, or nothing to fire at, but on the outskirts, the greener troops were keen for some sport. A tank shell burst well behind the jeep. The ground shook. Another tank raised its barrel, a turret-spotter could be seen on his radio.

"They're closing in," Vince warned, throwing the jeep's gear into reverse.

"No." Peters saw through his binoculars more Chinese tanks appearing from behind houses in the middle of Kingston. It was a defensive move, and if they were firing at faraway jeeps, they were bored. Tanks. He had none. Shrugging, he thankfully added, "Shit aim, though."

"Not for long."

"Fast as you can, get in and we'll get Romano out."

Vince naturally hesitated, put the gear into first and flattened the accelerator.

Romano sat up, watching. A tank crossed a street, moving behind a weather beaten house. Troopers followed it, fanning out, securing the outskirts of Kingston. No place for a man to die, Romano thought, got to his feet and limped behind another tree-trunk, heard an engine whine and spied along the road. He gasped. A jeep was accelerating, swerving, now decelerating, right to him. He scanned the bush, he could run, but heard a familiar voice.

"Hurry up fatty!" Peters yelled.

Romano ran onto the road and Peters hauled him in. Vince u-turned the jeep and they sped south.

"The Virgin Mary told you to come!" Romano lunged at a rifle in the back seat and swung to Kingston firing wildly. "Dogs!"

Though the escape was bumpy, Peters sat in quiet contemplation. "I think you got one."

"Ergh!" Romano held himself steady. Crimson gravel rash covered his forearms and shoulders. Patches of black, ash and burns, smeared his clothes. He was twitching, scatter-brained and vicious. He snarled, "They have not beaten me!"

Peters patted him on the shoulder. "But it was close."

Romano held his head in hands, beyond cursing, thinking of Emelda cutting onions, tears welling in his swollen eyes.

The jeep stopped on the hill again. They looked to Kingston: it was darkened under the thick smoke, gloomy and messier than it had ever been.

"Providence?" Vince asked.

"No." Peters said, his tone thick. "We defend from the Arubai River, pivot on Sunny Bridge. We come face to face with them on our grounds…"

Romano panted and with a new grit, "So we fry them all?"

"In good time. We'll set a little trap. It's the only way."

"It better be good," Romano snarled, "*Fucking* good."


DEAR TANYA, Matthews typed into his satphone keypad and observed diligently from the fork of the gum tree he was covertly propped in. The new observation post was closer to the road and still offered a view of Kingston. He reconnoitred from the gentle western ranges to the northern smoke rising from the invaded town, the eastern sea, to the south and the small outline of Providence, the last known destination of his boss, Major Krue.

At the base of the tree Tom and Corrie hunched over a meagre fire, cooking rice on a metal plate, sprinkling in curry powder and chunks of snake they had caught. Matthews knew his posting as spotter for things near and afar did not encompass sending personal messages, but the world, as it appeared from the north, was burning, and what if the fire came south, across the road spanning the Arubai River, a few hundred metres to the north west (the main purpose of this observation position) and devoured him? Who would know they were here? What good is the military at recording a man's thoughts? And as if they'd know he was sending a very personal message to his lover's mobile phone, all the way down in Tasmania. He spied down to the ground. Their position was atop a gully and well protected by lantana. If anyone tried to come through he'd hear their struggle with the mongrel bush from a mile away.

> *I miss you and think of you everyday. I am in*
> *Queensland, behind enemy lines, Matty xxx.*

He pressed send and riding on this brief satisfaction pondered what else there was to say. The smoke over Kingston thinned then expanded as a warehouse or something large and combustible took light. He scanned the sky above for bombers but saw nothing, only the hovering of crows and hawks picking at that god-awful patch of road north of the river. At night the smell seemed to creep all over the lands and invade every pore of a man's body so that he awoke covered in the grizzly putrid aroma and had to wash himself in the murky brown salty silty waters of the Arubai river. Then he saw a jeep speeding from the north, heading towards the bridge over the Arubai river.

He called down, "*Aaaark!*"

He saw the driver concentrating on the road, militia checking the sides of the road, then Romano, looking crushed in the back, and a white man: the target? He swung his rifle and adjusted the sight but at 300 metres it was tricky. He could try with a volley but the jeep's now erratic path, behind trees, dodging dead things on the road; what use would it be. It would be a go, he thought, and if he got him they could be gone, because the wind from the east had changed to the north and he could smell not only burnt bodies, but the smoke of Kingston. He closed his eyes and prayed for something to stop it all. What could do it, he wondered, maybe rain. Before he could wish, a message came back.

*My poor baby! Tanya X*

# Dawn

Dawn, overcast, it rained torrentially hard yet the people of Providence were up and gathered and gossiped at the few eyewitness reports. The chance of escape was in their minds until the winds blew too hard for the merchants to set sail in the boats and the roads west and south flooded. The relentless sheets of rain eventually drowned some of the panic. Militia roamed the streets and houses rounding up the able-bodied males and females and were handed a rifle and taught to load and aim at soggy targets of bundled hay or wooden palings on the beach. Callaghan kept up the pace of preparation. Civilians could not rest under fear's blanket. Some saw Peters, shook hands with the man, left him to his mobilisation. He instilled pride, saluted the new militia recruits and shot away to the front, a front which technically didn't exist. At dusk, Providence hushed, tired by hysteria, and mourning for those who would most probably never return from Kingston.

From her balcony, during the brief breaks of downpour, Krue strained her ears to the wind and heard the marching orders for teens as young as fourteen drilling on the hard sands of the beach, shivering, the mixed-emotions of their mothers seeping down from the dunes. Into the night the whine of heavy trucks and splutters of dirt bikes cut through the puddles in Providence announcing the next phase, complete and urgent mobilisation. Later the clouds blanketed the stars.

She sat on the couch and flicked through television channels like a square eyed junky. Destruction and terror splattered onto the glitzy international news desks detailing a general consensus of Pacific Doom by showing segments of pre-packaged and digestible apocalypse; forecasts by suited analysts, old updates, re-runs of Chinese propaganda happy-policing clips of liberating battalions and thankful peasants, high level bombers annihilating a Chinese Navy depot in Java and then a uranium processing plant in the Northern Territory, plus the cliché Indonesian-come-Australian farmers on their knees flying a Red Crescent handkerchief with the Port of Darwin as a scenic backdrop. Then to illustrate the shit going on close by, a lanky Barbie with a buffy hair-do waved a stick pointer to red arrows on pastel maps magically pronging North Queensland. Then over to the crooked fingers pointed across the floor of the U.N., humble faced diplomats and stuttering interpreters chasing their tails in a sea of set arguments. It was rounded up by a ten second humanitarian special: Five-million Chinese children starved in the coldest winter in thirteen years. Trade *could* have saved them. But *you* didn't. "Trade is impossible in a world riddled by petty wars." General Zhing is quoted, scheming his next master stroke, "Only peace can promote fairer trade."

Krue was interested and un-impressed. Half the world faced death, the other half faced it as couch potatoes. Each time she looked around to escape the screen, the walls moved in closer like thick steel vault walls sliding on ball-bearings... Sealed in silence... For all she knew, the Chinese could be a thousand miles away... Or, she was in the eye of their cyclone.

STARS ?

Tom, Corrie and Matthews hid in a dense gully close to Sunny Bridge. During the morning they had sunken into the mud and evaded two militia patrols with ease and had grown quite comfortable with their surroundings. In the beginning, when they were younger, they would slide into the bush and note that each time they nudged a branch its rustling would alert all the branches, and all the leaves would hang attentively. Now the three were the branches, the trunks, the worming roots and the imprinted dirt. They hardly spoke, and often for hours two would sit in separate positions in silence observing the entrances to the gully. Droplets of water dripped from oiled leaves to their shoulders and soaked them to their mud-caked boots.

Matthews was resolute to finish and to get back south as if the entire affair was an exercise back at the training grounds. He could march back into the air-conditioned barracks, wash up, then hit the local bar. Playing jungle fighter was fun enough but isolating and strangely dominating: You become the bush and it controls you. It sprouts invisible vines that coil into your ear at night and you waken to find – hang on, movement. From his concealed haunt he watched the road and the bridge, mainly militia sentries helping the frazzled civilians come refugees who straggled from the north. A new batch were passing through, wretched and wounded beings. Then the militia blocked the bridge with tree trunks and sat atop scooping rice from coconut shells. They casually shooed away civilians and refugees to come back later. Lunch is lunch. Matthews slithered down into the gully. He drew his two companions together for a special lunch of dried beef and vitamin-enhanced cordial mixed with rain water.

"What about 'em?" Corrie's eyes monitored the direction of the bridge.

"Lunching. Haven't seen Peters, either."

Only he had seen Peters, but was it really him or who he wanted to see? Who else could sit so proudly in this time of trouble.

"And Major Krue?" Matthews then asked Tom and the radio.

"They can't have buried her," Tom said optimistically. "And before we know it," he ran his thumb over the soggy disintegrating map spread out before them, "We could be in Chinese territory."

Matthews agreed, a thin though obvious smile, "It'd wipe out the purpose of our mission, wouldn't it."

"Not if Peters still has his nuke," Corrie added. "Mad fucker."

Matthews scented a multiplication of impending isolation. No one wanted to become a Chinese Prisoner or a prisoner of anyone. "We can ask their headquarters in Providence, they speak English. They'd know we were here anyway."

Tom said, "I bet they got more than us to deal with."

"They do. What's their frequency?"

"It's programmed in. Should we ask *Overlord* first?"

"No," Matthews said firmly, "It's Krue's orders not to. We'll see if we can speak to her. I bet they have her satphone."

Corrie sighed. "You reckon she's still alive?"

"Hope so."

Tom shrugged. "And what if China jumps on Providence through here?"

There was nothing to say. They listened, birds above fluffed wet weathers.

Matthews spoke as surely as he ever had in his short life, "We are in a world of shit, and Major Katherine Krue, she can't be K-I-A... She owes it to get us out of here. Right? And I have to know."


Creton thumped on Krue's door and yelled something guttural.

She threw on her clothes, fastened her belt, muttered *wanker* and swung open the door. "You two," she said pleasantly, "I thought it was the Chinese coming to rescue me."

Creton blushed.

Marcus, with dark rings under his eyes, stepped away form the thug's side. "So you are funny. The bank, Callaghan wants you," he said fluidly, then part mystified, "Some surprise for you."


Outside the bank a line of customers contemplated raising their fists to those inside, a protest that they should withdraw their precious savings. They attentively watched the tall frame of Krue bound up the stairs, through the guarded doors, and straight into

Callaghan's sights, and with a hopeful smile, figured she may do some good.

Callaghan briskly led her into the radio room, checked to see all was currently under control and testified in an uncertain tone, "We're a little busy this morning… Things are a bit complicated…"

"Understood."

"Good," he said and suddenly darted to his office to take a call from the militia. Krue's eyes systematically studied the hardware around her, and whilst waiting for Callaghan to return, watched Eric's keen interest in the screen before him.

"Not meaning to interfere, can I ask what are you doing?" she asked.

He only leaned closer, his hand guiding a mouse to zoom in on the messy layout of a foreign city before him.

"Still preparing for a showdown with China?"

Eric stressfully hummed to himself. "The One-Shot Big-Bang Theory."

"Big Bang? Since when did you deal with theories outside your own universe?"

"We supposedly only deal with certainties, but I'm sceptical if it could work: so many links in the daisy-chain need mending." He nervously stated, "Who knows *if* the Beijing Ninety-Six is operational."

Krue was startled, "What?"

"I won't be working for the Chinese. Mention the word 'freelance tech-head' and quick smart," Eric clicked his tongue to his pallet like the cocking of a pistol. "Treason. Healthy kid like me," he thumped his chest, "They'd put my kidneys in ice and sell them to their frail Party Leaders. No doubt if they could cryogenically freeze my head," and he tapped his crown, "They could cut out the smart bits and feed the rebel bits to the dogs. *Shit*. I could be good for them but it's all gone wrong. I took the job here because what the hell was I suppose to do? It's just a job!" He glowed. "Now it's coming back ten times worse. Have you heard of the Chinese curse: May you live in interesting times?"

"Does it end with 'Or would you rather live in boring times?'"

Eric smugly nodded, "I guess it's all a pain threshold."

Krue's eyes were quick to catch the map of the world on the wall. Callaghan must have put it there as a joke, it was all wrong because when she examined it, the lettering was surprisingly small for Western cities; Beijing was the centre of the world, borders were shifted with China's distinct propaganda irony, but the science of longitude and latitude remained factual. It wasn't newly updated to their latest conquests, it was a measure of their launching pad pre-war; North Korea and Vietnam were shanty provinces of China, Tokyo a mere neighbouring village on a thin island when compared to the bold black sphere of Beijing. Taiwan, well it was common knowledge to any peasant that it was China. She checked from the co-ordinates of the expanded city on Eric's screen to the map on the wall: Beijing.

Eric the Hong-Kong tech-head refugee fed the co-ordinates into a separate computer which spat it through the antennae atop of the bank and was picked up by Peters's nuclear missile launcher out of town. Eric scanned the layout of the mega-city for a central point.

"Does the nuke have the distance?" she asked, as if it wouldn't.

"Should do," he profoundly boasted.

"And you're happy to commit mass-slaughter? Pushing buttons, following orders, like you haven't got anything better to do?"

"You haven't killed him, so, yes," he fathomed and stretched to Marcus, "Your turn to take over. M-L-T three should be online, position five."

"You boys are playing – I don't believe this one bit. You're dreaming you can launch a nuclear attack." She stabbed her crooked index finger at them and snarled, "Demented little shits."

"Major, Missy, Whatever..." Marcus abstractedly and patiently explained, "If it's anything to you, we just see this as a computer game. That city doesn't exist – I've never been there... Ignorance is a primalistic bliss. You have to accept that in this day and age."

"You're little fucking evil henchmen. Where's your pride?"

"Pride," Marcus dismissively grinned, wrinkling the purple rings under his eyes, "Peters wants to go out in flames, not only him, *them*. Isn't that sweet? We don't have any pride. We're caught in the middle."

"So you're suicidal now."

"... Wouldn't you be if this was all that mattered?" Eric answered for himself and Marcus, "This is the best of our 'interesting' lives,"

"As we know it," Marcus stressed.

Krue scolded, "Naïve fucks!"

She turned on her heel to face Callaghan's office. Jintana and Callaghan petted each other and embraced. Jintana worried so much that age began to show. She squeezed Callaghan's shoulder with her fingernails as he warmed her back with his flat hand, mumbling encouragement and issuing orders to militia over the radio. She wiped a tear and palmed her hair back. Krue felt an urge to smash their cute cuddling, but then again she was free for the moment. Beside her Marcus quietly sat at his work. His terminal was a multipurpose communications hub, most definitely connected to Peters's sole nuke. Why couldn't Smacker do away with this? And not Peters? Did Smacker know? *What am I doing here,* she asked herself. Where's that satphone now? Turn it on, target activation, leave it here and run.

"You want to blow this place up, don't you?" Eric snickered.

She cast him an iced smile.

Marcus turned blank, "Too late."

"One here," she imitated with her finger a missile dropping from the sky to where she stood, "And all his cards tumble."

"Nope. Peters has a mobile command." Eric cheekily quipped.

Marcus delivered the gag-line, "Because we're expendable."

"I know that," Krue said.

"We got three lives." Eric broke free from his computer and inclined his head to the wall, and the vault behind it, "I asked if we could put the hardware in there so that if something did happen to the bank, we wouldn't lose the important tools of the trade, or ourselves."

"Nice idea," Marcus ungraciously yawned, "But how we going to drill holes through that fucking thing for the power supply and cords? And working in there so long, we'd suffocate."

"Hey, it's an idea." Eric returned to his work, tapping away, boasting, "I think we won't get hit though, not here."

Krue tapped her boot on the floor.

"We're valuable, aren't we Miss Krue?" Eric continued, "We're an extension of Free Australia. *That's* why you're here: It'd be a waste to blow us up."

"You're a little deluded cunt."

"No, it's just like in a game of chess. We might be a pawn, or a castle, or *who cares* – but we've been kept around. We play some part. And maybe you're the Queen."

She cast him a sympathetic stare then marched straight into Callaghan's office.

"Why was I called?" she demanded.

"Oh,"

Krue watched the embarrassed Jintana shift away from Callaghan's loose embrace, "What? I'm here… And you're…"

"Your lads called in."

"My lads?"

Callaghan slapped his field radio, "Yeah. Bit of a surprise, but given the scenario, I understood. Real nice guys. They asked if you were in. Well mannered and all. Sounds like really *sincere* guys. If they're looking for some real action they can join Team Peters. The militia is recruiting."

"Who spoke to them?"

"I did. An hour ago."

"I must radio them, they'll continue their mission if I don't."

"Can I trust you on that?"

"Yes."

"I doubt you'd change their objective anyway..." He chewed on a pencil, "Would you like me to deliver a little message?"

"That would be less than satisfactory, I thank you."

Callaghan bit the lid off a biro and paused his hand over a notepad, "To anyone in particular?"

"Tom, Dick, and Harry."

"Funny." Scribbling, "Tom, Dick, and Harry. How about... I'm having a fine time holed up in the lovely beach at Providence. Peters thinks I'm cute, and I'm not going anywhere. By the way, China invaded Kingston."

"Sounds fine to me." Krue shrugged. "It's the truth."

"Does it hurt – the truth?"

"To them it won't."

"Join the club. As we know it shit has hit the fan. We're unexpectedly busy... This place is, well you can sense it, so time to put you back under lock and key."

Jintana took hold of the moment, "I'll take her."

"And take Creton too, can't have the little Major escaping right at this opportune moment."

"I wouldn't call this moment opportune. It's horrible." Krue denounced the air of the bank and the waiting people out the front. "They'll riot – you don't have their money do you?" She pointed out to them, ready to make another lasting point, and saw they were stepping back, brightening up.

Callaghan said lowly, "Half of them have got nothing in our vault anyway. Opportunists." A radio on his desk beeped. He picked up the handset. "Yep, it's me... ... Bread and circuses... I see... Sure, minus the bread? ... Hmm... Now?" He unexpectedly leapt out of his chair and peered through the foyer, "You mean right now? Holy fuck are you a show pony!" He placed the handset down and proudly stuck his thumbs under his armpits, leaning back, a wondrous illumination shining from his face to Krue, "That fucker's *mad*. I'll show you! Out the front! Everybody!"

Standing on the steps of the sandstone bank with Callaghan, Eric and Marcus, the first thing Krue noticed was an imminent sense of gloom in the form of swollen storm clouds concealing the sky and sun. The bellies of these monstrosities were ghastly grey and moving at a sluggish rate denying spy satellites a view to earth. Over a thousand civilians from the town and around the farms, loyal subjects, gathered around the main intersection of Providence jostling for position to voice their concerns, some persistently pointing at the bank. Apart from gossip and the rash movements of militia and mobilisation from the day and night before, there was no hard evidence that the Chinese could be contained. Then when the usual produce from Kingston and the northern regions of Peters's robust state failed to arrive for morning markets, the implications of the new war hit home. The people were sullenly moping about, concealing their shattered trust in the security they had helped create. Hearing of flooded roads and rough seas had only made them worse. There was no escape. The looming clouds above could only work to one man's advantage. It was in this window of opportunity that Colonel Peters displayed his weapons of mass destruction.

First came his armoured personnel carrier crammed with gun-totting, leaf-covered Tonkas who were by no means afraid of the soft drifting rain. Then came two missile trucks driven by bearded surviving Task Force Seven whites. These trucks were the standard launch platforms for the favoured Fudos. Each was loaded with two missiles and ready to blast off. The third vehicle, driven by another whitey from Task Force Seven, was a huge Mac Truck hailing a trailer with a twenty metre long intercontinental ballistic missile laying in a cradle, which at a moment's notice, could be activated into a fifteen minute launch sequence. The cradle would be winched upright, and the missile thus aimed for the sky, would rumble to life and blast off. It was the finale which sent every civilian and refugee cheering. They danced in circles around the small procession, singing, and praising Peters as he stood on the trailer and patted the missile as if it were a trusted, domesticated yet ferocious pet. Even the local dogs were there, wagging tails, happy to be part of the fun and cheering. There were no speeches, only cheers of good luck blown in the form of kisses to the missiles. Peters waved farewell, and with a column of two hundred militia, some as green as spring leaves, behind him, the procession rumbled north out of Providence with a diminishing trail of cheering, flower throwing, children.

Peters smiled over his people and at the brief sight of Krue cast a rigid salute. Krue could not help but to grin. Here was a master unto himself and the roll of fate, off to hold back a tide, even though, Krue grimaced, the tide would roll back of its own will sooner or later. The true strength in China lay in its isolation behind stone walls. Anything outside was disposable. Every gambler knows that.

Jintana had watched from inside the bank. She saw the gaiety in Eric's stride as he bound down to the lead armoured personnel carrier and huddled inside with his equipment. This was the first time she had seen all three missiles trucks together. Even to a girl uneducated in the modern lances of war she was very exasperated. She shuffled down the steps glaring with an over-enthusiastic interest at the mighty objects rolling away. She returned to the sandstone stairs feeling light as a feather and nabbed Krue by the arm, "Walk with me, quickly... Back to your penthouse... Quickly." They broke free from the straggling dispersing crowd and made towards the beach. Heavy sparse specks of rain hit their skin.

Creton lumbered behind, careful to noose them in his sight as cheering, celebrating civilians milled between them farewelling their only hope of salvation – fire from the sky. Creton liked to keep Jintana and Krue's buttocks close, fuelling the dream of molesting either one, or both. Two pairs of cheeks raised pale and sweaty in the moonlight for his delight, thrusting and busting, slapp'n. Now's the time. He could die tomorrow, a bullet in his gut, and it'd been a long-time since the bam-bam with a good woman. Grinning wickedly, rubbing the tip of his stubby penis in his filthy pants, he drooled as Krue in mid-stride twisted to Jintana, her proud breasts swaying to a halt under her tight black T-shirt. Wearing that, Creton reckoned, she's got it coming.

"I need a radio," Krue propositioned to Jintana, shivering as the sea-breeze flickered her stray hairs. "My soldiers will kill Peters and Callaghan unless I call them. Without them all this," she pried deep into Jintana's eyes and meaning all that surrounds, "Will be destroyed! You need me to save you too."

Jintana's eyes said nothing.

Krue challenged Creton, "Don't act so dumb! I know you can hear me. You know what I'm saying!"

He stepped back and pretended to pick his nose.

"No, James wouldn't want that... I'll ask him later – but not from me," Jintana passed a fleeting glance to Creton, looking over Krue with cocky admiration. "You must stay out of sight Katherine... No man is making sense here! Go up! Now! Please!"

Krue paused, swung her head around from the beach to the streets of Providence, "I don't want to die here," and marching before Jintana into the foyer, cast her hands to the grey heavens, half-shouting, "This is so fucking frustrating!"

Creton followed, mentally erect.

Jintana shuffled behind nibbling her thumb.

The roar of the waves ceased as the foyer doors closed behind.

"Why can't anyone wake up?" Krue screamed, her shrill voice echoing off the walls into her ears. She jogged up the stairs to let off steam and then racing out on her balcony opened her mouth to cry to the sea wind but the cold wet lashes calmed her, her skin was wet and clammy, and a shiver ran down her spine.

Tom scrolled the message on the radio display, frowning.

"Get me out of here," Corrie interpreted it.

"You think that's her?"

"I smell a trap."

"Wake up. We're in a trap. No word and that's what we get: Holidaying."

"We could move towards Providence. At least we'll have a better view."

"Maybe. It's dangerous. Closer to Krue."

"Closer to Peters too. Providence is all he's got now."

"He's got the bridge... If we only had..." Matthews shied from saying it.

Tom erased the message from the radio's memory, "More of ourselves?"

Corrie felt fatigued. Stress had kept them awake. He felt like a ghost. He was fading and fumbling. "Would *Overlord* send another Team?"

Matthews rebutted, "So they can end up like us? It's us verse who knows what." With his knees hunched up to his chin in the midst of their dense scrap of forest, he reminded, "Let's get to basics. We're still alive."

"Yeah and living life to the fullest." Tom switched the radio off, whining, "But we're dying by the day mate. This is *fucked*,"

Matthews nodded, "An' we go *mental* here. What have we done here – Nothing."

Corrie said, "Hell, yes, what have we achieved so far?"

"Fuck all," Tom gauged, "So I reckon we kill him."

With a snide hiss Matthews cut Tom short. They listened for an intruder disturbing the approaches to the gully around them. There were people aimlessly trudging by, their feet sloshing in muddy holes, potentially laying an ambush, or refugees emerging from having swum the river. Then as it came it passed and after ten minutes of absolute silence, and after Corrie had silently crawled from end to end of the gully, they conferred again.

"This is fucked. Kill him."


North of Providence at purposely unmarked crossroads, Peters stood atop his armoured personnel carrier staring up to the bellies of grey clouds above, oblivious to the large droplets of rain slamming onto his face and forming rivulets down his neck. He had a few more hours of cover. Assembled before him were the drivers of the weapons of terror.

"Billy," he called and checked down to see that Eric was feeding the finer points of what he had to say into a laptop, "M-L-T One is to go up, stick to the roads on Jacinda Mountain, east side, facing Kingston and Sunny Bridge."

"Got it," Billy saluted, nodded his head forward, shaking rain droplets from his bushy beard. Kingston, he frowned, would not burn in this weather. That had disturbed Peters.

"Wayne,"

"Yes Sir." Wayne called up. He, like the other low-key Task Force Seven survivors, was vacant eyed, nervy, yet trusted to drive a Fudo missile truck.

"Hit the granite belt," Peters turned towards the granite belt, a few kilometres north and west. "Should the shit hit the fan you'll launch at the main body of the Chinese."

"Yes sir."

"Stevey,"

"Ya," Stevey called from the bonnet of the Mac that hauled the inter-continental Beijing Ninety-Six.

"You're gonna' ring south right around Providence during the night and set up on the range, south of Jacinda Mountain. Concealment is the top priority."

"Sure thing."

Peters admired the clouds. In the previous minute they appeared to thin, not excessively, yet enough to trouble him. He called down to the assembled men, "We're holding at Sunny Bridge. Get in position as soon as possible before these clouds disappear. If you do see a break in the clouds take immediate cover. There's an abundance of spy satellites these days and they got nothing to do but watch. Questions?"

Stevey raised his hand. "Do I need to set-up for a launch?"

Peters pointed down to Billy and Wayne, "You two will, have some space for the lift-off blast." He rested his hands on his hips and faced the column of his weapons, focussing on the tip of the Beijing Ninety-Six. He rubbed his stubbled cheeks, wondering if it actually worked, yet plumed his chest all the same, "Stevey, no. If you set her up for launch you take a larger risk of exposing yourself. However, if I call you, you might need to. So be close to a clearing. That's it."

And then they saluted him as casual as they could, yet sunken in their hearts screamed the conflicting feeling that this could be the last time they amassed as a formidable force, with a unified purpose.

# Action

Those were the days when sorties and poached eggs and hot showers and the smell of raw oxygen from the face mask blended into one streamlined indecipherable existence. And after briefings, de-briefings, correlating sorties and tallying he was astutely aware that down there under the wing were a hundred thousand perished souls put there by his thumb pressing the red button, easing the stick up, after-burning and atomising their asses. Doug heard that the worst case scenario was three months and the Chinese could be here sprinting across his runway and he'd be out of aviation fuel, grounded, fighting on his feet for once, jack-hammering a double-barrel K-41 into the hordes.

Until the calamity came to disrupt his routine, his effort to save the nation had been an enduring two missions a day harassing the Chinese Navy fleeing the Coral Sea. They had come so far, deployed their army buddies, and were set to prowl for more territories to exploit along the way from where they'd come. However, the Chinese Navy were now paying the price for chewing off more than they could handle and treading where Indonesia had already bled. With all the Chinese Armed forces on land cut off from their little empire and destined to perish, plus Cyclone Sandra creating havoc for both sides in and above the Coral Sea, Doug's superiors generously granted him eight hours leave.

For this afternoon he'd succumbed to the desires of the daughter of the Mayor of Ipswich, the closest town to Amberley Airbase. Doug and Suzie had taken the motel approach and lay in bed gazing out the window to the freckled granite buildings on the town's main street, each in their own thoughts. Suzie's slender legs suddenly straddled Doug's hips. She clutched his chest and feverishly ran her eyes over his broad shoulders. With a forceful stare she announced mandatory romping and sheet scrunching till sunset. However, there was dinner with her father tonight at some propaganda function. For Doug it would be an immorally devastating function. The Mayor pins a ribbon and thanks him, "For such a fine job, protecting our country from greedy peasants. Every time you drop a load of bombs, we're thinking of the good you do."

"If only I could tell you that for the last week what has kept me alive is not dropping loads of bombs... I been dreaming about your little Angel. She's what keeps me up there,"

"Doug." Suzie pried, her glowing eyes and smooth cheeks flexing into the first physical signs of a woman's intuition, "What's wrong?"

His eyes sprang open from a mix of intertwining dreams. Fresh was the father pinning the medal, or was it floating on a wing as it floated on the sea, defying its weight. I should be sinking. He reached for a glass of gin and stale tonic water and gulped it hard.

"Ahhhh."

"Raid the bar-fridge!" She raided the bar-fridge. "Ol' Timbo' the owner won't give two shits. This could be *it*, you know. Watch." She downed a mini-bottle of Bundaberg Rum. "Haaah!" She cat-licked up his neck. "All mine," and full of girlish glee, "For four and a half hours! Fuckity-fuck fuck!"

She bounced up and down in all sorts of manoeuvres, her soft milky breasts hovering over him.

"Suzie: crazy Suzie." He languished under her spell. "Don't go changing."

She smiled, "C'mon Doug *you're* the star. Now fuck me!"

"If you put it that way." They were at it like rabbits until his satphone beeped from within the folds of his clothes crinkled at the side of the bed. He wasn't scheduled, but it had to be –

She squealed, "Don't go! Don't leave me here like this! Don't be such a patriotic bastard! I'm tell'n ya to stay!"

They thrashed about in the bed for another forty minutes.

Then he calmly kissed her naked body, satisfyingly spread-eagled on the bed, "Tell Daddy I'm saving the world – can't make it."

"And me?"

"I'll be home'n'hosed before too long."

"Roger that!"


At the airbase Doug sat in the underground Tactical Operations Room with his Navigator, Willy.

"Get yer end in?"

"Yep," Willy pawed his stubbled face. "The wife was glad to have me. The kids thought I was Santa Clause or something… You?"

"Suzie."

"She sounds like a regular now."

"Less time coaxing. More time fellatioing."

"Can't forget the Latin."

"When this is over I'm gonna' pin her down and impregnate her."

"That easy huh?"

Doug looked dead ahead. "Easy."

Willy excitedly squeezed his hands together then unzipped his breast pocket. "I got around to that quote."

"… The quote! How much?"

"Have a peek."

He showed Doug a list; the vessels, tanks, trucks, men by the hundreds, they had reported as destroyed in all their sorties since invasion day.

Willy grinned, "And best of all there's this guy in strategy who allocated a cost to everything. There was a spreadsheet already set up. It's his pet hobby. Bastard's only got one arm."

"Booby trap?"

"Tindal."

Doug thought back, Tindal airbase in the Northern Territory. A lifetime ago. He read the sheet, "Streuth – this is the shit."

"Yeah, well he hasn't got much else to live for. Lost an arm *and* a leg. Check it out Doug, end to end."

At the top of the list was the most recent, an 'unfortunate incident' as the diplomats would say blubbering for forgiveness, but to Doug it was a Chinese frigate, alone and departing the Coral Sea, that had locked on to him and let loose too many warning shots, enough to sever the uneasy pact. They clobbered it with a laser guided bomb and it took all night to sink. On the left hand side of the sheet was its price, forty million.

"And that's a cheap frigate," Willy expertly pointed out. "Ex-Soviet."

"Probably why we sunk it: No chance." Maybe there were survivors swimming in shark infested stormy waters. He continued reading. "Where's the SAM sites in Brisbane? Definitely earned our money on those."

"They're counted as Anti-Aircraft hardware. Next category."

Doug scanned to the end of the list. "Impressive."

"He thinks we might rack up one billion in global carnage if we survive another few months."

"I'm sure we can stay alive for that. What's it now?"

"Seven-fifty-nine – *million*."

"Not bad. Arms dealers should give us a commission. What about Scotty from Six Squadron. How's he fairing?"

"Just under seven-hundred million."

"Better keep ahead of him then. You know how he likes a challenge."

Both men sat waiting for the next mission. Operations staff were busy tracking the Chinese Fleet, a Cyclone, a new disease outbreak in a neighbouring refugee camp, sorting recon data from the satellites and deducting which available targets should be marked for imminent destruction as soon as the rains passed.

"What about damage to non-legitimate territory?" Doug wondered, "Targets of no military value?"

Willy crouched forward, as he did staring into the targeting screen in the bomber, "We'll have to speak to Jesus H Christ about that."


Wayne drove the Fudo missile launcher truck in a measured manner up the steep and tight roads of the granite belt. Pre-war he was a courier, pre that he was an avid dirt-bike rider. It seemed that though he had perfect legs he was genetically disposed to travelling on wheels and rolling over the earth. He laughed at that thought as the clouds sunk to smother the land and his passenger, a quiet Tonka, pressed his face to the windscreen and remarked in poor English at the tempo of flashes of lightning.

"Could be in for a show," Wayne remarked.

"Show?"

"It's very pretty, very pretty. Keep watching."

He slipped into second gear as they slowly powered up a slope that curved around the peak of a rocky set of hills. The muddy road was screaming out for maintenance – a luxury that only a proper civilisation could offer. The mud on their boots was testament that they had already been bogged but were well prepared. Nestled between the two Fudo missiles in the back were planks of hard wood, chains for the front winch, a camouflage net for perfect weather. Nearing the apex of the curve Wayne shelved the truck into the safe side of the road, right up to the rocky wall, so close he could reach out and touch the trickling water. Looking to the other side he saw the Tonka engrossed in the view the hill offered; through sheets of rain they could see from the road's edge down to the extent of the beautiful granite belt. Large boulders protruded from the earth, slim gum trees in between, one taking a lightning strike as the fury of Cyclone Sandra spread from sea to land. For half a second the granite belt appeared in electric blue, illuminated from end to end, a surreal bony landscape. Wayne turned back to the muddy road. On the wall side of the slippery road was a fallen clump of mud. He swerved tightly around it, careful not to veer to the edge off the road, and once passed it, corrected himself to glide along the wall and was briefly flash blinded as above them, on the peak of the hill, a large gum tree lost a branch to a lightning strike. The glowing stumped branch rolled down the muddy hill bringing a meagre avalanche of sizeable rocks and came to rest metres ahead, on the road beside the moistened wall of earth.

Wayne eased to a halt and waited until his frazzled nerves settled. Then he and the Tonka jumped out into the rain and dragged the large branch to the edge, and though slippery at the edge of the road, they pointed it off and pushed it off until its weight pulled it over and they heard it disappear into a muddy ravine below. There was not much foliage to break its fall: bare earth and granite. From where they had launched the branch an indent remained at the lip of the road overlooking the granite belt. Water coming down from the hill soon found a more direct escape to below and within seconds the indent resembled a wet bite taken from the road, the road gradually washing away to the hungry ravine below. Wayne started the truck up again and seeing the debris of rocks carried down by the branch next to the rocky wall, expertly steered around. His back wheel jutted out to the sinking, increasing indent at the edge of the road, and for a second became bogged. He typically revved the truck, hoping that one short burst would set them free, but the wheel sank a few inches, the truck's weight compressing the weak muddy road, the foundations on which the road was packed shifted, rain water pouring through minute cracks, lubricating faults. Suddenly the entire road fell through; forming an avalanche. As the truck tipped back and rolled into the ravine the Tonka and Wayne braced. Mud and rocks blasted their windscreen. Broken, concussed, and upside down, they came to rest in a wildly flowing creek. The dark silty water quickly filled the truck's cabin and they drowned, upside down, hearing it trickle into their ears.

Eric hunkered over the keyboard, his short stubby fingers dancing merrily, eyes vigilantly locked on the code running across the screen. He had hacked a route from their bank up to a rogue *Black Tide* satellite down to Fiji's University, cloaked himself in a bogus Academic I.D. and logged on to an orbiting French space station, straight down to San Francisco and bounced across the city to the US Pacific Naval Command Firewall. Security was tight as a digital Fort Knox tonight. He shut down. Co-worker Marcus double-checked their contact with the missiles launchers spread out in the region. He waited patiently for one more.

"San Fran's gone maximum security."

"Yeah, Chinese have been over-loading the wired world with mega-bogus packets of crap jamming servers left, right and central... They're not getting what they want. Wait till the cunts bring out the ionising cannon." Marcus sighed to his screen. Perhaps the missing MLT was too deep into the granite belt to be reached by radio or the storm interfered with the signal. But, he figured, Wayne came good in the end, every time.

Eric heard a tap-tap and thought the roof had sprung a leak. He looked over his shoulder.

Peters was sopping wet, silently standing behind them. In the foyer three of his drenched Tonkas stood silently, united and void of emotion, armed to the teeth and looking gruesome with camouflage cream streaked over their bodies.

A shiver rippled through Eric

"Working late," Peters winked, browsing the screens.

Marcus spun from his console, "Overtime for you too?" He cheekily poked his head to the vault.

"Everyone that counts is working around the clock and it's the Bounty Hunter's pay-day."

Eric found the courage to joke, "Could he do one last job on a certain Chinese General?"

"Tried. He said No… Any news?"

"Cyclone Sandra halted the action in the Coral Sea. She's moving out like a left hook now." Marcus reported. "You?"

"Fortifying Sunny Bridge."

Marcus and Eric frowned suspiciously at one another. Was Kingston now officially off the map? Is this what history is?

"Here he is." Peters said.

Malo entered the foyer, a stockman's coat draped over his forearm dripping the rain. "Eh blow this rain off brother," he half-yelled, "I'm goin' walk-about. I get fucking muddy boots, I go no-shoes I step on land-mines. No tap dancing." Under his coat was a sexy machine-gun and long arm sniper rifle.

"You want ya' pocket money first?" Peters led him to the vault and heaved the thick metal door wide open.

"I gotta' find somewhere to spend it you know," Malo joked.

"There's more than enough men out there to rob you of it. But before you go to spend, you can sit out the storm."

Marcus and Eric watched as Peters and Malo slipped into the vault. Malo, was the eeriest being either had come across. He didn't appear like the killer he was renowned to be.

Inside the chilled vault Peters flicked a light switch. Malo stood coolly fixated at the range of wealth on the steel shelves; various sized ingots of gold and silver, wads of currencies, trays of jewels and jewellery, microprocessors and exotic weapons, all stolen, exchanged and ransacked from years of war. He recognised a few.

Malo said, "Must be hard work, mate."

"Some of it was here before I came, it was the inheritance that enabled me to establish this pit into a society. We've built on it. Hit the four million mark this week."

Malo poked his nose along the trays. "Fancy stuff. Some of it, wouldn't know what to do with it."

"Like most men," Peters remarked, his voice jaded with a strange irony.

Malo then abruptly stood back and pointed to a shadowed far wall and heavy shelves. Small pearls and diamonds, bonds, handguns and a grenade sized Semtex H detonator. He picked it up and admired the device, a simple adjustable timer and push button. "Take out a tank with one of these. I'll give ya' fifty for it."

Peters removed the Semtex H detonator from Malo's hands. "Callaghan likes that thing close by, in case you know what."

"Understood... *Brrr* It's cold in here." He slapped a wall. "Thick, like a tomb. What can you pay me in?"

"Gold." Peters decreed. "Bonds go up and down and they don't mature for twenty years. Jemmy brought them in from some Pacific trader thinking they'd be good for toilet paper. Fucking dickheads. Could be real, could be shit."

"So you cash 'em in twenty-years time?"

"Yeah," Peters nodded, "Euro though. Got to get to Europe first."

"Give us a couple," Malo snatched out, "You'll see. I'll come back in a flash personal jet, the Malo Machine: black, sleek, with a spa bath out the back and a double bed and Miss Sweden."

"Sure, and don't forget me when you're up there." Peters gave him ten bonds, each supposedly worth a thousand euros, shaking his hand, trying to imagine twenty years into the future but then smugly congratulated, "If you can think that far ahead you deserve it."

"No it'd make good dunny-paper," Malo slid them safely into a water-proof inner pocket. "What else can you pay me in?"

Peters checked the gold, Callaghan had coded them. "Gold?"

Malo nodded. "White-yellow-black man speaks the one golden language."

Peters picked up two bars. "These equal your fee."

Malo held the bars and grinned. "Nice. Right size, too."

"How long before you come back?"

"... What you thinking in that wicked mind of yours?"

"The strangers up north will be cleaned up in a week or less."

"Yeah?"

"I'm working on a solution – something quick."

"Might camp out on Jacinda Mountain, watch the fireworks eh?" Malo said with an expectant smile.

"Keep your eyes open."

"Never closed," Malo winked, slid the two gold bars into his coat, "These will drown me if I swim the rivers come flood time." Paid up, he relaxed and out of curiosity ran his eyes along the length of the shelf coming to rest on a coarse faded paper decorated with a basic picture – amid the hi-tech stuff and glittering booty it looked plain, out of place and interesting. It had been used to wrap valuables and now lay there, discarded. He snatched it and marvelled at the face, an amused smile kinking the ends of his lips, growing into a bold grin so malevolent he slapped his thigh.

"What's that?" Peters cocked his head to scan the faded bounty notice.

"This that white sheila I seen today!" Malo rejoiced. "She must be it!" He pegged the paper to Peters's chest. "She's the white devil. Yellow-fella think you white-devil. Fuck'n'bullshit. This sheila – see that? Fifty thousand! She'll cost you an arm and a leg. She's cost a lot of yellow-devils their heads!"

Peters studied it closely. Issued by some Warlord in Broome, representing an alliance stretching to Kakadu and Mt Isa, from three months ago.

Malo crudely asked, "You want me to do her in?"

"No... She's got something about her,"

"You're thinking with your dick."

"So what?"

"She's a dangerous one. Do her in. We go halves. That's twenty-five each."

Peters folded the paper in half, half again, and held it between two fingers, "As if we'd get paid. Besides, we'd have to cart her head to the other side of the continent."

Malo frowned, "Nah. We take photos. Email them."

Peters led him out, "You're got some serious gold on you, you don't need anything else to play on your mind. Going walk-about?"

"Not too far."

"*Sure...* Good move. Shit's coming down."

They stepped towards the doors to the bank, each deep in thought.

"Don't worry 'bout me." Malo paused and turned to all, even the Tonkas, "See you next time. See ya' Marcus! Hey Eric! See ya' next week! Hey Captain Callaghan!"

Callaghan stumbled out of his office with a radio in his hand and a map in the other, "Hey what?"

"I'm going brother!"

"Where you going, brother?"

"I'm goin' walk-about mate."

"Lucky you. Come back now, ya' hear?"

Malo waved, "Sure brother!" and with those lasting words stepped outside into the pouring rain and submerged into the night.

Peters stood, thinking precariously: Malo goes walk-about right now and being an aboriginal may be on to something – an intuition – of what? Of living twenty years in the future?

Callaghan said to Peters, "I knows he's the best investment we have for on the ground intelligence, but he commands such a hefty sum. The guy can live off the land if he wants. He doesn't need money."

"Who said aboriginals know nothing about commerce? Staying here?"

Callaghan rubbed his eyes. "Trying to trade in some food from the farms. All the carts are bogged down, so yeah. How's the new border?"

"Secure. I've got spies on Kingston. The Chinese aren't moving out yet. I'll be going up to the bridge in the morning."

Callaghan asked, "Are you staying in town tonight?"

Peters tapped the folded paper into the knuckles of his other hand, "Yeah. I'll find somewhere safe."


The night-duty militia man was woken out of a doze and ordered to return to his shanty barracks. The visitor then unlocked the door, knocked on it lightly and with a cold wet hand pushed his way into the dark living room.

Krue heard the click of the door of an unannounced entry then the soft footsteps of someone else making their way down the dark stairs. She and the visitor observed each other from across the living room. She had rolled straight out of bed in a sheet with her Berretta pistol cloaked under it, the muzzle paused by her belly.

He stood with rugged apprehension, staring from the form beneath the sheet to the weapon now held rigidly to her side. He stepped closer.

She remained transfixed. She placed the pistol on the table.

He stepped closer again.

Lightening out to sea cast pure illumination and she saw Peters, brandishing a crude grin, his wet and curled hair still dripping, his blue eyes grey.

"If you're still here in the morning I'll kill you," she advised him. He nodded, and followed her.

# Wake Up Call

The next morning Krue buzzed around the kitchen, twirled to the frying-pan cracking in two eggs, sliced tomatoes on the bench, grilled toast, squeezed lemon juice into a glass of ice cubes. She ate on the balcony to a magnificently clear sky, watching seagulls bobbing on the sparkling waves. Afterwards she showered. Drying her hair, peering at her steamy reflection, a light knock came from the door.

Jintana, wearing a dark blue sarong, bowed her head before entering, stepped by her host to the table and planted herself there, her elbows holding up her troubled head. She was so dark she could have turned day to night.

"My god. Woke up on the wrong side of the bed this morning?"

"No." Jintana sulked. "Of all the places in this world the Chinese come *here*."

"I'm not surprised: What goes on around here is a magnet for any type of order."

Jintana's eyes levelled on to Krue. "Peters is in town. Did you see him?"

Krue bit into a succulent tomato, "… Yes."

"I heard you," Jintana frugally commended her friend, "Do not fall for him – for any of them!"

Krue wiped away a droplet of tomato juice running from her lip to her chin. "Who said *I* was falling? How *teenage*."

Jintana remained resolute, scrutinising the beautiful blue sky above, "I have."

Krue relaxed, withdrew a nail filer from her top pocket and silently flashed her growing nails, then one by one, examined the edges, filing finer edges and points. Jintana watched on admiringly.

"You have nothing to say to me?" Jintana asked.

"Maybe it's good for you, for us," Krue examined her other hand, "One shouldn't deny affection in these times. Get it when you can – I say."

After lunch, Two Stars Ghan walked with a proud stride and an air of impeccable invincibility. He checked into one of the numerous pubs on Gallipoli Street with Chiang to enjoy a drink with several of the fine soldiers of the 177th Brigade. They poured beers from kegs, trying in earnest to keep the cooling system working. The decor of the pub seemed very outlandish, lavish, antique, or plainly alien. And like a temple, the ancient essence would have to be preserved for historical purposes.

Chiang coltishly laughed and raised his glass, "To frontiers conquered and pirates decimated."

"Cheers!"

Ghan surveyed the cheery, celebrating troops. "This is very good... Aren't you glad we came here and weren't dropped off at some hellhole island in the Pacific?

"Exactly!" Chiang's cheery face drained his beer and he stumbled to the bar. A Supply Sergeant poured from a flat keg. Chiang took two beers and sat down, explaining to Ghan, "I have nothing to complain about... Look, what we drink now is a local brew. It's nice."

"Not bad," Ghan said, "But we could be drinking pig piss and wouldn't know the difference."

"I haven't died yet, so let's celebrate."

"True." After another sip Ghan felt the stress of the previous days blurring. The torrential rain hampering patrols outside Kingston, and the lack of communication with the Third Fleet, and the fact it was retreating from the Coral Sea, had taken its toll. But he couldn't let it show. Not now. Not ever. He was actually missing his superiors. Maybe it was the bad weather. They will return. They have to. His eyes roamed the pub, taking in the delight of a foreign drinking den, the décor, the tables, the pin ups on the walls, the face in a large blue poster.

"Is that Peters?" he called to the back wall of the pub where five Intelligence Officers played a jovial game of darts. They were sombre faced because the soldier's had bayoneted the whores of the town last night in some moralistic cleansing purge. There were only a few left, and beaten up at that. The men needed raw flesh.

"Peters?" Chiang echoed with perfect clarity.

"Yes..." Ghan awed at the propaganda poster, drawing him to Peters's screen-printed hardened face and hollow eyes. Written in English in the lower third of the portrait poster, in bold, was the slogan to which he stood for: *All for Providence.* A variety of Asian interpretations ran down the sides like margins, white lettering against the ultramarine blue background. An icon, that like this pub, had survived the rummaging of two invasions.

"That's Colonel Peters... Commander of Providence."

"Ah, my enemy." Ghan covertly studied the image. "Interesting."

Between organising the patrols and screaming at his HQ staff to contact the Third Fleet however they could (they did find a pirate's satphone and called the Navy in Beijing, but even that call was cut short, having come from an un-reliable source) Ghan had an hour briefing with his intelligence officers as to what lay outside of this third-world shit-heap Port of Kingston, named by some emancipated German immigrant one hundred and eighty-nine years ago (his original preference of name was Kaiser Town but was voted down by the majority of Irish settlers). The only information in hard copy came from the 'Australasian Pacification Manual' issued by the New Exterior Ministry, describing Colonel Peters as a *Pirate masterminding punitive land and sea operations in Indonesian Occupied Queensland. A ruthless, cowardly, genocidal, prejudiced, outcast, an insult to Chinese and Global values, an unfair trader and exporter of produce to the Philippines, Taiwan, Singapore and Papua New Guinea. Provider of a port of call for the lowest of pirates to roam the Pacific. If captured alive, this glorified bandit is to be executed, publicly if possible, no trial necessary in the Motherland, but the Motherland is to take all credit for the above mentioned execution.*

The manual was three months old and tainted by politically inspired detestation at the rot in the Pacific. But somewhere up the chain, so far up Ghan couldn't and wouldn't bother to comprehend, this Peters was on their Hit List. He sipped heartily. This Peters was on *his* Hit List, a list one name long. A sadist. A glorified bandit. Well, welcome to the world of modern war, just like a feudal crisis of the past.

Ghan wondered, having taken Colonel Peters's largest port of trade, if the job was actually complete. Tactically, yes, but a town for pirates and bandits could soon enough be the next town too. Then Ghan understood the shift from armoured movement to global policing. Chase the enemy. The slamming of his fist spelt order to the chaos and anarchy of feral, apocalyptic, uncharted Queensland. He sat on a stool in heavy contemplation, his gaze firmly out the window to the blue sky, the burnt husks of warehouses, and down to the wharf where the *Margarita* was preparing to sail to China.

Chiang said, "Colonel Peters was the pervert Lieutenant Ling spoke to on the radio."

"I know." Ghan stood up, his steely eyes surveyed his troops, and he cast a sneer to the poster of Peters, roaring, "This pirate, bandit, Warlord – whatever – will be wiped out and his comrades scattered like leaves in the wind! His buildings demolished and the caves he hides in, crushed!"

The troops straightened up and glared at the poster of Peters, crowding around it and mocking the austere pose. The contrast of crisp blue on white of the eyes created an eerie magnetism, and any way one looked at it, those penetrating eyes followed you around the room. Ghan strutted with scissor-leg precision to the Intelligence Officers playing darts, clicking his fingers for them to hand the slim projectiles into his palm.

Ghan decreed, "We are here to control these lands."

The troops cheered.

Ghan continued, a rising tone of vengeance, "Tomorrow we smash his illegitimate militia - *peasants*! We rid these lands of the rot that is plaguing our peaceful Pacific!"

"Tomorrow!" the troops cheered. After all, they were bored of this shit-heap. The victory, though climatic, was empty compared to the battles they had been taught of that raged in and out of China for over eight thousand years of written history.

Ghan stepped three meters from the poster of Peters, paused, weighing the darts in his hand, "Over-glorified bandit, killer of innocent men, women and children, can not stand against a steel-hearted army!"

The troops eagerly gulped their beers.

Chiang cheered, pretending to squash a sizeable bug under his rubber boot. "Warlords throughout the Pacific are the instigators of senseless wars!"

"We fight for peace!" Ghan yelled. He swivelled his head to the poster and threw - The dart sailed before their eyes hitting the ear. Second try, Ghan hit the left eye, third and final shot, hit the other eye's black pupil. But Peters's heavy gaze remained intact. Determined, enveloped in a cruel and a twitching stare with gritted teeth, Ghan spoke though constipated through anger, "Scourge of the Pacific! *Our* peaceful, beautiful Pacific!"

Chiang applauded Ghan's effort, "Sir, we've got the firepower!"

Ghan plucked out the darts, "When he is done with, the whole world will know of our crusade and of our bravery... We will not be forgotten." He handed a dart to Ling, his most trusted Intelligence Officer, "To prepare the way, you will leave Kingston, and go under the cover of night behind Colonel Peters's lines and report back to advancing frontline units by dawn of tomorrow. Surprise is our essence!"

"Yes!" Ling gasped, "My heart is abound with honour to be on such a glorious step forward for the Chinese Army!"

"You will be honoured alongside those of the Great March!"

"Divine!"

"Go now Lieutenant Ling before the sun sets, and when it sleeps, guide yourself by the stars. You are elite Lieutenant Ling because you are highly adaptable."

"I will appear as a local refugee of Providence!"

"Yes! You are a master of disguise!" Chiang congratulated to Ling.

"I was trained as a Statistical Analyst, but, I will strive hard."

"Good! Now go with the knowledge that every step forward is a step closer to peace!"


On the northern side of Sunny Bridge Peters strolled through distressed refugees. They were massing in large hungry groups by the roadside, looking up and down, north or south, for an avenue to flee. They can't cross the bridge, barricaded by his orders. They can't move north, the Chinese are coming. Peters saw hundreds, and guessed there were thousands more in the bush. They were not survivors of the fireball, they were recent additions and had traversed many a differing roads in the plight south. Some had odd wounds; bites, scratches, caked blood from crude shotguns and machetes, and though terrified of the white-man, yellow militia and the blend of cut-throats in the regions they had fled through, they came here for protection.

Vince kept to Peters's side, "I think the Chinese have been at them."

"Why wouldn't they. Only friends they've got are the ones they educate."

"Are you willing to be educated?"

"Like them?" Peters looked down his nose to the wretches. "I haven't got the resources to deal with them. It's the several thousand psycho Chinese up north that are on my mind."

"Verses our two-hundred?"

"Call it ten to one." He faced up to the bright blue clear sky, "I hope the Fudos are concealed."

Vince reported, "Wayne, still no contact."

Peters tilted his dejected countenance to the earth and the overlaying sets of muddy footprints sinking into puddles.

"What do you think?" Vince worried.

"Until he calls in, consider him dead." Peters turned to his armoured personnel carrier, hidden on the southern side of the bridge. After running through the mathematics he decided, "One missile short. *Bugger*. I need some cannon fodder."

"For what?"

"To keep the Chinese occupied and annoyed."

"Recruit refugees?" Vince proposed, "They can be tricked."

"Not in a hurry though. They'd only turn against us. Fodder, that's all they're good for. Give the Chinese something to chew on."

Vince suspiciously eyed the refugees, "Can you control them in such a way?"

"No. They'll just be in the way and that'll create enough of a headache for our Chinese chums. But also, let some of the refugees into Providence. They'll create a cushion should the shit get too close."

Vince was flustered with disbelief.

"We'll open the bridge for some of the night. I mean, it's proof we are providers of protection. And then I bet within a few hours there'll be just as many waiting here in the way of the Chinese."

"You are a man of sober compassion,"

"No," Peters felt offended and showed Vince an imaginary pocket calculator, "If only two thousand refugees are causing stampedes either side of the bridge, I am a man of calculation. That's another ten targets for each Chinese soldier to have to aim at instead of us."

Tom had crawled down to the Arubai River for water. Left was Sunny Bridge and on the opposing bank refugees were washing and shitting into the river. The rains receded quickly and filthy water would not do. Then he saw the top light brown hair of the only white man on the north side. He was taller than his military partner, he was also pointing out the approaches to the bridge and masterminding something. Tom remained silent. Should he tell Matthews? Matthews only wanted out of here. Corrie? Corrie wanted Krue back. Tom didn't want to be overrun by hordes of Chinese. He slithered back up the muddy bank, empty-handed but full of quiet thoughts. From the northern side of the bridge a herd of refugees picked themselves up and marched straight across at the beckoning of the white man, the primary target. In this break, the noise of their plight, Tom easily and quickly slid back into the seclusion of the gully. If he had his rifle, after one clean shot they'd be free.

Krue watched the sun set, hope waning into disillusion, exhausted from probing every fact and eventuality. It was a bore. There was no action. On the balcony all she could do was wait, and wait she did.

The militia were shouting again. Orders. She heard a whine, they'd hit someone. Well, she muddled, that wasn't nice. She looked over the balcony and had to look away, then back again. Trickling onto the beach from within town, herded by young militia armed with rifles and clubs, were refugees. They were obviously not citizens. She remained fixated, studying them, as the sun was swallowed by the earth and the first stars came out to play.

They were ordered to sit on the beach, several hundred, sorted into loose tribal groups, huddling, scared and beaten. They knew in their starving little hearts that life should never have eventuated to this. A few were the rich and middle-class city dwellers fleeing oppression, but most were just the poor, on the run. When the militia were busy the refuges meandered up and down the beach and around the units. Some waded into the waves with hand reels, rods, or a spear. There was some hungry moaning going on. Mothers gathered children. Fathers dished out the last rice from faded plastic bags. A few small fires flared and they squatted closer to watch the flames. Some saw Krue and faced up to her, refining a pleading stare for something she couldn't provide. In her heart there was no hope. With a malicious grin she stared back: Peters was pawning these suckers. The Chinese will swarm in here like a plague. They won't know who is a refugee and who is a militia. Guerrilla war is best fought with an abundance of civilians in between.

It was dark now and Krue went to turn on a light but it didn't work. Mandatory blackout. She didn't mind. Back to her balcony she admired the stars. They twinkled vigilantly, each individually lonely with a particular glimmer that soaked a human's cry for attention rather than negate or oppress it. And then a purple shooting star scooped under the moon. That flare from the heavens requited a single wish to be granted by the Gods of the Universe. She made one. Then she felt mentally exhausted and was ready to retire and recap the day before she fell to sleep. But in a sullen correlation, those on the beach bleated their pain, first the women leaving sentimental songs unfinished, hitting a dull, slow, burning note, haunting the ears of the fellow disheartened, then they simultaneously moaned up and down, unified grief directed to their captors, the sea or the stars? The combined primal groan jammed Krue's thoughts. A cold shiver rippled through her body. Who can sleep with that going on?

She moved off the balcony to try the lights again and like all the lights in Providence, no luck. Her eyes adjusted quickly to the dark interior. By blacking-out Providence, what had Peters announced? She patiently guided herself to her pack on the bed. Her hand slid into a side pocket and retrieved a lighter. She flicked the lid and pressed the charger, cupping the blue bulb of gas with her hand, directing the light to her bed. There was a leather belt uncoiled next to the pack. Her army belt was around her waist. Creton stood tensely by the wall pretending to be a curtain shadow within the folds of the hanging fabric. The top of his pants were unbuttoned. He removed one hand from his groin and clenched it into a fist, breathed deep, held his gut tight under a looming bulky rib cage, and lunged forward with a premeditative, maniac, growl.

With the flick of her thumb she cast the room into darkness.

She rolled on to her back and drew her knees to her chin. Creton came crashing over the bed, springs squeaking, half his body falling on top of her. Using her thigh muscles she pushed and held his body up with one leg, then with her free boot she stabbed tip-toe kicks to the edges of his eye socket and temple. The pain threshold tested, he recoiled off onto the other side of the bed yelling horrendously loud and clear, "*Biiiiiitch!*"

Her eyes were re-adjusting to darkness again. Krue leapt for the door but bounced hard into the wall and flopped disorientated to the floor. Creton flashed a torch over her as she drunkenly crawled on all fours tilting to her sides. The black barrel of his gun probed into the beam of light from behind the torch.

"You get it now *Biiiiiitch!*!"

"Ahh, "

"Panties!" Creton satisfactorily grunted, the brief beating he suffered now justified. "Panties!"

It was going to be rape, Krue sank, sanity sliding like a mulch of meat off a slanted steel tray into the fucked-up bucket. He had the gun, she, somewhere to stick it. Just another side of town she had to see first hand.

"Peters will know," she warned as the light edged closer. "He and I are *lovers!*"

"He pay *me* to kill *you*…" He cast the room into darkness, kicked her where head meets neck and ear and announced "He wants you to die in pain! Fifty-thousand dollars of pain!" She fell forward spinning out of her mind. He planted his foot on her buttock, squashing it into the carpet, trying to part her cheeks under his weight. Krue's eyes bulged, the pressure surging, popping. A pain in the cranium, maybe he could knock her out and do it cold.

"But I said *No!* No pain!" Creton huffed to himself, "But I give *you* pain! *Fucking* pain."

She instinctively whimpered, purposely futile, "Please! I'll do anything! Please! Don't hurt me! I am good girl! Good girl do *bad things!*"

"Cry like a whore!" He lifted his foot and slid it under her crotch. "I hear *pussy* stories. Suck. Fuck. And suck." His tongue smacked his lips then his pallet, "You fuck Peters? Army Whore. You fuck me."

"Okay," she grimaced. With a burning stare into the darkness she knelt with her back to him. He'd do it doggy. However he did it, for the moment she wouldn't have to look him in the face. She wouldn't have to see it, feel it, yes. She wouldn't even hear her last shot. He'd kill her humanely, to the back of the head, *ciao Bella*.

Creton unevenly pulled his pants down and fondled his erection. "Down!" He whacked her buttock with the gun barrel. "Suck *me!*"

A foul taste came to her mouth. After one good suck there'd be millions of Cretons swimming in her mouth. She stood and turned to him, kneeling to unlace her boots as fast as possible before he slid his groin up to her mouth again, offering her a smelly infected grotty penis as reward for submission. He'd cum in seconds, she knew it, and like all desperadoes, afterwards the pain of immaturity would over-ride any morality and like a shameless one-night rub he'd be gone but not before killing her. He'd go to his drinking den and tell tall tales of his ecstatic night. He'd have to cart her head to a deceased warlord to claim a forgotten bounty. They'd want to know she died humiliated. He could most certainly say so.

She fell backwards, hopelessly, struggling to get one boot off, and then a trouser leg, and her underpants. He enjoyed her flight to undress and stood over her casually masturbating then refraining from exciting himself, watching her through a cone of the torch light. She stood, caressing a hand to his belly and lightly, warily pushing the extremes of frigid, pushing him back to the bed. He shone the torch on her hands, the gun barrel resting on her shoulder, stretched himself back with a sense of decadent satisfaction. She wanted to fuck him, just like he thought so!

Krue said timidly, croaking and afraid, "Let me do my job properly... You were right. I am a whore for an army that does not love me."

He rightly growled and rested the gun barrel on her other shoulder. If it were to blow off so close the sound would slap her ear drums into tattered biological vapour.

"We do everything!" Creton barked. "Everything..."

Krue hurriedly untied her other boot, drawing the laces rhythmically, dancing, pouting her breasts from under the black T-shirt.

"Titties! Mine! And your ass – what happened to your ass!" he demanded.

Krue involuntarily blushed and sulked, "A bullet."

Creton announced with glee, "Mine!"

Krue slid her last boot off, the panties, and was naked bar the black T-shirt. At this point his mind was blown out by her pubic hair. It existed, the white-woman had a different pussy and he would be one of the few to taste it.

"I've never," Krue whimpered, "*Ever* done it with such a long man."

"Yagh!" He was ecstatic and suspicious. He knew he was in no way large but to hear it, even so falsely, that was the finishing touch!

She hovered over him, thinking: Stall that festering yellow tongue peeping out of his lips with stark breasts or straddle the sick monster. Breasts... She slid her hips forward, rubbing herself over his penis and leant forward, bowing over, to take her shirt off. His torch shone on the breasts to be. She curled under the length of the rifle and with her left hand, accidentally elbowed his gun forearm away. As he jerked it back, her right hand cut through the dark, driving her index and middle fingers into his mouth. He suckled, she withdrew them wet, and wriggled that arm out of the shirt, carelessly tossing it over his gun elbow. He licked his lips as her slimy finger tips parted, raised up in the dark, then curved through the air slicing like knives into his eyes – gouging, twisting, and piercing under the eyelids, hooking the whites out of their sockets. She then dived into him, away from the gun barrel.

Creton screamed, flexing his arms, a single rifle shot deafening them. She hunched up, kneed his groin then rolled onto his gun arm, twisting on her back, flicking her legs to kick his free arm and chin. She wouldn't break any bones or grapple the gun from his iron grit. He tried to bear hug her but she slithered out and off the bed. He screamed. She held her breath. Her enforced silence choked her, and a mere breath away from coughing, Creton rolled around on the bed in his agonising pain, fraught with fear, wailing to the world that he was blind and the cursed bitch would die, "With my long dick in your mouth! I can see you! I smell your cunt!" He blindly swung the rifle around the darkened silent room, searching, sniffing, "You!"

"Stop it!" Jintana whispered in a pathetic, panic stricken tone from the doorway.

Creton fired. *Crack!*

"*Eeeeegh!*" Jintana dropped to the floor. Krue snuck forward, her hip-bone rolling over the torch. She popped up to the bed and flashed it directly into Creton's bleeding eyes. He was blinded, frightened, flooded by pain and shaking. Krue shone the torch on Jintana, bleeding and alive, fragments of the wall blasted by the bullet had sprayed like a wing of shrapnel into one side of her thigh. She whimpered. Creton swung and fired another shot into the wall. It ricocheted into the living room. Creton shuffled back to the wall, swiping the gun before him and cursing to make her say something.

Krue silently moved to his flank and launched a pillow at the other wall. He struck wildly and scrunched it like a rag. She knuckled in the dark for his temple with one hand and found his gun with the other. He twisted to her and took a fist into his nose. The bridge collapsed. He gurgled warm blood and pulled the trigger. The bullet passed through the wall and split a brick. Krue slammed his nose again and twisted his gun arm by twisting the stock. Creton belted at her head in the darkness but she was elusive. She looped her finger into the trigger, sharing it with his sweating index digits. His other arm flexed and landed a punch into her ear which sent her launching backwards but not before squeezing the trigger. A bullet struck the opposing wall. She slanted the rifle down, squeezed the trigger, the bullet pulverising a bone in Creton's foot. Still, he held the gun, an iron fist welded by pain. She clambered over him and swivelled the stock thus twisting his wrist. He punched her in the back repeatedly, seeking the kidneys. She twisted the rifle harder but in his grip it was like twisting his arm off. He yelled. As the gun barrel passed over his gruelling gasps she squeezed the sweaty trigger again. A bullet hole appeared in the wall beside his neck, the aroma of his burnt skin stung Krue's nostrils. His retarded gun arm buckled throwing her aim far, his other arm gripped her neck and squeezed. She hugged the gun and directed it into his ribs. Scrunch that trigger! A flame puffed up from the shot mattress. And again! Bones cracked, blood sprayed over her forearms and breasts. His finger was harder to budge from the trigger as through a punctured torso he sucked in an inferno of doomed power. She elbowed his temple, one, twice, thrice, harder for a forth until pain sprang up her arm. Creton's grip went limp. He slumped. She stood over him on the bed and with the heel of her foot slammed his forehead, once, twice, and thrice so hard she fell forward into the bludgeoned but warm mess, his half-erect penis symbolically sliding up between her buttocks.

With the rifle now securely in her hands and fury driving her, Creton ended propped against the wall, his torso ruptured by two more shots. Krue stood over him, victoriously sneering, gagging for breath. She jumped off the bed and found the torch, directing the light to Jintana, who kneeled and pulled up her kimono to stare at her wounds and the naked blood-smeared Krue.

"Let's get out of here."

"Agh," Jintana picked out a splinter, "Did he …?"

"I'm fine. I'm on fire. That fucker sums up this place, doesn't it?" She yelled to Creton. "*Fucking fucker!*"

"Callaghan's not here." Jintana whimpered and by torchlight burnt to her memory was the bludgeoned body. "I could have warned you! I'm sorry! Sorry! He is a *bad* man!"

Krue scowled as proof of mockery of Jintana's sense of mistrust, "Forget it. Is James at the bank?"

"I don't know." Jintana swayed her head, "Maybe he has gone?"

"What?"

"*Home.*"

Home. Creton off the leash as the ship goes gurgling down.

"Sleep in my bedroom," Jintana begged. "We can't go outside. Too dangerous."

"Sure… You might just be protecting me." Krue checked her naked self.

Jintana shone the light as Krue washed blood from her stomach, navel, finger tips, wrists, arms, the wrinkles in her inner elbows, thighs, knees, splatters on her toes and under her toe-nails. It crept in where it could.

"Are you bleeding?"

Krue turned in the shower, "Bruised. Aching. That was close. I can't do this shit anymore. That *fucker.*"

Jintana shone the light to Krue's feet to see the blood run between the toes, then up again, admiring the cleansed, sculptured body.

"What's going on?"

"People are outside…. So many Katherine… Scavengers. Rats."

Krue wringed water from her hair and ruggedly dried herself. "Are there guards downstairs?"

"Two." Jintana replied, thankful, then clasped her leg.

Krue hissed to Creton, "Dead *fucker.*" She pulled up her pants, tied her boots and found her rifle and pistol stashed under the bed. "Let's get Creton out of here and down *there* as a message to any of his buddies."

"How – he's *dead.*"

They rolled Creton up in bedroom sheets, dragged him to the balcony and after several efforts of heaving pushed him off the edge. In the dark, behind the dunes, the body bounced once. Asian languages chattered softly interpreting why this carcass had come from the heavens just as their previous meagre meal wore off. The first scrawny hand of many felt up Creton's unwrapped chunky thigh and returned with a blunt rusty knife. Krue could hear them four stories down scurrying for cooking cans or the odd piece of ply wood or fallen branch.

"Come." Jintana urged, dragging Krue's pack across the living room floor, palming her hand flatly to the dark walls, "Demons everywhere."

Krue turned to the stars scattered across the sky then looked to the beach.

"Hurry!" Jintana rushed, her small frame lugging Krue's pack to the door. "Come to my unit... No one dares go there."

"And outside? We have no idea of what's outside."

"Come," Jintana pleaded, "Here is *evil*, come!"

They quickly made their way downstairs, Jintana still clasping her leg and suppressing her will to cry. Inside, after Krue had barricade the door, she lay Jintana down on the floor and shone the torch over the blood stained kimono covering the wounded thigh.

"Where's the pain?"

Jintana pointed to the obvious, sat up, and together they unwrapped the kimono all the way up to her belly. Her naked hips, honey yellow skin, soft inner thighs and rounded knees seemed untouched. At the front of one thigh Krue fingered around the small wounds, pinching at the skin, trying to squeeze at the bits blasted in there. Jintana instinctively slid her hand over her sex, her other hand tenderly gripped Krue's wrist, "I will not die?"

"Not from that, I think I've found a bit..." Krue squeezed at a perfectly built stretch of muscle and extracted out a sizeable fragment. Jintana screamed, and continued screaming and whining until she passed out. Krue bandaged her leg with a silk scarf, a flimsy synthetic *Made in China* tag flicking against her thumb.

# New World Order

Marcus paused the conversation. "You hear that?"

Staccato gunfire. And again. No return. Probably up into the air.

Callaghan sighed. "Crowd control for the tourists."

"Well, continue."

Callaghan and Marcus were in his office, sipping camomile tea, listening to Doc Nelson's report. The windows of the bank had been blanketed, and inside lamps and locally made candles added an unfamiliar though harmonious balance to their surroundings.

"There's too many to make any effort to save them… And there'll be more making straight to the hospital," Doc Nelson worried. "They come into town, crowding the streets with their bullshit commotion about United Nations protection and looking for Embassies and when they see they aren't fooling no one they beg. The locals don't know what to do. Help them or ignore them? They're all legitimate refugees and it's the first time they've run helter-skelter into somewhere *civilised*. And, they're deluded to think we really are *civilised*. *This* has the potential to tear the place apart."

"Let's get to basics…" Callaghan dug a clump of wax from his ear, "Who is causing the commotion and who thinks they're righteous enough to expect civilised protection? Is it one mongrel mob or all of them?"

Doc Nelson grumbled, "That's not the point. We have to treat them as one group; there's no diversified charity when we're stretched to the limits!"

"But they're behaving on the beach?"

"Most are but for how long, who knows?" Doc Nelson levelled his sombre gaze up to the map of Queensland, behind Callaghan's desk, tracing the route off Highway Five into Providence. "It's a leak that will turn into a flood. Peters must secure that bridge. You don't know who the hell is in this crowd, where they came from, and we can't feed them. This is the *end*. They've been told all this *compassion* shit by some northerly warlord,"

"Kai," Callaghan guessed. "Such a smart arse."

"And the Chinese situation isn't helping either. You'd think the massacre last week would have done something but they think it won't happen to them."

Marcus recalled, "All along the coast of Queensland, if they hadn't found food they wouldn't be here, would they?"

"Exactly. In the scheme of things we're softer on waste management than other regimes; all these refugees coming have no fucking idea of reality but much of possibilities; international relief, Western niceness... It's so outdated! They've been told fat lies." Doc Nelson rubbed his face. "As soon as I shut the door to the hospital they go nuts terrorising the locals for food and water until the militia round them up send them to the beach. Bullets or bread rolls, that's what it comes down to."

"They go to the hospital first – because," Callaghan stammered, "It's a beacon; a humanitarian safe haven. It's their weakness!"

"And if it wasn't for the militia presence it'd be riot city, we gotta' get them in one place and make them stay. They can't be wandering all over town breeding disease and crime in search for salvation. Every means we've used before has just fallen to pieces."

The three sat in gentlemanly contemplation, the feint shuffling of those outside who they judged and sentenced, compounding their thinking into ruthless absolutes.

"But the threat of China is making them more desperate: We are the devil they know."

"Well, remove China from the equation and you still have them here."

"Peters wants them here. Fodder."

Marcus theorised, "The ground floor of the beachside units is empty. Tell them there's a hospital there, offering treatment and protection, and that'll clear the streets. They'll have no excuse to wander around."

"Plausible," Callaghan agreed, "With a bogus beachside hospital, the militia are validated to enforce a curfew, thus containing the refugees to the beach."

"They're all diseased, poor little fuckers... And if they're bunched together too long they'll cross-infect," Doc Nelson warned. "We could get them to have a swim. Salt water will do them some good."

"They haven't got that weird disease that broke out in Kingston last year? Fucking awful shit to have. Gooey bodies *everywhere*."

"That was something mutant and flesh eating but *sexual*. Not that. Cholera's on the cards. T-B too. Lot's of dysentery."

"I could smell that. And that's another fine reason to get them off the streets too." Callaghan composed himself for a formal decree, "Never be afraid to end charity but remember Peters wants them in Providence. The best we can do is give them a wash, make them wait, throw some vitamins down their throats, see what happens with the Chinks up north, and then send them south to breed and multiply – whatever they do. Pushing them out of the streets onto the beach so we can keep the peace in Providence – that's our top priority. Other than that we do nothing. Since when did we give welfare to refugees!" And disbelieving at their excess of benevolence, "Are we eye to eye, gentleman?"

"All the way." Nelson grimaced and saluted.

"But since they weren't the original threat," Marcus snidely reminded, "They're not the problem."

"No, they're the outcome, and are they helping us? We're in control of this town and those refugees, they're body armour should Providence came under the Chinese crunch. We'll play Nurse. They'll play Patient." Callaghan tilted his head, his eyes rolling the other direction, his pace jarred but well meaning, "What else can they expect? Two acres and a welfare cheque? After the shit hits the fan and they've cleaned the walls they can go on to wherever they were going..." His voice trailed off, his promises spelling out a destiny inexplicably tied in with an inevitable death.

Ling was making history. Over his summer invasion uniform he wore a dirty, long-sleeved cotton shirt and grubby, baggy pants with twin thin peeling speed stripes. Comrades applied dirt smudges, rustled his hair to the flare of apocalyptic feral and saluted him farewell. The lone spy posthumously saluted the tank turrets and well-wishing guards posted at Kingston's defences. Alone on the road with the inky night ahead, his feet precariously plodded to the drum of the unknown. After a few hours walking, well away from the presence of his army, he encountered the scattered refugees from all over Asia; families, mixed lots, struggling, escaping, fearfully exhausted, or asleep by the road. Some would sit up on their knees begging for water. Ling would imitate a compassionate sulk. By the light of a magnificent array of stars he saw their eyes drooped dejectedly to the ground. This is, he struggled to hide his sense of abandonment, the human condition we were all warned about.

Ling moved quickly. Silence descended upon the road like an impenetrable mist. There were few others to share the lonely trek. Maybe there were ravaging animals quick to pick the living from the dead; Human sized cats, carnivorous kangaroos, wolves and vultures. The stench of their feasting was very overpowering. He tied a rag around his head, shunned the vile stench and marched forward even as his striding rhythm was broken by decayed beings creaking underfoot. For an eternity it dragged on, and for all the moonlit skulls that lay in clumps, shone minute stars. He sweated, short of breath, paranoia exhausting him, near collapsing. Demons swam in his mind; the futility of this mission... Ghan, why this? Why? The Third Fleet have retreated, not vanished, why do this?... The furthermost frontier from his homeland – A mass grave! He could turn back and forewarn them of the macabre path. Oh the diseases here! The men that would die from this rotting marsh of flesh! Or he could leave the road and travel through the bush, haunted by man-eating kangaroos and the buggery of pirates acting on the orders of Colonel Peters! None of this is real. Dead men tell no tales. See through the bluff. I am honoured to be here to destroy the instigators of this deplorable example of the human condition.

He combined all his courage and pushed on along the road. Feeling his way with the tip of his sandals he kept his head triumphantly held high and his gaze to the heavens was rewarded. A wishing star. Out here in a graveyard wilderness, his soul among many passed, Ling knew the touch of life was there for him to grasp. The death did not worry him now, for proud and brave he would survive. Quick marching and hard tempered he began kicking aside the wrecks of lives and soon enough it was clear road and forest at either side. Sweet smelling eucalyptus.

Refugees coming out of the woods gathered their courage to move on further into the south. Would they find another road of genocide? Ling led them cautiously, grouping a motley crew with another then more. After snowballing strength in numbers they halted at a bridge, their tired eyes searching into the dead of the night. Ling smiled. This must be the Arubai River. There was Sunny Bridge. No guards in sight. Some scurrying refugees crossed to and fro unsure which way to go. As dawn broke Ling decided to cross with thirty or so, a pilgrimage for safety and peace.

Once across he saw armed bandits watching the steady flow of refugees warily watching him. Hadn't he led these feeble people over the bridge and now under the stares of bandits they looked to him as if to blame for their approaching deaths! Bandits barked. He could only retreat. He would act as though a loved one was abandoned on the other side of the bridge and he would take his time, not too anxious. They nabbed him by the scruff of the neck. Bandits barricaded the southern side of the bridge. Refugees on the north side threw their hands up in confusion. A white man struck him with a bare knuckle. He blacked out.

Two Stars Ghan found an atlas in a plundered library. He sat on the rear of a tank with the world in his lap and the fresh morning sun on his back. He flicked through the pages, the lands he would never see, the lands he left, and rested his finger on the Queensland Coast. Kingston was a dot. Chiang looked on and read another name; Providence, another dot. Two insignificant dots. Between them a thin blue line ran to the sea; the Arubai River. About a thousand kilometres south was a sprawl of dots joined together, Brisbane, and a thousand kilometres south was a thicker sprawl, Sydney. Turning back a few pages, Beijing was a very large black circle, and Chiang noted that all the people in Beijing equalled all the people in Australia, the latter roughly the same in area size as China. Ghan elatedly imagined the route to Melbourne. From Melbourne to Tasmania would require another amphibious assault. Then to Antarctica, a conquest of foe and nature, un-tapping an abundance of fresh water, plutonium, gold and a multitude of mineral riches. Chiang scoffed but his mind was more on the day's gigantic task. Wearing a boyish smile, Ghan closed the atlas, stood tall, stepped up and held his hand up into the air. Before him his army had formed up in a long tight column at the outskirts of Kingston. The tanks turrets were positioned to cover 360° around the column, the troops were well fed and keen to move on to greater victories, and the weather was perfect. Ghan turned and pointed his arm down Highway Five. A journey of a thousand miles starts with a single step…

Peters dissected Krue's reasoning. It was easy for her to say, much like admiring an actor on stage – but it wasn't their reality. He surveyed the southern side of Sunny Bridge and soaked the morning sun and crisp air. This is where he would meet the enemy, this double-lane hundred metre span of old government-grey cement, supported by cement pylons fingering into the Arubai. On the southern side he positioned his militia behind freshly-felled tree trunks, safely barricading his end of the bridge. Along the river banks, for several kilometres up and downstream, he positioned them with precise directives – shoot any uniformed soldier that dare swims. His reserves were setting up mortar positions down and off to the sides of the road, aiming across the river. Waiting, he avidly frowned, is taxing.

On the road, back from the barricade, he sat at a simple fold-up card table and ate boiled egg and grilled fish for breakfast. It was good. Romano finished his meal, burped and spread his feet on two spare chairs, running his eyes up and down the bridge, twenty meters away. They sat listening to radio reports and plotting positions on their rudimentary maps. On the northern side, growing in numbers, where a thousand plus refugees from the globe. No one dared cross the bridge, not with mean-ass militia guarding from the other end.

Romano said, "What if they don't come?"

"Then we're lucky. But look at him."

Peters moved to the side of the road and inspected in a ditch, bundled and guarded by Hoochi, a puffy black eyed Chinese prisoner. Under a pitiful disguise was a Chinese Army tunic. When the militia were scanning the influx of refugees into Providence, they noticed that everyone was tired, some diseased, a few collapsing, many crying, all terrified yet this one man was the only one that seemed to know what he was doing and marching with an animated pride like he *enjoyed* it.

Peters dragged the prisoner up to the card table, opposite from Romano.

Romano was exceedingly nasty, "Send that filth back!" He grimaced at the abandoned on the other side. "Slice the tongue of some dying rats... Give me nine tongues! And we pierce them with a rope and make him wear it like a necklace. Send him to his master!"

"And say what? ... He's saying it just by being here. Speak English? C'mon talk, Dead Man."

Ling hung in Peters's grasp, able to understand the words, but the heady mix of the thousands of slain on the road, Ghan's Army, and this bandit, added up to something horrible.

Romano purred. "You think you're smart, huh?"

Peters slapped Ling about, "Say something... Don't think you're smart by playing dumb."

"He is a spy! Just kill it."

"Reconnaissance from the north. His legs are covered in that filthy muck. Walked from Kingston!"

"He won't talk."

"Was he the only one..."

"I told you to shut the bridge." Romano meticulously ran the tip of his finger along their line of defence, the river. "There will be more."

Peters emitted a muffled laugh. "Maybe he was sent to assassinate – like our nasty friend Major Krue."

"Him? Too dumb."

"They're on their way," Peters screwed his face into a pinched mess, "En masse." He plainly asked to the prisoner, "Got anything to say?"

Ling defiantly swayed his head.

"O-K you will not talk." Romano cocked his pistol. "We have much to do."

Two Stars Ghan and Chiang rushed to the front of the halted convoy. What Ghan saw stunned him as much as the leading platoon of conscripts. It was ghastly. Some turned north to the comforting power of the column of tanks and troops assembled behind them, yet the vision of rotting, burnt and bloated bodies, stretching south down the road, had stained their impressionable minds for eternity. Complimenting that, was the dawning of horror on the faces of their comrades, observing what the halt was about, now staring in solemn disbelief at the organised massacre on the road before them.

Ghan stroked his goatee, admiring the hindrance. He called an emergency meeting and within minutes the Brigade Company Commanders assembled at the front of the convoy. Metres away was the slick of flesh.

Ghan looked each of them in the eye, "I was told the devil's greatest work was to make you believe he does not exist... But this... Remember it well... This is proof he does exist and we're here to *destroy* him."

"Is it the only road to Providence," one asked, "Is it logical to venture too far from our only source of supplies in Kingston?"

Ghan efficiently confronted the cowardice, "And where does Kingston lead back to, hah?"

The Company Commanders did not answer.

Ghan staunchly turned his back to the impromptu meeting and with a blunt face to the road of death before him, decreed, tensing his entire chest and throat, "Warlord Peters greets us with the promise of death – but who has he slaughtered!"

"The innocent." Chiang exasperatingly sighed.

Ghan thrust his hands at the road, "And what does it take to stage such hell? I could make a mess like that! Give me humans and gasoline and we could decorate any road! We go on! We are not fooled. Forward march!"

"Yes Sir!" they cheered.

"We will be greater men for passing through this noose!"

As Ghan led his Brigade through and the deeper in, it wrenched and twisted their minds, and he sensed an evil far more sinister than the sights his brothers may be witnessing elsewhere on China's Frontiers. Troops threw their morning breakfast up on their pants, the sickly road, and the sweaty backs of the man marching in front. As they were sick more comrades vomited, and once one man started from a section, entire companies of a hundred men would shrivel to that ghastly state adding to the swaggering, regurgitating, proud procession.

Ghan grouched. "You sick pansies - Do you see me?" Calling to the marching troops, "I am fit!" Waving away the stench and bodies underfoot by flapping his hand, "It is all in the mind!" He rattled his fist on his helmet. "The mind!"

"Yes Master!" Chiang agreed and shouted down three subordinates to pass the message back along the column of troops and tanks. "It is all in the mind!"

They spewed half as much. The pace quickened. The heat became stifling. They quick marched knowing that sooner or later the march of death would end. And though they came from the most populated country, they knew there are only so many human beings on the planet.

"Sunny Bridge, we will stop there." Ghan pointed down to his map, his sweating finger leaving a feint fingerprinted smudge on the thin blue line wandering from the mountains to the sea, roughly in between the two insignificant dots, "And bath in the Arubai River! This stench will be washed away!"

Chiang pitched to his side splattering his breakfast over a skull eyeing him from its putrid puddle. He dry reached, his teary-eyes staring into vacant sockets, "Yes Two Stars Ghan!"


The power came back on but Callaghan had not come home during the night. Jintana tossed and turned in bed as outside the moans of the refugees swelling into Providence grew frightfully coarser in the cold hours before dawn.

Krue slept on the living room before the barricaded door. At dawn from the balcony she saw the wretches huddled behind dunes and sprawled on the hard sand. Some had carved Creton up and now roasted, his spirit was carried by the wind. Some refugees waded into the sea, waving their scrawny arms and calling to fleeing junks, dinghies, and beat-up yachts. The sea-faring had enough trouble giving themselves assistance. The hopeful on the beach would splash in the surf, calling and finally succumbing to abandonment to those they didn't know or owed nothing too, they cursed the sand, their feet for taking them here, and the depth of this misery. The tired young militia looked on, resolute that no one would leave the beach.

Krue recounted the curse, *may you live in interesting times*. The smell of Creton wafted up to the third level unit and hung outside the balcony like a ghost. After checking the sturdiness of the door she went back to sleep in the master bedroom. It didn't work. In all her waking years it had been a badge of honour that she could fall to sleep at any given moment. This morning was different. The collective of doomed individuals on the beach moaning and cannibalising knew before Krue realised, that today was *the* day. She felt its presence in the air, a firmness and certainty, a calm before the storm.

She could hear clangs in the kitchen as Jintana made breakfast. Lined on the bench were plates of bacon and eggs, toast, sliced overripe tomatoes, canned pineapple juice, wafer crisps imported from Taiwan's finest food chain. Jintana was shaken but cooking kept her calmly in denial. Her dreams during the night had consisted of all her family members, including grandma in a bleak creaseless hospital gown, and a dozen dead relatives whom she'd never seen, gaily holding hands in a circle standing on a black soiled field. "Jintana! You come home! You come work for us! We make good deal, seventy percent! You thirty percent! Good deal!" This was dream talk, complete nonsense that loving people like that should barter for her return like apprentice pimps. She could not utter a single word in defence. They demanded her return. They threw cabbage at her, and banana leaf, and soggy condoms, and finally, little plastic smiling Buddha's. Back to reality, dropping swabs of butter into a frying-pan was an illusion of runny life on a hot plate. Shaking salt on the rims of plates a reminder of scant meals to come. It would be hard for farmers to trade in more food. Jintana sulked, this meal could be the last real meal for a long time.

"Smells fantastic." Krue surprised her.

Jintana artfully cracked an egg with one hand onto the frying-pan, "He must have stayed at the bank. So very busy, many many people not knowing what to do, why should I know, why?"

"What?"

"He works all hours at that bank. *Work work work!*"

Krue was hungry. "Sure."

Jintana swayed her head. "I suffer." Her eyes squinted tight and a tear welled. "I suffer for him; for them. And for many it's all over. Too many."

Krue reached out and stroked Jintana's long black hair. "Don't forget how far you've come… Both of us deserve better than this place…"

Jintana nodded, indifferent. "Coffee?"

"Later," Krue said, excusing herself to make use of the en-suite. She washed her face in the basin and thought of the bedroom upstairs, an abattoir, and what if she were to spend another week there. A month? A month or less and it'd be accommodation for a new ruler. She had indulged in the current ruler. Risky, fun, but worth it. She looked at herself in the mirror. "Deal with it." She then imagined living here parallel to Jintana and strung out by a man that was hardly there in a land that might not exist much longer: Post or Pre Apocalyptic Housewives, interesting in a suicidal kind of way. But for now it was crunch time. It was all going down and not to plan.

She dried, came out and couldn't believe her eyes.

At the head of the kitchen table sat Callaghan, tired but heartily diving his fork into breakfast. Jintana devotedly topped up his pineapple juice. Coffee steamed from a mug on the edge of the table by an empty chair. Krue sat and suggestively glanced over his fatigued, red rimmed, hungry eyes.

"Heard you endured a rough night?" Callaghan jested, pulling bacon off his fork with his teeth. "Sorry."

Krue sipped her coffee, purportedly listening to some moans from the beach below. As the silence at the table grew unnerving she casually announced, "Wait till it happens to you,"

"Ouch. I'm proud of you for punishing him so accordingly. If he had just tried knocking you *off* instead of *up*, it could-"

"He didn't get a chance."

"Indulgence cost him his life."

"Goes with the territory… Tell that to your band of cut-throats."

"I will."

Krue poured a half glass of pineapple juice and watched the sediments drift to the bottom. Maybe she was dead, upstairs, face down, bleeding from every orifice. Maybe she wouldn't have to hear the screams from outside. This was all borrowed time. Even her crew, who by now would think they were deserted, were borrowed for a futile cause. Make contact.

"Busy in your little office?" Krue asked in a disinterested way. "Everything under control? Has Peters sent the Chinese retreating yet?"

"You're such a laugh! Ho-hum. Where else would I be in this lovely little crisis. What else can Peters be doing. I think he wants to thank you,"

Krue blushed. "For what?"

"For warning him. If you hadn't been sent here, he wouldn't have taken the China threat for real. Who sent you *knew*. The *players*." He jerked his thumb skyward. "They know, *every* time."

She felt intellectually violated and numb. "Well, we're all here now. Tool late to howl about it. Is this town secure?"

"Ha! Hear about the renovations downstairs?"

"No,"

"The ground floor of this place will be a dodgy hospital for the refugees. They need somewhere to flee and complain so we'll throw 'em all on the beach. How's that for welfare? Better than sitting in the bush so the militia have to drag them out... Or Turkey Shoot. No! The Chinese are into that now. Same ballgame, different players. I reckon with this beach-welfare we may pull a swifty. If we can keep it going, get some foreign correspondents in, we'll call in the United Nations for hand-out relief. I heard they issue Independence Certificates if you got the starving numbers and you show that you care. It's called Internationally Recognised Statehood by Numbers."

"You're fucking crazy." She drank her juice. "Have you slept?"

"A few hours in my office."

"You need rest," Jintana comforted him, "Eat, then sleep. You must."

"No, I have to see if this hospital is working. Doc Nelson's down there playing phoney Red Cross. Miss Krue, are you sure you're alright; I mean, Creton was a scary big bugger. If you're split to bits, Doc Nelson can sew you up,"

Krue curled her fist and planted it on the table. "Wrong smart ass! *I* fucked him up in a way you can never ever imagine! and No! I am not fucking all right! You are demented like your Colonel! It's getting to *me*."

Callaghan swallowed, pretended to swallow twice, and raised his glass to his adversary, "So, I'm on your hit list too?"

"No." She didn't know. Then the idea came to her, go for gore, kill them all. With Jintana she'd make it simple (a bullet through the head). Maybe Krue's emotions registered outside her own mind.

"How do you live this life?" Callaghan asked, "I mean you and Jintana are up to your knees in shit, I just don't understand why you two haven't escaped – all in theory! I'd flee if I were you."

Krue looked to Jintana and dryly answered for her, "Because we live with it, as you do, and we're in this together."


Emelda sat on her couch, alone. The wind had changed years ago; worry had sculptured her face and it had became a trance and the deafening isolation didn't help either. Excuses may come and go but this was her duty, self-imposed, hardly beneficial to anyone else, perhaps intoxicating to a greedy little part of herself. Then an unannounced knock on the front door; a heavy patient sound, each knock rattled the house, the sound booming down the hallways. She rushed to the front, opened the door and hugged the guest then quickly led him to her couch but he would not partake in worrying.

"I've been thinking of you!"

Malo's lips formed a malleable smile.

"Going west again?"

"Where the sun sets," he explained, the prediction of Providence written over his face, "They can't get me there."

Emelda flatly inquired, "You won't see Peters kick the Chinese out?"

Malo's slender hand ran through his curly hair, "Bin'a *long* time out here."

"I see. You have news?"

"Walk-about news only. Time for you to stay west too. You got farmer friends, they're good people. I'll take you there. C'mon."

She withheld a shriek of panic, carefully forming her words, staring into some distance, at some scene she had no say in, "And Romano... Tell me," her hand gripped Malo's shoulder, her other hand covered her eyes, "It's dangerous, it must be... Poor Romano."

"Oh he's not *dead*. Nah: he's still kicking."

"But why tell me to go west?"

Malo winked, "When white fellas and yellow fellas come from the sea and they meet, things get out of control. They just love a good punch up."

She sat perfectly still and read the things he worried about, the severity of the approaching battle, how he foresaw before all others and remained disciplined and simplistic to let little show.

"We go, then I go up mountain," Malo plotted their avoidance, "Not *our* fight. Let 'em 'ave it out."

She agreed, stood, packed her bags and stood on her front veranda staring east, rotating north, Malo at the stairs, his eyes and ears soaking the ambience from the mountains. They were calling him back.


Two garages and the ground floor unit became a make-shift medical drop-in-centre. Three petite ladies from Burma, trained by Doc Nelson, served as nurses. They looked neat and clean and clinical in white aprons, injecting a clear liquid to in-patients and then giving them a polished red apple or a bruised orange. Doc Nelson diagnosed complicated cases, referring them to wait out on the beach for more treatment. The patients, the fit to survive the perilous journeys from all over Asia, were apprehensive but thankful for Western-style medical-attention prescribed by a white Doctor. They were pumped with some formula and assured it either made them miraculously healthy or immortally safe from numerous diseases. Their clothes were stained with weeks of travelling and over their shoulders they carried bags with few belongings. The majority were evidently thankful to be a stride ahead of the Chinese, and in the face of such fear, word spread that Peters had The Bomb.

Everyone knew what The Bomb was. India and Pakistan paid their dues dearly for having too many Bombs. It was bad news to both sides. Now China was stepping into a zone where the local Warlord had The Bomb it was so obvious the Chinese would pull back. All this is not worth A Bomb.

A thousand of them squatted on the beach, a hundred milled at the quasi-hospital. Northwards, they were dots, crawling on the beach as it curved to the horizon. This could only be interpreted as more refugees coming from the north.

On the balcony, Krue packed her pistol, ammunition, her rifle, imagining a disguise for herself. She could just pass as Asian, having a quarter of their blood. The faces on the beach weren't close enough to compare to the memory of her grandmother's high cheekbones, the old matron was proudly from Mongolia. So Krue guessed China was in her gene pool and she could on just a quarter or less, if it came to the crunch, plead loyalty. Another reason to be sent this far? Fuckers.

Callaghan came out of the bedroom, cocky, scrutinising Jintana's demands. "You're safe here. The guards are on the door and downstairs – I don't know what you're complaining about: what more could you want? And you've got Krue, armed and fucking dangerous!"

"But I want to come with you!" Jintana pleaded, hugging his hips.

"There's so many ruffians and anarchists and sick people out there and I'm the only policeman! I have to go to that friggin' beach and check that it's secure or it could turn into absolute fucking..." He bit his knuckle, imagining the extremes, "Just understand, Jintana, please!"

"Everywhere is dangerous! If I was with you I would be safe? Yes?"

Callaghan held her, "I love you but I don't want you near it at all. I don't want some fucker taking you hostage, taking aim at your pretty face. Do you understand?"

Jintana wiped away a tear, "I'm scared James. I had nightmares! I have never been so scared!"

"Will you take care of her?" Callaghan propositioned Krue, "Seeing you're not going anywhere."

"I'm waiting too," Krue testified, sharply stepping to Jintana and peeling her hands off Callaghan's hip as she sunk to her knees. "But I can see you have got something *important* to do here."

"One of you understands," he huffed, slipped away, slammed the door behind and jogged down the stairs to ground level. The sick and broken greeted him with eyes spiked like thorny bristles. Doc Nelson bent over pondering the fate of a dehydrated Malay girl. Lost eyes locked to his as he scanned over her body for signs of contagious sores and infected wounds. Apart from scratches, she was physically strained but fit to survive and desperately lonely.

"Bit late to send her out to a farm." Callaghan frowned. "Another time and place and she'd live like a Princess. Don't need another nurse?"

"Nah. To the beach." Doc Nelson handed her a banana and an apple from a hessian sack at his side, then pointed her directly to the surf.

"Special one huh?"

Doc Nelson apathetically explained, "Got to give hope to some of them."

"Why her?"

"She's fit and young. Anyone over thirty-five I couldn't give a shit about."

"Right." Callaghan watched with interest as the Malay girl meandered to the dunes. "Wait till you're thirty-five then. There's thousand out there to lend a heart too, why should you give individuals special attention now? But you got a plan for euthanasia, eh?"

"*No...*" Doc Nelson held his hand high to pause the next in-patient. "Are they staying on the beach?"

"We're trying. Marcus is down there. Crowd control."

"Keep your eyes peeled, they're desperate."

"Hell yeah."

Doc Nelson stared resolutely to them, "We'll have to move the dying on soon, we don't want them dropping like flies near here. Then there's the solution, do we have a solution yet?"

Callaghan, hands on his hips, face sagging and squinting at the sunlit beach, said, "The Arabs say '*It is written*' and that's history, fate, all in one bunch. For these people they know it but they can't *read* it yet."

"And Peters knows what's going?"

"Too concerned with you know what."

"And you?"

"I'm here to check things out. That's all I can do."

He walked over the dunes and scoured the beach crowded with refugees dozing or patiently dying in the morning sun. Obviously many had run through the night, the breath of the Chinese chilling their unwashed necks. He breathed, thankful of the sea. Mothers led naked children to the waves, wringing out clothes, scrubbing behind ears. Marcus and three militia moved along the beach pushing refugees to sit on the ground unless they were undertaking a useful task. They were easy to control, almost obliged to be told what to do. This form of crowd control made it easy for Callaghan to catch up to Marcus, fifty meters and walking away. But the eyes of the refugees trailed him, determining if he were friend or foe, provider or thief. They saw his water bottle on his belt, a rifle slung over his back and radio in his hand. He felt like the luckiest guy in the world.

He heard the *duff-duff* of bare feet accelerating on white sand. He spun round, raising his arm to block whoever was chasing him and tripped on a skeletal refugee. A knife-wielding scrawny refugee, dressed in non-descript khaki pants and faded shirt, leapt on him. Callaghan pitched and rolled and tumbled into another three refugees, leapt into the air, swung his gun in a wide circle to clonk his vicious assailant but it was too late. The assailant monkey-swung behind.

Refugees sat up, warily observing the struggle, unsure who to pin their hopes and desires on.

The assailant's arm locked around Callaghan's neck and drew a knife up under the throat. Callaghan felt it dig in, tilted forward, holding the assailant's knife arm, reversed into a failed backflip, landing both of them on the assailant's back. Bleeding and mad with fear, Callaghan rolled off the young man and punched him fair in the head then tried for his gun, it was slung from his side and in the sand, but his left arm pathetically jolted and twitched. Splatters of red stuck to his forearm. The knife was lodged in his left shoulder on a slant. Then came the pain.

Callaghan rolled away and with his other hand levelled his rifle at the assailant, now up and speedily attacking again. Both were in mid-stride, one staggering back, the other attacking, and Callaghan was lucky, not sharp, to pulverise a knee-cap. Ligaments and bone sprayed into the air. The attacker hopped madly on one leg then flopped face first and lay like a starfish, in shock. Callaghan squatted and aimed again. Refugees wriggled from the line of fire.

Krue blinked at the gun shot and rushed to the balcony. She stood alert as a stick insect, her eyes narrowed exactly to the sound of one delirious man's slaughter. Jintana bit at her knuckles as her lover stood, wobbling, dropped his rifle, waved to her from the beach grinning like an idiot, mechanically trying to pluck a six-inch knife out of his shoulder, and hollering something that was incomprehensible. At his feet a man squirmed on his side in circles on blood smudged sand, now holding his bloodied knee-cap up to his chin. The refugees parted for Marcus and militia charging to the rescue.

Callaghan kicked the man in the ribs, rolled him over, then in the stomach. The scream switched to a curdling wail.

"Just the one?" Marcus asked, both eyeing the refugees, "Only one?"

"He was after *me!*" Feeling over his shoulder, the blade was wedged and packed in by tight muscle. "He knew who I was..."

The attacker's teeth clenched with the youthful fury that his wild task was shamefully incomplete. He screamed. The militia shot him twice, either side of the heart.

Bleeding and charged with adrenalin, Callaghan faltered on his knees. "I'm cool... We're cool..." He wasn't cool. He'd been like this on the beach before and looking around, was distinctly reminded of calculating death tolls. Where were the bodies of the Task Force Seven men and the militia? Did the tide take them out, did the undertow roll them to the sea bed? Didn't their bodies roll back on the beach in three days time, mauled by crabs?

"Let's move out of here. Can you walk?" Marcus tugged at him, "C'mon – snap out of it!"

"I," he balanced on his knees and winced, "How the fuck do I get this out?"

"Hmm. This requires some thought." Marcus touched the blade of the knife.

"*Sheezus!*"

Militia shooed the refugees away with gun toting threats creating a ten metre circle around the crime scene.

Callaghan moaned deliriously to two approaching female figures. "Oh no, she's coming... And her too." He could easily make out Jintana; her nimble figure skimmed over the beach like a dragon fly over the ponds. But Krue, sleek yet padded with a slim flak jacket, loaded with grenades on a belt and a K-41 rifle over her back, carrying her small pack, her boots scaring refugees out of her way, made him wonder if he were to be stomped on. It all became blurry and doubling, spinning, fading out. He flopped forward on his face.

10:03. His sub-conscious pulled the plug on the conscious. Callaghan dreamt... Lucky it wasn't a grenade... Cool water lapped his waist as attentive voices circled above. Fading in and out were machine-guns then a hush, a ka-boom, and as if trapped in a box under a violent explosion, his ears were ringing, what thoughts remained calculating how many breaths he had left. *I'm claustrophobic*, he gasped! It was too dark to make out much, but Jintana was close and unafraid. The dream time, so good.

"Doc, he's out."

"Weak as piss and lucky as hell. You hear a sucking lung wound?"

They listened. A few refugees chattered, inspecting, debating, worrying.

"Nope."

"Stand back!" That was Krue to the refugees, then: "If they take a step this way I'll kill them."

Callaghan could feel someone was at his shirt with a knife, slicing it into removable tatters.

"Oh James!" Jintana shrieked, her little knees hitting the sand beside his ear and her fingers stroking his outstretched arm.

"I got an idea."

They picked up his limbs to slip off the sleeves then throw water on the wound. The knife was firmly in place.

"Hell, it's nothing," Doc Nelson inspected the wound.

Callaghan woke refreshed, topless, one cheek on the wet sand, drops of sea water running over his clammy forehead, focussing on the sun blinding bright beach and perfectly still refugee figurines. Tender hands and knees rigidly held him face down. Back to sleep. So much easier. Yet his eyelids parted at the refugees silently marvelling. They didn't flinch with his spasms of pain. They'd seen this shit before, like pain you'd find in Dante's Hell was all second nature.

"Hold him down!" Krue called, shifting her shins and body weight on to Callaghan's free arm.

"Careful, he'll squirm!" Doc Nelson fore-warned.

Krue planted one hand firmly on Callaghan's head, palming his cheek in the sand. He could see the audience of refugees, watching with beady stairs as though they wanted him to die, a gaunt and united hatred of his existence contrasted by their satisfaction in his agony. Krue yanked the knife out and the pain died. Callaghan screamed all the same, shutting his eyes and popping veins in his neck. He screamed until he was blue in the face. Krue relaxed her grip. He sprang to his knees, sat upright, ashamed and inspired.

"*Whooagh!*"

Doc Nelson asked, "Are you all right?"

"Bloody fantastic! Couldn't be better."

"We need disinfectant for your wound." Doc Nelson persisted, accepting the knife from Krue.

Callaghan mauled to his audience, casting a hand to them and fluttering his fingers northwards up the beach, "Go back! I can't feed you! I am not Jesus!"

Krue stepped out of Callaghan's peripheral vision.

The dead assassin endured Callaghan's disgust, "Who sent him, Canberra or Canton? Who was he?"

"Could be anyone," Marcus guessed, "He must've thought you were Colonel Peters."

"Oh yeah, because to *them* all white people just look the *same*." Callaghan howled to the sky. "Stitch me up!"

Doc Nelson and Jintana led him by the elbows off the beach. Marcus and the militia followed, and Krue trailed, her head hung slyly low

At the non-hospital, Doc Nelson rudimentarily stitched up Callaghan's shoulder. Jintana fretted and patted his forehead.

"Some drugs... Where's a joint. It hurts, Doc." Callaghan complained. Refugees eyed this white man with curiosity. Marcus and militia men tried to keep them at bay. "Look at 'em," he hissed, "Starving. They understand pain. Crazy world we live in... Where did it all go so wrong..."

Jintana reassured him, parting his fringe, "Be calm, my love.."

He rolled his eyes, "Yes, my darling."

"I love you too much to let you die like them,"

Doc Nelson, bent with concentration, studying the flaps of skin and looping of stitches, interrupted, "Can't your romantics wait? Don't move."

Callaghan twitched. "Thanks."

"You're doing fine, complaining, but fine," Doc Nelson said.

"I'm fine."

Jintana soothed him, wiping remnants of sand from his cheek, "Better now?"

He winked at her, stating his thought, "My darling, what are we going to do."

She didn't know. In her eyes he was as desperate as she had ever been.

"And where's little Miss Krue," he suddenly sneered. "She's gone?" He thrashed his head from side to side. "Slut! Any chance! Ouch!"

"Hold still!"

They found her at the bank directing the barrel of her pistol at Eric's head. She spoke in a precise manner into the radio. She removed the headphones on sight of Callaghan's pinched figure; caught in jerks with a bandaged shoulder and sidekick Marcus; terse at shooting her and taking out Eric too. Callaghan didn't even bother to raise his gun. He marched up to her, grabbed her gun and yanked the headphones down her neck. Eric, relieved, slumped on his desk as the radio respondent signed off, "See you when we see you."

"Bad girl!" Callaghan slapped her across the face. He shuddered, "Wicked little witch!"

"I had to," she apologised, leant over the radio, swiftly twisted the frequency dial and rested her hand on Eric's shoulder, "He was at gunpoint, big deal. He wouldn't let me otherwise."

"I know he wouldn't, because he's a good boy, isn't he? I thought you were to stay in your beach front apartment? No! You run off!" He asked to the radio. "Who was that?"

Krue's lips were sealed, forming a narcissistic smirk.

Eric hid his sorry head from Callaghan recounting her urgent message. "I only heard her transmission – I thinks she was talking about a wedding or something – bells and rings."

"I was ordering them to observe the situation at hand," Krue saliently testified.

"Don't shit me like *that!* They're ready to make a kill, aren't they Missy?"

"If that's your perception of observe."

"You're pushing it, bitch!" Callaghan pointed to Marcus to keep Krue covered and then sat in his office chair to think. Providence is a whisker from becoming a putrid example of global overcrowding and mayhem. If he knew what the situation for tomorrow would be, or even this afternoon, he could plan things. Like genocide, or supervising the construction of rudimentary refugee camps for United Nations bleeding hearts Observers to observe, so that Western Countries who were not at war and thus alienated from the shit could parachute in canned food for the slaves. The slaves, Callaghan mused, I'm a slave. To what. To couch potatoes sitting at home in countries not at war but yearn for something to care for? A slave to Krue? To Peters? To Jintana? To the starving Malay girl? To the dead attacker? Callaghan yelled, his voice a giant blow torch scorching throughout the bank, "O-K: All this shit is still manageable but the fun times are over! I'm off to see Peters *right* now because I wouldn't mind knowing exactly what the fuck's going on! I want to see it all for myself!"

They stared at the enraged figure, petrified of him, but he was calming himself, looking logical and calculating what to expect.

"Take me with you!" Krue demanded coarsely.

Callaghan sized her presumption of importance.

She persisted, "You know we see eye to eye. We both need to know what Peters is doing!"

He simmered, playing her game out, his good hand felt over the stitches.

Jintana busied herself searching his office for a shirt.

Krue malevolently added: "You know the worst that can happen."

As Jintana helped him into a shirt, he rolled his eyes closed and wished to remain that way eternally, "Yes... And what do you do when nightmares become realities?"

Krue nodded.

Callaghan blurted, partially apologetically but mostly vehemently, "I have to see it for myself, I need to know exactly what the hell is going on," He faced Krue, demanding, "And if you can make a worthwhile difference, without adding any airy-fairy peace-love-and-happiness bullshit, or military-minded kill-them-all crap, you might just survive!"


Having noted the formative scouts rummaging through the gully and the familiar sight of Romano re-checking machine-gun positions to cover the bridge, the crew vanished from their gully. They headed deeper into thick bush, south of the river and east of the highway, until finally they found a suitable hill from which to observe the bridge and its surroundings. Just as they were making themselves comfortable the call came through. Tom could hardly believe she was alive. They crouched under branches, in their newly acquired position, Tom staring into and Matthews and Corrie's rigidly set eyes.

"What did she say?" Matthews whispered.

Tom recounted and decoded. "Eliminate his Command."

All three slowly tuned to the bridge, now over half a kilometre away. They could see and hear the protesting refugees gathering on the northern side, the militia at the southern blockade shouting back, and first traces of movement from the far north; the heat from tank exhaust fumes slightly bended the light above them into a simmering thin layer, a signature. They were heading for Peters, who had been seen numerous times, too hard to hit, fortifying the bridge.

"Ready?" Matthew asked.

Corrie breathed steadily, totally sure of himself, "I'm ready."

Tom growled, "Bring it on!"


Smacker peered into the dark and cold well that was his third coffee of the morning. "Play it again."

The radio operator looked to Mrs Benson, who nodded her approval. Crackling voices stained by the physics of distance conversed with a strained urgent flow. There was a timer, recorded ten minutes ago. Smacker recognised the first voice.

Krue: "Voodoo Child, Voodoo Child this is Krue."

Eleven seconds of static.

Krue: "Voodoo Child, Krue. Voodoo Child, Krue.

Three seconds static, feint interference by fishermen.

Voodoo Child: "You're O-K?"

Krue: "No. Remember the romance?"

Voodoo Child: "Yeah… Looks like a good catch… Is he wearing the ring?"

Krue: "Did the fiancée?"

Seven seconds static. Arguing fishmongers reached a pitch.

Voodoo Child: "Do we hear wedding bells?"

Krue: "Did I?"

Five seconds static.

Voodoo Child: "Absolutely?"

Krue: "Fucking oath. Oh shit here we go,"

Voodoo Child: "See you when we see you."

3rd Male: "Bad girl!"

SFX: *Slap!*

3rd Male: "Wicked little witch!"

Krue: "I had to."

Resolved fishermen joking faintly in the middle of the Pacific.

"What do you make of it?" Mrs Benson asked, concerned not to be overtly upset.

Smacker sucked on his lip. Sounded a bit personal for his liking. The Third voice was familiar too. That little fucking weasel Callaghan. He should have been the Primary Target *then* Peters.

"And there's this." Mrs sat him at the computer screen and opened a new window, a live image from a Royal Navy satellite. "The Chinese are on the move."

Smacker peered glumly and then as the caffeine kicked in he was enthralled at the coverage and resolution of the images: A crystal clear birds-eye view of columns of Chinese Troops amassing in Kingston. Next, they marched south, the advance troops leading tanks, their turrets in a defensive setting. Next, the troops halted at a devastated section of road, wondering how to proceed over thousands of decimated humans.

She said, "Next."

Zoom in, downloading, the latest high-resolution picture dithered in of Sunny Bridge. Troops and militia were plotted on either side, the northern force pushing a herd of black-headed civilians against the river bank.

# A Step Forward

11:49 AM. Ghan's two-thousand strong force halted in a kilometre long column on Highway Five leading up to Sunny Bridge. Leading reconnaissance platoons found the bridge approaches swamped with dispirited refugees and the bridge blocked by bandits.

Ghan organised a forward observation post, plotting a bombardment, quietly moving up his thirty-eight tanks and arranging them out of sight of the bandits. His troops rested, squatting cross-legged by the side of the road, glad to be far from their pilgrimage through the field of bones, wondering, how can a beautiful land be so savage?

"Two Stars Ghan! Lieutenant Ling has not been found…"

Ghan rosily suggested, "He is across the bridge, waiting for us to cross. As I sent him there I will see to return him: We leave no man behind."

That quote, his squatted troops noted, was uplifting because eating at their hearts was the molten fear; how could one *not* want to run away and escape this madness, even if you had to leave your best friend, dying.

Peters and Romano sat partially shaded from the sun by an overhanging branch from a gum tree, each man entangled in his thoughts. Romano could smell eucalyptus and recalled how Emelda dabbed tea-tree oil on his scratches after a hard day of people killing. She would glare intensely at the wounds, wondering if it were a defensive or offensive scratch from someone condemned, or just a brush with lantana, her voice caressing and consoling for the minor injury. She had radioed to say she was seeking protection with one of the farming families. But were they safe? Only Malo could claim any real heritage to this land, and apart from him, every man, woman, child, and imported dog had a lesser reason for living. With one look over to the opposing river bank Romano could see more arrivals. There was no end.

Peters was ruminating: What would an invading army from China want out here? Land? Migration? Lunacy? Plunder? Anarchy? A diversion? All adequate answers as to why Task Force Seven had arrived, why General Sumatra and his brothers had fought and why the British Empire had come too. He then probed the outcome, trade. Minerals. Oil. Food. Gold. They knew of the gold. Gold came from three sources: mining, trade and plunder. In Queensland it was no secret that Colonel Peters inherited gold as capital, and Sumatra had amassed that gold from his own thievery. It made perfect sense that future attempts would be made and the Chinese, having been digging for gold in Australia as long as the whites had, saw an easy justification to come all the way to Providence, nab the current $4 million and go home. Perhaps there was some other mineral deposit yet to be clawed out of this old barren land. Still, Peters was baffled. What price do you put on the value of Ghan and his men? Two-thousand dollars per man? Surely it cost more than that to train them, to manufacture weapons, ammunition, pay their drill instructors, ship them out here and back safely. Or, Peters figured, their worth is to be written off, like he was by his own kind, like the convicts sent out here by the British. It's a cruel example to threaten those left behind, the start and end of a lucky country.

Ling was dead at their feet. Sunny Bridge was blocked. Militia raised their rifles at irate refugees trying to cross south. Those unlucky enough to be on the other side ran off into the woods as Chinese troops moved in. Dispersing shots were fired.

"This," Peters said prophetically, "Is it."

Romano stiffened. "I heard tanks."

Peters wiped a thin sheen of sweat from his forehead. "Yeah they got tanks... They're not messing around." The worrying refugees bolted out of sight. Peters's last glimpse of them were the slow and sick cripples scurrying down and sinking into the cool mud of the river. He *tsked* at a few rifle cracks and yelps. "Here come the scouts."

"Shoot on sight – we must! They move fast!"

Peters grimaced. "First up, out with the white flag."

Romano shook his head. "And him?"

There was the dead Chinese spy cleanly executed after a messy interrogation.

"Intimidation," Peters clapped his hands for the attention of two favoured militia. They were finely tuned twenty-three year old ex-Gurkhas and wasted no time in lifting the body and tossing it into the scrub at the side of the road then whisking back to behind the barricade. Peters stood at their sides facing down Sunny Bridge waving a white tea-towel tied to the butt of his gun.

Vince, overseer of the barricade, propped one leg up onto the logs, rocking himself back and forth.

"What do you feel over there?" Peters asked.

Vince observed across the bridge. Abruptly advancing along the road were the first Chinese troops he'd ever faced, and for Peters, including, from behind a white tea-towel. As the Chinese saw their enemy, they thrust their chests out, ready to take lead, shrapnel, buckets of shit, because they are mean sons-of-bitches and had just walked through a rotten hell. Before that, they'd stormed a port after one month cramped in a troop ship listening to looped propaganda announcements. Not a very pleasant way to travel to war but an excellent reason to avenge those you were taught to be at pains with.

"Like a hungry fire," Vince noted, exhausting his English vocabulary, "See everyone *run run run*. The Chinese come like swarm of locusts, *eat eat eat* all in the way."

"Streuth."

"Like a flood, they have the *mass* of nature."

Peters, a tone of respect notably in his pitch, said, "Making history."

Vince was endeared to project the severity, "Do you know what you're doing?"

"Yes: Stopping them with guns or diplomacy."

"We are an obstacle in *their* way." Vince's foot stomped on the wooden barricade, "Perhaps what they want we can't give."

"We?"

"You're not alone," Vince reminded his friend.

"If I can't get some peace happening with these nutcases, it'll be a nasty fight to the finish."

"We can survive this. Their face is brave," Vince pointed to a single Chinese scout crouching by the road across the bridge. The face *was* brave, and the eyes white hot. "And the harder it is set the higher the fear driving them. They want this matter done with. That's what I feel."

"And they got the numbers." Peters waved the white tea-towel precariously higher, "So my good friend, do you have faith that what I'm doing is right?" He regretted not being able to mow them down at first sight. See exactly how hard these hordes charged into spitt'n lead and other flesh-fucking extremities. With two napalm missiles on stand-by on Jacinda Mountain, a radio call away, he could try and arrange their funerals in one swoop. Or, deal. If they want trade, any trade, they'll have to give something, *anything*. Appropriation of the wealth in Providence by any other means would be plain robbery. A section of Chinese soldiers trotted up to the bridge carrying a high calibre machine-gun and tripod.

Peters waved to them, friendly and banefully cheerful.

The greeting party secured their side of the bridge and from under the rim of their helmets, decorated with mismatched gum tree leaves and prehistoric ferns, they discerningly watched Peters wave the flag franticly higher.

"I they shoot me… Nuke 'em…"

Vince grinned. "What else can you do?"

"Exactly." Peters admired the enemy, squat in a defensive position to pour fire should they immediately storm the bridge. Peters fired a shot from his gun and waved that white tea-towel across his face as if fanning his fiery temperament to that of a painful truce. The invaders huddled closer to their high calibre machine-gun and sent a runner to their superiors back down the road. In stereotypical fashion Peters stood down from the barricade with the rifle levelled out from his hip, the tea-towel drooping off the barrel to the bridge.

"I think they're scared shitless, Vince."

"They think the same of you."

Romano cautioned from the card table, "Do not sell Providence… You are dealing with the Chinese… They have been masters of business for five thousands years!"

Peters snapped, "Why aren't you up here!"

Romano lay his hands on the table. "The Chinese can come to me."

Peters returned his gaze to the bridge. Across the span of concrete was the tip of the tentacle of the World's Largest Armed Forces. A Chinese corporal raced across the bridge and confronted Peters at the barricade. He offered a full cigarette packet for imminent barter, prompting to Peters with a buck-toothed charming smile that it was a good deal, possibly the best he'd get today.

"Thanks mate," Peters marvelled, taking a smoke, the corporal smartly flicked out a lighter, a cheaply cloned zippo gadget that played a tune when the lid popped and spouted instantaneous windproof flame. On one side was a portrait of some Chinese Superhero with a cheery smile. Peters puffed on the cheap smoke and faintly recognised the grainy one-byte tune. "Flight of the Valkyries?"

The corporal offered his crappy gadget lighter for trade, confident that their new found friendship would work favourably in the future.

"I don't have anything." Peters told him.

Vince took a packet of 555 cigarettes from his pocket and offered it for the crappy lighter. The corporal took Peters's hand, placed the lighter in it, then took Vince's packet of 555s, pointed from one to the other and grinned that they now had to work out who owed what, and bolted back to his side of the bridge showing off his new smoking pleasure to the machine-gun crew.

"What was that?" Peters asked.

Vince sighed. "I don't know. Friendly though."

Peters swayed his head and walked to the card table, throwing the crappy lighter to Romano. "How's that?"

"Aaargh!" Romano howled, hearing the electronic tune as he flipped the lid, "What an annoying sound! Is that Mao Tzu Dong?"

"It's not Mao."

Romano studied the picture. "Who is it?"

"It's General Zhing! Supreme Commander of the Chinese Military Machine!" Peters frowned, "A pop icon!"

"Bah!" Romano cursed, tossing the lighter into the centre of the table. "You traded fine cigarettes for a box of matches with a childish music tune. See the Chinese know how to rip you off!"

Peters conceded. "Oh get *fucked*. The little opportunist made an effort."

"Every man does, when he wants to prove something."

There was no time to reply. Peters's attention shifted to the stylish entrance of two Chinese Military Battlefield Brasses dolled up with ceremonial ribbons on their chest, blood-mucked boots, shiny belts, shiny pistols and emotionless faces.

Colonel Chiang and Two Stars Ghan, escorted by two of the tallest troops of the 177th Brigade, the Red Dragon Flag fluttering over their heads, proudly marched across Sunny Bridge as if they owned it. Approaching an opening in the barricade made by two sturdy militia, Ghan palmed the objects of obstruction away as if they were magical gates.

The militia pitied the show of arrogance, immediately checking out the two following flag bearing troopers and the rate of their ware. They appeared proud, sunburnt, dirty, wreaking of dried crusty vomit and corpse swiped boots. And if it wasn't for the excitement of invading, they'd rather be back in China's embrace sucking on a plastic Coca-Cola nipple.

Peters whispered, "So *serious*."

"What *are* they doing here?" Romano asked, his horror of their professionalism masked by a sense of starry-eyed wonderment.

"They look hard to crush but once it's done they'll be begging for mercy."

His bottom lip jutted out, Romano pettily dismissed them, "What do they expect so far from their own lands? Wine and blowjobs?"

Peters met his adversaries like a true gentleman. He shook their hands, Ghan first, and politely smiled from ear to ear, "G'day fellas."

Ghan and Chiang remained rigid and apprehensive at this Third World six-foot something bandit. Peters forgave their naivety and led them to the card table. Ghan and Chiang sat, suspiciously scowlish of their host, an anxious distressed act orientated at worming Peters's problems more so than their own.

"Do you speak Mandarin or Cantonese?" Peters asked Romano.

Romano's eyes narrowed with an intense hate, "No."

Ghan discretely conversed to Chiang, "*Say something or this is all useless!*"

Chiang proudly and urgently introduced his leader in poor but improving English, "Two Star General Ghan. Commander. One-Seven-Seven Brigade. He speaks no English. I interpret. Speak. Please."

Ghan sat back with a smug smile, confident that Chiang was apt for the job.

Peters concentrated. "I am Colonel Patrick Peters, Commander of Providence. I am part of an Alliance of Independent Warlords stretching from the Northern Territory to Queensland and the Coral Sea."

Chiang translated, slow, then quickening, then reiterating.

Ghan half-interestedly raised his eyebrows. Yes, the bandit! This is our reason to venture this far! He has changed from the mystical being in the poster into something humane and frail, weaker in stature, his eyes portray only desperateness. This is no great villain, this is a mad man in the wilderness, or an old tiger that is too blind to hunt the young prey.

Peters locked on to Ghan, "You've heard of me?"

Chiang asked, Ghan cheerfully confirmed, muttering something Peters couldn't understand yet uncomfortably grinned at.

"I understand that you, representing the Chinese Army, want to enter my region... A very interesting scenario."

"Yes!" Chiang responded, gleeful that Peters did somewhat understand their presence.

"Excellent."

"Excellent?"

"*Good.* I know what you're after. But I won't let you. You are not liberating or exploring any further and if you chose to, I'll use nuclear retaliation."

Chiang blinked, contemplatively tipping his head back, releasing an agonising sigh to the sky, "Ah – *nuclear* retaliation."

"Yes. And I have surface-to-surface missiles aimed at your forces on the other side of the bridge." Peters held his radio handset to his chest. "I call, you die. Your Brigade stops here. If you have anything else to say, tell me now. I am sure we can come to a mutual and peaceful agreement – trade, perhaps."

Chiang frowned and took some time explaining in a measured way to Ghan the precise meaning of the bandit's dialogue.

Ghan nodded amicably, appraising Peters with a firm nod, and recalled that in all his training and briefings there were no instructions on dealing with desperate bandits at the edge of colliding civilisations armed with nuclear weapons. But were the weapons inter-continental or just battlefield? Ghan's mind raced: They send me out here to deal with *this!* Yes, interesting.

He quietly conferred with Chiang, their voices restricted to bland monotones, in-decipherable of emotions. *"What he claims to be or offer does not concern us, nor his threats with weapons we can not see... He has halted our advance onto Providence with words – words! There is no tactful understanding of the gravity of the situation. The fool is signing his death warrant with each syllable! Our duty is to police these lands of Warlords and Pirates and Bandits and that is more important than his petty claims of sovereignty and military muscle!"*

*"Yes sir."*

*"See how he stares at us? See his men – they are not an army. They are partisans, and partisans without political will are bandits! All this talk is entertaining but hindering our progress."*

*"I understand."*

*"If he had any intelligence his forces would melt into the wilderness and let us through yet he wants to make a show of himself. Ask him if he really wishes to stall our conquest of Providence. We have come far by sea, he must not understand the regional power plays beyond his own little shithole. Tell him."*

Chiang had to think hard and fast, he looked troubled, and flipping through a phase book didn't help. After a few minutes he managed to explain: "Who you are, your weapons, your ideals, does not matter to Two Stars Ghan. We have come from China. It is *very* far. Ghan says you misunderstand how important you are. We have orders to go to Providence. Our progress is important. We have come to police the Pacific of piracy at the request of the world that lives in *peace.*"

"Really?" Peters deliberated. "Well, if we'd known that before…"

Chiang symbolically cast his hand over the table, layering on Ghan's wisdom, "Peace is our mandate."

Peters simmered. "Lies!"

"It is a lie if you hear it." Chiang flipped through his phrase book. "When man sees it… *We* sit before you. Is that a lie?"

Peters's smouldering eyes flicked from Chiang's diplomatic brilliance to Ghan, brooding, "A journey of a thousand miles starts with a single step, and though you be a long way from home, a single step forward will be your last."

Chiang translated, trying to keep the poetry intact.

Ghan's limited grasp of English was returning, only slightly. Still, he quietly scolded Chiang, *"China is policing the Pacific. We have a duty; duty and orders from a unified peaceful state many times larger than what despicable shit we see here."*

"General Ghan," Chiang spoke squarely to Peters and Romano, "Uses very strong words. We are policing for the benefit of many. We follow the orders of a very *big* peaceful society. And here, we know it is not nice. All is broken. Must be fixed."

"Completely fucking lost in translation…" Peters shook his head. "We're having a communication problem."

Chiang knew that term. "Yes! Communication problem!"

"This is useless. You know, I know, any pretext by an aggressor will do!" Peters uncontrollably. "You're testing my patience!"

*"What did you say to make him do that?"* Ghan nudged Chiang, *"What was that about? Are you unnerving him? Very good Chiang. You are doing well my friend! What did you say to him?"*

*"I said,"* Chiang blushed and bit down his grin to portray only a stony face, *"I am not sure, many things."*

*"Impressive."* Ghan smiled directly to his adversary. *"Tell this bandit that I know there are political ramifications from this military action and I'm certain what we do here today is validated by the… United Nations… No… The … We're part of it… Chiang?"*

*"The G-8?"*

*"No… The United Nations Security Council."* Ghan cleared his throat and reiterated, *"Tell him that we are approved by them."*

*"Is it true?"*

*"Yes; It was a small concern."*

*"But he's a bandit, Ghan. What does he care? He despises them."*

*"So do we, but tell him. It might make him angry again!"*

Chiang formulated the words. "Colonel Peters, the United Nations Security Council asked China to police the Pacific. They asked us to make peace."

"And I'm the King of France."

"Please, explain."

Ghan interjected, *"Chiang, don't answer his questions. Tell him that as it is our duty, we can only move onwards,"* fluttering his hand forward, *"No bargaining backwards."*

Chiang expressively strained every syllable, "Forward is our *only* path. We are cleansing the lands. The world wishes it so."

"You follow some fucking warped global rationale that I certainly haven't heard of. Subsequently,"

"Ah, what?"

"Listen: I don't care what your excuse is for being here but you want to enter my region after you've destroyed my Port. This land is mine," Peters boasted, "I have nowhere to retreat to. I will obliterate your forces with my nuclear weapons. Do you know of my capabilities? Death." He flexed his fist and kissed the air. "A dirty, painful, death."

Chiang hurriedly conferred.

Ghan had heard none of Peters's capabilities. Zhing or his Intelligence apparatus would have mentioned something if it was important.

"*Ruses – tactful – but ruses.*"

"*Two Stars Ghan, you are a very observant leader. Perhaps we are being too generous with our honesty with this demented bandit.*"

"*Not at all. Tell him this…*"

Peters and Romano tuned their ears to Ghan extolling the virtues of this mission to Chiang, who translated.

"We tolerate the diversity of individuals and cultures in distant lands," Chiang explained, then obnoxiously sourly, "And we know you as a renegade bandit isolated from your own country. Do not fool yourself. You are of no importance."

"I understand that very well. And the same for you. Does Ghan know that? He is of no importance to me."

Chiang asked.

Ghan did not doubt his *own* importance for he was history. And of Peters's importance? "*Look around Chiang, he is too glorified to be legitimate. See his peasant bandits; revolutionaries for what? We were sent with an obtainable objective. Do not involve us in pity for these bandit causes.*"

"*So he is of no importance?*"

"*Exactly.*" Ghan's tight smile was directed purely at Peters.

Chiang explained, "Colonel Peters, you are of no importance to us."

"Then why are you sitting here talking to me if I am of no importance?" Peters responded with good humour, "Look at your boots – you have seen my work. That'll be you, *Dead*. Why didn't you attack? You are here talking! Stop this bullshit of importance and mandates. No more lies!"

Chiang related nothing to Ghan, and glared at Peters, "You are angering Two Stars Ghan! No insolence!"

Underneath the table, Ghan excitedly knocked his knees together.

Peters's jaw fell in disbelief. "Now you listen to me! Because of my importance and your mission here I want you to know I can wipe out Beijing, just like this." He clicked his fingers and placed the radio temporarily to his cheek. "If that's what you want, I can deliver it."

"Now *you* lie!" Chiang said sagely, "I see no nuclear weapons!"

"Just because you can't see it, doesn't mean it's not there."

Romano raised his chin at Chiang, "I have seen it, a Beijing Ninety-Six. Very nice. It cost a quarter of a million U-S dollars."

"*They have a Beijing Ninety-Six,*" Chiang shuddered.

Ghan felt a welling in his chest, and in safer climates, he would have laughed, but today, he could only frown, and deeply, "*Those Beijing Ninety-Sixes could never work... What were the Taiwanese thinking when they made them? Anyway, if I was him, I would say the same. All we want is Providence, he knows that?*"

"*Too well,*"

"*And the fool wants to stand in our way? A conflict will be very bloody.*"

"*It is his decision.*"

Ghan tapped his finger on the table. "*Let him say what he wants. Maybe pride is burning him alive. If he wants to stand in our way he has to have reason and his reason will be his weakness.*"

"*His reason is pride...*"

"*Chiang, look at him... Don't be so obvious... He does not want to die, does he? If he did, we'd be fighting them, yes? Find his reason for not fighting and that is his weakness.*"

"*Yes Ghan.*" Chiang's eyes skirted between Romano and Peters, "Ghan appreciates that we can talk."

Peters understood, "I do too."

"And, we want talk to lead to peace. A peace where we don't have to die."

"Really?" Peters's spoke matter-of-factly: "My Army. Your Army. We don't have to kill each other. Too much war has pacified me so now I want to deal with you." He toyed with the crappy lighter, flipping the lid to his adversaries. "One of your soldiers came forward and traded this. I see that opportunity is in you. And if Ghan understands how far away he is from Beijing, he'll know that business is different down here. We don't fight like the armies of Asia. This is a land of opportunity." He shone a jaded though confident, enlightening smile. "Even though you are obedient to your superiors, remember where they have sent you. This is the end of the earth, they have no idea what exists here, but you do."

Chiang translated persistently until he was sure Ghan had all the details. Ghan wanted to know the type of opportunity, what is opportunity other than what he and his troops offer? Deliverance from maniac bandits?

"First, you will not die. If your army has plans to trade with these lands, deal with me and I will open a trading port to boost the economies of both our peoples."

When Chiang told this to Ghan, Ghan appeared enlightened and pleased to have navigated a difficult situation. *"Chiang! Oh! If we were sent here to trade we would be doing so! Instead, we have been sent here to conquer!"* Ghan wore an exultant smile. *"He wants to trade with us! And we invade his trading Port! No wonder he's angry!"*

*"Do we take him seriously?"*

*"For his sake, yes. To adapt our duty of policing to trading would require us to contact the Third Fleet or even General Zhing."*

*"Yes, they would like to know of our progress,"*

*"The bandit's proposition of trade is a ruse we can take advantage of. Make it known that I will ask our superiors and they will direct any political decisions."*

*"Political?"* Chiang brightened.

*"War governs trade and trade governs politics,"* Ghan said, *"We are in this war to police which creates peace and thus opportunity for trade, the latter we should explore first and foremost. True?"*

"Yes, but what of the military objective?" Chiang twisted to Ghan.

Ghan's stern face partially bowed to shade from the overbearing sun. A small trickle of sweat skidded from behind his ear, down his neck, under his collar. Are great merchants famous? No.

Peters, suspicious of their secretive chatter, informed them, "I know you understand that trade is the only peaceful solution."

Chiang told Ghan.

Ghan cheerily smiled to Peters, *"Chiang, look him in the eyes as I do, tell him I will confer with my superiors on the prospects of trade as a means of peace. It sounds promising."*

Chiang, relieved at the prospect of a peaceful day, translated to the best of his ability, "Two Stars Ghan will contact our superiors on the prospects of trading so that we can make peace." He saw a crooked limb poking out of the scrub at the side of the road, recognised the standard issue bloodied uniform, contour of flung lifeless limbs, and Ling poised: lips ajar, swollen eyes shut in tight consternation; crushed and destroyed. "We will consult with our High Command for a, ah… Decision. We will consult with our High Command for a strategic and political *decision*."

Peters, over-estimating Chiang's words, asked, "So there will be a political decision? Impressive! We have progress! No more killing. You like that? I do."

Romano turned away to hide his consternation. Fairytales!

"Yes. There has been enough killing. China is very tolerant," Chiang said and discretely conferred with Ghan: "*See the fate of Lieutenant Ling!*"

Ghan had seen dead Ling a minute before. Small change, Napoleon would say. "*This Colonel Peters prides his prey like cheap jewellery. See past his trickery. Believe half of what you see and none of what you hear. Look this bandit in the eye – do not falter – make a polite farewell like you want to see him again. That's what he wants to see. It is preposterous that we have even been speaking to him, that is a form of flattery in itself. It feeds his ego. That is good.*"

Chiang curtly explained their predicament to Peters, locking eyes, "We value your friendship and will see you again very soon. We need guidance from our superiors before continuing our movements. We hope you please understand."

"I understand…"

"So we wait?" Romano scrutinised the invaders. "How long?"

Chiang appropriately asked Ghan, who plainly flapped his hand south, "*What we want to do first is secure peace. They'll like that. Make them feel comfortable.*"

Chiang then stood and formally bowed, "Please await our word. We are happy to have made peace."

"So be it." Peters replied, "I have your word and the means to burn you bodies to ash."

Chiang translated to Ghan.

Ghan sat there, quite solemn, his vexation growing, "*Burn us to ash? What a charming and dangerous man. Now he thinks I fear him. I like it.*"

"*You fear him?*"

"*I want him to think so. This has been extremely interesting. I thought they would surrender or try to buy us. Let's go. I've seen enough to know what to do.*"

"Colonel Peters," Chiang stood and rigidly leaned forward to shake hands, "We will depart now."

"Thank you for talking," Peters told them, "It has been an honour."

Ghan, Chiang and the two troops saluted their opponents, briskly marched through the barricade back across the bridge disappearing into the ranks of their spear-head unit of crack troops in section formations poised to assault the bridge. As Ghan vanished around the bend of the road all signs of his military sunk into the bush. Refugees surfaced from the river banks waiting to cross. The tears for mercy ran down their bodies only moistening the mud where they stood. Then from the sky a flock a galahs descended, wheeling across the river and perching on the bridge. Chinese spotters, Peters and his militia, and the refugees in between, watched the birds. The galahs however, after some chirping and ruffling of feathers, took off, heading west, forming a flurry of grey and pink against the sky.

Over a hundred metres down the road from the meeting were the commandos, crawling into position, concealed under a dark overhanging branch, camouflaged, hidden from the militia who nervously faced the north. This area was deemed pivotal to the unfolding events. Propped on his elbows, dripping sweat under his camouflage hessian and attached twigs and branches, through foggy binoculars, softly blowing away a persistent mosquito, Matthews spied the end of the meeting.

"That *was* the Chinese," he squinted and quivered, "With Peters, Romano…"

"Doing?" Tom whispered.

He waited, Peters and Romano sat figuratively in their chairs as militia blockaded the bridge after the departure of the Chinese officers.

"Chinese brass. Shit."

The three breathed at one with the bush, surveying the aftermath of the scene. The flight of the galahs seemed surreal and was thankfully short-lived.

Tom urged, "Krue wants us to do him in."

"I didn't see no ring on him. And if he's surrendering to the Chinese?" Corrie slowly counter-whispered. "Something's gotta' give."

Tom plugged in a radio earphone, clasping it with his palm to the side of his head straining to hear friendly air-traffic, "We can call in the bombers. Fuck 'em all up."

"Bonze idea, mate. Radio in the position. He's not moving."

Corrie lightly clicked his fingers. "*Shah!*"

Hurtling from the south, braking out of a bend in the road, decelerated a speeding jeep. The driver dropped a gear. The engine whined. The jeep passed the trio like a blur and then attracting their focus was the long blown brown hair, the sun-kissed tips flicked out with speedy fanfare. Tyres screeched and tail-lights flashed. It halted halfway between the trio and the card table. Callaghan and Krue eagerly alighted, immediately marching towards Peters, who halted their abrasive arrival by defensively holding his palms up in protest.

"This is fucked up," Matthews cursed. Cradling his rifle, he measured the distance and adjusted the sights. Breath in. Out. "So easy... Standing tall now... Shaking hands..."

"Call in the bombers?"

"No! We don't know what..." She'd be gunned down, blown up, either way, lost in the fog of war.

Before Callaghan or Krue could report of the impending collapse of Providence, Peters held them steadily with a stern gaze, "I just met with the Chinese, Two Stars Ghan."

Callaghan's hands flew to his head in a stupor, an act which installed in Peters less faith. "Two Stars *what?*"

"Their commander."

"What are they doing?" Krue looked over the span of Sunny Bridge to the anxious refugees, over their heads to the bobbing green helmets of Chinese troops. They tipped on their toes, mirroring the ominous stare to Krue. She could smell the fear and was perplexed that bullets hadn't started flying yet.

"Supposedly they're talking to their superiors and if they say yes to trade we can sort something peaceful out." He wearily turned to the bridge. "And if they're playing global enforcer, I blow Two Stars Ghan high into the sky."

"Hang on, whoa..." Callaghan stuttered. "After what they did to Kingston they don't look like a Trade Mission to me! They're here to kill pirates! That's you and I!"

"We're more than pirates..." Peters crossed his arms and rested his closed eyes in the sunshine, confident that if there was an attack, he would have warning, and in the meantime he had to act that peace, whatever that meant, was holding.

Krue continued the tempo, "You trust them?"

"Hell no! Take a second not to fuck with my head – Something you seem to value on your *diplomatic* mission. I know exactly what's going on."

"What's going on?" she asked calculatedly, part terrified.

"They know that if they push me they get the bullet. Final!"

Krue smartly composed herself. "You said they might trade... What does that mean?"

Callaghan warned. "Crazy shit's been happening in Providence. Too many refugees are running around, civilians are fleeing, a bit of looting, Creton took a shot," and shrugged *as if you would*, "At Krue."

Krue gloatingly piped in, "I killed him."

Peters could see she was bruised. He was more interested in the bandage under Callaghan's shirt, "And you?"

"Some prissy assassin... Dead."

"You're both lucky. Was he Chinese?"

"I don't know!" Callaghan flexed his shoulder to feel the pain, and infuriated, "But what is happening here? If we don't know it's hard to make plans and Providence could be ripped apart just waiting! Things are falling to pieces!"

Peters adroitly faced north. "Yeah, well, this is it. We're facing the Chinese. That's our reality. Things are breaking apart, that's what this is, nothing less."

Krue stood with her arms on her hips. A dead Chinese trooper lay in the bush, that grinning idiot Romano sat at the card table peering into a map, a barricade of tree trunks and anti-tank mines blocked the bridge, militia boys nervously spotted new Chinese troops positions across the river.

Callaghan pried, "What's this trade talk? Let me in on that."

"They wanted to roll over us but we settled on some prospect of trade. They'll contact their superiors."

Krue pedantically asked, "And if there's *no* trade?"

Peters, anchored to Krue with solemn admiration, postured, "When was it ever going to be right?"

"Get to the point!"

His eyes were set like stone. "I can handle anything I know the capabilities of but you," he menacingly twisted to Callaghan, "What's the point in bringing *her* up here? Did you want me to shoot her? Is that it? You think it'd made a difference?"

"No, well, maybe. It could be beneficial," Callaghan argued indignantly, "It'd make *my* day easier."

"No, she's an asset," he corrected his friend, "An insurance policy."

"*She* held Eric at gunpoint and radioed her crew of commandos to observe *you* which in my book means take a *shot*."

They looked over her and shunned the attractive traits to glare at the strategic wickedness.

"They're still working this mission as much as I am," she reminded Peters, "What did this Ghan say?"

Peters just watched the bridge. About now Ghan would be deliberating.

Krue persisted, "Are you bluffing them?"

He answered deadpan and robust, "No bluff. This is what happens."

She cast her eyes to the mad man she had legitimised by preferring to play diplomat with. She had her handgun. The rifle was in the jeep.

"Katherine," Peters placed an arm around her lower-back, the tip of his finger prodding her pistol, "No one can say you didn't try and that we didn't try. My advice is simple: Get out of here."

"To where?" She twisted out of his arm and to the bridge. Unseen tanks were moving up but Peters pretended to be oblivious. Two militia spotters ran up to Romano and reported something urgent. He took the news with a brave face but underneath could feel the fabrics of this little enclave shredded to bits. Even Callaghan portrayed the agony, not of not knowing, but knowing that what was coming would be messy. Peters barked commands to militia in the bush at the side of the road. They nodded and crawled away to the mortar pits. Krue felt strangely vulnerable standing in the open, like an invitation, when across the river there had to be keen snipers.

"Maybe you don't know what you're doing?" she said.

Peters swayed his head. "You don't get it. I'm ready to take them on regardless of what they do."

"Peters," Krue's steely eyes zeroed in, her face serene and tranquil, her presence of absolute servility to a greater cause, unshakeable, "I want to go to the Chinese. I'll win you peace easier than you can. Trust me."

From the table Romano chuckled abrasively, "Yes off you go to the Chinese! You'd fetch a good price to a Chinese General! See, we trade!"

Peters's head tilted up, praise intertwined with scepticism, admiring her. "You think you can get peace? With them? With *me* around?"

"You are up against tanks!"

"So?" Peters flustered with boyish excitement, "I'm waiting for them to bring up their forces into a nice juicy target ready to come rolling across that bridge... Don't look so horrified; you've called in missile strikes. I bet you *love* it."

She seethed, "I don't want to see you annihilated for something that in a week's time matters for nothing. That's reality."

"I know what," Peters boasted, one hand resting on her shoulder. "I have left them no option but to tackle this bridge and so they should if they're worth their salt. I know they're going to do it but when they realise I want them to do *that* – they'll come back with something different. Trust me. Trade is a gentleman's excuse not to die."

Krue swiftly reprimanded him: "The only thing you have to trade you won't."

He shifted from her angered glare. "They know that. It's up to them to gauge if *they're* worth it. Get it in to your head: It's up to them."

"Run, save yourself."

"Can't you see what this means to me?"

"Us," Callaghan tersely stressed, "Destruction *is* group therapy."

"I'm in it too." Romano assured them, "No more running! We defend!"

Krue said, "You're fighting over this?"

They looked around them. Just a bridge.

Krue said, "Blow the bloody bridge – deny them a route!"

"And divide this region? I can't build a bridge, I need that one."

"It'll be the end of you!"

Callaghan calmly agreed, "Listen, what the hell else are we to do? Move out for them to come in and set up their own little state and obedient people to plant rice to send back to a country that can't support its own? They wouldn't know shit what to do with this land either way. They're not having it. They're not imposing order or religion or whatever the fuck they've invented. We have to stop them now or everything goes to shit! This is what we do here!"

Peters added, "This is my role in the world."

Krue asked, "And you'll use your nuke?"

"As a last resort. I don't want fallout any more than you do."

"Great. Then what have I tried to warn you about?"

Callaghan exhaled, "Shut the fuck up before you bite a bullet!"

Krue fronted to Peters; he was fighting the impulse to slap her into submission, gritting his teeth.

"You know my position, you've always known it."

Krue demanded, "Something can be done to stop this!"

"No, nothing can stop it," Romano weighted his gun in his hand, one eye sizing up Peters objectifying Krue. I want to kill her, Romano telepathically zapped to him, I deserve the privilege.

Peters faced the bridge. The solemn prelude to battle descended as the hand of death cups the spirit from the dying.

"I don't want to die here," Krue admitted, "I'm telling you we can stop this!"

Peters smacked his lips. "If you're as good as you say you are, and now that you're in the one place on earth where proving your worth is fundamental to survival, perhaps there is one thing that can stop this... Vince!"

Vince jogged from the barricade towards them. "Colonel! No trade today?"

The light in Peters's eyes were electric. "Major Katherine Krue, thank you for sacrificing yourself for the prosperity and everlasting peace for an illegitimate region. Your days as a warrior woman are over. I'll notify your headquarters in Canberra. Congratulations, you are now a Diplomat."

"What?"

"You're so smart, go *reason* with the Chinese. Tell them to turn back and start marching north."

Callaghan caustically intervened, "You trust her?"

Peters asked, "Major Krue, you're up to it?"

She said nothing.

"Your gun," he commanded.

She handed her pistol to him.

"Vince, take her across to General Ghan and explain she is a Diplomat; a sign of goodwill," Peters speedily briefed him, "And make sure *you* come back!"

Vince nodded, took Krue by the wrist and led her over the barricade. She shook away his tight hand and together they walked across the bridge, side by side.

All three saw it and couldn't quite hear it.

"Maybe she's cutting a deal?" Matthews vaguely speculated.

"Better her than us," Tom said.

Corrie recoiled. "Shit is *going* down."

Krue and Vince crossed the bridge and were enveloped by a surprised infantry section.

Matthews felt ill, "And if they do her in?"

They froze, she was gone and she might not come back, and then it was them verses Colonel Peters, his militia and the Chinese Army.

Tom toyed with the radio, "We need air support."

Matthews gravely nodded. Distaste burnt his dry pallet at the sight of Callaghan, Peters and Romano relaxing at the card table merrily lighting up cigarettes, an annoying catchy electrical tune faintly floating on the wind, mixing with Tom's softly spoken call into the radio, "V*oodoo Child* requests air support, *Voodoo...*"

Ghan and Chiang inspected the assembling of his force from a convoy into a robust assault unit. Ghan strode with pride, sniffing the rolls of fumes puffing from the tank exhausts, listening to the clinks of knee-mortars assembled and aimed, the troops forming up and the nervous hush of medics waiting for wounded men. Troops applied camouflage cream, squatted around platoon leaders who made models of the bridge out of sticks and orchestrated their part of the attack. Grenades were primed, rifles fixed with bayonets, tank crews sat on turrets smoking, writing letters.

"The Third Fleet has not made radio contact in twenty-seven hours... Nothing." Chiang held his eyes on the pin-dots of sweat glistening in the palm of his hand. "Two Stars Ghan, we have come so far, so victoriously."

Ghan placed his satphone between them. The screen was lit but there was no signal. He symbolically stated, "All those satellites, so much trust we had in them, how technology has come to command man."

Chiang's stressed, "We are very alone in a strange land."

Ghan knew the Third Fleet was out in the Coral Sea battling it out and their fleet of satellites were probably obliterated by superior Western weapons. History. Something grand must come of this investment.

"We are stranded." Chiang admitted.

Ghan sounded strangely upbeat, "Yes, but we were sent to take Kingston and we did. We were ordered to Providence and we are on our way. We have a job to do, stranded or not."

"But we can not discuss the prospects of trade, maybe peace?"

"There is no peace!" Ghan vehemently decreed. "As for our superiors, as the bandit said, they have sent us so far away and do not know what goes on! Now see what we achieve in uncharted territory on our own Chiang, and then we will command our superiors with our success. Until then General Zhing relies on our obedience. He trusts our resourcefulness to make the whole. Otherwise, our Army would not be at its full potential. We will continue our mission for we are an instrumental part of the army, as it is instrumental to establishing peace."

"And the prospect of trade?"

"Trade with bandits," Ghan shook his head, "More pain than gain."

"So there is no need to contact our superiors?"

"Exactly."

"And without their guidance... Who, but you decides the end of the day?"

"Myself, and if I were to die, the honour would pass to you."

They arrived at the brigade's makeshift headquarters, off from the road, shaded and concealed by ghostly grey gum trees, two trucks in a clearing and a hive of busy staff. They could smell something in the air, something momentous. Ghan stood by a table, their only map of the region laid out before him. Company Commanders arrived, saluted, tensed and watched Ghan's hand hover over the map, the bridge, fingers splayed, pushing south.

On the outside he was all steel but internally, Ghan gulped, he was thinking – not raw calculations but sloppy ruminations. His training had not covered this type of obstacle, yes a bridge was a bridge and his forces were assembled to take it by storm, intact, and push on, but the aftermath was peculiar. Peters's ruse was a mix of peasant/bandit bluff and big-balls hardware. The concept of nuclear retaliation was absurd, for as the frontlines were so close any battlefield nuclear weapon would damage both sides. And, what man out here can strike Beijing? Perhaps, Ghan reflected, he was sent to take out Peters who actually did threaten Beijing. Ghan lay his hand flat on the table and stared at the bridge. Peters was waiting: a last stand in a doomed time? Ghan needed guidance, and from his breast pocket he slipped out his little red friend, *The Art of War II*, by General Zhing.

Meanwhile, Chiang crouched beside two radio operators. They had contact with a platoon left to garrison Kingston. Those in Kingston had no contact with the Third Fleet either. Chiang looked to his leader.

Ghan thumbed a dog-eared page, reading: *By discovering the enemy's dispositions and remaining invisible ourselves, we can keep our forces concentrated, while the enemy's must be divided.* Then his mind wandered, his trance disintegrated into the dust at his feet. There is no saving wisdom, only action.

Chiang's cautious and poetic tone seemed to float in from behind, "Is a victory far from home really a victory, Sir?"

"If a tree falls in a forest and no one is there to hear it, the *trees* hear it."

"Even so, we are like a lighthouse with no light."

Ghan said nothing, staring into the shadows cast by company commanders conferring over their only maps of the region. They were excited, drawing heavily on cigarettes, discussing acceptable losses in return for ground taken. One obnoxiously went as far as forty percent.

"Colonel Chiang… I see the courage in your face for you think with your eyes open. Don't dissect this day for we were sent here for a reason, perhaps the reason is far beyond our comprehension. We face an enemy. The only question in our minds should be, how do we deal such a man?" Ghan majestically stroked his goatee, "What is he thinking?"

Chiang glared spitefully.

Ghan clasped his friend, "You spoke to him… What does he think?"

"In his heart is something dark."

"And his mind?"

"Strategy. A dangerous mix."

Ghan methodically agreed. "He knows we know this. So, what to do? Trade with thieves? Peace with bandits? Disobey our orders, shame our country?"

"Regardless of the bandit, see how far we have come – how far can we go after Providence?"

"Our objective is Providence." Ghan now whispered, "To take it now would be a great victory – only then will we be acknowledged by our superiors and then they have to get us out of here!"

Chiang felt cold, lonely and immobile.

Ghan turned, his lone lock of black hair whipping out, calling his tank captains and headquarters staff, "Attention!" Standing hands on hips, sucking his belly in and jousting his shoulders up and forward, inhaling the winds of the world into his lungs then blowing words of fury like a foghorn, "We are the army, we are here, and we are here to conquer! We cross the river! This is *our* Long March! Tell that to the unborn!"

A messenger ran straight up to Chiang, staring nervously at Ghan. "Yes?"

"A woman from the Australia Army has asked to see you, Sir."

"Thank God she's gone!" Callaghan howled. "That infectious creature!"

"She will tell all to Ghan," Romano complained, one eye scouring the Chinese positions. "We should have shot her dead. I will, you know. Look at me. These eyes do those things."

"I couldn't think of her that way," Peters apologised but exonerated his decision with a simplistic frown. "She has that *power* to interfere, and to Ghan, isolated from his masters, she just may bring peace!"

Callaghan mused. "… If they piss off, yes."

"I can't change that mongrel and his superiors and whatever drives them this far – So send him a muse. It's the same war, different weapons."

"Ah this is crazy!" Callaghan cackled. "She can't solve this. Us, his tanks, one river between us." Turning to the Chinese river bank, "Snipers. I can feel it." His wound cramped. "I got a bad feeling."

"O-K, let's get some cover. Ease down a bit... Ghan will have to consider a lot more with Krue around. We just sit and wait. We can't appear afraid."

"Easy to clean 'em in a mess."

Corrie held the cross-hairs on Callaghan, swung to Romano, then back to Peters. The trio suddenly stood up and sauntered off the road into the bush.

"Not good," Matthews said, "If there's an attack, we're fucked."

Tom added, "But if any firing breaks out who's to notice us popping off the high-command? Who cares how many holes we fill 'em with."

"Think fellas. Then who's to stop the Chinese?"

"Shit."

"Hot shit."

"Yeah, anyone see if the keys are in that jeep?"

The jeep was halfway between them and the card table, an affordable escape vehicle in the right circumstance.

Vince and Krue were escorted past tanks, intrigued troopers, mortar platoons, a medical armoured personnel carrier, all busily preparing for a massive attack. A Sergeant guarded them. The messenger came running back. Krue and Vince were hurried onwards.

A majority of the troops were aged between sixteen and nineteen, mentally preparing for the rigours of battle, chanting a war-cry, re-checking weapons, orders, hand-signals, and which direction to fan out once they crossed the bridge. The sight of buxom Krue broke their concentration; some commanders lost their tempers. Her breasts, medium sized in the world, appeared gigantic like melons and soft as clouds. Many of the troops had not seen a white woman in the flesh in all their lives, and traced the fine curves of the cut of her eyes, lips and cheek bones. Of beautiful western creatures the most they had seen were the glossy muses; movie stars, magazine centrefolds and billboard girls advertising alcoholic and cancerous products few could afford but were eager to devour. What they knew about the Western Woman was simple; the West was won by the men because the women demanded it. Yet here was a soldier. She showed no fear, this calm state reinforced by their awe of her.

Vince grimaced.

Krue's mind raced. Too many troops. Over a thousand. She shut her eyes and opened them with a question, "Vince, why are you here?"

The troops escorting them listened to her peculiar sounding voice.

"Here?" Vince asked, surprised, as together they were surrounded and going somewhere, hopefully to the right person.

"How did you end up here?"

He carefully formulated his words, "I am a Gurkha, a soldier for life with the burden of war and the shame of surrender. Life is bad at home… There is no home, no family… So a soldier sails across the seas and finds Providence and Colonel Peters… A lost soldier has an ideal to fight for."

"An ideal?"

"To exist, to be, we all wish to make something. Some actually find it." He wryly smiled on his good fortune.

Their guards became suspicious. One padded Krue's body for weapons.

"Fuck off," she snarled at the guard, he stepped back. "What does he expect me to say to the Chinese?"

"You are his last hope for peace."

"*I'm* the last hope?" she gasped. "For the preservation of *his ideal*. His *people*. Their *history*. What's left of my *ass*. *Fucking* bastard."

"He has faith in you. He said you are very courageous for coming here from so far away. He knows that."

"Sure."

They were led off the road, between trees. Vince and Krue shared an uncertain and sorrowful look. Execution. But then they saw a mob of hierarchy approaching them, trucks, staff and order.

Krue straightened her back and looked dead-ahead. Several officers closed in on her and shuffled her to a table. She recognised the region on the map.

Chiang coltishly hailed, "Colonel Chiang of the One Seven-Seven Brigade!"

Krue sensed his lust for superiority and sharply saluted him, "Welcome to Australia, Colonel Chiang. Major Katherine Krue, Australian Army."

Chiang noted her curt discipline and enunciated English tuned specifically to his ear. "We have met Colonel Peters. Why are you here?" Turning to Vince, "And this bandit?"

Vince matched Krue's sharp military tone, "Vinh Goh Lok! Colonel Peters's Personal Guards. I have escorted the Major here to speak directly to General Ghan! She represents the Australian Government and not the Warlord Colonel Peters. She is a respected and experienced Diplomat in Occupied Australian affairs! She is hear to talk of peace!"

Chiang studied the adorable diplomat, top to bottom and up again.

Two Stars Ghan fronted up to Krue, *"A woman interrupting our preparations! Where did she come from!"*

*"Across the bridge,"* Chiang informed. *"An Australian Army Diplomat."*

*"The Australian Army is here? But they are so weak! What the hell is going on?"*

*"She is a messenger..."*

*"The diplomats had their time and now we've been sent to deal with reality..."* Ghan lifted a lock of Krue's hair and marvelled at the fine sandy tips. *"It is gold like silk,"* he told the gathered troops, loud and abrasively, a warning shot over Krue's shoulder. *"We shall have a golden haired mistress each!"* They applauded. *"Fair skinned maids to serve our children! We came here to conquer and reap rewards!"*

Krue endured the mockery, stood six inches taller than him and looking over his head spoke unfalteringly to Chiang, "I am a Diplomat for the Australian Army. If I do not return, Colonel Peters will launch a missile strike," she encompassed them all in one graceful sweep of her arm. The troops marvelled as her eyes briefly passed them over, then she wickedly kissed the air, "Your forces will be destroyed."

Chiang snappily translated.

Ghan stepped back, astonished, admiring her full figure. If his troops needed reason to cross the bridge, she was it.

She roared, "I have come to make peace! I am a diplomat!!"

The troops inquisitively shuffled closer.

Chiang said, *"Sir, a Diplomat of Peace. Very strange, and threatening."*

Ghan dismissed her, *"A Diplomat of Peace – Diplomat of War: the same! And she is a warrior, not to be trusted! Look at her!"*

Chiang locked his eyes into Krue's, his English tardy but forward, "I fear, you and I, what we feel in our hearts, will not be heard," and then for Ghan's entertainment, asked loudly, "What peace do you offer?"

"A ceasefire," Krue proudly sang.

Chiang told Ghan, who asked, pounding one fist into the other, "*Only after the conquest of Providence will we have peace in this land! That's our objective! Anything short of that is defeat!*"

The troops cheered him, making Chiang's translation barely audible.

Krue snarled, "You are mistaken! You're mission is not what you think!"

Chiang translated and whispered into Ghan's, "*She may be a ruse, but she has good intentions.*"

"*I can see that. What does she want from us?*"

Chiang asked and received a bright though unbelievable reply.

"Go back to China. Head north or die here!" she animatedly yelled to the troops crowded around her. "Go north to your families! Providence is not worth your lives! I know! I've been there!"

Chiang carefully translated to Ghan who heeded and yelled his reply to his hearty troops now laughing at Krue.

"Then who will destroy this bandit who kills refugees; this pirate that plunders from the sea; and this Colonel Peters that wages war when a world should be at peace!" Chiang retaliated, bitterly and partially apologetic, to Krue.

"I will kill him," Krue gladly announced, "As I have done before in the name of peace!"

Chiang fluidly translated to all and they fell presumptuously silent.

Ghan marched short contemplative steps before Krue, his hand contemplatively up in the air, "*So she is asking to take the glory of destroying the bandits! We are not tourists! We have a duty! We are warriors of peace! We need no diplomat! Why come this far for a woman's job! It is not one woman's job! It is every man's job to bring peace!*"

Chiang translated to Krue.

Krue begrudgingly swallowed Ghan's rhetoric and braced herself. A weight lifted off her shoulder. It dissipated into the air and fell like a mist on all the dumb faces on this side and the other side of the river. She rallied them, "If you do not let me kill Colonel Peters, and if you do not head north," she wickedly smiled, illuminating the perverse fires in her eyes, "I will watch two armies attack! There will be peace after your short lived war and these lands of Australia will become free of war... And I will be happy!"

Chiang appeared grave and serious, telling Ghan and the troops, "*If we do not let her kill Colonel Peters, she is to watch two armies fight and then there will be peace in Australia! She will be happy.*"

"*I can see she will be very happy...Strange diplomacy... She's invited us, on behalf of Australia, to battle! What a cunning ruse,*" Ghan gallantly assumed. He merrily applauded her. *"Why are there not more diplomats like this one?"*

Krue quietly grimaced to Vince. "I can't do shit."

Vince said between clenched teeth, "I can't let you kill my commander."

The eyes of the troops zoned in on her. She said loudly, "If you do not want to fight, Colonel Chiang, you and I can make contact with the Australian Army Headquarters and arrange a compromise to the slaughter of so many men and innocent refugees. I have my duty too, the same as you, the elimination of Colonel Peters, and peace."

Once translated, Ghan asked Chiang, *"She has not eliminated him. It is too tough for one woman!"*

Chiang translated to Krue.

She protested, "Without your threat there was no need to kill him... Your presence creates a great disturbance. Now Colonel Peters must die."

Chiang explained to Ghan. It sounded plausible. He studied Krue, his troops, the map, the bridge. His words ran so fast Chiang had trouble translating.

"He thanks you for your honesty and commitment to peace... He says you are one... Pirates are many... It is not just the man but the bandits... Many! You can not kill them all. We will enforce peace! Save yourself for what is left of Australia!"

Evidently the troopers agreed with Ghan, they clapped him, cheered him, and commended Krue for her luminosity...

Ghan took centre stage, decreeing, *"Men! Be the heroes we are! We will not let this white woman negate our right to wage war and steal not only glory but our rewards! How can a man sleep at night when a woman has told him what to do and who to be!"*

They cheered, up, up again and down.

Krue raised her arm up to the sky like Caesar greeting centurions. The troops hushed, and Ghan, greatly impressed and honoured, stood firm to hear her words via Chiang, "My enemy's enemy is my friend and if I do not kill *our* enemy, if you wish to carry out the dirty task," she carefully waited for Chiang to translate the pious keynotes, "My fate is to witness your victory! I am happy because afterwards there will be peace as day follows night."

Chiang hurriedly translated, excited at would come next...

"Men of the Chinese One Seven-Seventh Brigade, fighting under the glorious Two Stars General Ghan," Krue worked them with a wink to Chiang. "Today you will fight like true warriors."

The troops roared with applause at this fine woman.

"And for those that survive, after today you will all know how well you have lived and the true price for Peace!"

Hot on the heels of Chiang's perfect translation, the troops cheered, the roar carried over to Sunny Bridge. Ghan smittenly clapped his golden haired muse.

Peters was disturbed by the cheers from the north, imagining Krue and Vince butchered in a few minutes of peasant frenzy and the bits stuck on bayonets, bobbing up in the air for all the troops to cheer. Having once been 'out there' and beset by isolation and savagery it was a struggle to think in a sane way. Peters straightened himself as the latest cheers struck a chord. She was buying time, but he was already prepared. She was pleading to Ghan on Peters's behalf. It would make no difference. Whoever sent Ghan out here did so to be sure he never came back. There were no deals. But, there was hope.

He forced a weathered smile to the northern side then frowned and stared into his palms; he had held her mangled buttock there. He had not seen the imperfection but the crude indenture reminded him of a bite, not too large and uncomfortable, but deformed enough to send a shiver up his spine. His battle scars were lively things, he could flex a muscle or turn into a mirror and glare, but Krue's wound touched vanity yet she was back to risk it all. She too lived as though already dead.

He sighed.

Callaghan's discerning eyes measured from the bridge to his jeep. "You think she's coming back?"

Peters countenance was drained and fading. "Maybe."

"I've got an idea. Here me out. Kill them all now! Launch!"

Then their ears prickled at the intertwining sounds the wind carried from the north; the rumbling of tank engines vibrated the bridge and exhaust clouds floated above the tree line; Battle-cries… A chorus up and up and down; the rasps of platoon sergeants assembling troops along the column.

"This will be a long day." Peters tucked his fingers under his tongue and made a shrill whistle.

Militia sprang into action, hauling anti-tank mines onto the road. Romano and Callaghan squatted in the bush, praying but to different gods. Militia perched behind tree trunks aiming their rifles to the focal point of the day, a bridge too close.

Peters bravely walked behind the barricade, raising his head over to see further across the bridge and down the road. The Corporal who traded him the lighter gave a silly wave, the machine-gun crew were squatting like bronze statures, impervious to time and bullets. Peters could see nought of what they were to throw at him but he knew they lay there coiled like a snake. Perfect.

"Oh my god," Matthews moaned.

Corrie sniffed. "Tanks. Infantry."

"Thousands of them." Tom winced.

"We got to move," Corrie said.

Matthews whispered, "Hold on. Play it cool. Anything can happen."

Krue had run dry of words and faced the troops. Coupled with the taking of Kingston and the march of death, now this pep talk of nothing but death and glory, they were ready, to her pleasure, to do her job.

"*In five minutes we attack!*" Ghan hailed his troops.

On the road she could hear the message spread. Troops assembled in respective units. Tank crews sealed their turret hatches and raised cannons to the sky. Mortar men squatted by the weapons ready to drop shells. The few medics attached to the headquarters stood their place against empty stretchers.

"When are you attacking?" she asked, instinctively scanning the sky.

"In four and a half minutes!" Chiang kneaded his hands together. Mechanical mobilisation had reached its final stages. He stepped next to Krue, breathed in the sweet sweat from her burnt cream complexion, and said, "Ghan has one last question: From what side do you wish to see the arrival of peace?"

She timidly bit at her lip.

Chiang inferred, "You have faith in neither side?"

She turned to him. "I must flee south to my superiors in Canberra. I will inform the Chinese embassy of your exploits."

He bounced backwards, "The Chinese Embassy in Canberra?"

"I will bring news of the victor of this campaign. I will leave through Colonel Peters's region."

"Are you a soldier of Peters!"

"No! Diplomat!"

Chiang didn't believe her. He conferred with Ghan for a sharp second, they looked in doubt, "Ghan believes you are something different, a witch: casting spells."

Strangely, Ghan then re-explained to Chiang, then resumed his final briefings with his headquarters staff.

"Or an Angel," Chiang smiled.

"If I were, you'd be heading home."

"The troops are under your spell that they are dying and fighting for peace… They want you at their side. Why let you leave?"

"Who is to write history in case all of you die?"

Chiang translated this to Ghan, who nodded once, looked to his watch, and simply waved Krue and Vince away to the south, rambling, "*Colonel Chiang, your fraternising with this diplomat distracts from the job at hand. Send them back now! If they are bandits it will be rewarding to kill them. That act will show our troops I call the shots. Inform her that if she really has any say in history, to tell the world who we are and why we're here.*"

Bluntly, coarsely, Chiang explained, "Ghan says you must go now but remember this: Who we are and why we're here! You must tell your people that. Run now!"

She did, Vince hot on her heels, past platoons of troops shuffling forward and tanks rumbling the earth. Her boots dashed through the air and rounding a bend she huffed with relief at Sunny Bridge: at the abandoned barricade there was not a soul to be seen. Peters, Krue was mortified to think, had retreated. Had he sunk into the bush like a good revolutionary partisan should? With Vince behind her she felt an inkling of betrayal, both expendable ruses to drag out the enemy to give Peters enough time to stack the deck and run! How many seconds were left? Callaghan's jeep was down to the side of the road, partially concealed.

"It's her!" was Matthews's jubilant whisper as Krue clambered over the barricade and hop-scotched past numerous anti-tank mines placed like overturned dinner plates on the road.

Vince led her off the road into the bush. In the darkness of the sub-tropical roots and ferns was the assemblage of Peters's field command at the flank of the bridge. Militia peered ominously to the oncoming attack. Romano and Callaghan drew heavily on cigarettes. Overwhelmed but cool and commanding was Peters and his instrumental field radio held up to his poised lips, his cold eyes warming at the vision of a panting Krue.

"Check A-O-K," Eric chirped over the radio. "Any movement?"

"Krue?" Peters asked her. "Do we have a deal?"

She fell forward, hands on knees, panting. "Fuck you. It's a," rushed for air. "An all-out assault!"

"Game over!" Callaghan shrieked.

Peters growled, "They're fucked!"

"I tried, it's *impossible!*" Krue panted. "You'll have to find out for yourself if it's all worth it."

"Exactly!" Peters gripped her, "Welcome to my world!"

She looked to Callaghan, Romano, Vince, Hoochi in the shadows, and the cast of sucker militia and Tonkas, the few white men who had survived Task Force Seven's foray into anarchy so far, staring intrepidly to the bridge.

With robotic precision Peters spoke into the radio, "Standby launch."

Those that had seen his methods for annihilating masses knew it would be messy, a far more uglier scene than obliterating nomadic peasants brandishing antique rifles.

Peters tossed Krue her pistol.

Callaghan unashamedly panicked. "Fuck me I'm out of here. You handle the bridge, I'm handling the town." His exhaling smoke mixed with the light penetrating through the canopy. "You know I'm no soldier!"

"Go then!" Peters commanded. His eyes were on the bridge. "And Katherine?"

"I'm leaving too! I must get back."

His mouth turned down but his eyes were lit up. "I,"

First one shot in the air, then twenty, shattered the fragile prelude. Troops across the river emptied their rifles and machine-guns, each covering a section of bush.

Krue slide behind a tree trunk.

The first spray of bullets flew over their heads, dropping a few branches and mincing leaves. Birds fled and the air stung with searing sounds. Militia returned fire, sweeping across the Chinese positions.

Peters screamed to Callaghan and Krue, "Go!"

Romano rose from behind a log and aimed his rifle, "Come to me..."

The first tank appeared, troops at its side and behind.

Krue shouted, fiery and piercing, "Just don't nuke 'em!"

Peters palmed her away, artfully aiming from around a tree trunk, firing concentrated bursts at the charging Chinese.

Callaghan led the way out, through the bush, keeping parallel to the road, heading to the jeep. He was cursing, muttering, maddened with anger. Krue's pulse raced as bullets randomly crossed their path or thwacked off tree trunks. She turned and saw the sledge-hammer assault: Tanks sped across the bridge, behind them charged eager, screaming troops. Deep in the bush, Peters stood tall and mighty, his fingers tight over the radio handset: "Target: Northern Side of Sunny Bridge. Fire!"

# Who Dares Wins

At the bank, Eric hesitatingly confirmed, "M-L-T to launch, target north side Sunny Bridge."

Jintana stood in a state of paranoia verging on convulsion. Marcus nervously fingered the trigger of his rifle as he also edged a mouse on its pad, dragging the cursor across a digital map, not that he could concentrate or effectively appear to. Jemmy and five cut-throat pirates waited at the front of the bank, concealing small-arms, dressed in typical pirate work clothes of salty bleached singlets and trousers with numerous zipper pockets, carrying empty sports bags over their bare sun-baked shoulders. They waited for nothing in particular, as if their presence was justified that the setting was a bank and service was what they were after but as can be seen, there were other matters to attend to. Marcus was shaking like a leaf. No man, not even Malo, could out shoot them. Those seedy bastards were toughened nomadic rascals, born on a boat, wed on a boat, lose their virginity on a boat, die on a boat and what are they doing on land?

Eric radioed the mobile missile launcher, "Fire!"

The high-pitched reply dulled the fear purging in Eric's veins.

"Initiating launch sequence now!"

Jemmy grinned. The Chinese will be twice as angry. As a missile is to soar into the sky from the eastern side of Jacinda Mountain, he moved on Providence, "Hands up Nancy Boy."

Jintana clasped her hands to her cheeks and purposely bowed to the floor. Jemmy and pirates spread into the back of the bank tearing out chords connecting radio equipment. Sparks flew, contact with the outside world was lost.

Eric stuttered, "No! Take what you want! Please! Don't destroy this! No!"

"Peters has gone too far," Jemmy prophesied to Marcus and Eric, "He'll be dead soon … You know what I am doing here… No fucking around!"

Marcus and Eric immediately complied.

Jemmy pressed himself against Jintana's quivering body, "Open the vault."

The missile launcher truck was manned solely by Billy. He sat on the cabin of the truck with a two foot telescope resting between his knees, spying and gaping down to Sunny Bridge and the frenetic movement below. He witnessed it, minutely and remote, but the grizzly fight rattled him to the core. Then the call came. He leapt off the cabin roof, leaving the radio handset dangling by the open door, ran to the rear control panel and noticed the bush eerily silent; he figured mellow breezes hushed the trees. He stood back and admired the Fudo; the robust fuselage, the polished fins, the napalm warhead, a package, ready to rocket. Time was precious, and getting to work, he then saw five, frail yet energetic, young men of the Fang Tribe, emerging from the bush with spears, a rifle, a hessian sack and a hacked-off kangaroos leg.

"I am with Peters!" Billy hollered. They silently approached, quickly surrounding him. He raced to the front of the truck, pulled out a 12-gauge shotgun and levelled it to their punitive chests. They ignored the weapon, advancing on the bigger weapon. "Don't touch that!" he yelled.

The Fang nodded at him, wicked smiles of chiselled teeth, then like monkeys sprung up and clambered over the missile truck. Three prayed to the fuselage, one balanced atop the warhead and wiped the bloody hind leg on the pinnacle. Droplets ran down the silvery belly. The fifth stood on the truck tray and from his hessian sack decorated the missiles with vibrant wattles, cockatoo feathers, a cup of breast milk from a fifteen year old mother.

"Hurry then!" Billy flipped open a metal hatch to the control panel. He inserted and turned the key, power, circuitry warm-up. "Stay clear!" He checked the target co-ordinates had come through on the outdated LCD screen. "You beauty!... O-K... *Forgive me for sins I may commit...*" With one finger he pushed the red button. "Run!"

The Fang obeyed, slid off and watched from behind tree trunks.

Billy checked the fuel valves weren't leaking or blocked, and then ran for cover. "Can you count?" They couldn't understand him. "One minute. I'll count up, one, two, three... No, I'll count down... Fifty-five, fifty-four..."

Mechanical arms raised the missile to the sky, its thrusters vibrated, the truck shook, toxic smoke curled from the rockets. Birds stretched their wings and shuffled along branches for a better look.

"Aw' she'll be a real rippa' this one!"


The lead tank of the first wave accelerated onto the bridge and broke through the barricade, sending trunks and branches across the road and into the air. The tank continued onto a bed of anti-tank mines, jumped a foot backwards as explosions split its front tracks, a spray of hot metal splashed forward.

Militia cheered at the smoking wreck.

Two tanks followed over Sunny Bridge. Troops ran behind them, hunched over, hurling grenades and firing indiscriminately into the bush at concealed militia. There was confusion as with the lead tank immobilised, the following tanks rammed into it, reversed, and tried again. Scores of troops panning out off the bridge, some lugging away anti-tank mines or making a mad dash for the bush, were gunned down, forming withering piles on the road.

At the observation post of the bridge, Ghan cowered down and signalled the forward mortar platoons to adjust their aim. He stepped onto the road in clear view of the bridge, with three spotters, and pointed to the left, right, and hazed road beyond the bridge, then with a hand flat to the ground ordered it to be wiped clean. As they turned to retreat for better cover he saw the bandit's only known vehicle escaping. He reached for his pistol and fired a volley over the heads of his charging troops then refrained; for there was the golden haired angel escaping. He fired at bandit positions until he was empty, changed clips, stray shots whirred in all directions, his ears were ringing. His heart was pumping. A tide was turning. He steadied himself. This must go on.

"Sir!" a company commander's red face impeded, "The bridge?"

Ghan punched him in the shoulder, "Attack!" and repeated himself until the commander's hundred men had filed past onto the bridge and onto the other side and were shot to bits. Through the sprays of blood, whirls of smoke pushed out from grenade blasts, he saw the golden haired angel again.

Callaghan reversed back onto the road and planted the accelerator. Three bullets riddled the rear panels as they lurched forward. Krue braced herself, thrown back and forth, as Callaghan slammed on the brakes, gripping the steering-wheel, skidding to a swerved halt. Green guerrillas Tom and Corrie menacingly blocked the road with rifles aimed to his head. Matthews, dirty, gaunt, unshaven and brave, jumped in the back and cowering from the bullets, held his grimy knife to Callaghan's three-day growth throat, "Hey Sunshine, we're hitching a ride."

To Tom and Corrie the smoking and rumbling bridge, stalled battling tanks and hordes of Chinese troops was an immediate threat yet spectacular testament to the war they had conjured during their training. They held their fingers on the triggers and dropped a half dozen of the invaders each. Mortar shells sailed down emitting a spine tingling whistle that exploded over the bush. Militia mortars retaliated. Chinese tanks, well out of sight, fired up into the air, their shells sporadically hitting the road. A triple succession of blasts shock-waved from fiery craters in front of and behind the jeep. Tom and Corrie leapt in the back and franticly curled up in their seats for cover. All were temporarily deafened. Matthews removed the knife from Callaghan's throat and shouted like a wide mouthed puppet, "Go! Go! Go!"

Callaghan took one look at Krue, she was petrified but pointing south, and planted his foot on the accelerator. Rubble sprays showered the bonnet. A puff of smoke blew over. For the next ten seconds, an eternity, bullets and shrapnel pursued the jeep. A shell split trees apart in the bush. Birds flocked into the air. The windscreen shattered. Corrie poked his finger through a hole in the crotch of his pants. Then the smell of smoke disappeared and apart from the receding crackling of weapons at the bridge the road was quiet and dark. A few refugees struggled along Highway Five, loners looking north to witness the commotion; obviously living in interesting times. The jeep hurtled towards them sending their frail bodies aside.

Krue hugged her men as best she could, "Thank God!"

"That *was* the mince-maker!" Tom marvelled, his head back, wind flushing debris from his grotty hair.

Corrie, inundated with adrenaline, retained a façade of alertness, "Let's get the fuck away…"

Matthews's young countenance had been replaced by a man's mind; hardened, broken, and as a result the wound that youth and innocence is, healed over. He remained rigid as Krue squeezed him.

"You're all in one piece!"

"*Same.*" His stately mouth spoke softly and stolidly, "They aren't stopping."

They heard a growing wave of gunfire. No shot or volley stood out, it was mixed and flowed like an orchestrated racket of destruction.

Krue held on to Matthews. She measured an inch between index finger and thumb, "That fucking close we are,"

"No," Corrie measured from the hole in his pants to his scrotum and showed all a half centimetre between thumb and index finger, "*That fucking* close."

Krue deftly examined the hole. "That'd put you outta' action in more ways than one. God that was nuts!"

Callaghan gritted his teeth and banged his steering wheel, "*Ohhh yeah* you're all fucking regular psychos aren't you – cool as cucumbers – shit!!! You shit me off! Get back there and save your country!"

Krue screamed, "Shut up!"

"Major! You want an air strike?" Matthews shouted as the wind rushed by tearing at his words.

"Not yet. Peters has done it himself. Watch the sky, and if you see a blinding light shut your eyes."

"There'll be none of that nuke shit... What now, Missy?" Callaghan asked, loathing, but the wind soothed his frazzled nerves. "This is your patrol! Christ! I expected the cavalry! But we're all fucked – you know *that*: What's your next trick?"

She slid into her seat with her mind on the road ahead, "Probably saving your life."

"My life," Callaghan heckled, watching the speedometer rise to 150 around a blind corner. "And what a fucking fortunate life."


Two Stars Ghan saw his bridge bottle-necked by the lead tank, disabled and blocking the southern outage. Behind it the two stalled tanks were sitting ducks, so too over two hundred men cowering there for cover, bravely aiming indiscriminately at bandits safe and concealed spitting fire from the river bank. Any troops that had so far made it to the southern side had been picked off like little ducklings. Ghan took charge. Waving the Red Dragon Flag he jostled along the bridge into his blocked mess of troops and tanks. He saw bullet holes in their cheap helmets, he slid on a layer of spent cartridges rolling on the bitumen like a sea of ball-bearings, screamed orders to a few shell shocked, threw some hand signals to mortar spotters, fired his pistol into the banks of the Arubai River. Mortar shells lobbed to the bandits at the rate of five per minute forcing them deeper into the bush. Ghan wanted his enemy out there, he wanted the whites of their eyes, he wanted a bayonet in their gut. He climbed the second stalled tank and waved the flag high over his head thinking nothing of the bandit's bullets. He pulled open the tank turret hatch and yelled at its driver, "Forward you blind bitch!"

The driver faltered. "We are jammed in General!"

"Ram forward! That is the way south! Ram!"


Peters's forces scurried deeper into the bush, away from the bridge, some curving around towards the river bank. On their side of the bank, down or up stream, they picked off troops charging over the bridge.

"Him!" he snarled at the heroic figure atop the tank waving the red flag. "It's Ghan! Direct fire to the lead!"

But fanned out by fear and dispersed from the incoming mortars, his men had little knowledge of his command. Peters crawled through mud and mangrove to the bank of the Arubai River for a better aim. Ghan cowered behind a tank turret. Difficult. Peters raked fire along the bridge, pinning down charging troops. Also on the river bank three militia pumped shotgun rounds at bunched troops squashed on the bridge. The entire scene was fogged by cordite, white smoke from burning synthetic uniforms, smoke grenades and a pungent humidity. Refugees tried swimming the river, but once in the middle, they deemed both sides too dangerous and thus floated downstream. Peters aimed at Ghan again.

The tank driver rotated the turret barrel to starboard. Ghan's angered face glowed from the hatch above, "Forward!" His thigh had been peppered by shot, gun smoke stung his eyes, specks of shrapnel dug into his back. "Ram or Die! Just like Saigon!"

"Yes General!"

Ghan slid off the tank. A bullet pinged the metal where he had just been. The tank reversed back squashing three wounded wailing troops then lurched forward. "Forward!" Ghan screamed, hoisting the flag into the air as the tank charged the lead tank blocking the bridge. There was the grinding of metal on metal scraping on bitumen, digging up clumps of tar and mulching bodies under tracks. Even for the might of the engine, the dead tank remained a dead dilemma and would not budge. Troops squeezed through, and as they charged onto the southern side they fell in the face of their own exploding mortar shells. Ghan stumbled over and found himself facing scores of dead and dying troops trampled like olive green wriggling maggots. He waved to the north for more troops to advance, and fearless as they were, they rushed. The ram tank reversed, squashed more troops, and rammed again but with little luck. The dead tank budged a mere foot. The obliterated barricade was now buried under dead. Ghan held the flag high as a signal for all troops to pour down from the northern side. Shotgun blasts shredded his flag leaving it a mere red camouflage net.

"Forward! Kill the bandits!"

Half of his two-thousand strong force were still on the north side waiting to push through and none of his tanks had crossed. The ramming tank reversed, squashed, revved to punch forward. With all the commotion of his second big battle Ghan didn't see the Fudo dropping out of the sky.

Peters scurried away from the river bank and a lone militia teenager pulled him deeper into the bush. Apart from the Chinese troops probing with searching fire, there was no concentrated action, yet the ring of carnage stung the air; wounded wailed, foliage smouldered, mortar shrapnel ripped through the bush, and on the road grenades exploded. Vince, covered in grime and camouflage, pounced from behind a tree and tapped Peters to look up. Trailing an exhaust smudge was the descending Fudo.

The area just north of the brigade was scorched by a burst of heat, followed by a billowing wave of splashing napalm. Tanks and troops were smothered, burnt, and then rocked by exploding fuel tanks and munitions. The ferocity diminished as the heat panned against the thick and flammable bush. More secondary explosions sent debris into the air: body parts, mortar shell cases, water bottles and molten red helmets. Troops frantically leapt off Sunny Bridge for the water below. The ram tank heaved forward, belted the dead tank, spinning it out of the way off to the roadside. Troops surged forward as the ram tank rumbled forward with the furore of a wounded bull released.

Ghan stumbled across the bridge, over the bodies and into thick smoke and an eerie silence. His ears were ringing but he could distinctly hear a far-away battle. Troops slumped at his feet, dead and wounded, then he found the living, advancing into the bush, spotting the bandits, firing earnestly. He tried to find section commanders. Two more tanks crossed the bridge and charged a hundred meters before halting, waiting for troops to catch up. There were no more mortar shells wreaking havoc, the launching positions having been wiped clean by the mammoth explosion from the sky. That was no bluff. He felt like in a dream, floating through a surreal landscape, and picked up a rifle and sprayed into the bush. He smelt smoke, blood, tree sap, pulverised leaves and burning metal. On the northern side Chiang wept for the rear of the brigade. Flames engulfed them, mortar crews exploded with their shells. The fires swept south and soon enough any man and machine on the northern side was rushing across the bridge.

"Attack!" Ghan called to the survivors racing towards him.

Roars rose from behind as hundreds of men escaping the smoking pit of the north clambered across the bridge, some on top of tanks, making it to the southern side fighting down the road, advancing with the smouldering air of hell-forged gladiators.

The bandits had retreated into the bush.

"To Providence!" Ghan screamed, striding into the battle-haze.

Those of his headquarters staff that had come to the forward observation point earlier, were all that remained. More typists than gung-ho warriors, they protectively circled him, firing bullets at the muzzle-flashes of sly bandits.

"Come and fight! Fight!"

Twenty meters up the road to the side, five of his troops knelt and fed belts of ammunition into a heavy machine-gun. A lone bandit leapt from the trees and belly flopped between them with a grenade in each hand. Vince exploded. The five troops gyrated up into the air and flopped to the crated ground like rag-dolls. Ghan was thrown flat on his face again, his teeth grating the insides of his cheeks. Tank cannons from behind shot shells south. Ahead the road was littered with an international mix of corpses. His troops advanced. Ghan aimed his pistol, shouting, "Victory!!" Platoons of petrified troops ran past him taking up the forward positions with a naive vigour, vanishing into clouds of smoke. "Victory!" he called to them as they ran head-first, faster and faster, into the fiery edges of the perilous new frontier.

"You come with me." Jemmy commanded. Jintana turned away like an ignorant animal shunning its predator. Jemmy slapped her. She turned stone cold. "It is safer with me."

She twitched, shattered.

Jemmy slapped her again. "No more chances! Come now or die!"

"No!"

He clenched his bile yellow teeth, all the more filthier under the white-collar hum of fluorescent lights and pale wallpaper. His pirates hastily rummaged inside the vault, her delicate hands had spun the dial entertaining them to a worthy heist. Marcus and Eric were blind-folded and on their knees, counting the last seconds of their lives. Outside fear molested the town as word spread: Peters has launched against the Chinese.

A tear raced from Jintana's puffy eye to the line of her jaw. She wiped it with her silk clad shoulder. "No more running!"

He grappled her wrist, pulling her to him, "We have boats waiting to take us away... With gold we can go to Noumea – I have a contact! You stay: You die!" She cried. He slapped her again. She snarled straight back into his face, resonating the sting. "Dumb whore!" he cursed, dragging her away from the vault.

"Callaghan'll be fucking you up" Marcus blindly shuffled on his knees. A pirate, swinging a bag of gold bars, elbowed him into the wall. "Ugh!"

Jemmy laughed, kicking Marcus in the gut, "I've never fought their wars. I serve no one and I take as they do."

"You have what you want!" Jintana pleaded, "Now run! Save yourself!"

"Here is something I don't need!" Jemmy clicked his finger and pointed to the computer screens and radio equipment.

The pirates joyfully blazed their guns and shredded the technology that they had not understood nor would ever need to. Computers cracked, shattered and disintegrated throwing up a fine mist of blasted plastic and silicon.


Outside the bank locals and refugees ran amuck. If they listened carefully they heard the tanks firing.

The jeep moved at a jutting pace through breaks in the crowded street, created by Matthews roaring, *"Run! Run! Jau! Jau! Chay! Chay!"*

Krue observed the civilians and refugees scurrying in search of family, belongings or an escape route. Opportunists had began obligatory looting; breaking into shops, robbing the merchants, running off leaving a trail of dropped valuables. Crime and dismay was spreading. Providence was, she shivered, eating into itself. Tom, Matthews and Corrie noted that this was the worst side of the town on their first and final visit.

"These fuckers will pay..." Callaghan whispered and ploughed into a hobbling procession of refugees. They scatted down a side-street. "Keep them panicking. That's how you gotta do it. Half the time they've done it to themselves," and he added as an afterthought, "by the time they reach us they're fucking animals."

She bitterly reminded him. "You're as fucked as they are, whitey."

"What are you trying to do?" Callaghan asked as they arrived at the bank. "Demoralise me? You're the failure, baby. Thanks for all your *reasoning*! War is insane and you tried to unravel a few mysteries! Failure!"

"I haven't failed shit."

Callaghan looked up at the bank and saw no militia on the door; they weren't inside looking out, they were most probably running into the hills, least likely fighting the Chinese. He felt weak, and drooping on the sandstone steps, had to force himself up and to follow what ever happened, through.

Krue was at his ear, "And you'll help me, you know why?"

"Bullshit I will."

In one swift move she straightened her arm, levelled her pistol to his temple. "Let's go."


Strained under the weight of their loot, the pirates clambered halfway across the foyer towards the front glass doors when Jemmy called, "Stop... We leave nothing." He tugged the blindfolds off Eric and Marcus. "Your lives are finished! You push buttons! Look at me, cowards!"

Marcus screamed, "Arsehole! Fuck you!"

Jemmy hooked up one flared nostril, kicked him in the groin, then breathed the foul fear of death to Eric, "Look at that whore on your way to hell! An expensive whore you were never good enough to take!"

They intuitively turned to Jintana, *please smile at us. Please! Our last memory!*

Jintana's eyes spoke of that incongruous pity she was destined to feel every few years, each pain a point in her life, each crisis a slayer of good men as she stood by, the witness, her life saved by the craft of selling her soul, or the chance that someone may be there to buy it. Her hands clasped to her heart. Her face elongated in lost hope, forever changed, as she realised she was next.

Eric squirmed, "Jemmy! I can work for you! *You know!* I can work for you! 'Asia is our oyster!' Remember?"

Jemmy cackled, "It was in *your* time – not mine."

His pirates faced to the rear of the bank, keen to witness the dual execution.

Eric's square eyes accustomed to playing computer soldiers were startled and openly wept. "But I'm one of you... You! *Black Tide!*"

At the mention of the syndicate, Jemmy wiped his brow, "We'll *never* be promoted... The elders only look after their own..."

"You'll never make it to Noumea!" Marcus yelled to amuse himself. "Never! And if you do they'll know who you are! You're shark bait!"

"And you won't see me fail, Marcus. But poor Eric," Jemmy pitied, admiring the shot-up computer consoles. "I need no computers... *Phst!* They piss me off." With a carefree flair he waved his gun over his head. "When will you learn you can't eat a microchip, Eric?"

"I," Eric sobbed.

Marcus muttered, "And after how many cheap bourbons did it take to come up with that? *You're a fucking poet now!* Jemmy you've got your gold now fuck off!"

"White boy shut the fuck up! I am giving you just enough dignity in your death to make your life worth something – not nothing! *Look at the whore!*"

Eric shuffled inches forward to Jemmy's kneecaps. "If I am no use, why waste the bullet?"

"And who's to tell the rest of the world how tough you are?" Marcus sarcastically added, "Your dignified departure is to let us live. You can do it! Go on! Run you fucker!"

Jemmy outstretched his arm and aimed at Marcus. It was in these seconds that Jemmy was at his cut-throat finest. Marcus succumbed to the stark black and whites of life and saw only black. This is death, not at the hands of a romantic band of South Pacific Pirates feeding the poor islanders and saving them from global warming, but a gruesome gang of looters. Then for what reason did Marcus smile, Jemmy faltered, now that was disrespect, or, acceptance, and therefore dignity. Jemmy cast a rueful stare to Jintana to check if his atmospheric level of testosterone still held her deeply entranced. Her head was cocked to the entrance and he could see little pumping veins under her lovely honey skin, her entire neck glistening with sweat, her petite hips flat against the vault, her stomach sucked in. He then heard a familiar though strained voice from the entrance. A voice that automatically inspired obedience.

"This isn't some fucking Bangkok bar!" Callaghan shouted, staggering in time with Krue, her pistol nudged against his neck. "This is the bank of Providence! Where are your allegiances!" Callaghan barked to the pirates, each slyly lowering their bags of loot for greater grasp of defensive weapons.

Three commandos, their uniforms layered with thin intermingling films of dried silt and jungle grime, their eyes white and alert peering from their darkened faces, their rock-solid mosquito-bitten hands moulded around their high-powered weapons, each mans' finger a millimetre away from pulling a trigger, stood at Krue's side, mute as creatures of the night, still like figurines, having silently emerged through the front door. They spied their immediate enemy – pirates; tattooed, blood-thirsty and young.

Jintana begged to all, "No guns!"

Jemmy relaxed his taunt gun arm and frugally tilted his head back, "Greetings Major Krue. I had twenty-thousand reasons to kill you,"

"It's a fifty grand bounty fee. No, you're here for the big score." Her point blank aim on Callaghan slackened. "I can understand that."

Callaghan slipped away from her. "O-K! No fast moves! It's a stand off! I'm alive let's keep it that way! We can work this out!"

"Shut up!" Krue mechanically levelled her pistol to Jemmy's sternum, obliging, "Put your guns down."

"You are mistaken," Jemmy spoke directly to her, blending an exotically intelligent tone into his crude voice, "We come for the gold... We worked for gold, not for a few jolly white men. I am no slave! Yes, I am robbing," he shook his head, doubtful she would understand, "I leave my way – you leave your way. You are no bandit, no *Police* too. You are a soldier. This is none of your business. You must kill Peters! Go kill him."

"Maybe you're the smartest man in these parts,"

"I never went for the bounty on your head," he informed her, the flicker in his eyes betraying the fact that he should have. "I am the only man that has been fair! Let me leave with what I have earnt – and we will not die. Easy deal. No complication."

Krue's steady aim was fixed but her eyes panned the terrain; the pirates used every point of distress or showmanship to slowly reach for their guns. And the Bounty. If he had known, how many others had known. Fuck it. Disengage the situation. Don't think. Matthews is to my left, *too* trigger happy.

"We have an understanding?" Jemmy asked her, dignified.

"Yes," she flatly replied, lowered her gun to hip-level, loosely but poignantly trained on his groin.

"Many will thank you, Major," Jemmy appreciatively smiled at the easy peace. It worked. She smiled, relaxed enough to look away.

He took a step back. His gun arm tensed and arced up to Krue.

Marcus, behind, bound at feet and wrist, seeing the step back, uncoiled as fast as he could, torpedoing his head at the back of Jemmy's legs to thwart the aim.

Jemmy felt his body jolt forward and still squeezed the trigger, aiming from the hip for the glow of skin just below Krue's neck, fleshy and clear. The bullet brushed through loose strands of her long hair and struck the front glass door, spraying minuscule shards out over the steps of the bank. Jemmy tried to aim again but was walloped backwards, his sense of time warped, landing on his back, half lying on top of Marcus. He felt bare, bloody and void. He looked over himself, his groin had disappeared – shot out. The guns stopped firing. It was seconds ago, or minutes ago, his eyes rolled. He was shaking, exhausted, his trigger finger still pulling in.

Tom, Corrie, and Matthews systematically nailed the five pirates. Weapons, loot and bodies tumbled to the floor. Jintana hid under a desk. She could see Jemmy and Marcus, Jemmy still alive, imagining he had a gun in his hand, firing at the sky. Krue lined up the dreamy face and finished him off, one between the eyes. She stepped closer. The original bullet into Jemmy's groin had exited taking everything with it but lodged itself in Marcus's head. He lay curled on his side, involuntarily wriggling. Krue tapped a bullet into the back of his head.

A bullet had hit Eric in the chest. She looked to Tom, Corrie then Matthews. They were scanning the sprays of blood on the carpet, clouds of cordite in the air, and gold sparkling from split bags in the loose embrace of twitching pirate limbs. The bank was a chipped and splintered, torn-up, blood-splattered, slaughter-house.

"That was good," Krue said deathly softly, her eyes fixed on the pirates, studying the hands that may try for a weapon again.

"Fuck me dead," Tom panted in complete amazement.

Corrie's eyes proudly glared at the macabre scene, "Sweet."

"Does anyone give a fuck about me?" Callaghan snarled, "Anyone?"

Jintana came out of her hiding place, trudging over dead pirates and discarded gold, to her lover.

# The Noose

Five hard won kilometres south of Sunny Bridge on Highway Five, Ghan grunted pain, satisfaction and confidence. A medic crouched by his thigh plucking out ball-bearings. Ghan focussed his binoculars to the south and the smoking wreck of the bandits' only known vehicle, an armoured personnel carrier. His tanks had trapped it as it tried to flee south. Bandits, some of them white men, had leapt from it. Two were gunned down, two fled into the bush.

"You will not be able to walk tomorrow," the medic advised, injected a shot of morphine, explaining, "It will cramp during the night, Sir."

Ghan's focus was not on *tomorrow* or *walking*. "Campaigns are won in one day, battles are won in fifteen minutes. Make sure I can walk today, for today we are *alive...*"

"Yes Sir."

Ghan lit a cigarette and surveyed this new territory. Parallel to the road were grey gum trees, home to screeching sulphur-crested cockatoos. From the far east the sky threatened with heavy swollen clouds. Around him the surviving headquarters, medics, regrouping troops, a few distraught mortar platoons and twenty tanks formed a loose convoy, progressing south at a cautiously tardigrade pace. The further they ventured the less resistance they found. There were bandit snipers in the woods, and as his troops pursued them they only became entangled in the game of thwarting his drive on Providence. This Peters was drawing him out, dividing him, diminishing his strength. Ghan hobbled on his bandaged leg to the lead of the convoy, congratulating his troops on the way and when at the front called an immediate halt. The lead tank did not stop. He stood rigid in front of it. The tank slammed its brakes. Ghan scaled the blood smeared front and up to the turret and faced north to the remnants of the 177th Brigade. He clapped his hands loudly three times and waited for the column to finally halt. Sergeants shouted the troops to form up in two neat columns for Ghan's inspection.

"Snipers?" a spotted called up to him.

He sniffed the air and flapped a hand to the south. The most able bodied troops hastily secured the road ahead. Back to the north, Ghan saw that the walking wounded were following. He had deemed it responsible to leave them there, but obviously they wanted to partake in the final thrust. Very good, he smugly smiled.

Chiang came jostling through the battle-hardened convoy to the side of the tank and rocked with the shock, "Ghan have we stopped? New orders?"

"Are you fearful?" Ghan sternly examined him.

Chiang swayed his burnt head and crossed his blistered forearms, "Never!"

Ghan, with added elevation from atop the tank, sucked in his cheeks at the spirals of smoke spindling up from the north, the dying fires, the cremation of their comrades. Before him was his surviving convoy, perhaps a third of his infantry and half the tanks. Though they were ashen and blood stained, most slightly wounded in some way, they stood in perfect columns expectantly facing up to him.

"We are now warriors born from the Great Battle of Sunny Bridge!" he shouted, holding an erect finger to the sky.

They cheered ecstatically.

Ghan saluted them. "Now we regroup! See the enemy? No! They shoot and run! They become nuisance! Why do they not stand and fight! They want us to chase them into the wilderness! No! We regroup and we take Providence. Our enemy has fled, he is cunning, waiting... Yet to admit defeat! He will only do so when we attack his pride! His home!"

At the northern fringe of Providence Peters and Romano paused from their frantic retreat. Peters's quick breathing scratched his dry throat, he was covered in cuts and scratches, a tattered Task Force Seven uniform, a smoking AK-47 across his lap. He held his face in his burnt palms and swallowed the nauseating feeling from the bridge. They had run eight kilometres through bush and only on the road when it was safe. In that time the sun had moved across the sky and he knew that before night came, an eternity away, the day would be decided. Fragments of shrapnel had peppered down his back and legs, he figured he had a day of fight before requiring surgery.

Romano's former retreat from Kingston had prepared him. He sat with a straight back calculating if he could run to his farm and plant something, anything, just so he could claim to be anything other than a warrior in this madness and when he died, go to heaven a farmer.

"The Fudo got quite a few," Peters reminisced, wincing, his eyes searching out the launch position on Jacinda Mountain.

"It did. But an army with tanks," Romano acknowledged, with a neat salute, the puffing and bleeding militia rushing into Providence on the back of utilities or on their feet. "Difficult..."

"Aye…" Peters counted how many militia emerged, less than a hundred. Highway Five would be hard to defend. Only Providence itself could stand against the invasion. "Ghan won't stop… He's closing in for his kill."

"We must defend from the houses…" Romano spoke of the urban fringe of Providence.

Worried locals stood at front doors. Old men and women were distraught at their militia fleeing, their eyes hung precariously to the smoke columns rising from the northern horizon, smudged west across the blue sky by an increasing coolish easterly sea-wind.

Peters turned to Romano with a look that both of them were still in control, "We must give the women and children the chance to fight."

Romano's heart dropped, it flopped onto the ground and wriggled before his eyes like a fish. "The children?"

"They won't care. There are thousands of refugees in the town. Ghan will kill 'em all to get to us. Tell them that, they have to fight to survive."

Romano patiently fumbled for his next phrase, and clenching his fists, "Do we have to fight that *way*?"

"What else can we do? Surrender would be execution! To run, we would be hunted!"

A chill from the sea blew through Romano's shirt cooling and prickling the sweat on his back. "So many die anyway…"

Several kilometres to the north, Ghan's first advancing tanks crept over low hills and raised their turrets to cover the road leading into Providence. Suddenly their puttering machine-guns could be heard. Trickles of refugees, fleeing from the path of the machines, were easily downed or scattered.

Romano placed his hands together as one, perfectly perpendicular to the sky, "Fear not what God gives, but what he takes. Let God intervene to take this vermin away."

The tank cannons fired, puffs of smoke betrayed their positions, lobbing shots immaculately into the streets of Providence. A pole fell. Children screamed. Dogs barked. A rifle fired in retaliation.

Peters flinched, "Hail Mary."

"And they've improved their shot." Romano noted.

"Little fucks. I have to show 'em who's daddy."

"I have no radio. Everything is scattered!"

"The bank." Peters said, "I've got one missile left. Maybe I'll be doing more than giving it to this Ghan fuck… There's the world too. Napalming wasn't enough, 'eh? I'll be at the bank."

Romano objected, "Defend our Providence! That's all we have to do! No nukes," and he examined the word, is that how we pronounce it, and with his two fingers carved an iconic mushroom cloud on the horizon where the Chinese came from, "It will not make a difference here."

"Right." Peters grimaced and planted his hands on his thighs, bracing himself to stand up. "Romano, position the militia in the houses." Peters measured the distance of the slowly advancing tanks. "Stall the Chinese at every possible point. I'll be lobbing another Fudo into the mêlée. We have to slow them, make them group up into a target... You understand? No nukes in our backyard, I promise." And tinkering, squeezing sustenance from a snide thought, "Think global solutions for a local problem."

And Romano smiled, "Very funny."

"But not funny enough, hey?"

The attacking tanks in the distance halted, troops ran to catch up.

Peters reminded his friend. "You saw Kingston."

The refugees in Providence fled in every possible direction. Some clambered on to roofs for a panoramic glimpse of ensuing doom, the smaller and less nourished wriggled into man-holes, a darkness and loneliness, where at least it was figured, the danger would trample overhead and pass. Processions in a united front of pacifying notions wandered west into the farmlands but in this time of need the farmers did not need extra help, competition, or any form of threat. The farmers killed them on the roads and left the bodies in ditches waiting for the war to the north to recede. A few of the plain crazy refugees did venture north with the hope that being part or full Chinese, the invading Chinese troops would embrace them. The troops, under Ghan's orders, warned them to stay clear. The majority of refugees headed south as a disorganised mob. Many had fled their countries for fear of invasion or counter invasion. Now they felt haunted that fate was hounding them. So on they ran, blindly, to the unknown ends of the earth.

The bodies of Jemmy and his pirate buddies were thrown down the stairs of the bank. The town looked deserted but some opportunist souls, taking a gamble with time, scavenged for supplies in the houses and stores.

Tom and Corrie stood guard at the entrance of the bank eyeing the relic of the *Dead Head Pub*. Sprightly looters darting across the intersection warily acknowledged the dead bodies posted outside the bank and ran faster. Inside, the gold bars and wads of currency were piled in the foyer forming an impressive glittery pile of booty.

Callaghan inspected another loot bag, "Where was he going? He might have been on to a good escape route."

"Noumea," Jintana swallowed hard, "He wanted me to come…" Crying, imitating a pistol and clicking it to her head she briefly relived the strain and squeezed Callaghan.

He cradled her delicate head in his hands. "You're all shaken up… He's dead now, long overdue, I know, but now it's done."

"Yes,"

"No one will hurt you now – look me in the eyes,"

Krue studied the rear offices and equipment. Bullets had burrowed through cases of circuits and chips leaving a mess of obliterated prickly technological bits and splintered hardware. The hub of communications were finished with, so too the operators. Eric lay on the floor biting a leather belt, fighting the pain of his fractured ribs and a punctured lung. Matthews covered the bullet hole with a plastic folder sleeve, murmuring to Krue, "This isn't any use…"

Callaghan briefly cuffed Jintana's eyes as he followed the blood trail where he had dragged Jemmy's mauled body across the foyer out to the steps. He whispered, "It's all over. I'm sure."

She whimpered pathetically on his shoulder.

Krue turned from the mess inside the bank to Callaghan with a hard, determined, searching stare.

Eric cried, trickling blood down the side of his mouth, "Doc Nelson! He's – Ugh!"

"Settle, hold still…" Matthews knelt down to Eric's arm and plunged in a syringe full of diluted morphine, "Just relax… Oi! … Be calm… Better?"

Krue squatted to the crying man's side and wiped his sweaty fringe off his clammy forehead, "It's a bad one Eric. I'm not lying."

"You know my name," Eric's ghastly face contorted to a frightening pitch as he bit the pain, *this is it!* tensed, then as a wave of calm ceased the aching in his torso, his pupils wandered over the ceiling then daintily circled about Krue's face. He determinedly croaked, "You can help me…"

With a matronly smile and kind blue eyes shining, she said, "I shall, Eric, the best I can."

Matthews stepped away to face the entrance as a wild mob of teenage green militia rushed by. Corrie and Tom crouched at the broken glass door hoping they wouldn't be disturbed.

Krue leant closer to Eric and breathed on his burning reddish cheeks.

He looked up to her.

"You're not going to die," Krue inspected the shot-up computers and radio equipment. "If you want to live, you must tell me where the nuclear missile launcher is."

Eric's eyes rolled to his useless computers then to the ceiling, filled with bullet holes. "He never tells us."

"You're lying,"

"He's not!" Callaghan called to her. "And I don't either."

They heard the familiar scream of an incoming shell.

"They're here – the fuckers are here!" Callaghan ducked under his desk.


Ghan had gained a foothold on the northern outskirts. His troops secured half-demolished houses and surviving mortar platoons commenced the pounding of inner-Providence. The softening up would keep the bandits occupied while Ghan organised a spearheard force of five tanks to blitzkrieg down the main road into the middle of his objective. Step two, his remaining several hundred troops and tanks would advance, eliminating all aggressors, under the cover of a light smoke screen, and in no time at all meet up with the five tanks in the centre. Step three would be the same process to secure the southern side of the town.

"May I ride with the first wave of tanks!" Chiang propositioned Ghan at their roadside headquarters on the outskirts of Providence.

Mortar bombs *flomped!* into the air. Crews waited for signals from their forward spotters. Ghan spied down the main street through binoculars and winced at two ragged refugees cart-wheeling across the road as an abandoned car was blasted by a falling shell. He saw thin silhouettes dashing behind doorways, an uneasy quiet as compared to the momentous carnage and rage encountered crossing the bridge. Ghan knew there would be nuisance bandit gun and rocket emplacements to be neutralised, probably make-shift urban warfare traps. It could take days, perhaps a week, but he had only hours.

"Sir!"

"… Do you realise the dangers, Chiang. You are an efficient and dear soldier, and my prized second in command." Ghan reasoned the bandits were cornered, resistance could be substantial. General Zhing would be very proud of him. Strategically, logically, morally and ethically, the tempo Ghan orchestrated for was a perfect consolidation of military might and fear. His enemy had partially regrouped in the town, at least they were prepared to fight an urban war lasting *his* several hours rather than a guerrilla war that may continue for months. Yes, he marvelled, cornered.

The five tanks were lined up in a convoy formation, each barrel facing a different assertive direction. Ghan positioned his remaining fifteen tanks in a tight arc around northern Providence, their barrels raised, ready to drop smoke-screen shells into the town.

"It has been an honour." Chiang recounted, "I have no family back in Shanghai. You have a daughter and an adorable wife. Nothing would turn my stomach more than to see the relatives of a brave, heroic, commander... Sob at his death ...."

"I will remember that. Look into the town... A brave man needs to lead the way in there. You are that man, making history."

It was a pretty sight compared to the polluted, multi-layered, condensed shit heaps they had risen from. The plumes of smoke, the bodies lying on the roads, the mortar holes in roofs and steadily burning houses enveloped them with an eerie sense of satisfaction. As much as they were attracted to this beachside town, the only means to express it was to tarnish it, and to really impress themselves, enter it with arms outstretched like bulldozers. Scouts that had probed into the town now returned: bandits were everywhere but mostly in-experienced.

"It is your choice."

Chiang made a note of scanning ahead with his binoculars. He saw the mess, the rationale behind their entire mission, the looting refugees that upset so much of the Pacific. He judged the distance to his target again; a perilous sprint. "I have a request, Sir. Make it an order that I capture this town!"

Ghan's arm extended forward, his erect index finger pointed directly over the centre of Providence, his voice thundering, "Colonel Chiang, you will lead the first attack and win Providence! Victory!"

"Yes Sir!"

When the first volley of mortars landed Krue, Callaghan and Jintana stood in a spasm of mortification. Matthews, Tom and Corrie, drawing from their short experience in urban warfare, determined they were not in danger yet.

Matthews announced, "Coming from the north."

Callaghan flustered, "Don't you get it? The Chinese are softening us up!"

Krue arrested Jintana and Callaghan with a commanding stare, "How many missiles did he launch?"

"What?" Callaghan asked.

"One." Jintana sobbed.

"It's true…" Eric croaked, vainly holding up one finger, "A Fudo…"

Krue appreciatively smiled, standing over his bleeding pale body, "Look at me."

He did, grateful and exasperated.

"I'll shoot your balls off if you don't tell me where the mobile nuke is."

"Uh!"

"The Beijing Ninety-Six!"

Tears bubbled over his cheeks. "I don't know! I don't know! We never knew! What – No! – Aaaagh! … South… Maybe ten kilometres… South west… Maybe…Ah… It is… But don't tell him,"

Krue popped one bullet into his stuttering skull and calmly continued business, "Matthews, contact Smacker. Callaghan, drag the body outside."

Callaghan lugged dead Eric, feet first, onto the street. Eric, he prayed to the cooling body, the neat hole in the forehead, the closed placid eyes that had seen so much for such a young life, any other intelligent man would have run, but thank god you were there. We did it Eric, Callaghan smiled and hauled harder and faster out the doors and down the stairs, didn't you always want to have a go at the Chinks? You couldn't ever love them after what they did to you. You lucky bastard. Your life was complete. *There!* I'll put you next to poor Marcus. Brothers in Arms. Callaghan looked at the pile of corpses and quickly realised that most of his friends in town where there. He crouched beside them and looked over the disintegrating town. The air tingled; similar to before the attack on the bridge and before that, riding in the landing craft to the beach. A swelling of pride kept him there, lingering in the danger, to taste the oncoming apocalypse. This is it, he decided. A round of shells hit the road and houses. Smoke spread, smothering Providence in an acrid fog. Refugees and looters continued to scatter helter-skelter, emerging from one spot and racing to another.

Callaghan crept back into the bank and covered Jintana's ears, holding her head to his heart. An explosion next door rocked the walls, unsettling plaster and dust. They knew that ten metres closer and all could be different. Callaghan shook it off. Smacker, he cursed. Hate boiled through his veins and steamed out his pores until an ice-blue cool sweat of disciplined vehemence dropped his temperament to tenaciously mild on the outside, but on the inner, plain fucking neurotic.

Tom and Corrie guarded the door both-ways; alternatively surprised at the ghostly looted town under bombardment and Callaghan's impatient moves.

"Check that out!" Corrie spied up the street.

Tom pressed his face to the broken door; a militia boy lead other boys north along the street of scattered debris and bodies, each hauling a rocket propelled grenade or a rifle.

"Major," Matthews called. "We're on."

Krue stood guard over Callaghan, relaying her message to Matthews. "Fucking excellent. Communication is: One. Possible nuke launcher ten clicks south west from Providence. Two. Have secured the headquarters of Providence and its Second In Command."

Callaghan seethed, "Don't forget who saved you!"

"Three, *Voodoo Child* is to be airlifted out of here with *Blue Tongue* giving support. We need a long distance chopper or a V-L-O."

Jintana's heart trembled.

"And Smacker will listen to you? He'll get you out?" Callaghan objected. "After you've served your purpose? He's the inhumane bastard!"

"Right he is, but he does listen to me because I do want to return," Krue needlessly justified herself.

"You succeeded with your little mission?"

Her motion did not falter. "You're talking to me about success?"

Callaghan heckled her, "You haven't done shit."

Krue bypassed Jintana and slammed the butt of her handgun into Callaghan's gut.

He doubled up, winded, gasping. "We're about to get captured – Let's get the fuck out of here! *Who* gives a fuck about that piece of junk nuke!"

Halfway between Ghan's advancing tanks and the bank, on the main road that connected the two extremities, Peters mustered his remaining forces of thirty men. What was left were the pack animals of his militia, those that could not survive without each other, those that would give themselves to breaking the effort of the invaders. He positioned them in smouldering houses and behind up-turned cars, ready to spring into action. He saw five tanks forming up ready to hurtle towards him, their exhausts forming a rising smoke column against the afternoon sunset.

"Romano!"

Romano eagerly called out from a window of a ransacked brick house. "You still here!"

"Yeah... No... Take out the lead tanks and block the road. I'll make it back to the bank!"

"I see! One more missile! One!" Romano threw the weight of his arm to the northern approaches where the Chinese had obviously amassed what remained, "Quickly! They will move up soon, I will try to stop them. Then you burn them!"

"Will do," Peters saluted and ran towards the bank. Though this was his town, and far from laying claim to have built it, he had inherited it in reasonable order and felt pity that if he did bequeath it, Providence would be a husk of its former self. On the main road was an abundance of carnage, craters, bodies, belongings, marauding dogs, a twisted bicycle, even an orphaned half-white baby serenely staring up to the sky. How a few hours can change everything. His pace peaked at a hearty run, half a mile to go. The street was vacant. Creeping pain jolted his body. Behind him the first advancing tank met Romano's rocket launcher. Two loud explosions racketed the town. The remaining tanks swivelled their turrets searching for an enemy. Peters heard searching firing, demolishing the holes that the defenders crawled in and out of. Then he was thrown into the air by an explosion and came crashing onto the road. His body was rattled and aching but his head hurt the most, a sorry pain gripped his cranium and wouldn't let go.

"Ahh!"

He turned to his left. Two civilian boys carried the sagging body of their wounded father, the best baker in town, from out of a shanty doorway. The father was too heavy for the boys and wailed from some terminal wound.

"Ahh!"

The sons hoisted their father up but he sagged, his spine scraping on the footpath. Peters stormed up to them, wrenched the sons from their father and pointed to the abandoned baby down the street, now crying, then pointed an escape route east. He slapped them hard on the backs and they ran for the baby. Peters then ran on. The pain was gone. He *was* pain.

In a courteous, curt and precise manner, Matthews detailed their position, that of the nuke, the request for evacuation. A radio operator in the Canberra H-Q replied in a flat yet urgent tone. The communication strength fluctuated. The signal up from Providence to a surviving satellite and down to Canberra was frequently interrupted.

"*Blue Tongue* en route."

"*Blue Tongue* on its way!" Matthews cheered to Krue.

"Excellent! Ready to roll?" She then aimed her pistol at Callaghan's knee caps. "I'll leave you here hobbling if you don't tell me where my satphone is."

He pointed to his office, "All you had to was ask nicely. Top drawer."

A ripple of explosions shook the bank. She found her satphone, turned it on and flicked the red button. The longitude and latitude was registered. She said to her men, "Red is on. In one minute, we're out of here." Krue then turned to Callaghan, cowering with Jintana. "So you run?"

"We have to!" Callaghan bit at his knuckle, "They're not taking prisoners."

"Go south," Krue suggested.

"Take me!" Jintana pleaded to Krue from Callaghan's grip.

Callaghan eyed the loot on the floor in the foyer. The tips of Jintana's fingers dug into his flesh…

Coming down from Mach 2.2. Wisps of cloud slid off the swing-wing's tips. Willy tweaked the focus of their targeting camera onto the town.

"Now… Phew… Hmm. It's rough down there."

"Closer look?"

"Surprise fly-by. Sure."

The fighter bomber swooped down. On the main street three Chinese light-tanks charged. Two were smoking wrecks at a northern intersection. Flowing into Providence from the north were hundreds of troops and more tanks, awkwardly halted at corners awaiting directions, their heads tipped back caught by the vulture in the sky.

Doug whistled. "We got enough H-E and incendiary to wipe this place out."

Willy scrutinised the view, zooming in. "Type eighty tanks… Can't see any Z-S-U fifty-sevens."

"Message coming through.…"

Doug and Willy listened to the radio relay: "From: *Overlord*. Voodoo Child is in Providence."

Doug jolted. "Get her out. Chinese assault in progress!"

"Wait on her signal."

"Will do…" The fighter bomber circled high in the sky, expectant, surveying.

Another message came through: "*Blue Tongue… Recon ten klicks south of Providence for one mobile missile launcher. I repeat…*"

Two Stars Ghan saw up to the centre of the town, Chiang's thrust was working perfectly. Troops were following up, making good progress. He then gave the order for the remainder of his army to storm in and ramp up the tempo.

The troops were now veterans, the tanks their pet beasts. There was little resistance. Along the main road Ghan saw a burning hospital, its front flowery garden intact but littered with bandit wounded. He even saw another white man, dead on the driveway. That greatly impressed Ghan. He could cut into the Asiatic race as much as he liked, and the Asian mind-game cares little for inter-Asian slaughter, but killing whites, now that was something impressive. East meets West. Visions of this gratitude were to continue.

Suddenly the commander of the company of troops which Ghan marched with, held him still and pointed toward the main intersection, now only a few hundred metres away, partially cloaked in twirling smoke.

"Our troops are there, see?"

Ghan saw the familiar helmets securing the intersection. He saw one piggy-backing the other down this way. Very few casualties indeed.

"Radio ahead, tell Colonel Chiang I'm nearly there."

A spotter from atop a tank cried, "Fighter bomber!"

All troops, upon seeing the sly bomber pass them over, dispersed for immediate cover leaving Ghan staring scornfully up to the sky then down to the town he had half taken and its ravished empty streets. He clambered atop a tank and in the silence following the jet's turbines passing, yelled up and down the street, "Men of the One hundred and Seventy-Seventh Brigade! We go on! Victory is in our hands! Victory!"

*Victory, victory*, his words bounced off shattered walls, echoed by platoon sergeants, ricocheting along the remnants of the brigade.

# Mercy

Jintana slipped from Callaghan's arms and threw herself at Krue's boots, "Take us! Please! Don't leave us to the Chinese!"

Krue unctuously stepped back.

"We can take the gold!" Callaghan picked up a bag of loot and stood poised as if he was ready to run several kilometres with his shiny ball and chain. "And I'll pay my way to be innocent!"

"You'd never make it, carrying that," Krue said, "And if you did, you'd face a War Crimes Trial."

His nostrils snarled, "Agh! Go then! Take her with you! Go on Jintana!"

Jintana unsteadily hovered, horrified at the sacrifices, but then mortified by another.

A twin-turbine jet passed over, the screeching of its engines permeating into and vibrating the weakened town.

Corrie spun to the entrance, searching the sky, but swiftly aimed his gun to the steps, "Fuck, it's him!"

Peters's staggered up the last step, thumped and smudged his bleeding hands on the broken glass door, defiantly staring up to Tom and Corrie, who guarded his every move. By virtue of his survival he was allowed to enter. He surveyed the ruins of his command; bullet holes, blood pools, gold and loot, destroyed technology, Jintana obediently beside Krue, not to mention the mess of corpses he had stepped over outside. He was in shock, wired and wild, blinking in disbelief, or calculating some last ditch fighting finesse.

"Snap out of it, Colonel." Krue ordered.

He faced her, plainly defiant. "I need a radio."

"Where's your nuke?"

His eyes roved about the mess, he had a nuke, on a truck, to the south west, and no means of communicating with it. "What does that matter… We have to escape!"

Krue levelled her pistol to his heart, "You know I can't leave until I account for it."

Peters glared from her cold eyes to Callaghan; both his palms opened up to the heavens in weary contemplation.

Tom called from the entrance, scuttling away, bullets zipping down the road. "Armoured!"

Three tanks crashed through the street and swung to a stop in triangle formation, commanding the intersection. Between them grey smoke from spent smoke shells formed a murky obliqueness. In neighbouring blocks, fires raged like miniature sunsets, each dancing amid the smoke. Somewhere, a militia boy pinned down a squad of troopers with a spray of rifle fire. Two grenades silenced him. Providence burnt. They were trapped.

Krue scolded Peters and Callaghan. "You're incapable of launching your fucking little nuclear missile and now I'm cornered!"

Peters moaned, part delirious.

Callaghan erupted, "We can take the gold Peters, and run, and start again!"

He muttered back, "They're outside…"

"My jeep's outside," Callaghan protested, "Let's get out! It's worth trying!"

With his boot, Peters nudged a gold bar, merely flipping it over. Corrie and Tom guarded him, he acknowledged them with a rueful wink. "We're all going to die,' he predicted, "So go out like fighting men… This is it! What are you waiting for!"

Krue ordered, "Tom, Corrie guard them against that wall… Matthews watch the front. Is there a basement or a bomb shelter?"

Matthews watched the three Chinese tanks eerily guard the intersection and any traffic on the adjoining roads. Through a break in the smoke, he tensed as Chinese troops edged closer, smoking guns aimed at suspicious windows and doorways, firing searching shots, booting their way through the urban war zone.

A familiar militia boy tried breaching the streets and was easily cut to pieces outside the *Dead Head Pub*. The smoke rolled over again, briefly concealing the intersection.

"Fools." Peters demanded, "Give me a fucking radio so I can blow 'em to stone age! I can lob one missile at them, I have one left, trust me,"

Krue observed the street – smoke, metal, debris. "You had your chance."

Romano crawled up the bank stairs and softly rattled his fists against the fractured glass, hounding his eyes inside. From the intersection a barrage of gunshots rattled shop windows. Romano crawled into a shivering ball, his hands clasping protectively over his large head.

Krue accepted that one step out there was imminent death, but twitched, "Get him in, disarm him,"

Matthews quietly pulled him in and swiftly stripped him of weapons.

"You…!" Romano howled, "And him… And her!" Like a violent little sharp toothed animal he relentlessly tugged back at his gun, "Bah!"

"Shut up!" Krue ordered.

His neck and shoulders were splattered with blood and caked in ash. "Peters?" Behind him was a scurry through near-death. "We are dead meat here!"

Callaghan rounded on him. "Should've shot her when you had the chance."

Romano saw the sports bags and spilt loot, "Thieves… Who?"

"Not I." Peters masked his anger and suspicion towards Callaghan.

"Jemmy," Callaghan explained, "Krue got him."

"Matthews, call *Blue Tongue*. Create a diversion," Krue spoke quickly.

"On it."

Peters berated her. "Let us out and fight!"

"Oi," She trained her gun on his head. "See the loot, place it all back in that vault. Understand?"

"You need us-"

She aimed to the wall. *Bang!*

Peters's jaw dropped, a bullet hole was in the roof just above his head, "Damn it woman, whatever!"

She then crept to the shattered doors and inspected the smoked-over heavens.

"What are you doing then?" Peters asked, less contrived and more appreciative, hurriedly lugging the gold back into the vault.

"They'll find us," her eyes shifted to the murky silhouettes of Chinese troops outside, "Not if we get to them first."

"So you're taking me back?"

"Be thankful I haven't shot you."


Minutes earlier, through the smoke, Hoochi and Romano had one last dash to make from the path of the stomping Chinese. Under the cover of smoke Hoochi lost site of Romano, ran into the side of a tank and held his breath. Chinese whispers turned to orders. He saw two mistaking him for one of them. Hoochi ran. Machine-guns obliterated his legs. Moaning, rolling on crumbling ground, he blacked out…

"Cease fire!" Ghan screamed. "Bring me that bandit!"

They dragged Hoochi inside the *Dead Head Pub*. He dreamily smiled at the familiar smell of stale beer stained in the wood and spilt liquors in the cracks, hopefully a scent of cheap perfume too…

Chiang knelt down and studied him. In brutish English he shouted, "Where is their headquarters! Speak or die!"

"*Aaaaghk!*"

"Medic! Attend to this man's legs!" Ghan called and then grilled Chiang, "You must save his life before you can bribe it!"

"But this is a bandit! See how his eyes roll – he knows what we want!"

Two medics knelt at Hoochi's chewed up legs and pondered how to begin the amputations. They looked to Ghan. He pointed bluntly to the legs and said, "Save them, for now." They speedily wrapped bandages around the thighs and removed a grenade from Hoochi's belt.

Chiang tipped sips of water in his mouth, "Your legs will survive, brave bandit! You will walk, you will run!"

"Bandit?" Hoochi stuttered, dribbles rolling down cheeks, "I am no bandit! I kill bandits for a living!" He tried lifting his legs, nothing. Shattered shins, white bones and blasted away flesh. He feinted.


Peters and Callaghan stood at the door of the vault. The gold was back in the cavern of steel walls. Even though outside was awash with debris, inside the vault was the familiar, stale, scent of wealth.

Krue ordered Romano, then Jintana, Callaghan and Peters, "Get in."

Corrie guarded them, "In! In! Step out and I'll blow your fucking head off."

Tom impulsively tightened the straps on his flak jacket then scanned the skies from behind the smashed entrance, "Mid altitude stand-by."

Matthews attached a bayonet to his rifle, "*Yea though I walk through the Valley of the Shadow of Death, I shall fear no Evil for I am the meanest,*"

Jintana screamed: "Take me!"

Krue hollered, "Control your woman!"

Peters and Callaghan grudgingly nursed Jintana inside the vault.

"Sit tight and you may survive this," Krue advised.

"Don't close the door! Don't close the door!" Jintana pleaded.

Peters scorned, "Don't leave us in here! Take us with you!"

Callaghan called, "Don't you have a fucking soul! You want to see us die! That's fucking beautiful isn't it!" he screamed to the roof of the vault and shivered when his ears began to ring incessantly.

Krue's body faced the shattered glass doors and the murky sky, while her eyes sized up the sturdiness of the vault and the open door.

She cruelly stared at Peters, Callaghan, Jintana and Romano, squashed into the crowded metal cell where oxygen would expire within hours. As the eyes are the window to the soul, those in the vault saw her dark blue iris morph into a shallow, pale, watery glow, fierce and defiant as a newborn sun.

She said, severely and sternly, "Trust me."

Peters stood by the door of the vault, ruminating, nodded courteously, amicably and gentlemanly, digesting her command. For a fraction of a second, between the two, shone an intense, verging on pleasurable, yet accelerating into a derisively and vehement stare, until she abruptly and callously called to her men, "Shut it."

Matthews and Tom's combined weights heaved the heavy door closed. They shoved a chair against it and stood nervously back, ears strained to the mêlée outside.

"Rock'n'roll. Load up," she said chirpily. The four of them replaced their K-41 magazines with full ammunition clips. "Don't hold back when we blast our way out."

The four inside the vault lapsed into expired slouches against shelving units packed with the spoils of anarchy; bars of gold, weapons parts, a jar of diamonds, wads of money, a boomerang, and one Semtex H hand-held detonator. They could hear little from outside.

"Fuck!" Callaghan cursed, cradling Jintana in the darkness. He called out, his voice echoing inside, "She can hear us, she knows it!"

Peters forced a contrived laugh, faced the cold metal door and whispered, "Don't die out there – Alone!"

Krue patted her pocket for the satphone. It was working. She looked to Matthews. He nodded. She stepped into Callaghan's office and tossed it on his table.

"Now we evacuate."

Matthews, Tom and Corrie stood in a petrified manner between the vault and the entrance. They could see part of a tank in the intersection and hear approaching searching gunfire.

Krue swiftly addressed them, brimming with a strange pride, her tone tainted and excited by the impending doom, "We got one chance. *Blue Tongue?*"

Tom turned the radio on his back to her.

She picked up the handset, "*Blue Tongue* this is *Voodoo Child* – come in."

The radio beeped, Doug's voice was distorted but direct, "*Voodoo Child*... Um... Very hot on the ground... What do you need down there?"

"We're holed up in the centre. What's it look like?"

"One column, armoured and assault troops... Regrouping in the town..."

"Is the south safe? We need an exit."

"Ah, that's your best bet."

"We need covering fire for that."

"What flavour?"

Krue fleetingly examined the intersection, "Hell... Something to sting... Once we're out you can level the place."

"And the nuke... *Overlord* wants to know about the nuke, over."

Krue cringed, "Ten klicks south or south-west. That's all I could find out."

Willy peered into the radar screen searching for an elusive blimp to signify a metallic object hidden in the hills.

Doug said, "We're searching for it, needle in a haystack out here."

"I don't care about the fucking nuke just get us the fuck out of here!"

Dreams. Shock. Cold and hot in one wave. Hoochi woke up. Still alive. The gnawing pain was wrapped in rolls of bandages. He was unsure how much of his legs were left.

Chiang looked over him, fatherly and polite, gracefully lighting a cigarette. "Where is the headquarters, brave bandit?"

Hoochi dazed, "Huh?"

Chiang gripped Hoochi by the shoulders, shaking him, the cigarette between his lips, exhaling a steady stream at Hoochi's bleeding nostrils. "You know!" He slapped Hoochi. "We know you know!"

"Destroyed..." Hoochi murmured.

"Lying!" Chiang screamed, high-pitched.

"... No lie,"

"You lie!"

"I *not* lie,"

"You lie!" Chiang walloped Hoochi in the head with a right hook. "Where? You tell!"

Ghan snappily clicked his fingers for Chiang to stop.

"Burning..." Hoochi rambled, "Fires. Peters,"

Ghan planted his knee onto Hoochi's chest, nuzzled the muzzle of his gun into the shoulder, and pried into the eyes of the doomed-soul, "*Peters!*"

Hoochi muffled his surprise with a whimper and fondly remembered, "Ahh Colonel Peters…"

Ghan shouted in his native tongue, "*You know! You know!*" And raised his gun as if to smash it down on Hoochi's nose. "*You will tell!*"

Chiang intervened. "Colonel Peters, that is all: Where is he?"

Hoochi thrashed his head side to side, crying, "The bank!… Across the road! Now leave me alone! Leave me alone!"

"The bank." Chiang recounted. "It must be very close."

Ghan angered, "*And where are the bandits?*" A shiver raced down his back. The roar of that twin-turbine fighter bomber air-breaking, diving. He hobbled into the intersection and hailed his troops, "Shoot it down!"

They raised their guns northward.

The fighter bomber descended out to sea, came in along the beach, looped out again and came in low from the north.

"Street harassment as ordered."

"Kiss the road."

"But not the toad. Afterburner and twenty-mil. North to South."

Willy checked both fuel gauges, "Five seconds only."

"Not the centre of town, can't singe *Voodoo Child*." Doug reminded, "Don't want no fried beaver."

The fighter bomber slowed, almost to a stalling speed, and at a frightening low level, rattling the foundations of buildings for miles around with its blowtorching thrusters.

Two Stars Ghan raised a rifle at the approaching fighter bomber and instinct intervened. He ducked behind a tank. 20mm cannon fire hosed a hail-storm of destruction, eating into and peeling the Chinese column into fleeing halves. From the tail of the jet a spurt of fuel shot out, igniting with the turbine exhaust, leaving a scorching flaming trail a hundred meters long in its wake.

Ghan shat his pants. He'd heard of it. It wasn't doctrine, but he had been warned of this practise. The Western World Slash and Burn Tactic. The afterburner was a gigantic torch, scorching the Chinese along the road with more carnage than the peppering of bullets. Ghan could hear it heading his way and leapt from behind the tank, over the road and straight into the *Dead Head Pub* and behind the bar. Medics, Chiang, and fear ridden troops dropped to the floor. The walls, stools, and shot glasses rattled. Ghan wriggled, covering his precious face from the flames that would come rolling from the hellish ignition. His troops wailed in deathly anticipation.

"We will survive!" Ghan screamed. A wave of heat sucked at the oxygen in the air. His goatee smouldered.

As they neared the intersection Doug gently pulled up. "Visual?"

"Hot. Real hot."

"How much, you think?"

"Couple of hundred thousand, every dollar counts."

The fighter bomber gained altitude, thundering into a greying afternoon sky. Several hundred troops and tanks lay in a gully of flames boarded by burning houses. Ghan cowered a few seconds longer in the heat wave. The devils may be playing tricks on his mind. No screams for his own combustion. Mercy?

"Deliverance!" he finally rejoiced. But his lock of hair smouldered. He clasped it, extinguishing the embers.

Slicks of smoke washed up the road and into the intersection. Ghan cautiously stepped out of the pub into a flaming wash-out of orange and yellow marking the path of the afterburner. The atmosphere smothering Providence was a smoky cavern.

"Colonel Chiang!" he coughed.

"Yes Ghan – We survived!"

"We go on! Men of the One-hundred and Seventy-Seventh Brigade! Form up!"

Ghan, Chiang and a tight ring of surviving troopers gathered in the intersection behind the protection of the three tanks. Mixes of smoke concealed their views in all directions.

"Men! Hurry!" Ghan called to the burnt out road north. A few coughing troops clambered from neighbouring houses eager to escape the flickering flames, quite surprised at their miraculous survival.

Ghan cried, "Faster!"

An easterly gust crept up the coast thinning the smoke but breathing wasn't any easier. The sky above was orange but they weren't sure if it was the sunset or impending doom.

"Sergeant!" Chiang called into the gathered twenty troops, "Get your troops ready to attack!"

"They are not my unit," the Sergeant explained, turning to the new faces, the only faces that remained of the 177th Brigade, "We are ready!"

"There!" one called, sending a spray of bullets into a haze of smoke obscuring a shot-up sandstone building across the intersection. Four khaki soldiers, whites, dived into a jeep parked outside. Two in the rear, and the golden haired angel standing in the passenger seat, raised their rifles at the troops and fired.

Ghan cried, unevenly aiming his pistol at her. "Attack!"

His troops, choking on smoke, some with tears running from their stinging eyes, enduring the smell of their burnt hair and the aroma of roasted flesh and a town set alight, shakily fired at the jeep as it accelerated south. One trooper dropped like a sack into himself. Ghan scuttled to the wounded man, took the rifle and from a shoulder position tracked the jeep, firing widely then zeroing in. One of the khaki soldiers firing from the rear was punched backwards. The troops continued their tempo although the speeding target was progressively smaller and more erratic. Another figure wailed from the jeep. The golden haired angel tossed back a grenade but not without a farewell volley, striking down the trooper closest to Ghan. The distant grenade spun on the road and puffed out a concealing smoke screen.

The turret of a tank in the intersection rotated, the barrel raised, discharged. The ground shook. Delicate near-destroyed structures collapsed throwing up clouds of dust and ash. Nearby troops rolled in pain cupping their ears.

"Cease fire!" Chiang called into one of the only surviving radios. He too was temporarily deafened.

Out of sight to the south the shell landed.

The tank turret popped open. The tank commander waved his hands, calling, "Two Stars Ghan! Two Stars Ghan!"

"My ears are ringing you fool!"

"We can pursue it!" the tank commander yelled, stabbing his finger southward.

Ghan grinned. "*Yes!* Destroy her! But watch the sky!"

The tank commander saluted and pulled his hatch down. Moans from burnt and deafened troopers were drowned as the tank eagerly rumbled south. Those that remained lowered their weapons and watched it sink into the smoke.

"Form up!" Chiang ordered the few troops to coherently survive. "Hurry! We are so close!"

Ghan pointed his men towards the steps of the bank and screamed, "Advance! There!"

They saw the structure, and bent over rushed towards it, descending into a fresh wave of solid smoke deluging over Providence. From near and afar refugees cried, surviving and wounded troopers scattered them with shot. In a brief break, the gentle roar of the ocean waves rolled across the battered town.

Brigadier Tolken, Colonel Smacker, and an assortment of staff crowded the large screens viewing the invasion of Providence from the lenses of spy satellites until the fighter bomber's fiery path ignited a parallel row of buildings along the road into inextinguishable infernos. Within minutes smoke covered the entire town, bleeding west. The spy satellite switched to infra-red mode yet only displayed globules of flames and explosions rather than military movements. Minutes later, high-level cloud concealed the entire region with a front as Cyclone Sandra's fury lashed back into play.

Tolken and Smacker stood perplexed, wishing that with their rushed breaths they could blow down there to reveal if the Chinese had ventured farther, had halted, retreated, or melted into the flames.

Tolken's anxiety was growing. He crossed his arms. "Is Colonel Peters in there?"

Mrs Benson retained a matronly gaze over the operation. She spoke into the radio. "*Voodoo Child*, come in. *Voodoo Child*, this is *Overlord*, come in." Her repeated requests were unanswered. She looked up and realised a tight crowd hanging on her every vowel and anxious glare at the silence from the battlefield. She cast her eye over the information before her; the visuals, the reports, the updates.

"What's the update on the Chinese Navy?" she asked.

An intelligence office answered, "Routed from the Coral Sea."

"And their forces in Townsville and Cairns?"

"No reports. Cut off."

Tolken intervened, "What we're seeing now is a milestone in global conquest. They've reached Providence, Colonel Peters beckoned them there."

Mrs Benson shrewdly agreed. "Where he is we don't' know, but Major Krue's satphone targeting location is activated. She may have escaped. Maybe not. But she has identified a target. Continue. Then we must track down the primary – the nuclear weapon."

Doug's pulse raced. "Verify that."

"*Blue Tongue*, this is *Overlord*. We have an active target."

"Yes *Overlord*, verify the location."

"Centre of Providence. I repeat: Centre of Providence."

"Yes… Are there any friendlies in the area?"

Doug powered the fighter bomber through the sky, circling in a wide arc out to sea again, steadily rising to ten-thousand feet for another pass.

The radio replied, "No friendlies. Proceed. Out."

Doug's hands stiffened. Had she escaped. For the carnage, the billions, the losses, the cost, he tried to shut out the imposing thought if he'd ever destroyed something on his side and if a cost is associated or is it marked as a kill never to be spoken of, or noted on his report which didn't matter because by calculation he had outlasted most pilots. Inevitably his number was up. He was fearless. He was emotionless, but she was down there.

"Circle out to sea then make another run for the nuke,"

Willy cautioned, "Can do… See that front?"

Doug, in his haste, had not seen the wall of high-level clouds rolling in from the east and only now saw it's torrential intoxication. Any flames he cast would be suppressed by the oncoming tropical storm. "A little search then we take out the town. Confirm that *Overlord*?"


Ghan's fingers evenly spread out pushing against the wafting white smoke. His hands floated forward, level with his half-blind crawling across this foreign land. Impatiently stabbing one hand lower to the ground, his fingertips scraped fragments of glass on stone steps and swiped over the skin on a cold, slippery forehead, traced the contour down the bridge of a broken nose, a rubbery cheek, mangy hair covering a rubbery ear that led to the bare skin of a lifeless neck, a collar bone and the fraying strap of a burnt singlet. The glow of a yellow hand flare danced behind him. Its dissipating burst of phosphorous light blended into the smoke forming a mist of peachy orange like a wintry morning apparition. Ghan withdrew his hand from the body of Jemmy and studied the stairs before him, then over his shoulder, expectant to find his troops, a column two-thousand strong, yet under twenty had made it this far.

Chiang headed them, waved the flare above his head, the platoon of survivors jogged from the protection of the tanks to the sprightly yellow glow. "We are ready!"

"This must be it!" Ghan decreed, hoisting his good leg up three steps, pointing his blood-smeared fingers to the shattered glass door of the bank and the stately sandstone walls. He stood poised and admiringly staring in at the shot up, smoke filled interior, deciding, this is our objective and once taken signifies the closing of battle! "Follow me!" He cheered, "Victory is in our hands!"

In the silence and dark of four thick, chilled, metal walls the rumblings outside attracted curiosity. Peters squatted on the floor, hunched and maddened. The whine of the jet had gone. He had certainly heard the Chinese firing at Krue as she escaped, but did she make it? He ran his hands over the gold bars, unable to see the gleam. Cursed gold. He held his lower lip between his teeth and thought backwards. He had found the gold like this, some bandits had tried to steal it as Sumatra's body bled into the sand. Had Sumatra stumbled upon the gold as Peters had? Is this the gold that builds empires, is traded at each major turn, used as collateral, in a world where life, perishable materials, bullets and the labour of man, are all miniscule in comparison.

Jintana asked, her tone firm, "How long?"

"Don't know." Callaghan reckoned, "Your little friend Krue has gone back to Papa."

Romano sparked with jubilation. "We escape!"

"I've never heard an afterburner before," Callaghan impulsively edged the vault door ajar a mere inch. "Nasty. Who could survive that?"

Peters reminisced, "You have to be lucky. *Shh!*"

They heard the crackling of burning and light footsteps on shards of glass sifting through the carnage.

Peters whispered, climbing Callaghan's shoulder, "Someone's inside...."

Romano shuffled to the rear of the vault, although anywhere in there was safe against the inflicting carnage outside. He shivered. His bloody wounds were coagulating.

Jintana's red-rimmed eyes adjusted to the gloom and tranquilly accepted what was to unfold. *Here we go again.*

Romano whispered, "Don't open the door! Please!"

"Sh!" Peters ordered.

Callaghan and Peters looked through the slim opening with detrimental interest. A haze hung in the bank. Smoke seemed cemented in the air outside the glass door. Then a probing spray of bullets obliterated what remained of the glass door. Bits and pieces of the bank roof hung by twisted wire, winding, swaying and sizzling. A stun grenade flew in and bounced about in the foyer. The explosion rolled over the front desks, spilling tills laden with coins. The vault briefly reverberated. The shelves inside rattled.

Peters bowed his head in a frank acceptance and blinking, staring back out, witnessed the smoky entrance of Two Stars Ghan, cautiously stomping with a bleeding leg, a wide commanding path into the bank, heralding "*This is history!*"

Colonel Chiang and five soldiers followed, smoothly stepping through with crisp confidence and hardened bravado.

Ghan stood over the cherry red stains on the floor, determining that like the corpses outside, these were part of fresh organised killings, and on a closer inspection, head-wound executions. He scrunched his face, probing the bank. "*Infighting among the bandits! What enemy is this! How can they fight me when they fight among themselves! Chiang, do we have any photographers?*"

"*Dead. Lost at the bridge... Look!*"

They observed the sabotaged radio equipment, obliterated computers and bullet-chipped walls, tracing the path of spent shells and debris.

Chiang knelt down and cupped a handful of coins, mixed currencies, pocketed a few and stood to show Ghan, "*This is the bank. General Ghan – peasant bandits leave nothing but this!*"

Ghan nervously reached behind and tugged at his lone lock, curling it around his cheek, smelling the burnt ends. In a few more weeks it would be long enough to kiss and then it would remind him of his wife's hair. His leg hurt. It was cramping.

"*So this is Policing the Pacific of Pirates?*" Chiang sighed, lighting a cigarette.

"*Who are the real bandits!*" Ghan shifted his weight to his good leg. "*The Diplomat?*"

"*That woman?*" Chiang asked the stillness.

Ghan mellowed, "*She was here...*"

Chiang tossed his handful of coins to the scene, "*Then she is nothing but a common thief!*"

"*Where is the method here?*" Ghan asked himself, facing his troops.

The troops gripped their rifles. At least the assault was over.

Chiang assured his superior, "*We will find method.*"

"*To come this far...*" Ghan hobbled around the mess, inspecting the shell casings, destroyed technology, useless money and clumps of flesh. He found on an office, intact, and though messy with paperwork, gave some sign of the end of business here. On the wall was the map of Queensland, the Warlord's territory and trading routes clearly marked. "*Their headquarters…*" he summarised. In the tinted glass window was his reflection, the stature of a fearless warrior: high boots, the rose-tinted but multi-stained uniform, the bandaged leg, the goatee beard burnt into a motley patch anchoring his commanding, blistered features into a noble façade. "*Of the thousands of miles and restless nights…*" he spoke to himself in a poetic manner, "*Of blood we shed on a foreign land,*" his fist unfurled to the mess of the bank, the coins, strewn paperwork, spent shells, blasted body bits and silicon. "*I enter as a victor – a saviour – to the ruins of the day.*" His sad eyes lowered. He could not adequately stare at his figure, he was now just an observer of history, and let his eyes falter into the background of the office; a desk, cigarettes, chewed pens, crinkled notes, crude documents of a defunct civilisation, and a pin-sized red light that flashed on, off, on, off. He slowly picked up the slim, black, metallic satphone and held back the instinct to hurl it against the map of Queensland on the wall. Two thousand men, far for this!

A wide eyed trooper stood a few feet back from the vault and observed everyone else occupied in inquisitive rummaging and petty looting through the abandoned remains. He slung his rifle over his shoulder and quietly shifted the chair aside and pulled open the door of the vault. No one paid him any attention, and fearing he'd have to share any spoils, he then discretely peeked his head around to look in. He saw strangers huddling, exhaling a breath of terror under fresh light. He was seventeen and docile bar what he knew about conscripted service in the world's largest army and the life of a son of a small-time pig-farmer in a backwards, arid province. He saw glittering elements of wealth on the shelves and these strange people, the fair skinned being the most mysterious, and these were the enemy he had been drilled to hate, appearing extremely appreciative for his interest.

Jintana instinctively shied from his newly acquired manly stare and mocked some innocent, depraved and ravenous, plea for escape that only he could appropriately offer.

Callaghan blinked at the Chinaman with a frank brotherly smile, "G'day *Mate!*"

Peters spoke diplomatically, "Hello. You speak English? … Peace."

The trooper's mind was over-ridden with stimuli. In a fluid move he swung his rifle and aimed at their chests, his tongue speedily dancing between his pallet and lips. "Hans yup! – Hans yup! – Yankee Die! Hans yup!"

"*Don't hurt us!*" Jintana pleaded.

At the squeal of a female, Chiang rushed to the vault and stood beside the trooper (dwarfing the boy) and venomously pointing to Peters and Romano, "*Ghan! We have prisoners!*"

"*What?*" Ghan harked, *prisoners* were an abstract thought.

"*Look!*"

Ghan hobbled over thinking who the hell wants prisoners and shoved the trooper aside. Those in the vault were cornered, fear darkening their faces. He snorted, still holding the blinking-red satphone.

He turned to his troops and Chiang, "*A headquarters... Complete with bandits and gadgets! So, there is a prize.*"

The young trooper pried the vault door open enough so every man could see inside. Ghan stepped to a closer view. These bandits were nothing but an insipid motley brotherhood of scoundrels standing in a mess of loot! The leader, Colonel Peters appeared morosely fatigued, a burden even as a prisoner. There was that Asian bandit too, Romano, standing with his hands behind his back, behind a very elegant woman – no doubt a whore to scum. She stood fragilely, hunched bare-shoulders, hand-over-hand half concealing over her crotch a black spherical object that blinked a green pin dot of light. Another white man, angered and vicious, leered like a castrated dog. Two Stars Ghan, descendant of Mongolian Herdsman, Crusader for the Chinese Army, leered to Colonel Peters.

"You!" Chiang prompted them to speak.

Colonel Peters performed an immaculately gracious bow to General Ghan, "Congratulations on my defeat."

"*What is he saying?*"

"*Congratulations on his defeat,*" Chiang explained disdainfully.

"*Congratulations? Fucking mad man.*"

"I surrender," Peters spoke loudly and fluidly. They looked him over, searching for a ruse. "I have been deceived... I was betrayed,"

Callaghan cursed, "Yes, it's all your fucking fault."

Peters shot to his comrade a silencing glare.

Chiang translated to Ghan as best he could.

"*Betrayed?*" Ghan asked Chiang to extract.

"The Australian Government placed a traitor among us..." Peters sourly explained, "She claimed to be a *diplomat*. She has escaped."

Chiang translated, unsure what though. It was very confusing.

Ghan nodded along. There were a million pieces to a giant jigsaw puzzle. The general becomes a cop who becomes a game show contestant. What was the evidence: This maniac bandit. A treacherous diplomat that escaped. *She* may have been responsible for the jet attack and if she were capable of that, then the missile at the bridge. Her escape had led him here to this bandit lair. So, one light cast out to sea causes two ships to collide! All eyes where on Ghan as he sorted the rubbish from the reality, his thumb and forefinger rubbing the bristle on his chin. Interesting, but the reality was war: dirty and still unfinished.

A trooper at the entrance called in, "*The jet is back!*"

Ghan waved that piece of information away. What was left of his brigade to destroy?

The jet powered to the south.

Callaghan patiently picked the right second to step to Ghan, "We can serve you well..." He smugly smiled and raised his eyebrows invitingly to Ghan then opened his hands to the gold on the floor of the vault. "The ways in this land are much different to any other in the Pacific Region."

As Chiang translated Callaghan's offer, Jintana shyly opened her mouth, her fists were held before her and over a gadget, her lips worming in Ghan's native tongue, "*Please do not hurt us, we mean no harm! Please! Trust the white-devils!*"

"*Trust the white-devils? Look at you! Prisoner!*" Chiang hissed back.

"*Trust me! Trust me!*" Jintana pleaded.

"*Silence!*" Ghan studied them. The journey and the costly battles netted him an enemy and now it was captured in a cage to admire like a trophy – but what if no one can see the trophy? He could cart them back to China – that would be something, like a great explorer returning with a collection of specimens. He tossed the satphone to the vault floor. The infamous pirates of the Pacific. No running. A few riches to take. Standing at the doorway, bemused but his fuse burning by the second, he drew his pistol and let it hang by his side. Baggage.

Chiang asked, "*Can I shoot one too?*"

"*Prisoners,*" Ghan exhaustingly sighed, "*Their lives are leverage.*"

"*For what?*"

"*We may take them back... I don't know... We will know soon enough.*"

Chiang took charge. "You are prisoners of the Chinese Army One-Seventy-Seventh Brigade,"

Peters cursed, waving away Chiang, "Fuck that shit off!"

Jintana's eyelids fluttered to Ghan's scurrilous gaze, "*Do not kill us!*"

Ghan looked blankly at the black sphere in her hands, held over her crotch, to the satphone he had discarded.

Romano snatched the satphone like a beggar stealing from the apple cart. "I've seen this, it is from that Krue!"

Callaghan grabbed it and snappily turned it over before his eyes. The casing was an antennae, and in his palm, he could almost feel the pulse throbbing through his forearm, turning his body into an extension of the antennae, bouncing bytes of longitude and latitude data into orbit. "It's on... Activated!"

Peters stared, a stupendous grin freezing his face, "Bitch! Target beacon!"

"Traitor!" Romano growled.

Callaghan switched it off. "We're *fucked.*"

"The witch!" Jintana hissed.

"She *is* an assassin," Peters noted with added authority, staring back to Ghan, "And I am a target... Look! She wants to kill me."

Ghan feared the change of expression in Peters. "*What is going on?*"

"Stop!" Chiang stuttered.

Peters heralded at the top of his voice with amazing clarity and acceptance, "We're about to be blown to pieces!"

Jintana switched to Ghan's tongue, "*Trust the white-devils! The fire from the sky! It comes!*"

Ghan, Chiang and the troopers looked on with muddled bemusement. The cornered bandits in the vault then fell into a unified, unfathomable and remorseful silence.

"*They have lost their minds,*" Chiang whispered to Ghan.

"*Trickery,*" Ghan abrasively grunted. "*We come so far to see artisans, we could have stayed home...*"

"*No! We will die!*" Jintana wailed.

Callaghan's finger played thoughtfully with his lip, smiling to Peters. "I knew she'd like you in a weird *fucked up* way."

Peters swayed his head. "Perhaps... And with women – you just never know."

Callaghan candidly slapped the thick steely walls of the vault, "But we do, we do."

"This is as good a bomb shelter as any." Peters then reached to the door to pull it closed, screaming to Chiang and Ghan, "Don't try to stop me..."

The fighter bomber passed over. The custodian of the Beijing-Ninety-Six, Stevey, and three Tonkas, stood rigidly by the massive missile launcher. Stevey broke first. The fighter bomber thrusters dipped behind a neighbouring ridge like a thunder-clap and he knew, when it came back, his precious truck on their sensitive radar, Peters's precious missile and the jungle-bunny Tonkas, would be engulfed in a napalm bath.

"Run! Down to the stream!"

The Tonkas poised their rifles to the expected path of the fighter bomber yet wondered how to effectively shoot down a supersonic craft.

"No! Run! Follow me!"

They followed him away from the dirt road that meandered between two lush hills, into the undergrowth, wriggled under a fallen trunk and into the muddy waters of a stream. Stevey stood half-submerged shrieking to their missile launcher barely visible through the foliage. His eyes narrowed on the tip of the missile, the uranium tipped warhead he had admired for many lonely days and nights, ashamed to cowardly leave it to such a fate.

"Steady..." Willy checked his screen, the digitised image of the Beijing-Ninety-Six, carefully configuring the target for an air-to-ground missile.

Doug winced, "C'mon... Sitting pretty."

"Steady ... We're locked... Firing... In she goes... and ... Ah fuck! It missed!"

"What?"

"It fucking missed... you jolted!"

Doug scrutinised his gloved hands perfectly still on the stick yet pulling out of the attack, "No fucking way! I'm Cool Hand Doug!"

"Bullshit! I felt it shake and I lost the missile!"

"Where did it hit?"

"I don't fucking know!"

The radio interrupted, "*Blue Tongue*, what's the,"

Doug turned it off.

Willy briefly closed his eyes. "We got time for another run?"

"We have to... Diving in from the west,"

"Outta' the sun?"

"Yeah. Are they shooting at us?"

"Not sure." Willy leant into the screen. It fogged up from his breath. "Missile armed..."

"What happened to the first?"

"It missed by a metre ... Hit a tree... Snapped it in half. Jesus..."

"The launcher..."

"There…She's a big girl. How much ya' reckon?"

"Five million?"

"Maybe two… Old junk, I reckon. Locked on."

"I'm steady."

Willy said, "Hit the deck a bit,"

"Like that…"

The fighter bomber hugged the earth. From under it's wing the air-to-ground missile blasted off and darted ahead.

"Fired." Willy watched his missile careen into frame towards the image of the target, slipping between the launcher's rear axle and explode, jolting the vehicle. "Bingo!" He concentrated. "Hang on… No secondary explosions…"

"Huh?"

"We hit it but it didn't blow! For fuck's sake! Circle around again…"

Doug fumed. He felt like a novice, in training, hitting cardboard cut-outs.

Willy blinked. The missile truck was damaged, the rear a smoking wreck, but the intercontinental nuclear missile supposedly full of flammable rocket fuel, remained cradled in it's launcher unharmed. "Ah! C'mon around again – rip it up with the cannon."

Doug nodded, "Right," and carved over the terrain, pulling in tight, bearing down on the launcher and pressed his thumb on the trigger. The 20mm cannon sliced the Beijing Ninety-Six in half, the nose keeling over and hitting the ground, smoking. The fuselage lit up, searing hot gas spurting into the air, falling, burning out the launcher.

Willy thumped his thigh, "I don't think that was real, I expected something huge-"

"What?"

"Mobile missile launchers, that size, the secondary explosion is huge. That was… I think it was a dud. It could never have gotten off the ground."

"Shit. How much you reckon? A thousand bucks?"

"Maybe… Back to town."

Doug turned the radio on: "*Blue Tongue* has destroyed Primary Target: Mobile Launcher…"

"Excellent. We can breath easy now!" Overlord roared.

"Yeah… Primary is taken out, *Overlord*. We're going in for a preliminary pass of Providence, north to south. Out…" Seconds later, "… What we got down there?"

Willy discernibly peered into his screen. "Smoke's thinned out... North side; aye they're fucked... Middle; action. South; ... A T eighty tank is creeping south! Gutsy bugger. It's fired a few salvos ahead."

"Target," Doug requested. They cleared Providence and slowed to cover the southern approaches. "A volley? Can we nail it?"

"Nah... More... Civilians by the bucket-load... One jeep, could be *Voodoo Child*, heading south... Thousands of refugees..."

"They're clear of the impact area?"

"Maybe... Circle back. We got storm and fuel warnings."

"Shit."

"Yeah."


The roar of the fighter bomber overhead throttled them to the bone.

"Oh it's g-g-good to hear that!" Corrie groaned.

Matthews skidded the jeep around a blind corner tilting on two wheels as a tank's cannon fire tore apart the road behind them.

Corrie lifted his head and flattened his hand over the bite-sized chunk taken out of his rib cage. Blood frothed on his lips. "Eh... It don't hurt... *Yet*."

To his side, bracing with the rolls of the jeep, Tom pained with each breath, his eyes widening at the pursuing silhouette of the pursuing tank, "Uh-*haaa*....You're awake... Nah! You'll be fine mate. *Uh-haaaa*... It's your ticket ... Out of here – check this out..."

"Tom?"

"*Ah*... I got mine here," he waved his forearm in front of Corrie's half-closed eyes. The hand was limply grotesque and bloody, a bullet hole in the back and out the palm on a slant. He was bleeding down to his elbows and dripping over his rifle. "The fuckers winged me. My chest aches..."

"I got one..."

"You reckon?"

"Yeah I'm sure... An' they got me."

Krue's voice sounded directions to the driver, Matthews, "Shake 'em,"

"Our shooting days aren't over yet," Tom yelled, "Incoming!"

They ducked.

Fleeing south out of Providence the tempo of the Chinese advance had halted, but not their influential firepower. The jeep squished a corpse, swerved out of control, heading into a fleeing mob.

Matthews sat bolt upright grappling with the steering, his foot firmly on the accelerator, demonically charging his way along the pot-holed, muddy road. The mob split before him. Another shell came down off the road in a sugarcane field flipping clumps of the rich brown soil into the air startling refugees out of nearby fields onto the road to run south as fast as possible. The hell followed them, endeared to their endurance, out pacing and running them down. The jeep couldn't run the scared herd down – a leg was stuck under a mudguard. Matthews yelled "Brace ya self!" and reversed over a ditch, dislodged the leg and powered back onto the road. Krue saw the hopeless spectacle and the washed out faces of the refugees who now accepted the soldiers as part of their plight. A scare crept up Krue's spine – they were now part of the misery. She shook her head, praying for another avenue other than this crowded road.

"Into the field!" she ordered.

They flattened a path into the sugarcane, half-circling to create confusing twists for any pursuers, driving deeper and deeper into a sweeter pasture. She turned to Tom and Corrie in the back to grab the radio. The two soldiers ached, half-blinded, scratching clumps of hot bitumen from their smouldering fatigues and ducking from sweet stinging sugarcane whiplash. The roadside had blown up in their faces. Their ears rang. Time slowed. The smoke dispersed. They were submerged in a green field and partially deaf.

Corrie hunched over cursing, "Let me out!"

"Jesus!" Krue sunk. "Stop! Stop!"

Matthews turned off from his last direction, halting at an earth wall separating fields. Krue doused Tom and Corrie with sloshes of water from a canteen.

Tom coughed, cradling his arm.

Krue scanned the sky and foreground of ripe green sugarcane. It was a wondrous day hinting of an approaching easterly afternoon storm. The ruins of Providence were less than a kilometre behind. The fighter bomber circled, encompassing the ends of the horizon in its gradually descending and tightening spiralling pattern.

"Right on!" She extended the aerial and tilted her head to the earpiece. "*Blue Tongue, Voodoo Child.* Come in over… *Blue Tongue,* this is *Voodoo Child.*"

"I feel it now," Corrie gasped, "I'm in shock, Oh fuck… Ohhhh,"

Tom searched the sugarcane for an enemy. With his good arm he propped his rifle between his knees and fingered the dent in his flak jacket. "I get it now… I've broken some ribs…" He traced the indenture of the bullet's impact. "I'm a lucky bastard!"

"*Blue Tongue*, this is *Voodoo Child*. Satphone activated as target. Come in *Blue Tongue* this is *Voodoo Child*, we've got two wounded."

Matthews stood up out of the driver's seat, searching erratically over the sea of sugarcane around them. Either the tank had rumbled past or was lurking behind. "Anyone following? Anyone see how we got in here?"

They listened. Silence. The tank halted. From the road, somewhere through the sugarcane, refugees picked themselves up and moaned south. Corrie spasmed. Matthews leant over to check the exit of the bullet wound – the chunk out of the rib cage. A shattered bone protruded from the exposed flesh.

"What's the deal, Matty?" Corrie frothed blood.

"Maybe give up smoking,"

"Bastard." Corrie gasped. "Slack, rich bastard."

Tom saliently scanned the sky, humming to himself, his fractured arm shaking, pain fingering through his torso, "Fella's, I'm done for... I'm *fucked up*..."

Krue persistently called into the radio, "*Blue Tongue* this is *Voodoo Child*, come in over."

Nothing. No static, no fuzz, and no reply.

"C'mon *Blue Tongue*..." She looked over the radio; no battery charge, a blank LCD panel, the casing cracked by a bullet, "Fuck!"

The fighter bomber looped out over the sea.

"No signal from *Voodoo Child*," Willy sighed.

Doug grunted. "Was that her heading south?"

"Everyone is escaping south."

"O-K... *Overlord*... Request immediate extraction of four commandos, location south of Providence... Evacuate A-S-A-P. L-Z is hot."

Tolken's grainy voice crackled on the radio, "*Blue Tongue*, will do... What's the E-T-A of strike, over."

"Is she in there, or close, we might wipe her out," Doug urged.

Willy added, "*Overlord* the centre of Providence is occupied with Chinese Infantry and three... Uh... Seven tanks. No positive v-v of *Voodoo Child*. Do we proceed?"

There was a pause. Underground, in the safest bunker in the world, Smacker, Tolken and Mrs Benson, plus the hangers-on, surveyed the confusion.

Mrs Benson shut her eyes, knowing Tolken was waiting on her. She said, "Proceed."

"Yes, proceed." Tolken sounded off.

Mrs Benson then beckoned another staffer, "Get me Airforce. Dispatch a rescue unit up there immediately. We can't leave anyone up there, again."


"This is it," Krue told her soldiers, motherly hugging their shoulders. They crouched behind the jeep, partially shielded from the direction of Providence. "An air strike has been called in... That jet is sizing up the target zone. I don't know if we're far enough, it'll be *nasty*."

"Nuclear!" Matthew horrifically objected.

Corrie howled in disbelief, "*Ohhhh ma God!*"

Tom saluted Krue, "You don't mess around 'eh miss?"

"Fuck no," Krue said, held them together and stared squarely into their frightened eyes, "In case we do die, remember-"

The fighter bomber swept on Providence.

Matthews gaped, boyishly astonished, "Oh my,"

Krue outstretched her arms and embraced them, squeezing up to her and against each other, "Don't look. The flash is blinding. We'll survive it. We'll survive it-"

"Pray," someone asked, their voice shaken and scared, stretched.

"Pray." Krue admitted, and prayed, "Oh God!"

*"Yea though I walk into the Shadow of the Valley of Death, I shall fear no Evil, for,"*


Hoochi slithered out of the pub and onto the footpath at the intersection. The battle was over. Tanks in the intersection ceased fire. Ash settled on the road. Hoochi coughed, peering through the haze, struggling on his elbows and taking deep breaths of the vile air. He saw the cracked burning shops and shattered glass over the cratered streets of Providence. Victorious Chinese troops tipped their dull green dome helmets salutary to the sky. The few remaining disillusioned civilians and looters hovered in doorways or on their knees bowing like sombre grey statues to the captors. Burnt surviving troops gave a weak smile, they had survived. Ceasefire. He rolled his head back to the heavens racing over in a rich swirl of beautiful, high and swollen dark storm clouds. Then he saw a bird swoop down like an eagle from the heavens, and as his tired eyes rolled closed, he dreamt it was coming to take him away.

Outside was the roar of diving fighter bomber. Peters's eyes met with Callaghan.

Peters maniacally launched himself to Ghan, "Out!"

"Silence!" Chiang screamed back.

"Fuck you!" Callaghan wailed.

"*Bandits!*" Ghan barged into the vault and whacked Callaghan in the chest with the butt of his gun and threatened Peters, "*You are a prisoner!*"

Chiang made a hasty interpretation.

Jintana shuddered.

"*Take them outside!*" Ghan curtly ordered his troops.

"Outside!" Chiang told Peters.

Callaghan, moaning, stepped half out of the vault and using the door handle of the vault for support, gasped, then fell backwards, dragging the door with him. But an audience of troops wouldn't allow it. They held it open. Their hungry eyes glowed in preparation for an orgy of bandit's blood.

Ghan aimed his pistol right between Peters's eyes, "*Troopers! I want this one alive!*"

The troops in unison saluted *Sir!*

Jintana elbowed through to Ghan, presenting a Semtex H detonator under his nose, professing in eloquent mandarin, "*This will kill you, me, everything. Stand away!*"

Ghan noted the green flickering light of the detonator, Jintana's unflinching eyes, and palmed her to the side.

A teenage trooper falteringly called from the entrance, "*Two Stars Ghan! A jet attack!*" but knew that how ever he pushed his frail voice and his young legs the descending weapons would outrun him.

Two troopers from outside ran into the bank screaming hysterically.

"I will not die in here!" Romano barged out of the claustrophobic vault, tackling into three troops, who gripped him by the shoulders and threw him over onto the upturned reception desks and impetuously plunged their bayonets into his belly. Romano's eyes bulged, he clutched at his wounds and tried to kick his murderers away.

In the vault Ghan shifted his pistol from Callaghan to Jintana to Peters as they heard their accomplice die, Romano's incomprehensible words gurgling through the bank.

Chiang, thinking Ghan had those in the vault subdued, stood back from the vault door, drawing a dagger to take a gutsy plunge into Romano.

With Chiang's attention shifted to simple blood lust, Peters sharply elbowed Ghan in the head and kicked out the bandaged leg. Callaghan grabbed the pistol. Ghan toppled down. Peters then lunged at the door handle and pulled it shut, sealing the vault in darkness as Tom, Corrie, Matthews and Krue sang, *"Not gonna die. Not Gonna Die! Yeah we're not gonna' die! Not gonna die!"*

Ghan was trapped in the darkness and silence. Breaths were on him, hands held him down, bending his arms behind his back. Struggling would only be out of spite.

He could hear Chiang banging his bloody dagger on the door outside, a dull *cling! cling! cling!*

The intersection was the focus for the centralised carpet-bombing, each of the twelve falling bombs guided to form a descending, dilating disc. The first six to detonate were a mix of high explosives, blasting and tearing structures into flammable bits. The second six popped, each creating expanding rings of flames that linked and morphed, forming a wide, molten, mark of destructive success. In seconds Providence was torn up, eaten by heat and flattened; wiped clean from geography, the eyes of aviators, the prayers of the inhabitants, and the desires of conquerors. The burning remains threw up a blanket of smoke, the fires below choked for oxygen and sucking at the clouds above, found them heavy and burdened by tropical humidity.

The jeep served as a barricade against the shockwaves. On the side facing the impact the tires expanded and popped, the paint flaked into the air and the shattered windscreen disintegrated into shards. As for those who sought shelter, Krue's black shirt peeled open and the skin on her back scalded. The thick curls of Corrie's hair silently burnt to his scalp and sacrificing the tough skin on the palm of his left hand, doused the cindering coils. Matthews tore off his smouldering flak jacket and shirt, squinting at the wave of heat expelled from the epicentre; a glowing band of dirty orange, brightening up the sky. Krue, bent over to escape the initial blast, painfully straightened her back and faced the aftermath. Being on the outskirts of its hell, its shifting glow painted on her stunned face, she observed the town excessively torched into the stone age; mushrooms with fireball heads ascended into the air after disintegrating houses and incinerating buildings, leaving flickering flames to scavenge the blackened remains. She warily turned a full circle, watching a filthy, inky fog rolling towards them, sucked along by the lingering wave of the blast. Corrie coughed. She knelt to his side and passed her eyes over the wound. He'd live, but not as well. She searched in his pack for gauze, a bandage, a shot.

Likewise, Matthews peered along Tom's crooked arm, wondering what to strap to it or to let it bleed itself. Tom ominously blinked at the acrid fog and flakes of falling ash.

Krue faced the fog. She detected a new aroma, something flammable and completely organic. Squinting her smoke-strained eyes into the dark atmosphere, patiently peering into the receding waves of ash and smoke, she traced the morphing outlines of flames, advancing through the fields of sugarcane, spilling across and below her horizon. In the aftermath of the initial explosion and heat, the sugarcane had ignited. Fires waltzed across fields like an approaching ripple. Krue predicted that they too would soon be engulfed by her own demise. She looked for a saviour from the sky and saw only an impending fiery roof shining down; the glow of approaching flames illuminated on the bellies of the heavy clouds above.

Corrie coughed, winced, bowed his head to the earth and wiped blood from his lips. He sickly convulsed, his eyes distractedly examining Tom and the sky.

Krue arched back and prayed for an escape from the rapidly approaching walls of flame and enveloping, thick, choking smoke. Her head rolled zombie-like as tears sprinted over her taught cheeks washing tracks into her ashen face. She flopped forward onto her knees, doubled up, rubbing her face into the flattened sugarcane. It was cool, and burrowing her fingers deeper, it was moist. She sobbed as Matthews stood up and faltered at the world burning before him, and Tom and Corrie tilted their faces to the hell above and felt the fingertip of the Grim Reaper approvingly rubbing their foreheads, marking them for a consumption by fires too infernal to outrun. Before Krue could cry to them to try to flee from the encroaching flaming fields, droplets coated in ashes tapped at her shoulders and arms, one drop hitting her nose and running to her lip. She tasted it; a cinder coating for a perfectly succulent droplet. Sudden, ear-splitting, distant thunder claps from out to sea charged closer to shore. Lightning bolts painted their weathered camouflaged faces into ultraviolet contrasts set against their dark pupils. Krue marvelled at sheets of soothing tropical rains building up and washing down in waves where heat once reigned. Dense grey clouds of smoke were pelted by falling rain the size of thimbles. The red glow of Providence shimmered and faltered.

She lay exhaustingly sprawled on her stomach, drenched and gasping that she could easily drown with her fingers clawing into sloppy mud. She slanted her body to the sky, parted her lips, and tasted the tropical rain trickling over her tongue. Thrashing winds washed the grime off her face and arms. Her eyes flimsily scanned the sky, marvelling at the lightning bolts illuminating the veins and circuitry of the souls of gods.

The storm passed, rolling over and to the west.

They recovered what senses remained, and soaked, sat in a circle, exhausted. All was quiet and strangely tranquil. Corrie was pale, half knocked out, but stable. Tom was morbidly accepting that one arm lost was better than a life.

Matthews toyed with his satphone, "I'm sending our location to Overlord. Can we get out of her now?"

Krue's face was a fusion of shock and awe. She could only nod.

He tapped in a few commands and waited.

"So," Tom exhaled, "Is that it? Is that what we were dropped in here for? Nothing else popping up on your agenda, Major?"

Corrie's head rolled. "What you want Tom, a marching band?"

"I can't believe we've survived." Matthews stated. "Lucky, huh."

Krue frowned, "Yeah, now let's hope we can get the fuck out of here."

They waited. The sky was clearing. There were no shots, no wails, just the wind blowing steadily from the sea. Their nerves were atomised and hearts thudding to a primal beat. They were vulnerable, helpless and discarded in time. Krue had few thoughts, or energy. She huddled into herself, expectant of the trek to come.

"I hear something," Matthews said softly, standing and scanning to the east.

Tom queasily croaked, "Me too. One of us, or them?"

The vertical lift off jets careened in from the sea, the lead zoning in on the jeep. It hovered, circled around, the other two secured the area, then the lead descended and flattened the sugarcane. Matthews led Tom and Corrie under and into the craft. He bundled them in then twisted to haul Krue into the hold but she smartly stood back, her body facing him, her head turned to the town. Embedded in her memory was a paradise engulfed by flames, fire beaten by a storm and now from the glistening sugarcane a thick mist ascended and smothered the land. She stared into the craft. Inside, they were fiercely prying with their eyes to flee. Krue graciously smiled, her free hand carefully clasped at the curvature to be of her belly, and she wondered as she stepped up to her vehicle of escape, for all that one man was capable of, including her own play in this world, was she escaping with not only herself intact, but the seed of an ideal, yet a reminder of the evil of men and woman, evils never to be doubted.

# Epilogue

For the first day he sat patiently on Jacinda Mountain pondering down to what remained. When the weather was clearer he saw that the town had been heeled into the earth by some demon, leaving an ashen footprint that led in no particular direction. When the wind came in from the sea, he could smell the destruction. In the meantime he enjoyed considerable kinship with the Fang Tribe. He showed them how the mountain supplied food as only a true bushman would know. They were grateful. They offered him some of their finest warriors to accompany him when he did depart but he had no need for company. They offered him their finest lady, he did not decline, but only smiled, and said he would fetch her later, but not before thoughtfully impregnating her now.

On the way in he met farmers returning to the fields, gathering lost flock, planting, continuing their existence, and digging graves. All took cover when a swarm of white-fella helicopters mapped the region of Providence in a grid pattern. In the afternoon they found something of interest in the south-west and proceeded to circle it, descend and secure it. Within an hour a much larger helicopter came and hauled the crumpled and blackened cylindrical cargo up into the sky and straining with the load, limped past Jacinda Mountain, then peeled to the east, crawling like a bug over a blue floor to a grey military ship sitting stately on the horizon.

He then ventured further through the farmlands and encountered grim reminders of slaughters that continued unabated. Refugees, and now returning Indonesian soldiers, were shot at from a distance. For him this was of little concern. He visited a few of the farmers who over bread and soup expressed interest in hiring him as interim or head protector, but he kindly refused and continued.

After resting up for a night he walked into the incinerated soul of the town he knew so well to study the flow of human traffic and climatise to the overpowering acrid smell of wet ash. Refugees still trickled from the north and returning Indonesian soldiers, some by the hundred, swelled into Providence from the south and quickly moved on, without so much as a whisper of warning at the juncture. He wondered if the two tides ever spoke of where they had been or where they going, and if it mattered. There was come general consensus that heading west was not an option. He saw none of the signs that any formidable force remained. Even the tallest building, the four storey unit block, was blasted away. On the outskirts all the houses were at best half burnt; missing roofs and walls, or at worst completely flattened into a jumble of charred broken beams. Standing in the middle of the intersection it was different. The tar had been torched into the dirt. Tanks remained intact, apart from the scars of internal explosions that over-turned them off the road. A few black bony limbs flopped out hatches but there was no flesh for maggots to infest. He walked to the beach to find the units palmed over the sand like an aeroplane crash, the spray of debris, bricks, ashen trusses and disfigured furniture thrown across the beach like a slick that slid under the surf. He watched the sea for sign of the white man. Nothing at all on the horizon, only seagulls bobbing on the backs of waves. With a hunch he reckoned they wouldn't come yet, about turned and picked his way through the black bones and ruins for the bank.

The steps were intact and layered with flatly fried human and immaculately melted beads of glass from the front doors. The blackened sandstone structure was intact from a distance though on close inspection he could see it had weathered the brief fireball and fractured. The roof was blown away in a thousand pieces over the countryside leaving unstable walls. Where there was a front reception desk resembled an ashen flaking log, and of the technology was now a mess of shrivelled metals and crumbled cement. Ribs of a large chest protruded from a sodden sludge of ash. Other bones, skulls, helmets and warped rifle barrels resembled only what they were; an incendiary graveyard of the unrecognisable. He turned to the vault, surprisingly upright but on a slight slant, exposed and naked to the blackened wilderness, its roof bare to the sun. The surface layers of polished metal had flaked from the heat revealing a matt, leaden-grey, iron core. He circled it with admiration, and scowling back to the intersection, waved away two inquisitive Chinese troopers. They had survived unscathed or had intentionally escaped the terror responsible for the carnage from here to Sunny Bridge. They had wandered looking for comrades, but all they found were the wounded, and all the wounded found was death. The two troopers paused, and though they were too far away to see the dark brown eagle eyes, they knew by the chills emanating from their hearts to their boots, this scavenging stranger's willingness to act on the simple laws of nature in this alien land – the weak don't survive. He carried a long hunting rifle, a handgun, was as dark as a cavern, every move about him announced his hunterly ease in a time and place he rightly called his own.

He stood before the vault, running his fine fingers over the door, measuring it against its former self. He pulled the lever handle down and lugged hard; the hinges squeaked like an ancient abandoned machine of the industrial revolution, the heavy door swung out. The noise had disturbed nothing. He stepped to the entrance, his eyes following a ray of sunshine inside, revealing upturned shelves, a few discarded pearls and coins and other scraps of plunder. He pulled out several shelves, throwing them over his shoulder. He had seen this junk before and now he had a particular fever. His hands speedily plucked through the remaining belongings: useless currencies, not so precious jewels, stubbed out cigarettes, microchips and bits for machines he'd never heard of, plus a few coins hidden in corners. He palmed his forehead and hungrily moaned. There was nothing of value here, not even good for memories. He surveyed the aftermath: Wiped out. He pulled at his short coils of hair, sweated, and fondly asked the empty vault as if it were a good friend and always had been but was now wronged, "Who has been here first, eh?"

Standing inside and in the shade he felt beset by an immense loneliness and turned to the sea, visible beyond the flattened blackened town. He stepped out. A straggle of sickly and frightful refugees quickened their pace on the road, a black path, moving on south. They had never seen the likes of Providence and feared that in their fleeing the old world this may actually be the new world. He cast them a cruel stare yet when they whimpered forgiveness he dismissed those kind as looters, as he dismissed any newcomer as a looter, and he wondered if those who knew precisely what to loot had even survived the war they had caused. He heaved the door closed and with a knife sturdily held in both hands, studied the iron core. His crude short swipes with the tip of the blade scrapped thin legible lines, M-A-L-O, and, T-H-E L-A-S-T A-B-O-R-I-G-I-N-A-L.

The shrill feeling of metal on metal reverberated through his spine. He methodically finished his work and stood back to briefly admire the crude inscription. He sheathed his knife, unslung his rifle to hip level and hastily fled, his wild eyes probing forward and to his flanks for traces of the old character of the town in the flattened, dark, surreal terrain. He moved with sure-footed steps, skipping and hopping between and over the spread of mixed mounds and splays of debris, speedily sinking into the safety of the drab green bush and its mystical sanctuary. As he ducked under branches and wriggled into the mazes in near impenetrable forests, clambering up over craggy ranges and resting in the cool shade offered by hidden pristine waterfalls, he shunned craning his neck towards the stain of the demolished town blotting the exquisite coastline.

Someone, at the peak of the fury, knew what they were doing and had generously helped themselves to the spoils of war but they, he smiled of his growing enlightenment, had saved him of that burden, a very unnecessary burden. So in all kindness he thanked his generous enemies, but he knew, as time moves on and comes back again like the waves from the sea, he was sure to see them again, some day.

www.ingramcontent.com/pod-product-compliance
Lightning Source LLC
Chambersburg PA
CBHW031141050726
47495CB00018B/276